LAST TRAIN TO GLORYHOLE
(OR 'THE SHAKEN SLEEPERS')

by

Keith Price

**Grosvenor House
Publishing Limited**

This book is published by
Grosvenor House Publishing Ltd
28-30 High Street, Guildford, Surrey, GU1 3EL.
www.grosvenorhousepublishing.co.uk

A CIP record for this book
is available from the British Library

ISBN 978-1-78148-621-4

Dedication:

*For Alison, hoping it might help
bring us back together*

To Pen-Y-Fan

You stand so proud and noble against the lightening sky,
The rising sun trims your skirts with gold,
The dawning day, for you, no mystery holds,
It will pass as countless days gone by
    And be no more.

You stand erect, defiant against the gathering storm,
The thunderous clouds a bonnet for your brow,
The mighty winds do not your shoulders bow,
While we of weaker, mortal, human flesh
    Are tossed and blown.

You stand so silent, peaceful before the evening sky,
The moon and stars caress your form with light,
The features of your face are veiled by night,
You stand eternal, constant, to the end of time -
    We live and die.

                            – Charles Harvey

CHAPTER 1

I remember it as if it were yesterday. One night in late winter, and just months before her death, my mother told me how, during the war, and on the very night of her own mother's funeral, she had retired early to her bed only to be awoken and terrified out of her wits by the sight of her mother - the grandmother I never knew - standing at the foot of her bed, dressed in the very clothes that she had just been buried in.

I well recall how I shuddered, then leaned towards her and carefully poured the last of Beryl's *Carling Black Label* into the half-pint glass she held out for me, and, watching the foaming bubbles rise, and listening to them fizz, pondered for some moments over her startling revelation. I stared into Beryl's thin, rouged, but coarsely lined face, and I recall how I seemed to see my mother in a completely new light. As she sat forward in the chair, I sipped long and hard from my own golden glass, then watched pityingly as she leaned even further forward so as to turn on the television. Now seventy-nine - and just months from her abrupt demise - I was alarmed that she could barely manage to switch the set on, let alone turn the knob in her frail fingers to increase the volume.

'God, Mam! What did she do?' I asked her, shouting now above the noisy TV-commercial that was playing. Beryl rested her frothing glass on the window-sill beside her and turned and looked at me askance, almost as though I were a stranger, or worse, some newly-arrived preacher from a chapel she avoided, and who had just walked in uninvited from off the street. 'Why, she went away of course!' she replied sharply. Yes, that was all she said, for soon after that the cat perched on the slanting, slate roof signified the beginning of her favourite soap.

Strange as it may sound, up until then I had believed every single thing my mother had ever told me. How, for instance, when a child, she told me that it was imperative that I got a smallpox-vaccination, and she had had us queue up two-and-a-half times round the clinic, and for the best part of a day, in order to obtain it; that, shockingly, I had failed the simple music-test at school to be loaned out the shiny, semi-precious, wooden recorder of my dreams, that even tone-deaf Lorraine Morgan got given; that I was to be punished at home for calling a half-German boy at school 'a bloody Nazi!'; and, worst by far, that I needed to wear glasses! The very shame of it. And me, like my Uncle Bryn from Penydarren decades before, a future Arsenal and Wales footballer at the very least. Ever since when I have concluded that this last declaration of hers was most likely an apt and rightful punishment for the unforgivable nature of the, plainly racist, penultimate one. After all, I soon learned from David Trott's mother's own lips (in the hushed private office of the Junior School headmistress, no less) that Greta and her future husband had travelled across land and sea, with neither sleep nor luggage, all the way to England, then to Wales, in their efforts to escape the tyrant Hitler, and not at all, as I had announced shrilly in the school dining-hall the previous day, to spy for him!

Yes, it transpired that my dear mother had been right about all the things that I still regard as the key parameters of my childhood, and many more things besides. But of course I didn't believe for one moment what she told me on that particular winter evening in her steamy back-parlour about her mother's ghost. Indeed how could anyone with an ounce of sound judgement accept such abject nonsense? I asked myself. I had enjoyed a grammar-school education for heaven's sake, and had supped, conversed, and even argued with the best. I decided that my beloved Beryl had unquestionably dissembled that night, and so had deceived me for the very first time in my life, and, looking back, it may be that, subconsciously, I was never quite able to forgive her for it.

The following day, on returning to my home just a few miles up the valley, I soon discovered that my mother's tale had upset me considerably: for the second time I now felt deeply betrayed by a woman whom I loved. Beryl died that April before I even got the chance to revisit the matter with her, and this time perhaps get her to admit to the truth. However, maybe I should have shown greater consideration for her, considering the mean and solitary nature of her death - her sudden heart-attack, her ignominious fall from an easy-chair, the abject, prostrate hiatus before her unfortunate discovery on the floor of the room by the young delivery-boy from the shop across the road - but, like a fool, I was headstrong and self-righteous. Beryl had deceived me about her own mother, I told myself, and, as if to confirm *the lie*, during the weeks after her death I noted how she never appeared to *me* once, even though, in my inimitable grief, I must have summoned her daily.

So my dear mother Beryl May went out of my life for good, in what seemed to me a sort of fictional, smoky haze of disappointment, her final words of note to me an unforgivable sham. At least that was the view I took of the matter back then. But I have long since wondered whether her bizarre assertion was in fact *the lie* that I had then pronounced it to be, or whether, unbeknown to both of us, Beryl was simply one whose vision *'through a glass darkly'* was unexpectedly, miraculously perhaps, unimpaired and crystal-clear. Yes, for my sins, this is the bitter question that I now find myself pondering at least once daily, with or without a darkened glass of ale to aid or cloud my insight. Do such people exist? I often wonder. And if so, was my mother one of them?

The ruddy-faced, bespectacled old lady, her dark, curly head bent low over the sheet-music, pumped her narrow, veined, leather-clad feet on the pedals, as if for dear life, and the bulky, black harmonium responded grudgingly, gasping out in laboured tones the pungent chords and scales of a hymn that the body of assembled mourners all knew, in the biblical sense, to their very souls, and sang out once again with traditional gusto. *'Love divine, all loves excelling,'* they sang - man and boy, girl and woman.

3

On this occasion I sang only to stay abreast of them, and not in some vain attempt to out-shine them, as on one, much earlier, childhood visit to *Bethel* that I found I could still faintly recall. This particular hymn was, somewhat strangely, a favourite song of ours at weddings too, I recollected, holding up the single-sheet programme before my fast dampening, lately cataract-shrouded, eyes, in an effort to make out its timeless lines. But it was at a funeral once again that bent Agnes played it for us on that late March day - the sunny, yet sombre, morning of my elder brother Sam's second - yes, second - and, God Willing, his final, burial.

The screw-fastened pine box, bearing on its gleaming, amber surface a wreath of red, white and yellow flowers, and wound about with a black-and-white woollen, football scarf - the word *'Martyrs'* stitched across it in large block letters - had been wheeled in from the rear of the room on its squeaking, wooden trellis by two of the most solemn-looking gentlemen ever to don charcoal suits and matching black beards. This anomalous action, I felt, they seemed to effect rather too much in the manner of manoeuvring a wayward shopping-trolley for my liking, but at least I felt to a degree placated by the expert way in which the strange, narrow, overburdened tricycle became parked and secured. With two vertical bolts along its foremost legs, the coffin now sat firmly at rest, straddling the polished middle-aisle rather like a wooden ship in a dry-dock. It lay just ten or so feet before the raised lectern, from behind which the aged, shaggy-haired, Welsh preacher sang out to us his earnest and eternal soul, while staring downwards in due reverence, his large, steady fingers cleaning diligently in his off-white, creased handkerchief his pair of tiny, round-lensed spectacles, his large, flared nostrils sniffling up the first signs of a Spring-cold.

Between verses I turned my head to gaze around the large room. Yes, all my close family were there, I saw, even the remoter strands, comprising, most notably, a long line of young children in white shirts and blouses, all flaunting crisply-ironed tails that flapped back over pert, black-cotton buttocks, some adorned with silver dog-chains, key-fobs, or exposed zips which gleamed brightly in the morning sunlight that streamed in on their tender forms through the tall, trellised windows to one side of the room. If I had felt inclined to make the effort I might have recognised a few of them - or the identity of their parents, at the very least - but my weary and distracted mind only skimmed along the rows from head to head, summarising how, in the cavernous epochs between family interments, the unremitting round of coupling, conception and reproduction proceeded at its all too familiar pace, and the Cook and Rees families could now be seen to be growing quite alarmingly, rather than fizzling out, as I once believed they might conceivably do, given the curious nature of the calamitous chain of events which we in our portion of our dear valley had all had to endure.

I turned and looked behind me to the rear of the church, and quickly registered that none of the actual killers had turned up this time. Yes, they would have other plans, naturally, I told myself. Well they had certainly attended that first time, I recalled, except that, back then, I had no idea what it was that they had actually done, and so had little reason to question their presence, or the seemingly authentic offerings of empathy and contrition which each one had taken great pains to make me. Yes, it was only much later that it became clear to me that, between the four of them, they had endeavoured to affect innocence by jointly conspiring to hide the truth of what had actually taken place on that fateful day in October 1974, just a fortnight or so before the bleak, eighth anniversary of the terrible disaster which befell us at the village-school that Sam and I had once attended just a few short streets away, and which it had proved impossible for anyone in the community to shrug off, or even to tuck away temporarily, as one might an embarrassing love-letter, or a cotton leek, or a folded, felt daffodil, pressed in amongst sundry needles, buttons and cotton-reels in a much-loved corner of the linen-drawer.

'People often like to give God credit,' the white-haired pastor suddenly bellowed out from behind his lectern, holding high in his hands a wooden bowl filled to overflowing with fluttering notes, and with a painful, almost wicked, smile emanating our way through brown, gritted teeth. 'But I see you folk have seen fit to give Him cash! And I've little doubt that He will bless you all accordingly, and many times over, for your humble, kind gesture.'

I shook my head at the glaring incongruity of his remark, and glanced up at the black, wooden clock on the wall just above the pastor's head. I blinked my blurred eyes in disbelief, then regarded it again for confirmation. Its wide-splayed hands informed me that it was now exactly a-quarter-past-nine; just as it had been back then, I thought! Suddenly I realised that today was a Friday too, although on this occasion an unseasonably bright and sunny one, which had at least attempted to enlighten the mournful mood that had entered the room on the squeaking heels of the Sunday-best-dressed congregation's shuffling footsteps, and had deepened still further with every stern, uttered word of God, each minor key, each sniffled sigh.

As so often before, my mind drifted back to that first tragic Friday in question. I recalled how an off-duty fire-man had later told me how none of the clocks - in any classroom, office or changing-room - had ever lived, or ticked, a moment longer than 'a-quarter-past-nine.' How on earth could they? I mused, when, after all, the hushed, but shuffling, columns and rows of dishevelled, jumper-ed and cardigan-ed, young time-learners were now long gone - the sternly ordered, stool-raised, winders of clocks forever now departed, perhaps to some timeless realm far, far away.

An ice-cold tear suddenly fell onto my cheek. I dabbed it away with a fore-finger, gazed down at my feet, and reflected on how, for all those poor children's parents and siblings, and for all their many friends and loved-ones, an entire life-time must surely have ceased that day at precisely 'nine-fifteen,' and how, for so many of my fellow countrymen, that famous, fab, cool, Beatle decade had been swiftly curtailed at just 'sixty-six.'

Then, looking down, I saw it. A small, frail, brown money-spider suddenly emerged from out of the red, cloth seat of the chair that stood vacant before me, and promptly toppled lightly to the polished floor below, then nimbly regained its frenzied gait, and marched on boldly between my black, laced-up shoes, and away to safety beneath my chair. I smiled inwardly at the creature's dogged boldness, looked up at the clock once again, and then suddenly recalled how 'nine-fifteen' had to have been the time when my very own concussed, or, at the very least, sleeping, head had been rudely shaken awake, and my all-too-cocky, yet tender, young life inexplicably spared.

Searching in vain between the flapping legs of my black trousers for a last sight of the fleeing arachnid, it suddenly dawned on me how *just two legs* had proved sufficient for my salvation on that bleak and rainy, fateful day. And, boy, back then, I thought, was I able to shift on them!

But what I didn't realise at the time was that one of the four killers was actually present there all along, standing beside the passenger-door of her tan Passat, which she had parked adroitly just across the road from the chapel. '*Anne of Green Gables*,' I had often enjoyed calling her during our youth, since the green-doored, little house on the hill that she had grown up in, along with her mother and younger siblings, was to my young, impressionable mind reminiscent of the mansion in the novel that we had shared class-reading of in our first year at Grammar School. This was during the days when I discovered that I loved her in a different way, more deeply perhaps, than I had loved the dusky, tantalizing Rebecca from the Secondary Modern School, whom Anne somehow managed to repeatedly scare off about as effortlessly as she might have swished a money-spider from a radiator.

Looking up and down the main road, Anne listened to the echoing tones of the ancient, Welsh hymn, and construed that, for her, there was little that was divine or celestial either in its music or its lyrics. She drew thinly on her cigarette for the final time, and then adeptly stubbed it out on the multi-cracked pavement with the heel of her long, black stiletto. What on earth had possessed her to wear these uncomfortable shoes, anyway? she asked herself, with more than the usual tinge of frustration and self-loathing. After all she hadn't even planned on stepping inside the chapel, or indeed within the walled confines of the hill-cemetery later on, where Sam's crumbling body - his, by now, long disjointed and overly poked-over corpse - would soon be lowered down and buried in the good Welsh earth for the second sad time in almost forty years.

A young couple - the first fruits of the congregation's impending mass-exit - idled out of the wooden double-doors, skirted the surrounding wall, and rounded the corner in search of their tightly-parked transport, while two teenage girls, arm-in-arm, in white blouses and black, pleated trousers, dashed between passing cars to cross the main road towards where Anne stood. 'Don't go getting yourself killed mow, Megan!' one screamed, hurrying back to the middle of the carriage-way so as to grasp the hand of her far less lissom companion, and pull her, rather grudgingly, to the welcome safety of the opposite footpath.

For fear they might recognise her, and perhaps report her presence over tea and sandwiches to the assembled family at the customary post-funeral gathering, Anne ducked inside her car, nimbly shifted her bottom across to the driver's seat, and switched on the engine. Glancing in the mirror at the ageing face she had made up as best she could that morning, Anne soon became aware of someone knocking feebly at the window on the passenger-side of the vehicle. On looking out, she saw that it was one of the two young girls. Anne froze for an instant, but a second bout of knocking finally persuaded her to reach down to her lap and press the black, plastic button that would gradually lower a steamy window to the world.

'You couldn't take us to the cemetery could you, lady?' the pretty girl enquired, her companion's head turned away in apparent shame. 'I can see from how you're dressed that you must be going there yourself, yes?'

Anne thought for a moment, then let the two girls inside. 'Of course. It's the least I can do,' she told them, realising in an instant what else her words might indicate in a different context, and how, for her own tortured mind, this was an absolute truth, and something which might yet assuage a tiny portion of the guilt she had always felt, that she had mercilessly killed a man, and had knowingly buried the guilt of it far deeper than his own broken body would soon be plunged. Out of sight, out of mind, she had many times been wont to tell herself comfortingly; and, hopefully, still out of all suspicion too, she reflected. Anne reversed her car into an adjoining street, regained the main road, and drove away north, the glowing outline of the Brecon Beacons soon supplying a sudden, glorious backdrop, to her mind a glowing halo, for her first, and perhaps, solitary act of propitiation.

'I could kill for a fag, Megan,' the bottle-blond girl in the back of the car suddenly exclaimed. Open-mouthed, Anne held on steadily to the driving-wheel with her right hand, and, to the evident satisfaction of both girls, adeptly flicked open a packet of Silk-Cut with her left.

'Should I lower the window again?' the girl called Megan enquired from the passenger-seat, turning now to glance side-long at Anne's thin, lined, and too heavily blusher-ed face.

'No - that's O.K. You only live once, right?' replied Anne. She pursed her lips and decided not to even contemplate this, her second, incongruous comment in minutes. 'Say - can you light me one?' she asked her young companion. 'Funerals do make you tense, I always feel.'

'Sure thing,' the girl in the back replied. 'We might as well all go together, right, Megan?'

The tea and sandwiches had finally all been snatched up and consumed, the cups and plates washed and stacked to drain in the enamel sink of the back-kitchen, and all the family-members and other assembled guests had long gone home. Weary from the day's activities, and reluctant to socialise any longer, I once again found myself hidden away upstairs, and trawling through the swirling ocean of my sad remembrance: '*My Back Pages*,' my namesake, and one time hero, Bobby had called them, and so, naturally, I felt so inclined, at least mentally, to title them also.

I scanned the tiny thumbnail square that featured my ten-year, curly, fair, bespectacled face. The rumours that had swept the school back then, though denied by me repeatedly, (and too often over-vigorously,) were indeed true: I had indeed been named after a poet. And yet in my terrible teens I chose to be somewhat economical with the truth, denied my classmates' assertions as bogus, and, instead, elected to re-brand myself after the world's greatest living songwriter. That was cooler by far, I judged back then, in what were labelled '*the swinging sixties*.' And anyway, my conscience could scarcely be pricked by doing something that few could claim a fallacious act in one so tender in years - I was barely twelve, after all, and still in the formative stages of honing and fine-tuning my, as yet, unripe skills of self-delusion and fraud.

Names and their meanings were so crucial to a boy's image and self-worth back then, I recalled, and indeed, to my mind, seemed more than half the battle. Although I had read and enjoyed much of the great dead poet's written work, the brilliant, crinkly-haired, though pug- nosed, and invariably monochrome, smoking bard had fortunately looked nothing at all like me, I judged, and so, understandably, I therefore felt no desire whatsoever to ape him or any of his curious mannerisms, whatever they might have been.

But the other Dylan, well, he was a different matter completely, I judged. Yes. I felt sure that I could take on his mantle as lightly and as carelessly as he himself had done, and, likewise, amble nimbly through the slushy, Buick-strewn streets of New York and New Jersey, or, in my case perhaps, nearby Newport and Newbridge with the best of them, armed, if not with a guitar-case, then perhaps with a portable typewriter clutched securely in my right hand.

Yes, the two great men's names were the same, and I cannot deny that I went on to find each of their unique creative spirits inspiring, but I quickly realised that the name Arthur Dylan Thomas Cook was one that was as likely to set me travelling as writing, as my father Derek's parents were often keen to inform me. And indeed, largely by way of hitched motorway rides and the occasional coach, to Cardiff, London, and other great cities much farther afield, it certainly had done, but then again, one might say that *by train* it brought me right back down to earth again.

'*Bobby,*' the girls in County School had called me - two rude sisters from Pant '*Bobby Shafto,*' even. But the boys all called me '*Cooksy,*' naturally - '*Crafty Cooksy*' the bolder, meaner ones preferring. And '*The Prophet Elisha,*' one thin, swatty lad called Delwyn, with a squished nose and no front teeth, announced one time to all and sundry on the school-bus back home. I raised my fist, and studied again the small scar on my middle knuckle – an indelible testimony, both to the times, and to the deplorable quality of dentistry in The Valleys back then. Delwyn had earned the surname '*Dentures*' soon after that I recalled, and, yes, his renaming had caused me pain.

But it was not his classmates that the hapless Delwyn snarled at in the school-photograph I now held in my fingers, but in the general direction of the camera-man, for whose class-portrait we had grouped together in the July of 1966, in four shambling, tiered rows erected on the bare, grit-strewn, white-lined yard, long since gone, where nowadays stood a peaceful, tree-studded, memorial garden, within which, in pride of place, was the plaque that Queen Elizabeth herself had travelled all the way there to unveil, amidst those all too familiar, grey perimeter-walls.

My bent knees trembled from a combination of the cold and their cramped position on the thinly carpeted floor, but I was determined to remain there for as long as I could manage, or at least until I felt I had done service to the tender, but bitter-sweet, memories I still retained. Holding up the larger, creased, landscape black-and-white snap at an acute angle so as to view it in the final, faint light from the setting sun that now flared orange and dying through the bedroom window, my weary eyes darted left and right along the four separate tiers of laughing, smiling faces. Then my gaze paused at each one if only to judge whether that particular dead child could relate to me his, or her, personal tale of smothered hope and starved ambition.

'Brenda, Byron, Stephen - oh, and there's Anne!' I proclaimed joylessly. At every fleeting glance I somehow felt I could still make out the echoing voice that each hair-blown child sang out in its high, shrill, dutiful reply. *'Present, Sir.'* And, stranger yet, it now almost seemed as if I myself were our dear, departed Mr. Jones, undertaking the banal, twice-daily ritual that was our registration. 'Arthur Cook? Are you listening, boy?' 'Yes Sir!' 'Well, why don't you answer me, then?' 'Because -' 'Yes? Yes - Cook! Out with it, lad!' 'Because - because you're dead, Sir! No offence intended, you understand.' 'And none taken, neither, boy,' the balding, suited, old form-tutor seemed to reply from his grave, his thick, square glasses gleaming in the morning light.

My eyes welled still further as I realised with astonishment how the names of each and every one of my classmates were as clearly etched in my memory today as they were still on that broad, grey, weathered, slate-stone tribute that sat within the hillside shrine, less than four short miles from where I now bent kneeling in remembrance of it.

Not that *everyone* died in the tragedy, of course. I recalled how quite a lot of the children survived the turgid, black torrent that ploughed down the mountain on that fateful day, and somehow, to my mind quite miraculously, went on to live lives that mattered, that counted for something, and who even managed to enrich the lives of other, more fortunate, souls, who resided worlds away from the unfortunate Merthyr Valley, as well as, of course, the lives of their living contemporaries who still resided here, and who shared many of the same desperate memories that they did.

And yes, that certainly included me, of course, I mused, smiling. I had escaped Aberfan in a physical sense, even though I freely admit that, in the emotional sense, I had found it impossible to fully break out and flee the deep-clefted slough of despond that my brother and I were born into, and that, alive and kicking, I was plainly still heir to. Although dead today, Sam was, thank God, very much alive on that sombre day, I recalled - that wet and dreary Friday shortly after he turned thirteen, when he was given permission by the teachers of the grammar-school he attended to return to his junior-school, and share with its pupils and teachers alike his experiences; the week-day morn he dragged me out by my heels from under a steaming, lifeless, unimaginably putrid mire of saturated carbon, coal-grit, crushed glass and leaves, that my choking, fast-expiring brain must have already begun to feel surprisingly at home in.

Shivering suddenly at the lucidity of my recollection, I got to my feet and buttoned up my suit-jacket, then slipped the photograph back into its plastic cover once again. I swayed to the right, and, immobilised with cramp, fell sideways onto the bed, where I lay back and recalled how Sam and I, like two overgrown moles blessed with sudden sight, had gripped hands and clambered through a shattered, pane-less window, then trudged through a school-yard we had formerly loved and knew so well, yet now found unaccountably lain waste, and as alien to us as the surface of Titan. Our filthy, clutched hands once again slipped apart, I recalled how we had scrambled unsteadily and erratically over twisted benches and milk-crates, dustbin lids and school-bags, all seemingly afloat, yet unmoving, in what resembled, to my young and demented mind at least, a fast-setting sea of dark-chocolate slurry.

Clambering up Sam's bent back, and, seconds later, perched alongside him atop a fractured, stone wall, to the door-stepping wives of Moy Road I feel sure we most have resembled a pair of ragged chimney-sweeps bent on escaping from the slavery of some dank, grey Victorian manor.

'Hey! You boys get down off there!' I recalled one woman had shouted. 'Head for the hills, you guys!' she might have better advised us, as John Wayne or The Lone Ranger would surely have commanded to camera in similar circumstances. And so we two shabby cow-pokes tumbled onto the flag-stoned pavement, leapt quickly to our feet, and dashed headlong for home - our haven of love and hope, in a sloping, terraced row, thankfully spared from that sad, Michaelmas-Term sacrifice, or retribution perhaps, delivered upon us innocent children and teachers by that cold, wet, coal-black, low-sweeping, Passover angel.

Yes, my saviour angel that day had been Sam. I rolled my head over on the pillow and closed my eyes, and recalled how, one Saturday afternoon in the autumn of '69, and the

South African rugby team having arrived in Swansea, he and I had gone along together to see the controversial, 'all-white' representative side take on the city's best. Grasping a half-time pasty in my left hand and a plastic cup of hot tea in the other, I recalled having had to jump back a step or two so as to dodge the duffle-coated torso of a young, bespectacled student in a multi-striped scarf being cruelly tossed over the railings towards us, and then how Sam had soon after dried my clothes and even retrieved my flying pasty for me. The timid, try-less game may have tottered to a close that day, I recalled, but my own conversion seemed bang on target, as was Sam's; our political senses becoming pricked and transformed in little more than a flash.

If, as many claim, the seeds of future events are carried within ourselves, then surely the truth about the past is to be found in the writings recorded by us all back then. I quickly thumbed through the pages of my one and only remaining diary from the time. With a sharp intake of breath I saw that the final words I had recorded inside it were written in red ink, and so was hesitant to turn over the final page and read what, if anything, I might have followed it with. Instead I quickly thumbed back to page-one. '1964!' That obviously explained the diary's unusual thickness, I mused: it was a five-year one, of course. I hesitated a moment yet still flicked over the pages to 'October 1966.' I noted how most slots on the double-pages lacked an entry of any kind. Then on the 21st stood a single word - Disaster! And on the 22nd. three solitary phrases - 'Yet more rain,' 'Toll rises,' and, finally, 'Clearing up will most likely take forever.' A future historian would most probably have surmised that the school's drains had flooded, and so might never have guessed the truth: the tragic truth that 144 young children and their teachers had perished while seated in pairs at their oak-hewn, ink-welled desks, in what transpired to be their terminal head-count in this life, but doubtless their initial registration in the next.

Once the only town of any notable size in Wales - in industrial terms its very capital - Merthyr Tydfil has a history based upon iron, steam-coal and trains. Having travelled far and wide, I knew only too well how so few people outside Wales were aware that the first steam train ever to run on rails ('*The Penydarren Locomotive*') was built in Merthyr, and, in 1804 - little more than a year before the Battle of Trafalgar, in fact, and fully eight years prior to the more famous run of George Stephenson's '*Rocket*' - had rattled along on its iron track, and, carrying a cargo of iron southwards along the sinuous Taff Valley, reached a point almost halfway to distant Cardiff. It is said that the local people were so terrified at the train's shuddering, steam-shrouded passing that they turned aside to shield their eyes and scurried rapidly for cover, whereas some braver-hearted folk chanced their arms, and their lives no doubt, and boldly leapt aboard its veritable 'caravan' of jangling trucks for what would prove to be '*the journey of a lifetime.*'

The actual steam-engine, both built and driven by the pioneering engineer Richard Trevithick, and ably assisted by skilled, local engineer Rees Jones, is believed by many to have long lain buried in the sloping ground at Penydarren, very close to the site of the old ironworks, where every one of its metal parts, and also the prototype, black rails that it ran upon, were forged.

Very well acquainted, as I recall I was in my teens, with the major facts of both transport development and local history, and having learned everything there was to know about the historic event itself, I can remember venturing to the location alone one late-October night, the small spade and rock-hammer in my shoulder-bag being the solitary tools that I took with me with which I planned to unearth history.

I was filled with high hopes of a monumental discovery only to find myself ambushed and chased away by a gang of boys from Trevithick Street, who, it appeared, were convinced I was trying to raid items from their planned, and already towering, bonfire. Indeed the monstrous tyre that overtook me and, thundering by, almost flattened me, as I sprinted for my life down the steep, grassy slope towards the Morlais Brook, I took to be a staple component of the same, and one of several that the Penydarren gang had clearly stolen from the nearby bus-garage in order to fuel their intended Guy Fawkes' conflagration.

In the welcome twilight I managed to escape their clutches, but, while joyously scampering off in the direction of Penyard, I only succeeded in walking right into the arms of the very first girl that I ever truly came to care dearly for. Gwen, the small, dusky, brown-eyed beauty told me her name was. I told her that mine was Rod - it wasn't, obviously - but I found it seemed to matter little in the long run. So thoroughly captivated was I with this strange, new creature that it was hardly surprising that we teamed up, and spent a couple of winter months in each other's company, celebrating together Hallowe'en, Bonfire Night, then Christmas and the New Year.

But contact between us understandably began to wither when the schools went back after the break, and the nightly grind of Grammar-School homework began to kick in once again, and then suddenly ceased altogether when I discovered, quite by chance, that she and her family had moved to live further up the valley. Yet, unbeknown to the pair of us, our paths were happily destined to cross once again as adults, and that resulting from her husband's untimely, and quite unexpected, disappearance.

March brown set in soon after four in the afternoon, and by five had already climbed down the flocked paper that was beginning to peel off the cold bedroom's walls. Outside the picture-window darkness gradually overtook the pavements, and began to isolate the street-lamps that lined the inhabited, living side of Cemetery Road.

Winter was almost behind us once again, thank-fully it had proved a far from harsh one, even by modern-day standards, and very unlike any that I had known as a boy. I well recalled how winter days appeared to be far longer back then, how their water-channels and rain-gutters seemed always to be brimming, and dangerously poised for overflow, their winds stronger and more blustery, their snow blizzards thicker and more fierce, their frosts keener than grief.

I turned over once again and lay on my side, shut my eyes, and allowed myself to scamper back through my book of memories to the front-door of our tiny, terraced cottage in the early morning, where my first task before school had always been to bring in the milk. I recalled how the glass bottles deposited on our door-steps at the passing of the horse-drawn cart seemed always to crack and spill their cream with the very first snows; the drifts outside our door invariably letter-box deep and largely impassable, and the folded *Daily Herald*, hanging from its draughty, metal opening, either dripped with the moisture of the falling snowflakes, or was completely sodden through.

It was in that same little house in Aberfan that my grandfather Charlie had finally succumbed to the extremes of a dour, ash-flicked life and died. The second stroke in as many years had already knocked out his respiratory centre and left his right side paralysed. Everyone in the street was aware that he was barely able to speak, or even open his eyes, although they knew he could still hear our tearful voices, and could yet still move the calloused fingers of his left hand, that once could strum a banjo of a Saturday night in *The Mackintosh, The Labour Club* and *The Cardigan Arms* in Dowlais with the very best of them.

I recalled how, on what proved to be his final evening among us, I had detected a blackened hole in the thumb-nail of his rigid right hand that I strangely sensed would now lack the time necessary to work its way out, however many hours or days he might have remaining, and however much longer after death a dead man's nails were said to continue to grow. And I fondly remembered too how, at the end of that long night, and barely minutes before the welcome sunrise, I felt moved to lean across the blood-stained and phlegm-encrusted pillow to caress his furrowed brow, only to find that his temple was already as cold as the corrie-d, mountain-ice on nearby *Pen-y-Fan*.

My dearest Grandad, (whom we all lovingly addressed as *Dad-cu,*) had breathed his last in those early hours before school began, and so had left me - his youngest grandson, and his ofttimes acolyte - to spit and cough and curse away the day on his behalf, and to poach and proffer, pilfer and plunder, and, as was his wont to do before me, walk the weary world of Wales alone.

I stood up and walked across to the window of the room, and gazed out across the narrow road to the broad side-gate of the cemetery just as its janitor Ivor Coles locked it up for the night with his great, clinking bunch of keys that your average cat-burglar might have given up his fence for. The vast grave-yard's narrow, dusky lane ran on up the hill to where Sam's recently re-opened, and now, once again, refilled, and bouquet-strewn grave lay, just a few feet at most from the stony path, as well as to those other, more monumental mounds and memorials that housed, now and forever, the remains of many of my former family-members, among them my own dear mother.

My mind drifted back just six or seven hours this time, to the moment when I had bent my back up there to scatter a handful of soil atop Sam's coffin for the second time in almost forty years. A crowd of friends and relations had stood around in black attire, accompanied by the odd local journalist, who had more than likely been required to attend purely on account of the very unusual nature of the interment.

I had watched a group of starlings swoop down on a colony of hapless insects, that were understandably oblivious to their lack of camouflage, as they ventured out of the grass-verge and across the grey, tarmacadam lane. And it was back down this same lane, towards the hill-top home in which I now stood, that we had all either driven or strolled, after paying our last respects to my dead brother, before taking time to acknowledge, and tearfully embrace, those distant relatives who had, by now, become almost strangers to us all. having travelled there from as far flung locations as West Wales and England, and so needed to leave early in order to get home again the same day.

The scene from my window was now one of supreme stillness and peace, with just the rising, yellow moon to light up the vast, undulating field of death that for many years now

I had, through my second marriage to my darling Gwen, elected to live alongside. The eerie creaking of the gate, as it was dragged to in Ivor Coles' iron grip, and the horrible clunk of its ultimate closure, saw no one running towards it this evening, I mused, in their desperate efforts to escape the embarrassing predicament of another dreaded lock-in. And yet I felt sure I could still glimpse one solitary figure in the far distance, making her stooping way from the site of my brother's grave, and gracelessly stumbling away in the direction of the narrow, precipitous path that led down to the furthermost gate of the cemetery - still as yet unchained - and near which I felt sure her VW Passat must be parked.

I strained my weak eyes to the limit in my efforts to be sure. The great shadow cast by the March murmur of starlings, continually circling and folding around itself overhead, did little to assist me, but I opened up the window and, with field-glasses in hand, persisted. Yes, it was one of Sam's killers all right, I told myself, in fact the very one I had at one time loved and lain with, at a time when we had each found ourselves released from the precepts of first-marriage, and whom, at the time, I had unexpectedly put in the family-way. And then, again with the aid of my trusty binoculars, I was finally able to satisfy myself that, alone and under cover of semi-darkness, and clearly in shame for what she had done, the very first female friend I had ever known had returned at long last to her victim's grave, and, much like the money spider I had witnessed in church that morning, was now creeping her weary way home again.

CHAPTER 2

'Bye, Anne! I'll be back after the staff-meeting. Around five, I expect.'

Hearing no hint of the expected reply, Drew slammed the front-door and, package tucked tightly under his arm, walked down the path to his BMW, spinning round briefly, keys in hand, so as to take in a full, sweeping view of the empty terraced-house that stood next door to his own. He noticed how the letter-box was now even more jammed full of mail than it had been the last time he had looked, and he silently told himself that he would need to go up the path and force it all inside again, either that evening when he returned, or, at the latest, the following day.

Drew hurled the clump of string-tied sketch-books into the car's leather back-seat, followed by his empty looking brief-case, climbed inside, tilted down, then, (spying his brown eyes looking back at him,) re-set to its default position the broad rear-view mirror, and switched on the ignition. The tones of Roy Orbison's *'Candy Man'* rang out to dispel the morning-fog, and disrupt, for just a second or two, the wondrous, trilling song of the tree-dwelling blue tits and robins that, unlike Drew and his wife of fifteen years, were the rightful residents, the legitimate owner-occupiers you could say, of this, most southerly, quarter of Powys - or *Breconshire*, as it was more familiarly known in those parts - the rural, relatively peaceful, and ofttimes glorious, upper reaches of the largely urban and industrial Taff Vale.

Smoothing down flat with his long, thin fingers what little remained of the curly, fair locks, that had for decades crowned, if not adorned, his pronounced, tanned forehead,

Drew donned his brown-tinted driving-glasses and instantly felt himself once again. With a firmly depressed, right, leather lace-up he accelerated his much cherished, three-litre saloon-car down the hill, and away from the short row of terraced homes that sat adjacent to his own. The loud, booming blast from the vehicle's double-exhaust duct belched out a swirling cloud of gas and steam that raised a thick layer of dust from the crevasses in the carriageway and adjoining pavement, and rattled the tall, slanted estate-agent's *'SOLD'* sign, which stood, forlornly flapping like a cardboard flag of surrender, pinned for dear life to the wooden fence that fronted the house next to his own.

Within seconds Drew had sped past the village-sign that read *'Glo-Ar-Ol,'* and rounded the hair-pin bend which led one down alongside a fenced-off tract of the precipitous valley-side and towards the old, stone bridge that traversed the river's torrential waterfall, and which bore almost as many cracks in its grey walls as it did limestone blocks. One of the largest and most conspicuous of these cracks, Drew recalled, as he changed down into first-gear, happened to have been of his own creation, and this painfully embarrassing recollection swiftly caused him to grimace, just as it had done on virtually every previous morning of his working life.

Window agape, Drew coasted silently towards the bridge so that he could listen to the gushing sound of the river's youthful torrent, with its many-pooled cataract, that flowed in the deep gash beneath its ancient, limestone structure. Once the sleek, black body of his BMW had slid through the tight gap and then rounded the right-hand bend at a snail's pace, Drew kept the car in low gear, and then, foot down, thrust it powerfully up the steep incline of the opposing valley-side, past the solitary cottage, whose exterior wall was the road's kerbside, thrashing it on through the rising hair-pins in much the same way that he believed he had seen the great Sebastien Loeb do one school-day morning a year or so before, most probably on his way to the *Spar Shop* or *Asda* for an early snack, before returning to his check-point in the mountain forests just north of there, and resuming his quest for yet another *World Rally Championship*.

Leaving the gaping limestone-quarry, and the even loftier ruins of the hill-top Norman castle, behind, and to his left, Drew now caught sight of the rising sun for the first time that morning, and felt, as in recent times he frequently did, that the day ahead would be the thrilling Thursday that thankfully followed what had, yet again, been another woeful Wednesday. At last changing up into fourth, Drew took the bull by the horns and shot past a line of four or five aged, shaggy sheep that were approaching, single-file, where a footpath might one day be constructed, no doubt returning from some late-night watering hole, or perhaps another rough night on the town. Drew smiled proudly at his anthropomorphic conception as he coasted his car down the gentler slope towards inhabited Wales again - to his mind the world of worries and work, yet, for the vast and growing minority in the Kingdom of Coalition, the land of the enveloping dole-queue.

But for Drew Cillick the world that his gleaming chariot was fast approaching was a world of teaching and learning, of classroom celebrity and staff-room stardom. At *Pennant Comprehensive* he felt he had found the very medium in which to glean for himself a large portion of what his wife and two children no longer gave him - an untainted self-image of wisdom and grace, the garnished status of a minor icon, and, more vitally in recent years, a necessary reason to simply go on living. No longer, Drew mused, would he permit himself to feel like a piece of paper that had once had coherent writing on it, but had since been through the wash.

As he sped along the hill-road within sight of the cemetery wherein his former college-friend's recently exhumed, and now re-interred, body now lay finally at peace, Drew changed down and slowed his comfortable, gleaming car to a crawl. He then closed his eyes, (as he didn't even realise he had been doing twice-daily for some considerable time now,) and once again asked the God he didn't even believe existed to forgive both him and his second wife Anne for their cruel and callous murder, almost forty years before, of poor, unfortunate Sam Cook.

The purple-tinged panoply of the three major peaks of *The Brecon Beacons* had by now become clearly visible through the broad, curtained picture-window of Anne's large lounge. Outside it a bright orange helicopter, with the loud, incessant buzz of a furious hornet, suddenly swooped low overhead, scattering the morning's songbirds from the very branches of the trees they nested in. Through the open door to the adjoining room, Anne watched, blinking, and quite horrified at the sight. She then moved in quickly from the kitchen, carrying in her slender, bare arms a bright-yellow breakfast-tray, on which she had carelessly, but understandably, spilt a little of the cereal milk on hearing the cursed rotor-blades sweeping nearer once again, and, with a deafening hum, shuddering the very walls of her precious, much loved, country home.

'Chris!' Anne shouted at the top of her voice. 'Chris! It's time for school, you know. Come on now, there's a good boy. You know, my lad, I wouldn't be surprised if that orange thing flying around outside wasn't one of those new-fangled drones sent out to check up on you, because - well because I'm sure I couldn't see any driver.'

A five second pause, during which both mother and teenage son separately contemplated this, then the boy replied weakly from his bedroom upstairs, 'But Mam - can't I go in tomorrow?'

'You'll be there again tomorrow, my lad,' replied his mother. 'Don't you worry about that now. Because I'm certainly not having the nonsense we had last term, I can tell you.' Quieter this time, and to herself, 'Bullying, indeed. The size on the boy!'

'They're homophobic, I tell you,' her son announced.

'Huh! No more than you are, my lad,' she responded with a shake of her pretty head.

'What!' he cried. 'But you know I'm gay, Mam. Didn't I tell you already?'

'Yeah. And so was Henry Tudor I heard. But that never stopped him, the old goat.' Then more quietly to herself, 'Last term it was his weight, and now it's his - his orientation.'

'You shouldn't make fun, Mam,' she heard her son complain. 'Really, you shouldn't.'

'Don't you remember your Dad telling you how he went through the same baloney when he was your age?' she told him. 'It's only natural for a growing boy, after all. He had a crush on loads of his teachers, he told us. Especially that shaggy-maned Music master with the curly-handled cane and the strange penchant for pentatonics and Percy Grainger.'

'Mam - listen!' Chris went on. 'Is that why you - why you cane Drew some nights?'

'What was that!' Anne yelled out, staring, open-mouthed, at the ceiling that separated them.

'I'm never asleep before midnight, you know,' he countered.

'Don't be a silly billy,' Anne called out, eyes wide. 'Your Dad deserves to get his bottom smacked every so often. He can be a very naughty man you know.' Her eyes lit up. 'One time he even chased me right the way round - anyway, never you mind about all that. Say - are you coming downstairs today or what? Daddy Drew must have gone off to work almost an hour ago.'

To the accompaniment of feet banging on the ceiling, Anne heard her son demand, 'Mam, why do you call him that?'

'You mean Drew?' she replied. 'Because it's his name, of course, dear. Drew. Though I admit it's incredibly comical, given his job I mean. But there again I suppose we both have odd names, don't we? My middle name is Florence, for all the good it's ever done me at *The Willows*.'

Anne's son Chris suddenly walked into the room, still dressed in his black dressing-gown and pyjamas, his dark hair a-frazzle. 'I don't mean *Drew*, Mam - I mean *Dad*. Why do you say that?'

Anne turned and looked at her teenage son askance. Her blue eyes suddenly flared. 'Look, we had all that out last week, didn't we?' She handed the boy a comb. 'Get your blazer and jeans on, and - and get to school right now!'

'Oh, but Mam, can't you drive me?' he pleaded, dragging the comb across his head.

Anne banged her little fists down on the table, and turned and stared straight at him.

At this Chris turned his whole body away from her. 'O.K., O.K. Just don't spear me again with those - those scary eyes you've got, please, Mam.'

'Whatever do you mean?' Anne asked him, first scowling, then smiling thinly. 'Drew is always saying how he loves my blue eyes. They're beautiful, he's always telling me. And *he* should know if anyone should. Artists know what beautiful things look like, don't they?'

'Well, not all of them,' put in Chris. '*He* certainly doesn't, for a start. Didn't he tell you he had to go to *Specsavers* last Saturday? I bet he didn't, did he, Mam?'

'*Specsavers!*' exclaimed Anne.

'That's what I said,' Chris told her. 'And when he was there guess who he bumped into?'

'Oh, I don't know,' his mother replied, plainly alarmed at this news. 'Who?'

'Everybody,' Chris told with a laugh. 'Get it?' The boy swiftly ducked and turned away as Anne picked up an apple from the table and hurled it at him, but only succeeded in striking the sofa. Then, recalling something, she ran towards the sofa and reached behind it for the cane she always kept there, and, bending it adroitly between her hands like a practised school-master, proceeded to chase her son out of the room with it, and back again up the carpeted stairs.

Dressed in skinny, black jeans, black trainers and a black fleeced-jacket, Chris, walked out of his end-of-terraced house and slammed the front-door behind him in his customary, care-free fashion. He suddenly halted on the footpath and watched, intrigued, as a large furniture-van slowed down, then pulled up in the road outside. Chris pulled the gate shut behind him, and, after spinning round a few times to take in the unexpected scene, he began to walk off briskly in the direction of a pretty, red-haired girl in full school-uniform, who, having just climbed out of a battered, old car, now stood further down the road, clearly waiting for him. Chris approached and kissed the girl on the neck, patted her bottom affectionately, and shouldered her bulging school-bag for her.

The pair then walked off together, hand-in-hand, as happy as two young larks.

From the front-bedroom window above and behind them, Anne watched on like a hawk. She was no less intrigued than her son was at the large van that now sat, parked, outside in the road. Suddenly the orange helicopter began returning, and very soon, whirring as loudly as before, hovered overhead, scattering loose leaves and twigs all around. Anne felt compelled to shut out the noise which had interfered with her subtle act of spying, and, after reaching up and slamming the window, and setting the catch, she quickly moved back a little from the glass, and watched the developing action from behind the safety of a thin, red-flowered curtain.

Anne soon hurried downstairs and went into the front-parlour, believing that this might be a much better vantage-point from which to view and assess the new arrivals, whom she felt would most likely turn out to be her new neighbours. But her decision was sadly the wrong one, as she found she was now only able to make out the hats and caps of the three men above the flat summit of the hedge, one of whom was clearly just the driver, and another his removals-assistant. Straining now on tiptoe, Anne longed to see a female head appear, but, gaze as hard as she dare, there didn't appear to be one. Oh, dear, she thought, surely it wasn't going to be a single male resident again, like the last but one gentleman they had had, she mused unhappily, grimacing at the despondent memory she still harboured of the wheel-chair bound sergeant who had got injured in Iraq, and who had had to go off to Cardiff for the more constant care she had always known he desperately required. Decent and friendly though he was, this was no place for Sergeant O'Keefe or for any of his solitary, secluded kind, she told herself.

Minutes later, dressed now with just an unbuttoned grey macintosh covering her navy-blue uniform, Anne shut tight and locked her blue front-door and walked hesitantly down the flag-stoned path. Conscious all of a sudden that she might be being watched from the neighbouring house, she thought better of peering over the adjoining hedge, and instead, closing the gate on the latch, she approached her small red Nissan Micra that sat parked at the kerbside, and, after depositing her bag on its passenger-seat, she climbed inside, belted herself in securely, started the engine, and, after gazing briefly into the rear-view mirror, drove cautiously away.

The noise of the car's engine still audible in the distance, an old, white-haired man, clearly waiting for Anne to leave, suddenly emerged from his new front-door, tipped over to the ground the 'Sold' sign that stood right beside it, and spun round to confront the set of a dozen or so cardboard boxes that still remained to be carried into the house, and which had been left scattered over his crazy paving by the disappointingly lazy, now departed, removals-men.

With the largest of the boxes in his arms, the old man forced the door open wide with a knee, and walked, with stumbling gait, into a hall-way that was still bestrewn with a multitude of junk advertising-bills and letters. Some minutes later, and noticeably wearied by the task-in-hand, he returned outside to collect the next box. It was clearly going to be a taxing day for the elderly gent, and it wasn't long before he took out a large white handkerchief from his trousers-pocket in order to wipe away the beads of sweat that were already covering his wrinkled forehead. The old man's keen blue eyes scanned once again the exterior scene around him, although there now seemed little for him to take in, apart from the surrounding hedges and his new, sparse front-garden, which at first sight seemed to comprise little more than two large mounds of dry, brown soil and an assortment of small, coarse-grained stones.

'Old red sandstone,' the old man mumbled to himself, dipping his head briefly to examine by sight and by trembling hand the debris scattered beneath him. 'And limestone too, of course. In fact some *Lithostrotion*, if I'm not mistaken,' he continued, his mouth falling open, his blue eyes flashing. 'And *Lonsdaleia floriformis* in the coarser rocks. Mm, now that's very interesting, that is.'

The elderly gent straightened up once again and folded the handkerchief he held into squares, then slipped it back into the pocket of his trousers, and approached, with due trepidation, a particularly large box of clothes and folded curtains that lay beside the door-step, its bundled contents now, at least partially, spilled out onto the footpath. He moved to the side, looked up, then rubbed his coarsely-veined hand across a stone tablet attached to the house-wall, around five or so feet off the ground, and that once had clearly displayed a house-name that was no longer there. '*Coral*, I think I shall call it,' he announced proudly to himself. '*Coral,* yes. After the first dog we ever owned. Our family's prize Springer Spaniel. Oh, there's lovely you were, girl.'

Deep within the slate-grey shadows of the unlit, and relatively dingy, Art Room, Drew was sitting in his favourite, black swivel-chair, and with his black, leather shoes perched high before him on his paint-stained, brown, wooden desk. The finest examples of his students' paintings adorned the three, otherwise bare, pastel-painted walls that enclosed him, along with several of the most vibrant and colourful fruits of his own imagination, so fashioning a working space which, but for the rows of tables that comprised its production-line, seemed to resemble some cavernous, neglected store-room, largely abandoned and rarely illumined, perhaps somewhere deep within the bowels of London's *Tate Gallery* itself.

Sipping coffee from a large mug, and taking occasional mouthfuls from a buttered-bun which was filled to over-flowing with red salmon, the Head of Art at Pennant Comp. sat reading the day's *Guardian*. Swaying back and forth, he happily sniggered away at the many stories he read reported in it, and which, to his mind, succeeded only in illustrating how futile were the efforts of politicians and salaried officials to pronounce their wisdom on behalf of the very people who had elected, and so chosen, to employ them, yet who only managed to convince everyone of the fact that they acted very largely out of gratuitous self-interest, if not from wanton arrogance.

'*Coalition*, indeed,' the seated man announced scornfully, 'What coalition?'

Drew then laughed loudly at the thought that suddenly entered his clever, energetic brain. 'All they are is a temporary, make-shift government, already Con-Dem-ned as much in aspiration as in name.' He read on a little. 'God! And *we* all thought Thatcher was bad!' Shaking his head in disbelief, he folded the paper over, removed his new, round reading-glasses, then sat back and began singing a song out loud, 'The first cut is the deepest - baby I know.' He chuckled once again on hearing the odd pitch and tone of his lowest note, then continued, 'The first cut is the -'

Suddenly his step-son Chris walked in to the room, and picked up off the desk and rudely donned Drew's new glasses. Then taking a harmonica out of the man's jacket-pocket, he began playing a piercing and rather raucous blues-riff that, in key and genre, failed utterly to match its original.

'Do you mind, young man! Can't you see I'm having my break,' Drew told him firmly, dragging from a cigarette, then laying it back in its former, tilted position in a small, discoloured, white saucer on the corner of his desk.

'Morning, Drew,' Chris replied flippantly, then choosing to play two bars or so of '*Mercy*.'

'Oh, I see. So *Dad* is defunct these days, then,' his step-father replied dispassionately. 'Well, if you wish, Chris – if you wish. Anything to minimise family discord, that's what I say. What can I do for you, er…son? Cigarette?'

'You are supposed to be a teacher, you know,' Chris told him, tossing the ill-fitting spectacles back onto the desk.

'I'll have you know I've been a teacher for thirty-six long years, young man,' Drew told him. 'Ten alone within this particular hub of learning - and I can honestly say that not once have I let rules interfere with my practices, or with any of my personal pleasures, however frowned upon they might be by those who, ever so lightly, grasp onto, and barely retain the reins of power.'

'Well, not by me,' his step-son told him. Chris took the burning cigarette from the saucer and inhaled deeply from it. The scrunched-up face he made betrayed his distaste.

'You! No, not by *you*, obviously,' Drew announced, snatching back the cigarette. 'Don't think I don't know about all that weed you used to horde up in our loft, young man. But don't concern yourself on that score. I wouldn't dream of ever telling your mum. Sorry - *Mammy*, I mean.' Chris watched as Drew calmly replaced the cigarette on the saucer. 'By the way, is there something I can do for you? I'm surprised you aren't outside searching for *Solaris* or *The Great Bear*.'

'In the daytime!' said Chris disdainfully. 'No. You should know - an old man has moved in next-door.'

'And?' Drew replied sharply. 'That would be er....Gerald Philips - History. Started Monday morning. New term - new teacher. Same ol' same ol'.'

Chris walked around and picked up a colourful poster that was lying on a table. '*Idle talk costs lives*,' he read out. 'No, I mean, at home. You know, on the other side of ours.'

'Really? Say - are you being serious?' Drew pursed his lips tightly. 'Oh, dear. Now I suppose I shall have to start keeping the music down.'

'Hey, isn't that funny?' exclaimed Chris, turning, his nut-brown eyes flashing at the seated man.

'What's funny?' asked Drew.

'I somehow feel that *I* should be the one to be saying that. About keeping the music down.'

'Mm. How droll,' his step-father replied. 'But that's not music you play, remember, Chris,' 'That's - that's battle-flack.'

'Oh, really? And your stuff is -'

'Cultural history, dear friend. Our musical heritage. World-spinning sounds. The music of the spheres.'

'Balls!' Chris responded, picking up and hurling a snapped crayon straight into the dust-bin.

'Balls. Spheres. Well, I suppose that's more or less the same thing, wouldn't you say?' Drew told him. 'You do possess *some* musical talent, at least, young man. But do you really think that without Miles there'd ever have been an Eminem or a Jay-Z or a - a Tinie Tempah, even?

'But what exactly is world-spinning about that trumpeter guy?' asked Chris. 'Was he Welsh?

'Who?' Drew asked.

'Miles Davis. He's not Carla Davies' dad, is he? Now there's a girl with awesome talent. *And* she's Welsh. *And* she attended this school for her last two years, I heard.'

'Well, that last part is true, at least. Her dad is a semi-local man, who, many years ago, sent her here from their home in *The Beacons*. Yes, she developed her talent in this valley, it's true, but the difference between her and Miles is colossal. Our Carla may have won herself a Brit, dear boy, but Miles Davis is international.' He spun round on his chair as if to emphasise the point, and depressed the switch on a tape-machine which stood, unevenly, on the shelf behind his desk.

'And dead,' Chris informed him bluntly.

'Well, yes. There is that, of course,' said Drew. 'But such is the way of the world, my boy. He's been gone for over twenty years now, but the music he made has a quality that will most likely last an eternity. You young chaps can learn a lot from this sort of music, you know. Take time out and listen. Hark!' Eyes closed and biting into his lower lip, Drew sat, clearly absorbed in listening attentively to the introduction to track-one. 'It's '*Kind Of Blue*,'' he told his son.

'Is it? Where on earth are you looking?' Chris asked him. 'Because I can't see anything.'

'The album,' said Drew. '*So What?*' That's the name of the tune you can hear, by the way. *So What?*'' He half-closed his brown eyes so that they vanished into the shadows of the lashes.

'My take, exactly. So what?' Chris sniggered, nevertheless imitating Drew's odd far-away look. 'You know, I think I'll stick to my own sounds, thanks anyway. But I guess you could always give your Miles a blast later tonight, if you like. To welcome our new neighbour to *Gloryhole*, I mean.'

'You know, I might just do that,' said Drew, smiling broadly. 'It's good to share, right?'

'That's what I always say,' the boy retorted smartly. Chris took two cigarettes from his step-dad's packet and walked off towards the door with them. From outside it Drew could hear the high voices of young children approaching down the corridor, and so quickly stubbed out the cigarette-end in the saucer alongside about four or five others that already lay there, curled-up, shrivelled and decaying. He picked up an open diary, and scanned it to ascertain which class it was that he was about to teach an Art lesson to, and walked over to the window and opened it as wide as it would go, then swishing the fetid air fiercely in a roughly horizontal plane with both of his arms.

Spinning round suddenly to face front, and inhaling deeply, Drew called out to the empty room. 'O.K., Seven-GD! Line up quietly!' He lifted from a table and wafted, with great, giant swoops, an enormous, closed drawing-pad, and then, somewhat languorously, approached the door. 'And I don't want anyone complaining about the window either. I have a feeling that that boy who just walked out may have been smoking a crafty fag, if I'm not mistaken. What do you think, Megan?'

The small, round, spotty, sweat-glistened faces of young girls and boys began to appear like unfolding, pink flowers in the doorway, awaiting now only the teacher's command to enter. The shrewd smirks and facial contortions, and the general boisterous laughter that ensued left none among them in any doubt as to who was, in fact, the true source of the still swirling cigarette-smoke and its abiding stench.

For Drew this was yet another daily occurrence of the ironical kind, which, as always, caused him to smile broadly with the inner satisfaction it supplied him. No. Rules or not, he would never have wanted it any other way. There were very few things in his life that he was ashamed of, after all, except perhaps the scratched, tin-banger which his wife drove, and which barely passed for a motor car, and the patched black jeans and jacket that his son wore; although, had he still been a sixth-former himself, Drew knew only too well that he would most probably have attired himself in much the same way, except that he would most probably have worn extended side-burns, as Bradley Wiggins now did, and donned a garish, pastel cravat, as was his custom back in the day.

As the slim, blue-blazered children finally entered the classroom, pushing and shoving each other playfully as they did so, and without fear of sanction, Drew smiled to himself, turned, and picked up two paint-brushes from a shelf and began beating out the time to the jazz music that still so joyfully filled his room. Yes, he still adored his job, he mused, and, despite its very many faults and failings, he even loved his present school. But strangest of all, and most probably since around the time that his wife had told him that their former college-friend Sam had been reburied the previous day in Pant Cemetery, Drew discovered that he was suddenly in love with life all over again.

CHAPTER 3

A divine, exquisite vision-in-blue to so many of its guests, Anne walked slowly into the lounge of 'The Willows Nursing Home' holding tightly, and with an acutely angled grip, the tremulous hand of a gentleman whose age was as deeply bewildering as his lop-sided hair-cut, his frayed, grey cotton-shirt, and the purple, round-necked jumper that hung loosely about his hips. Turning her body right round, Anne leaned down and fluffed for the aged man the cream, padded seat-cushion that lay there, then eased him back, gently and lovingly, into, what was for him, the deepest and most comfortable of easy-chairs.

'There you are, bach,' Anne told him tenderly. 'All fed and watered now, aren't we?'

'And by your almighty hand, isn't it, Annie love?' the old man replied swiftly, a wicked smile suddenly beaming across his rosy, glowing, but heavily wrinkled face. Anne shook her head with genuine pity, then picked up and held out a piece of cherry-cake for him to bite into. The man duly obliged, and, with the few teeth he still retained, carefully and methodically chewed every morsel of cherry, and every single crumb, until the cake was thoroughly devoured.

'Oh, you're such a flirt, Mervyn John,' Anne told him. 'Nobody would ever know you were ninety-six.'

'He's rude, he is,' the cardigan-clad dear sitting next to him suddenly announced through a stern and unforgiving expression that Anne recalled her own mother had worn for at least the last eight years of her fraught and beleaguered life. 'Isn't he, girls?' the old lady proceeded to ask her seated, similarly attired companions, many of whom were barely able to hear a single word of what the woman was saying, let alone comprehend it.

'I didn't mean it like that, Babs. Fair play, now,' Mervyn told the old woman apologetically, turning slowly to face her. 'Anyway, you know full well you'll always be the only bird for me, girl.'

'Oh, that's all right, then,' Babs responded, forcing a strange, coiled smile out between her hair-lined top lip and her grizzled chin. 'Though you won't get watered by me, that's for sure, Mervyn John, even though your hands are covered in psoriasis, and that English baggage Joycie on the night-shift might have slipped another one of them vee-ag-a-ra biscuits in your tea. Common, that was of her, if you ask me. Though I dare say it's a pity her old man ran off back to Worcester when he did.' She suddenly took out of her mouth her dentures, placed them on the table beside her, and picked up a piece of the cherry-cake herself, and bit into it with the most infinite care, and yet clearly, from the anguished expression she very soon made, more than a little painfully.

The back-door of the terraced-house slowly opened, and the old man called Tom emerged tentatively into the daylight, the back of his right hand suddenly shooting up so as to shade his keen, but weary, blue eyes from the sudden glare of the sun, which by this time was at its height, and already bathing the small, still largely leafless, trees that edged the steep slopes of the surrounding river-valley in a rich, vibrant fusion of dappled sunlight.

Tom took out a handkerchief from the side-pocket of his long, tweed overcoat and used it to wipe the drops of gleaming perspiration from his tanned, freckled forehead, and then plodded erratically across his new, tangled, grassy lawn towards the wire back-fence, at which point a clear vista of the enormous, grey railway-viaduct lay opened up majestically before him. Still shading his eyes, Tom gazed down towards the base of one of the viaduct's six great plinths in the valley below, hugely impressed, as he recalled he always was, by the bridge's solid, stone structure, and especially by the broad, Romanesque curves of its seven splendid arches.

The old man allowed his gaze to rise up the limestone columns to the wide, walled path that ran away from him along the top of the bridge, and where once had run a double-railway track that he remembered well. Close to the right-hand wall a man's head could now be clearly seen moving rapidly just above the parapet of the vast structure - too fast, he thought, for a rambler, and clearly a tad slow for a sprinter. Tom rubbed his dim eyes with his knuckles in a muddle of bemused wonder and deliberation, until it finally dawned on him what it was that he was actually beholding.

Many years after the steam-engines had ceased running along this route, and the two railway tracks and their points had been taken up, miles of tarmac had been laid down where the line had once been, and a new cycle-way was opened up for the use of the general public, and which is still known locally as '*The Taff Trail*.' Tom understood now: the travelling head his eyes followed was clearly that of a solitary cyclist, who was peddling leisurely westwards towards him, having just skirted, on this level, but winding route that ran parallel to the Upper Taff River, a towering escarpment of sheer, grey cliffs. Tom saw that these cliffs majestically rose up to, and, around the time of its construction in medieval times, had offered protection to, the elevated, Norman ruins of *The Morlais Castle*, which these days still sat peering down from its lofty hill that seemed almost to caress the creamy, cotton-bud, cumulus clouds that gently floated past it across the Spring sky.

With a trembling hand Tom lifted up a loose, waist-high length of wire, and eased his tired body gently through the back-fence of his kitchen-garden, and then more or less staggered his way out onto the steep, grassy bank which lay just beyond it. He was now able to see down to the river itself, and he smiled at its simple beauty. Picking up a weathered sheep's skull, Tom then took a quick look behind to ensure he wasn't being watched, and sat himself down carefully, though a tad painfully, beside the trunk of a tall oak-tree, and placed the strange grey object alongside him. Once comfortable, he then reached into his coat-pocket and took out a small tin-box, and, adeptly fixing the lid beneath its base, began rolling for himself a cigarette.

Within minutes the seated old man felt himself to be in another world completely - a realm of calm serenity and bliss. He closed his eyes and thanked his Maker for the same. Then, as the trilling sounds of the nesting birds in the trees above and around him amplified to the point of ecstasy, Tom stubbed out his stogie on a large stone, leaned his back against the thick, gnarled tree-trunk, and, even more quickly than he expected, fell fast asleep.

In the spare, but cosy, lounge of the Cillick household jazz music was playing quietly as Drew sat back in his favourite armchair, scanning an art-book, and sketching on a plain sheet of paper that he had secured with a paper-clip inside it. He paused and looked across at his wife who was seated peacefully on the sofa, repairing a button on her uniform, and then at Chris who was sitting at the dining-table, seemingly working on his homework. Drew suddenly reached down, and, clasping in his hand the remote-control for the stereo sound-system, raised the volume on it quite considerably, then swiftly dropped the hand-set back to its original position beneath the cushion where he always kept it.

'Darling, do you think that's wise?' Anne asked him, without looking up.

'Sorry?' Drew retorted with a smile. 'I can't hear you above the music.'

'Yes, I'm not surprised you can't,' she told him. 'There again, perhaps he's deaf.'

'Or maybe he's gone out,' her husband added helpfully.

'Oh, so you *can* hear me then?' Anne announced, looking directly into her husband's eyes, and clearly exposing for all to see yet another of his childish capers.

Chris slammed shut the textbook he was reading, and addressed his parents in the calm, deliberate manner that he always used to stifle any glowing embers of family discord that his fast maturing mind detected. 'He was out digging in the garden earlier. Did I tell you?' he said.

'Really?' replied his mother. 'So you got to see him then, Chris? Tell us - what does our latest next-door neighbour look like?

'Oh, I don't know,' he told her. 'Normal size for an old man, I'd say. He was wearing a waist-coat.'

'In the garden!' his mother asked him.

'Poor form, poor form,' said Drew, shaking his head a little. 'The chap is clearly a blackguard. I dare say you probably caught him trying to dispose of the bones.'

'Bones! What bones?' his wife enquired, staring at him, and making a face.

'You know, the body,' Drew told her, with a serious look that belied his black humour.

Her son stood up to join the fray. 'Oh, Mam, you must know how murderers almost always make use of their own gardens,' Chris informed her helpfully.

'I make use of my own garden,' Anne told him sternly. 'So does that make *me* a murderer?' She was feeling out-gunned again by the pincer-movement of the two men in the household, and suddenly wished that her daughter Bethan hadn't recently gone off to live with that awful man in town with the ice-cream van, that sat on bricks month after month in the street of prefabricated homes round the corner from her husband's school, and that had been erected just after the war, and with a projected life-span of twenty years, but had already celebrated its diamond anniversary. And how embarrassing that had to be for her son, too, she thought: having to walk past it as often as he did, even if Drew - Bethan's step-father - didn't appear to care a rat's behind about the shame of it.

'Look,' Anne told her husband, 'I can't seem to concentrate while you're playing your Miles, dear. Can't you just take him upstairs or something?'

'But he's been dead for nigh on twenty years, love,' Drew told her, barely able to contain his laughter.

'And it's world-turning music, Mam,' Chris added, smiling at his step-father, who by now was grimacing with the pain of it all. 'Didn't Dad mention that?'

'Really?' Anne retorted, smirking. 'Well, it's turning me, all right, I can tell you. Can't we hear something different for a change? A - a voice, maybe? Or another instrument, even?'

'O.K., if you like,' Drew told her. 'How about Dinah Washington? Or Benny Carter, maybe? Ben Webster? Coleman Hawkins? I know - Coltrane?'

'Say, isn't that what Grandad used to work on, Mam?' put in Chris mischievously.

'The coal train?' said Anne. 'He certainly did, Chris - when the line was still running over *The Seven Arches* back in the Sixties,' his mother told him with feeling. 'And your Uncle Ern was a coal-man too, remember. He used to deliver with a horse-and-cart back then, of course, and in those days they'd just drop a ton of it right outside your front-door first thing in the morning, and you and your whole family would spend the next few hours, rain or shine, just filling up bucket after bucket, and scurrying back and forth, until you had finally managed to cart it all inside.'

'Wow! How *Third World!*' Chris ejaculated, mouth agape, and clearly visualising the quaint, misty, historical scene his mother had so sharply portrayed for him.

'How do you mean *Third World!*' Anne bellowed back at him. 'It wasn't at all. No. It was lovely back then, actually - it really was.' By now she was positively beaming with the poignant recollection of it all. 'I tell you, those were the days, Chris. We even got our fresh milk off the horses,' she added.

Her son fell silent, trying to picture this most unusual - to him, thoroughly unfeasible - method of milk-production.

By now Drew was sitting with his head in his hands. 'What a family I've gone and shackled myself up with, eh!' he cried out in desperation. 'God help me! That's all I can say,'

'Hey - what was that!' Anne suddenly called out, leaping to her feet.

'What?' asked Drew, reducing the volume of the music. 'I didn't hear anything.'

'That,' replied his wife. 'Hey! You must have heard it that time, Drew, surely? Chris?'

'I heard something,' her son retorted. 'I thought it sounded a bit like a - like a -'

'Drill!' Anne replied sharply.

'Yes, that's what I thought,' Chris informed her. 'A drill of sorts.'

'God! There it is again,' Anne announced. 'Hear it? Hear it?'

'Oh yes, I can hear it now,' Drew told her. 'A bloody funny drill that, though, don't you think? It's very -'

'High-pitched,' replied Chris. 'Like - almost like somebody screaming.'

'Eugh!' Anne cried. 'It's fair making my flesh creep, I can tell you. You know, it sounds very much as if - as if -'

'You know, perhaps he's got the dentist round,' said Chris, poking his index-finger into his open mouth in simulation.

Both his parents suddenly stared straight at him. Their response told him that, yes, that is precisely what the Cillick family were all now collectively surmising.

Drew turned round to face his wife, and reached out, and tenderly clasped her round her shoulders. 'Anne, what was the title of that - of that very first film I took you to see, soon after we met?' he asked. 'You know - that horrible, scary one. Laurence Olivier, wasn't it?'

' *'Rebecca'* - yes?' she asked, watching him shake his sweet, curly head in reply.

'Or do you mean *'Spartacus?'* enquired Chris. 'I believe I've watched both of them on-line.'

'No dear,' his mother replied in hushed tomes, suddenly placing her free hand across her face. 'Gosh! I think your Dad means - I think you mean…. *'Marathon Man,'* don't you darling?'

'Yes, of course. *Marathon Man,'* Drew announced, smiling. *'That's* the film I was thinking of. Well, God help us if we end up discovering we've got some crazy Neo-Nazi living next-door to us, that's all I can say.'

'But that would be fantastic,' Chris told them firmly, his face beaming. 'Then we'd simply *have* to move house this time, and no two ways about it.'

Through the living-room wall the screeching, manic wail of the drill unexpectedly started up once more, and the family Cillick felt compelled to cover all six of their ears in a swift, synchronised movement. Their anxious looks and shared frowns confirmed that the noise was unquestionably a lot louder this time round.

Throwing down her sewing in despair, Anne suddenly rushed over to the television-set in the corner of the room, and turned it on at full-volume. 'A neo-Nazi, did you say!' she shrieked out in horror. 'As a neighbour! God alive! No. I tell you, I won't let it happen.'

'No, that would make life in *Gloryhole* almost unbearable for us again, wouldn't it?' her husband told her. 'And, you know, it's possible it could even turn out to be worse than when the paedo was holed up in there.'

Dressed in grey waistcoat and patched jeans, and with a pair of National-Health reading-glasses perched crookedly on the bridge of his hawk-shaped nose, Tom knelt on the floor of his new bedroom, taking out various items from their cardboard boxes, and putting them inside two small cupboards which sat against the wall that separated his home from that of his new neighbours. Reaching down into the empty box he took out a large brown envelope which was all that remained inside, and then tossed the empty box up and behind him onto the bed. Removing the shiny sheet of paper from the inside of the envelope, Tom read aloud the words typed boldly at its heading in proud, blue italics, and which made up the title of the, still pristine, document.

'*Degree Certificate for Dentistry - University of Wales, University College Cardiff - Thomas Davies,*' he read out proudly, stopping for a moment or two to dab his right eye gently with a wavering fore-finger, overcome, as he suddenly was, with the sheer, unanticipated emotion of the moment.

Opening up the second box, Tom reached down and dug his hands deep into its packed interior, in search of something that he was just as determined to find. Pausing briefly on its discovery, he then removed from within it a similar envelope, of a similar colour to the last one, but this time of a much smaller size, and gazed at it for ten seconds or more, and with obvious trepidation, before finally electing to remove the solitary, folded sheet of white paper which was contained inside. Tom then read silently to himself the opening two paragraphs that were written there without moving a single muscle, and then, in a voice which seemed to express his sense of personal shame, spoke aloud the single statement which sat written emboldened at the very end of it, and which announced, in official language, '*the same Thomas Davies is therefore barred from practising Dentistry forthwith.*'

A minute or two later, suddenly aware that there was no longer any cause to fret or make haste in this new home he had found for himself in the fresh, rural setting he had carefully selected in which he could live out his final days, Tom climbed painfully to his feet. He walked unsteadily over to the rocking-chair that he had just an hour or so earlier set up in the corner of the room, and which, in the days that followed, he knew would offer him a long-cherished view out over the upper Taff Valley, towards the great, limestone railway-viaduct which had for many years straddled his imagination, and had ofttimes haunted his nightly dreams and daytime reveries, ever since the sad, and sudden, death, years earlier, of his dearly loved wife, Carys.

Tom eased himself down into the chair, and, replacing his readers with his pair of regular, day-to-day spectacles, which sat where he had set them on the sparse dressing-table alongside him, he gazed out, through damp, squinting eyes, over the brow of the naked, cream-coloured, eyeless, sheep's skull which he had just placed on the bare window-sill, into the fast dimming light of evening. Yes, the long-term tenants of the village cemetery near their family-home in Talybont had certainly gained a gem in my Carys, he told himself wistfully. And, closing his eyes, he prayed to his God that it wouldn't be too long now before he himself would become boxed-up, lowered, and placed lovingly not more than an inch or so above her, and well within arms-reach, of his one true love's fruitful, ever faithful, and once glorious body.

Yes - only then would he be truly happy, Tom told himself, nodding contentedly, and then smiling broadly at the sight before him of the bright, new row of gleaming grey fillings, caps and crowns that now adorned the sheep-skull's gaping mouth, and which, to Tom, refuted, and indeed clearly belied, the slander and the libel and the hateful calumny of it all. Only then, in my death, would justice be truly served, the old man reflected; only then could the injustice, the patent abomination of the matter be finally erased and forgotten, and the wretched, cold case, which had tragically jolted, and then ultimately put paid to the hard-earned career that he had once adored, be signed and sealed, nailed down, and buried forever.

After almost an hour or so of dithering, Anne finally plucked up sufficient courage, opened the patio-door as wide as it would go, and strode out into the back-garden, quickly grasping, then clutching to her bosom, the assorted, slightly embarrassing, items of multi-coloured underwear which she had pegged up on the line there much earlier in the day. To her horror, Anne quickly saw that the old man, who was her strange, new neighbour, was still to be found out there, crouching low down, and pottering about on a quite different patch of ground very close to the house-wall, and collecting from it an assortment of small rocks and stones which he seemed to be dropping into a small cloth-bag that hung loosely from his neck and shoulders. Seeing him standing alone there, Anne began to feel a little sorry for him, but not quite as much as for herself, since the last of her shameful knickers hung very close to their adjoining fence, and so she was forced, very much against her will, to move within a few feet of his thin, bent, overcoated form in order to retrieve them. Yet her neighbour soon looked up, and so all was lost.

Anne emitted a broad, beaming smile which she normally reserved for the vicar of *Vaynor Church*, and, far more frequently, for the young people who called every Saturday morning without fail, to engage her on the topic of *The Book Of Revelation*, and, perhaps unsurprisingly, on the frequency of the bus service into town and the fact that it happened to stop right outside their Kingdom Hall. Anne waited until her neighbour had registered who she might be, and then commenced to address his kneeling form.

'Hello there!' she announced brightly. 'I'm Anne.'

'Yes, I can see' Tom replied, a tad strangely, slowly rising to his feet. 'I'm called Tom. Tom Davies, I am, you see.'

Anne watched the beads of sweat run off the man's long, hooked nose, then winced a little, recalling suddenly how so many of the men at *The Willows* often told her the strangest things in a similar, eccentric fashion, and often responded to her questions and comments in a way that instantly betrayed to her their diminishing powers of memory and deliberation. For reasons that she could never really comprehend, this always made Anne feel terribly angry, and her present fury was becoming palpable. She could only think that this might be because it caused her to recall, and perhaps subconsciously relive, the experiences that she had to endure as a young woman when her own father fell sick, and was ultimately confined to bed for many months, before he finally succumbed to the debilitating and degenerative condition known to the Welsh as *'Dust'*, and which finally overpowered his skeletal frame, and caused his death shortly after his sixtieth birthday. There had been no question of a birthday-cake for Dad back then, she told herself, and for the second year running, they commemorated the event with just the same soup-and-complan, liquid diet, which, by that stage, was all that the ex-miner's blocked gullet would allow passage to. Anne reflected on how the next day happened to be the anniversary of her father's passing. Like everyone else, Joe had entered into life as a baby, she told herself, although, to her horror and dismay, it was very like a baby that he had been forced to leave it.

Sensing that she might be on the point of weeping, and, fearing that Tom would notice, and perhaps ask her about it, Anne turned aside, and gazed into the semi-distance, at the great, grey viaduct, now barely visible between the swaying branches of the trees. The customary early evening breeze now swept in from that easterly quarter, and its advent promptly chilled the warm, trickling runnels that had emerged from the corners of both of her eyes.

Whatever happened now, Anne told herself, she would simply take the basket and gather up the rest of her laundry items, and slip away silently with them to the safety of her steamy kitchen, where a lamb stew - Drew's favourite supper - was already beginning to boil. But what Tom did next meant that, far from fleeing the scene, she would be forced to spin round and face him again, and once more seek out the sunken, blood-shot eyes which had previously caused her a degree of revulsion, reminding her, as they did, of her dead father's own.

'You were always my favourite girl, you know,' Tom suddenly told Anne, standing now, and gripping tightly with his bony hands the wire-fence that split in two their almost identical back-gardens. 'Always - always,' he continued, his wayward, mysterious words now rising up and spinning through Anne's brain like the circling clouds of condensed breath that emerged from his deep-lined, crooked mouth, and seemed to her now to swirl up high above them both, towards the brick-chimney that sat, perhaps a tad ungainly, above his terraced house.

Anne suddenly felt she was about to faint, and so, head down, rushed away to her open back-door, there to grasp firmly the wooden frame, trailing socks and pants all over the grass as she did so. Who on earth was this strange old man? Anne asked herself. And what on earth did he mean by his random, bizarre comment? Only when she was once again safe inside the house did she feel able to begin to contemplate the meaning of the words that he had uttered.

Anne drew closed behind her the kitchen-curtain, and then stared at the small, rectangular, black-and-white school photograph which now appeared in her eye-line on the wall alongside it. Anne slowly reached up, and, with a trembling forefinger, tenderly touched the tiny head of a young, dark-haired girl in a long, billowing skirt, who, holding tightly to a girlfriend's shoulder, smiled up at the world before her with a beaming, but innocently toothless, grin. Anne moved in closer, and gently rubbed her own front tooth with the very same digit, and stood staring in wonder at how peculiar, and how gauche and unattractive she had looked back then.

Anne spun round and walked into her living-room, and then turned towards a wooden shelf in the corner of the room. From it she collected a large, black album titled *'Anne's Scrapbook,'* and quickly skimmed through it until she reached a page which she already knew as intimately in her mind's eye as in her dreams, and which featured a cello-taped, paper photograph of a Sixties,' uniformed, and helmeted policeman. The bobby was carrying securely in his sturdy arms a shy, delicate, tender bundle that was a young girl, who had been rescued by the patiently searching miners just minutes earlier, alone, covered in rubble, but miraculously still alive.

Anne blinked repeatedly in anticipation as, with trembling fingers, she very carefully unfolded the crisp, cracked, and somewhat discoloured, printed report from a daily newspaper of the time, which she still remembered having once glued onto the book's broad, black page. Its smudged headline read - *'144 DEAD AT JUNIOR SCHOOL IN ABERFAN.'*

The road that ran uphill past Anne Cillick's house and the two other, more modest, cottages that adjoined and preceded it, crossed over an old, stone bridge, beneath which lay, and at a perfect right-angle to it, the old station-halt, and from which point the course of the old double railway-line ran away westwards, into a swirl of green fields, and eastwards, across the great limestone viaduct, known locally as *The Seven Arches*. The north side-wall of the Cillick dwelling, therefore, stood perched high above the old line's cycle-track that lay below it, while the views to the east from the windows of the family's back-bedrooms, taking in as they did the whole, deep and forested valley, were not only beautiful but breathtaking.

In the evening's gathering gloom a pair of young lovers sluggishly walked up the hill together across the road from the short, terraced row, moving in and out of the shadows thrown upon them by the tree-trunks that grew alongside the curve of the bend. The slim girl, who was walking on the inside of her taller companion, was in the process of telling the boy a story.

'Honest, Chris. Well, *I* believe her, anyway,' the girl told him. 'She said she got grabbed by him as he was giving her something off his milk-float.' She suddenly made a gruesome face. 'The dirty old bugger!'

'Semi, or full-fat, Rhi?' asked Chris, turning towards her, a wicked grin sweeping right across his handsome face.

'A belt is what he needs if you ask me. What? Oh, you're disgusting, you are,' replied Rhiannon, slapping him tenderly on the shoulder.

A vehicle suddenly pulled up on the road behind them, and the pair spun round as one to see who it might be. Two policemen in uniform soon emerged from their police-car and walked up the path of the adjoining house to the Cillick home, briefly knocked on the door, then entered. The young couple slipped from their hiding-place among the bushes, and, hand-in-hand, and still in partial school-uniform, began to cross over the road. But Chris suddenly pushed the girl back a few steps and up against a tree, and proceeded to kiss her roughly on the neck. Rhiannon squealed once, but then chose to accept his clumsy, but passionate, advances.

'I can't,' Rhiannon told him. 'You know that. Not here, anyway. And I'm not going with you down the line again, that's for sure.'

Chris recoiled his head a little so that he could look deeply into her blue, copper-sulphate eyes, made his customary disgruntled face, and felt confident that that might be all that was required. He was right. Rhiannon grasped his ears and pulled his head down once more, until his face was as close as she could get it to her own. There the two lovers paused, hair entwined, buttocks mutually grasped, tongues protruding slightly over lips and chin.

The two policemen emerged again from the house opposite them, but this time with an ancient companion, whom they guided, with a firmly gripped arm, down the path and into their car. Hearing the car-lock open with a squeal, Chris and Rhiannon suddenly broke off their clinch, and watched intently as all three men drove away down the hill that the couple had just walked up, on towards the hair-pin bend, and thence left towards the waterfalls and the road to town.

'Wow! That was quick,' Chris announced, laughing. 'The old fella only got here yesterday. I guess they must have been tracking him with that helicopter we saw. All the way up the valley, I wouldn't wonder.'

'Then he's probably from Cardiff,' said Rhiannon, glumly.

'Maybe. Or from England,' added Chris, his sparkling brown eyes now filled with mischief. 'He probably never paid the right money at the bridge.'

'The Severn Crossing?' she asked him. 'Yeah, perhaps he broke through the barrier like on *'Gavin and -'*

'But after first murdering the woman in the booth with a Molotov Cocktail,' the wide-eyed boy added imaginatively.

'Yeah. Or a W-K-D,' suggested Rhiannon. 'One bang on the bonce with one of them and -'

'Splat!' shouted Chris, mimicking an exploding cranium, and then wobbling about helplessly. 'Aye, they should always keep their pull-up windows shut, if you ask me, girl. I know for sure that the guy who brings my weed across it is never unarmed, and always keeps a steak-knife in his glove-compartment.'

'Eh? But I thought they used a grinder,' Rhiannon retorted, scrunching up her nose with bewilderment.

'Not for the drugs, babe,' Chris responded. 'Not for the weed. No, for the - in case they pass a stray cow on the carriageway, you know? And they fancy a quick sirloin-and-chips.'

'Stop it, Chris!' screamed Rhiannon, slapping him on the back. 'You know very well how much I adore cows.'

'I know, I know - you said your great-grandad was a farmer once,' Chris replied, grasping her swinging hand to save himself from more pain. 'I love them too, you know. Oh yes, I think they're delicious.' He ducked again, then raised his head aloft. 'Rhiannon - can I ask you something?' he asked her.

'About cows? 'Course you can,' she said. 'I know all about them - their colours, their lactation, their breeding, everything.'

'Their breeding? Oh, good,' replied Chris. 'Tell me, babe - if your cow was Friesan, would you get her a Jersey?'

'Well, that would depend on a number of things,' she told him, visualizing in her mind's eye a large brown bull she had once seen her grandfather releasing into a field for the sole purpose.

'If they made them that big, I mean,' added Chris, pouting his lips to stop himself from breaking out giggling. 'Jerseys, I mean. A polo-neck would look good, don't you think?' Unable to help himself, Chris started laughing, but this time he made sure he pinned back Rhiannon's arms to prevent her from retaliating. 'You know, I believe that's why I love you so much, babe.'

'You mean because I love cows?' asked Rhiannon, smiling, and suddenly embracing him.

'Yes, that's probably it,' he replied, grinning. 'Because, if people don't love them then I dare say they could all die out before long, couldn't they?' He rolled his shirt-sleeves a little higher.

'Why? Are they endangered, then?' she asked, more than a little perturbed by his comment.

'What? You mean you didn't know that?' Chris enquired, feigning horror. 'I'm very surprised, Rhiannon, especially as you seem to know so much about them.'

Rhiannon was seventeen, the same age as Chris was, but, because she had failed dreadfully in her GCSE examinations, she had been persuaded to re-take them all, and had elected to leave Chris's class and year, and move back to join the Year-Eleven class below her, whose students were therefore a year younger than she was.

Chris embraced his red-haired lover and drew her with him towards the open gate across from his home, and then down the short path that led to the deserted station-halt. There, turning smartly through a semi-circle, and ambling arm-in-arm past the north side of his home, Chris walked Rhiannon eastwards onto, then across, the lofty viaduct. As they slowly proceeded, he decided to tell her a bit more about the subject which seemed to fascinate her so much.

'Listen, Rhiannon,' said Chris, 'three of the most endangered species living in Britain today happen to be cows, and - and pandas, oh - and dinosaurs. You know, I nearly forgot those altogether.' As the sudden breeze that swept up the valley sent strands of his long black hair all about his face, Chris suddenly lost interest in his teasing tale. 'Say, have you got any crisps left?' he asked her. 'I'm starving, and I don't plan on going in for a while, yet. How about you?'

'I'm not eating today, I've decided,' Rhiannon told him firmly, taking a small packet from her pocket and handing it over to him. 'Chris, do you mean - do you mean you aren't going to go home *at all* tonight?'

'No, you see I don't see any reason to.' he replied, taking his fiery-headed girl's slim, pale hand firmly in his own, and pulling her even closer. 'How about you? Say, let's do what we did the other day, shall we?'

'And what's that?' enquired Rhiannon, starting to tremble with a mixture of fear and anticipation, as it gradually dawned on her what it was that he was proposing.

'Let's go down the line,' replied Chris, tugging both of her hands down firmly inside his own.

The confident, boyish smile that followed these words, and which set Rhiannon's heart beating faster, she quickly sensed was too much for her to consider offering up even the faintest of objections. So, unlike on the previous occasion, she didn't protest. And so, with tousled heads dipped, and slim, bare arms gripped tenderly round each other's waists, the two young people continued strolling eastwards along the dusty, tarmacadam lane that ran across the top of the great, seven-arched viaduct, into the teeth of a gathering breeze, and away from the setting sun, which quickly threw their long, single shadow way ahead of them down the line of the ancient railway-track, and, with just a single zig-zag, caused by the structure's perimeter walls, right on over the side of the head-high, stone parapet, and away faintly into the distant woods.

The entrance to the tunnel was now little more than a huge, round, concrete wall with a steel door at its base, which was supposed to be locked shut, but was invariably left wide open for intruders and ordinary passers-by to peer in, sniff the dank, humid air inside, and think better of interrupting their pleasant country stroll for a dim, cavernous step back in time.

In the Sixties this wide, curved passageway beneath the limesone hill provided a route by which steam-trains were able to reach the industrial town of Dowlais, and so carry away from it, in a long caravan of open trucks, both its steam-coal and its iron and steel products, for which the locality was rightly renowned right across the world. Indeed in early Victorian Times the *Dowlais Ironworks* had been the largest ironworks on the planet, and the very rails that the trains ran on from Dowlais towards Cardiff, to London, to Paris, and even further afield towards Berlin, Moscow, and Outer Mongolia for that matter, were all etched indelibly with the small Welsh town's famous name, the term *Dowlais Steel* being, as Isambard Kingdom Brunel had claimed at the time, nothing less than a by-word for quality product.

The steel-door creaked like a banshee as it was pushed open, and soon Chris's head peered out into the darkness which by now had enveloped the entire river valley, and which would inevitably make their one-mile walk back rather more harrowing than before. After Chris, emerged Rhiannon, holding on to her lover's shoulder with her left hand, while in her right she carried her scarf and blazer, from the pockets of which hung limply her blue-and-green striped tie and blue tights. Chris swung the door shut behind them, and the pounding clang of its closure echoed eerily around them, causing unseen sheep to gallop away raucously along the track, or to scramble noisily up the hill's steep slope in the direction of the castle for their very salvation.

'It's O.K., babe,' Chris assured her. 'It's just the pesky sheep. I think there's only two of them. You know, they've probably been doing much the same as we have, if you ask me, only amongst the trees.' He turned towards Rhiannon and giggled heartily at the thought, but quickly saw that she wasn't quite as amused as he plainly was. 'I'm sorry, babe. I forgot - you only know about cows, don't you? And horses, of course, since your dad's got two of them, you tell me.'

Rhiannon's ice-blue eyes met his own. 'I don't want to come here again, Chris,' she told him firmly, bending now, and lifting one bare leg up onto the bank so as to pull on her tights. 'And anyway, I bet this is where you brought Pippa Jenkins that time. And don't go denying it, neither, Chris, because I got to hear all about it. Do you know she told everyone on *Facebook* that you two went all the way? What? You didn't know? I thought not.' Rhiannon picked specks of grit from the netted fabric as she pulled the blue hose up around her hips and waist. 'Only I didn't know she meant all the bloody way down here. God! It's no wonder she's your ex now, is it?'

'It wasn't like that,' retorted Chris, sharply. 'It was the other way round, completely. In fact, let's not even talk about her, Rhiannon. She was - she was just to*o easy* if you want to know the truth. She was, I'm telling you. Pippa Jenkins, pah!' He shook his head at the memory and pointed at the bricked-up wall of the tunnel. 'You know, we didn't even have to go inside there. And, if I remember, it wasn't even properly dark. Christ! I could tell she didn't care *where* it happened. Just that it -' Chris suddenly tossed a stone at the steel door and it clanged loudly, reverberating starkly throughout the surrounding, now deathly silent, valley. 'You know, I thought that maybe I *would*. But I guess it's different when it's your first time, isn't it?'

'Is it?' replied Rhiannon bitterly. 'Chris, will you promise me you won't make me next time?'

'But I thought you liked it, Rhi?' he asked her, now disgruntled somewhat by her comment.

'Make me come down the tunnel again, I mean....not the other thing,' she replied, crossly. 'God, we had to walk for ages just to get here.

'But it's not really that far, babe,' Chris announced. 'And it was still light when we first arrived. Anyway, nobody could ever bother us inside the tunnel, could they?'

'Oh, really? Except the ghost, perhaps,' Rhiannon told him, throwing on her scarf, doing up every button of her school-blazer, and turning up its narrow collar against the stiff, cold breeze that now swept up at them round the curve of the wide river vale. 'After all, the tunnel runs under the cemetery, doesn't it?'

'What ghost?' Chris asked her. 'Whose ghost do you mean, babe? Aw, don't tell me you actually believe that old wives' tale, Rhiannon? Nobody else does, so why should you?'

'Well, he *was* my uncle, for a start, wasn't he?' she told him, biting into her lip.

'Yes, but you never even met the man,' Chris retorted scornfully. 'Your Uncle Sam is about as relevant to us now as - as, say, J-F-K, or John-the-Baptist, if you want my opinion.'

'Look, I can't say I do, as it goes, Chris,' she retorted. 'I don't happen to want your opinion at all. Really, please don't talk about my Uncle Sam like that,' she pleaded, taking both his hands in hers. 'He was my dad's only brother, after all, you know. And everyone says he saved my dad's life when they were just young boys, back in that school that got destroyed, down in Aberfan.'

'O.K, O.K., but my Mam went there too, remember,' put in Chris, by way of balancing things, but he could easily tell that Rhiannon wasn't really listening to him any longer.

'And anyway,' she continued, 'his body only got re-buried again the other day. And I was there, remember. We all were. Listen - I know you didn't go, Chris, but did I tell you I saw your mother, rambling about over in the cemetery some time later that evening? Creeping away like some vagabond between the grave-stones, she was, I swear. Like a - like some criminal. Why on earth was she doing that, Chris? Do you know?'

'What the hell are you talking about, Rhiannon?' the boy retorted sharply. 'That couldn't have been my Mam. She said she went to work as usual that day, so I guess you must be mistaken.'

'Really?' said Rhiannon, suddenly dropping his hand, and walking on ahead of him onto the rough, stony, cycle-way that comprised their route back towards the Gloryhole-viaduct. Not many seconds later she had turned the corner and was gone.

'You know, it's not just reading-glasses you need, babe,' Chris called after her. 'God help you in your driving-test next week. Yeah. I mean it, babe. Crash! Bang!' Chuckling loudly to himself, he reached the corner, and looked about him in both directions, but in the black darkness the boy could see neither hide nor hair of his pretty, young lover, and had no idea where she had gone to. 'Where are you babe?' he shouted, but his blood froze when just his own deep, urgent voice echoed back at him, and much louder now than he had expected. 'Rhiannon!' Chris called out, but less shrilly this time. 'You'll get lost, you know. And without me I bet you'll never find the way. Though you just need to keep to the cycle-path, you do. Rhiannon! Babe, please don't go!'

The large ram that Chris suddenly saw standing stolidly in the path, staring back at him, made the hairs on his head stand up. The robust animal's complete lack of temerity in response to his repeated calls to 'skidaddle!' finally caused Chris to clamber his way up onto the bank, and to creep all the way round him amongst the trees in a sort of broad semi-circle. To the boy's relief he finally sighted Rhiannon, flashing a torch at him from about fifty yards farther up the track, and so, although his legs now ached sharply at the joints, Chris dashed off in her direction, not once daring to turn and look back from whence he had come, at the stone-faced, hoary, old creature that had somehow managed to scare the boy witless.

A second, much leaner sheep suddenly ambled across the track and took up position alongside her male companion, and the two animals turned their heads in unison, and watched, as the two young lovers, of a different, perhaps more primitive, species completely, walked away from them, now arm-in-arm once more, in the direction of *The Seven Arches*.

CHAPTER 4

The incessant drizzle had coated the black head-stone in a myriad of bright, silver, pearl-droplets, reflecting liberally the light from the broad, bright, white-clouded sky which covered Pant just as thinly as it enveloped the upper Taff Vale and the broad sweep of The Brecon Beacons to the north. I laid the parcel of chrysanthemums - Sam's favourite flowers - on the narrow, grass-less mound, beneath which his recently recovered, re-examined, and re-packaged corpse now lay at rest for the second time, and then stood upright and still alongside it, so as to pay a personal tribute to the courageous elder brother I had lost in tragic circumstances when he was a final-year student at University College Swansea. I myself had failed to achieve the grades *I* needed to get there, and instead, out of frustration, took a job as a guard on the railway.

The car-horn blared out a sullen note, and I was suddenly aware that my daughter Rhiannon, who was sitting less than thirty feet from me, in smart clothes she had no desire to dampen, let alone allow to get soaked through, had become eager for my return. The yellow, second-hand Ford Fiesta she sat inside I had bought over a week before, and, once I had got it repaired and serviced, I planned to give her as a reward for having passed her driving-test at the first attempt. And this she had now achieved. Yes, despite what many of her school-friends had predicted, and recalling how more successful they had been in their GCSE exams than she had, I always kept faith in my only daughter that she would surprise us all on the day itself, perhaps because it was I who had given her her first half-a-dozen lessons.

'It was only the man's request for me 'to turn the car round' which threw me, Dad,' she had told me, as we sat together in my Rover earlier that morning, and I delivered my triumphant girl back home again to her nerve-wracked mother.

'How do you mean?' I had asked.

'Well, you always told me to do 'a three-point turn,' didn't you? But apparently that is not what it is called these days. Derrh! You have 'to turn the car round,' is what you have to do. Honest. And so to avoid driving up over the kerb, which 'three points' would undoubtedly have forced me to do in the dreadfully narrow lane we were in, I took six or seven goes at least, and, odd though it must have looked to the people who stood around watching, I can only think the examiner must have rewarded me as much for my patience as for anything else.'

'Though that mini you squeezed yourself into didn't harm your chances a lot, I bet,' I told her with a grin.

'Yes, perhaps that was the best car the school could have given me, as it turned out,' she replied oddly. 'Though the wipers were a lot faster than in this car, and squeaked annoyingly from start to finish.' She stretched out a bare arm and imitated their accelerated swing so as to illustrate the point.

I had turned round and was staring back into her lovely face and her flashing blue eyes that were a clear image of my own. 'I was talking about the dress you've got on, Rhiannon, not the car,' I told her, shaking my head from side to side. 'That damn mini-skirt that you're barely wearing today. Did you really think it was appropriate under the circumstances?'

'Well, I guess we'll never know, will we?' she responded, taking from the glove-compartment her prized pass-form, and studying it avidly once again, before emitting a high-pitched giggle. 'Do you know, Dad, I reckon that a lot of older men are so very extraordinary that it might even have been the deciding factor.'

'Well, knowing Alwyn Lloyd myself - that's the man who just tested you - I think you may have a good point there, girl,' I told her. 'Do you know since his wife ran off to Devon with the Avon girl, his success-record with females has become little short of legendary in these parts. And I don't just mean in driving-tests, either. But, at the end of the day, I guess we all feel rather sorry for the old bugger more than anything.' The silence that followed caused me to reflect on my last comment. 'Of course, I'm not referring to *you*, love. Please don't you go think I'm insinuating -'

'I should hope not, too,' retorted Rhiannon, affecting wounded pride as nobly as her mother invariably did. 'As you're always telling me, I'm much too young yet to even *think* of having a boyfriend.'

'And let's keep it like that, shall we?' I told her, turning briefly, and staring deeply into the pair of beautiful, ice-blue eyes she even boasted I had given her. What I saw in them told me all I needed to know at that moment. My lovely daughter had indeed arrived at that dangerous age - that emotional, sexual watershed that all humankind must needs approach, and then traverse - and both her mother and I were fully aware of the fact.

As I walked back to the car from Sam's grave, and opened the passenger-door to sit, wet and bedraggled, beside a legally driving Rhiannon, I pondered on how she was the blessed fruit of my second marriage, and quite unlike the son I had fathered just a year or so before her with a woman I had long ago lost, and then briefly met and loved again. I mused on how, many years before, Anne and I had attended school together in Aberfan, and even later on at Merthyr County, in the days when grammar schools were slowly turning into comprehensives, and Latin, Woodwork, and Technical Drawing - my favourite subjects at the time - were already being phased-out, and replaced by the likes of Spanish, Design Technology, and Computer Studies.

Though separated when we both left school at eighteen, and she went off to study at Swansea University, I well remember how Anne Morgan frequently filled my thoughts back then. But these days, now that she was married for the second time, and sharing her life with the slightly older Drew, and living up the valley in *Gloryhole*, I normally just ran into her at the check-outs in *Asda*, or on the odd occasion that we happened to be in town at the same time, and I caught sight of her shopping at some clothes-shop in the High Street. But of course I had recently seen her again just days before in this very spot just across from our house, apparently skulking away from my brother's grave under the cover of semi-darkness, and dashing for the little iron gate that I could very nearly make out, just down the steep hill from there.

I dare say the pain of what had happened back in 1974 still shrouded the lives of those involved in my brother's untimely death almost as much as it had for those affected by the tragic events at our old primary school in Aberfan just eight short years earlier; and for no one more than myself, perhaps. Would I ever finally begin to forgive? I asked myself. Could I even contemplate attempting it? Even nearly forty years on, I found it was still very much in the balance. I might already be dead and buried, and lying beside the path here, I told myself, before the blame - that was rightly theirs, but which, oddly, I myself now felt - could be finally cast aside, and before the injustice of what happened back then could finally be forgotten

As we approached the cemetery-gate that sat across from our home, Rhiannon suddenly slowed the car down and brought it to a halt. She turned and looked across at me with a genuine loving tenderness that I knew well and could feel in my very bones.

'Dad - I need to tell you something,' she began. 'I know it sounds awful saying this, but I didn't come up here with you today for Uncle Sam's sake. Can you forgive me, do you think?'

'Well, I think I might have guessed that, as it goes, the way you're all dressed up again, sweet,' I replied, with a chuckle.

'No, Dad, you don't understand what I mean. I brought you with me so that I could tell you something, something important. You see, Dad, I'm going out with a boy these days, and I think - no, I know - that I love him.'

'But how can that be?' I asked her, shocked beyond belief. 'You, in love, Rhiannon! But you're barely seventeen, for God's sake.'

'I know, Dad,' replied my daughter, 'but I feel that I already love him like - well, like you say you love our Mam, you know. There, I've said it.' She averted her eyes from mine and started up the engine once again.

'But Rhiannon, aren't you going to tell me who this fellow is?' I asked, turning and staring straight at her. 'As your father, I have a right to know at least that fact, don't you think?'

'No, not necessarily,' she replied timidly. 'Because if you knew, Dad, then - then I feel you might try to -'

'Put a stop to it?' I asked her. 'But I wouldn't want to do that sweetheart, would I? Now why would I want to do that? After all, it's your decision, isn't it? And it's your choice. And, anyway, I know you'd only grow to resent me for it.'

'No, don't be silly, Dad,' retorted Rhiannon. Then, hesitating, she went on, 'Though it's true that I might, I suppose.'

'You're getting to be a big girl now,' I told her. 'Doing so well at school now, passing your test and everything. Perhaps it's time I let you - we let you - make lots more decisions for yourself, and even make lots of mistakes too, of course. And then you can reflect on them, and perhaps even laugh at them when the time comes, as we all find we do sooner or later. Yes, only in that way will you find you really grow, my love. And I want you to grow, Rhiannon, even if it means, one day, that you grow away from me - away from your mother and me. Like in Gibran's poem, you know? The living arrows we parents send - no, that the Great Archer dispatches *through us*.'

'Bless you, Dad,' my tearful daughter whispered, then leaned across, and softly kissed my damp cheek. I dare say I must have smiled at her gesture just then. But later on I decided that her kiss was probably her way of trying to placate me a little, and of keeping things sound, and together, and even, I guess, of maintaining her silence about the awful, painful secret of who precisely this first lover in her life actually was.

No, my Rhiannon didn't disclose to me who her young lover was - not then, nor even in the weeks that followed - and by the time her mother and I finally found out, well, it was far too late for us to do anything about it.

The, diminutive, curly-haired, brown-eyed brunette called Gwen Havard was a Roman Catholic when I first met her, and remained one, despite the fact that, in me - her second husband - she married a solid, old *Welsh chapel-man*, although one who, unlike her, believed passionately that you needn't feel you have to go anywhere special on a Sunday to remain true to your beliefs, and still live your life in the unyielding hope of salvation. Now, after twenty years together, and Sunday mornings having become for us a cherished time of mutual love, extended sleep and tranquillity, Gwen and I gradually developed what was, for us, a way of life that followed the principles of, for want of a better description, the archetypal British Christian belief-system. This, I contend, is founded, simply and succinctly, on a love for God and a love for others, whom we should endeavour to treat just as we would want ourselves to be treated by them.

For Gwen and me family love came first, of course, followed by love and respect for our neighbours, and in this regard, thankfully, the people of Pant were, by and large, the sort of people you would be prepared to walk miles to give your last *Rolo* to, unless, that is, they already had chocolate stains running down their faces, or, just as unlikely, chose to refuse the offer.

Already a divorcee, I happened to have been living alone in a modest two-up-two-down just round the corner from her in Pant Road when I discovered that Gwen Havard was one such neighbour of mine. When I came across her by accident, for the first time since we were teenagers, I found that she was living with her husband Richard in a great big house on Cemetery Road - the house which, with my agreement, she later chose to name *Caerleon*. In the years when he was still working, tall, beefy, Gloucestershire-born, Richard - or Dick as he was more familiarly known - worked as a book-maker during the day, and as a bingo-caller at night. What with Gwen managing her own hair-salon just a mile or so down the road in Dowlais, the couple made more than enough money to comfortably raise a daughter called Sarah Olwen, and also to purchase for themselves the lovely, traditional, four-bedroom villa that she and I now happily share together, and which is located almost opposite to one set of the cemetery-gates.

But the good life for the family Havard came to an abrupt end soon after Dick was found to be cheating on Gwen with a skinny usherette at Merthyr's *Castle Cinema* called Vera, who was just half his age, and who had originally been employed there for general duties, such as handing out bingo-cards and checking the toilets for loiterers, but, after just a few weeks, ended up sitting alongside the man himself on-stage, and collecting up and mustering his coloured balls for him in slender, white, fishnet gloves, and slipping them, singly and lovingly, into their allotted positions. Aided no doubt by her long, horsehair mane of sparkling, blond tresses, and by her wider-than-wide, white, euthymolised smile, Vera nightly cast an enchanting spell, no less effectively on her Dick than on the captive, largely superannuated, audience, who marked their cards while gossiping loudly and drinking weak lager at the tables down below them.

With a practised finger-grip, no doubt perfected in a quiet corner of some local cricket-field, Vera made the stream of coloured spheres spin, and cascade, and spill out their rich rewards to hushed acclaim. And so adeptly, and so fruitfully did she effect her magic that the star-prize she quickly claimed for herself were twin boys, born just two bingo-rounds apart. Very like their famous namesakes, after whom they were obviously named, Eric and Ernie shared a bed together and thrived, and they continued to enrich their parents' lives with a surfeit of love and laughter for many years to come, even after their father earned himself the sack for misappropriation of takings, and the new family were forced to move south temporarily into a damp, poky flat a dozen or so miles down the valley in Pontypridd.

Back in Pant, Gwen unsurprisingly grew to despise her daughter's father about as quickly as an abandoned woman is entitled to. And not much later, in fact just a few short months after the courts took over where heated negotiations fell short, she divorced his sorry arse in Merthyr Crown Court, soon after being awarded sole custody, not just of Sarah Olwen, but of the salon, the house, and of its only other occupant - the fast-balding budgerigar called Joey - who merrily scattered *Trill* about him and slammed his little, silver bell all the way through it all. And that was where, less than six months later, and with heavy and hesitant tread, I found myself stepping in.

I confess I loved Gwen never more than when she bore me our beautiful, flame-haired daughter. Initially my wife and her mother Doris toyed with the idea of calling the child Philomena, which Gwen told me happened to be her own confirmation name, but I quickly said I wasn't having it, and, fortuitously, common sense seemed to have won through in the end. 'We're certainly not naming my only daughter after your *altar ego*,' I told her firmly, breaking out in laughter at my spontaneous, yet wholly unintended, quip. Fortunately Gwen saw the funny side, as well as displaying a measure of common sense, and we agreed to name the girl Rhiannon, providing that our next sprog was christened with a name which hailed from Irish legend, rather than Welsh, so as to compensate. To this proposal I gladly agreed, and yet no second issue was forthcoming, though we tried and tried with commendable dedication. And so Rhiannon - the flame-haired girl from *The Mabinogion* - has proved to be our solitary child.

I must admit that I am forever grateful that Rhiannon developed an early aversion for all things pious, and has, to this day, apparently only ventured willingly inside a church, Catholic or otherwise, on secular excursions - usually school journeys, and sundry carol-services at Christmas time. You see it is my view that organised religion, with its false, or at least, questionable, supremacy of high church, and its long out-dated strictures, is something that a sensitive child needs to be incubated from at an early age, in much the same way that we keep puppies safe by preventing them from dashing out into the main road. Churches are, after all, dreadfully stone-cold places, where warm feelings and positive attitudes towards others are not easy things to develop, let alone sustain. Although not a view shared by my wife, naturally, at least this has long been my own contention, and I would go so far as to maintain that the only thing that a church ever gave to me, (crammed full, as they all seem to be, with wooden altars and polished pews,) was an embarrassingly thin, shiny patch in the seat of my suit-trousers. Now I have no doubt that my Gwen would maintain that there was more than one gaping hole in such a thread-bare argument, but, at least, for the twenty or so years that we have lived together as man-and-wife, she has, thankfully, waived her right to contest it.

My elder brother Sam once told me that, if he should die before me, and had the good fortune to enter into *an after-life*, then he would be sure to send me back a message to tell me so! Needless to say this missive from above was still to arrive. 'And what if there *is* no after-life?' I had asked him. I well recall his queer response. 'Then you will simply never get to hear from me again, will you, little brother? Nor, indeed, I you. But, not only that, you will also come to appreciate how it isn't just dust that returns to dust, when all is said and done, but indeed all forms of matter, and every type of human progress, and, most perturbing of all, perhaps, *time itself*.' I stared at him gob-smacked. 'Picture *Big Ben*, Dyl, tumbling into a bottomless, black abyss.' I did so. Soon after that he smiled at me, then turned and walked off to buy some more fags. He was a clever boy, by all accounts, my brother Sam, with a keen understanding of Physics, though for my part, I admit I didn't understand any of it.

Although I was still in school when he made me this strange pledge in his study-bedroom at University College Swansea, it seemed to me to be something that a dead person might just be capable of carrying out, and so I looked forward to the possibility of participating in the exercise, never imagining that his passing would take place just the following autumn on the occasion of his twenty-first birthday, and but a week after he enrolled for the final year of his Physics degree. But, even though Sam is deceased, our mutual endeavour has now become more than a little complicated by the fact that, as his dead body has since had to be disinterred - as the police claimed 'in the interests of scientific enquiry,' (and, it is said, following a tip-off or two on *Twitter*) - then, irrespective of the truth or otherwise of the hypothesis we undertook to test, I *did* sort of get to see him again after all!

But, now that Sam was returned for good to his former resting-place in the hill-top cemetery that lay barely twenty yards from my family home, I still cherished a hope that the object of our joint experiment, bizzare though it obviously sounds, might still one day come to some satisfactory conclusion. By this I mean that I might get to find out ahead of times where I was going to spend the greater part of eternity, and whether or not I would get the opportunity to share that sojourn in the company of my beloved brother - the invaluable soulmate of my youth, as well as my ofttimes protector. You see, despite being lost to me when he was tragically killed near here at just twenty-one, I doubt to this day that there could ever have been anyone who so greatly impacted the lives of his family and friends as my big brother Sam had done.

In Merthyr town-centre Rhiannon was stood, standing and eating, at the curved corner of Church Street when Chris's mother suddenly walked out of the library and instantly clocked her standing there with a hot-dog clutched in her hand. The girl spun round in the hope of disguising both her face and the greasy fast-food, as well as the rather risque outfit she had chosen to wear that morning, but sadly it was too late. Anne paused for a few seconds to tuck her books inside her bag, then slowly approached the corner and called out her name.

'Hello, Rhiannon,' she announced, with just a flicker of a smile. 'How are you? Are you waitng for someone?'

'Oh, hello,' Rhiannon replied, turning and smiling broadly at Anne. 'I was waiting for the library to open, actually.' Behind her back she adeptly, and surreptitiously, tucked the wrapper containing the hot-dog into the belt of her jacket.

'It's already open, dear,' Anne replied, holding up her bag, filled to the brim with fresh books. 'That's where I've just come from, see.' Then catching sight of her son crossing the road from *Lloyds Bank,* she said, 'Gosh! Here is my boy

Chris! Why, he looks like he's been in the bank to get some money. Not for more of those coffee-bags again, I hope. You know, Rhiannon, I never even knew he had any money.' She giggled at her remark, then suddenly realised what the reason might be for Rhiannon's waiting there, and said, 'Oh, I see, you're not on your own, after all, then? And fancy my son leaving you out here in the cold, *and* it's starting to rain, too. Dearie me.' Anne began to put up her brolly for shelter. 'I've a good mind to have a word with him.'

'Please don't,' pleaded Rhiannon, spinning round and forcing a half-smile at her illicit lover as he reached the pavement, then suddenly took in who it was that had run into her at the corner.

'Mam, you - you know Rhiannon, don't you?' Chris sheepishly enquired of his mother.

'Of course I do, love,' Anne responded. 'Well, as your school-friend, anyway. Although she's in the year below you these days, right?' Chris nodded. 'Well, any more than that and I guess you'll have to tell me about it, won't you?'

'Eh? What's there to tell you about?' Chris asked, clearly getting tetchy. 'We just had to come down into town to get - to get -'

'Brushes for Art,' Rhiannon told his mother firmly, sensing her boyfriend's considerable embarrassment, and deftly producing a small bag from her coat-pocket which she waved at his mother by way of explanation, but which actually contained make-up.

'Brushes! But your Dad's got thousands of brushes,' Anne told Chris, narrowing her eyes. 'He practically smokes the damn things.'

'But they're for me, Mrs. Cillick,' said Rhiannon, with a smile. 'Don't you know that I do Art with Mr. Cillick these days? But I would never ask a school-friend for - for gifts, or such like.'

Placated somewhat, Anne smiled back at her. 'No, you don't want to go doing that, do you, love?' she told her. 'You could give a boy the wrong idea completely by doing that. But then why is he out getting things for you, Rhiannon?' asked

Anne with a carefully composed smile on her face. 'Why, you've got legs yourself, haven't you? Don't take offence like. I mean, I know you have two, like everyone else - even me - and very nice legs they are, too, dear. I mean yours, of course, not mine. But why is that? That's what I want to know. Tell me, Rhiannon, please.'

All the time Chris's mother kept gabbling on so, Rhiannon kept her body turned sideways and just smiled in a fixed, wincing fashion at her secret lover. And then, seeing him starting to stare down at the ground, and sensing his reluctance, or inability, to assist her in any way, turned and looked back at his mother, and, biting into her lip, and realising she was starting to perspire profusely, searched her poor, demented brain for a suitable reply - any reply - that might settle everything, and perhaps pacify the insufferable woman. But Rhiannon couldn't think of a single one, and then found she couldn't even remember what the question was.

'My Dad says they were a gift from Nanny Beryl,' Rhiannon suddenly told her tormentor, yet instantly sensing that the explanation she came out with perhaps wasn't at all satisfactory.

'The brushes!' exclaimed Anne, bewildered. 'But how could she? I mean, hasn't your Granny Beryl been dead since - well, since long before you were born, dear? Explain, would you, because I have to say I don't understand.'

'My legs, I mean,' replied Rhiannon. 'My legs are *hers*, my dad told me.' She suddenly realised that she was now beginning to feel faint, and believed she might even topple over onto the pavement any second. In truth, Rhiannon so wanted to just reach out a hand to Chris for some comfort, or assistance, but, for his sake alone, she decided she wasn't going to let him down whatever happened, and whatever nonsense his infernal mother came out with, or whatever stupid face she might choose to pull in doing so.

Legs, brushes – this was becoming all too much. Rhiannon's thinking mind seemed now to be just about on the point of closing down, and her slim, cold legs, that she had got from her Nan, suddenly seemed to be as much use to her as they were to that old, dead dear who had bequeathed them. In a fast darkening corner of her visual perspective she watched *Lloyds Bank* begin to suffer a similar fate to what she recalled its company had suffered a few years earlier, except that in its current decline it appeared to be merging physically with both *Nat West* and *Cash Generators* in a bizarre, unsettling, crossroad amalgamation that made no sense to her.

What on earth was this? Rhiannon asked herself, as a strange buzzing noise began sounding inside her ears. Why, the whole financial world of Wales appeared to be toppling sideways like a deck-of-cards, just as the whole universe of Rhiannon Cook felt like it was spinning and sinking into oblivion. She blinked three or four times in an attempt to trigger some powers of apprehension, but she could swiftly tell that it didn't seem to make things the tiniest bit clearer.

Then a single thought struck her like a jolt of electric current. Could this particular credit-crunch in Merthyr High Street be related to the, strangely painless, collision her head had made with the iron fence behind her? she wondered. As yet she couldn't tell for sure, but she felt that if she chose to do A-level Economics next year instead of Music, then perhaps everything would make more sense to her. Rhiannon then rolled over onto her back, and her smart, new jacket fell wide open at the front.

Soon a greasy, curved length of brown sausage, liberally covered in, what appeared to be, bright-red blood, was all that filled Rhiannon's immediate field-of-vision. Then the cold, slender hand that tugged at the neck of her blouse, scattering several silver buttons across the pavement, seemed to possess its own queer, amplified voice that was pleading loudly, 'Lie on your side, girl, and for heaven's sake try to cover your chest up!'

Yes, this definitely had to be done, Rhiannon told herself, but, try as she might, she quickly realised that she wasn't able to move a solitary muscle, and the only reply she found she was able to give was, 'Yes, I already know I'm a slut, Mrs. Cillick, and - and you're right to think I deserve to go straight to hell!'

Science on a wet afternoon, he thought. How on earth am I supposed to put up with it? A pensive, unusually depressed, Chris sat staring out of the first-floor window at the classroom directly across the grass in the Maths Block, where Rhiannon usually sat watching him like a feeding hawk at this exact time every week while studying GCSE Maths, but where, at present, her chair now stood empty, and was being used as a temporary receptacle for what appeared to be two drying anoraks and a boot-bag.

Chris's teacher, Mrs. Hussain, was standing close at hand, waving her purple-nailed hands about, and talking to his table-group in her usual, unnecessarily harrying fashion. But Chris wasn't at all interested in anatomy - not on paper, at any rate - and bemoaned the fact that the year-group had moved on from the science-units on astronomy, light and sound that they had touched on in the early Spring Term, having the previous Autumn exhausted fuel and power completely, ironically, perhaps, without having tackled 'green issues.'

What's the matter, Chris?' the teacher suddenly asked him, leaning forward and emitting the most annoying and fakest of smiles, that each time, quite literally, set his teeth on edge. The word going round the Sixth-Form Common Room had been that Mrs. Hussain was now divorced from her husband, and that Chris's dad was the new object of her affections. So, out of familial loyalty, if nothing else, Chris was determined he wasn't going to be smiling back at her under any circumstances. Instead he decided, for now at least, that honesty would be the best policy, and replied abruptly that he simply couldn't understand what the group were expected to do.

'Tell him, April,' the teacher retorted, gripping the shoulder of a bespectacled student sat just across from him, and whose eyes lit up like a startled rabbit.

'Well, it's just a starter-task for the new unit, right Miss?' the studious girl replied. 'And, so as to provide a bench-mark for future learning, I think it's called, you have to - we each have to - link up with arrows the different parts of both the male and female bodies with the written term in the margin which relates to, or describes them. Do you get it now, Chris? It's hardly rocket-science,' the cocky girl added with a smile.

'God, I wish it was though,' he replied cryptically. 'After all, that's precisely what I chose the subject for. And light, and sound.'

'It may not exactly be your cup of tea. Chris,' Mrs. Hussain told him with that insufferable smile again. 'But you see I can't possibly be certain about what I need to be teaching you for the remainder of this term if you don't first inform me what it is you already know and can do.'

But why not? Chris asked himself. Teachers had schemes-of-work that they were obliged to stick to, didn't they? His dad certainly did, because he had shown him them. Yes, sadly this had the distinct feel of a lesson that was unnecessary, or just a pathetic excuse for the lazy, rotund woman, with the dodgy fashion sense and the questionable oral hygiene, to take it easy, and coast through the dreary afternoon until the final bell. Yes, two hours of pure torture this would clearly prove to be, Chris told himself, so he would naturally need to find a way of escape. Chris realised it wasn't going to prove to be easy but he was determined to try. Yes, this would be his own personal lesson-objective for today, he mused, grinning, not some silly anatomy labelling.

'Let me see what you've completed already, can I, Chris?' the teacher continued. Female faces, full of supposedly banned mascara and lip-gloss, stared up at him. There was plainly no time to say no. Mrs. Hussain dragged Chris's paper towards her and spun it round so that now the whole group could see his hapless efforts too. From the extent of April's and Daisy's sniggers alone Chris just knew that the denouement of all denouements was about to arrive.

'Oh, dear,' the teacher began, in a tone almost as ironical as her knee-length black cardigan and trainers. 'So you think that females have testes, then, Chris! Mm. Now I'd say that would make life interesting, don't you think, ladies?' The group of girls laughed sadistically, yet harmonically, at the teacher's curt, yet risque, remark. Yes, it seemed that the dreaded woman in black had won them all over in a trice, and plainly at his expense. And now, he thought, it might well prove an arduous task for him to win them back again.

'Oh, I thought that particular picture was of the boy,' Chris told the woman timidly. 'Sorry, I should have labelled it 'vagina.' '

'Wrong again!' the mad woman repeated, shaking her head this time, so much so that three- and-a half-feet of straight, black hair whipped across some of the girls' faces, and yet none of them chose to move a muscle, or voice any objection. 'Tell him what that is actually called, girls,' the teacher commanded.

'Vulva!' came the chorus-ed reply. Not a single one of the girls said another word, yet their combined stares in his direction simply spoke volumes, and slayed him completely.

Chris was on his own from here on in, and he knew it. Now he was more determined than ever to spring himself from this bear-trap - this ursine, no feline, no bovine stall, that by now he felt tightly tethered inside. Chris found that he couldn't look anyone in the face, and so instead he stared down at the two anatomical sketches for some jot of inspiration - some opening, perhaps, by which to squeeze through. But the opening - the particular aperture - at which he found himself staring happened to be the urethra on the end of a man's cock, and he couldn't, for the life of him, see a glimmer of hope for him down there.

Chris glanced at the tall, slender sketch of *Everywoman* standing asexually alongside it and thought instantly of Rhiannon. Except for the rather hirsute lower exterior, it certainly did remind him of the soft, pink folds of the girl he had in recent weeks grown to adore. What did it matter if she happened to be his relation? he told himself. Yes, what if she did turn out to be the step-sister he had heard Daddy Drew talking to his mother about while he played hide-and-seek with a young friend in the rambling flower-garden of Cyfarthfa Park just five or so years earlier? This, after all, was the real reason that he had found it impossible to stand up for her in front of his mother in town last Saturday, he mused, because she knew far more about it than he did, even if Rhiannon knew absolutely nothing.

Chris continued to study the paper. It was indeed a beautiful pudenda, he told himself, and one that he decided he was entitled to stand up for. His eyes looked up. The females at his table were all still staring at him, much as if the teacher had asked him another stupid question and they were awaiting an equally inane reply. Chris suddenly decided that he didn't feel like disappointing them. No, not at all. In fact he decided that he would give them all precisely what they wanted, even the students idling on the adjoining table, and the other groups of boys and girls scattered in the far corners of the room, who had no idea whatsoever of his pain. Well, here goes, he told himself. Never before had he felt more entitled to scream out the *c*-word for the opening that it presented him. So he did. He just sat back on the stool and let it come.

'*Cunt!*' shouted Chris abruptly, and closed his eyes to fully experience the class's reaction.

'Who is!' Denver Probert suddenly bellowed from the adjoining table.

'Who is he calling a cunt, Denver?' Denver's equally thick-set brother Dallas enquired from way across the other side of the lab.

'You two,' a girl told them mischievously. 'He said you *both* were.'

Oh, my God, it was Fat Ange! Chris told himself, giggling. What a stirrer that girl could be. And yet, as always, he still adored her, and instantly forgave her for it, because it was the sort of blatant lie that Chris knew that he would have claimed for himself, if he had been in her position, and given half the chance.

'Fat Ange with the equally wide flange!' Chris called out blindly but gleefully. He knew full well that Ange would be utterly shocked by this, but would most likely smile proudly at it, nevertheless - that's just how she was - but at least Chris now knew for certain that it was going to truly kick off. He just hoped Brynmor wouldn't decide to hit him in the face again. He had done so in a rugger match the term before, and Chris's jaw had never felt quite the same since.

Now whereabouts was the nearest male teacher? Chris asked himself nervously. He knew that Mr. Dobie always went for refuge to the library on a Monday, and he was sure that the female student with the nose-piercing was the only other teacher on the floor. Then it was definitely on, he decided. Yes, Carina Hussain had more chance of one of her beloved, six-inch, pink, plastic bananas piercing one of her plain, unribbed condoms than of her managing to stop him in his tracks today, he thought.

Chris felt that about half of the boys present would probably stand by him, but that there would still be a total massacre in the laboratory all the same, and so he had best get plenty of glass-ware and a few of the acid bottles stacked up behind him just in case. So he jumped to his feet, then nimbly leapt up onto the bench, and reached up to the shelf high above it in order to secure for himself his ammunition.

As expected, the Proberts came at him like the prop-forward combination the boys always were in a maul of a Saturday morning, and, to the sound of shattering glass, Chris suddenly felt himself flying, feet first, from the shattered window, down through the cool, damp air, and into the long, wet grass that covered the ground below. Rolling through a full circle into the thick, sharp bushes, and ending up with his multi-grazed head under a privet hedge, Chris quickly scrambled to his feet and ran for the school-gate. Although largely unhurt, he felt he now had the excuse that he sought, and, he quickly decided that, if he ran hard over *The Bryniau* moorland at the cross-country pace he was accustomed to, then down past the castle, and over the viaduct, then he might just make it home before either one of his working parents did.

But as Chris's legs began to tire, and, sadly, well before he had even reached *The Bryniau*, he instead took the undulating road that wound its way east towards Pant Cemetery, and, walking boldly with his torn jacket under his arm, past the rugby pitch where he had scored his first try for the school, (despite landing, as he had done, in a steamy green pile of sheep manure,) paid a surprise call on his truant and ailing lover, who, in night-dress and slippers, explained that she had only just risen from bed, yet nevertheless got dressed on his account, and decided that she would go out walking with him wherever it was he decided to take her.

Leaning, with the palms of his hands on a long, stout piece of wood, Tom at long last stood on the very summit of the hill where the Normans had built their once soaring, cream-coloured, limestone castle, and which now lay all about him in abject ruin. Still breathing heavily from the long, hard climb up the stony path, which wound its way round to the top, he blinked continually as he looked all about him, and surveyed what features he could still recall from his last visit there, which he knew had to have been well over thirty years before, and not very long after the last train chugged its way across the viaduct that he could see below him, on its passage from Brecon in the north, through *Gloryhole,* and right around in a giant semi-circle and down into the Merthyr Valley, that now lay to his left, from which direction the sun was holding sway.

Nowadays it seemed only the castle's ancient crypt remained to venture inside, and this Tom had earlier adjudged to be as much a vast, dripping cave as a holy room. Yes, he had felt deeply saddened to find it just a dank, stepped cellar, rather than the proud, twelve-walled chapel which the revered, continental Christians from Normandy had initially constructed, and then ordained for spiritual purposes, in this wild, western outpost of empire almost a thousand years before.

Yet it was not so much the distinctive architecture, nor the way in which the rocks had been dressed in cuboid forms and fused together, which fascinated Tom most of all, but the very rocks themselves, and the hilly outcrop out of which they had been plucked. He therefore ambled right round the steep, circuitous perimeter, and, occasionally stooping low, turned over much of the grey, tumbled rubble in his search for ancient, sea-living creatures of the shell-fish kind. Within minutes Tom was thrilled to have found brachiopods aplenty, but, try as he might, he was unable to find any of the crinoidal sea-lilies and sea-urchins that were always his prime goal when he worked limestone sedimentaries such as these, and, to him, this felt a crushing disappointment. Nevertheless, Tom filled his knapsack with a dozen or so large stones that were chock-full of shell-casts and other such delights, along with one enormous jaw-bone, which was clearly not any kind of fossil per se, but was all that remained of a hapless sheep that had tumbled to its death from an overhanging ledge on the vertical cliffs nearby. Imagining the sudden avalanche of loose rock that might have accompanied its fall, Tom's thoughts suddenly turned to Aberfan.

An hour later, (by which time his tears had finally dried in the wind,) as Tom made his steep, precarious descent back towards viaduct and home, he paused for breath many times, and then stopped completely in order to investigate *The Key-hole Cave*, which he soon discovered was possessed of two entrances, and not just the one that the handbook he had consulted about the the area's geology, had reported. On peering down from the cliff-top into what appeared to be a sort of blow-hole at the cave's lofty rear, the old man soon concluded that the aperture was much more likely to have been made by man, rather than produced naturally, (as the handbook again had claimed,) and he was thrilled to discover, during his subsequent examination of the cave from the inside, that his assumption in this regard did, in fact, appear to be borne out.

With a great deal more pain than he had imagined possible, Tom bent his aching joints, and sat his, plainly ageing, body down astride a large, smooth rock, which he fortuitously found lying right beside the key-hole shaped cave-entrance, after which the queer rock-feature had taken its name. Sipping the final drops of cool water from his plastic bottle, he chuckled quietly to himself, recalling how, just minutes before, he had witnessed a solitary, shaggy sheep emerge head first from out of the lofty, upper exit, then skip on to graze at a yet higher altitude, and well within the castle's domain. Biting his lip as he pondered this, Tom soon came to the conclusion that, with regard to the feature's formation, perhaps nature might indeed have played a vital role after all, but in nothing like the manner that he, or indeed the handbook, had previously imagined!

Gazing north towards the distant Brecon Beacons, and then westwards, to where the afternoon sun peered out from amidst a woolly blanket of cumulus clouds, Tom felt that he could just make out the distinct and separate, but clearly related, shapes of two people who seemed to be making their way towards him across the, once great, railway-viaduct, at the far end of which his new cottage-home was located. Who the two individuals might be was a mystery to him, but, if they were indeed a couple, as he thought, then he figured that the male of the pair was most likely the one who had dashed on ahead of his companion, and now stood idly flinging stones over the top of its stone parapet and down into the fast-flowing river, which, though unseen from where Tom presently sat, he well knew lay around a hundred feet or so directly below it.

Tom rubbed his stubbly chin and smiled broadly at the sight: he envied the young male his youth, his vigour, his fearless, care-free spirit, and his healthy exuberance. He and his girl were probably newly returned from school, he mused, and most likely making hay in the Spring afternoon's gradually fading sunlight, in much the same way, he tenderly recalled, that he and his childhood love, and future wife, Carys, had ofttimes done in the shadow-strewn hours after the home-bell had sounded at the tiny village-school they had both attended in his native, Breconshire home, not many miles away to the north. Tom wiped away the tear that came rolling down his cheek as he pondered what the said woman had meant to him during the twenty or more years that they had lived together as man-and-wife. And he wept again for their parting, and their divorce, and the immense distance that the dreadfully sad circumstances had put between them. And finally, he wept bitterly for Carys's cruel, painful, and protracted death.

'What film are you showing them, then?' Anne asked Gareth, as she carefully guided the wheel-chair bearing the crazy-haired, elderly lady in the shawl into the already crowded common-room. 'We hope it's something fun today - something exciting, don't we, Doris?'

'Aye, something romantic, I hope,' the old woman replied, wiping her wet chin with the bib that was still hanging from her neck. 'But not too sexy, you know. It's the middle of the afternoon, after all, and things don't ever get hot around here until after all the men have been fed and rested and had their tablets.'

'It's '*Camelot*,' ' Gareth informed them, moving away from the plasma-screen with the slender remote in his hand.. 'Vanessa Redgrave, Richard Harris, you know.'

'Oh, I do like him,' Doris told them, licking her dry lips with an even drier-looking tongue. 'I just hope he wears his right size tights this time, that's all. My dead husband - God rest his soul - never looked quite right in mine, I felt, whatever colour he wore. But he just wouldn't take telling, you know.'

'O.K.,' said Gareth grinning at Anne with his eyes, but with his palm endeavouring to cover his mouth.

'Patrick was six-feet-four and a scaffolder, you see. And you can just imagine how awfully windy it can get when you're sitting on top of a tower-block or a pointy church-spire, can't you?'

'Painful, too, I'd imagine,' Gareth replied in a quieter voice that this time only Anne could make out.

'Oh, look! Here comes your daughter to see you, cariad,' announced Anne, suddenly tensing up, and wondering how she might get away quickly from the infernal little woman who was approaching quickly on her little, booted legs. After all, she was married, unhappily, by some accounts, to Rhiannon's dad Arthur Dylan - a man who had expressed his love for Anne on two separate occasions during her lifetime, and to whom she had returned the favour more than abundantly just the once, to the extent that, completely unbeknown to his wife Gwen, Arthur, (or Dyl as he was far better known,) was the real father of Anne's only son Chris.

'They told me you're watching *Camelot*,' said Gwen, with an angry look on her face. 'Well, we'll sit this one out, if you don't mind, folks. I mean making a trivial song-and-dance out of our cultural heritage is not at all my idea of an afternoon's entertainment. What do you say, Mam?'

'But what about the men in tights?' Doris asked her daughter, with a look of sincere appeal in her eyes.

'Tights! But the men never wore tights back then, mother,' Gwen told her sharply. 'That's all that slushy Anglo-French, medieval interpretation for you, that is. They've gone and turned our cultural history into a silly love-story between some poncy English king in drag and his pointy-hatted, bejewelled queen. What a total travesty, eh? Whoever heard of such nonsense.'

'Whatever do you mean?' Anne asked her, just as the large room's lights were being dimmed.

'I mean that all that Camelot crap is just so, so fake, dear,' Gwen shot back.

'But isn't Camelot somewhere down in Cornwall?' asked Anne. 'I'm sure I read that.'

'Correction - it's at Glastonbury,' Gareth chimed in. 'Near to where they hold the music festival, you know.'

'Pfuhh! Then you clearly don't know your own history, young man,' replied Gwen, shaking her head about with authority.

'Why *my own*?' enquired Gareth, determined now not to let the matter drop.

'*Why!*' Gwen snapped back. 'I'll tell you *why*. Because Arthur was a Welshman like you and I, and a tribal chieftain to boot, who united a whole host of disparate Celtic tribes under his brave, courageous leadership. And Arthur never spoke any English, either, I'll have you know.'

'Didn't he?' asked Gareth.

'Of course not,' Gwen retorted. 'How on earth could he? Back then English hadn't been invented!'

'You know, I never knew that,' interjected Anne.

'And Arthur was never a king, neither,' continued Gwen. 'There's no record of him ever having been crowned, for a start. And as for Arthur's castle - his court, if you like – well, it has recently been verified as having been located in the very place my father's family hail from.'

'Where's that? Do you mean Newport?' Anne suggested, almost tempted to say Ireland.

'Caerleon, yes,' Gwen told her. 'Right on the banks of the River Usk down there, on the outskirts of the town. And, you know, they've just discovered Caerleon's ancient trading port there too, and found out that it was far, far grander than they had ever imagined.'

'Well, I never,' uttered Anne, mouth agape. 'Why, you live and learn, don't you, Gareth?'

'So you mean that Camelot is just some Anglo-French, medieval scam of sorts,' said Gareth.

'Absolutely,' replied Gwen. 'As are all the French names you find in the slushy re-write. In truth they went and made a right pig's ear of the actual facts in Arthur's story just to satisfy the romantic appetite of the slushy French folk, and of the medieval English many centuries later,'

'You mean long after he had died,' said Anne.

'If you like, dear. If you really believe that he *is* dead,' said Gwen.

'You mean - you don't mean you still believe he -'

'But that nice Richard Harris is Irish, Gwen,' Doris told her daughter forcefully but to no real purpose. 'Oh, please, love. Can't I just see what he's wearing on his lovely long legs? Please. Please, Gwen. Pretty please.'

The music that suddenly filled the room told everyone that the film was beginning. A hush gradually began to settle on all the aged, chatty, coughing, comfortably seated residents of *The Willows* care home, but a surly, stubborn Gwen turned her mother's wheel-chair right round, and steered, a markedly less than contented, Doris straight out of the common-room, and back down the long, shiny corridor she had just minutes before arrived along, towards her distant, poky single-room.

With genuine sympathy, Anne watched the shawl-covered back of Doris as the speeding passenger was gracelessly chauffered from the scene, yet glancing back twice despairingly, before her taxi finally careered round a tight corner and disappeared completely from sight. 'Poor dear,' said Anne. 'She'll never get to see what Arthur was wearing on his lovely legs after all.'

'Yes, poor Doris. But you know it's lucky her mother didn't show up for the film I showed last week, that's all I can say,' Gareth informed her with a grin, grasping her tenderly by the hand.

'Why is that?' enquired Anne, smiling.

'Don't you remember?' Gareth asked her. 'We showed them '*Monty Python And The Holy Grail.*'

The bespectacled old man took the prized, recently polished, sheep's jaw-bone from his knapsack, and promptly waved it before him towards the powerful wind that blew into his face from out of the high peaks of The Brecon Beacons to the north. He smiled, believing that he now knew the power that an ancient Welsh tribal chief must feel, exhorting his brave men to advance before him and drive back the hated Norman invader, so as to maintain independence, and the control which this implied over their native soil, their farms, their farm produce. The fossil finds may have been disappointing today, Tom told himself, but this last discovery, albeit clearly a contemporaneous one, was indeed something that he felt he could get his teeth into!

The old man laughed aloud, suddenly apprehending the sheer audacity of this last reflection. He peered into the distance. 'And death to all of the Latin tongue!' he bellowed out as loudly as he could manage before his tender throat promptly seized up in pain, and he succumbed to a horrible bout of coughing.

As Tom wheezed and spluttered helplessly, the echo of his deep, baritone voice could still be heard clearly right across the valley, which now lay, very gradually, darkening before him. The sheep nearby all turned their heads sharply to study him, their heavy coats shivering as they did so, one or two urinating resonantly into the short grass beneath them with palpable fear.

Just a few seconds later the distant, slim, male and female figures, which were by now making their way abreast of each other along the former railway-track, and towards the nearby woods, halted, and seemed to peer out in his direction.

Although Tom could not quite see half as well as they could, he was able to tell that the boy with the gleaming, silver telescope was shaking his head with apparent disdain, and calling the flame-haired, young girl, whom Tom could see was carrying a bulky, black box, to his side, so as to share with her his new, magnified perspective, and his personal opinion concerning the old fool he now beheld upon the hill.

Tom watched the slim-figured girl intently. He already felt he knew exactly the thoughts that filled her mind, and he also knew that she would very soon fall out with the boy, who now stood behind her, having just handed her his telescope. After briefly ruminatng once more over his own long-lost love and marriage, Tom heaved a deep sigh, realising full well how, within that very hour, the slim, young girl's hopes of love would literally come crashing down with the trees.

Chris carried the bulky, black radio-recorder into the deepest part of Vaynor Woods, placed the item snugly at the foot of a tree, turned on some music at full-blast, then took the axe from his shoulder-bag and began chopping. The noise he created was instantly deafening, so much so that he wasn't able to hear Rhiannon's sweet, high tones calling out to him from behind, and imploring him to kindly tell her what on earth the point was in his bizarre behaviour.

'Chris! Chris! What do you think you're doing!' she pleaded, folding away his little, silver telescope and staring across in his direction. 'You know this isn't at all like you, don't you? And you told me last week how you can't even stand woodwork.'

Rhiannon approached apprehensively as her dark-haired lover carried on clubbing at the tree, finally finding herself becoming increasingly engrossed, and more than a little admiring, of his unfamiliar vigour, and even of his detached, self-absorbed attitude, as he went about carving a great, gaping notch near the base of the naked tree-trunk, little more than a foot or so above the soft, loose carpet of nettles, leaves, and bracken that surrounded it.

Chris had already stripped off his shirt, and now stood tall, his lean body brown, and liberally covered in beads of sweat, the odour of which, Rhiannon decided, smelt deliciously male and strong. She sat herself down on the horizontal, fallen trunk of an even larger tree, which she imagined he might perhaps have chopped down in a similar fashion on some previous occasion when he spent his spare time alone in the woods. Suddenly spying something exquisite in the long grass, she reached down and examined a beautiful, but frayed, long-discarded, satin glove.

The audio-tape that was playing *Eminem* at full-volume had already begun to infuriate her, and so Rhiannon walked over to the machine and flicked up the switch which instantly delivered them *Radio One* instead. A song off an album she had at home by Adele - was playing, and so Rhiannon smiled at her good fortune and resumed her seat. Yes, this was much more her kind of music, she told herself. She began to imagine what it must be like to have someone waiting ages and ages for you on your very own doorstep, but, however much she considered it, she somehow couldn't quite see any boy she knew, Chris included, being that placid and patient, much less romantic. Did such boys actually exist? she pondered. If they did, then she certainly didn't expect to encounter any of them in the close-knit Welsh valley she lived in. If truth be told, Rhiannon mused, she occasionally felt ecstatic if her boyfriend actually turned up to meet her on time, and was frequently grateful that he had decided to show up at all.

A few minuutes later the mind-numbing racket of the chopping suddenly ceased, and Chris walked over to the recorder and switched it off. He threw down the axe, and began to dry off his torso by rubbing himself vigorously in his crumpled shirt, gazng across at his girl as he did so. Just then he felt that Rhiannon looked so pretty, and so loyal to him, sat there as she was, waiting patiently for him to complete his task and move across and join her. Chris bent low and took from his bag a large ball of twine and unrolled it a little, then paused and looked up again. Watching Rhiannon slapping her two pretty knees together, and twirling the long tresses of her red hair securely behind her ears, he decided that it was now time to tell her why he had brought her there that day, although he felt a distinct urge to tease her just a little first.

Rhiannon looked up and noticed him watching her, and so, folding up the teen-magazine she had been reading, called over in his direction. 'Do you know you can adopt a jaguar for just two pounds a month?' she said. 'Isn't that amazing? I must remember to tell Dad.'

'Really? But won't it just mess up your house something dreadful?' replied Chris, grinning.

'It's just an ad, silly!' Rhiannon told him. 'You know - for *endangered animals*. My Aunt Ada used to adopt quite a lot of wild creatures. Then she met Bamber!' she announced, emitting a noise that resembled a snarl. 'We all told her it wasn't going to last, and do you know that once they had finished their relationship, and he had removed from the house everything he had bought while they were together, he told her he wanted her implants back. Can you imagine it? God! You could never be *that* crass, could you, Chris?'

'Oh, I don't know,' her mischievous lover replied. 'If I tried, I reckon I could. '*Crass Chris.*' I actually quite like that moniker as it goes. Sounds cool. Anyway, if you remember, Rhiannon, it was only a day or so after we first started going out that I made you take your tits out, right?' he told her, grinning. 'So how is that any different?'

Rhiannon jumped up and reached out a fist to strike him, but he swiftly spun away from her. She sat down again. 'But boobs is just - well, they're just boobs, aren't they?' she told him. 'But *implants*, for God's sake! Well, I mean they're -'

'Bags of alien fluid unnaturally forced under a woman's breast muscles and skin,' shot back Chris. 'Poisonous, even. That Bamber fella did your aunt a favour, if you ask me,' he went on, bending at the waist and forcing the axe back inside his shoulder-bag, and then walking over to where Rhiannon sat waiting for him, her pretty, tanned knees now set slightly apart.

'Well, no, he didn't do her any favour, as it happens,' she told him. 'because my Aunt simply refused to return them. And can you blame her? After all, they were *hers*, not *his*. Bamber - her rich, but crazy, boyfriend - had just paid for them, that's all.'

'God - they're only breast-implants we're talking about, babe,' said Chris. 'Anyway, do you want to know what I'd feel like if I ever did what he did to a woman?'

'What?' asked Rhiannon.

'A bit of a tit, as it goes.'

'Ha, ha - very funny,' said Rhiannon. 'That's so hilarious, that is.' She leaned her head to the side and stared at him. Hey - are you're making fun of me again, Chris? You are, aren't you?

'No, not at all. Why would I do that, babe?' he asked, suddenly leaning down and grasping her head, and then kissing her full on the lips. Pulling back again he said, 'Do you remember the time you didn't believe me when I told you how the robin was the most reliant of birds?' He tilted his head to the side and smiled at Rhiannon's quite helpless level of discernment. Even this comment was plainly way over her head, he thought, and yet, just then, he found he couldn't help himself. Yes, Chris realised that he still loved Rhiannon's wonderful, unpredictable, girly innocence more than anything else he had so far discovered about her. He crouched close to her seated form and pressed his knee up against hers, then, quite without warning, his muddy right hand began to drift down inside her brassiere, almost as if it had a mind of its own.

Permitting his plunging, kneading, most tender of embraces, Rhiannon looked up into her boyfriend's eyes, and stymied his second kiss momentarily, by asking him, 'Chris, why did you chop down two trees that don't even belong to you?'

'Two! Only one, sweetheart,' he replied, mysteriously. Then added, 'The other tree I've been hacking at today we're about to pull down between us.'

'You and I are going to do that! Are you mad?' she asked. Rhiannon pointed over his shoulder. 'But surely that one is practically down already, isn't it?'

'It is,' he replied. 'But it won't finally crash to the ground until we begin to leave the woods.'

'Won't it?' she enquired, now extremely curious to find out what her lover was actually aiming to achieve with all his hard slog and perspiration. With her forefinger she lovingly wiped a bead of sweat off Chris's rib-cage

'No. it won't,' he replied. 'Look - Rhiannon. I'll show you, shall I?'

Chris jumped up and approached the tottering tree, and spun a few rolls of strong twine around its trunk. He then picked up the radio-recorder, but, instead of carrying it away from the scene, he pressed down a few of its buttons, replaced it on the ground a few paces from the tree, and began to disguise its presence beneath a camouflage of small branches and a handful of grass fronds. Then, still holding tightly onto the ball of twine, Chris slowly retreated back towards Rhiannon, and reached out his hand for her to take it from him.

'Hey! What do you think you're doing?' she asked, jumping to her feet.

'Just hold it, Rhi!' he commanded, before suddenly spinning round and racing off into the distance, his semi-naked torso quickly disappearing behind a clump of trees, where he paused for a moment, and called back to her. 'Just don't lose your grip now, that's all,' he reiterated, 'otherwise we'll just have to tie it all over again.'

Rhiannon was none the wiser, but, feeling that it was now high time that they did in fact make their way home, she decided to comply with his odd request. 'You know, sometimes, Chris Cillick, you just make me want to scream,' she told him, smiling.

'Scream all you want, babe!' replied Chris, turning, and then ambling away down the slope into the valley bottom, where, once found, the narrow path would thence lead him on homewards, towards *The Seven Arches* and his supper. 'You're in a thick forest, remember!' he hollered back at her. 'So who the heck is going to hear you? Don't you get it?' He felt she couldn't have. 'If you're on your own, and there's nobody there to hear the sound you make -'

'Oh, I see. You know I think I get what you're trying to do now,' Rhiannon called back at him, smiling, and suddenly feeling quite admiring of his ingenuity, and now almost as fascinated as he clearly was to see how this strange, homemade Physics experiment of his own devising might actually turn out. 'You're not as thick as you look, Christopher Cillick,' she remarked to no one, giggling away to herself at her use of a phrase that Chris had, more than once, used about her. 'But, I will say this - you are definitely the fittest boy that *I've* ever known, and no mistake.'

A crow squawked agonisingly from a branch above Rhiannon's head, and she halted and peered up at it, hoping that it wasn't about to foul her. Yes, there's little doubt about how fit you are, she mused. I'll grant you that, Christopher Gareth Cillick, student, lover, future professor, husband. And do you know, young man, I believe you might even turn out to be one who could conceivably change the world with his hands behind his back, or with one hand behind your back, and the other one pressed snugly in mine, perhaps, she told herself, smiling. 'Rhiannon Cillick,' she whispered softly to the crow, then giggled once again as she deigned to repeat it in the face of superstition, adding, 'And Christopher Cillick I do believe that you'll be there for life.'

Gliding through the undergrowth deep in thought, Rhiannon suddenly let slip the ball of twine from her pale, delicate hands, and, in retrieving it, and lifting it again from out of the long grass, momentarily caught sight of the flashed-up image in her mind's eye of her handsome, semi-naked lover catching, and supporting the trunk of a giant, slanting tree between his tanned, tight-muscled legs. Shocked, and more than a little ashamed of her stark, sensual reverie, Rhiannon began laughing loudly, and somewhat uncontrollably, to just herself and the odd crow, in the seemingly uncharted, deep, dark bowels of Vaynor Woods; the wonderful, mysterious woods that were to her - to Rhiannon Charlotte Cook, seventeen years young, and only daughter of Arthur Dylan Thomas Cook and Gwen Philomena Cook of Caerleon, Cemetery Road, Pant, Merthyr Tydfil - the hitherto, now, and foreverafter, sweet-scented, lush, green playground of both her own, and her brilliant, fearless, handsome first-lover's youth.

Rhiannon followed her sweetheart's trail down the shadowy, tree-covered hill towards the river, and when she finally caught sight of Chris, watching her slyly from among the trees, and with a ball of strong twine held firmly in his own grip, she sat herself down in the long grass, took up the slack on her own ball, and pulled as hard as she could with both hands. Then pausing for breath, and so as to assess the situation, she giggled quietly once more, realising that, although she could hear absolutely nothing in the woods that lay before her, that that didn't necessarily mean that something fundamental hadn't happened in there.

Chris soon skipped out of his makeshift lair and rejoined his girl, sitting close up behind her on the ground, knees wrapped tightly round her hips, and tenderly pecked her on the neck. Then together they gently intertwined their two separate spools to create one enormous, now much stronger, more powerful, line, and, heels set, and with considerable strain, and much puffing and panting, the youthful, laughing, care-free couple, unwittingly, began to pull their love apart.

CHAPTER 5

Without question the most talented sixth-form student ever to attend Pennant Comprehensive School, Carla Steel hadn't become a successful recording artist purely by chance. She understood only too well how music was in her very soul, and was convinced that she had acquired her talent from her mother, who had only recently passed away in her house in the Home Counties from the cancer which had long riddled her tired and aching body. And, in deference to her mother's family, she had chosen to call herself by *their* family name, rather than by her birth-name - her father's name, Davies - the surname of the man who had chosen to stay out of her life after her Mam elected to move from their family home in a small village in rural Breconshire to reside alone not many miles from where her daughter Carla was living in London, during that special time when she was preparing to record her first, her break-through, album.

It was already late afternoon, and Carla Steel was now returning home to Wales for the first time in years, hopefully to reunite, and perhaps even bond once again, with her father, just a few months after taking him completely by surprise, and sending him by post a six-figure cheque, large enough for him to buy himself the quiet, country home that he always craved, and which he could now happily live, then die, in. And now in his seventy-sixth year, and with failing health a genuine problem, Carla knew only too well that her father Tom might not have very long left to him on this Earth, but, since she knew she wasn't the sort of person who could forever hold a grudge, she felt confident that, by going to see him, she might at last be able to forgive and forget, or at least move their fractured relationship on to a new, perhaps more tender, footing.

As she gazed out of the window of the train from London at the contented group of swans that seemed to circle endlessly round each other on the glistening waters of the River Thames near Reading, Carla reminded herself how the nature and the variety of her young life's joys and tribulations had been what had yielded up for her the nutritious food upon which her musical abilities had voraciously fed, and that therefore, to Carla, her music was unquestionably her life.

On the two previous occasions that she had returned to her homeland Carla had elected to stay at a plush, five-star hotel on the outskirts of Cardiff, but this time she had decided to book herself into a relatively small motel in the heart of The Brecon Beacons, where she knew the air would do service to her lungs, and the lofty peaks would hopefully maintain her buoyant spirits, and perhaps even provide her with some sort of creative stimulus. The guitar-case she carried on her back on her stop-off for food in the centre of Merthyr was all the proof the town's populace required to claim that the unmistakable, raven-haired, poet-minstrel had finally come home. To them it seemed to signify that her busy life on the road was done, most likely overtaken, superseded even, by her instinctive, feminine need to finally settle down, and perhaps pair up with a nice, dependable, local-born member of the opposite sex, and, like the majority of Welsh women around her age get herself married and bear fruit.

But babies and love happened to be the last things on the attractive young woman's mind. Carla was in her home area purely for a reconciliation, and, as she deposited her leather-clad burden in the boot of the black Vauxhall Vectra outside Merthyr Station, and paid the driver his generous tip in advance, she was thinking only of waterfalls and Welsh-cakes, lofty peaks and rambling, and soft, Welsh water at last, and the thick, soapy lather that one could easily make with it at bath-time. But, gazing out at the figures on the bridge that were hurrying and scuttling across the River Taff for the comfort of hearth and home, most of all Carla was thinking about sleep - hours and hours of dreamy, peaceful, deep, forgiving sleep.

The crunching sound of the sandstone shingle, grinding itself ever smaller beneath the taxi's wheels, as it pulled slowly into the motel car-park, gradually woke Carla from her brief, head-lolling nap, and warned her that her weary legs would soon be required to perform yet one more act - that of bearing her in the direction of 'Reception.' Inhaling deeply the cool, clean air that swept in from the west as she slipped from the car onto the bottom step of five that led up to the door, Carla momentarly felt enlivened, and thought that, if she could only concentrate long and hard enough, she might just be able to pour herself a hot, steamy bath and perhaps fall soundly asleep within it, head tilted to one side, and satisfactorily clear of its warm, comforting bubbles.

Leaning her body against the tall, chestnut desk, Carla paused, looking around her for a moment or two so as to take in the comparative solitude of her sparse, new surroundings, before finally writng the name 'Davies C.' into the motel-register, as she had done now for the greater portion of her adult life. Once handed the room-keys, and being directed to her ground-floor apartment by an aged lady in a long cardigan and trainers, who drew her two items of luggage behind her on a trolley, the singer entered the suite through its polished door, guitar-case in hand, and flopped herself down beside all three on the pink eiderdown of the large, curtained bed, to drift, almost instantly, into the deep, forgiving slumber she so desperately craved.

It was well past one in the morning when Carla finally woke up again, and, after depositing her instrument and her unopened suitcases inside the closet, lay back down again - this time beneath the thick, warm blankets - and slept, and dreamed on, for at least seven hours more.

'Oh, I see now. So home is where the art is,' Drew announced, with a smile. The class were Year-Nines, - Mrs. Llewellyn's form - so he guessed that none of them would get it. They didn't disappoint him.

'Yes, Sir,' a boy at the nearest table replied. 'I'm afraid I must have left it by my X-box in my bedroom. Sorry, Mr. Cillick.'

'You do your Art homework in your bedroom, Ashley?' retorted Drew. 'Blimey! So where do you take your girlfriend, young man? To the garden-shed?'

'I don't have one, Sir,' the fast reddening boy responded.

'A girlfriend?'

'No, a garden-shed, Sir,' Ashley answered with a grin. 'You know you're hilariously funny sometimes, Mr. Cillick. Er - not! My girlfriend is in Year Ten, Sir. Marilyn Morgan?'

'Marilyn Morgan,' Drew repeated, rubbing his pointed chin. 'Oh, I see. My, my, Ashley. Well done, by the way, boy.' Many pupils laughed at this familiar aside. 'You know, Ashley, I think you and I have something in common, after all. You see, it seems that older women have always hopelessly succumbed to my charms too, young man, although I can't really explain why.' More laughter ensued. 'The homework is not of her, though, is it? It was supposed to be a still-life, young man, and I can assure you Marilyn Morgan has never sat still for five minutes in her entire life. Just watch. She'll be in here looking for a pen for Maths again any moment now.'

'Sir - guess who Nessa fancies,' said a curly red-haired girl sitting opposite Ashley on the front-table.

'I do not!' the horrified, brunette girl sitting beside her ejaculated.

'She hasn't even said *who*, yet, Nessa. Give the girl a chance,' said Drew. 'O.K. We're all ears, Catherine.'

There followed a short pause, during which Drew took the pile of homework sheets he had collected to his desk, and then returned to face the class. 'Er - you *are* goimg to tell us, aren't you, Catherine? You know, I can feel my ears expanding as we speak.' Many children laughed at this. 'Don't be afraid, girl. Say, what's the matter?'

'I'm afraid - I'm afraid you might get angry with me, Mr. Cillick,' Catherine told him.

'You mean - you don't mean she fancies *me*!' he bellowed, and stared straight into the face of the red-faced girl sitting beside her. 'God, Nessa - how sad is that, my dear!'

'No, Sir, not you,' Nessa replied, clearly wincing at her teacher's typically risque suggestion..

'Who, then?' asked Drew.

'Tell him, Ness,' Catherine urged her friend. 'It's O.K. Mrs. Llewellyn already knows, *and* everyone else in here.' Then looking at Drew, 'She fancies Chris, Sir.'

'Chris!' exclaimed Drew, thinking fast. 'You don't mean the school-keeper!'

'No, Sir. Chris, your son, Sir,' announced Catherine. 'Sir, tell her - tell her it's hopeless, will you, Mr. Cillick? She's gone completely mad with love for him since watching rugby-training last Tuesday evening. She said she thinks he's ever so lush, Sir.'

At this comment Nessa suddenly let her head drop and began to sob.

'Oh, please don't go crying, Nessa,' Drew told her, moving closer. 'Look, if it's any consolation to you, young lady, I understand that my boy Chris isn't seeing anyone at the moment. Apart from his usual boyfriends, of course.' The class laughed again as one, and even Nessa seemed to jiggle her fallen head a little at the sheer stupidity of it. 'There again, don't go quoting me on that, now, *Nine Double-L.*'

'But *he is*, Sir,' Catherine and Nessa told him in unison.

'What? My Chris! Is he?' asked Drew, somewhat surprised.

'Yes, Sir,' Catherine told him. 'He's going out with that ginger girl in Year Eleven who stayed back a year. What's her name, again?' She spun round for enlightenment on the matter.

'Rhiannon Cook!' at least half the entire class responded helpfully.

'Didn't you even know, Sir?' Nessa asked him, sensing his surprise and dismay.

'Er - no. Actually I - I hadn't noticed,' came Drew's hushed reply.

'Sir hadn't even noticed, you lot!' Catherine turned and announced vociferously to the class, seemingly to elicit him some degree of sympathy. 'Sorry. Mr. Cillick, Sir. I can understand how you might want better for your son than - than *that.*'

At this, a tall girl with long, straight blond hair and glasses in the corner decided to chip in her five-pennyworth. 'But now that you know all about it, Mr. Cillick,' she said, 'don't you think that they go really well together?' Catherine's mouth fell wide open as she spun round to watch her.

'I - I don't know, I really don't. I never thought about it,' Drew answered, looking up to check the clock, and realising that he still had almost fifty minutes left before he could even get himself to the staff-room, which is where he now so wanted to be. Yes, Drew suddenly felt a desperate need for a calming coffee and a cigarette, and a decent break from the busy, noisy classroom, so as to consider the impact of the news he had just discovered, totally by chance, in what was only his second lesson of the day. This wasn't his worst, nightmare scenario, he kept telling himself, by way of encouragement, but there was no denying that it was pretty damn close.

'I'm not being cruel to you, Vanessa,' the girl in the corner continued, 'but I think it's the ideal combination, don't you? Dark, with fair. Brown eyes with blue. I mean, isn't that perfect?' A few girls nodded. 'Like me and - and Justin Bieber. The ideal marriage, even though I say so myself.'

'Well, I just think you are trying to be cruel, Angharad,' Catherine called out, raising her brows in a perfect v-shape and giving the bespectacled girl *the evils*. 'Isn't she, Sir? And she doesn't even seem to care a fig about how my best friend feels. Now that's just not right, is it Mr. Cillick? Mr. Cillick. Mr. Cillick! Sir - where are you going?'

Drew was in a total daze. He felt he needed to ring Anne right away, and so he collected his packet of cigarettes and his mobile-phone from the desk-drawer and spun round, and, opening the classroom-door with a deft, right-foot kick just below the handle, walked straight out. As he did so he almost collided with Marilyn Morgan, who happened to be standing outside the door.

'Mr. Cillick, can you help me Sir?' she said, a pleading look on her heavily mascarra-ed face.

'What? Of course I can, Marilyn,' he told her. 'There's a whole selection of them lying on my desk. Take what you like girl, yeah?'

Walking off into the room, Marilyn suddenly turned round to gaze at him again, and said, 'Sir, you're so kind, do you know that?'

'Am I?' Drew retorted, biting his top lip nervously, and inspecting closely the lettering on the fire-extinguisher on the wall, thereby feigning distraction.

'Yes, Sir. Mr. Cillick - what's wrong Sir?' she enquired. 'Because I can see that something is. I'm right, yeah? Let me help you, please. Just tell me what I can do for you, Sir, and I'll do it.'

'Oh, I don't know,' Drew replied, thinking fast. 'Well, I suppose there is something you can do for me, as it happens, Marilyn. Though I don't like to impose.'

'Just say it, Sir,' the pretty. diminutive girl replied, approaching him and staring into his face.

'I need someone sensible to watch my class for a little while. Sit at the front, you know?'

'Oh, I can do that!' she told him, smiling. 'Brill! What are they supposed to be getting on with?'

'It's 'Life-drawing,' as it goes,' he replied. 'The materials are all laid out at the front. Just hand them out and get the class to draw whoever is sitting opposite them, would you?'

'You just to leave it to me, Sir,' Marilyn told him, beaming in anticipation, and noticing the cigarettes in his hand. 'Look, you just go and have a ciggy and put your feet up and relax for a bit,' she added. 'Because, you know, Mr. Cillick Sir, I also plan to be a teacher one day.'

'You're very kind, Marilyn,' Drew retorted, smiling back at her. 'And don't worry, I'll pop in and see Mr. Collins-Maths and tell him you're presently helping me in my room, O.K.?'

'Thank you, Sir,' answered Marilyn. 'Though I imagine he'll have already guessed I won't be back for a while. You see I always do a bit of a tour of the school about this time of the morning.'

'Oh, and Marilyn,' Drew said, now already half-way down the corridor, but turning back.

'Yes Sir?'

'You can always let Ashley Rees draw *you*, if you like.' Drew winked at her once, then turned and walked away as the girl from Year Ten punched the air with pure joy.

Tom Davies lay in his single-bed beside a cold hot-water bottle and with a fresh pair of pants in his right hand, wondering if the daughter he adored, but had not seen for almost ten years now, had arrived from London as planned, and would decide to visit him in the next day or so. But the old man need not have worried his grey head about it, since, unbeknown to him, the thirty-one year old Carla was already on her way, in a 'Royston's' mini-cab, travelling less than incognito - apart from the obligatory 'shades,' of course, and the trade-mark, large, black, furry hat she had recently taken to wearing - dressed in a simple skirt and jumper beneath her brand-new, long, grey, cashmere overcoat.

Suddenly hearing the sound of a car-door slam, Tom arose, and, pulling on a threadbare dressing-gown to shield him from the Spring chill, he edged his way over towards the window to try to see out. From this vantage-point he soon caught sight of his only daughter dismissing her cab back down the hill, pushing open his squeaky iron-gate, and, in her short, but languorous, stride, making her way up towards his new front-door. Realising that he wasn't going to be able to make it downstairs in time to greet her when she knocked, Tom quickly raised his front-window as high as it would go, and leaning out, and with a mixture of love and anticipation, peered down upon his daughter's sweet, covered head, and the black, flowing tresses of the scarf which, from above, seemed to circle freely around it.

Hearing the horrible, grating noise that the window made above her, Carla looked up, and addressed the man in tones which, sadly, he could no longer recognise. God, it had been that long, Tom told himself. He nevertheless concluded that the voice of the girl he could barely see without his glasses on was indeed the lovely daughter that he and his dear, departed, ex-wife had borne and raised in love, and christened Carla.

Tom suddenly had a brain-wave. He picked up his spare door-keys from the dresser, and then leaned out once more and threw them down onto the lawn beside his daughter's feet. 'There you go Carla! Come in out of the cold, won't you!' he called down to her, and he smiled nervously to himself as she swiftly responded by unlocking the front-door and shuffling inside.

Wiping her feet on the door-mat, Carla looked about her. Yes, it was a lot smaller inside the house than she had expected, she mused, and, for a moment or two, as she surveyed the cold, bare lounge, she felt that perhaps her unexpected gift to him had proved to be a less than generous one. After all, she pondered, she was now an A-list celebrity, a high earner, and a very rich woman, and could easily have housed her father in far greater luxury than this rather humble, three-bedroom, terraced property that he himself had chosen to settle for.

Carla laid her fur-hat on the old oak-table in the middle of the living-room and went looking for the kitchen, which she soon discovered was at the rear of the house. She checked in each of the wall-cupboards for a hint of a snack of some kind, but, sadly, discovered none. Then, peeking inside the fridge at the seemingly perspiring, cling-filmed plate of pink salmon that sat sadly in its state of solitary confinement on the top-shelf, she concluded that there was little doubt that an elderly, single man lived alone there, and one who clearly didn't eat a great deal, and probably had to scrimp and save just to make ends meet. Then suddenly sensing the odour that betrayed the fact it needed a good cleaning out, she swiftly slammed shut the door of the fridge, then turned towards the high-pitched, squeaking sound she took to be the kitchen-door opening. It was then that she saw Tom walk in

'Oh, Dad!' exclaimed Carla, biting sharply into her bottom-lip, and staring at his thin, drawn, bespectacled face, and the grey-fringed, balding pate that sat above it, trying her utmost to recall it. Beneath his dressing-gown his grey sweater hung from him in great hanging folds and bulges. 'It's been such a long time, Dad,' she announced, trembling all over, and not at all sure what else to say to him.

Tom approached his daughter with a sudden, flapping shuffle of rubber-soled slippers over linoleum, and embraced her slim body tightly in his firm, but bony grasp. Tears of pure joy began to well out from his creased, mole-speckled eyes very like a mountain-spring. Her body felt to him very much as it did when he had embraced her the last time at Cardiff Airport, ten or so years before, except that, now that she was finally back, he was determined that he would do all in his power not to ever let her get away from him again. No, never again, he told himself firmly.

Carla folded her shorter form into her father's breast, and allowed his tears to dampen freely the high collar of the purple, woollen jumper that she wore. A long, protracted embrace of this kind was the very least she could do for her own father, she mused, as, ever so gradually, she began to loosen her hold, and endeavoured to ease his aged form, gently and lovingly, back into the large, wooden rocking-chair that sat invitingly alongside the kitchen-table. When she saw that Tom was comfortably settled, and staring up at her through tearful eyes, Carla pulled up a stool and sat herself down facing him, took out a large white handkerchief from her pocket, placed his spectacles carefully on the table-top, and gently dried her father's face. She couldn't tell him just then, but this was something she had dreamed of doing for him ever since she was a young girl, and so she savoured the sweet moment to the max, and finally, gently cleaning his concave lenses in a paper-tissue, she began to feel that soon she might start crying too.

'Oh, Dad,' Carla said again. 'How old you have got, love.'

'I know. And how lovely *you've* got,' he responded, now smiling serenely into her bright, blue eyes that he had always felt much resembled his own.

'Tell me - have you managed to settle in to your new home yet?' Carla asked him. 'I see you need to stock up a little in the provisions department. Is that all you've got - cold meats and lard and pink salmon? There was a time, I remember, when you insisted on red.'

'How many years is it, Carla?' Tom asked his daughter, feeling that whatever answer she gave him would be just the right one.

'I don't know for sure,' she replied. 'Ten, maybe? Eleven? I'm thirty-one now. But let's not think about it, shall we?'

'And Carys is gone since -'

'Last May,' she told him. Now she finally *was* going to cry, she thought. Mention of her dead mother always seemed to do this to her. Carla stood up and turned, as if to look out of the window, and her damp, but lustrous eyes suddenly took in the staggering sight of the vast, limestone viaduct, standing imperiously behind the little house in all its late-morning glory. 'Oh, Dad!' she shrieked. 'What a lovely view you have here. Is it - is it really the -'

'Yes, *The Seven Arches*,' he replied, getting up from his chair and joining her, and placing his arm around her shoulder, as he remembered he had often done when she was a sad young girl who needed comforting, or reassuring, or just a lift up in the air and a spin round. 'You know these days you can easily ramble away from it for miles in either direction, if you want, girl, except I feel that down that way - eastwards – I've discovered is by far the best.'

Gripping her father's thin, veined hand in hers, Carla asked, 'And is that *Morlais Castle* I can see up there?'

'It is,' he responded. 'See - that's where that cave is that's shaped just like a key-hole, do you remember? And up-river,' he told her, pointing down to the left of it, 'where the fiery kingfishers fly, and the trout we searched for always seemed to need a good tickling now and again, is that rickety old bridge that takes you back up the steep path to old Vaynor Church.'

'Oh, I remember now,' his daughter told him, smiling. 'And isn't that where that old iron-master is buried, under the biggest chunk of rock I've ever seen in my life?' she asked him, the sudden flash of the memory's image now causing her blue eyes to sparkle, as Tom recalled they often did when he took her on long walks through the wild and windy Brecon Beacons as a child.

'Yes. Just in case the miserable, old devil ever decided to try climbing back out again, I bet,' he told her, smiling.

His daughter smiled too at the sudden recollection of this old wives' tale about the long-gone, wicked iron-master. 'And I remember, too,' she went on, 'that bizarre inscription on the outside-wall of the church, that tells of the local woman who lived through the reigns of eight different monarchs.'

She gazed into his eyes again. 'I'm right, aren't I, Dad?' she pleaded. 'It was eight wasn't it?' Tom nodded. 'Well, can you just imagine that?'

'Yes, and whose husband, I recall, was a great deal younger than she was,' he replied chuckling.

'The very opposite of you and Mam,' Carla told him, with a precocious grin, and a twitch of her nose that still seemed to speak her love for him.

Yes, his beloved daughter certainly possessed his nose, Tom pondered A bit of a shame for her, that, though, he thought. 'What do you mean - the very opposite of me and your mother?' he enquired softly. 'We were - we were just seven years apart, is all we were - Carys and me.' He bit sharply into his top lip, and fought hard to stop himself from welling up again. 'You know, I have never loved anyone like I loved your mother, Carla. And I'm damn sure I never will again.'

Carla decided that she wasn't going to tease him again, but still couldn't resist taking it just one little step further. 'Oh, I bet you've got yourself a lover tucked away somewhere round here, Dad. Yeah? It was always your way, as I recall. Or at least that's what my Mam used to say.'

'She said a lot of things - your mother,' Tom replied. '*Some* of them true, of course.'

'How diplomatic you're sounding, these days,' said his daughter, a little sarcastically. 'Do you mean to tell me that those things she used to say about you were lies after all, then?'

'No, dear,' he replied. 'Just - just exaggerations, that's all. I was much younger then, remember. I had plenty of money, friends, status.'

'Status!' stammered Carla, suddenly looking into his eyes. 'What's that when it's at home? Well, I'd say you don't seem to have a great deal of status about you at the moment, do you, Dad?' To her mind, her father's sense of taste was for ever a dark spot in Carla's vision. 'Why, look at all this old furniture for a start. It's practically Victorian.'

'But isn't that good?' he joked.

'No, it isn't,' she retorted. 'I can see I shall need to get you some new stuff, for sure, and then we can shove all this old rubbish up in the loft where it truly belongs.'

Tom started laughing. 'Well, you can try if you like, young lady, but you'll never manage to get that hatch open,' he told her. 'The removals' men tried for me, and they couldn't budge it an inch, so *we* certainly shan't be able to.'

'Well, we shall see, anyway,' Carla told him. 'We've got plenty of time. Hey Dad! Look at that man running over the bridge down there! God - he's fair bombing along, isn't he?'

Tom started laughing. 'That's a man on a bicycle, sweetheart,' he told her. 'You can only see his top half above the parapet, do you see. The old railway-line is a long-distance cycle-track these days, you know. I gather you can cycle all the way to Cardiff along it if you're that way inclined. I did - I did tell you that's where I've been living these last few years, didn't I, love?'

'Cardiff? Oh, Dad,' of course you did,' she replied. 'Derrh! I must have written to you there more than twice, didn't I?'

'O.K., O.K.,' Tom retorted. 'It's just that these days I'm a bit more forgetful than I used to be, sweet. Now what was I saying?'

'I don't remember. You see, I'm a bit more forgetful than I used to be,' Carla told him, grinning like the Cheshire-cat, as she once again cuddled his frail body to her.

'You know, I can still remember the line as it was when I was young,' Tom told her. 'And all the steam-trains that crossed it in both directions, pulling their long, open trucks full of iron and steel, and coal, and limestone - the cream-coloured rock cut from the quarry in the hill over there - which supplied them with the flux they used in all the blast-furnaces in Merthyr and Dowlais, and Cardiff even, so enabling them to manufacture, first the iron, then, later on, the steel, that was always, along with coal, the staple of our region's economy.'

After telling her his history lesson, Tom suddenly began feeling weary, and so he sat back down in the rocking-chair, and made Carla sit down again on the stool beside it. 'And I can remember, too, how the passenger steam-trains that used to travel up from Dowlais and Pant and over the viaduct often used to stop at the little station-halt just over the road from the front of this house. You know, Carla, we could wander down there later if you like, and then, perhaps, cross over the viaduct, then go up along the river again until we reach that same rickety, wooden bridge. The views are truly wonderful from the viaduct at this time of the year, before the trees get too thick and green and start obscuring the view. And it's not going to rain today, either.'

'Did they say so on The News, then?' she asked him.

'No, I don't often turn on The News, love,' her father replied, rather sheepishly.

'And yet you still know that, do you?' his daughter enquired, suddenly sitting up, and staring deep into his ice-blue eyes, her mouth beginning to fall open. 'Because, if I recall, it was drizzling earlier when I got in the taxi.' Tom looked down. 'Tell me, honestly, Dad. Do you - do you still do - *all that*?' Carla asked. She wanted the truth from him now, and not some shallow reply. 'Can you really, truly *forecast events*? Can you, Dad? Or is it just like Mam said, and what I've always thought, too - just a load of old - old bollocks?' She watched Tom as he stroked the long, white hairs that ran up his thin forearm. 'You know, you can tell me now, Dad,' she went on. 'Confession is good for the soul, remember,' as my Mam never seemed to tire of telling me.'

Tom looked over his shoulder and gazed out at the high, grey castle-ruins in the distance, perched way above, and beyond, the point where the old train-line curved to the left below its precipitous, protective slopes, and where the rail-cutting carved its way round to the north and skirted Vaynor Woods, where, a few days earlier, he had watched on helplessly, as a young couple who ventured there in the evening twilight, conspired together, unknowingly, to pull their love-tree down; and where the tape-recorder, which the boy had left hidden away in the bushes, now lay totally crushed under the impact of the fallen tree.

'Listen Carla - I just feel there are certain things it's best not to - not to interfere in,' he told her, attempting the sharpest of smiles, but not quite pulling it off. And, at that, he decided to refrain from revealing any more to her, since the little she already knew about the *gift* he knew full well he possessed she certainly didn't want to believe, and, anything more that he told her, he realised she was unlikely to appreciate hearing about. His sweet daughter was so very like her mother Carys, after all, he pondered.

In Carla's eyes, he would, most likely, forever remain a disappointment, Tom told himself. And anyway, why should he bother attempting to dispel, or even interfere with, the lifelong assessment of his character that a fast-maturing Carla had gradually built up for herself in the years when she lived not many miles from her mother's home in the green-belt near London. And why should he try to change it with - with positive things? After all, hadn't his daughter twice memorialised his failings, both as a husband and a father, in songs she had written, and hadn't both creations proved to be two of the most popular tracks on her first two albums?

And, to top this off, Tom felt sure that, by now, he knew exactly what the bulk of Carla's millions of fans already thought of him, and he could even hazard a guess at what they would most likely want to do to him, should they discover - Heaven forfend - that he was, in fact, still alive, and, worse, perhaps, where it was that he presently resided. But even though Tom realised that his daughter's up-coming, fourth CD would soon turn out to be, by far, her most successful and lucrative, he also knew only too well that, whatever powers he possessed, he still would not be able to live long enough to enjoy and share its glittering success with her.

'Liar! Liar! Pant's on fire! Throw on trees and build it higher!'
The two screeching boys from Year-Nine turned on their heels and sprinted headlong behind the hedge so as not to be recognised by her, although a shocked Rhiannon had a fair idea of their identity, since they were in the same house that she was in, and had often sat together on the far side of the room when she and the other officers had addressed the children, and tried to encourage them to be even more bold

and hard working, so as to defend the spurious honour of the red house known as *Crawshay*. Carrying her little leather-case in her hand, and trying to maintain her composure, Rhiannon walked on past the crowded library, and the Food Tech. Block, where the hot, savoury aroma of the after-school cooking club wafted out seductively, and then disappeared inside the brand-new Music Block, where she had a flute-rehearsal with a group of fellow students of differeing ages who were, to all intents and purposes, the core of the P.S.O., namely *The Pennant School Orchestra*.

With a look of simple pride on her face, Rhiannon unpacked her shining instrument quickly, but with loving care, and then picked up and carried, one-handed, an already erected music-stand, with her paper-score precariously balanced upon it, into the very centre of the room, where a few like-minded male and female musicians, all younger than herself, were already rehearsing the *G Major Concerto* by Vivaldi. It wasn't long before Rhiannon began to ponder the annoying incident that had just occurred in the playground, and how it might easily have ruined her day completely had she not got something as uplifting, and as challenging, as this - the school's music-club, and its upcoming *Annual Concert*-preparations - to look forward to.

Since the day that Chris had dumped her, (a text-based action that Rhiannon regarded as having been executed with a minimum of compassion or regret,) she had made up her mind that no boy - nay, no mere male - was going to hold sway in her life ever again, with the sole exception, that is, of her own dear father. Although her mother had not been well recently, and the strain within the family-unit appeared at times to be at breaking point, her dad remained, as always, the central pillar of her life, and the constant fount of her, much needed, reassurance.

Despite having recently been made redundant from his job as a guard on the railway at the age of fifty-six, and now unemployed for the first time in his life, Rhiannon realised that he was still managing to maintain the household by carrying out a variety of jobs that needed doing for both neighbours and friends, and was just about able to restrain himself from taking the ignominious ride downtown, that many of his age simply couldn't avoid, to the local Job-Cemtre, and claiming the benefits that he was otherwise fully entitled to. Unusual though this might seem, at a time of severe austerity, and recurrent Con-Dem self-congratulation at the sharpness of the misery they were inflicting, Rhiannon respected her father's humbling, unconventional course of action, knowing in her heart that she would forever gladly defend him with her life.

Rhiannon blew her nose and paused for thought. She couldn't really understand why the two young boys who had screamed out their taunts at her had then turned tail and acted as timidly as they had done, since she was just a girl, after all, and clearly weaker than the pair of them, and, of course, quite alone. How she perceived it was that, when boys were hanging around in pairs, or, far worse, in small groups, they were far more apt to seek to impress each other, either with their fake courage, or their stupidity, or often both at the same time, the result then being that she often felt absolutely terrified by the sight of them when grouped together.

In recent months Rhiannon had begun to abhor the fact that just about everyone in *Crawshay House*, then in the entire school, now seemed to know where she came from. And, no doubt, having seen her parents standing alongside her on 'parents' evenings' and 'open-days,' and having witnessed how desperately unpredictable, some might even say eccentric, her mother had sadly become in recent years, (a fact her dad seemed to have put down to possible bi-polar issues of an age-degenerative kind, of which her mother was, quite naturally, unaware,) Rhiannon unsurprisingly began to feel more and more self-conscious in the face of their gaze.

The sprawling, undulating village of Pant, where her family lived, was seen by some of those at her school as a less urban, more rural, perhaps more yokel, community than the adjoining towns of Dowlais and Merthyr to the south, although certainly not as rustic and behind-the-times as *Gloryhole,* Vaynor and Pontsticill in the more hilly north were generally perceived, even though very few children, except Chris that is, chose to travel to Pennant from so far afield, and that only because his dad happened to teach Art there.

Despite its rather odd name, Pant was a place that Rhiannon was exceedingly proud of, and a community she knew she would be very loath to move away from in two years time, when she would hopefully be graduating from school and going off somewhere else to futher her career.

Eyes lightly closed, her body firmly poised, but ever so slightly twisted to one side, Rhiannon cradled her pierced, silver rod in a horizontal plane between her pursed, hollow-whistling lips and her two slender hands, whose nails were no longer tinted, nor even varnished, and whose fingers wore no ring, but that given her by her dad when she recently reached the age of seventeen. Playing sweetly, and, for the first time, by heart, the Vivaldi second-movement's hypnotic, swaying legato melody, Rhiannon suddenly felt as free and weightless as the chattering, melodious blue tits she had seen darting from bough to bough among the trees of Vaynor Woods, the time she last snuck along there after school with Chris - that time of - of love.

As Rhiannon circularly breathed her way through the oscillating, many-trilled, cascades of the ancient, haunting piece, that for Jenny, the young organist, seemed to go on forever, but for Rhiannon never quite long enough, she pondered over how she now wanted her future life to be. The joyous music that, to the flautist seemed to emanate from her very being, certainly did seem to aid her into viewing her current life much more clearly, and even seemed to assist her in beginning to draw the conclusions that might yet define her future actions, if not her life.

Yes, in a way life was very like a forest, Rhiannon told herself, as she shook a loose strand of her fiery, red hair from out of her eyes, and, holding head and flute high, began to play with heightened sensitivity the exquisite, final section of the concerto. And as with some of the more timorous birds who nested and lived within a forest's lush, organic system, her inclination in future days would be to flit timidly amongst only the canopy's loftier, safer branches; patient and alone, yet still triumphantly alive.

And so Rhiannon mused on, her back now arched divinely, as the wondrous music that inspired her florid train of thought slowed to its serene finale. Lips tightly pursed, the flautist pledged herself to henceforth shun the thicker, greener bushes, and the seductive long grass of the lower realms, which hitherto she had explored only hand-in-hand, and mouth-to-mouth, with man; and in whose domain, after all, the devilish magpie and the carrion crow hold sway, and where as tender a heart as hers would, as like as not, become too easily tumbled to the ground, pecked, pierced through, and torn, and left to rot, in situ, like some long-discarded, satin glove.

A curled-up Carla slept soundly and silently in the small bedroom at the back of the house, while her father, asleep on his back at the front, was a veritable symphony of whistling, snoring, and raucous, seemingly choking, noises. Tom suddenly choked himself awake with a bizarre, but strangely familiar thought in his brain, and words on his lips, that said, 'Old urologists never die, they only peter out.' He opened his eyes and chuckled loudly at the strange, old, witticism which he had just unaccountably recalled, then, second later, when reality finally registered, the old man reached out a frantic hand, and patted and felt the cotton sheet upon which his spindly old body lay, so as to verify that he hadn't, in fact, wet himself.

Dry, and now suitably reassured, Tom suddenly remembered that he presently had company in his little house by the bridge - the sweet company that his heart had long desired. He lay back and smiled serenely at his good fortune, then closed his eyes and tried to summarise what his daughter Carla's life must have been like for her up to this point in time, and the part that her native Wales might have played in it.

Tom reminded himself that it was against the wishes of his wife Carys that he had elected to send Carla to school at Pennant. Having himself had to commute to Merthyr daily from his Breconshire villlage, and, while there, having been told of the school's good academic reputation and its friendly environment, he quickly chose to act and enrolled her there, and had long since known that the decision he had made to move her had been the right one. Tom recalled how Carla had thoroughly enjoyed her brief time at the school, and, once she had passed all her GCSE's, was one day sat down and told by her music teacher - an acclaimed choir-master called Omri.Jones - that he believed she possessed all the essential qualities to succeed in music as a full-time career, providing that she was prepared to put her mind to it.

Tom recalled how he had laughed aloud when Carla had recounted to him this observation, not because it seemed comical or unrealistic, but because it confirmed what he himself thought of Carla's astonishing musical ability. He remembered having sat down with Mr. Jones at a parents' evening later that year, and, while Carla was off speaking with some of her friends in the orchestra, he had held a deep conversation with the bearded, old man, and which, to his complete surprise, he found he could now recall almost word for word.

'As far back as I can recall, Mr. Jones, my Carla was always musical,' he had told the man. 'You know I remember how she began to play Mozart at about the same age as Mozart had begun to play Mozart.'

'Do you mean on the violin or on the piano?' a stunned Mr. Jones had responded.

'No, no - on the stereo-gram,' Tom had replied with a smile. 'Forgive me, Sir, but you see, I bought a job-lot of the composer's finest symphonies and concertos on twelve-inch discs from a warehouse somewhere down in Cardiff, and I rememder how Carla used to like to listen to them when she was writing, or playing with the cat, or colouring in her picture-books. You know, I can even remember her, eyes closed, lying in the bath with the door open.'

The Head of Music looked up with something of a start. 'Er - too much information there, I think, Mr. Davies,' he retorted, using his handkerchief to wipe up the drops of tea he had spilt.

'How do you mean?' Tom had asked, a tad confused. 'No, you see, Carla showed very early signs of appreciating, and, seemingy, even understanding, musical compositions, but, though Carys and I paid for her to get piano lessons with a lady in Brecon, it was a small guitar that took her eye, in the window of a shop across from the cathedral, as it goes, and so we went straight in there and got it for her, on hire-purchase, of course. And since then I believe that Carla has never really looked back. Music - well, it all seems to come so naturally to her, don't you agree?'

Tom recalled how Mr. Jones had nodded, and then smiled in accord with his own summation. 'I believe that, one day soon, Carla will make all of us in Merthyr very, very proud,' the old chap had told him. 'And I, for one, can't wait to see it, should the Good Lord grant that I live that long.'

Tom could still remember how he had felt huge satisfaction with what he had heard that night, and no small amount of pride, but then recalled how the old teacher had gone and dropped dead suddenly the following term, and so was never actually able to see the predictions he had made about the young girl's future come true.

And yet so it had proved, in spades. Carla Steel, as she was soon to become known to us, went on to release three universally acclaimed solo-albums in less than ten years - all of which went platinum - and made enough money from her astonishing success to purchase houses in London and Rhodes, a flat in New York, and now, at last - Tom chuckled heartily at this - even a humble, three-bedroom terraced property in a hamlet known affectionately to its local residents as *Gloryhole,* for the benefit of her dear old dad.

Tom eased his thin torso into a position where he was very nearly lying on his side and waited to see what the effect might be. So far so good, he told himself. All in all, he thought, he had good days, and he had bad days. Still, even the worst morning, was considerably better than the best night. The man's nights were nowadays very often like long, drawn-out periods of severe torture; indeed if he were locked up in Guantanamo. Tom felt he couldn't really have fared much worse. And, what is more, even his mental clarity seemed to depend on something as simple as whether he had lain on his back or his side for the duration of the night.

The multiple sclerosis which Tom now suffered from had developed quite quickly soon after he returned from a spell working abroad. Around that time Carys had moved away to the Home Counties, and, with Carla's help of course, had bought herself a nice house in the country.

Tom recalled how a year earlier he decided that he needed to get away from the UK in order to deal with the emotional pain and the mental anguish he was feeling, and so first moved abroad to take up a job teaching English in Taiwan, and there worked in a small school in Taipei called, in translation, '*Happy Tongues*,' where he would teach boys and girls during the daytime followed by their parents in the night. Despite the low wages, he had enjoyed the life there, and he felt it had probably served its purpose of, at least to some extent, rehabilitating him mentally.

Then the great earthquake hit! Tom had never given a thought to the possibility that this might happen, and the unexpected event shattered a lot more than the tall building in the northern suburb of *Shi-lin* that he shared with his fellow-teachers. This six-storey structure was severely split apart by the jolt, although, quite miraculously, everyone who was inside at the time managed to get out alive. But despite his deliverance, Tom, not unsurprisingly, felt he was not prepared to carry on working there, and so, just a day or so later, he took himself off to the airport and purchased a seat on the first plane he could board that would get him off the island.

Via a long, circuitous tour that took in Thailand, Australia, Peru, and then Mexico, Tom finally arrived at, and settled on, the Caribbean island of Tobago, where he discovered that he was able to purchase a wooden house near the sea relatively cheaply. And so that is what he did, and he ended up residing there for a just over a year, quite alone, and yet a popular and accepted member of the local community nevertheless, often pulling teeth and treating oral infections in exchange for gifts of fuel, food and drink, the use of a donkey, motor-cycle, and such like. All in all, everything seemed to be going well. That was until Tom went and fell in love.

Carol was a widow, or so she had told him, but her husband Benjamin was, in fact, still alive and well, and living with their sons on the nearby island of Trinidad. Then one day, when Tom was away in town buying provisions, Carol's husband arrived back on the island, with the sole purpose of reclaiming his side of the marital bargain, or, failing that, of at least driving out her new lover. But the, now much wealthier, Carol, who had convinced herself that she now loved her older, but wiser and more talented, Welsh partner, wasn't having it, and repeatedly repelled her husband's still flourishing advances, including his train of strange, but generous, gifts that arrived in a single delivery by postal-van, including lipsticks, cheese, see-through underwear, and potted-plants. And so, perhaps unsurprisingly, Benjamin felt forced to resort to the only course of action he now believed was left open to him.

The spell that the old lady from the hill cast on Tom happened on two separate occasions, he recalled. The first occurred at the outer, perimeter fence of his property when Tom was home alone, and when two large dogs belonging to a very tall man he had never met before called Benjamin were found to have trespassed onto his property, and Tom had had to brandish a gun just to let everyone know that the land they were straying onto was his. The old lady in black certainly didn't seem to appreciate this, and soon began waving her thin arms about, and declaring, in patois that he couldn't interpret, whatever it was she needed to get off her chest.

Of course Tom had no idea that this strange speech might be of significance, but when the same old biddy carried out the same, strange performance close to the beach-market less than a week later, Tom decided that maybe his Caribbean sabbatical could be coming to an end. Then one morning, on hearing a car-door slam, Tom rose to find that his paramour Carol had disappeared from his house with her property in a clutch of bags, and, just days later, Tom elected to take a slow boat to Trinidad, and a flight to Miami, and thence flew back home again to Europe. No, Tom told himself, he had never been one for drawn-out periods of deliberation.

Tom found that the MS had set into his body not long after that, and, over the years, it degenerated to the point where, these days, he was grateful that he still retained the powers to read, write, and move about slowly. He understandably had to desist from driving cars - changing gears, and using the hand-brake, being functions that were well nigh impossible using just his right, his strongest, hand alone. Then, in the last year or so, having decided that it would be best all round for him to live, and, ultimately, to die alone, he made the difficult decision to ask his daughter for help for the first time ever. To his great surprise, Carla soon wrote back to inform him that she would provide him with whatever cash amount he felt he required, and so Tom was able to purchase for himself the humble, rural abode in which he now resided.

And when Tom paid a visit with an estate-agent to the all-too-familiar, little hamlet of *Glo-Ar-Ol* for the first time in decades, and he saw, from the frost-fringed, back-window, not only the resplendent stone-viaduct that he so vividly recalled from earlier, much happier times, but who the dark-haired, middle-aged woman happened to be who resided with her family right next-door, Tom decided that this simply had to be the place where he was meant to dwell.

Life at home with my wife Gwen had become extremely fraught, to say the least, but now that Spring had arrived, and with it the sort of temperatures that were more akin to the month of August than April, I decided that I was able to come away from *Caerleon* of an evening just to take a break from it all. Hill-walking was my chosen therapy.

From the most northerly point of the limestone castle's crumbling walls on *Morlais Hill*, I looked down and surveyed the sight of the majestic viaduct which, running away from me towards the north-west, crossed its lovely valley, and then gazed beyond it towards the little hamlet of *Gloryhole,* and the fast-greening mountains of *The Beacons* that lay, piled high like a scattering of great, lime-coloured pillows, both above and beyond it.

Pulling my jacket-collar a little tighter round me in the face of the cool evening-breeze that blew in from the northern quarter, and whistled its way amongst the ruins of the once great fortress, I contemplated all the historical information that my wife Gwen had bombarded me with over the last few years, during the period which coincided with what I had come to regard as her time of protracted, mental deterioration.

It was on the orders of the Norman-English king Edward 1 that *Morlais Castle* had been built, I remember her telling me. And it had been that same king, known as '*Longshanks*' by friend and foe alike, who had one time, somewhat bizarrely, commanded that the tombs at Glastonbury of my more notorious namesake, Arthur, and his wife Guinnevere, be opened up, and the contents removed and transplanted in a far more ornate receptacle, that has henceforth been left in its place at that same location.

Gwen told me that the reflected glory which King Edward believed that this action would bring him, by way of his performing such a monumental, albeit sacrilegious, disinterment of the one time great Celtic chieftain, (from whom Edward, highly spuriously, of course, claimed descent,) was most probably the key factor in his decision to proceed with it. But even more important than that, or so my wife had insisted, and repeated to me countless times, was the fact that he could now, as had his father - Henry-the-Second - attempted to do before him, remind the Welsh people, in the most stark fashion possible, that their beloved Arthur was indeed dead, and gone forever, and so was no longer able to be summoned by them to their aid, and, spiritually, at least, lead them in their rebellion against the despised Norman, now English, invaders.

'But, isn't he?' I asked Gwen the very first time she had told me all this. 'Dead and gone, I mean. Arthur.'

'Of course he isn't, silly,' was her astonishing reply. 'After all, the two skeletons in the tomb in Glastonbury that Edward opened up weren't really theirs, were they?'

'Weren't they?' I enquired, mouth agape, and as clueless as before.

'Of course, they weren't,' she continued. 'Do you really think that, if the skeletons housed there hadn't already been known, and accepted by everyone at the time, to be complete fakes, the Welsh wouldn't have disinterred them themselves, and carried Arthur off across the Bristol Channel once more, and back to his own homeland? It stands to reason, don't you think?'

'Well, yes, I can see your point,' I told her, admiring the logic of the argument she was making. 'So were Arthur's remains buried somewhere else, then?'

'What are you talking about?' my wife replied, glaring at me in the oddest fashion. 'There aren't any remains that *could* be buried, are there?'

'No remains!' I asked, somewhat aghast. 'But how come?'

'How come? Because Arthur is still alive, my love. And he is with us here in Wales, even today,' was my wife's calm, and worryingly assured, response.

'Is he?' I asked, astounded by her declaration. 'Is he, really? Well, where is he now, then?'

'Why, what a silly question, darling,' she replied, smiling serenely. 'And from *you* of all people, Why, he's living in Caerleon, of course, dear, where he's meant to be.'

'In *Caerleon!* Do you mean - do you mean he's down in Newport then?' I asked.

'Not Newport, silly.' Gwen retorted, her eyes closing, her thoughts now seemingly transported, and leaning her body forward and spreading her arms wide to enclose me. 'He's living here with me.'

'With you!' I ejaculated.

'Yes, with his Gwenhwyfar - his beloved wife's original, un-corrupted name. Although she'll always answer to Gwen to you, naturally, my love.'

'Gwenhwyfar? Gwenhwyfar! Oh, I see,' I told her. 'Not Guinnevere, then? Because I guess that's the name you tell me the French or the English went and changed it to, and continued to call her when they rewrote the most famous of Arthur's stories during the later, medieval times.'

'It is, my love,' she replied. 'And the name Guinnevere is what is called 'a corruption,' and there have been far, far too many of those in this traditional Welsh tale for my liking.' She spun round again, this time indicating with a sweeping arm the lounge we were standing in. 'And, God willing, my love,' she told me slowly, 'Arthur will go on living here with me until the day that I die.'

I looked back at my wife askance. Surely Gwen was having me on, I thought. 'Oh, will he now?' I asked her, smiling at the thought that suddenly came to me of the rather more crowded table this would inevitably create for us at breakfast-time.

'Of course, he will,' Gwen declared firmly. She leaned in close to me and proceeded to kiss me on my cheek. 'Why on earth wouldn't you, dear? You're very happy living here in *Caerleon* with your Gwen, aren't you?' And, to my utter astonishment, and almost as if bewitched, she suddenly reached out and grasped my right hand firmly in hers, and placed it deep inside her woollen jumper, then, studying my flushing face, said brazenly, 'Yes, I thought you were, dear.'

When had it happened that her father had become the child who went to bed early? Carla asked herself; the one who was now calling down to her for help from his bed upstairs. When on earth had this magnetic-pole of life switched exactly? Gripping the bannister, she swung her body around it and shouted up, 'What is it, Dad? Do you need help getting your sweater on again? Make sure you're decent this time, won't you, because I'm coming up.'

Carla began to make her way up the staircase to assist him, moving slippers, an empty polythene-bag, and a plastic box containing a dust-pan and brush into the corner near the foot so that she could pass by, and so that in future her dad might reach the front-door from time to time without tripping over. He had, in just a matter of a few weeks, Carla felt, managed to create a home-life for himself that seemed to scream out *'sick old man barely able to cope any more.'*

Once she had satisfied herself that Tom was properly dressed and more or less ready for a trip to the super-market, Carla peeked out of his bedroom-window to verify that the mini-cab she had summoned had already shown up.

She decided that the sun-glasses she always chose to wear in all weathers when out and about in London might look equally chic for a sunny morning such as it was, and so Carla pinned them high on her forehead, helped her father button up his overcoat, and, within a short time, the rather unlikely pair locked the door and set off.

For well over an hour father and daughter walked arm-in-arm around the twenty or so aisles that comprised *Asda's* vast shopping-floor, and gathered up in a large trolley all the provisions they imagined they might need for the week ahead, then slowly made their way towards the tills.

'Have you swiped your card?' the automated voice at the check-out asked him.

'No, I bloody haven't!' Tom replied in anger. 'The cheeky bugger! They sent it me through the post like everybody else.'

Carla shook her head and smiled at him. 'They mean you need to push it - swipe it - through the groove, Dad,' she told him, 'otherwise your purchases won't go through you see.'

'What a palaver, eh?' shot back Tom. 'I don't see why we couldn't have gone through the normal check-out, Carla, love. I know there's a queue, but it isn't any longer than normal, is it?'

'I know, Dad, but this is how I always do my food-shopping in London. It's quicker, for a start.'

'As your mother was apt to remind me, not everything that's quicker is a brilliant idea, you know,' he told her.

'Tell me about it,' Carla replied, giggling. 'You know, I've always found that in a race to orgasm the man will invariably win.'

But her aged father wasn't referring to anything of the sort. He had heard her cute reply, but as she was his daughter, he didn't feel able to look her in the eyes, less acknowledge it. 'You know, I don't actually know what you're talking about half the time, girl,' he told her, studying the new receipt in his hand, which he couldn't read without his other glasses, then looking away. 'But, seeing as how you seem to have succeeded in your career so quickly, and - and so effortlessly, perhaps the least I should do is listen to what you have to say every now and again.'

In the taxi back to *Gloryhole,* Carla began to contemplate this last observation her father had made. She recalled how years before she had moved into a poky little flat in Fulham, with views over a school playground, in order to concentrate on writing new material, and put down higher quality, more professional demos. And yet, from that moment, she recalled, it had still taken her almost three years to actually achieve her first big break. That had been the most trying time of her life, she reminded herself, and it was fortunate that her dad knew next to nothing about it. She had initially left Oxford for London in order to find herself, but after after just six months she was virtually suicidal. She had found herself all right, she thought - found herself utterly alone.

Her first album, entitled *'Introducing Carla Steel,'* had been by far the hardest task she had ever had to undertake, despite the fact that more than half of its songs were composed when she was still at school in Pennant. Although she regarded her short spell studying Music and Literature at Oxford as having been misguided and pointless, and the three years in Fulham that followed taxing, laborious, and so stressful that resorting to using substances to mask the pain she felt was more or less inevitable, the warm reception she received upon the record's release, by music fans and critics alike, took her genuinely by surprise, and had made her instantly realise that the tough decisions she had taken, and the sacrifices she had made to get where she was, had finally all been worthwhile.

Fame followed fast behind. Initial visits to a diaspora of music-festivals in The States helped get Carla's music heard far more widely, and her album-sales swiftly quintupled as a result. Soon it seemed that people the world over simply could not get enough of Carla Steel. As one noted critic wrote at the time, *'The Welsh girl's sudden and unexpected rise to fame has been nothing less than meteoric. It was very much as if there were some colour previously missing from our musical spectrum, and Carla alone possessed it and supplied us with it. In fact it seemed that Carla Steel was indeed that colour.'*

Yes, the young girl from Talybont, via Merthyr, had done it. And, quite unexpectedly, and somewhat bizarrely, she promptly forgot all about the folk who had helped her get started, those who had made it possible for her, and whom she really ought to have thanked, but instead she neglecred even to contact again. In hindsight, however, this was now her deepest regret, she told herself, that she had acted so selfishly and so arrogantly while under the spotlight, too often believing the hype which the music papers piled on, all the nonsense she had read about the natural flair and sensitivity she appeared to possess being some sort of bi-product of her Welsh heritage and its cultural landscape: a certain something they had claimed must be *'in the water.'*

There was probably just as much chance of it being *'in the rain,'* of course, Carla told herself, gazing at the ponds that sat alongside the main road, known locally as 'The Heads-of-the-Valleys Road, along which they now drove. Carla looked up at the bright, blue sky overhead. Well, there was certainly no rain around today anyway, she thought. And there was no rain or even cloud in prospect for the remainder of the week, the weather-forecast suggesting that 2011 was going to turn out to be a far warmer, drier year than any of the previous ones had been. Well, this would be a welcome change for Wales, anyway, she mused, and even for herself perhaps, since her own personal plans were simply to lie low, and remain in *Gloryhole* with her father for an indeterminate period, while Charlie Furlong - her agent back in London - dealt with the issues and complications that had arisen from her recent cancelled concert-tour, and at least until she had a clearer idea about what her father's precise medical prognosis turned out to be, and what his immediate prospects were. Well, these were Carla's immediate plans, anyway.

CHAPTER 6

It wasn't that Rhiannon had really done anything to upset him, or to cause him to suddenly hate her, Chris told himself. For a start, he felt she had never so much as looked at another boy in that way, and he knew she would most likely keep to the promise he had persuaded her to make him, and that she simply never would. No, it was just that he suddenly felt an animosity of some kind towards the girl that he found he genuinely couldn't explain, and, such was its ferocity, and, perhaps, its inevitability, that he decided that he wasn't even going to bother to attempt to rationalise it, or try to explain it, or even dwell on it too often, if he could actually manage that.

With the fingers of his right hand, Chris pulled the thin, brown thread of tape from the plastic cassette-case that he held in his left, and let it drift of its own accord down onto the duvet, at the same time, and certainly without wishing to, recalling almost everything he knew about Rhiannon. On the evening in the woods when he was intimate with her for just the third time, he recalled how, in the very motions of their coupling amongst the rushes and the lush grass of the moist river-island hidden deep within the woods, his urgently dipping head had become filled with strange, malevolent thoughts that he had never before experienced, and his flared nostrils with odours which, henceforth, he forever would relate, not to love-making, or even to the sweet girl who had been the object of his love, but to failure, to lies, to self-deception and self-loathing.

Chris recalled clearly how, lying prone on his damp, muddy palms, just inches above his lover's splayed torso, he had begun experiencing that same strange, nauseous feeling he could recall having experienced whenever, at his mother's request, he had agreed to shell peas for her, and had decided to taste first one, then another, and frequently ended up consuming a goodly portion of the collander, leaving little more than a handful for the saucepan and the evening's dinner. To his keen senses that feeling was unquestionably a horrible, sickly one, and right now it was one that he could not help but associate in his mind with Rhiannon.

In addition, Chris winced horribly each time he recalled the sharp reprimand that his mother had given him after she discovered, possibly from his step-father, where it was that he had been spending virtually all of his after-school time in recent weeks, and with whom. For years there was little doubt that Rhiannon Cook had been a sort of *persona non grata* in the Cillick household, and for reasons that Chris initially had very little idea about, except that it appeared to relate in some way to who the girl's parents were, or perhaps to the way that her family lived their lives down in Pant, but other than that it was all a complete mystery to him. Then, quite out of the blue, he got to overhear the truth.

Having quickly lost interest in the laborious task he had just set himself, Chris pushed the unspooled trail of audio-tape completely off the bed, and was now sitting quite alone on his duvet, legs-crossed, watching the flaming, satsuma sun go down over the fields beyond the old station-halt, and smoking a home-made joint of a particularly fine girth, while carefully blowing the smoke from it clear out of the bedroom-window that was pinned wide open before him.

Just then Chris saw a dark-haired woman in sun-glasses, who, in some respects, resembled Carla Steel, the singer, ambling very slowly towards him down the road from Vaynor, and appearing to be escorting by the arm an ancient-looking man, who looked remarkably like his new neighbour. Almost instinctively, Chris's nimble fingers adjusted the button on his i-pod, and, within seconds, he found that he could hear the powerful strains of Carla's own languid, soulful voice, singing a song called *'Don't walk on by me,'* that had recently taken the music-charts by storm. 'Either that is Carla Steel, or this is some powerful shit!' Chris told himself, chuckling loudly, and squinting a few times, so as to clear his bleary eyes and verify the facts.

The bizarre synchronicity of the sight of the singer and the unmistakable sound of her voice pulsing at his ear-drums soon began causing his head to spin. 'Ah! So amazing coincidences do happen, after all,' he mumbled to himself quietly, sniggering a little, since, in truth, he realised that this one was, to a large extent, self-created. Chris leapt up from the bed and pressed his face against the window-pane, and watched as the sorely mis-matched pair approached the row of terraced houses by crossing over the little road-bridge that was built across the old railway-line, (but now traversed the cycle-way,) and, seconds later, opened, then closed behind them with a loud, right-rollicking clang, the iron-gate of the cottage contiguous to his own.

Chris stubbed out his stogie and rushed to the bathroom to fetch the step-ladder. Dragging it out into the hallway, and placing it firmly and squarely below the hatch to the attic, he leapt up it, unfastened the metal catch above his head, and nimbly climbed aloft, swiftly pulling the ladder up behind him, and was gone from sight within a matter of seconds. Once in the attic, Chris switched on the large torch which he kept hidden below some felt in the near corner, and silently edged his way towards the adjoining wall. From beside the brick-work he found that he could already make out the sound of two voices conversing in the house next-door, and this became much clearer once he had reached down and opened up a hinged panel at the base of the wall and expertly crawled his way through it.

Once inside the neighbouring loft, and torch-in-hand, Chris used his foot to edge a large bucket of sand close up next to an even larger one, whose weight already prevented the hatch from being forced open from below. Then he bent his body low and tore a strip of cellotape from the wooden floor, and, peering down through the hole beneath it, he found that he could easily make out a female form, standing before the mirror in the bathroom down below, and engaged in removing her make-up. And yes, he could easily tell that the girl beneath his gawping gaze was indeed the famous, local-born, singer that he had minutes earlier assumed she might be.

Chris was astounded. However, what he saw Carla do next, with a sharp dip of her dark, curly head, a sweep of a credit-card held in her right hand, and a grip on a thin plastic tube with her left, caused Chris to jump a fraction, and to tip over onto its side a square container filled with cannabis plants, which were already a few feet in height and almost ready for harvesting. With a measure of both luck and skill, Chrs just managed to save a second turned-up tray from crashing to the attic-floor, but the shock of the near-miss was enough to persuade him to make a swift exit, again through the gaping panel in the adjoining wall by which he had just arrived.

But, in turning, Chris suddenly found himself dazzled for a moment by the array of powerful lights which were both standing, and hanging down, but now seemed to be spinning all around him. He began feeling nauseous from breathing in the stale gas that filled the air, and which the rushing air-con. was desperately attempting to clear out through the corrugated, plastic pipe he had recently fitted into the roof. So, squinting uncontrollably, and making a huge effort to hold his breath, Chris ducked his head down, and squirmed back through the hinged-panel and returned once again to the safety of his own home. And, despite the sudden fit of panic that had overcome him while up aloft, he already felt he now had the bare bones of a new plan fomenting nicely within his sharp brain. And so, he told himself, mock-examinations, school generally, and especially the annoying business of Rhiannon Cook could easily wait until another time.

'Well, as a family back in Penyard, we did have the one thing money couldn't buy,' Gwen told the woman shopkeeper, who, at six-feet, stood almost a foot taller than herself.

'And what was that?' Zeta asked her, holding a metal pot in one hand, and forcing one lever up, then a second lever down with the other hand.

'Poverty,' Gwen told her, then repeated the word much louder in a vain attempt to rise above the explosive, gushing noise which the quaint, hand-operated machine suddenly made, and which sounded to her very like a steam-train, and which continued for some considerable time, and, again like a steam-train, soon emitted a cloud of vapour that briefly shrouded the two middle-aged women from each other's sight.

Mrs. Jones-the-Caff, as Zeta was known, shook with laughter at this typical example of Gwen's dry humour, then pointed at the spillage of frothing cappucino from the cup she held in her hand and, shaking her head from side to side by way of apology, proceeded to make her old friend a second cup. And so the loud, arcane process of coffee-production began all over again.

'But now that my husband has just this week started working again, Zeta, at least I can afford to get you and me both a cup,' Gwen told the proprietor. She turned and sat down at the table in the very first booth behind her and waited for Zeta to come over, when she was finished, and serve her. First cleaning assiduously the plastic-coated surface before her with a paper-tissue that she took from her pocket, Gwen stood the large, glass sugar-dispenser in the very middle of the table, and then very carefully placed the silver salt and pepper pots, and similarly the circular mustard and ketchup trays, at equi-distant and opposing right-angles from it, and then sat back so as to assess the effect created. Seemingly pleased with her effort, Gwen smiled broadly.

'Here you go, love,' said Zeta, sitting down opposite her friend, a striped tea-towel draped over her shoulder, and placing Gwen's cup of cappucino on the table in front of her and the second one before herself. 'You don't mind if I join you, do you, pet? It's nice to take a break sometimes, isn't it? Normally at this time of the day, I'm run off my feet. But it's raining, see.'

Zeta took the sugar-dispenser from the middle of the table and poured about a spoonful of sugar from it into her cup. Then, suddenly noticing the strange, elaborate shape which all the condiments had been arranged into, she decided to place the tall glass item back precisely where she had found it, in the very centre of the wagon-wheel shaped framework. 'Say, do you remember when we used to live in the same street together back in Penyard, Gwen?' Zeta asked her brunch companion. 'Six of us lot in an end-of-terrace we called '*Casa Mea*,' and you and your parents - Patrick and Doris was it? - in a two-up-two-down only a few doors away.'

'And you were just a year ahead of me in the Catholic Junior School,' said Gwen, 'but later on I remember you left long before I did from *Bishop Hedley*.'

'That's because I was never as clever as you, though, was I Gwen?' Zeta told her old school-friend, smiling. 'And I already knew I was always going to work in the caff eventually. Though you stayed on to do your A-levels, didn't you?'

'I did, Zet,' Gwen told her friend. 'Altogether I took History Welsh, and Geography. And it was History that I went on and got my degree in at Abertstwyth. And, do you know, in my final year I got to stay with three other girls in the prettiest little cottage you ever saw right down by the sea.'

'Aw, there's lovely,' said Zeta, recalling the sand-and-pebble beach she had played on when, as a child, she had stayed at the same resort with a group of other families of Italian descent. 'Why History, then, Gwen?' asked Zeta. 'Did you always like old things, then?' She suddenly dipped her head and winced. 'Sorry, pet, I've just remembered how your last husband was quite a few years older than you, wasn't he?' However hard she tried, Zeta fell about giggling.

Gwen inhaled deeply, taking exception to this witless comment about her first marriage, but decided that she wasn't going to show it; after all, she hadn't so far been asked to pay for the two cappucinos she had ordered. No, she decided she would endeavour to maintain her dignity, and carry on regardless. 'Well it might have been all the castles that won me over in the very beginning, I think,' said Gwen, answering the original question Zeta had posed her.

'Oh, I see. Well, I can easily believe that,' said Zeta. 'There's some lovely castles in Wales, aren't there?' A short pause ensued while Zeta pulled her tights up, one leg at a time. 'Say, Gwen, do you remember how we used to go to the *Castle Cinema* on a Saturday afternoon?' she continued.

'And how they always seemed to cram us all together in the front two rows. Do you remember? Why was that, do you think?'

Gwen stared straight at her, and suddenly recalled the reason why Zeta had left *Bishop Hedley* a very long time before she had. She bent her head and sipped from the frothy, chocolate-speckled cup, still seething with anger from her earlier observation, but allowing the other woman to take the discussion on further again if she felt so inclined.

'Tell me - does History still interest you, then, Gwen?' enquired Zeta. 'Henry-the-Eighth and all that.'

'Yes, it does, Zet,' Gwen replied. 'Though I can't stand all that later, Tudor and Stuart, la-de-da, costume-drama crap, if I'm honest with you.'

Zeta's jaw fell open. 'Tudor and Stuart!' she repeated. She was suddenly mystified as to why the woman sitting opposite her had just mentioned the names of the homosexual couple who had been in for ice-cream sundaes less than an hour before she herself had walked in.

'Six wives, indeed,' Gwen went on.

'Oh, I know. That's not normal, is it?' said Zeta, wondering if the most famous of the Henrys might have been a Mormon.

'And the willful destruction of all those beautiful Catholic churches and monasteries.'

'And wasn't he married to a nice Catholic woman at the time, too?' enquired Zeta. 'Although I heard he was cheating on her something rotten by all accounts.'

'That Catherine of Aragon, well, she should have, er -'

'Cut his balls off, right?' snapped back Zeta. 'Because I know I would have done.'

Despite herself, Gwen found herself chuckling at Zeta's response. 'I was going to say - she should have refused to divorce the man. It was anathema to all Catholics, after all. But he probably would have chopped her head off anyway, if she hadn't done what he'd demanded. You see, the man was a sexist pig, to be quite blunt, Zeta. Forcing a poor Catholic woman to do what the Pope says she's not supposed to do, indeed. Why. that's utterly disgusting, right?'

'Aye, the dirty old bugger!' ejaculated Zeta, misinterpreting her comment spectacularly. 'My Mario wouldn't dare go round there even if I'd just got out the bath. Would yours, Gwen?'

'Get divorced, I'm talking about,' said Gwen, suddenly apprehending what the pickled brain belonging to the gauche, brunette woman seated across from her was thinking.

'Oh, I see, of course,' stammered Zeta. 'The ginger bugger! I could never stand him, myself. I don't know why they spent so much time teaching us about him, do you? Six wives, indeed. Spanish and German and English and God knows what else. And what didn't he like about Italian women? That's what I want to know. Couldn't the man have squeezed in a cuddly, brown-eyed, bambina? And I'm sure *she'd* have given him a son. Seven's a lucky number, after all.'

By now Gwen felt she had had just about enough of this senseless confab with her childhood friend. She remembered now why it was she normally went to *Zanelli's* for coffee when she found herself in town, and a sudden shower upset her plans. But the beverage before her was still too hot for her to finish just yet, so she decided to bite her tongue and make just one more effort. 'To be honest, Zeta,' she said, 'these days I find I'm only really interested in Arthur.'

Zeta stared at her, plainly confused. 'Oh, you mean *King Arthur!* For a second then, I thought you meant -'

'Look, Zeta, the man was never a king, O.K.?' retorted Gwen, feeling herself getting angrier by the minute. 'He was a chief. Not a king - a chief.'

'Oh, I'm sorry, pet,' retorted Zeta, feeling embarrassed and not knowing what else to say. .

'Arthur's the greatest leader we ever had here in Wales. He was born here, remember, and, though some will no doubt say different, he is still living here with us today.'

'In Merthyr!' ejaculated Zeta, licking her lips nervously. 'Surely not, pet.'

'No, no – up in Pant,' Gwen told her.

'Pant! Where you live! He's living in Pant, is he?' Zeta enquired, her hand shooting up to her mouth. 'Well, I never.'

'Until the day that he finally emerges, that is, to lead us bravely on the field once more.'

'In the *Rugby World Cup*, do you mean?' said Zeta, picking up the sugar-dispenser, cleaning its surface with her tea-towel, and putting it back nearer the edge of the table.

'Zeta! What on earth do you think you're doing, love?' Gwen screamed. 'He's *living* in there!'

Terrified, the shopkeeper stared, wide-eyed, at her petite friend. 'Who - pet?' she enquired. 'You're not - surely you're not telling me that King Arthur is stuck inside one of my -'

Gwen suddenly reached over and snatched the dispenser out of Zeta's hands, and placed it back in the very centre of her defensive arrangement. Zeta was at a complete loss about what to do, so, reluctantly she got to her feet, and edged away from the table. 'Look, I'd better be getting on with my job, Gwen,' she told her old friend, without looking back. 'But it's been really lovely seeing you again after all this time. In fact, now I think of it, I don't believe I've seen you since that night we went to the *Ex-Club* with all the girls for that show. Wasn't your ex-husband performing that night? Dick, is it? What was it he did again, pet? Stand-up comedy, was it?'

'He was a bingo-caller,' Gwen retorted, frowning.

'No, I mean that particular night, pet,' Zeta continued. 'I know he used to call out numbers during the week, but on that particular Saturday night we all went there together for something else, didn't we? Another kind of show entirely, I'm sure. What was it he did when he wasn't doing the bingo and robbing all the customers, pet? Do you remember? 'Cause I'm damned if I can.'

By now Gwen was raging. She stood up and walked towards the door, turning back only to leave her empty cup on the counter. 'Zeta Carini, I haven't got a bloody clue what the hell you're talking about,' she bawled. 'I can't remember ever going anywhere with you on any evening, as it goes. And why on earth *would I*, for heaven's sake? This is about the closest we've ever been since we lived a few doors apart up in Corporation Road.'

'Corporation Street,' Zeta corrected her, smiling thinly. 'And the surname isn't Carini any more, is it? No, love. It's Jones. Plain Jones. Though it was Carini back then, of course.'

'Quite,' retorted Gwen. 'But you know, Zeta, your name may have changed love, but you're still as thick and stupid now as you were back then. A total plank, in fact. And now I think about it, the only test I recall you ever passing in school was a pregnancy-test,' Gwen continued, all the time eye-balling the shopkeeper aggressively. 'And even that one I guess you expected to fail.'

A silence fell on the *Café Giotto,* broken only by the drone of the morning-traffic passing by on the High Street, then braking sharply on the wet surface before filing round the junction with Glebeland Street.

'You'll call again, won't you. pet?' remarked Zeta, turning completely away from her and washing out the cups in the sink. 'I'm sure Martin and the kids will be pleased to know that you're keeping well, at any rate.' She continued to ignore Gwen, and, as she set the dried cups back on the shelf behind her, and turned away to lay the tea-towel back on the rail to dry, Gwen turned about, and, pausing only to put up her umbrella, slipped out of the shop, and sallied off into the morning crowd.

Seconds later Zeta's husband Martin quietly walked in to the cafe, bearing two large bags of supplies in his burly arms. Oblivious to his arrival, Zeta carried on much as before. 'Aye, and you can take the condiments home with you, as well, if you like, pet,' she exclaimed. 'After all you don't want to go leaving King Arthur in the sugar, now, do you?' Martin stood still, and, mouth agape, stared at his lanky wife from behind. 'You know, if you like, I'll try and get you a massive, great, round table for the next time you come in here,' he heard her say with a snigger.

Martin shook his head about, then went round the counter and placed the heavy bags on the floor. He then turned and stared deeply into his wife's eyes. 'You know, I'm getting a bit worried about you, Zeta,' he told her. 'Say, you haven't been at the *Babychams* again, have you?'

It was already past six o'clock, and Rhiannon climbed up onto the stage by the short, winding staircase, took the flute from her bag, and dragged a music-stand across to where she knew she would be sitting for the concert. Placing two sheets of music on top of it, she then licked her lips, pursed them, and began to play the harmony section of a jazz piece by Duke Ellington, entitled 'Sophisticated Lady.' By now Rhiannon knew it well, and she felt that she played it almost perfectly this time, and without a single mistake. Two boys from her year suddenly ran up to join her, and took out from their cases two very different looking saxophones, and began playing the song's main melody, while Rhiannon stood to the side of them, watching them admiringly, and sipping water from the plastic bottle that she gripped tightly in her hand.

Rhiannon looked over and saw a group of girls approaching the stage, and quickly noticed how glamorously dressed they all were compared to the usual, grubby school-uniform which she was still wearing. She now wished that she had skipped revision-classes too, and had gone home and spent an hour alone in her bedroom, by way of preparation for the musical soiree that was soon to follow. Rhiannon decided to remove her tie and undo a couple of buttons, and then adjusted her skirt-band so that the blouse she wore now fell loosely around it. This was about as much as she could do under the circumstances, she told herself, and, anyway, Chris had seen her in far worse shape that this before, and had still wanted to share her company, and even do a darn sight more than that! Perhaps she really was a naturally pretty girl, after all, she mused, as so many of her friends and family were often kind enough to tell her.

Rhiannon turned to study the second piece which sat on her music-stand. It was a Carla Steel song, and the school-band were going to be playing the tune together, but without anyone singing the words. It was called 'Heaven Scent,' and was one of Rhiannon's favourites. To her mind, it wasn't like any of Carla's other famous pop-songs - it had an unusual bossa-nova feel to it for a start, and there was clearly a deep meaning attached - and, as she began practising it, many of the other musicians took advantage of this welcome opportunity to join in and rehearse along with her.

Before very long the school-hall began filling up with teachers and a whole host of parents, including her mother Gwen, and also quite a few students from the upper-school, amongst them Chris, his fake-blonde friend Pippa Jenkins, and the school-hussy - Pippa's friend, Suzie Amos - all of whom elected to sit together in seats just across the aisle from Rhiannon's mother.

Suddenly Rhiannon saw Mrs. Roberts approach the lectern, stick-in-hand, which told her that Mr. Conway, their music teacher and regular conductor, wasn't going to be joining them tonight after all. Rhiannon was a little concerned at this, but understood that Mrs. Roberts would do her very best to keep them all together, and deliver the evening's musical programme as intended.

The evening wasn't really so much a concert as yet another welcome opportunity for the talented students of Pennant to show what they had been learning throughout the year in a wide range of school-subjects, including music - Rhiannon's personal favourite. When the initial introductions were done, and a boy from Rhiannon's year - Year Eleven - had recited, by heart, a strange poem about clocks and other related stuff, the band got the opportunity to play the first song of the night, which was so familiar to them all that no music-score was really required.

'And did those feet in ancient times,' sang the audience - 'walk upon England's rugby team,' sang the boys on stage, and quite a few in the audience. The adults present recognised this break with tradition and many of them giggled a little, having sung it that way themselves at school, as did Rhiannon one time, even though she now usually tried to sing the original words. Bows and arrows, swords and spears, and Jesus Christ himself walking around England for heaven's sake! To her mind, this was every bit as ludicrous as the tales of Paddington Bear and Peter Pan. But she had actually seen a 'mental fight' one time, she recollected. It was in Asda, late one Saturday evening just before Christmas, and it certainly wasn't a pretty sight to behold. It happened to be the day when treble points were awarded for just the one day only, and she could clearly recall the two mental-looking women involved being unceremoniously hand-cuffed by police-officers on account of the fracas, and getting taken away in their large, white van.

The would-be anthem's final verse rang out. *'Til we have built Jerusalem - in England's green and pleasant land,'* the rows of singers sang. As the audience members closed their hymn-books and sat down again, Rhiannon pondered over where this pleasant, green region they had just sung about might actually be, and, given the times when the song was written, whether it could, in fact, refer to Wales. Although, she pondered, the Lake District is very nice in summer, and there are parts of Yorkshire to the west and north of Leeds that are very like some of the finest Welsh Valleys, and every bit as beautiful, she felt, as the one that she was happy to be living in. It was undoubtedly a lovely hymn nevertheless, she mused, and would seem a far more appropriate song for English rugby fans to be singing than some quirky, old, Negro spiritual about chariots and the River Jordan, and angels chasing around after you, of all things.

The Duke Ellington went well, even though Mrs. Roberts forgot to let them repeat the last chorus at a decreasing tempo, as had originally been planned. After this the Drama Club's *'Scenes from Under Milk Wood'* was completed, to loud applause and considerable wolf-whistling, aimed, she imagined, at the brazen Polly Garter, played by Pippa Jenkins' sister Britney, who, in a ripped, seemingly see-through, white blouse, daubed with red, lipstick circles for nipples, easily succeeded in shaming her family-name even further than it had been already by her shameful elder sister.

Then, at last, it was the time for Rhiannon and the school-band to play the audience the well- known Carla Steel song, and hopefully restore normality once again. Rhiannon stood up and began playing the song's lengthy intro, but a few sudden screams of excitement from the side of the stage told her that something unexpected was happening. Then, to loud applause and widespread cat-calls, her music teacher

Bob Conway entered the auditorium, and walked onto the stage hand-in-hand with none other than Carla Steel herself!

The buzz in the hall was unlike anything she had heard before, but, though shaking with understandable trepidation, Rhiannon decided that she dare not pause the music even for a second, and risk ruining the intended effect, and so she carried on regardless, and, with her busy fingers trembling uncontrollably, she played the last few bars up to the point where the lyrics normally began. Just then, and only a few feet away from her swaying, tilted shoulder, she heard the great Carla Steel herself begin strumming her electric-guitar, and singing in her unique, powerful voice the words of her song 'Heaven Scent.' For a duration of close to four minutes thereafter you could literally have heard a pin drop in the crowded, excited auditorium.

Down in the audience Chris's eyes were standing out on stalks. An under-dressed Britney Jenkins had done nothing to rouse his libido, nor indeed did the proximity of her sister Pippa, who was, after all, an ex-lover and his present consort, but the exquisite sight and sound of this mature, glamorous, international singing-star literally popped the boy's cork for him. Chris already knew how to play five or six different major-chords on both piano and guitar, and had written a couple of tunes that made him feel like it was time he formed his own thrash-band, and yet this majestic female standing before him, her dark, curly head bent slightly over her *Fender Stratocaster*, could clearly play any chord imaginable to the human ear, while, quite stupendously, singing all of the song's lyrics at the same time!

This was, without doubt, by far the most incredible feeling Chris had experienced in his seventeen long years of life, and, at that moment, all he really knew was that he desperately wanted to experience it further and far more intensely. This truly captivating female deity, who seemed often to be looking over in his direction, was, for Chris, the epitome of grace and beauty. Her glorious voice alone seemed to transport him to regions he felt Columbus and Magellan had never dreamed of reaching, and her wondrous form to heights that Hilary and

Tensing had never attained. And the sheer economy of Carla's song, which was quite clearly the story of her own life experience, was such that every single line she delivered was, for him, at any rate, a unique thought divinely expressed, every single sound produced, a matchless statement of love.

Yes, this surely had to be the music of love that the duke in Shakespeare's 'Twelfth Night' had raved poetically about, Chris told himself, as the audience finally rose to its feet to applaud the finest musical talent that the school, the town, and indeed its valley had ever produced. And the feelings he felt he had already developed for Carla were, for Chris, from the heart and of the heart. Indeed, with the sheer power of the emotions he was presently experiencing, Chris believed he could quite easily write the woman a heartfelt love-song to match the one he felt she had just sung to him, and that he would gladly leap up on stage beside her that very instant, clothed or naked, and, on bended knees even, sing it, with genuine meaning, to her very soul.

To Chris's eyes, Carla Steel stood perfectly alone on stage that evening, and young, neglected Rhiannon Cook, poor girl, was relegated to a place somewhere far behind her, as well as to some time-period in his deep and distant past. Solo, or indeed accompanied, Carla Steel, this sublime, dusky, honey-toned, angel now seemed as real as roses to him, a shining star, and most truly heaven sent. And, as Chris stood alone in the centre of the, still applauding, audience, and watched the players on the stage flock franticallly around her - the happy, giggling girls over-joyed simply to hug her slight, busty frame, the flush-faced boys, wired-up like light-bulbs, and as frenetic as meerkats, safely sated by simply stroking her gleaming guitar - Chris felt very much as if the woman had now supplanted the girl, and as though the budding, divine love that he now felt coursing thickly through his veins was already transforming the adolescent boy, he had hitherto unquestionably been, into the man.

Every day that Anne got up early she seemed to leave most of her hormones in bed. And this Sunday morning was no exception. Within hours of the day beginning she had already fallen out with her husband because her son Chris desperately wanted to use the bathroom. But his step-father felt he had waited long enough for the privilege, thank you very much, (following Anne's lengthy preparations for her over-time shift at the care-home,) and was now locked away inside, and determined to repel all intruders, especially Chris, so as to repeat, if he could manage it, his feat of the previous Sunday, and languish in the warm, soapy balm of his long, pastel-green bath-tub for an hour at the very least.

Drew eased himself back and raised the Welsh tabloid-newspaper just above the level of the suds that covered his slim, but hairy chest, and began to read; and to Drew, the local news that week seemed to be unusually hilarious. There was the semi-detached house in Swansea that, from the front, bore a striking resemblance to Adolf Hitler; the five-legged lamb on a farm in nearby Penderyn with an extra spring in his step; and the pensioner from somewhere down the valley who, having sadly died alone, had apparently got gradually eaten up by her mass of rescued strays. Well, well, Drew thought, with a smile, even the most loyal, best-behaved dogs must get sick of over-cooked, meaty chunks after a while. Yes, surely all God's creatures valued a change, and even he got tired of curries some weeks.

Drew turned next to the British national papers in the anticipation of more serious comment, sipped his coffee, inhaled the smoke from his Rothmans, and read on. 'Man escapes prison when wife sends fax ordering his release,' *The Mirror* informed him. He chuckled raucously at that one, and reached over again to the toilet seat-cover for a second publication. *The Mail* reported how oral sex was now a bigger cause of throat cancer than tobacco. Drew pondered this. But surely that had to apply just as equally to men as to women, he mused. Mm, there again, perhaps not. Drew laid his head against the rim of the tub, closed his eyes, and let his mind drift back in time, but, however hard he tried, he couldn't even recall the last time that his loving, long-term co-habitee had felt impelled to cross the nut-bush city-limits in an effort to please him!

Drew read on. The headline he made out just below the last one reported that possessing a pot-belly significantly raises a man's risk of blindness later in life. He thought for a moment, then held the newspaper as far away from his eyes as he could manage and tried to read the small-print. Spilling water all over the carpeted floor, Drew slowly turned his twisted, dripping torso towards the wall, in an effort to regard himself in the full-length mirror that clung to it, but was now edged with broad corners of condensation that barely allowed him to see. Mm. He could remember being younger and looking a damn sight worse, he told himself. Yes, he looked quite fine for his age, he concluded, and if he could just maintain his weekly jog, and his twice-daily walk to the Spar-shop near school for the likes of gum, chocolate, lighter-fuel and cigarettes, then he saw no reason why he shouldn't be able to see his way to seventy, at the very least, even if, by that time, most of his egg-shaped head's flowing locks had fallen out, and what hair still remained hanging there might leave him looking a little like Father Christmas.

Three loud bangs suddenly sounded high above Drew's head, the stumbling footfall in the empty loft disturbing his weekend peace and tranquility. What on earth was the foolish boy up to now? he wondered. Was Chris 'trippin' again, he asked himself with a chuckle. Drew contemplated how his son was by now beginning to tax his powers in so many areas, and he already felt that the nefarious activities by which he attempted to acquire some extra cash for himself, as well as his all too secretive love-life, left him wide-open to falling foul of the same mistakes that he himself had made at that vulnerable age. And now that a bog-standard, university education at practically every red-brick institution throughout the land was soon to cost a fortune under the crazy plans of the, already discredited, 'Con-Dem' Coalition Government, (despite their ministers' initial promises to the contrary that had swindled them their seats in the recent general election,) Drew thought that he might now struggle to even get Chris out of the house at all in eighteen months time, when the boy finally finished school, and, as he had told Anne many times, ought to be aiming to stand on his own two feet and seek pastures new.

Drew threw down the newspaper he was holding, lay back in the tub, and listened even more attentively. Yes, he could still hear sounds of human movement overhead, and he decided that, when he was next a tad grubby, and on the point of taking a bath, he would venture up into the dusty loft minutes beforehand, and find out what it was that Chris was actually getting up to.

Shaking his head, Drew recalled the time, just a few years before, when he had found a half- finished joint up there, and lit up and smoked a good portion of it himself, before climbing down again and joyfully berating his step-son about the perils of dabbling in drugs! Drew turned again and smiled into the wall-mirror, and chuckled sadistically at the memory. On account of the struggle and outrageous self-sacrifice that was involved in child-rearing, he believed that parents and teachers alike were, at least at times, entitled to be hypocritical, and so he therefore felt not an iota of guilt about what he had done, just a profound sense of self-satisfaction. Perhaps he would find some more of the stuff up there the next time too, Drew pondered, although he seriously hoped that Chris was becoming more discerning these days, and that anything he did stumble upon would be of a far higher grade, and not as bitter and mouldy as the last one was.

In the loft Chris forced opened the panel in the wall, and again crept inside his neighbour's attic. He could already clearly hear that someone was on the phone in the room below, and the only female it could possibly be, he told himself, was Carla Steel. He was of course correct. Peeling off the tape, and staring down through the hole in the floor-board, he could clearly see the singer, dressed in a fetching, blue, silk dressing-gown, and with a blue towel-turban heaped over her head, sitting on the side of the bath-tub and addressing someone in Welsh.

It was at times like this that Chris wished that he had paid far more attention during his Welsh language lessons he had

had at school, because the only thing disclosed in her conversation that he could truly fathom was a mobile-phone number, which Carla repeated on two separate occasions, enabling Chris to memorise it. He quickly made up his mind to ring it some time in the near future, and hopefully find out a lot more about who Carla's acquaintance might be. After all, he told himself, it could turn out to be another famous celebrity, or, even better than that perhaps, the singer's personal dealer.

Chris smiled broadly at this thought, and spun round to check out the present height of the different varieties of skunk that were growing, tall and green, in a myriad of separate pots and trays laid out behind him. He then reached down and grasped a plastic-bottle off the floor, and began squeezing some of the fluid into a few of the pots whose plant-cultures looked like they were most in need of it. Yes, he told himself with a chuckle, squeezing repeatedly, and turning over several of the broader leaves which sprang out impressively from their main stalks, an appreciation of 'cultural differences' was something that he felt certain he was developing fast, and this fact his liberal leaning step-father would surely be proud of, if only he knew!

Anne happened to be walking around in town one afternoon when Zeta Jones - nee Carini - suddenly stepped out of her family's café, gripped her hand, and pulled her forcibly inside. Anne smiled at her old friend's impertinence, but put it down, as she had in the past, to the woman's Latin temperament, coupled with the fact that, in her opinion, Zita had never been the sharpest knife in the drawer, even in the evening cookery-classes they had attended together at the local college, where knives in drawers were expected to be sharp, or else were of precious little use.

There was just the one table vacant, and that at the rear of the steam-filled room, and so, making her husband aware that she would be busy with a customer for a while, the female proprietor led Anne over towards it, and bade her sit down in the seat just across from her.

'What will you have, pet?' Zeta asked her, holding up the brown-smeared plastic card that sat on the table, headed '*Menu.*'

'Oh, that's O.K., Zet,' Anne replied. 'It's only an hour or so since I had my lunch. What is it, love? I dare say it must be important or I'm sure you wouldn't have abducted me like this.'

'Well, I'm not sure it's earth-shattering, pet,' Zeta told her, 'but I'll wager you'll still thank me anyway for telling you.'

'Fire away, girl!' said Anne.

'Gwen Cook,' said Zeta. 'Havard, as was.'

'What about her?'

'She's not exactly on your Christmas card list, right?'

'It's still only April, Zeta,' shot back Anne, grinning.

'Oh, you know what I mean,' continued Zeta. 'Didn't you and Gwen's husband have a thing going one time? Although this was long before you and your Drew got together, naturally.'

'Well, of course it was,' Anne told her, slightly offended that her lanky friend would even consider that she might have behaved in such a way since she got married. 'I think it was about eighteen years ago, for heaven's sake. And Dyl is a good man, Zeta. I wasn't really myself around that time. I was on a course of prozac, for a start. And my Bethan's dad had walked out on us, do you remember?'

'Of course I do,' her friend replied. 'And, if you recall, we were all there for you at the time, right? But I didn't really want to talk about that time in your life, love. No, no. This was something else completely. Something that happened just three or four years ago, as it goes.'

'Go on,' said Anne, now totally intrigued.

'I believe it was in 2007, on my birthday if I'm not mistaken. Do you remember how we girls all went out for the night?'

'That wasn't *The Dream Boys*, was it?' asked Anne, smiling, then shaking her head.

'Do you mind!' stammered Zeta, colouring, 'If you did see those lot back around that time then I'm sure it wasn't me who went with you. No, no, it was the night when we went to *The Ex.Club. The Ex-Servicemen's Club,* I mean. Say, Anne - can you remember what it was we all went there to see?' Zeta suddenly jumped to her feet and pulled up her tights, a leg at a time

'Gosh! How would I know?' replied Anne. 'I bet we must have gone out on the booze on a fair few occasions around that time.'

'Well, let me give you a clue, shall I?' said Zeta. 'It was the night that Gwen went with us. Gwen Cook. Now do you remember?'

'Well, yes, I think I do,' said Anne, biting her lip, and making a strange, wheezing noise.

'It wasn't for bingo, was it?' Zeta asked her.

'Zeta, I never went to bingo in my whole life!' Anne told her. 'No, I think it was a special show of some kind.'

'Cerys Matthews?' asked Zeta.

'Who? No, that was much later. It was some kind of show with, er - what do you call it now?'

'What? Live music?' asked Zeta. Anne shook her head. 'Karaoke? Nudity?'

'Definitely not,' Anne told her. 'None of those, I'm sure.'

'Well, what then?' enquired Zeta. 'Can you remember? Try and remember, pet, will you?' Zeta lifted a long leg in the air and pulled up one side of her hose again, but Anne was too engrossed in thought to notice, less comment on it, although an elderly gent at the next table spilled some of his tea all over the table.

'I'm not sure what the show was that was on that night, Zeta, but I certainly recall that there was...er, what's it called now?'

'Audience participation?'

'Aye, that's it.'

'Really? You know, *I* thought there was, too,' Zeta told her, licking her lips and becoming more animated. 'So tell me - how did we participate exactly?'

'*We* didn't,' replied Anne. 'You and me, I mean.'

'Who, then?' asked Zeta, lowering her eye-brows.

'If I remember rightly, it was Gwen,' Anne told her.

'But not *just* Gwen?'

'No, not *just* Gwen,' Anne continued. 'But I can remember she was definitely one of the people who went up onto the stage that night. Loose Linda was another one, and Maggie Scratch, so I'm guessing it must have been something pretty disgusting, don't you think?' Eyes wide, her friend nodded in agreement. 'But tell me, Zeta - why on earth would you want to know about that night at *The Ex Club*, all these years later?'

Carla studied her father. So gaunt had he now become that his grey sweater hung from him in great, rolling folds and bulges, much as if he were an up-ended log, or an old, wooden chair.

'Who invented electricity, Dad?' enquired his daughter, who was sitting comfortably on the sofa just across from him, with her feet curled under her, and clutching a pencil and a crossword-puzzle book on her lap.

Tom glared back at his daughter, clearly disgruntled at her question. 'Why, God did, I guess, dear,' he replied, shaking his head with disappointment. He suddenly sat forward so as to address her, his narrow shoulders hunched, his hands visibly trembling. 'Carla, dear - I am shocked that you don't seem to have learned anything in all those early years when your dear mother used to take you to chapel each Sunday back in the village.'

'Oh, really? Except how to play the piano, the organ, the bass, *and* the guitar,' she replied, grinning, 'and even the drums after a fashion. It didn't exactly disadvantage me a great deal, now did it, Dad?' Carla closed the magazine and placed it on the seat beside her. 'If you want to know, I believe the chapel was the basis of all my musical ability,' she told him. 'And where do you think I learned how to write poetry, and even develop the lyrics to some of my very first songs. All in all, I reckon you and Mam couldn't have done any better for me, Dad, had you been some music-mogul, or a multi-millionaire even, instead of a - instead of a -'

'A frustrated, failed dentist, who - who had to settle for being an underpaid medical assistant,' he replied with feeling.

'And had to simply *make do* all my life since, instead of developing a proper career and prospering, as your dear mother must have expected I would do, and indeed as you yourself have managed to do wonderfully.'

'Money-wise, I may have prospered,' Carla responded. 'But there have been very many dark days along the way as well, if you want to know the truth.'

'Sweetheart, do you mind if I ask you something?' Tom enquired of his daughter tenderly, leaning forward again, his orange mug of coffee, wobbling a little, in his bent, veined hand.

'Of course you can, Dad,' Carla replied, moving to sit closer to him, and stroking his speckly, wrinkled forehead with her fingers. She feared his question, and so subtly changed the subject. 'Do you really believe coffee tastes better in a mug that's orange, Dad?' she asked him, smiling.

'Did you ever take drugs?' Tom enquired earnestly. 'Did you, love? Because if you did, you can tell me now you know. It's O.K. You can, Carla. Honestly.'

Finally the moment had arrived that Carla had been dreading all her adult life. And, now that it had, she certainly didn't intend to lie to her Dad about the facts, although she realised how the truth might just finish him off, or at least sadly malign their newly re-kindled relationship. 'Oh, Dad,' she mumbled softly, rather like a loving, forgiving parent, and exactly as her mother had done to her many times before. 'You really don't have to worry on that score, you know.'

'Well, I'm glad,' Tom told her with a smile, then turned away, and gazed out of the window at the tall trees that stood across the road. But the old man could tell that it had slipped his daughter's mind that her father possessed a special gift that his daughter didn't appear to have inherited. Tom turned back and looked deep into Carla's beautiful blue eyes, and very soon gleaned all the knowledge from her that he felt he needed to learn, of the pain that her life in the spot-light had involved, and of the terrible pain caused by the men who had lived with her, and used her, and hurt her, and of all the substances she had consumed, and abused, in her frantic attempts simply to cope with the sequence of disapointments that befell her, and, in the end, perhaps helped get her through them.

And, despite it all, Tom knew that he truly loved his daughter just as he had loved her all her life, and as he had indeed loved the son he had also had - Will, her much older brother - and who had died when still a youth, because of *his* foolish actions, and not *hers* - no, not because of Carla at all, as she had always supposed - in that vast, deep, mysterious lake that sat, brooding, just a few short miles from the house where the two of them now sat conversing together.

Gifted like him, or not, Carla could usually tell when her father was contemplating her brother's death. She leaned down and placed her slim body very close to his, and hugged him long and hard, until their concordant, plenteous tears, and his shuddering sobs which followed, were sung out and were finally at an end. Then her father was at last able to lean back and snooze again in the great, cushioned belly of the big yellow sofa, and Carla could take herself upstairs once more to replenish her daily needs, and climb into her soft, warm bed and sleep again, this time perchance to dream, of happier times to come for the pair of them.

And as Carla entered the bathroom, pulled the cord, and sat herself down once again on the side of the gleaming, off-white bath-tub, and stretched her hands over onto the flat, raised back of the gleaming, off-white wash-basin that stood alongside it, she contemplated sadly how this deadened cycle of shared, agonising pain certainly did not appear to have any end to it.

CHAPTER 7

Chris had rung the number twice already. The first time his mother had walked into the bedroom to collect his soiled shirts, and complain once again about the coffee-beans he stored in bags beneath his bed but never seemed to use, and so he was reluctantly forced to abandon the task. The second time someone had answered, but chose not to speak. His last dealer - Dai Blaze - had done that same thing many times in the past when he had called him up to get 'something for the weekend,' Chris mused, and so he thought little of it, feeling sure that he would be bound to succeed in making contact with the guy, sooner rather than later. And in a way he was right.

Chris closed his bedroom-door and flopped himself down on an armchair near the window. He rang the number for the third time and waited, but when a girl answered he wasn't at all sure what to do. He presumed she was a friend of Carla, but wasn't clear how he could establish that. Then he had an idea.

'Hello,' he began. 'I've got to drop something off for Carla. Tell me - can you accept it?'

'Well, I should be able to,' the female voice on the other end of the line replied.

'Good,' Chris told her. 'Where *are* you exactly?'

'You need to tell me what it is first,' the girl commanded, 'then I'll see what I can do.'

'It's - well, it's some shit, actually,' Chris informed her, a tad abashed he was being so blunt.

'You mean for the garden?' the woman asked.

Chris was confused. 'Look - I'm not bothered where she does it,' he told her. 'She can smoke it in *Asda's* as far as I'm concerned. Say - we're talking high quality skunk, here, lady. Fresh off the bone, do you get me?'

'Fresh off the bone!' the girl repeated with a slight giggle. 'What is your name, by the way?' she enquired.

'Er - call me Chris,' he advised her.

'Oh. Is that your real name, then?' she asked.

Chris realised how foolish he had been, and said, 'Of course not. Do you think I'm stupid or something? Say, what is your name?'

'What do you mean - 'what is *my name*?' ' she asked him.

'Well, is that a hard question, lady? I mean -' He started laughing at her stupidity. 'Listen - you need to tell me who I'm dealing with here. Otherwise we can't do business, you get me?'

'Oh, I see. O.K.,' she responded politely. 'Look - you can call me Carla, if you like.'

'Can I, now?' Chris asked, with a chuckle. 'O.K. then, er - Carla. You're in the Merthyr area, right?'

'Yes, that's right,' she told him.

Chris heard a strange noise that sounded very like she had opened her purse with her free hand and dropped all the money she had inside it onto the surface of a table close to her.

'Do you happen to know *Pontsticill Reservoir*, at all?' Chris enquired.

'Yes, I believe I do,' she told him, now sounding as if she was counting out all her cash.

'You do? Good,' he told her. 'Then I'll meet you there with the stuff at seven tonight, yeah? Listen - I promise you won't be disappointed - er, Carla.'

'And you're going to drive there, yes, Chris?' she asked, making a quiet sound like she was giggling into her hand.

'Of course,' he replied, realising he had better not tell her he didn't own a car, and hadn't yet even managed to pass his driving-test. 'But - but, as I'll be already parked-up in the village, you won't get to see me in the motor at all. No, I'll be on foot when you first see me. On the dam, yeah? At the tower-end. By the way I'll be wearing a white Swansea football shirt with - with -'

' - with *Chris* on the back, yes?'

This reply took Chris completely by surprise. 'Do you know it does, as a matter of fact,' he answered, as calmly as he could manage. 'As well as a big number nine.' He suddenly realised that the girl had tricked him into revealing his true identity, but he felt sure he knew just how to manage that too. 'You see - I *am* called Chris, as it goes, so you - so you already know me, and so you already know you can trust me, yeah?'

'That's good, Chris.' the girl replied. 'Seven, then, yes?'

'No - nine,' he told her firmly. 'A big black one.'

'*The time*, Chris,' she said, giggling again. 'Say - can I ask you something? How come you knew that, er - that my friend Carla needed some dope, anyway?'

'You being serious?' Chris replied, laughing. 'She *is* Carla Steel, right?'

A few seconds silence. 'No, I mean that she needed some right now,' she continued.

'Listen, lady - you don't actually need to know that,' he told her. 'It's a secret, you see. As is my address and - and my supplier, and my car-registration and everything else.' What was he saying? Chris asked himself. He could sense that, by now, his nerves were definitely beginning to get the better of him.

'Oh, O.K., then, Chris,' the girl replied. 'Look, I know Carla will be delighted if your stuff turns out to be top-quality, as you claim it is, and I guess she will probably want me to give you a great stack of cash for it. So why don't you bring a load of your gear along?'

'A shit-load you mean?' Chris giggled back. 'O.K., then.' he said, thinking fast. 'Yeah, I might just do that. Look - she certainly won't be disappointed, you can tell her. Remember it's -'

'Fresh off the bone,' she said, finishing the tele-sales advert for him, although he wasn't actually intending to say that. 'And I'm fresh off the phone right now, so I'll be seeing you later on, Chris. Bye, then.'

'Bye,' said Chris, terminating the call, throwing his phone down onto the bed, and leaping up and down with excitement. Seconds later he was running off to the bathroom to get the ladder.

In the house next-door Carla tossed her phone down onto the bed and checked the clock. She saw that it was almost six o'clock already. Dressed only in her silk robe, she walked over to the window, opened it, and looked out across the back-garden at *The Seven Arches*, and at the lovely Taff Valley in the distance, and slowly moved her eyes a mile or so to the left to where she knew the vast reservoir was located, far behind the hill and the trees that presently obscured it. It was a place she rarely chose to visit on the odd occasion that she came back to Wales, but on this particular evening she felt the desperate need to get out of the house for an hour or so, and perhaps take a welcome break from the task of caring non-stop for her sick father.

So distant was the lake from her father's home that Carla realised she would need to get a cab to make the rendez-vous. Minutes later, after getting properly dressed, and with the taxi on its way, Carla went over to the window to close it, and was more than a little surprised to see the wiry youth who lived next-door hurrying away at a trot across the viaduct, and off into the deepening gloom before her. She contemplated how she had only seen him once or twice before, and didn't even know the boy's name, but she smiled, admiring what she observed of his young, but manly, vigour, his resolve, and his fleetness of foot. Just then her train of thought was suddenly broken by the sound of a mature, female voice yelling out from the window in the neighbouring house that was opened up right next to her own.

'Chris!' the voice shrieked. 'Chris - where on earth do you think you're running off to at this time of night? It's Sunday night, for heaven's sake. You've got school in the morning, remember. And you told us you've still got homework to do.'

Carla laughed aloud, realising instantly what it was that had happened. She followed keenly the boy's galloping, scarlet-jacketed form, but not once did she witness the said Chris turn round to reply to his mother, nor even so much as to glance back in her direction. No, she thought, the callow youth was off on his wild, solo mission to make some bread for himself, and she knew that he wasn't going to let even a mother's concerns for him hold him back. In that respect, thought Carla, he seemed to be very like how she herself had been at his age. She watched as his scuttling form left the bridge and disappeared round the bend in the direction of the woods, the long-abandoned tunnel, and the slowly rising valley that lay beyond it. Yes, she pondered, in a way the boy-next-door seemed to possess her much-admired strength of purpose, and most likely the type of impulsive, instinctive spirit that was at the heart of her own creative urges.

To Carla, who securely latched the windows shut, and drew the pastel curtains closed before them, the thought of buying a quantity of cannabis off a school sixth-former, who lived right next-door to her, was almost too hilarious for words. Ordinarily, she told herself, this would be the type of crazy exploit she would steer well clear of in the neighbourhood she lived in back in London. Still, she knew she was desperately in need of some puff, so, when the cab finally arrived, she paid the driver up front, with a handsome tip into the bargain, and climbed inside its sparse, but musty, interior, and raced off in the night to the secret rendez-vous at the head of the very same lake where her brother Will had tragically lost his life at her own hand years earlier.

That Sunday evening I remember I had left my daughter Rhiannon in the living room with her homework, and had taken the car to the lower gate of the cemetery so that I could leave some fresh flowers for my brother Sam, and pop over to visit long-deceased boxer Johnny Owen on the way back down the hill. I got back into the car and then drove north again, past the little narrow-gauge railway station, whose car-park sign bore a display announcing that it was soon going to be open to the public most days, now that the Spring Bank Holiday was well behind us.

I soon pulled up just after the narrow bend, and proudly sat myself down on the famous stone - *The Prince's Seat* - from which prime view-point the sight of the valley of the Upper

Taff is truly sublime, as the river curves its way west and away from you, carving out its impressive, ever deepening, elbow-of-capture as it does so, and flowing on again through Vaynor Woods, and up against the sandstone hill that supports *Gloryhole,* to run beneath the great viaduct there. Thereafter the river speeds down through its brief, thrilling course of waterfalls, cataracts and rock-pools, then, slowing once more at *The Blue Pool,* continues on for a couple of miles more towards Cefn, and then bends south through Merthyr, then towards faraway Cardiff and the sea.

Below me, and hidden away just off the main track of *The Taff Trail* - the former steam-railway line - lay the site of my elder brother's tragic death. I let my eye drift left, towards the steep path down which, in 1974, I well remember I had run to find him, once the news of his death was abroad, and once the perpetrators had cowardly fled the murder scene, to cower, and hide, and shamefully lie and conspire, and so escape the blame that was theirs alone. I recalled again how three young ambulance-men and I had carried Sam's broken body on a stretcher back up to this very spot, then, along the road by which I had just come, had transported it in a white van to *St.Tydfil's Hospital,* where Sam was officially pronounced dead.

Sadly the actual cause of Sam's death was unknown. His young torso bore no signs of his having been run down or assaulted, either on, or close to, the railway-line on which it was found, but the multitude of marks on his bruised, scarred hands, arms and legs bore witness to a violent struggle that had clearly ensued, a point which had been repeatedly denied by all who had accompanied him on the country walk that day, and the afternoon picnic, the purpose of which had been to celebrate his twenty-first birthday. But, instead of celebration, the booze-fuelled festivities had only heralded the tragic termination of Sam's short life.

For my part. forgetting, let alone forgiving, had been well nigh impossible. The killers were, after all, his closest compatriots - college friends, no less - and I had met, and knew well, each of them. Indeed one - Anne - but a few months my junior, had once been my closest companion at school, where she had intermittently even answered to the sobriquet *'Dyl's girl.'* Anne was the only one of the four whom I ever chose to see again, and that many years later, when her daughter Bethan's father deserted her, and I fancied I might be able to help her out, and ended up comforting her more intensely than I ever intended. But that brief, passionate relationship had terminated abruptly after she reunited with, and soon after, married a man whom she and my brother Sam had been friends with at university - an Englishman from Exeter, via Cardiff, called Drew Cillick, who was presently my daughter Rhiannon's Art teacher at Pennant High School.

With my car's windows open wide, and the evening breeze streaming in and carressing my face and temples from both sides, I eased back and listened to the Dire Straits' album *'Brothers In Arms'* on the car-stereo system, as I skirted the limestone hill to my right called *The Twynau,* and once again drove north towards the rural haven known as Pontsticill village.

Passing under the old railway bridge, I was soon faced with the usual choice between taking the left-hand turn, which crossed the Taff River at one of its prettier spots, followed by the short, but steep climb up the hill towards the village, or else taking the much longer, winding route that first invites the driver right down towards the water's edge, and then takes him up once again along the longer, and much gentler incline, past the cottages and wooden barns on the limestone hillside to the right, towards the reservoir's colossal dam, and the vast, sinuous lake of fresh water that, fortuitously, it held back for the best part of three or four miles.

I well remember that it was just after six when I drove across the great dam in the direction of its stone tower, rounded the hairpin-bend, entered the hill-top village, and parked up for my customary Sunday-evening drink in *The Butcher's Arms.* I can even recall that, despite the fine weather, it was more crowded than usual inside the pub that evening, and that I therefore stood for some considerable time at the bar, admiring on the wall before me the array of framed images of all the famous, local sportsmen and women that our valley had produced over the years, such as boxers Johnny Owen, and Howard Winstone, and Eddie Thomas - the latter's late manager, who had trained and guided him to winning a world-title - and even Joe Calzhage, the modern-day equivalent, who hailed from a neighbouring valley, but had achieved unrivalled fame by having never lost a single fight in his entire fifteen-year career, and who had only recently hung up his gloves as an undefeated world-champion.

'*The Merthyr Match-stick*, they called him,' the young red-headed barmaid declared, pointing up at the photograph of Bantam-weight Johnny Owen, and smiling at his lean, but pugnacious figure. 'He died in the ring, they say,' she added, pouring me my third, and final, frothing drink into a straight pint-glass.

'Yes, I can remember it well,' I told the barmaid with a sigh, pointing at the first image. 'World-title fight in Los Angeles, nineteen-eighty,' I told her. 'The lad just happened to walk into the most powerful hook ever thrown by man, and fell heavily to the canvas, completely concussed, and more or less deceased already some say. I only just went over to see him about an hour ago.'

'Eh?' the girl asked, confused by my statement. 'Oh, his grave, you mean?'

'Well, aye,' I retorted. 'What do you think I meant, girl? His ghost?'

'Well I wasn't sure for a minute then,' she replied, her brows arched widely. 'Talking of ghosts, Dyl, the folk living round here tell me they've seen plenty of 'em over the years. Including the one of that man who perished in the closed-up tunnel down your way. But you'll pardon me if I just drop it there, won't you, as I find I get terrified these days just thinking about it.'

I decided it was best to shut up and finish my beer. You see, little did the girl know but she was clearly referring to my brother Sam. And so I quickly finished my pint, slipped on my coat again, and, by the light of the solitary street-lamp, sauntered my way back to my parked car.

Chris was so shocked that he literally fell out of his tree when he saw who it was who had actually turned up to meet him on the narrow, country road that ran across the dam. From his shadowy lair he watched like a hawk as the pretty, dark-haired woman, whom the whole world knew so well and admired so much, stepped out of her cab, which straightaway drove off, then turned and walked languidly towards the stolid embankment-wall. There. standing up on tip-toe, she gazed above and beyond it into the far distance, perchance to see a trout fly, (just as Chris himself had done minutes earlier,) and seeking out the once-memorized-never-forgotten, though by this time barely visible, outline of the mountain landscape known as The Brecon Beacons.

To Carla's mind, the long, whale-backed outline of the three lofty peaks, known to walkers everywhere as 'The Fans,' could not help but resonate forever in the native's living memory, she mused, in a similar way to the trilling song of the skylark, or an old Welsh hymn, or even the narrow-gauge, steam-train that gently runs its way along there from Pant to this day. The unique, serrated mountain-profile had countless times enlivened for her the long hours of a care-worn city life, much as if it were a throbbing, long-loved vein which ran joyfully through the collective unconscious of all the people who inhabited the lovely Taff Valley, including those, such as her own dead brother, who had gone before, and no doubt those mortals who were yet to come.

Her long, black hair circling her like a spinning veil, Carla spun round on the empty road, perhaps seeking out some human interraction, but the warbling sounds of the birds in the trees were all that she found to sustain her. Soon Carla began to shiver, discovering how alone she felt in this wild, exposed location, where she now stood for the first time since it had happened. She glanced down at the deep, dark water beneath the gloomy tower, and saw how the water-level was presently twenty feet at least above the level of the beach on which she and Will had fished for trout, then picnicked happily, on that summer afternoon many years before. Suddenly Carla felt something akin to a night-terror begin to overtake her, and. feeling nauseous, she dropped to her knees, and began to weep bitter tears that she knew only she could cry. After all, Carla told herself in a sort of silent scream, she believed that it had been her own stupid actions that had resulted in the needless death of her brother - her father's beloved, only son, Will.

Though a striking success in the eyes of her army of fans, her fellow musicians, and music-critics right across the world, Carla saw clearly how she had been nothing less than a desperate failure in the realm of her personal life, in terms of love and relationships, and in terms of her family's aspirations for her as their only daughter, and therefore as a potential creator of new life. Indeed, for years now she had felt that, instead of helping Tom and Carys to become the grandparents they had every right to anticipate they one day might become, tragically the sum of her efforts was that she had cost them a son. And, she told herself through gritted teeth and painful sobs, her poor mother had plainly withered appreciably and noticeably as a result of it. In contrast, her father, far more resilient and self-assured, and much less obsessed with filial devotion and responsibility as he unquestionably was, had taken the matter of Will's death much more in his stride, had lived on into old age, and now, if you listened to what he had to say on the subject, 'stood on the brink of the ultimate discovery that defined and united all life on Earth.'

The crouching Carla started at the scuffling sound of a squirrel, or a fox, perhaps, moving about amongst the golden leaves that formed a crinkled carpet, from which emerged the tall, slender pines that bordered each side of the narrow road leading towards *Pontsticill* village. In an effort to identify the cause, Carla screwed up her eyes for optimum effect and stared into the gloom. Amidst the deepening shadows she felt that she could make out the gleam of a white, polythene-bag at human hip-level, a flash of red above it, and two, adjacent white trainers sitting much closer to the ground. Then surely it had to be Chris, she told herself.

Carla stood up and approached the side of the road and peered even more intently into the shadows, until she was sure she could make out the boy's slim, open-coated form, and what she felt were his flowing, dark curls. She paused near the fence, waiting for him to be the first to speak, but, when nothing of the sort occurred, Carla concluded that it was clearly down to her to break the eerie, evening silence with the first human sound.

'Chris - yeah?' Carla asked, smiling at the trail of leaves that traversed his clothes and hair. 'What on earth are you doing *in there*?'

'Christ! She didn't have to make you come yourself, surely?' said Chris, stumbling quickly out of the trees, plastic-bag in hand, and squeezing his slim torso between the vertical bars of the iron fence, then ambling out into the middle of the road to join her.

'But that was me!' Carla told him, smiling. 'You rang my own personal mobile. Where on earth did you get my number from? Eh? Listening over the fence, right? You know you've got some nerve young man. Say, are you some kind of stalker then? Because I've had quite a few of those over the years, I can tell you.'

'No way!' Chris responded sharply, genuinely embarrassed at the comment, and from her of all people. 'I'm a - I'm a dealer,' he told her, and he opened up his bag so that she could peer inside and so verify his claim.

'Of course you are, Chris,' Carla replied, with a smirk. And what she saw when she looked inside the bag didn't impress her any more than his demeanour had. 'Do you mean a car-dealer?' she asked. Dismayed, he looked down. 'Where's your car, by the way? Getting valeted? Circling the block? Taking a leak?'

'My car!' stammered Chris, pulling his bag back, and feeling both flustered and more than a little intimidated by her .

'How old are you, anyway?' she enquired. 'Sixteen?'

'Seventeen,' he shot back. 'And I'll be eighteen soon.'

'I bet you haven't even got a driving-licence, let alone wheels,' she told him. 'I watched you dashing over the viaduct, by the way. Your mother was right. You ought to listen to her, you know, Chris. You've got school tomorrow, and there's probably still a stack of homework you haven't completed.'

'Did she say that? The bitch!' he ejaculated. 'She knows very well I did everything yesterday morning. Except the modes and minors. And she knows I can only do them when I'm at school. You see, we don't have room for a piano, according to her, not even a stand-up one.'

'You play piano?' Carla asked, brows raised.

'Key-boards. Yeah, of course I do,' he responded confidently. 'And guitar. Don't you believe me, then? You know, I can play most of your stuff, for a start.'

'Except the minor pieces, right?' said Carla, smiling at him. 'And that would be about half of it.'

'I don't - I don't have all the sheet-music,' he told her, by way of explanation. 'Your books aren't cheap, you know. I just can't afford it.'

'Is that why you're selling drugs, then, Chris? Yeah? Is it? Silly boy. Look, if you want my music, I could let you have all of it.'

'You mean - do you mean for some weed?' Chris asked her.

'Well, if you like. No, no. Forget the weed!' Carla answered firmly.'No. For nothing. Look, I'll give you money for the drugs if that's what you want.' She handed him a few notes and took the bag out of his hand. 'O.K.? You know, I bet you grow it in your parent's attic, don't you?'

Chris thought for a second. 'I don't actually,' he told her truthfully.

'That *Verve* song was right, you know,' she told him. The drugs *don't* work. Get yourself a girlfriend, why don't you? That's a lot safer. You're not a bad looking boy, you know. A bit on the skinny side, maybe. Wiry. But you'd pass muster.'

'I'm concentrated,' he shot back. 'Like Bob Dylan was at my age. That's what Rhiannon says, anyway.'

'Your sister?' Carla asked, bemused.

'My girlfriend. Well, my ex-girlfriend, as it goes,' he explained.

'Oh. And does Rhiannon know you sell drugs, Chris?' she asked. He narrowed his eyes at this observation. 'No? And what do you think she'd say if she found out you did?'

'But she's my ex, I told you.' he replied, grinning weakly.

'Of course she is, Chris,' responded Carla, staring directly into his rapidly squinting eyes. 'You know, I think you should ring her up again some time soon, that's what I think,' she added.

'Why?' pleaded Chris. 'There's plenty more fish, you know.'

'Oh, now that's a nice thing to say,' Carla told him. 'Most gallant of you, don't you think?'

'But Rhiannon is younger than me by almost a year,' he told her. 'She's barely legal.'

'Really?' replied Carla. 'So you're basically admitting you've been intimate with the girl, then. Yes? Dear me, Chris. All the more reason to ring her up and speak to her then, if you ask me. You know, I fear you're going to break poor Rhiannon's heart, if you're not careful, Chris.' The boy shrugged his shoulders, then looked away to the side. 'Now you wouldn't want to do that, would you?' Carla continued. 'Well, would you, Chris? No, of course you wouldn't.'

Chris shook his head, and, with fore-lock slightly bowed, turned and looked back in the petite, handsome girl's direction. What the hell was happening here? he asked himself, quickly flushing up. Why all these silly questions for a start? And why on earth did the great Carla Steel have an opinion about what he - Chris Cillick - even did with his life?

'No. I thought not,' Carla told him, answering her question for him. 'So take my advice, would you, Chris, and promise me you'll speak to the girl in the morning, O.K.? Will you do that, Chris?'

Chris quickly realised that he simply couldn't argue the point with her, and certainly couldn't relate to her the two linked, troubling dreams he had about Rhiannon on the night after they had been in the woods together. Instead, and against his better judgement, he found himself nodding to Carla in agreement with virtually every word that the singer spoke - every single suggestion that the adorable, talented and tremendously sexy woman happened to come up with.

'You're not a little boy any more, are you, Chris?' she asked him, reaching out to grasp his hand.

1 5 3

Chris smiled back at her and shook his head, then became aware of the sudden, warm stiffening that was taking place just below his waist-band. Horrified, he quickly turned his body to the side and stared out at the great, dark lake in the middle distance, in the hope that she wouldn't get to suspect anything, and in the greater hope, perhaps, that its cool, sheen-like surface might have a settling effect on his soaring libido. Chris breathed deeply and let the cool, evening breeze fan his burning cheeks and forehead. Then he watched, taken aback, as a gleaming trout leapt high into the night air, then slapped itself back into the water. Chris bit sharply into his top lip and squirmed. This was not at all what he'd anticipated taking place tonight, he told himself, turning to meet her gaze. Now what the hell was going to happen next?

The moon was full, but dark night had drawn in, and the cold breeze began to blow in through my open window from The Beacons to the north. I drove my car up the steep incline and left Ponsticill behind me, then changed down and sped along the only fast stretch on my route, and then braked hard as I began to enter the un-lit gloom of the two tight bends that ran down towards Vaynor. It was then that it happened. Yes, it was at that moment that my life was about to suffer a severe jolt, and, in all truth, was never to be quite the same again.

After rounding the first curve at little more than twenty miles per hour, I suddenly saw two figures walking ahead of me in the middle of the road. There were no footpaths alongside the narrow carriageway, and I could just make out that the two individuals were smoking a long cigarette between them, and idling their way along almost unconsciously, very like two drunken companions rendered hard of hearing, and possibly stupefied, by the effects of their indulgence.

I tried to steer my car to the side, but, sadly, it was too late. The loud thud on the front-wing told me that I had struck the male of the pair, and knocked him to the side of the road, and head-first into a fence that protected the vast sheep-field that stretched away for some considerable distance behind it.

How on earth could the pair not have seen me? I asked myself, angrily. In a tormented screech of brakes, I pulled up a few yards past them, leapt out, then instantly realised that I had been driving the last mile or so without any lights.

With a mixture of horror and self-blame, I grabbed a torch from the dash-board and sprinted over to where the fallen boy now lay upon his side. He was deposited, bleeding and bedraggled, upon a large, grassy bank, toppled over it somewhat uncomfortably, and with his two legs just above the level of his head. With his female companion's earnest help I managed to gather the boy up onto his back, and soon flashed my torch onto his face. Thankfully he was still alive, and he soon began breathing deeply, and opening his flickering eyes to look about him. I recognised him instantly. His name was Chris, and he was a close school-friend of my daughter Rhiannon.

The girl I also recognised a few minutes later as Carla Steel, (or Carla Davies - as the Merthyr Valley community had long known her,) whom I had seen performing on stage alongside Rhiannon and the rest of the school-band only a week or so before. The pungent odour that swept around us on the road-side as she cursed aloud, and screamed unrepeatable profanities at my alleged stupidity, and my lack of driving skills, told me more or less instantly that they had been smoking a cannabis-joint together, and this same item I soon saw the singer fling away into the long grass beside the poor young man's flattened torso. Whether or not the boy was stoned out of his mind that night, or whether his senses were just slightly impaired, as it appeared mine were, I could not say I cared overmuch. But I was nevertheless horrified at what I had done, especially as I could plainly see that it was my very own son that I had almost killed that night.

The room at *Prince Charles Hospital* was just off the ward in which many male patients seemed to be already asleep. Chris had a leg-wound and was concussed, and so presently asleep too, but thankfully, he was otherwise unscathed, and, when I heard that his parents had just driven up, I thought it best that I should leave. My bedside companion, Carla, showed no inclination to stay there a moment longer either, and so we walked off down the silent corridor together, took the lift down to the entrance, and in the bright moonlight made our way back to my car.

When we reached the main road I asked Carla where she would like me to take her, and to my surprise she said that she wanted to be driven back to *Gloryhole*, where, she informed me, she had been staying for a fortnight or so with her father. Minutes later, and still greatly surprised by her comment, I carved my way up, in first gear, from the eternally gushing *Blue Pool* towards the tight, hairpin-bend above it, and then, swinging right, motored right up to Chris's front-door, and let the singer out of the car.

Carla turned and waved goodbye to me, and I eased off the brake and drove on once more, and made my way home again by the longer route - the route along which the accident had occurred just a few hours before - via the now silent hill-top village of Pontsticill, and the steeply dropping lane that ran back south-east from it towards Pant.

Sitting in my car, in the full glare of the street-lamp that stood looming above me outside my front-door in Cemetery Road, I pondered long over the strange events of the evening just passed, and realised that it had all begun because I had quaffed a solitary pint of ale more than usual, and had simply forgotten to switch on my car-headlights before setting off for home and tragically colliding heavily with the hapless Chris Cillick. But just as strange, I felt, was the fact that Carla Steel had implied that she was staying with the boy and his mother Anne at her father's house, and so I quite naturally assumed that Chris, although well over ten years her junior, was, in fact, Carla's step-brother, and that she was presumably the daughter of Drew, the eccentric, somewhat refractory, Art teacher I had many times conversed with at Pennant.

There had long been rumours that, before his marriage to Anne, English-born Drew had fathered another child with someone while living in Cardiff, but, for some reason, I had always assumed it to be a son. But, in light of what I had just witnessed, it certainly appeared that Drew was the father of a woman whom the whole world knew and loved as Carla Steel. Well, the pair of them were both well-educated and artistically inclined, after all, I mused, and so I felt reluctant to question the sudden discovery I had made. And yet I was still unwilling to share what I had unearthed with another soul, not even with the other members of my family, well, at least not until I had myself confirmed its veracity.

CHAPTER 8

The Willows Care Home: a place where fifty shades of grey managed to live out the fag-end of their lives largely asexually, though frequently frustratingly, in fifty single-bedrooms geometrically arranged alongside each other on a single floor. In a rest-room that looked out on the garden at the rear of the building Anne sipped her jasmine-tea and read silently to herself one of the Sunday papers she had found lying on a table there.

'Is it fair that only people in England are being charged for prescriptions,' asked *The Mail on Sunday*, in its *'Today's Poll'* feature. Anne was feeling heartily sick of the pathetic lack of common sense implicit in this sort of shallow question, and which appeared to have been devised and presented with a specific, preconceived outcome presumed. Mail readers would no doubt reply that it wasn't fair, when all the Coalition Government had to do was bring in the same sort of bill that had been passed in the Celtic nations and then just about everyone in the U.K. would be happy. Anne felt that they might as well ask if it was right that the Welsh and the Scots decided against forcing their school-leavers to pay tuition fees, which, after all, those in her year at school who went on to attend Uni never had to pay anyway as young students, in the good old days when the local councils picked up the bill, and so charged the rate-payers accordingly. It was a self-financing method that appeared sensible and fair back then, she thought, so why wasn't it so any longer?

And the newspaper might as well ask why the Welsh had the nerve not to charge car-parking fees for people who were visiting their sick and dying loved-ones in hospital, or why supermarkets in Wales charged customers a small fee for each polythene-bag they chose to use. As far as Anne was concerned it was all a question of priorities. The priorities decided upon by the Celtic nations, and expressed through their specific assemblies and parliaments, simply appeared to be very different ones to those that the Coalition in Westminster chose to adopt for England. There they elected to spend their money on things she imagined perhaps they cherished more, and therefore prioritised. So why couldn't the London press acknowledge this fact, she wondered, and simply respect the rights of the Welsh people to choose for themselves what they wanted to spend their scarce resources on, and stop inciting their readers like this.

Anne sat back and pondered over what these priorities might be that the English committed their finance on instead. Well, there were all the road speed-cameras for a start, she thought, that seem to have sprung up on every conceivable by-way. And what about all those pot-holes that had opened up like earthquake-fissures on virtually all the main roads over the previous winter. Didn't it occur to the people with power that endlessly filling them in would simply prove expensive and futile? Anne wondered why, when repairing the road, the councils didn't choose to lay down the sort of surfaces that didn't suddenly peel off the road whenever winter temperatures fell below freezing. That way they might get to save themselves millions that they could then elect to spend on free prescriptions, hospital-parking, and the rest of the things that the Welsh did that those on the other side of Offa's Dyke seemed endlessly to complain about.

There was one area, however, where Anne thought the Welsh might like to prioritise soon, and which she bet the English already did. She had worked at the care-home for some years now, and was appalled at the poor standard of the facilities there, especially the depressing quality of the bedrooms and bathrooms provided for the use of the fifty old people who had invariably been forced to sell their homes in order to afford the extortionate charges that were made on them so as to finance their living costs. And, she mused, an improvement in the wages paid to those who worked there might even result in them not having to employ the less than dedicated, and, too often, far from patient, younger folk who had recently been despatched to them from the Jobcentre to work the shifts alongside her, they having been judged as failing to satisfy the new, harsher conditions by which the unemployed qualify for benefit payments.

Anne looked out of the wide bay-window and saw a large group of nurses, including Gareth, who, these days, seemed to be more or less in charge of the home, helping a group of aged women to seat themselves in the garden in an attempt to take advantage of the unseasonably warm Spring sunshine, which made *The Willows* feel more like Dubrovnik than Dowlais. Anne felt moved to smile at the respectful air of authority that Gareth seemed to display when around them. She suddenly recalled how the man had quite recently told her that he had fallen in love with her, but, by way of reply and rebuff, Anne had told him that, as she loved her husband dearly, she could never in a million years entertain such an idea. As ever, though, Gareth's attitude to her rebuke was both principled and generous, and she had told him how she felt it was so good of him to have even said such kind, loving words to her. Yes, there was nobody in her work-place whom Anne respected more than Gareth Marshalsea, and the sight of him showing kindness to the old and the dying alike was, for her, a most tender sight to behold.

All of a sudden Anne heard a male voice let out a fearsome shriek in a room just along the corridor from where she was taking her break. She leapt to her feet, and went out and hurried quickly along the passage-way in the direction from which she felt sure the sound had come, and very soon she found she could hear the voices of two young males talking animatedly together above a background of loud music.

Arriving at a partially-open door, Anne peered inside it, and could clearly see two young men in white jackets, sitting at a computer-screen, and apparently smoking two cannabis joints. She could see straightaway that they were the two work-experience students from Year-Eleven at Pennant School, who had only been working at the home for just a few days, and whose names she was still unsure of. Anne wondered what the two young boys could possibly be doing that seemed to arouse in them such a high level of excitement.

A calling-bell was being sounded inside the room the boys occupied, but, instead of responding immediately, as was the care-home's policy, they simply chose to ignore it. One of the pair, whom Anne believed was named Steffan, walked over to the window, forced it open, and tossed his smoking joint out into the flower-beds that were sited just outside. Then, seeing something that seemed to take his interest, he suddenly began laughing derisively at the group of old people on zimmer-frames, whom Gareth and the other nurses were patiently entertaining with songs, and stories, and pots of nice hot tea.

Steffan then spun round and, approaching his young friend at the computer, cursed loudly and repugnantly at the recurring sound of the bell. 'Aw, shut the fuck up, will you!' the boy suddenly screamed at the tannoy above his head.

Anne was horrified. She opened the door a little wider, peered in more intently, and soon found that she could just make out on the computer-screen a close-up of what appeared to be the moving face of an attractive young, dark-haired woman, whose music was playing loudly in the background. She quickly realised that the two boys were playing a video of the local-born singer known as Carla Steel. Anne watched, astonished, as the taller, much thinner youth, who was seated at the computer's keyboard, and who she suddenly remembered was called Jake, started squirming around oddly on his chair, and crudely simulating masturbation, while drinking what Anne pesumed was alcohol from a large, red tumbler.

Just then an old woman called Victoria very slowly approached the room's window from the area of the garden where Gareth was working, seemingly attracted there by the noise of the music inside. She raised her thin, frail, heavily wrinkled arms and pushed open the window a little further so as to peer inside, seemingly fascinated, not just by the music, but by the sight of the colourful, flashing video that was playing on the table-top screen.

'Who's that then?' she suddenly called out to the two boys. 'Who's that woman, there?'

'What the fuck do you want, you old slut?' the stouter boy called Steffan shouted back at her.

'I know her!' Victoria yelled back at him, pointing a trembling finger at the oscillating, singing face of Carla Steel.

'Course you do. She sang at your funeral,' Steffan replied, approaching the window at speed, and slamming it shut in the woman's face. Laughing aloud, he quickly returned to the computer and, grasping the mouse in his hand, minimised the video, and so revealed the web-page that lay beneath it. To Anne's straining eyes, it appeared to display the interior of someone's kitchen, inside which an armoury of guns and knives were laid out on a table. The two youths passed a second joint between them as they scribbled down information in a note-pad that they had laid open before them, presumably about the weapons that were on display.

The calling-bell sounded for a third time, accompanied by a frantic curse from a bed-ridden gentlemen in a bedroom nearby, and so Anne quietly pulled the door of the room closed, and, turning about, dashed off to see what it was that was troubling the old man.

'I'm sure I've got a screw loose, you know,' Tom announced, standing under the frame of the open back-door of his *Gloryhole* home.

'You didn't have to tell me that, Dad. I've always known,' replied Carla, with a smile.

The old man looked inside to where his daughter stood with her back to him, working at the bread-board. 'I'm talking about these sun-glasses, Carla,' he told her. There's no need to be so cheeky to your father, is there? It's this right arm, this shaky one here. It seems to be about to come off in my hand.'

'What's about to come off in your hand, Dad?' she asked him, then giggling quietly to herself at the crudity of the words she had used, and which she knew her father would never comprehend, as she laid the ham-slices on the buttered bread, and carefully folded each alternate slice on top.

'These old tinted specs I've got,' he replied. 'Why? What do you think I was talking about? Eh? You know you seem to have learned an awful lot since you've been up in that - that London, my girl. Much of it disgusting if you ask me.'

'Then perhaps *I won't* ask you,' she replied, spinning round with two plates full of sandwiches in her hands, and a cheeky grin on her face. 'You know, Dad, I wouldn't be surprised to find you think that some my song-lyrics are disgusting too, right? Do you, Dad? Tell me - do you?'

'I wouldn't really know,' he responded, taking one of the plates from her, and shuffling along in his carpet-slippers towards the iron table in the far corner of the garden-patio, where his daughter had suggested they could sit and enjoy the day's brunch together. 'I find I don't seem to have much time to listen to music.'

'Really? Not even mine?' Carla enquired from behind him, affecting a bruised ego. She walked over and joined her father at the table and sat down beside him. 'You've got all the time in the world these days, Dad. When the police leave you alone, I mean. You could do all sorts of things now that you're retired and have got a nice, brand-new home to live in. You could learn to cook properly for a start, or you could try painting some water-colours, or writing your memoirs, even.' The look of disgust that Tom instantly shot back at her still couldn't deter her from saying more. 'I know you've got a whole host of things you've done in your life that you must want to tell people about you know. For instance that story I recall you telling me as a child, about - about the little girl from Aberfan. I always remember that one, Dad, although I admit the precise details escape me.'

'What girl?' her father asked, staring angrily at her, and clearly regretting her having brought up the subject.

'Well, I never knew her name, did I?' replied Carla. 'I remember you always kept that to yourself. Don't go denying it now. And then there was that murder in America you helped their police solve, and without even going out of the country. How come you managed to do that?'

'Well, I didn't have a valid passport any longer, did I?' he replied. 'I'd have loved to have gone to the United States. Your

Aunt Sally lives over there, you know. In Detroit, she lives. Gosh, I haven't seen her since I was around twenty-one.'

'Well, I have,' Carla whispered in response.

'What was that you said?' he enquired, biting carefully, but a tad painfully, into his sandwich.

'Aw, nothing,' she replied. 'I - I did a concert in Detroit last year, you know. Perhaps - perhaps I should have invited her along, or something.'

'Oh, I doubt she would have gone, my love,' he told her. 'Sally was always such a grumpy old bugger at the best of times, and especially so after her Chesney died. And, as I recall, she can't hear any more, either, so it's probably a good thing you never did.'

Carla chuckled to herself, recalling, as if it were yesterday, the embarrassing row she had had in the 'green room' after the Detroit concert with her two female American cousins, who, it seemed, wanted to make a not inconsiderable sum of money from a pre-arranged magazine-interview they had set up for her the following day, and which carefully conceived plan Carla had knocked on the head as soon as she heard about it. But they weren't really family, anyway, Carla told herself. Family don't exploit each other like that, do they? Well, her father had never wanted to, anyway, and he was just about the only family she seemed to have left.

'Listen to this, Dad,' Carla told him, picking up the daily paper from the table, and reading a small headline that was inside it. 'Man escapes prison when wife sends fax ordering his release.' Now don't you think that's amazing?'

'What's a fax?' Tom asked her, suddenly coughing harshly, and spilling crumbs all down the front of his cardigan.

Carla stared at him and shook her head from side to side. She could understand her dad not knowing about texts and tweets and the like, but faxes! Wow - that was right out of the blue. She truly pitied her father so, but she realised that it was far too late to think about teaching this old dog any new tricks. There again, Carla thought, she still could throw a ball or two for him to catch, even now. 'Dad,' she began, 'you must have heard people saying - 'Get your facts straight, yeah? You must have.'

'Well, I dare say,' he responded, wiping himself down with his handkerchief. 'Get your facts straight. Aye.'

'Well, what it really means is - it means - you should straighten out the fax-machine.'

Tom stared across at his daughter. 'In case it falls off the table, like?' he asked, sipping his tea. He smiled at her. He fully realised his daughter was teasing him now, and yet he was so glad she was there for him at long last that he simply didn't care how much she exploited him.

'Yeah, that's right,' she told him. Carla smiled at the joke that she was convinced she had just played on him, then looked about her, at the rural scene over the fence, the little garden, the trees that surrounded it, and then at her wonderful father sitting contentedly before her. At this she felt a leap of joy in her very soul. 'You know I love you so much, Dad,' Carla told him slowly.

'I know, sweet,' Tom replied, a tear welling up in the corner of his eye, and another, more raucous cough than the first - a quite scary one this time - beginning to rise up in his swollen throat. 'But, you know, like I've been telling you lately, girl, love is all about letting go.'

In the last lesson of the day Drew walked around his classroom watching a dozen or so young children standing to do their work at different tables. They were all fully engrossed, happily engaged in printing large letters of their choice onto plain, white t-shirts.

A boy called Grant was talking to another boy called Dafydd. 'A pair of specs walks into a bar,' he told him, 'and the landlord says, 'Get out of here - you're off your face!' '

'I don't get it,' replied Dafydd, 'nor that one you said about the little horse with the long face.'

'Smiling to himself, Drew approached the table to view the two boys' work. 'Oh, you've gone and written it wrong again, Dafydd,' he told the smaller one. 'Couldn't you see that?'

'How do you mean?' asked a bemused Dafydd, looking up anxiously into his teacher's face.

'Well, you see the company's spelt F - C - U - K, not - not the way that you have just printed it.' Drew grinned. 'You won't be able to wear that around school, I'm afraid, my old mate.'

'Damn!' shrieked Dafydd angrily, stamping his foot on the floor and clearly hurting himself in the process. 'I'm sorry, Sir,' he added.

'It's O.K.,' Drew told him fondly.

'Dafydd is such a silly *c-nut* sometimes, isn't he, Sir?' said Grant, barely able to contain himself.

A group of girls at the next table began laughing at Dafydd's mistake, one especially loud girl crudely calling him 'a cock.'

'Excuse me, Hannah Jeffries!' Drew bellowed at her. 'Nobody hearing you would ever know that you lived in a vicarage, now would they?'

'No, Sir,' the girl replied, flushing up, and printing away. 'My parents would, though,' she added. Her friend leaned over and laughed with her at this seemingly clever riposte.

'Yeah, they came to see you once, didn't they?' called out Dafydd from the sink, where he now stood spreading out his shirt, and desperately trying to clean up the mistake he had made.

'Shut up - you!' Hannah screamed back at him. 'At least I can spell 'fuck,' you pillock. Oops! Sorry, Sir. Honest, I am.'

Suddenly a much older boy, who was wearing jeans and a t-shirt, walked into the room, and hurried away into the store-room that branched off it. Drew watched him arrive, considered for a moment what his sudden arrival might mean, then surreptitiously approached the half-closed door of his art-store, and peered inside. Drew could see the lanky boy, whose name was Jake, deep within the dark room, standing on a chair, and reaching up to collect a small bag from a high shelf above his head, and then swiftly stashing it inside the neck of his shirt. As Jake regained the floor and turned to leave, Drew squared-up to him and spoke.

'Shouldn't you be on work-experience, Jake?' he asked him. 'You and Steffan are at *The Willows* care-home, aren't you?'

'Oh, I just came back to get a few - a few paints,' the boy replied. 'You don't mind, do you? Those old fogies are just mad for it, you know. Painting, I mean.'

'Paints, yeah?' Drew asked him, thinking fast. 'All colours, or - or just *green*?' The two males stood and stared at each other.

'Yeah, just green,' Jake announced, with a forced smile.

Suddenly Jake's side-kick Steffan walked into the room, and, seeing his friend confronted, spun round and stood beside him.

'I'm not stupid, you know,' Drew added. 'Say, can I ask you boys something?'

''Course, you can,' Steffan replied on their behalf.

'Where are you growing it?'

'Where!' Steffan replied, grinning. 'You're asking *me*! Moi? Look, I think you need to ask the right guy that question, don't you?'

'Jake?' asked the teacher, turning and regarding his much taller, but thinner companion.

'Jake!' shrieked Steffan. 'Not Jake, for God's sake. No - Chris! Ask him, why don't you?'

'Chris! My Chris?' stammered Drew, clearly flustered. 'Look - he might have done it at one time a while back, but - but I checked out the loft just the other day, and it's completely empty. And I know there's nowhere else it could possibly be. So - so I really don't believe my son can be involved in any of this.'

'No? Really?' sneered Steffan. 'But he's *not* your son, is he?'

'What do you mean?' said Drew.

'We mean he's somebody else's son really, isn't he?' Jake cut in.

'And we found out who,' added Steffan, with a smile. 'Sorry, Drew, old boy. Drew-the-Art!'

'Drew-the-Pictures!' chimed in Jake, sniggering in unison with his partner-in-crime.

'Look - you two get out of here right now!' a livid Drew commanded, shifting his frame to stand alongside the, now open, door.

The two boys swaggered out into the classroom and grinned vindictively at many of the young, uniformed children, who were plainly concerned by their unexpected, and noisy, arrival.

Steffan suddenly spilled over a pot of coloured water that stood on a table-top. 'Oh, sorry about that, Mr. Cillick, Sir,' he said. 'We'd stay and clean it up, but, you see we've got a great deal to do -'

'A *great* deal, as it happens,' cut in Jake, giggling.

'Yeah, a really brilliant deal,' added Steffan, grinning.' By now the two boys were falling about laughing, arms around each other's shoulders.

'Look - when he gets back on his feet I won't have you messing up his life for him, you know,' the teacher told them.

'Your step-son?' said Jake, now as anxious to address the whole class, who were his captive audience, as the red-faced man he glared at.

'Yes, my step-son,' Drew answered. 'My boy Chris. I won't have you ruining *his* life. I'm telling you that straight.'

'I think he's telling us straight, Jake,' said Steffan, grinning again. 'What a mug, eh? But it's ruined already, isn't it, Drew? In fact, his life's been messed-up for ages now, old boy. And you know you're caught right up in it, too, Drew baby. Yes, yes, old man. Believe me, you are.'

'He's called Mr. Cillick,' little Dafydd suddenly called to them from across the room.

'Shut up, dick-head!' Steffan screamed, staring the young boy down.

'Anyway, this is all above your head, teacher,' announced Jake, beginning to smile at Drew.

'Way above - you get me?' added Steffan, chuckling maliciously, and pointing at him derisively.

'Do you mean it's - it's growing above the roof?' enquired Drew, more confused than ever now. 'But how can that be?'

'Only thing you can grow on a roof is mould,' little Dafydd told them all, with a smile.

'The dick-head's right, for once,' Steffan told everyone, spinning round to face them. 'And so - and so he wins a prize.'

'A prize!' repeated Dafydd excitedly. 'What prize? What? What do I get?'

Steffan suddenly walked across to him and tipped a jar of black water all over the boy's newly-printed, white T-shirt. 'You like water-colours, yeah?' the older boy asked him with a venomous look on his face that was pure malice.

Dafydd's chubby little body began shaking and he started to cry. Two of the girls in the class quickly ran over to comfort him.

'Like we said, Mr. Drew - this shit is way above yout head,' announced Jake, checking that his bag of drugs was well tucked in under his shirt for their impending exit. 'Any road, we're off back to work now.'

'Say - shall we give your love to Anne?' Steffan asked in a sinister tone, opening the door for him and Steffan to leave. 'Shall we, Daddy Drew? You know, most of the old blokes locked-up there already have, by the way. Only they're all too doped-up to even realise what they've been doing with her.'

The two youths laughed out loud, then left, slamming the classroom-door behuind them.

Dafydd suddenly hurried forward and embraced his quivering teacher round the chest. 'You're my favourite teacher, Mr. Cillick, Sir,' he told him through a flood of tears. 'And you know I'm really going to miss you when I go off to Special School, I really am.'

Without thinking about it, a number of girls followed Dafydd's lead and rushed over to their teacher to do the same.

The family's cat had completely disappeared and couldn't be found anywhere. Anne ran out into the back-garden and called out to her, 'Emily! Emily!' but no avail. 'God, I hope she hasn't fallen off the bridge!' she shrieked, running over to the fence, and staring eastwards into the mist that now shrouded the viaduct, as her husband and her limping son - both in shirt-sleeves - joined her on the patio.

'Don't worry, darling. Cats always fall on their feet,' Drew announced, illustrating the point with his two hands gliding down slowly like a parachute, then lowering his fingers and settling them on the wooden table-top.

'It's a hundred feet high, you clod,' Anne responded fiercely. 'She's bound to be dead unless she fell straight into the river. And even then. What's more the poor dear can't even swim.'

'I know it's sad, Mam, but cats have nine lives, remember,' Chris told her, walking round to embrace her. 'Even Persians. And if she did fall, and got crushed into a bloody pulp on the rocks down there, then she'll probably be back here again next week for her meals, though obviously with a brand-new make-over.'

'Though maybe not as a pussy,' Drew added quietly, as an after-thought.

'What are you talking about, you stupid boy!' Anne screamed at her son. 'How do you know this wasn't her *ninth life*? I mean her very last one. I'll never forgive myself if we ended her entire series through pure negligence, and she got finished off while living here with us in Wales.'

Her husband listened attentively, but couldn't quite fathom his wife's logic. 'If you want my opinion,' Drew told them reassuringly, but with a playful smirk on his face, 'I bet she's probably down there in the woods right now, doing what all felines like her enjoy doing sooner or later,'

'Behave, will you!' Anne shot back at him. 'Trust you to be thinking about *sex* at a time like this.'

'I'm only saying that if I was a cat -' Drew began explaining.

Anne was starting to get angry now. 'You know, Drew, don't think I didn't know where you were going with this, the moment you called our dear cat a pussy.'

'But that's precisely what she is, isn't she?' said Drew, brows aloft.

'She! Just listen to yourself,' shot back Anne. 'Our cat's name is Emily. And Emily is one of the family - right? *She*, indeed! She's not the cat's mother, you know.'

'Well, not yet, anyway, but if she's loping about where I said she is -' replied Drew, who, rightly seeing how livid his words were making his wife, instantly ducked his head to avoid getting struck by Anne's swinging right hand. It turned out to be the right move, but only just.

It was past seven o'clock already, and Chris had been hobbling up and down the only road in *Gloryhole*, knocking on doors and asking folk if they had seen his family's missing cat. As he arrived back where he had started, he realised there was only one house left to enquire at, and that was where Carla Steel was presently staying with her father. With more than a little trepidation, he walked up their path and rang the door-bell. There was no reply. He tried again. It didn't seem to be working, he told himself, so, instead, he rapped loudly at the front-door.

Eventually Carla slowly opened the door, and then stood back and stared at him. 'Why. it's you, Chris!' she exclaimed. 'Are you selling door-to-door these days, now, then?'

'Funny. We've lost the cat,' he told her.

'Well, *we* haven't got it,' Carla shot back.

Tom's head suddenly appeared round the door, and he stared at the boy until he thought he recognised who he might be. 'You're the chap from next-door, aren't you lad?' he said. 'Chris, is it? Do come inside. We're so slow around here that we're still having breakfast, I'm afraid. Brunch - my daughter calls it. Same thing. Would you care to join us?'

'Do you like muffins?' Carla asked him, sensing his dilemma, her eyebrows raised in anticipation of a positive response.

'Mm, yeah,' replied Chris, crossing the threshold, and following Carla's lead into the lounge, and thence into the kitchen. 'You know, your house is arranged very like ours,' he told them.

'Except yours is a lot cleaner, I bet,' Carla suggested, pointing out an empty chair for him to sit on at the table.

'Well, that's my mother for you,' Chris replied, taking his seat rather cautiously. 'She seems to clean up after people all day at work, and then feels compelled to continue in the same vein when she gets home. She works at *The Willows*, by the way.'

'Oh, I know it well,' answered Tom, who filled the kettle for them all to have some tea. 'It's in Dowlais, isn't it?

Near where the steel-works is, or used to be, at any rate. I had an aunt who lived in Dowlais. Do you know I can go back half a century and more, to when I used to stay with her there, and I can still remember how the night-skies used to get lit up a bright orange colour from the flares of the blast-furnaces that used to get fired up there both day and night during its hey-day. Yes, a beautiful orange, the sky used to be.'

'My dad's favourite colour,' chipped in Carla, with a smile.

'What was that, love?' enquired her father. 'Why, I can still remember how just getting to sleep at night could be a right battle back then, I can tell you.'

'Yeah, I learned about that big foundry in History,' Chris replied. 'And my mother told me about it too, although she actually grew up a few miles further down the valley.'

'In Aberfan, yes?' Tom added, warming the tea-pot under the hot-tap.

'Yes, that's right,' Chris replied. 'And I'm sure you know far more than I do about the terrible disaster that happened at the primary school down there, right? In 1966, I believe it was. It seems that the whole world was shaken up about it. Mr. Philips-History told us how people as far away as America and Japan and Australia sent loads of money to the fund set up for the benefit of all the bereaved and the survivors of the tragedy that happened in the village.'

'Of which I guess your mother was one?' cut in Carla.

Chris's head dropped slightly. 'She was, as a matter of fact, although she doesn't like to talk about it very much. But you can understand that, can't you? You see she lost most of her closest friends on that awful day.'

'Wow! That must have been crippling for her,' Carla responded with genuine empathy. 'Was she - was she one of those that got rescued, then?'

'No,' Chris told her firmly. 'No, the weird thing is - she didn't choose to go to school at all on that particular day - that Friday.'

'Do you mean - surely you're not saying she had a - a premonition, or something?' said Carla.

'I don't think so,' Chris told her. 'I remember her telling us that she had to go the clinic on that morning, about her teeth. And that when she got there - and I know you're not going to believe this, as my father certainly didn't - they told her she didn't need to have any dental work done after all. Her teeth were perfect, they said. But she thinks the man may have given her a little filling, anyway, she told us! Now doesn't that sound ridiculous? These days she even jokes about it probably being the only filling in her mouth that has never fallen out!'

'I once wrote a song about all that, you know. The tragedy, I mean,' Carla told him. 'But my Dad explained to me how the - the wound of Aberfan was still a very sore one - still raw and open, you know, even after all this time - and so I....shelved it. The music was never actually written down or demo-ed, although I sometimes feel I still have it up in my head somewhere.'

Tom sat himself down in the chair opposite Chris, closed his weary eyes for a few moments, then suddenly opened them once again, and gazed straight into the eyes of the handsome boy sitting across from him. 'She's in a dark tunnel, you know,' the old man told him strangely.

'My mother!' stammered Chris.

'No, Emily,' Tom replied, closing his eyes tight once again.

'Who's Emily?' Carla asked him.

'Our cat,' replied Chris 'Did I tell you her name, then, Mr. Davies? Well I guess I must have.'

'Yes, you must have,' Carla told him. 'When you first walked in, I think. Right Dad?'

Chris watched the old man's heavily lined face intently, wondering what he was now thinking, and what would be the next words to come out of his mouth. 'Which tunnel would that be that Emily's in, Mr. Davies?' he asked. Tom said nothing and kept his eyes tight shut. 'The one down the line, that runs under Pant, do you mean?'

'Well, I can't say for sure,' Tom replied slowly. 'But it is very dark there, and exceedingly wet.'

'You *know* that?' shot back Chris, his eyes wide open with shock. 'But if you're saying Emily is in a tunnel somewhere, how is it that you can know that? Do you mean you've actually seen her there?'

Tom gazed deep into the boy's eyes and nodded.

In the silence that ensued Chris felt that he was beginning to understand what was happening, and that the strange old man might actually possess a gift that it was best right now not to question - best to just accept, especially if it meant recovering his mother's precious cat for her. 'Is she - is she still alive?' Chris enquired, and waited until Tom opened his eyes again and responded.

'Emily couldn't swim, could she?' Tom told him sadly.

'I don't think so,' responded Chris anxiously. 'But I could check to be sure, if you like.' He made to get up.

Carla grasped him by the wrist and spoke. 'I think my Dad means - he is telling you she *couldn't*, Chris.'

'Oh, I see,' said Chris, sitting back down again. 'And is our Emily dead, then, Mr. Davies?' asked the boy, biting into his top lip, in dread of the man's impending response.

'Well, soon she is going to begin floating out of there - that I know,' the old man replied, his wrinkled eyes closed-up tight again. 'Just as soon - just as soon as the water-level rises sufficiently. But - yes - she is gone there now.'

'Gone there! Gone where?' asked Chris, confused, and now beginning to tremble like a leaf.

'On the last train,' Tom told him, now with his weary, glazed eyes wide open once more, and smiling jubilantly, almost joyously, right past him. 'That long, last train we all catch in the end.'

Rhiannon was walking along the road to school with two of her closest girl-friends, eating together from a packet of crisps, when up ran a short boy with dyed, blond hair, who tried to grab her round the waist. With her hands held high before her, she managed to push him away.

'Ger-off Brian!' Rhiannon shrieked. 'Prat!' She returned to addressing the two girls. 'Where was I? Oh, yeah. We had a wonderful Libyan teacher once called, er - er - Miss Ratah, I think her name was. Taught us R.E.'

'Yeah, of course you did,' Brian cut in. 'And we've got a Libyan boy in our class called Ben Ghazi. Rides a camel to school sometimes, he does.' The other two girls began giggling despite themselves. 'Always has Halal sandwiches in his lunch-box, and a tea-towel over his head that he usually pulls down when he's finished to wipe his mouth with.'

Rhiannon wanted to laugh, but decided she daren't. Brian had offended her and she wasn't prepared to put up with it. 'You're racist, that's what you are, Brian Flynn!' she told him.

'How am I?' the boy responded, moving towards her and bringing his freckled face up very close to hers.

'Without any feelings for anyone but yourself - that's how,' Rhiannon told him angrily. 'And your little brother Danny is even worse I reckon. *And* he does drugs. You're his older brother, you know, Brian. You should step in.' Plainly disgusted, she turned away

'What are you trying to say, Rhiannon?' the boy shot back at her, trying to get her attention once again.

Rhiannon ignored him completely, and instead grasped her friend's hand tightly. 'Let's walk on, shall we, Carmen?' she told her. 'Perhaps *then* the idiot will just go away. Say, what do you think, Sian?'

'Yeah, she's right, Brian,' said Sian. 'You're the one who needs to wipe your mouth with something.'

'Or *wash* it out - much better,' added Carmen, illustrating with her free hand the action required.

'And preferably with soap and water,' said Sian aggressively.

'Or maybe just the soap,' chipped in Carmen, turning to Sian and laughing out loud.

'Yeah, carbolic would be good,' said Sian, making such a horrible face that they could practically taste it. 'Eughh!'

'Or worse - Camay,' Brian called out, suddenly running along in front of the three of them, and trying to befriend them all again, in spite of their directed comments.

'Oh, I like Camay, I do,' cut in Rhiannon, stroking with her fingers her pale, but attractive face.

'Do you, Rhi? Oh, I don't,' Carmen told her.

'Nor me,' added Sian. 'Mind you, there's not a lot it can do with the face I've got, is there?'

'Well, that's true,' shot in Brian, preparing to duck any swing she might elect to take at him.

Instead Rhiannon ran after him so as to thump him on Sian's behalf, but, before she could strike him, Brian reached out and grabbed her arms tightly, and, with his superior power, managed to turn her slim body right round, and, while pinning her securely from behind, proceeded to first bite, and then kiss her voraciously on the back of the neck.

'Oh my God! He must love you, Rhi!' cried Carmen, gleefully. 'Do you, Brian? Do you love Rhiannon then? He won't admit it, but I bet he does, you know.'

'And I thought you loved *me*, Bri!' screamed Sian, chasing after him to hit him with her satchel, but instead watching the boy spin round and protect himself from harm with Rhiannon's struggling torso.

'Ger-off me, Brian!' screamed Rhiannon, making to pull away, but not quite succeeding.

'Yeah, you'd better, Brian,' added Carmen. 'She's going out with a gorgeous, really fit sixth-former, remember.'

'No, she's not,' said Brian assuredly.

'Tell him, Rhiannon,' said Sian, angrily.

'He's right, you know - I'm not,' Rhiannon told them. 'That's all over, that is.' Brian suddenly released her, and she stood up straight, pressed down her skirt, and carried on with her story. 'Chris went and dumped me in Vaynor Woods weeks ago now. And all because - all because it seems some stupid tree wouldn't obey his command, and some silly dreams he had about it.'

'A tree! He's not right in the head, he's not,' said Carmen supportively.

'Sadly that's what I think,' Rhiannon told her. 'Anyway, Chris dumped me all right.'

'He nev-er!' the two girls uttered in stunned harmony, mouths agape.

'It's true,' retorted Rhiannon. 'So I'm free to go out with whoever I like now, I suppose.'

Rhiannon looked around. All she could see was the rude, blonde-haired boy, standing stock-still before her, hoping against hope that she just might say *his* name. Rhiannon could sense her new power, and so stared right into the boy's eyes. 'Even - even -' she stammered, playfully.

'Brian Flynn!' shrieked Sian, in anger.

'Yes, even Brian Flynn, I suppose,' Rhiannon replied, turning to face them. 'Sure, why not?'

'Yeah, right,' said Carmen dismissively, beginning to fear for her best friend's sanity.

Rhiannon took a sideways glance at her prey, and then sauntered right up to hm. She paused for a moment, and then slowly wet her lips with her long, pink tongue. Her two friends quickly moved round in a circle so as to best observe what they feared, yet secretly hoped, was about to follow.

A little hesitantly, and with just gentle pecks to start with, the two young people began to kiss each other passionately on the lips. The clinch was prolonged, and was disturbed only by the sound of a distant dog squealing. The pretty, red-haired girl then suddenly pulled her head back from his, and started spinning round in the street, and warbling at the top of her voice a pop-song from the charts. *'Maybe you got messed up by someone in your past,'* Rhiannon sang, and then danced away along the pavement, singing to herself the remainder of the song by a Dionne someone-or-other that she could just about remember some of the words to.

'God! Just look at her!' called out Carmen, her hand now covering her mouth, and genuinely shocked.

'And listen to her!' added Sian. 'What is she like, eh? She must think she's Katherine Jenkins.'

When Carla walked into the house from her afternoon stroll the first thing she saw was the scribbled note lying on the table. *'I've been taken off by them to help the police with their enquiries,'* was all that the familiar, stuttering hand had penned.

Carla sat herself down on the sofa, and, before even removing her coat, looked up the number in the phone-book, and rang the police to find out why her father had been arrested. But her efforts were in vain, as the woman on the other end of the line insisted that she couldn't be of any help to her, since nobody with her father's name had been recorded.

After apologising for the error, Carla put the phone down and sat silently for a few minutes, contemplating what might have happened to her dad. If he hadn't been arrested, then where on earth had the police taken him, she asked herself. That is, of course, if they were actual policemen who had called at the house for him. She bit her lip and shuddered at this last, unlikely thought. The old man was so plainly unwell, after all, that removing him from his warm, comfortable home, and taking him whoever knows where was surely tantamount to abuse, she mused. 'Senile abuse, I'd call it,' Carla told herself out loud. 'But the Merthyr police wouldn't do that, surely. Unless - unless he was the only person who could possibly help them with something, that is. I wonder - I wonder if it's got anything to do with that cat. I wonder would Chris know?' she asked herself. 'Maybe the Cillicks are at such a loss about their Emily that they let them know what my Dad told Chris had happened to her. Yes, I suppose that might be it.'

So, closing the neighbouring gate quietly behind her, Carla tentatively walked up the short path to the Cillick house and rang the door-bell. She repeated the action three times, and even looked in at the window, but eventually she was forced to walk away. Everyone must be either at work or still at school, I guess, she told herself.

But as she spun round to close the gate and return home, she noticed a male face at the upstairs-window, and, deciding it looked like Chris's face, she returned to his door, and not long after found herself being let inside. Chris was barely able to walk, but he managed to stumble across to the sofa, and, with his sore, bandaged leg raised up on the cushion beside him, he listened to all of Carla's queries with commendable patience, and an obvious eagerness to be of help to her, but sadly shook his head in response to every single one.

'You know, I fear that perhaps those evil people who tried to blackmail me in London might have kidnapped him!' Carla screamed. 'Chris, what can I do?'

'What people?' the boy asked, getting tetchy.

'You know, dealers,' she told him. 'Real dealers, I mean. You see they got hold of film of me blazing weed and trying to score and everything. And the state I was in at the time you just would not believe. I have a still from it, a grainy photograph I got sent by them in the post. Want to take a look?' Carla opened her hand-bag and handed Chris the picture. She looked away.

'Oh my God!' the boy responded, shocked at what he saw. 'You mean they sent you this?' he asked.

'No, it's my ID. Derrh! Of course they did. I told you, didn't I?' Carla retorted, angrily. 'Along with a written demand for fifty grand.'

'And you paid them off?' he enquired.

'No. But I wish I had, though,' she answered, 'Now, I mean. They came round to my riverside flat.'

'Where was that?' he asked.

'In Fulham. Near the *River Café*. Though I guess you wouldn't know where that is, would you? They came round and tried to force their way in. At four in the morning, for Christ's sake! Can you believe it? For some reason or other I decided to pretend I was out.'

'Didn't you ring 9-9-9?' he asked.

'But how could I involve the police, with what they had on me?' replied Carla.

'Look - I see what you're saying, all right,' he told her. 'But I reckon you'd best call them up now, don't you think?'

'No way, Chris. How can I do that?' she asked. 'And, anyway, I already called.'

He stared at her. 'You didn't really, though, did you? Did you?' he persisted. 'Carla - you have to call them again, right now.' Chris picked up the house-phone from the table and held out its ear-piece for her. The buzzing drone that the telephone emitted pierced the silence in the room as Carla deliberated long and hard over what she should do.

'But I don't think I dare,' Carla told him. 'How on earth can I, for Christ's sake? You don't understand, Chris. I've got so much I stand to lose. So, so much. Say - you know I'm not kidding you, right?' She watched the boy's eyes suddenly flicker in apparent disbelief. 'Hey! Do you think I'm lying, then?'

'Carla,' said Chris, tilting his head to one side, and smiling at her with raised brows. Suddenly the phone's tone changed to one that quite startled the pair of them.

'What?' she asked.

Chris replaced the receiver, and, raising it once again for Carla to take out of his hand, said, 'The man is your dad, remember.'

'The Church of Christ is clearly split in two,' Tom announced from his seat in the corner of the bare room.

'Look, Mister Davies - we called you in today to see if you could help us to find the body of a woman in west London, who's been missing now for almost nine months,' the white-haired Sergeant Foley told him, 'and not to hear what your views are on religion or Christianity.'

'But I already told you where her body lies, didn't I?' explained Tom.

'But she's a young black woman, Tom, not an old-aged pensioner.' This the voice of a cockney policeman, called D.I. Dawson, who had driven all the way to Wales to meet this strange old man he had heard about, and who he had been told possessed a, so-called, *gift*.

'Well, could it be that she had visited somebody old, then?' Tom enquired. 'Her grandmother, perhaps?'

'No, no,' the Englishman replied. 'Our records say two of her grandparents still live in Kingston, Jamaica. And her grandparent over here died years ago.'

'I see. But which one?' Tom asked.

'Which one!'

'Well, we all have *two*, don't we?' the old man told him. 'I mean, does the other one live in a large communal building, do you think? A sheltered-housing complex, for example? And quite near the river?'

'Near the river! You mean the Thames?' Dawson enquired, brows raised.

'I don't know, officer. I never lived in London,' replied Tom, his eyes now closing tightly. 'There are - there are midges everywhere, I can see that.' He slapped his forehead. It was summer when she disappeared, yes?

'Late August, yes,' the cockney detective replied.

'Yes, I can see it's summer. And - and they are playing football near by. I can hear the shouts,' the old man went on.

'Of children?' asked Dawson.

'Them, too. No. No, a large crowd of people. Men in white shirts and shorts. Other men wearing stripes.'

'In a park, you mean?' the detective asked.

'Yes, but right across the other side. Across the water. Deep, deep water. And there are some people leaving too - trying to leave, at any rate - trying to drive away - but who can't get into their cars!'

'Why not?' D.I.Dawson asked, confused.

'It's the river's water. It has come too high. Men with long, striped scarves are screaming in their efforts to get inside their cars and drive off. 'Away! they are shouting, in a sort of - northern brogue. 'Away!'

'You know, then perhaps they could be Newcastle fans,' Dawson told him. 'Apparently the team were playing away in London one afternoon in August.'

'Across a river?' asked Tom.

'No, at Fulham,' Dawson told him.

'But is that across the water?' the old man enquired.

'Well, yes, I suppose it might be if you are looking - if you are looking from the southern side - the Putney side,' D.I. Dawson answered. Tom nodded at him approvingly 'And *are you*, Tom?'

'Am I what?' asked Tom.

'Looking across from Putney? From the south side of the Thames, I mean?' Tom paused for thought. The cockney officer turned away and rang a number on his mobile-phone, waited for a few seconds, and then pressed a button on it. 'Hello! Hello! Drinkwater? Hello there! I'm putting this on speaker-phone - do you understand? Would you make sure you do the same your end?'

The shrill, echoing voice of the man in London soon told them that he had obeyed D.I.Dawson's request. 'I've just done it, Sir,' Drinkwater informed them.

'Thank you, Dave,' said Dawson.

'Yes, I believe I may well be on the south bank of the river,' Tom announced. 'I know for a fact that the sun is at my back from all the shadows before me. There's a - there's a pier to the right, yes? And countless swans everywhere. And a man is stood by big blue railings, beside a stand - an easel - painting a picture of the river landscape to the right of where he is standing, and of the bridge and the two churches he can see in the distance.'

'And are *they* split in two, Mister Davies?' Sergeant Foley asked him, with a smile.

'Do you mean the churches?' asked Tom. 'Of course, not. That is - that's another death completely.'

'Sorry! Do you mean you're cross-deathing again?' asked Foley, turning to the London copper and chuckling loudly. Eventually getting his little joke, Dawson began laughing along with him.

Finally comprehending their silly joke too, Tom suddenly sprang to his feet and turned, as if to leave. 'Perhaps I'd best go, gentlemen,' he said abruptly. 'I am certainly no fetishist, you know. I came here in all good faith to help you, remember, and you tell me my daughter is waiting for me downstairs. Been there for ages, I understand. You realise that by now the poor girl must be wondering if I've been - if I've been arrested and charged with something.'

'You might still be if we discover you're bogus and are wasting our time,' said Foley. 'Even though we made you come here.'

'Your daughter is Carla Steel, isn't she, Sir?' D.I.Dawson enquired. 'Yes, I think I saw her.'

'Now there's a girl who's known to the police,' Foley told the detective. 'In London, I mean. Though we've never managed to pin anything on her whenever she's come back to Wales.'

'Known to the police! My Carla!' Tom told them firmly. 'No - I'm sure you're mistaken there.'

'But am I wrong in thinking she has a habit the tabloids have shown more than a passing interest in in recent years?' asked Foley.

Tom wondered what it might be. 'She has a nasty habit of singing, if that's what you mean,' he said, grinning. 'Been addicted to it since she was four, so she has.'

'If only it were just that,' the Welsh sergeant told him, his eye-brows raised aloft. 'In fact, your daughter -'

'Shut up a minute, would you, Foley!' commanded Dawson. 'No, please don't go, Mr. Davies. Sit down, please. Please, Sir.'

Tom looked about him at the uniformed group, amassed there on his behalf. 'Well, if you insist, Mr. Dawson,' he said, resuming his seat once more.

'Guys, I need the computer now,' Dawson told the two constables in the corner of the room. 'Google street-map Putney for me, someone. The stretch of the riverside in Putney right opposite Craven Cottage. Near to where the stream called Beverley Brook, if I remember right, flows in to the Thames from the south. Look for sheltered accommodation, would you?' He stared down at the screen before him. 'That's good. Now zoom in. More. More again. Yes - that could be it. What does the sign say? *Brierfield*? Does that say *Brierfield*? Dave, send someone to *Brierfield*. His mobile-phone blared incomprehensibly You mean there's someone near there already? Where? In Santanda Street? Good. And is he on speaker, too? Oh, he's been listening to us all along, has he? Excellent. Then send him into *Brierfield* right away if you would.' Then turning to Tom, he said, 'Take a look at this image on the computer, would you, Mr. Davies?'

'I'm sorry, but I am no good with - with those things,' the old man replied, resuming his seat. 'And I left my readers at home too. All I can tell you is what I can actually see, you know. In my head, I mean.'

The telephone began crackling, then Dave Drinkwater's voice on the other end suddenly became clearer. 'Our man at the scene has just gone through reception,' he told them.

'Thanks, Dave. And what *do* you see, Tom?' D.I.Dawson asked the aged Welshman who sat quietly in the corner of the room. 'What is it you *can* see right now?'

Tom blinked once and turned his head to the side. He suddenly saw his daughter standing just outside the door, with her face pressed up against the glass. He nevertheless dipped his head once again, closed his eyes, then spoke. 'Well, I walk in there from the road,' he began.

'Just tell the officer on the scene, Tom,' Dawson advised him. 'Speak into the phone, would you, Tom? It's just a mobile. The police officer is there right now, you see. At this *Brierfield*. Just tell him yourself, old boy, where to go, and what he should do.'

'Well, O.K., then,' said Tom, tentatively, closing his eyes tightly once more. 'Well, before you is a lovely garden, yes? A square garden, with - with roses in full bloom. No, that was then. Sorry. Anyhow, there are four arches on each side that all focus on this square garden, and, through each arch, there are two separate, and opposing, numbered doors. I hope that makes sense to you. Well, I walk - I mean, you should walk - right around the square, and then you enter the arch right opposite from where you started, you see, then turn and enter the door that stands to your right. Its number - its number is -'

'Five!' said a young male voice down the phone.

'That's right, young man - five,' Tom told him. 'My favourite number as it goes. Good show, well done. Well, by now you should have entered the tiny building where the old man lives, yes? O.K.? Well, he does, anyway. And can you see that there is a door inside the first one, and to your right?'

'The bedroom?' the young voice echoed shrilly through the ether.

'Yes. No. No, the one just before that,' Tom told him. 'The door for the tiny room where - where the fuel is stacked. It is a locked door that is very rarely opened.'

Suddenly the loud, oblique thud, of a wooden door being kicked-in, echoed eerily round the crowded room. Then silence. Dawson and Foley exchanged worried glances.

'There is no light inside, I know,' Tom announced calmly. 'But she is - she is under the coal.'

Within the interview-room they shared, everyone bent forward to hear the unmistakable sound of loose cobbles of coal being rolled about across a solid, stone floor.

'Under the coal is she? Good God alive!' cursed the Welsh sergeant, now gripping his grey, balding head in his hands.

'Yes, she is. But you won't be able to recognise her any longer, I'm afraid,' said Tom slowly. 'You see, there are so many - so many rats that live there, being so close to the river and all. And many of them have - have found their way inside, you know. And now they live there. It's their home, you see.'

'Aaargh!' shrieked the young police-officer on the other end of the phone. 'The mess! I'm sorry but I'm about to retch!'

'Don't worry, young man,' said Tom. 'Try not to be too scared. We are all with you, you see. And remember that the woman you seek isn't there any longer.' The policemen in the room suddenly exchanged sharp glances, clearly shocked at this. 'No, she's long gone, on the train.'

'On the train!' said Foley. 'What bloody train?'

'Do you mean - are you trying to say she's in heaven?' the distant young voice enquired.

'If you like,' said Tom. 'Trust me on this one, would you? You see, it's only - it's only her *shell* that you will discover there. Left behind, I mean.'

'Aaargh!' the young officer shrieked once more. They could all now clearly hear the unmistakable sound of the young policeman being sick, followed by his awful weeping. Each of the officers present in the room felt that they understood something of the young man's pain, and that he had by this time most likely sunk to his knees, or become slumped against a wall, paralysed with terror at the dreadful, torch-lit sight he had just exposed before his youthful eyes.

The door of the interview-room suddenly opened and Carla stumbled inside. Realising that she, too, must have been listening to the long-distance interchange, the sturdily built constable and his blond-haired companion in the corner rose to their feet and dashed across to help her.

Tom, his eyes still tightly closed, and seemingly unconcerned by his daughter's presence, simply carried on speaking to the young policeman who was alone in the hellish coal-shed almost two hundred miles away. 'Young man - what is your name?' the old man asked tenderly.

'Darim, Sir,' the youth replied. 'Can I tell you something? I'm scared, Sir. I'm terrified, in fact,' he continued. 'You see, it's the man who most likely lives here, Sir. He's just walked in on me.'

'What the hell do you mean, lad!' D.I.Dawson shrieked. 'Why, he must be three times your age. Remember you're a police-officer, for Christ's sake. Just pull yourself together, man.'

'I would do, Sir,' replied Darim. 'But, you see, just now he's standing right behind me with a gun stuck in the back of my head. And right this minute, Sir, I'm totally unarmed.' Foley and Dawson exchanged worried glances, then stared at Tom, as if for direction. 'And I see that he's not really much older than me at all. In fact I believe I know the man, as I'm sure you do too. Christ Jesus! I was never trained for this, Sir. Is there - is there anything I can do?'

'Allow me, Mr. Dawson, please,' Tom suddenly broke in. 'Listen, young man. I'm afraid there isn't, Darim. You can't do a single thing that could possibly stop it. Not now. No, not now.'

'Nothing at all!' exclaimed the terrified young constable.

'Not a thing,' said Tom. 'I'm very sorry that it's come to this, Darim. We all are. But take comfort from the fact that where you will be deployed to next, is the very place that each one of us hopes to reach one day, me included. In fact - in fact it's the place where your own late mother and her mother and father, your grandparents, presently stand awaiting you.'

'Christ! Don't go telling the boy that, you silly old fool!' exclaimed Sergeant Foley, jumping up, his arms outstretched, his mouth wide open, spittle splashed down his chin and uniform.

'What!' yelled Darim. 'Sir, do you mean -? Are you telling me that *it's - it's written?*'

'Darim, my friend, this is quite easily the most crucial moment of your short, but very brave life,' said Tom. 'God bless you, my boy,' he said softly. The old man then covered his ears with his hands and winced perceptibly, his eyes and nose wrinkled up tightly.

Carla covered her ears too, as a deathly silence fell on the interview-room, and several pairs of male eyes flashed about them their incredulity and their genuine fear. Then two loud shots rang out, and everybody screamed.

CHAPTER 9

The sudden shower was the last of several that had fallen that morning. Chris was wet through, but still determined to get there. His leg was already much stronger these days, and so he decided he would sprint the last hundred yards or so, trying, but failing, to imitate the stride of his hero, rugby player George North. On reaching the tunnel-entrance he quickly opened the swing-door and dashed inside, and then instantly zipped off the sopping jacket that his mother had bought him the previous Christmas, and which, sadly, had proved to be just shower-proof, instead of water-proof, as the label inside it had claimed, and so had allowed the storm's rain to seep in through the seams and bathe his clothed torso liberally in freezing-cold water all the way from his neck right down to his hips.

Chris switched on his torch, and quickly noticed that there was in fact a stream of sorts already flowing towards him inside the tunnel, presumably fed by dripping water from perhaps half-a-mile or so further down the way towards Pant. It seemed to flow along at little more than a snail's pace in the direction of the walled entrance by which he had just entered, and then out through an aperture at the side of the base, running from there down into the ditch at the side of the foot-path he had just run along, and thence down the much steeper incline into the Taff River itself, in the wooded valley that lay beyond.

'I can't see no cat,' Chris called out to himself. The echo that his voice created inside the tunnel was a lot deeper in pitch than he could ever have imagined it would be, and that scared him. 'I can't see any damn cat anywhere,' he repeated for better effect. Then a third time. bellowed out, 'Pussy, where are you? Emily! Emily!!'

The echoing voice Chris heard, seemingly in reply to his own, made him jump. It was deep, masculine, and a tad ghostly, to say the least. Chris switched off his torch to test his courage, then turned it straight back on again, for company as much as anything else, then decided to shine it directly ahead of him, down the long, arched tunnel that he imagined ran directly beneath the limestone hill, and the vast cemetery that lay beyond it, and perhaps even beneath the four-bedroomed house that bordered its southern perimeter, where Rhiannon lived, and most likely still pined for him, but where, oddly, he had never once been welcomed inside.

Chris decided to walk further on into the tunnel, and soon found that the gravel-path he trod, and the lofty, stone walls of the great cathedral-to-steam he passed through, veered by constant degree into a vast, sweeping curve that, as he advanced into the torch-light, seemed to be endlessly revealed anew before him. 'Nobody could possibly see my light on account of the bend,'.he whispered, largely to reassure himself. He was beginning to feel a little more confident now, and so he switched off his torch completely, and simply listened to the scrunching sound his two marching feet made as they gathered pace and propelled him further and deeper into the vast, horizontal abyss, the great vaulted portal, whose extent he had yet to fully comprehend, and whose terminus might just as easily be in hell as in Pant.

Twenty minutes later, and still with his torch in his pocket, Chris had not yet encountered a soul, and so the sudden shout he heard ahead of him, then the prolonged silence that followed it, disquieted him greatly. Just then he felt he could make out what appeared to be a faint light in the distance, which told him that, either he had reached an exit, or, far more likely, that there was human activity of some kind going on somewhere down the track. Then a minute or so later, as the distant light helped the tunnel acquire greater definition, he decided that it was most likely both. But who could it be down there? he asked himself, and so now began to feel a tad scared.

Just then the whirring noise of what sounded very like a motor-bike started up, and Chris could tell from its ever-increasing volume that it was plainly fast approaching him. His first thought was to run, but he quickly realised the utter futility of it. All he could do was stand stock-still - his back up against the slimy, rounded wall - and hope that the rider simply drove straight past him, although he knew that the chances of that happening were little more than zero.

The motor-cycle was on him in seconds, and soon came to a crunching halt before him, scattering a patch of the limestone chippings which covered almost the entire floor of the tunnel where once train-tracks had been. Chris saw that the helmet-less rider was none other than Steffan Jones, who was a pupil in Rhiannon's class at Pennant, although the boy from Dowlais was a year younger than both of them. Chris was very glad the rider hadn't been anyone older.

'Clicker! What are you doing down here?' Steffan yelled at him, above the cycle's roar. 'The meeting-place was meant to be in Pant, at the back of the junior-school, you know.'

It was only then that Chris remembered that that particular afternoon was meant to be the time for his latest planned sale of drugs to Steffan and his friend Jake, and that he had completely forgotten all about it, and so hadn't brought the large bag of prepared skunk along with him. With little time to think, he quickly invented a story.

'I came this way because of the rain. It's - it's much drier, and quicker, yeah?' Chris told him. 'But I only have a very small bag of bud on me today.' He reached into a pocket and took it out. 'I easily can get the rest for you tomorrow, if you like.'

'Whatever,' Steffan replied. 'Listen - give me what you've got with you, anyway.'

Chris handed him the small bag, which the younger, but tougher, boy held to his knee and examined. 'You're having a laugh, aren't you, Clicker?' Steffan told him. 'This thing is not even what 'the fuzz' call 'personal.' I can't give you fuck all for this, mate. Jesus!'

'Look - take it anyway,' said Chris. 'Then you can check that it's the usual quality, can't you? And I'll - and I'll meet you where you said tomorrow with a proper sack full.'

'No - not near the school,' said the biker, shaking his head. 'Different day - different place, remember? 'It'll be at *The Blue Pool* this time. Yeah - *The Blue Pool* - eight o'clock. O.K.? And don't go forgetting again, yeah? Right. See you then.'

'I'll be there,' Chris told him, now a little concerned because the rendez-vous was going to be so much closer to his home this time.

'But no torches, O.K.?' Steffan added, lifting up and turning his bike round so that it pointed in the direction from which he had come. Chris nodded. 'And just one more thing, Clicker. Your step-dad. He's such a cock, yeah?'

Chris nodded, as he had done several times before when asked the same question at school, then watched as the younger, much sturdier, lad soared off back down the tunnel, no doubt to rejoin Jake and his other compatriots from Pant and Dowlais. He then turned round and trudged back once again in the direction of the bricked-up, northern entrance to this once-vital, but now largely forgotten, railway tunnel, and, slamming the steel-door shut behind him, and pulling up, and tying, the knot on the hood of his sopping coat, set off west, once more to brave the cold, drenching rain of the upper Taff Valley on his route back towards *The Seven Arches* and home.

But about half-way along the track Chris suddenly recalled the two dreams he had had about Rhiannon, obviously because he was now passing close to the location in Vaynor Woods, where the events in the first of the dreams had taken place. He veered to his right, and, though finding it difficult in the gloom and the rain to stay upon it, followed a narrow path that soon took him down to the little wooden bridge which crossed over the Taff at one of its prettiest spots, and which soon brought him out onto the lovely grassy glade beyond it that had always been his favourite picnic-spot, whatever age or gender the person was he happened to be sharing it with.

Chris didn't feel that he was able to cross over the bridge, since the dream's image, that he recalled, still seemed so vivid and real to him. And so, leaning against a large oak-tree, ten feet or so above the river-bank, he stared across at the, now almost invisible, copse, and imagined that his dream was recurring right before his eyes, just as he continued to recall it.

It was the middle of the day, and Rhiannon was running away from him onto the wooden bridge that would take them both away from the river and up the steep hill towards Vaynor Church. Chris watched the lovely, flame-haired girl he adored turn lovingly towards him when she reached the other side. With her pale arm she motioned for him to follow her, and he did.

Everything, including Chris's love-life with Rhiannon, felt tranquil and idyllic. Together the pair walked through a pasture where beautiful white lambs gambolled carelessly about, frequently suckling on their mothers' teats, the small number of ewes being, quite naturally, far larger animals that possessed much shaggier coats of a darker, browner colour.

But out of the woods to his left strode a wild mammal that looked like a grey fox, but far more closely resembled a wolf: a creature that possessed dreadful, penetrating eyes, and flashing, gnashing teeth. The four-legged beast ran into the copse and quickly snatched up in its jaws a young, feeble lamb, and shook it about mercilessly, until its neck was utterly broken.

As the rest of the sheep scattered, Chris then clearly saw Rhiannon and himself, standing just apart from each other, gazing down from opposite sides of the path at the awful, bloody scenario that was taking place directly before them. Chris watched himself simply standing there, stunned, and powerless to prevent the innocent lamb's demise. Yes, tearful and afraid, his eyes blazing, his mouth wide open in horror at the grisly event he was witnessing, the image of himself that Chris beheld on the far side of the river was one of cowardly impotence, and it filled him with shame.

Rhiannon, on the other hand, arms wide apart, the fingers of her hands twisting with obvious excitement, stood close up, and stared down at the scene of slaughter before her, plainly thrilled at being able to witness its reality, and its inevitable, bloody conclusion. At that moment Chris sensed that the sweet girl he had thought he loved had morphed into a boy, whose dark face, stubble, and side-burns were not unlike his own. He felt instant hatred for the Rhiannon that he now beheld, and, without even reflecting on it, knew he could never again go near her.

The second dream Chris had had on that night he found he was now unable to recall. Just as well, he told himself, as he clambered back up the path, and, in the dank, cold woods, hurried off once more along the wet, stony cycle-way that stretched away before him towards *Gloryhole*.

The wind that rose up all of a sudden disturbed the sleeping girl so greatly that she pulled back her duvet and sat herself up in bed, and listened attentively to its sheer ferocity and power. It was whistling noisily through the roof-top, and she could even feel its keenness on her bare arms, and this made her shiver. Carla had long wanted to compose a song that reflected the essence of her homeland, and, at that very moment, she decided that *the wind* would be the theme that ran through it. She then recalled that she had just been dreaming about a '*Queen of the Bee-hive,*' and, after pondering the matter for a minute or so, she suddenly realised that she had simply been experiencing yet another dream about Amy Winehouse. She shook her head and laughed at the stark simplicity of the, much-lauded, wisdom of the *personal unconscious*. Yes, Jung had definitely got that right, she told herself.

The bedside-clock read four-thirty. Carla yawned, then breathed in deeply to replenish the expelled air. The smell that suddenly hit Carla's nostrils was unmistakable. She leapt out of bed and opened up the drawer in which she had taken to storing her stash of '*green.*' The odour from Chris's bags seemed to be seeping out somehow, she mused, although why it was happening she couldn't tell, and so she searched around for a tin that she could seal it all in.

Suddenly Carla heard her father's plaintive cry coming from his room next-door, and so she left her task and dashed in to see to him. She could see that his head was lolling halfway out of the bed, and could straightaway sense from his contorted face the agonising pain that he had to be experiencing just then. Carla found she could only cry to look at him, but she nevertheless approached his single-bed, and eased his thin torso back into place, under the covers again.

'How bad is it, Dad?' she asked him, tearfully, seeking for his hand to hold.

'Pass me my water, sweet, would you,' he replied hoarsely, licking his lips for soothing sake.

Carla reached across and fed him a mouthful of water from the glass, and saw how his grey, marbled eyes suddenly lit up for a second.

'You know, I don't reckon I'm long for this world, now, Carla,' he told her slowly. 'Every day - every night, now - the pain just gets worse and worse.'

On hearing those pitiable words, which she felt were almost cracking up her heart, there was just one thought on Carla's mind. She turned and ran back into her room, took one of the little bags from her drawer, opened it with her teeth, and, with the aid of a rizla paper, began to roll up a cannabis-joint. Once done, she lit it, and brought it, lovingly, to her father's bed.

'Inhale this, Dad,' she told him gently. 'It's a - it's a special pain-killer I went and got for you. Just breathe it in, would you, Dada, and soon, I guarantee, you'll be feeling a whole lot better.' Carla held the tip of the spliff firmly between her father's pale, cracked lips and bid him take a draw. The wind howled like a banshee round the stairs beyond the open door, but, no longer hearing it, Carla leaned over and bade him take another puff, then yet another again.

'Yes, I can see that it's already working,' Carla told him with a sweet, beaming smile. She gripped his thin, quivering hand in hers, and convinced herself that she could feel its growing warmth. Soon Carla could see him begin to smile his elation back at her, and so she realised that this was indeed the sort of pain-relief that her aged father's broken body now badly needed.

Was this then *'the breath of life,'* she asked herself with a smile, that she had often heard folk speak about as a young girl in the little chapel in *Talybont*, where her mother Carys had taken her to learn about God and Jesus in much happier times? *'The wind'* that swept in through the bolted door at Pentecost - was this it? mused Carla. Not the actual smoke, of course - not the drug - she told herself, but the swift, miraculous, surely heaven-sent, heaven-scented, respite that it plainly managed to bring to one in such desperate need. She leaned closer to her father's frail form, eager to know the answer, and to Carla, just then, it most certainly appeared to be so.

'Good. Now take a final draw, Dada,' she beckoned him. 'And inhale more deeply this time. Ye-es, that's it, my love. You're doing just great. Now pass it to me and just lie back and rest.'

'Stop bumpin' your gums and listen, will you!' Steffan ordered his partner-in-crime. 'I know it's starting to get dark already, and that bloody waterfall is a hell of a lot scarier than it was the last time we came here, but we can't just leave the bike out on the road, can we? It needs to go where we go, in case - well, in case the filth are planning to light us up and jump us. Our exit strategy - do you get it?' He watched as his friend nodded. 'Right. Come on, then. Push!'

Jake and Steffan stood either side of the silent, blue scrambling-bike. Together they guided it, with every fibre each possessed, up the steep, muddy incline, and along the narrow, winding path that, in the gloom, they could barely make out, right up to the point where it sloped down again, but even more steeply this time, towards the river-torrent, and its whirlpool of white, gushing water, that rotated beneath it like a giant turbine in the midst of its vast pool.

A little further up the hill, hidden from sight, and sheltered from the drizzling rain beneath the cover of a sheet of black canvas slung over a bush, Chris sat silently watching them. Hearing mention of the police, and seeing how the two boys were now acting, convinced him that he had best remain where he was for the time being, and listen further to their crazy conversation. .

'Clean!' stammered Jake. 'Of course he's clean! He's the guy at the top, right? So he's bound to be as clean as a whistle, mate. He's just got the one conviction for speed trafficking, I heard.'

'What! Then he's not clean, then, is he, dumb-ass?' Steffan told him. 'Trafficking *Speed*! I mean, that's some serious shit right there, wouldn't you say?'

'Do you think?' asked Jake. 'But he said he was just doing forty in a thirty zone. Why, that's no big deal, surely. I mean, *you* do that all the time.'

'Oh, you mean he was speeding!' said Steffan, laughing.

'In his Audi, yeah,' added Jake. 'What's so funny? Eh? Say - why are you laughing at me?' Jake watched as his burly pal rolled about. 'Steffan, can I ask you something?' he asked. 'Why on earth are we meeting Clicker all the way up here? We can't even sit straight, it's so bumpy.'

'Why, here? Why not?' said Steffan. 'Look, mate, this might seem just a patch of shitty, rat-infested ground on some lonely Welsh hill-side to you and me, mate, but, this is Heaven-on-Earth to an Afghan immigrant and his two wives and extended family. Remember there's two ways of looking at everything, you know. Take what we are doing right now, for example. I mean you probably see it all as just - as just buying and selling drugs, don't you?'

'But isn't that what it is?' enquired Jake, bemused. 'Well, that's what I think I signed up for, any road.'

'No, not at all,' responded Steffan. 'You see, mate, I'm more inclined to view it as 'care in the community' - a kind of general practice, if you like. The Big Society at work. Do you get me?'

'Do you mean us two are like - like doctors, then?' quipped his friend, not a great deal clearer about it than before.

'Yeah, you got it,' Steffan told him, picking up and lobbing a slab of fallen rock at a couple of crows that had hopped onto a fallen tree nearby, then, once they had flown off, flingng another into the cavernous, revolving pool thirty feet or so vertically below the soles of their feet. 'People take cannabis for all sorts of reasons, and for all sorts of illnesses, you see, including the extreme effects of motor-neurone disease.

MS, asthma, adenoidal cavities, and a whole shit-load more. I've been researching it all, see.'

'How about cancer?' enquired Jake.

'Yeah, cancer, too,' replied Steffan. 'And all the different kinds of cancers you can get, too.'

'You know, I think I can see your point now,' Jake told him, nodding. 'By the way, I know what you mean about there being two ways of looking at everything. I remember how everyone in my Primary School was shocked when they heard how I stuck photos of single breasts of different women on my bedroom-wall. 'Single breasts!' they'd say. 'What's up with you, Jake? What's wrong with *two tits*? Are you weird or something? Are you gay?' they used to ask me. 'No, I'm not gay,' I'd tell 'em, only I couldn't tell if they believed me or not. But what they didn't realise was that what I'd actually pasted up weren't tits at all, but colour close-ups of all the moons of all the planets in our Solar System, as viewed from the spacecrafts Voyager and - and Cassini.

'Christ!' shot back Steffan. 'Do you mean - do you mean the Italians have been up there?'

'I guess so,' said Jake. 'And you see the biggest and the darkest of the craters on them -'

'They took for nipples!' said Steffan, chuckling loudly, and slapping his skinnier friend across the back of the head.

'That's right,' said Jake, rubbing his skull and stifling a wail. He was genuinely glad that his companion seemed impressed with his tale. 'Say, Steffan - see that strange blob of yellow sitting up between those two clouds. You probably think that's the Moon, yeah? But it's not, you know.'

'It's not!' stammered Steffan. 'It's not the Moon? Listen, Jake, I'm not at all sure you're not a bigger tit than they all said you were.'

'No, I'm not,' countered Jake. 'No, that big yellow sphere up there is just *our* moon.' Jake told him with obvious passion. 'That there above us right now is our very own special satellite. And we only have one satellite.'

'You mean like you're mine,' said Steffan, his right hand high-fiving his partner's left.

'Yeah, that's it,' Jake told him smiling. 'Yeah. No. Well, not exactly. I'd say we were more *a pair* of satellites, really. Like - like Mars has two moons, you see. Different sizes, of course, yet equal, of equal value, if you get what I'm trying to say. Like - I don't know - like two crows sitting on a log,' he said, smiling, and pointing at where the two birds had sat together before being driven off by his friend's mad missile attack.

'Except them two were a mating pair, stupid,' Steffan corrected him, angrily. 'I mean, I know you often talk like a girl, Jane - I mean Jake - and - and you told me you like *'American Idol,'* and *'Dancing On Ice,'* but you're really a dude, you know, dumb-ass. Otherwise I wouldn't have got myself stuck up here with you on some bleedin' hillside under the moonlight, now would I?'

'No? Do you mean - are you saying that, if I was a bird, you wouldn't have come here tonight?' the lanky boy asked him.

'Eh?' retorted Steffan. ''Course I would have. 'Course I would, dumb-ass. I'm not gay, I'll have you know. Listen - you know what. I bet you I'd have probably shafted you at least twice by now, mate - condom, or no condom - if you had have been.'

'Would you really?' Jake enquired. 'Eugh! I'm not sure I like the sound of that, if I'm honest. You know, Steffan, you're already beginning to sound a lot gayer than you used to say I was.'

'Hey! Who's that!' Steffan suddenly shrieked, scurrying away from his companion, and up the steep slope at a rate of knots. He soon arrived at the strange, hanging contraption under which Chris sat, concealed. Steffan studied him for a while, not really knowing what to make of it. 'Say, mate - are you loitering within tent?' he asked, pointing at the dripping canvas-sheet, and laughing so loud that the cowering Chris wasn't sure whether to laugh along with him or stick his fingers in his ears.

'I was just sheltering here out of the rain,' Chris told him. 'I - I thought it was you two, but I couldn't be sure in the dark, you know, so I decided to stay shtumm for a while, just to be sure.'

'Christ - it's not that bleedin' dark, mate. You got the gear?' Steffan asked him.

'It's in the tree,' replied Chris, pointing to the side.

Steffan removed a large polythene-bag from the branch of the dwarf-elm that stood nearby, pulled it open and peered inside. 'That's sweet, that is, Clicker. Look - we'll pay you in two days, O.K.?

'Eh? Why not now?' enquired Chris, getting to his feet, and pulling the canvas-sheet down to the ground..

'Because we don't have the money right now, that's why. Don't get arse-y now,' Steffan told him, looking fiercely into the eyes of the older, but less powerful boy, anticipating a problem, but not really expecting any. 'You know very well you've got nobody else to sell it to, right?'

'Well, I have, as a matter of fact,' Chris announced, with the hint of a smirk on his face.

'Really?' Steffan snapped back. 'And I suppose they buy in bulk, like we do, yeah?'

'And pay top-dollar, like us, yeah?' added Jake, who, having just climbed up the slope, had arrived at his friend's side.

'Well, I always charge the same price, as it goes,' said Chris, rolling up the canvas, and pushing it under the tree.

'Well, Clicker, that's where your whole business-strategy falls flat on its face, you see,' Steffan told him. 'You should always charge the least amount for your best customers, and a damn sight more for everyone else. Didn't you do Business Studies?'

'What? No, I chose Music in that option-group,' the older boy told him.

'And a lot of good it did you, yeah?' Steffan retorted sharply. 'I mean I know you play bass and piano and that, but you're never going to play with *The Stereophonics,* are you now?' he told him, laughing.

'Or *The Lost Prophets,*' cut in Jake.

'Or Carla Steel, even,' Steffan added. 'Are you now, Clicker? Old Carla wouldn't give you the time of day, pal.'

'Probably not,' replied Chris, thinking fast, and taking care not to mention that, not only was the woman his new neighbour, but he actually knew her to speak to, and she was already his main customer for the skunk that she was totally unaware he grew in her own dad's loft.

'Probably not, he says,' Steffan repeated, looking at Jake, and chuckling along with him.

'Anyway,' Chris countered, wiping the mud from his hands onto the back of his jeans, 'I'm going to be forming my own band soon,'

'Really?' said Steffan. 'And where are you planning to be playing, Clicker? Glastonbury!'

'Well, you never know. That's where Carla Steel is going to be head-lining the summer after next, I heard.'

'Really? And how would you know that, Clicker?' the older boy asked him in reply. 'They haven't even announced the line-up yet. And why are you going on about Carla Steel, anyway? Do you fancy the bird, or something? We two always thought you batti-ed for the other team, as it goes, didn't we, Jake? Do you get it?'

Suddenly the raucous, unmistakable sound of a police-siren could be heard approaching down the steep road from the direction of the castle and Merthyr, and, without bye nor leave, the two younger boys dashed smartly back to where they had left their motor-cycle lying on its side near the cliff. Mounting it, and clutching onto each other for dear life, they then rode off down-river, along the course of the narrow path, that gradually climbed up the hill-side once more, then ran back down again steeply towards the shallow confluence with a narrower, tributary stream, which they sped across in a hail of spray, in their flight towards the distant village of Trefechan.

Chris found himself alone and abandoned, and, wetting himself with fear, and not knowing what else to do, ran off in the opposite direction to Steffan and Jake, towards the narrow stone-bridge, which the police-car was in the process of trying to negotiate at even less than the five miles-per-hour that the road-sign alongside it requested. He dashed out in front of the vehicle's blazing head-lights, veered sharply to his left, then began scampering up the vast stone stair-case, known to many as 'The Ninety-nine Steps,' that rose almost vertically out of the river-gorge, and which would, providing his leg didn't suddenly give up on him, take him back up again to *Gloryhole* and home.

Pounding his way up the steep climb, the jarring pain in Chris's leg soon caused him to slow up alarmingly. He quickly realised that the squad-car might quite easily have rounded the hair-pin bend, and already be at the summit of the steps to greet him when he finally arrived there, but, despite his sore leg, and a burning throat, he pressed on regardless, and, in little more than a minute or two, he finally managed to reach his lofty destination.

When he got out onto the road Chris could see that the police-vehicle hadn't yet arrived, although he was certainly able to hear its three-litre engine roaring like a tiger out of the darkness to his left, as it rounded the hair-pin bend before hurtling up the curved hill towards where he was now standing. He had just a few precious seconds to spare in which to dash up to his house, un-lock the front-door, and slip inside, and, though it was a close shave, he made it.

A few minutes later, staring at his flushed, perspiring face in the hall-mirror, Chris was ecstatic that he had actually managed to make it home at all. Yes, it had been a very close thing, he told himself, realising that he would need to be even more careful in the future, especially when Steffan and Jake were about. But at least he felt thrilled to have succeeded in selling well over of half his stock of newly-harvested skunk in just a solitary night. And, what with his brand- new market just over the garden-fence, where the customer had no qualms at all about paying top-dollar, Chris truly believed that he had embarked on a new and exciting career for himself.

The twin, dark, satanic call-centres stood side-by-side on the main road into town. It was time for my daughter Rhiannon to carry out her own fortnight's work-experience, and, wearing the short skirt and heels that I had thrice warned her against wearing, she stepped out of my car and marched boldly into the lofty 'Silver Excalibur' building, directly beneath its massive, 3-D, blue mobile-phone insignia, pierced by its iconic silver sword, that sat perched above the entrance on its vast, coal-black, illuminated screen.

I waved my arms, then tooted my horn in vain, but Rhiannon appeared to take no notice whatsoever. Yet, within a minute or so, my sweet, but serenely absent-minded, young girl was outside on the road once again, and, with a shake of her pretty head in my direction that acknowledged her mistake, now began walking, more circumspectly this time, into the more rectangular, and slightly less offensive monstrosity that stood bang next-door to it, its red fish insignia appearing to be switched off to reduce costs.

I drove north in the pursuit of relaxation, and after a brisk walk through the glories of the woods and the flower-beds of Cyfarthfa Park, I decided to drive out of town completely, and within twenty minutes or so had reached the village of Pontsticill, that I normally ventured to only on Sunday evenings, and parked my car outside. 'The Butcher's Arms,' next to a large beer-lorry that seemed to be completing its weekly delivery.

'Fill me up, buttercup,' I urged the young bar-maid, who soon returned my smile with interest.

'Bitter - Dyl?' she asked.

'Only with life,' I told her, grinning.

'Mug?'

I could easily have delivered her with yet another pointless wise-crack, but thought better of it this time. 'Straight glass,' I replied. 'And give me a couple of packets of crisps too, would you? Any flavours you like.'

I sipped my pint and looked around for a suitable place to sit myself down. The two boys seated at the table in the corner looked familiar to me. On studying them for a while I recalled that I had encountered them not very long after my daughter's parents' evening at Pennant just before Christmas, and had had some sort of altercation with the pair them afterwards in the street, the cause of which I could not now recall. Although it wasn't yet midday, the young pair seemed to me to be just as drunk and out of it as they had been back then.

'How long have we been waiting now?' the bigger one asked his companion. 'Three days, is it?'

The taller, much thinner boy shook his head, and flipped the beer-mat up into the air and caught it. 'I don't know, but it seems like forever,' he replied, 'Say, Steffan, on which planet in the Solar System is a day longer than a year?

'What! How on earth can a day be longer than a year, stupid?' retorted his friend with a glare.

'But I'm not talking about *on Earth,* though, am I?' responded Jake, with a smile.

'Aren't you?' asked Steffan, flummoxed.

'No. I told you, didn't I?' Jake continued. 'Go on - guess. On which planet is a day longer than a year?'

'I don't know - the Moon?' his friend shot back. 'Oh, no, you said that was a satellite, didn't you? Er - Ur-anus. That one's always good for a laugh, right?' He sipped his beer and tittered at the name contentedly.

'No, not Uranus, or your-anus' Jake told him, chuckling along with him. 'Try again.'

'Look, Jake - do I look like I'm interested in knowing any of your crap about Space?' asked Steffan. 'How come you're in bottom-set for almost every subject you do, and yet you know all this shit? You a secret nerd, or something?'

'Hey - I think *I* know,' I called to them from my stool beside the bar.

'Which is it, then, Grandad?' Steffan rudely enquired, with a sneer that suggested he had already recognised me too.

'Work it out,' I told him. 'You probably think of *a* day as *twenty-hour hours*, right?'

'Well, don't *you?*' shot back Steffan.

'No. No, that's just *our* day - a day on Earth, I mean,' I explained.

'Get to the point, will you?' the boy commanded.

'And I guess you probably think of *a year* as -'

'Three-hundred-and-sixty-five of 'em,' he retorted. 'Say - am I right? I am, aren't I?'

'When, actually, *a day* is the time it takes for us to -' I got up, squared my two feet on the bar-room floor, and then turned once right around in a circle, and promptly sat down again.

'Time it takes to what, Grandad?' asked Steffan, mystified. 'To act like a tit?'

'Spin!' Jake told him. 'Spin once round. Do you get it? And a year is the time it takes for -'

The skinny lad suddenly placed his pint-glass in the middle of the table they were sat at, and, in a wide sweeping arc, and, facing inwards, walked all the way round it, circling his friend in the process, and ending up back where his seat was. He beamed a smile at his scowling companion, opened his hands to him, and asked, 'Now does that make it any clearer?'

'Does it hell as like!' Steffan shot back. 'I think the two of you are bonkers, if you ask me. Say, aren't you Rhiannon Cook's old man, squire?'

'Well, *old* is debatable, as I'm sure you'll agree, but I happen to be her dad, yes,' I told him, half expecting what was soon to follow.

'Christ! She's a girl who gets about, don't you think?' he continued.

'Well, she's working in a call-centre in town this week, if that's what you mean,' I replied.

'That's not what I mean at all, and you know it, Grandad,' he told me. 'What I mean is, she isn't exactly - er - particular about who she goes with, is she? At one time she used to go out with me.'

'Well, I can't think why, exactly, but oddly you've proved your point, I suppose,' I responded with a chuckle. From behind I felt I heard the bar-maid join in with me. Just then I swear I glimpsed two white, cartoon-puffs of steam shooting out of the bigger lad's weirdly-shaped ears.

'Say, was that remark supposed to be smart, or something?' asked Steffan, clearly beginning to get himself worked up.

'No, not particularly,' I retorted.

'Well, I reckon you were trying to be clever,' he continued, determined not to lose face in front of his friend and, I dare say, the pretty young girl behind the bar. 'What do you reckon, Jake?'

'Well, I was, as it goes,' I told him. 'Trying to be clever, I mean. Right up until the time I had to leave school, that is. It was then I suddenly realised I had better find myself a proper job, and knuckle down and earn some bread like everybody else, or I could badly lose out. Because it's a lot tougher than you think out there in the real world, boys. It really is.'

'Old man must think he's a smart-ass, Jake,' Steffan responded with a smirk. 'Well, listen, old boy, I don't see no point in feeling I need to work my balls off like some poxy slave for fifteen or twenty grand a year just so's I can afford some poxy council-house and a couple of packets of fags. That's forced labour, that is. I mean, what's the point in that shit, eh? There's a lot easier ways of making dosh, right? I mean, I may still be young, but I bet I already know most of them.'

'Yeah? So why are you sitting here, then?' I asked him, my arms stretched wide.

Steffan lifted his mobile-phone off the table and waved it round so as to illustrate his point. 'Because this happens to be my office, mate, you know what I mean?' he retorted. 'This is where all my best deals go down. Yesterday *The Red Cow*, today *The Butcher's Arms*.'

'Tomorrow *Pennant High,* yeah? Then the junior schools, I wouldn't wonder. You know you must be so proud of yourselves.' I said, shaking my head about. 'Say - shouldn't you two be at school right now? Oh, of course, it's work-experience week, isn't it?'

'No, that was last month for us two,' cut in Jake. It was then I remembered that he was Griff Haines' son from Dowlais.

'Listen, mate, it's work-experience all year round for us two,' continued Steffan. 'And what better experience is there than sitting up here with a pint of ale and a packet of crisps, and -' Steffan's phone suddenly began screamng out - *'Stop lookin' at my mom, my mom, my mom! Stop lookin' at my mom!'* He picked it up and answered it, then immediately gazed back in my direction. 'Sorry about this, old boy - it's my secretary,' he told me, grinning.

'Or it could be his broker,' Jake suggested, sniggering.

I decided to have it out with him. 'Jake, you used to be top of the class back in junior school, do you remember?' I said. 'I can recall how you and my Rhiannon once made a power-point together about The Solar System, and you both showed it to us all in a parents' assembly. Superb, it was. And you taught us oldies so much that day that we didn't know. You know, you seemed to have such a flair for science and astronomy back then. So can I ask you something?'

'Sure, fire away,' Jake retorted.

'What the hell happened, mate? Did your rocket-boosters run out of fuel, or something?

'Now that's funny,' the scrawny lad answered with a smile.

'Listen, Jake, I feel the need to speak up because I can see that this rubbish isn't you, really, is it? It just isn't you, pal. You used to have so much going for you at one time, you really did.'

Jake's head dipped, and he drank up the last dregs from his pint-glass that I thought already looked empty. 'I still do, you know,' he told me.

'Do you really?' I asked him, truly wishing I could place an arm round his shoulder, as I recalled I had once done at a junior-school football tournament where he had once scored the winning goal. 'You know, I'd like to think so. I really would, mate.'

Jake suddenly turned his head away, then looked all around the room, I guess pretending that the tear obscuring his right eye wasn't really there.

'Jake, mate, I know you daren't say in front of your pal there, but do you know what I think?' I asked him.

'What do you think, Grandad?' said Steffan, breaking off his phone-conversation for a moment. 'Think it's going to rain later?'

'Well, Jake, what I believe is - it's never too late to change your mind about something,' I continued. 'And thereby change your life round, do you get me?'

'You know, I reckon Jake's happy with the mind he's already got,' said Steffan, closing his phone and gazing up venomously in my direction. Steffan had clearly decided it was his turn to boss the conversation. 'You know you're a lot like your grand-daughter, if you ask me, old man,' he quipped back. 'Do you want to know why?'

'Not particularly,' I told him. 'And she's not my grand-child. Rhiannon's my daughter. My only daughter, as it goes. If you like, she's the child of my old age, and I'm right proud of it. And I can tell you, young man, that that is one bond that can never be broken.'

'No?' Steffan countered. 'Well, dig this, Grandad. Her last boyfriend - Chris - is a well-known drug-dealer, and her latest one is a two-bit fraudster, who collects credit-cards for a living, and spends most of his spare time scamming old people out of their pensions and their life-savings. Tell me now, grandad - which of the two do you think she should settle for?'

'And what are you?' the barmaid suddenly called out, glowering at him. 'We've seen you - don't think we haven't - round the back, lighting up your damn spliffs, and leaving the stinking butts all over the ground for my kids to find.'

'And in the Gents, sniffing up your future prospects through a ten-pound note,' the thin old man in the corner suddenly chipped in, before dropping his cane walking-stick from his trembling hands to the floor with an almighty crash. 'My sister told me how you scared the living daylights out of most of the old women in *'The Willows'* in less than a week, what with your loud, raucous rap-crap, and your wacky-baccy, and your dirty web-cam in the ladies' loos. You should be right ashamed of yourselves, the pair of you. You know, if you was in school in my day they'd have whipped your arse for you, and no mistake.'

'Listen - I could kick yours for you, right now, if you want, old man,' Steffan told him fiercely.

'What do you want to lick my arse for, you fairy?' the old man replied, mis-hearing his comment quite spectacularly. He pointed a trembling finger in my direction, 'See that black-and-white photo above the bar there? The small one. Yeah? That's me just after the war, that is. I nearly won a British title back then, I did. And, as a boy your age, I fought in the Libyan

Desert in the Second-Wold War too. And, you know, I may be eighty-four now, but I'm damn sure I could still tip the pair of you on your spotty arses as soon as look at you.'

'Hey, Alf - you know we don't use language like that in here,' the barmaid told him, pulling up the hatch, and rushing round to collect all the empty glasses from the tables in the room.

'Come on, let's get out of here, Jake,' Steffan told his friend, rising, and walking briskly to the door, and holding it open for him. He waved his mobile-phone back at us. 'After all, we've got a living to make,' he shouted.

Through the large, latticed window I watched as the pair of sixteen-year olds marched off towards their parked, blue motor-cycle. Seconds later, as they rolled out of the pub car-park, and then raced off up the steep hill towards Vaynor, their turbo-charged roar of defiance could be heard right throughout the village, and even across the broad Taff Valley that lay beyond them.

'You've been to London, yeah?' Carla asked him, the cool breeze blowing her black curls away from her temples. 'Then can you remember that raucous, bare, windswept atmosphere left behind on the underground platform the second a tube-train has just gone?' She swept her arm across her body, and made a loud, whooshing noise. 'Very like a vacuum-cleaner that has just flushed out and sucked dry a small basement room or cellar, and has now moved off into the hall. Or, in the underground scenario, down the tube-tunnel a way. Well, I am trying to capture that, if anything,' she told him. 'But I'm kind of struggling to get it, you know.'

'Oh, I see. And is that why you chose a minor-key?' Chris asked her, watching her intently as Carla sat balancing her favourite, old, brown acoustic-guitar on her right knee, and strumming it just once with all five fingers, creating a stark, stinging chord, the like of which he had never heard before. The boy looked down and attempted to imitate the same sound on the guitar that he carried, trying four or five times without success, but eventually, after several more demonstrations by

Carla, managing to get it right. 'Hey - I think that's it,' he told her proudly.

Tom lay on the sofa in the kitchen, listening to the pair of young musicians who were presently sitting together out in his back-garden, and wishing he could get his old saxophone out of its box and go out and join in with them. But those days were long gone now, he told himsef sadly, and so would never again return, however much he pined for them.

'Play it again, sweetheart,' Tom called out to his daughter. She did. 'Wow! You know, Chris, I bought her that guitar when she was twelve,' he announced proudly, and smiled at the sudden thought he had of the pretty young girl sitting in their little Breconshire chapel at Christmas and playing *'All Through The Night'* for the small congregation. There's lovely she had looked back then, he thought, laughing quietly to himself. Tom thought to mention it, but the two young people were having far too much fun for him to want to bother them with the same, and so he adjusted his fat pillow, lay back on the couch, and tried to snooze off once again.

'What's the song about, by the way?' Chris asked Carla, smoothing down the green t-shirt he now wore, and which pronounced for the world, first on its front, and then its back - 'I'M SO BROKE - I CAN'T EVEN PAY ATTENTION.'

'The song? Oh, it's about a young couple who have nowhere to live but a bench deep inside a tube-station,' Carla told him, strumming out a second chord that well complemented the first.

Chris tried to imitate that one too. 'And when it's finished, what are planning to call it?' he enquired, as he tried again.

'The Sleepers,' Carla told him. 'Yes, *'The Sleepers,'* or something close to that, anyway. You see, they live their lives quite apart above ground during the day-time, but each night their love is once again rekindled and shared together, deep, deep down below the sleeping city.' She played the two chords consecutively for the very first time, and the boy instantly recognised the true genius of the lovely, modest, hugely talented woman who sat, head bent, before him.

'And the noisy, squeaky trains that screech and stop, and soon after leave -' he began.

'And that shake the sleeping couple, and buffet them with their sheer power,' she told him, 'but rarely ever wake them out of their dreams - out of the pure, unfettered love that the couple know and share.'

'I see now. You know, Carla, that's the part of the train I always like best,' announced Chris, trying to blend together as well as she had done the two new chords he had just learned. 'The first place I always go to.'

'What part is that?' asked Carla, observing his futile efforts, but smiling at his patience.

'The buff-et,' retorted Chris, laughing. 'I could eat a sandwich or something right now, as it goes. Listen, Carla, I think I'm going to just pop over the fence and see if my Mum is in, O.K.? Yeah?'

'You mean you're goimg to make like a tree and leave?' she asked, grinning up at him.

Chris smiled at her clever reply. 'I like it,' he told her. 'Yeah - listen. I promise I'll be back in a tick. Well, not exactly inside a tick, but I'm sure you know what I mean.'

Half opening his eyes once more, Tom heard the clever play-on-words that the two young people toyed with, but only partially understood, since strange, deep thoughts of his own, solitary, long-dead, son - Carla's much older brother Will - drifted through his waning consciousness. And all he really knew just then was that a green-tinted sleep was beginning to overtake his tired, but no longer aching, bones, and was about to send him into his afternoon 'Dreamland' on board the long, silent subway-train of his own creation.

Occasionally peering round the door to check on him, Carla played on, creating, then replaying, whatever chords her nimble fingers chanced upon, until her bullion-vault memory finally closed up its flap, and she could at last move on to trying out some more. She felt content that she could be with her father in his home at this incredibly difficult time for him, well aware that he was trying his best to channel all his desires into the numbered days - the mayfly lifetime - that he believed he still had allotted him. Her dad had always been so very different to the rest of their family, mused Carla - intrinsically good, dependable, and with a heart as big as a cathedral. And the more time she got to spend with him now, and the more closely she got to observe him, the more certain she was becoming that his ambition was not for this life alone.

Having reunited with him once again after far too many years apart, Carla was now determined to make up for lost time. The period that her father had remaining with her - however brief that might turn out to be - she had already decided she would endeavour to make a time of loving creation, during which, perhaps, with Chris's help, she might hopefully get to write some of the finest music of her lifetime. Well, at least I'm determined to try to, she told herself, scribbling some notation down on the sheet that lay on the iron-table beside her, perhaps as much for my dear father's sake as for my own.

Carla leaned forward and peered again at Tom's crumpled, sleeping form, which lay inside, perched, somewhat precariously, upon the front edge of the small kitchen-sofa. Yes, I shall use this precious down-time to compose some special music if I can, she pondered, smiling at her good fortune in this respect, yet fearing, and somehow knowing, deep within her very soul, that her father's sudden crash, when it eventually came, would, for her, most likely resemble the last bar - the tragic final chord, perhaps - of the most bitter of life's symphonies.

'However friendly they were, he wasn't going to let anyone near his stash of green, I can tell you,' the tall, hirsute man with the deep brown eyes and the carefully cut, black beard told them, bending at the waist and tossing several sealed bags onto the ground beneath their feet. 'He'd have speared his own mother through the heart without thinking twice about it.'

'What was his problem, do you think, Volver?' Steffan asked the man.

'Anal retentive, wasn't he?' the tall, large-framed man told him in an accent Steffan knew was South African, but sounded, to many of the folk he dealt with, somewhere between Dutch and German. The denim-clad man used his thumbs to adroitly push his very long, black hair back behind his ears, from where, every few seconds, it seemed to come loose and fall like a curtain across his tanned, but heavily blotched and acne-scarred, face.

'Do you mean he stashed them up his bum, then?' asked Jake, a tad confused, to say the least.

'Big blocks of hash!' shrieked Volver. 'What's your mate talking about, Steffan? Is he all right?'

'I think I can see where he got mixed up, Volver,' Steffan told him. 'There are times when he can't seem to tell his arse from his elbow.'

'The elbow is the one in the middle of your arm, Jakie boy,' the lanky Afrikaner explained, grinning. 'The one you bend when you're sipping a pint, or having a tommy.'

'Ask him anything about outer space, and he'll be sure to know it,' Steffan said, smiling.

'O.K., then.' replied Volver, straightening up. 'I bet you can't tell us which two astronauts - apart from Tom Hanks, I mean - were on the calamitous *Apollo Thirteen* mission, which was the only one that never managed to land on the Moon.'

'Easy,' retorted Jake proudly. 'But Tom Hanks wasn't actually one of them, remember.'

'Do you think I didn't know that, dip-stick?' Volver retorted angrily, and turning to Steffan to share with him his sense of superiority. 'Mind you, he probably would have been, had he been born back then, don't you think?'

But Jake was busy thinking, and proceeded to answer the question posed. 'They were Jim Lovell -'

'Tom Hanks,' Volver explained, grinning.

'Jack Swigert.'

'Kevin Bacon - my personal favourite, as it goes.'

'And Fred Haise.'

'Er - some other actor I'd never heard of before.'

'Bill Paxton,' Jake told him, beaming. 'You must remember the sleazy car-salesman in *'True Lies,'* surely?'

'But I thought you said there were only three of them,' Steffan reminded him.

'There were!' the other two announced in unison.

'Oh, O.K., then,' responded Steffan, little the wiser. 'Say - how many large bags are you leaving us with, then, Volver?' Twelve, is it? And what's this one here with silver paper inside? Eh?' He looked up into the tall, bearded man's face. 'Do you figure - are you thinking - that we - we should be movng up a level all of a sudden then? Is that what you think?'

'Don't get so stressed, Steffan,' the foreigner told him, laying the palm of his long hand on the boy's cheek. 'It's on a sale-or-return basis, O.K.? Look - I realise you boys have only ever met me once before, but I'm going to be back here again in a fortnight, and hopefully once a week after that. And if you intend trying to save up in advance for those gigantic tuition-fees they have up in England now then you need to put the hard graft in right now, don't you? Because you'll soon find you've accrued a debt bigger than the average family mortgage before you even find someone you want to share a flat with. Life out there's not easy, you know, boys. Just look at me. I know I may look forty-five, but I'm only in my thirties.'

'But how on earth are we supposed to find buyers for all this lot you've left us?' asked Jake, suddenly acquiring a fresh insight, and marking how the tall, hirsute Afrikaner's own distinction seemed to wrap him round like a chill breath. 'Quite apart from the coke.'

Volver stood up to his full height and looked off into the distance. He shaded his eyes from the morning sun and pointed down into the green-edged, valley cleft below, at the long, parallel rows of terraced homes that made up the two contiguous communities of Merthyr and Dowlais, and the housing-estates that covered the hills, and told them, 'There's your market, boys. Go, be fruitful and multiply, subdue the Earth, and fill it with all your blessings.. He turned about. 'And in a fortnight I'll be back here with your money. It'll be in euros, by the way. And I'll also have a second consignment in the back of the car for you, all packed up and ready for sale, O.K.? Any questions? I thought not. Right, then I'm off back to civilisation. Well, Bristol, anyway. See ya!'

Donning his shades, the denim-jacketed South African got into his Audi coupe and sped off back down the narrow, winding mountain-road to the *Asda*-roundabout, and the Heads-of-the-Valleys road beyond it, which would eventually lead him, at break-neck speed he hoped, along the route that ran back east towards the English border.

With two large sacks hanging from their shoulders, the two boys soon climbed aboard their blue scrambler-bike, and began following after the drifting cloud of smoke and dust that the Afrikaner had left trailing in his wake in the cool, mountain air behind his fleeing motor.

'Who does that Volver guy think he is?' Jake shouted in Steffan's ear from behind. 'The Devil himself?'

His friend half-turned his head and screamed back at him, 'You'd better believe it!'

The drone of the banal, seemingly endless, chatter that seemed to pervade the whole room, chock-full of tele-typists, forced Rhiannon to get up again from the black, leather stool, (which they had chosen specially for her, but which she felt her bottom almost permanently stuck to,) and walk over to the huge window that looked out onto the bottom end of Merthyr. She was beginning ro wish she had accepted the opportunity she had been offered of working at the large leisure-centre she could just make out round to her left, except that that was where she heard all the jocks went, and where, inevitably, work-experience week would inevitably prove to be more exhaustive, if a lot less soul-destroying, than the call-centre in which she was presently based.

Gazing out into the afternoon sunlight, Rhiannon watched every motor-vehicle as it rounded the wide bend off the roundabout, then changed up and accelerated briefly past the front of her building, then drifted gently down to the smaller, much older '*Locomotive roundabout,*' from where the slow, inevitably tortuous, trek through the town-traffic would now begin.

It was the fourth car that approached from the main road which immediately caught Rhiannon's eye. For a start it looked familiar, and second, it pulled in suddenly, and halted on the double-yellow line just across from where she stood, face against the glass, looking down. Yes, it was her father's car, she told herself, but, oddly, it didn't seem to be her father who was driving it today, but some strange, unknown female in sun-glasses and a head-scarf. Rhiannon strained her eyes to try to make out the unknown woman's identity, but it wasn't until the diminutive little lady got out of the car, and began transporting a pot of paint and a large paint-brush across in her direction, that Rhiannon realised that it was none other than her mother.

Through the glass-pane the gob-smacked young girl soon saw Gwen pause outside the 'Silver Excalibur' building, which stood right next-door to her own, stare upwards at its broad facia, and, after setting her pot down on the grass, and carefully removing it's round lid, dip in her brush, and begin the task of daubing in red something that Rhiannon was unable to make out onto the plain, black wall before her.

Rhiannon was shocked beyond belief, and was reluctant even to turn round, in case someone else in the vast room had also seen what she had seen. Thankfully nobody had. She knew full well that she had to do something, but, not wanting to attract any attention, she calmly took her coffee-cup back to the kitchen, then walked slowly towards the door, taking care to smile at every person who looked in her direction, and even a few of those who didn't.

When she had passed out into the silent, carpeted corridor that overlooked the mezzanine and the spacious vestibule that sat beneath it, Rhiannon elected to wait for the lift rather than gallop off down the spiral staircase, and run the risk of toppling over disastrously in her strappy, five-inch heels. But, as luck would have it, this turned out to be the wrong choice completely, the lift, presently stationary at the top floor, clearly needing at least two minutes more to reach her.

On exiting the building, the tumult of the traffic at the busy junction hit Rhiannon like a speeding freight-train. She looked around her and quickly saw that the car and its driver - her mother, Gwen - had already departed, and all that was left behind was a wet brush and, alongside it, an empty pot, dripping splashes of blood-red paint down its side.

Embarrassed, and more than a little flustered, Rhiannon picked up both items, and, holding them well away from her pretty dress at arm's length, walked around more or less in a circle, searching for a waste-bin that she might safely deposit them in. But the poor girl soon found that there was none.

A man in a passing car suddenly screamed out abusively to her. 'You Welsh-Language protestors just make me sick!' then threw down on the seat beside him the mobile-phone he had been busy texting on, and raised his two fingers at her instead. What on earth did he mean? Rhiannon asked herself, reddening fast, and, tossing the two large, messy items she was carrying down onto the grass. Rubbing her soiled hands together, Rhiannon soon turned and looked up at the wall behind her, where, in large, scarlet characters she saw written the freshly-dripping word 'CALEDFWLCH.' But my mother doesn't even speak Welsh, Rhiannon told herself, so why on earth would she want to write up such a silly thing? And what the hell does that strange, almost unpronounceable, Welsh word actually mean, anyway? The girl turned and ran as fast as her stillettos would allow her back along the lawn to the neighbouring building she worked in, and then dashed headlong up its great, circular stairs. Reaching her work-station, she quickly clicked on the internet, and carefully typed into the *Google*-box the weird, Brythonic word her memory was unlikely to ever let her forget.

'In Welsh and British legend *Caledfwlch* is the name of Arthur's legendary sword, later called Excalibur,' she read out aloud. 'Christ alive! I know she's not been herself for a while, but why in hell's name would my mother -'

'Hey - I knew that!' her manager, Idris, announced from where he was standing, a few yards to her left, plastic coffee-cup in hand. '*Caled Fwlch*' he alliterated, splitting the term neatly in two. You see '*caled*' means 'hard,' he told her, approaching closer, and banging on his chest with his free hand, 'and *fwlch*, or *bwlch* means 'a pass.'

'Hard Pass!' exclaimed Rhiannon. 'That sounds like something in rugby, don't you think?'

'It certainly does,' the stout, bald-headed man replied, smiling. 'But I guess Arthur called it *Caledfwich* because -'

'Let me! Let me!' Rhiannon implored him. 'If Arthur was wielding it, then I imagine his enemies would find it well nigh impossible to pass him - to get past. Right?'

'Exactly. You got it, babe,' Idris told her, smiling again. 'Say - where on earth did you come across that word, then, Rhiannon? That's real, ancient Welsh, that is.'

Just then two young girls, carrying carrier-bags filled to the brim with sandwiches, sticky buns, and sundry snacks of various kinds, dashed into the room from the corridor. One of the pair suddenly walked over and addressed Idris.

'God, you'll never guess what some daft old bat went and scrawled on the front of the *Excalibur* building next-door, Mr. Evans!' she stammered, before bursting out laughing.

Chapter 10

'My uniform is but a rolled-up cloth I stash inside my bag,
My tie, a triangle of well-stained stripes of blue and green.
The only jewellery, my name-sake chain I catch upon my chest,
My indolent mind, a tangled web of thoughts obsessed and images obscene.
Who am I, dearest lady? Pray, do tell. To you, once loved,
who might this traveller seem?

Life's treasure is the latched-up box of memories I stow
'Neath bed wherein we once did writhe and write our love.
My breasts, two forest-fruits your tender lips did tight enclose.
My hips, that sunken freight your lissom body pressed, and thrice did rock above.
Who might I be, kind gentleman, who bathes her deepest thoughts in wishful streams?

Young lovers two, that's who these words describe, though parted now,
While time ensoaks the fabric that enfolds our loins
To test its denier-strength, its promise, and its surety,
Perchance to leave it stouter, whole, and free from joins.
Who could e'er gainsay young hope so, cannot love itself esteem.
Who would prise true love apart, may hell itself choke in between.'

Rhiannon smiled at the whispered words she had just read out, she now having managed to put all three verses together in less than half-an-hour of her first private-study session back in the school-library since returning from work-experience. She knew full well that Chris had somehow strained his damaged leg again and so was absent, indisposed at home, but accepted that she dare not attempt to contact him, since he had told her plainly, both by phone and text, that what they had had together was finally, and irrefutably, over.

But Rhiannon was of another opinion entirely. Oh, yes World, and you'd better believe it! she silently announced, by way of confirmation. Newly emboldened by her recent experience of work and real life in *Celtic Aquarium Solutions,* especially in the crazed, stiletto-ed swamp that passed for its typing-pool, she believed that, while she could still eat and breathe - oh, and wear a short skirt, a push-up bra, and apply daily her favourite Chanel mascara - there was still hope.

The bell for lesson-five sounded, so the girl folded the paper in her freshly manicured hands, stood up, and walked out of the room and along the radiant, sun-beamed corridor towards the Art Room, where her teacher, Mr. Cillick - Chris's father - would very soon be holding court.

The teacher wasn't in the room when Rhiannon walked in, but she noticed that, as was his custom, he had hung his frayed and patched-up brown sports-jacket over the back of the black swivel-chair which stood, as always, squarely behind his desk. Rhiannon smiled at her good fortune, and hovered above it nervously, deliberating furiously whether or not she should follow through with her plan, while her fellow-students wandered round and sought out their work from amongst the myriad of shelves, drawers, cupboards and chests that filled the lower parts of the peeling, pastel walls on two of the opposing sides of the vast classroom.

Nervously pinching a fold of her top-lip between her sharp front-teeth, Rhiannon looked down and quickly committed the three-verse missive to memory, and then, after silently whispering some words of a prayer her mother had often recited at times of doubt or stress, she carefully slipped into the father's jacket-pocket her literal expression of urgent, undying love for his darling, handsome son, which her tender, longing heart had just minutes before composed.

'Paracetamol doesn't cure headaches in Space,' the headline on page-four of the morning-paper declared in bold, but shaking type. Chris wasn't yet sure if it would work on Earth either, but he went into the bathroom anyway, and took another two in a glass of water, and sat on the toilet's lime-green seat, reading the remainder of the newspaper for an extended period, until the pain finally started to ebb away.

'Depressed man saws off his finger then eats it for dinner,' was the headline on page-six. Chris shook his head slowly. God - how disgusting! Wasn't there anything positive in the news today, he asked himself. He turned the pages until he reached the *'Music Section,'* wherein he was instantly shocked to see a surly-faced image of his new best friend Carla, holding her electric guitar across her naked thigh, and staring straight back at him. Well, he had seen that look for real only yesterday, he told himself, so nobody could question its authenticity. Sadly the two bottles of wine they had consumed when her father had finally retired to bed, and they were left kicking it in the kitchen, and jamming together on electric-piano and guitar, had rendered him in the sorry, hung-over state he was in right now.

Chris looked once again at the photo of Carla, then closed the paper and laid it down flat on the floor before him. *'His mobile-phone caught the sound of her scream in the woods,'* was the second-headline that he noticed at the foot of page-one. He picked up the paper again and read the article which he soon discovered concerned a man whose wife had been kidnapped, raped, tortured, then brutally killed in a forest somewhere in the north of England. Her husband was a drug-dealer it appeared, and he had failed to take seriously some warnings that a gang had been sending him via text-messages. 'Wow!' Chris shouted 'That's some scary shit, that is.'

'What's scary, Chris?' his mother called through the bathroom-door. 'You haven't gone and caught something again, have you? If you have, don't worry, darling. Doctor Pocock or Doctor Jain will take care of it for you, I'm sure, and I won't even need to come down the clinic with you.'

'Mam, what on earth are you talking about?' responded Chris angrily. 'It's just something I found in the paper, that's all.'

'Really?' she replied. 'Chris, dear - tell me something, will you? Why do men all seem to take the newspaper with them into the bathroom? You know I've never heard of a woman doing that.'

Chris suddenly remembered something, turned over to page-three, then quickly shut the paper once again and stuffed it behind the basin. 'I wouldn't know, Mam,' he replied. 'Ask Dad, why don't you. He's the teacher in the family, after all. As you're so often fond of saying, he knows just about everything there is to know about everything there is to know. And, you know, I bet *he* does it, too.'

'Does what? Chris, how dare you!' Anne replied, more than a little hurt. 'What are you implying about your step-father? He's a married man for heaven's sake. Look - get out of there now, will you? I desperately need the toilet.'

'But it's stuck to the floor, Mam,' Chris retorted, sniggering loudly. 'I'm sure I'll need a pair-of-gloves and a screw-driver, at the very least, if I'm ever going to shift it.'

'Out - I said!' Anne commanded him. 'And - and leave all the fittings where they are.'

Just then Chris thought he heard a foot-step in the loft above his head, and so he flushed the toilet and dashed out of the room, letting his mother past him as he went. He was suddenly in a frightful panic, and he only hoped that it wasn't the police who had paid him a visit. 'Oh, God! Let it be Carla - let it be Carla!' he repeated to himself, as he hopped about near the window in the front-bedroom, gazing down to check there wasn't a police-car in the road below. At least he couldn't see one anywhere, so perhaps he had mis-heard the sound, he told himself, as he lay back on his bed and pondered long and hard about the girl who lived next-door. It was that sexy picture in the paper that had started it, he mused. Feeling his blood rise, he turned onto his side.

Was he really too young for her? Chris asked himself. Well, she didn't seem to have any boyfriends, and she was quite easily the most alluring woman he had ever met. And you could probably count on one hand the number of men who had seen her emerging from the shower, as he had recently done. Chris didn't know whether he ought to feel fortunate on account of that, or accept that he should be rightfully damned to a brief life of misery and failure, and then a protracted spell in hell, as a result of the sweaty, libidinous feelings he undeniably felt for the girl, and which his demented mind had understandably, most likely erroneously, interpreted as love.

Chris turned onto his back, reached over to the radio, and switched on the local radio-station. Playing aloud was Carla's very first single release, which was, of course, no longer in 'The Charts,' but was regarded highly enough by the local disc-jockeys that they continued to play it at least once each day. 'You scream in the trees,' she sang, ' - in the trees where we found our love. But now it sounds more like a tease - to the girl who you rose above.' Chris felt he must have heard the song countless times over the years, but on this occasion he was taken aback by its lyrics - words which now seemed to him to somehow be freshly composed, and sung solely for his sake - his own personal experience - his own recent, brief relationship with Rhiannon.

Did Carla really write the words that I just heard? he asked himself, now in quite a fluster to find out the truth. He rifled through his bed-side drawer, found the CD that the song was on, and began playing it. But when it got to the song's chorus, he soon discovered that the lyrics were quite different to what he was convinced he had heard just minutes before.

'Holy cow! Is this how it starts?' an alarmed Chris asked himself, suddenly shaking his head about, and leaning across to see the somewhat distorted image of his drawn, worried face in the large mirror on the bedside table. Could this be the onset of short-term memory-loss, he wondered, and perhaps the related paranoia that were what his science-teacher at school had so graphically showed him and his class were the terrible, mental consequences - the inevitable scenario - of smoking large quantities of high-grade skunk on a regular basis, and which was even more worrying than the physical condition his class-mates jokingly referred to as 'skunk-eyes.'

This latter phenomenon, Chris told himself, he already knew Steffan and Jake, and a number of other of his school-colleagues, had developed to a greater or lesser degree, (including the Flynn brothers - Danny and Brian - who, like himself, were habitual users.) And now for the first time Chris was forced to concede that he could tell from his own bleary-eyed reflection which stared back at him that - yes - he had now also begun to be afflicted with it.

Or perhaps, thought Chris, swivelling his body round to retrieve the CD again, the problem was simply that he wasn't able to accurately recall the song's lyrics - the words he had listened to less than two minutes before. Yes, that could be it, he thought, smiling, since that must happen to everyone an awful lot of the time. Then, if that was indeed the case, he might not need to go and see someone about it after all. His A-level exams were now only just over a year away, and his whole future depended on the levels of the grades he achieved at the time, and so, he told himself, he would probably be better advised to put the brakes on, and start to get a firm grip on his usage. Yes, he would simply moderate it, that is what he'd do, he decided, since panicking about it, as he had just been doing, wasn't likely to help him one bit in the end.

The door to Chris's room opened slightly, and he instinctively called out Emily's name, forgetting that the cat had been gone now for weeks. Suddenly he recalled what Carla's father had told him about her whereabouts, and he was suddenly filled with a need to locate her, irrespective of whether she was dead, as the old man had suggested she was, or indeed still alive. Suddenly the thought struck him that perhaps it was Emily that was, in fact, the cause of the noise he had heard in the loft. Maybe the sound that he had heard had simply resembled a human foot-step, but had actually been their Persian cat moving about up there, as she had been used to doing. At least the notion sounded very plausible to him anyway. And if indeed it *was* Emily up there, he told himself, then he decided that some time later in the night, when his parents were fast asleep, he would endeavour to climb up there and fetch the poor thing down.

After almost half-an-hour of pushing and thumping and lifting, a precariously balanced Carla heard an enormous crash in the loft above her head, and straightaway discovered that she was able to force open the hatch for the very first time. Carefully maintaining her balance on the narrow, flat summit of the step-ladder, and slowly edging the top half of her body inside, the dazzlingly bright H.I.D. and sodium-lamps, and the extractor-fan's gushing sound, though disorientating in themselves, intrigued her right away. The step-ladder creaked eerily, and even wavered a little beneath her weight, but Carla found that she had enough courage, and possessed sufficient fascination with the strange, powerful, but familiar, odour that emerged from inside the room, to enable her to carry on and pull herself up. Within seconds she had finally managed to stand erect, and soon began to glance around her into the bright, glowing interior, where the cannabis-factory was clearly earning its corn by operating noisily at full-pelt.

'So this is where you grow it all, you wicked boy, you!' she exclaimed to herself, shaking her head about ruefully, but admiringly.

'Carla!' her father suddenly called out from below. 'Carla, dear. What are you doing?'

'It's all right, Dada,' she replied, looking down into the hall-way below her dangling feet, 'I'm just getting something from the loft for us. I won't be a minute, I promise.'

'But we've got nothing up there, sweetheart, I told you,' he retorted. 'Nobody has even set foot up there. And anyway, I thought they said it was stuck fast.'

Carla stood up on the attic-floor, and, with a slipper-ed foot, carefully pushed the hatch back into place. She then bent low and picked up the two large potted-plants, which she had earlier spilled onto their sides when she had forced her way in, and that she could now see boasted healthy, shiny-green leaf, and placed them in a safer location. Carla reached up on tip-toes and lifted the latch on the fan-light in the roof, so allowing a stream of cool, fresh air to drift in to the low room from outside, quite possibly, she mused, for the first time in a very long while.

All in all, Carla was staggered by the tremendous lengths to which Chris had gone to get his little business venture off the ground. Yes, this was a fully operational cannabis-farm if ever there was one, she told herself, and it was clear that the boy had taken full advantage of the many months, or years, perhaps, that the house next-door to his own had remained vacant, in order to convert its dusty attic into the *Aladdin's Cave* that it clearly now was for him. She was, however, at least heartened somewhat on seeing that the precious electricity-cables, without which none of this one-man enterprise would have been possible, were still connected to The Cillicks' own power-supply, and not to their own.

The many coloured balloons and little magical lanterns that caught Carla's eye surprised her just as much as everything else she saw there. They seemed to float as free as birds in the air-conditioned breeze that now rushed about them from all sides. Carla suddenly remembered that she had experienced something akin to this once before: she recalled it was the day when the record-company's chauffeur-driven car had broken down in the middle of the Severn Bridge, and she had sat back in the plush, yellow-leather, upholstered haven and let the sea-wind burst into her warm, insulated world like a great, fierce dragon's breath, and with such immense power that her floppy, cotton hat had soon flown out of the window, and had fallen, rolling and tumbling, into the dark, icy waters of the estuary's high-tide over two-hundred feet below her.

What *was* this place, anyway? Carla asked herself. Was it possible that this slant-roofed room, in some strange way, happened to mean a whole lot more to the boy next-door than just the roof-top hiding-place where he grew his drugs? Could this magical place in some weird way represent the play-room that the sweet boy had perhaps never had, or that he had once owned, but now sorely missed? She smiled at the curious scenario her imagination had just devised. To Carla's eyes, this strange, multi-coloured loft might easily be a place of sensual, if not actual, retreat, for someone who could never have imagined that it would so soon be discovered.

Carla lifted the hatch once again and soon heard her father's remote, sad voice complain. 'I'm not feeling too good, sweet. I think perhaps I'd better take a lie down. Perhaps it's the coffee.' Carla contemplated this last statement of his for a few moments, then turned again to survey the room, and swiftly registered the three large tubs of coffee-beans that the boy had set there in the hope of disguising the plantation's distinctive, clammy odour from anyone in the houses below. With her sharp finger-nails Carla nipped off some mature cannabis-leaves from a tall plant that grew in a large tray near the wall, folded them carefully in her deft fingers, and placed them, for short-term storage, stems-downward, in the sleeve of her grey, woollen jumper. Then, approaching the hatch once more, Carla eased her feet through the gap, and, slowly and cautiously, made her way down the step-ladder, and back into her father's house.

When I've finally got Dad off to sleep I think I'll come back up here again, and see if I can discover how crafty old Chris manages to get in himself, Carla told herself, smiling.

A blue-and-green uniformed Carmen was sitting on the bench just inside the school-gates, holding the tabloid newspaper - that had earlier held pie-and-chips - wide open before her, and addressing a similarly clad Rhiannon, who, having completed her work-experiennce week too, now stood facing her, paring her nails. 'Listen to this one, Rhi -' *'Don't wear uniform on the way to school - you'll attract perverts,' police advise girls.'* God streuth! What do they mean? 'Cause I bet you, if we took ours off right now we'd be far more likely to attract attention, don't you think? And not just Brian Flynn's, neither.'

'His grandad, for definite,' Rhiannon told her. 'Er - Trevor, I think his name is.'

'Oh. I'm not sure I know any Trevor,' replied Carmen, reading on.

''Course you do, Carmen,' her friend retorted, sitting down beside her. 'Trevor Paedo - they call him.'

'Oh, ye-es, I remember him now,' Carmen told her. 'Trevor Paedo. Right dirty old sod, he was. With his oxo-trousers, and his greasy sideburns, and his long, creepy moustache - you could spot him coming a mile off.'

'He'd be coming, all right,' said Rhiannon, looking into her friend's eyes. 'Know what I mean?'

'I know exactly what you mean,' said Carmen. 'The dirty old creep!'

'Say, didn't he used to live next-door to Chris up in Gloryhole?' Rhiannon asked. I'm sure he did, you know. There's another old bloke who's living there now, I've heard. God, I hope he's not one as well.'

'Why? Are you planning on going up there again?' Carmen asked, eyes wide. 'Surely not.'

'No!' retorted Rhiannon sharply.

'Are you thinking of getting back with Clicker, then? You do still like him, I know you do.'

'His name's Chris, Carmen! Not Clicker!' bawled Rhiannon. 'Don't go calling him that horrible nick-name again, please. He's not a dictaphone, you know.'

'I never said he was,' protested Carmen, clueless on the matter.

'And he's much nicer than Brian Flynn too, I found,' Rhiannon added. 'Talking of Chris, though, you know he damaged his leg badly, right? Although he's just come back to school now. Well, did I tell you what happened in the Medical Room when I had to go there Monday morning?' Carmen shook her head and waited to hear. 'Well, I was just passing this big stool,' Rhiannon told her.

'Now *that* can be very painful,' her friend replied, cringing noticeably.

'Eh? Shut up a minute!' Rhiannon told her. 'And he went and pushed me right onto it.'

'Onto what?' Carmen asked, confused again.

'The stool, of course!' retorted Rhiannon angrily. 'I just told you, didn't I? Jesus! I mean, Chris used to be my boyfriend. He was my first, and everything.'

'God, I wish I'd had a first,' Carmen told her, rolling her bottom lip over her top one to illustrate how glum the predicament, and her statement about it, made her feel..

'I know you're just saying that out of empathy,' said Rhiannon. She looked up into the air, recalling a particularly tender moment. 'You know, one time he sent me two sweet, little ducks and a bunch of sixty red roses. Did I tell you?'

'I don't think so,' her friend replied. 'I'd have remembered that. Do you mean through the post?'

'No - silly. On an e-card,' Rhiannon told her. 'And now - and now he's trying to murder me whenever he sees me. What the heck am I going to do?'

'Aw, come on, Rhi. It was only a push, remember,' Carmen reminded her. 'I wish some boy would push me over in the Medical Room.' She looked up, alarmed. 'Oh, I'm sorry. That sounds awful, doesn't it? *And* there's a bed in there too. God, I'm making myself out to be a right -'

'Push-over,' said Rhiannon, smiling at her, knowing that her reply had just prevented her friend from coming out with a far more disgusting expression.

'Yeah, I suppose so,' replied Carmen. Both girls laughed at the foolishness of it.

'Look - there he is now. There's Chris,' Rhiannon whispered, quickly looking down at her feet. 'Ooh, if I had a stool now.'

'Shall I go and get you one?' Carmen asked, grinning.

'Very funny,' Rhiannon told her. 'You know, I don't think he can have recognised me with my new hair. Or perhaps doesn't want to. Hey - where's he going? Let's follow him and watch where he goes, shall we?'

'Er - no,' Carmen told her firmly.

'Why not?' asked Rhiannon.

''Cause it looks like he's off to the toilet, that's why.'

'Oh, yeah,' Rhiannon replied, giggling. 'But listen - let's see where he goes for his lunch, shall we? I bet you he goes to meet that Pippa again, and I bet you he shares his lunch-box with her.'

'Ooh, what are you like?' said Carmen, chortling. 'Hey - listen. Salt and Pippa,' she added.

'Quite,' replied Rhiannon, convinced she could think up a much funnier insult if she put her mind to it.

'Rhiannon - can I ask you something?' said Carmen.

'Sure,' her friend replied.

'Please don't think I'm being intrusive or anything, please don't, but how many times did you two - I mean how many times was it, again, Rhi?' enquired Carmen, grasping her friend's arm to ease any pain there might be in the re-telling.

'Just three times,' answered Rhiannon, taking off a shoe, and rubbing her heel. 'Didn't I tell you?'

'Yes, you did,' Carmen replied. 'But carry on anyway.'

'Well, in the woods was the last time,' said Rhiannon, whispering, 'And the time before that was in the old tunnel.'

'Aah! God!' uttered a shocked Carmen. 'Say - doesn't that tunnel run under the cemetery? You'll go to hell if you're not careful, Rhiannon. You will, you know.'

'I hope not,' her friend replied, pulling the newspaper over her head, and hiding her eternal shame momentarily.

'But you said there was three, didn't you?' Carmen continued. 'So - so what was the very first time then?'

'I'm too ashamed to say,' retorted Rhiannon.

'Why?' said Carmen. 'It wasn't in - it wasn't in your bed, was it?'

Rhiannon took the paper from off her head, rolled it up into a semi-solid tube, and slapped her friend across the head with it. 'Well, it was almost as bad,' she told her.

'Where?' enquired Carmen.

'It was about a hundred yards or so from my house.'

'Nev-er!' stammered her companion, shocked, and showing it. 'Ooh look, Rhi! There he goes now!' said Carmen, spying Chris's sudden reappearance on the foot-path. 'He's going off to 'C-Block.' Oh, no! Isn't that where Pippa registers? Well, that seals it, then. Come on - I'm sure he hasn't seen us.' Carmen jumped up and tugged at Rhiannon's arm.

Rhiannon stood up and went with her, making as if to drag her feet. 'Carmen - did I tell you I sent him a poem?' she asked, as they ambled along the path together, arms clasped, and heads down and close together.

'No, I don't think so,' her friend replied. 'Oh, you mean an e-poem?'

'No - the real thing,' Rhiannon told her. 'You see, I felt I needed to tell him how I really felt about the two of us. Only - only now I think I did a very silly thing, you know.'

'What was that?' enquired Carmen.

'Well, I forgot to put it in an envelope,' Rhiannon told her. 'Think that'll make any difference?'

'I don't see why,' Carmen retorted. 'I never worry if I don't get an envelope with any of my birthday-cards or - or valentines even. After all, it's the message that counts, isn't it?'

'Do you really think?' Rhiannon asked her. 'Yeah, I suppose you're right. You know, everyone says I'm always worrying too much.'

'When I'm dead they won't need a coffin. They can just throw me over the cemetery-wall.'

The landlord and his barmaid laughed at my comment, but one customer took exceptiom to it. 'I work in Pant Cemetery, remember, Dyl,' said Jack Matthews. 'We have enough trouble with the crows dive-bombing us when we're digging up new plots, without damn bodies flying through the air at us as well.'

'But I only live across the road from it, Jack,' I told him. 'And funerals are so bloody expensive these days, aren't they, what with the rocketing cost of petrol and everything. I tell you if I still have a gasp of breath left in my lungs on the day I go, then I'll be sure to crawl my way over the road myself and just jump in.'

'Talking about graves, you know, a couple of months back I came across a pair of young lovers in the long grass up on the hill where we've just dug the new ones,' Jack told me. 'Well, they were still in a state of undress, and it seemed like they had, sort of, fallen asleep from their - their affections, you know. Well, I shook the lad by the shoulder, you know, as you would, and when he tried to swing for me, I well nigh stabbed the young bugger with my pitch-fork.'

'What's the world coming to, eh?' I said. 'Shagging in our cemetery. The dirty buggers!'

'Well, I reckon that *he* was. Skinny, curly-haired fella, he was. Them skunk eyes, you know. But the other one was - well, now don't take it the wrong way, Dyl - the other one, I was thinking - the pretty young girl whose shame was barely covered by a couple of wreaths - might just have been your Rhiannon.'

'Rhiannon!' I stammered. 'My Rhiannon! Naw! It can't have been. Jack. Are you sure about this?' I asked, my mouth wide open.

'As I live and breathe, yes, I swear it was your Rhiannon,' replied Jack. 'Listen, Dyl - how the hell could I be mistaken? I've known your daughter all her life, haven't I? Sorry, mate, 'cause I can see you're awfully disappointed. Say - you'll have another one, won't you, Dyl?' he asked.

'Daughter!' I stammered.

'Pint,' he answered, grinning.

I smiled at my error, and nodded my approval. Jack placed the two empty glasses on the counter. 'Fill me up. Buttercup,' he told the barmaid with a smirk. 'And less froth than the last time, if you don't mind, Betty. You gorgeous creature, you.'

I glanced across at Jack's eyes, watching the swaying, flowing movements of the girl's hips as she moved away from him, and then the earnest pull of her lovely bare arms on the wooden handle as she filled our glasses right up, and could tell that, despite his wizened old looks and his gammy leg, 'Digger' desired her even more than the beer she was pouring out for him.

'Thank God Betty didn't hear that last comment I made,' he said with a smile. 'Look - I'm not really the pervert you think I am, you know Dyl,' he told me. 'I know you've never really forgiven me over the business of Anne Cillick, as is. She was in my class in secondary school, remember, mate. Sat across the aisle from me in class all year, she did, and right opposite me in all my Art lessons. Oh, those Art lessons, Dyl. Each one of them was a sort of once-a-week liaison, you know - a silent tryst - where we feasted solely on each other's eyes, and stroked out all our mutual love on sugar-paper with wet, sticky paints that we mixed lovingly together in a shared finger-bowl.'

'Little wonder she married an Art Teacher, then, Jack,' I chipped in to lighten the tone.

Staring blankly out of the window, Jack seemed to ignore me completely. 'Two years we carried on altogether, you know, Dyl,' he reported to me proudly. Yes, he had plainly got it bad.

'Yes. she told me about it,' I said, accepting my new pint, and sipping its frothy peak.

'Took my cherry, too, she did,' he added, smiling. 'What a girl! I was a late starter, you see.'

'On my walk back we could always call in on her and get it back, if you like,' I said, leading him back to the table we shared..'Your cherry, I mean.'

Jack sat down at his table again. 'Say - did she take yours too, then?' he asked, drinking from his pint-glass more deeply than before.

'I wish she had,' I replied, taking a seat across from him. 'No, But I have to admit that Anne really was a very special girl. She had a whole host of unique qualities, so she did.'

'Oh, do you mean that thing she did with the tip of her tongue?' he asked, beginning to quiver.

'What the hell are you talking about?' I asked him. 'I mean her - her smile, her lovely smile. And her milky-white teeth, and - and that slight fall in her bosom when she, you know, took off her bra. What a woman, eh, Jack?'

'Aye, what a woman. Say, do you think we'll ever get over her, old boy? You and me,' asked Jack. I felt myself lost in thought for a moment. 'Though I can see you probably won't either, Dyl,' he told me. 'Women can have that effect, you know. Look at Helen, for instance.'

'You mean Helen-the-milk, from Pant Villas? Christ, Jack. So it wasn;'t just me, then.'

'Not her! No, the other one, Dyl,' he said. 'What was her name now? Oh, I know. Helen of Troy. Got taken away on a ship by her people's enemies, she did, and it started off a bloody long war, remember.' He looked over at the barmaid. 'Christ, I bet she would have looked damn good pulling a pint, don't you think? Anne Cillick, I'm talking about, Dyl.'

'You know I've recently been giving it some thought, Jack, and I think there are just two types of women,' I told him. 'First there's the girl who usually lives across the road, and who reminds you of your mother, but who you usually can't tell reminds you, if you know what I mean. Yes, she's so loving, and loyal, and she cooks a treat, that you'll probably end up marrying the girl because you find she's already inside your bones, you know, and it feels only right to do so.'

'Yes, I got sucked in by that one too, Dyl.' Jack cut in.

'Aye. And then there's the girl that lives over the fence next-door, and who sits on her lounger with as little on as that girl you always see in *'The Sun,'* and who you find you desire simply because *you* happen to be a man and *she* happens to be a girl. I mean, because of what you can get from her, you know. What you figure you need in that very special moment, so to speak. The dusky, dirty girl who feels just what you feel, and who would as likely quote verses from *The New Testament* as suggest you ever put on a condom.'

Jack laughed at this and said, 'And Anne is the second type, right? Was the second, I mean.'

'Do you think?' I asked him. 'No, Jack. I wouldn't say that. I happen to think Anne could be both women at different times of the week, you know. She was - how'd you say? - versatile.'

'You know, I like that word about her,' Jack continued, smiling into thin air. The beer had clearly got to him already, I could tell. He looked across at me and said, 'Dyl - did you ever wonder how on earth Anne got to be - got to be -'

'Saved?' I asked him, my eye-balls suddenly drifting left, then right, as my brain tried to fathom out what had made me speak that word.

'Aye,' he retorted. 'Saved. Not in the religious sense, of course.'

'Saved,' I said again, contemplating the strange sanctity of the word I uttered, and wondering why on earth I hadn't said *'spared'* instead, as I had done countless times before in bar-room discussions and family chats up and down the valley, and as I knew full well the whole world and his wife would most likely describe it. 'Saved,' I said again, 'from the disaster that killed all those children - those little departed friends of hers and mine.'

'Except for the ones who crawled out alive, that is,' he reminded me, smiling.

'Like me, you mean?' I said, staring down at the table. 'It was my brother Sam who saved me, remember, Jack. But, you know, what I could never work out is, how a girl who loved school so very much, and never missed a single day of it, that I can ever recall anyway, should be absent on the very morning the school had its life crushed out of it.'

There followed a long pause during which we both looked out of the pub-window at a young couple on a tandem trying to negotiate the steep hill, going down, and who were wobbling, and swerving from one side of the road to the other, in their jolly, joint efforts to do so.

'Dyl, can I ask you something?' Jack suddenly asked. 'Do you think their boy - do you think their Christopher - looks anything like me? Do you? You can be absolutely honest now, you know, Dyl. Because, you see, not very long before the time she got with child -'

'Jack, don't say another word,' I ordered him. I stood up and walked across to the bar, placed my elbow on it, and then turmed and stared straight back at him. I held his gaze for what must have been at least a minute, then said, 'You'll have a whisky-chaser with me, won't you, Jack? I know you want to. Let's forget about walking home tonight. We can always get a taxi back to Pant. You see, there's some things you and I need to talk about. And now's a good time I'd say.'

Soon after Anne found the poem in her husband's jacket she was so shocked that, without questioning the wisdom of it, she took off her coat and hat, and called Chris into the living-room, and shared the news with him. 'Chris, come and look at what I found in your Dad's pocket. You don't think he's seeing another woman, do you?' Tell me I'm being stupid, won't you?

'Daddy Drew!' her son retorted with horror. 'Aw, come on, Mam. Who'd want *him*?'

' Well, *I* did,' Anne replied. 'I do - I still do, I mean. But who do you think could be writing to him?'

'Let me see it,' Chris commanded her. 'Well, it's definitely a girl's handwriting, I can see that,' he told her calmly.

'Well, that's a comfort, at least,' said Anne ironically, peering over his shoulder at the looping blue words carefully set out on the lined paper. 'Do you think it's a school-uniform she's referring to? Blue and green *is* Pennant, isn't it?'

'Yes, but the staff don't wear it, do they, Mam?' he told her.

Anne looked into her son's face in horror. 'You mean - you mean you think this poem could be from a girl? A pupil? No, ne-ver. Let me see. Let me see. *'Images obscene,' '* she read aloud. 'Well, at least she admits she's got a dirty mind, doesn't she? The baggage.'

'I think she's saying *he* has,' put in Chris.

'Oh. Well, at least she's got that right,' she exclaimed. 'Though she's got a bloody nerve suggesting it, if you ask me.'

'Mam, I don't wish to shock you or anything, but the writing looks a lot like - like Rhiannon's,' said Chris, swiftly turning so as to examine his mother's reaction to this block-buster.

'Rhiannon Cook! What! But how can it be?' Anne replied, eyes wide, body shaking. 'He teaches her Art, for God's sake. And wasn't he her form-tutor last year?'

'Yes, he was,' her son replied.

Oh, hell's bells! And just look - she says she's had him *thrice* already. Good God alive! Drew will go to jail. I bet they'll lock your dad up, darling. They will, you know.'

'Step-father, Mam. Step-father,' Chris corrected her. 'But hang on - Rhiannon is over sixteen, now, remember.'

'Oh, so that's all right then, is it?' his mother asked him,

'No, but at least it's not illegal, Mam. In fact, in that case it's what they call *'consensual sex.' '*

'Oh, is it now? Is it, clever dick? Well, he didn't ask *my* consent, did he? Well, if the law can't punish him, then I'm damn sure I shall have to do it myself, won't I?'

Anne grabbed her purse from the table and took out some money. 'Look, I think you'd best make yourself scarce, young man. Here's a tenner. Go down the pub for an hour or two, or something, will you? But don't go getting paralytic again, or else. God alive! Just wait 'til he gets back. Just *wait* 'til your father gets home.'

'Do you mean - what's the meaning of the tribute carved on his stone?' I asked her. Rhiannon nodded, and waited patiently for my explanation. 'Well, you see Derek, my father - your grandfather - was serving in Iceland during the war,' I told her, placing the lovely bunch of flowers we'd brought beside his grave.

'In Iceland!' she replied, eyes wide. 'But I didn't know they had supermarkets back then, Dad,'

I got to my feet again and met her quizzical gaze. I felt this wasn't a terribly clever reply on her part in the circumstances, and I pitied her. 'The country - not the shop!' I exclaimed. 'Oh, Rhiannon. What are you like, eh?'

'Well, *I* didn't know what you meant, Dad, did I?' she responded, slightly hurt by my rebuke. 'Remember I dropped History for Child-Care.'

'For what?' I asked her. 'Child-Care! Is that a subject, then?'

'How do you mean?' she asked.

'Well, don't you need a baby to practise all that stuff on?'

'Well, Mrs. Coffey sometimes brings her grand-son Ryan in when she gets to have him off her step-daughter. The rest of the time we just make do with our dollies.'

'Dollies!' I stammered, making a face..

'Yeah. They're very realistic, Dad. They wee and poo, and can even throw tantrums if you know how to press their buttons.'

'Press their buttons!' I stammered. 'You don't mean -'

'I do,' she retorted. 'They've got these three tiny little switches under the curls on the back of their necks. The red one sends them into a sort of fit, while the yellow one and the brown one -'

'Have different functions completely?' I suggested.

'Exactly,' she replied, smiling sweetly at the comical perception that she could clearly tell our two minds now shared.

I decided to move our conversation onto more solemn things. 'Your Mam says she wants to lie just here, you know,' I told her.

'But she's not unwell in that way, Dad, surely?' she asked me.

'No, no, don't be silly,' I told her. 'I mean when her time finally comes. You know, love, if you ask her, she doesn't seem to think there's anything up with her at all. But, sadly, the doctor's got a completely different opinion, I'm afraid. Like me, he doesn't seem to know what the problem actually is, but he's convinced that something's definitely not right.'

'Yes, it certainly appears that way,' said Rhiannon. 'In fact I'm beginning to think that, perhaps mentally, she's beginning to get a lot worse.'

A skylark suddenly shot up and trilled majestically somewhere in the blinding, white clouds above us, and I looked up to see if I could pinpoint where it was hovering. 'It's a lovely spot here, don't you think, Rhiannon?' I said. 'Whenever our time comes, and whoever is first, your mother and I will be able to see The Beacons over the wall there, and hear all the birds, and even smell the trees and the wild flowers in the summertime.'

'If you've still got your senses, which I very much doubt,' she said, smiling. 'But if you do then you'll also have to put up with all the cars zooming along the road past the pub there, and all the visitors arriving in the car-park for the narrow-guage railway.'

Over the eastern, lower wall of the cemetery I could see that a long fleet of cars had arrived, which, for some strange reason, had elected not to venture inside. This puzzled me greatly as, to my eyes, it certainly resembled a funeral-cortege that had accidentally missed its turn, and had instead driven much further along the road. The cars then trailed onto a muddy track that led up to the largest sheep-field belonging to a neighbouring farm. I smiled at what seemed to me to be a monumental blunder on the part of the leading driver, but decided to pay them no further heed. Instead I took my daughter's hand and proceeded to walk with her back the short distance towards our family-home in Pant. Of course, neither of us was to know that the cortege of cars that we had seen driving past were actually involved in conducting a serious police investigation.

Anne and Chris gripped each other's hands tightly as they crept cautiously into the empty living-room of Tom's house from the back-kitchen, where the back-door still stood ajar. She then dragged her son, against his will it seemed, towards the large book-shelf beside the wall, from which she began taking out novels, and paper-backs, and other much larger books, which she started opening up individually, and whose contents she avidly scrutinised.

'We can't start moving things about, Mam,' Chris told her. 'It's bad enough that we've sneaked straight in here so soon after seeing them go out. Some of these are proper, expensive dentistry-books, you know.'

Anne looked into her son's eyes and said, 'You mean for a proper dentist, right?'

'Well, look at them,' he replied, helping her to slot them back into their rightful places, and at the correct angle, so that their slightest movement wouldn't get noticed. 'They must have cost the man a fortune all told, I reckon, even back in the days when he was a student.'

'Do you mean a student of dentistry, then?' she asked him. 'For someone who qualified to practise?'

'Well, what do you think?' Chris shot back. 'Derrh!'

'But he couldn't have been,' she replied. 'No, that's quite impossible, that is. Not from what Carla told you, anyway, about where they used to live, and the jobs he did to support her and her mother back when she was young.'

'Not a dentist! But why do you say that, Mam?' her son enquired, a puzzled look across his face.

'Well, take that silly sheep's skull we just saw, with all those holes drilled right round its jaw, for a start,' she explained to him, pointing back to the kitchen, where the sudden find had just caused the pair of them the surprise of their lives. 'What sort of dentist would ever resort to a crazy thing like that, eh?

It's quite absurd, is what it is, if you ask me. No, the old man is either mentally out of it, or he - or he just -'

'Or what, Mam?' Chris asked.

'Or perhaps he just never did make it as a dentist in the first place.'

'But now *you* are the one being absurd, Mam,' Chris told her, shaking his head, and pointing his finger, then running it along the neat row of dentistry text-books arrayed before them. 'Just look at these, won't you.'

'*Am* I being absurd, though? Anne asked, suddenly. turning round to stare into her son's eyes. 'Do you really think I am? Listen, Chris. You know how you always say to me - 'Mam, why do you always read those little books of childrens' stories that are written for the underfives?' And - 'Did you ever want to be a school-teacher, then?' '

'Yeah,' Chris answered her, smiling, 'And you always reply -'Of course not, dear. Whatever gave you that idea?' '

'Well, guess what, son of mine?' Anne continued, her eyes suddenly opening wide, and scaring him for a brief moment.

'What - Mam?' asked Chris.

'Your mother, was lying, dear,' she told him, biting her lower, quivering lip tightly so as to stop herself from crying.

'You were lying!' he asked, shocked by her comment.

Anne turned and sat herself down on a solid, wooden chair that stood with its back to the book-shelf. 'Yes, love, I'm afraid I was,' she told her son. 'You see, I always wished that I had been a teacher just like your step-dad, dear,' she told him in a voice that was audibly shaking. 'It had long been my ambition to teach 'Infants' ever since I was a very little girl back in Aberfan. I had a lovely teacher back there, you see, who was sadly lost. But, as the years went by, I was soon to discover - rather like - rather like I imagine old Tom, the would-be dentist here, discovered - that I just wasn't up to it.'

Carla sat next to her Dad in the back of the black police-car, waiting for the tractor, and the three loaded trailers it was slowly dragging behind it, to pull out of the sloping, green field they sat facing, and let the courtege of cars inside.

The constable with the bleach-blond hair pressed his foot on the accelerator, and forced the shuddering vehicle the pair were in onto the muddy path, and followed its course round to where it reached an aluminium fence which overlooked the sharp slope that dropped steeply into the deep, green, river-valley over a hundred feet below.

Carla could tell straightaway that her father didn't wish to get out of the car. Even when the other officer with the grey hair, the hook-nose, and the local accent opened the door for him, Tom's weak eyes looked back into his daughter's instead, and, without the need for words, told her plainly that the afternoon's excursion was all a wild goose-chase.

'Let me help you, Mr. Davies,' Sergeant Foley told Tom in as sympathetic a tone as he could muster, gently grasping the older man's thin, calloused wrist, and encouraging him to step out of the car and join him on the long grass.

'There's nobody here, you know,' Tom announced with bold assuredness from the back-seat, but then electing to step out of the car anyway, out of a sense of duty. 'I may be able to locate people over considerable distances away, as you've already witnessed, but even I can't conjour up a body for you if there simply isn't one around. Although I *can* certainly tell you where there are several others you might be interested in, if you like.'

'Bodies you mean! Where?' enquired the sergeant and the constable almost in unison.

'Just over that wall, back there,' the old man told them, smiling thinly. 'Pant Cemetery. Thousands of the buggers, if truth be told. And two or three freshly interred this morning, I think you'll find. Say - what was the boy's name again?' he asked the sergeant.

'Jake Haines,' Sergeant Foley replied, reading from a clip-board he was carrying. 'Sixteen-years old, thin, wiry, fair hair, and could be wearing a t-shirt, jeans and trainers. Missing from school for a week, and last seen two days ago at his home in Victoria Street, Dowlais.'

'You know, there are two boys over on the stone-seat who appear to match that description, Sir,' the bleach-blond constable suddenly announced, pointing them out to the sergeant and the others with his long arm outstretched.

'Yes, but they are alive, Ben,' Sergeant Foley replied, glaring at the younger officer with disdain. 'The boy we're searching for is probably dead. We believe he's been killed, you see. Therefore he'd be dead.'

'But how do you know that?' asked Carla, climbing out of the car and clutching her father's arm.

'How do we know that?' the sergeant repeated, staring deeply into the singer's lovely eyes. 'Because we have contacts in the druggie community, Miss. But you wouldn't know anything about that, I imagine.' He bit his lip and turned away from her at the sheer irony of his brass-necked comment.

'Well, actually, I do, as it goes,' Carla told him, to the sergeant's complete surprise. 'Five years ago I happened to get busted by an under-cover officer in west London. Only it turned out that the Met knew nothing about it. You see he was really acting on behalf of a tabloid Sunday newspaper. I dare say you know the rag I'm talking about. As a result I almost went to jail, and it scared the living daylights out of me. Nobody was really surprised when I decided it would be best all round to take a brief sabbatical from music completely soon after that. I didn't get to perform again for three years. I found I wasn't able to do anything except sit at home and write.'

'And your career - and the country, might I say - have benefitted enormously as a result, Miss Steel,' the sergeant replied. 'My grand-daughter has all your albums, you know. She's particularly fond of your second one. 'Candice Farm,' I believe it's called.'

'Yes, that's right,' said Carla, fearing what was coming.

'That's somewhere round here, isn't it, constable?' he asked, spinning round. 'Isn't it Miss Steel?' Foley could tell she wasn't going to oblige him. 'Tell me, young lady, what exactly went on there that made you decide to name your very own CD after it, if you don't mind me asking? As you must be aware, there have been countless blogs and rumours on the matter.'

'You really wouldn't want to know, Sergeant,' Carla told him, turning away to look west, along the line of the river's course, and way beyond towards the distant *Seven Arches*, and her father's home, which, though she couldn't presently see it round the obstructing hill that supported the castle, she knew sat perched, prettily but precariously, alongside it.

'No? But I think we actually might like to know,' Sergeant Foley responded. 'Listen - did you know that Dai - the poor farmer there - had to change the farm's name after your album went into *The Charts*. It is called *'Cwm Scwt'* now, I gather. A sad business that, if you ask me, because I can't for the life of me see as how that name's any better than the first one was.'

'There was never anything much to hide, Sergeant. That farmer happened to be a friend of the Davies family, that's all,' Carla told him with a thin smile, yet recognising from his stern, impassive look that Sergeant Foley wasn't buying any of it, and probably already knew about the vast majority of the scandalous activities that went on there when the weather was conducive.

Beginning to feel a little self-conscious, Carla turned round to check on her father.

Tom was standing just behind her, his wrinkled eyes closed, his body bent slightly to one side, an elbow leaning on the bonnet of the car. 'I am sorry to say I was wrong, Sergeant,' he said, 'The boy - Jake, did you say? - is in fact in the old railway-tunnel, deep down beneath us.' He is lying on his side on the stony ground, his arms stretched out, and - and inside his open mouth - ' Tom winced perceptibly at this point, and Carla thought he might be about to throw up.

'Yes?' said the bleach-blond constable, scribbling down all the old man's comments into his thin, black note-book as quickly as his young fingers allowed.

'His mouth has been filled with - it appears to be crammed full of -' Tom began. Then his hand shot up to his mouth and he spun round and vomited onto the side of the car. Carla rushed over to assist him.

'His bollocks!' stammered Sergeant Foley, staring at the old man, and nodding slightly so as to elicit from him a confirmation that he felt he barely needed. 'I'm right, yes, old boy? Say it, why don't you?'

'His private parts, yes,' Tom told him, as Carla held up his head in order to wipe his mouth clean. The old man suddenly pulled open the car's rear-door, and Carla, now pale as a sheet herself, helped him to climb back inside.

The two policemen shook their heads almost in unison, quickly realising that the long, blocked-up tunnel was the one place that they hadn't thought to look.

'Then it's similar to that one last month in Cardiff, Ben,' Sergeant Foley announced. 'The one in that enormous drain.'

'And I guess, if he's way down below us,' said the constable, pointing to the van at the end of the cortege labelled 'K-9,' 'then the dog we brought wouldn't have found him any sooner than anyone else would.'

'Yes, I guess that's true,' retorted Foley. 'As I said, Ben, it's virtually the same as what happened the last time, right? Which suggests to me that the killer could be one and the same. The tunnel-entrance is just down there through the trees, by the way,' he said pointing to the line of dwarf oaks and elms that skirted the precipitous edge of the rolling, boulder-strewn plateau that the squad of police-officers, in their long line of vehicles, were all now sat silently parked upon. 'Let's get the dog out of the van anyway, shall we,' continued the sergeant, 'and give the old boy a run. You see we'll need to go down there with a stretcher, and locate the fellow and bring him up.'

Merlyn Foley leaned on the open window of his car and peered inside. 'Well, it's a good thing you've managed to tell us exactly where to point the old fella, Mr. Davies, because I've noticed Cymro's no longer got the sniff that he once had.' He looked to the ground. and said quietly, 'Sixteen, isn't he?'

'The dog?' asked the young constable. 'No, he's got to be younger than that, surely.'

'No, the boy I'm talking about!' the sergeant told him sternly. 'Jake Haines we think the missing boy's called. Another bloody Valleys' coke-dealer, if our informant is correct.' He shook his head from side to side in frustration.

'You know, Ben, I'll be glad when next year comes, and I get to retire from this damn job, I really will.'

'Why's that, Sir?' asked Ben.

'Well, why do you think?' retorted Foley, dipping his head, stroking it with a sharp nail, and ruminating. 'Once again it's me that'll have to go and tell the poor lad's parents, you see.' He shook his head from side to side. 'And although I've never found it easy having to do that, even though it's a task you have to accept is part and parcel of the policeman's job, I'm definitely getting to hate it a lot more these days now that the poor buggers are getting to be so incredibly young.'

CHAPTER 11

Chris was wondering why he felt a great gaping hole in his existence these days, and he soon decided that the likely cause of it was the fact that Emily hadn't come home, and that he hadn't been able to locate her in any of the potential sites he knew about - underground, or otherwise. Annoyingly he believed that his mother held him responsible for the strange event, even though she had not once actually said so to his face. And this apparent dishonesty on her part to his mind illustrated the lack of trust she now had in him generally, and, perhaps, the absence of any genuine love for him, which he might find understandable had she found out about the use to which he had put next-door's loft, or that he had begun selling drugs once again, but which nevertheless undermined his self-confidence greatly.

A group of boys in rugby-practice had once called him *'a mummy's boy,'* and, although he had managed to get them to retract the slight almost immediately, through a mixture of bluster and physical exuberance on his part, he could now see quite clearly that they had been right all along, and that it was probably best just to acknowledge and accept the fact. The girls who came into his life had no realistic chance with him, he told himself with a shrug of the head; none of them, least of all Pippa or Rhiannon. This was largely because his mother had already met them, had swiftly summed them up, in that infernal all-seeing, all-knowing way of hers, and dismissed them both as sluts and harpies, and patently beneath him.

No. Pippa, Rhiannon and the other, younger ones, who seemed to plague him daily in the school-playground, stood no real chance of getting him to commit fully to them. The girls concerned were doomed even before they received their first valentine, their first bouquet, their first guitar-serenade, even if they ever got so far as to be invited to the home he shared with his family. Each would sooner or later have to admit that, though they might love him, they wouldn't be able to claim him for themselves. And Chris knew full well that this had all been his mother's doing, even if she would never acknowledge it, or probably even agree to discuss the subject.

Chris searched his brain for an example of how this all-consuming, all-singing, all-dancing love of his mother's had found expression in his life, so that he might, hopefully before long, relate it to Carla and glean her opinion. He tried to imagine her response when he told her of his concerns. 'I'd say it's almost as if you have a T-shirt on under your school-shirt that displays text that reads '*Property of Anne Cillick - kindly return after use.*' Yes, he told himself, Carla's response would almost certainly be along those lines, and he felt heartily glad that it would be.

Chris chuckled despairingly, then, suddenly sensing the greater than usual depth of the afternoon reverie that his waking mind had succumbed to, looked around him, and suddenly remembered that he wasn't alone.

Despite the pain caused by the tight bandage that he still wore on his right thigh, the piercing cramp that he felt in his buttocks, and the unmistakable, burgeoning onset of hemorrhoids just a centimetre or two away from that spot, Chris was spending his lunch-hour sitting on the uncarpeted floor of the dim and dusty science-corridor, once again holding hands with Pippa Jenkins. He reached up his free, right hand and rubbed a bleary eye.

Just then the seemingly oblivious, mini-skirted form that was Rhiannon Cook suddenly stepped over the two of them, then strode purposefully away into the illuminated end of the hallway, where the one o'clock sun streamed in powerfully, spreading its warmth horizontally, but slowly, up in the direction where the uniformed, newly-united, couple were awkwardly sitting.

'God! You can even see her bra - the peanut-smuggler!' Pippa suddenly announced, in a high, sneering tone, though too late, of course, for Chris to be able to catch a glimpse of the enticng sight himself. 'I reckon she's a student rep for *'We Buy Any Bra Dot Com,'* she told him, giggling. 'You know, I can't understand what you ever saw in her, Chris. And what pale, thin legs she's got, too - the lanky, old goose. Euggh!'

Chris eyed the slender calves he had once loved pass through the fire-door and walk out into the bright school-yard, from where cries of boys punting a rugby-ball back and forth pierced the afternoon air. From the jerking movements that her body made, he predicted that Pippa was far from done. Yes, another deprecating comment was plainly imminent, he felt, and so it was.

'You know, when she went to Switzerland with her German class last year, two girls from the hockey-team claimed she tried to get into bed with them. What do you think of that, Chris, eh? The dirty bitch! If she's not a full-on lesbian, then I'd say she has to be bi- , don't you think?'

Chris wasn't really listening to the vindictive diatribe emerging from the rose-painted, warbling mouth that moved thinly, and somewhat dementedly, just a foot or so from his, now throbbing, over-warm face. He knew from personal experience that Rhiannon wasn't anything but heterosexual, and calling the girl *'old'* like that was simply plain spiteful, since she had spent five years of the last six in the same year that he was in, until that sad day, almost a year ago now, when she was informed that her subject-levels and her test-grades were so disappointing that she needed to be kept back for a second year in Year Eleven. It turned out that he had been far more gutted than she was, Chris recalled, her dad quickly sensing that, in the long run, this would undoubtedly give his daughter the best possible chance of future success. And so it had proved, since she was not only leader of the school-band these days, but had been given an award that recognised her academic progress and achievements. And, only weeks before, Chris had shared in Rhiannon's joy and celebrated it with her with a weekend-meal at *'Nando's.'*

'You know, she's so dumb, that girl, that she took a scarf back to Debenhams because it was too tight.'

Leaning forward, and rubbing the cramp from the taut muscles of his bottom, Chris slowly got to his feet, looked down insightfully, for what would be the first and last time, at Pippa's lolling, bleach-blond skull, contrasted it instinctively with Rhiannon's finely shaped head and deliciously flowing tresses, shouldered his school-bag, and marched off towards the still-closing, glass fire-door. This he not only stopped in its tracks, but fairly took off its metal hinges, with an almighty, thumping, drop-kick, and, turning to the right, and breaking into a lumbering trot, hurried after his former girlfriend through the long line of regimentally parked-cars that bordered the playground.

In the leafy lane that circuited the astro-turf, Chris must have called Rhiannon's name a dozen times or more before she even deigned to look back once in his direction, and then only to verbally compare him to an orifice in which, sadly, he was presently experiencing the most severe of pains. It was four o'clock that afternoon before she finally chose to even address him by his name, and seven-thirty p.m. before she engaged him in any meaningful conversation.

In the deepening shadows at the side of the house that her mother had recently, and somewhat bizarrely, decided to name 'Caerleon,' (and so had attached a wooden board to its front-wall that, artlessly, declared the same,) Rhiannon told Chris that she definitely wasn't a girl for turning, and that taking a backward step in life was, and always had been, anathema to her, since it invariably led to bitterness and regret. She even declared things that she had hitherto kept from him, such as the fact that her friends had all warned her against getting back with him on account of the fact that he might, after all, be gay, that he unquestionably took drugs, and that he appeared to have caught a lethal dose of acne from the bottle-bronzed, but fast-peeling, Pippa Jenkins, and possibly a lot more besides.

All of this was, of course, true, Chris told her, turning, as he did so, to survey the back-garden with a far more relaxed, but characteristically mischievous, smile on his face. (He had never been properly invited inside her house in all the time he had known her.) Chris told her that he had meant to admit the truth to her of all the points she had just re-listed, but he found that whenever his phone hadn't needed re-charging, he was inexplicably out of credit.

Instead of replying, Rhiannon smiled a pinched grin at Chris's typically ludicrous confession, but closed the side-door anyway, stole away upstairs, and only dared gaze lovingly at him from her bedroom-window once he had negotiated safely the cemetery-wall, in a style very similar to what her high-jump instructor had called 'a western roll.' Removing her school-uniform, the girl continued to watch, wide-eyed, and with a mixture of wonder and trepidation, as her lover's lithe young body limped its way away from her through the green and yellow grass, typically threading its way in and out of the toppled, and standing, grave-stones, around statues of angels, turf-piles and tombs, finally disappearing from her line of sight as he traversed the hill and rounded the huge tree beside her grandfather's grave, (which, for Rhiannon, would now always have tender and erotic significance,) on his long and winding trek back to *Gloryhole*.

In the study of her house Anne stopped typing on her computer key-board, and once again unfolded the piece of paper that she had first discovered in the car on the way to *Sketchley's*, when she had taken some of Drew's school-clothes to be cleaned. Nervously folding down its four corners with her finger-nail, she recalled how she had dragged the grubby handkerchief out of a pocket, and as she did so, a few of Drew's inky pens, and the folded love-poem that encircled them, had literally fallen into her lap. It had made her cry at that moment, she recalled, and now it did so again.

Anne had meant to confront her husband about it, but, though she had confided in her son, and even succeeded in getting him out of the house, Drew hadn't returned home again until well after mother and son had gone off to bed, and so the matter had sat unresolved, suspended, not unlike a certain stale smell in one of the bedrooms in the house, which, if investigated, would more than likely require far more of her time and effort to clean up than she felt she could honestly manage at present.

This was the second time in their married life that this sort of thing had happened, Anne reminded herself. Rightly or wrongly, she had let the first one go. And anyway, just a week or two later the young, and overly pretty, French teacher had packed away her false-lashes and nails, her red, plastic tongue-piercing, and her coulottes, her *Cacherel* perfumes, and her eaux-de-colognes and fled back, by way of ferry, to Dieppe. And not a moment too soon, to Anne's mind. But forgiving her husband a second time was something that Anne had sworn to herself that she would never ever do. Perhaps her mother had been right about him after all, she pondered: perhaps Drew did possess both the stability, as well as the complexion, of sick.

'He can't do anything except paint,' her mother had shouted at her from the top of the stairs one day. 'His nails are so short he can't even undo a simple knot in his shoe-laces unless you've started it for him. And what good is Drew going to be if there's a flood in your house, for heaven's sake! He has no idea where the stop-tap is. He'll probably end up doing what Noah did, and let his whole house and family just float away to - to Babylon.'

'But we live on a hill, Mam,' Anne had told her, partially in his defence, but knowing in her heart of hearts that she was right.

'Then the house is sure to end up at the bottom of it - mark my words, girl,' Betty had told her. 'And, do you know, I'm not sure the man would even care, to be honest. Why is he like this, eh? Tell me. Look, I know he's English, but isn't his mother's family from near Swansea?'

'Mumbles,' Anne corrected her, for what it was worth.

'Yes, and that gets on my nerves, too,' Betty had added. 'Especially when he does it at table.'

'Mumbles, Mam! Mumbles by *'The Gower,'* Anne had told her. 'Got their own yacht, and everything.'

But Betty had carried on just as if her daughter hadn't spoken. 'You know, I can't see what you didn't like about Dillwyn Graff, the undertaker's son from Bedlinog. He had a steady job, so he did, a suit-allowance, shaved twice-a-day, and he was very, very good with the horses. And, unlike Drew, he always drove his car very carefully,' she told her daughter.

'Far too slowly, you mean, Mam,' Anne had replied. 'You wouldn't know how annoying it is to be stared at doing forty on the M.4.'

'Well, you can't be breaking the speed-limit if you're carrying a great big box in the back, now can you?' Betty had continued. 'What on earth would the traffic-police say, for a start, not to mention the dead's relatives? No, you missed a trick there with Dillwyn, young lady, and by now I'm sure you know it. Yes, you'd have been living in paradise by this time, so you would. Me, as well, perhaps, if he'd have had me. And in a house full of flowers, too. Nice.'

'That forever need watering,' Anne had retorted sharply. 'Instead, here I am surrounded by walls and walls of Drew's lovely paintings. And some of them are so romantic too, and so colourful, that you feel transported by them, so you do. *To The Gulag* and the beautiful *Algerian Pissoir* are my favourites. No, when all is said and done, I couldn't wish for better.'

Back then, that had shut Betty up, for a while at least, mused Anne, since she had agreed to attend their wedding, and had stood for the formal family-photographs alongside a very young Chris and the happy couple, and even smiled on occasions, when reminded to.

Anne turned her head so she could once again view the wonderful portrait on the wall that Drew had painted of the red-haired girl with the ringlets, but whose subject now suddenly looked to her remarkably like Rhiannon Cook. Then, gritting her teeth more than usual, she peered down at the three simple verses neatly written out in pen, and quite clearly conceived in the throes of love, and read each of the young girl's blue, flowing lines softly and lovingly to herself, as if she herself had felt urged to compose them.

Yes, Rhiannon might indeed have written this poem, she thought, on concluding, but, if she did, then what could be her reason for her spending so much time sneaking around with the teacher's own son? Anne's eyes suddenly lit up with comprehension. Why, so as to get closer to her Drew, of course, she proffered. I can't be certain, of course, but if this turns out to be true, and if the vain, middle-aged sick-bag I'm married to *has* fallen hook, line and sinker for her tender, but devious, ruse, as I fear he probably has, well, then I imagine that it's all over between us, Drew Cillick. Over and out, and no mistake, I'd say. If only I had some arsenic in the house then I'm sure I'd aquiesce to cooking your favourite stew for you tonight. And then I might need to make contact with that nice Dillwyn Graff after all, if only to bury your sorry arse in the morning.

Chris had read the story through twice now, but kept returning to the second paragraph. *'The body was that of fifteen-year old Danny Flynn, younger brother of Brian, and youngest child of thirty-five year old single-mother, Susan Flynn, of Edward Street, Pant, Merthyr Tydfil.'* Chris dropped the broad-sheet newspaper from his grip, and watched it fall to the carpeted floor in a more or less triangular heap of separating pages. For a few seconds he could only look down at the queer shape he had made, but didn't even recognise it as a mess that needed to be cleared up, as the dozen or so other patients in Doctor Jain's surgery, with their sick, red, glaring eyes, unquestionably did.

'Christopher Cillick!' the tannoy's high, feminine voice suddenly called out. Chris came to, slowly bent low, and in considerable pain, tried to gather up all of the newspaper's pages and put them back together again. Yes, there it was, he told himself, sitting back once again, and folding over page-one - the story of the killing of a younger boy from his own school, who had lived just a few hundred yards from the southern end of the bricked-up tunnel that Chris had visited three times in total now, and that the boy was finally discovered lying dead in.

'Are you next?' the old woman in the wheel-chair called across to him, with an anxious look on her drawn face that suggested that she knew he might well be. 'You're Anne Cillick's boy aren't you? Works in *The Willows*. Lovely girl, she is, aye. Ooh, you're the dead spit.'

Chris' mind was racing. 'I'm the what!' he stammered, not at all having followed what she was saying.

'You know, the spitting image,' she retorted. 'You've got her nose and everything.'

'Oh, he has, Margaret,' a middle-aged woman in the corner concurred. 'I was in big-school with Anne in County. Pretty, she always was, mind. But her nose - well, I'd say it was always a bone of contention.'

'Chris couldn't help but smile at this comment, then watched, rather alarmed, as two women in white coats approached from a side-room, bent over him, and put their huge, flabby arms round his shoulders.

'Shall we get you a wheel-chair, darling?' the one in the spectacles asked him. 'Or do you think you can manage it yourself? Eh? Do you want to try?'

'Oh, I can walk all right' Chris answered them. 'I got here all the way from *Gloryhole* without hardly any trouble at all.' He got to his feet and slowly walked forward, but halted again as he started to wobble. 'I'm much better on the grass,' he told them.

'Do you want your newspaper, sweetheart?' the shorter woman asked, studying the front-page as she lifted it. 'Oh, there's awful what happened down by the junior-school, isn't it?'

'I know,' her friend replied. 'They say the blade went right through his lung, the poor little mite.'

Chris swallowed, and straightaway felt he might have to throw up on the floor.

'And guess what they found in his mouth, Edith,' she went on. 'Oh, hang on. Let's wait 'til we've taken the boy in to doctor, shall we? Otherwise we'll have another right mess to clear up.'

The two women released Chris's arms, stood back, and let him walk on ahead of them, and by his own steam, into

Dr. Nita Jain's little office, smiling serenely at him as he went. Before he had fully closed the door behind him, Chris could hear Edith tell the other woman, 'Yes, I dare say they went to the same school, you see. And, you never know, perhaps they were a lot closer than that.'

Carla tugged gently on her father's dressing-gown, but could tell that he was already sleeping. She lovingly turned down the coverlet over his cold hands, and let him lie there on his back, so that he might fully absorb what remained of the pungent gas that still enveloped the large bedroom. Finally she picked up the joint and drew from it herself, and then, turning off the light, returned with it downstairs.

Carla too had a note to unfold and read, and which she had left open on the kitchen-table an hour or so before. And this one had arrived a day or so earlier in a more conventional fashion, by way of a post-man and a letter-box. In London she had had CCTV outside the house, she reminded herself, but here, in leafy *Gloryhole*, there wasn't even a camera to catch speeding motorists, let alone people who appeared to be threatening your life and that of your own dear father. But threaten them they seemed to be doing nevertheless. The scribbled letter, which she had read over an hour before she began tending to her father, had more or less said as much.

Yes, this is what you get if you are blessed with the curse of celebrity these days, Carla told herself. Determined to remain strong, she sat herself down on the sofa, picked up her guitar, and began strumming the very chords that had just come into her head. This one was a sad song, she told herself, almost a lament of farewell. She hoped it wouldn't be the last song she ever wrote with her father in mind, but feared that somehow it just might be.

Carla decided that she would stay up all night, if need be, just so that she could finish it. After all, it was her father's song, and not hers, she told herself, and she was now of the opinion, as was he, that the sick man was now entering the beginning of his last days with her. She called the song she created that night '*Shake Me From Sleeping,*' and, though never released, or even recorded, little did Carla realise that one day it would become one of her most famous songs of all, as, suitably inspired by its discovery on *You-tube*, and being encouraged by a local newspaper journalist to simply follow my nose, and advised by my evening-class tutor in creative-writing to simply jot down everything very much as I remembered it, I would one day get to write a whole book about it!

And then, just to top it all, one night soon after the following Christmas, I dreamt a strange, numinous dream that, on the very night that the girl's dad - Tom Davies - finally passed away, he flew down from the sky - from outer space, it seemed - and discovered that the choir of angels, clad in white, linen robes, that, along with his own deceased parents, his son Will, and his deceased wife Carys, greeted him when he stepped off the landing craft, were singing that very same song! Yes, it's the sort of story that's far, far stranger than fiction, I'm sure you'll agree, but I swear it was what I dreamt nevertheless. There again, I must admit I do sometimes dream the most peculiar things when I've spent the whole night out on the ale.

Standing pefectly still for many minutes, with his back to the windy parapet of the great viaduct, the coldness Chris felt seemed only to alter in increments of freezing. He had gone to school that day without a coat, and he now bitterly regretted it. He looked up as if for comfort. There were places in the sky where the clouds were parting very like the fingers of an enormous hand, once clasped, but now very slowly letting go. The enormous waxing, gibbous moon seemed suddenly to leap into one of these divisions, and instantly transfigured the river's valley beneath it with a glow that lit up every tree, bush and fern, every bird, lizard and rodent, indeed every living thing that concealed itself silently beneath its thick foliage, as well as those creatures that didn't, which included the man, cowering, but no longer concealed, at the top of the bank behind his family-home, and whom Chris could now clearly make out was holding a gun. .

What on earth is he doing there? Chris asked himself. Even from a distance he could see that the man seemed to be very tall, and was wrapped in a short coat, the hood of which seemed to have fallen forward and almost down to his eyes. And why was he standing as still as a statue on the narrow path just above where the train-tracks had once run, and where a steam-engine that had just crossed the viaduct in the old days would have needed to slow before passing under the road-bridge, and entering the former station-halt, that was nowadays barely a cracked, pock-marked platform, so weathered and broken up was the stone it was built of.

Chris knew that he was just a hundred yards or so from the safety of his family and home. To his left and right the shoulder-high limestone walls, (a hundred feet or so below which the River Taff ran on in babbling solitude,) far from offering him security, told him only that he was completely hemmed in. In fact, should the gun-man spot him, and walk onto the great bridge towards him, or, worse, if an accomplice of the man were suddenly to approach him from the rear, then he would have little option but to jump, and most certainly to his death. Chris shivered again, and turned and looked along the trackway by which he had arrived so as to ascertain that there was indeed no such person approaching behind him. Thankfully all that he could see there was the wide, grey, cycleway itself, curving away left into the great wood's darkness.

The illumination of the moonlight gradually increased once more, and Chris suddenly became aware of a second hooded figure, who, unlike the first, was bending low, close to the fence of his parents' back-garden, and clutching a longer implement of some kind in his hands. Chris narrowed his eyes and stared even more intently. The gleaming reflection that he soon glimpsed moving about urgently told him that the second, shorter figure was in fact busy cutting his way through the fence that belonged to his neighbour, Tom Davies.

Very soon Chris felt that he had more or less worked out what was happening, so he reached deep into his trouser-pocket, snatched up his mobile-phone, and key-ed in a nunber and rang it. Chris listened to it ring forlornly at least half-a-dozen times, then, thankfully, he heard Carla's sweet voice answer, 'Hi, Chris.'

'Lock all your doors, Carla,' he whisperted to her. 'Yes, that is what I said. And yes, I do have to talk like this. Then turn off all your lights and phone the police. There are two men at the back of your house, and they're both armed.'

'What! Are you being serious! What on earth do they want?' Carla asked him.

'How would I know?' Chris retorted. 'Carla, I'm really sorry if it's me that's sadly got you dragged into this, but it could be that they plan to kidnap you.'

When she was bored, or expecting a phone-call, as now, Rhiannon liked nothing better than to write her little poems. She sat on her bed in her coat and best shoes and knocked off one in less than five minutes. But, as she inserted the punctuation, she knew full well that her best friend would be absolutely livid when she got to read what it said about her. Rhiannon put down her pen, held up the paper, and read aloud what she had composed.

> 'Carmen McGra' (th,)
> Her eye travelled far,
> Her ear caught the faintest of sound.
> But tho' strident and tall,
> 'Twas no problem at all
> To trip over what lay on the ground.'

Rhiannon giggled loudly, imagining the shape her friend's face might gurn into, and the foul and abusive swear-words that would most likely fly from that great, tunnel-shaped hole Carmen possessed just under her nose, and which she invariably described as her 'cake-hole.' 'Oh, my God!' said Rhiannon. 'There could even be sputum!' At the very thought of it, she collapsed on her bed in a fit of laughter.

Suddenly her mobile-phone, which lay on the bedside-table, sprang into life, tinnily bawling out the latest rendering from Adele. From the next bedroom she heard her mother shriek, 'Answer it, Rhiannon! Perhaps Carmen can't get permission to go, after all.' At this Rhiannon's face made its very own gurn. 'Her dad's on the social, remember, love. Do you remember how Arthur found him that job, and then the silly man had the nerve to just -'

'Why do you *call* him that, Mam?' Rhiannon asked her, getting up from the bed.

'Who, love? Dad?' Gwen replied, sounding surprised.

'Of course, Dad. His first name may be Arthur, but the whole world and his wife call him Dyl, Mam - me included - and they always have done, as far as I can recall.'

'And?' Gwen cut in, clearly narked by her comment.

'And *you've* always called him Dyl, too, Mam, as far back as I can remember. But for the last couple of years you've been calling him Arthur, and I must say it's incredibly weird and incredibly annoying for me, as I'm sure it must be far more annoying again for my dad.' Then, much more quietly, 'But, there again, you've not been well recently, have you? And he does love you, and so I guess he's far too nice to just tell you to - stop doing it, you bitch!'

Anticipating a further response from her mother, yet not getting one, Rhiannon answered the ringing phone, but discovered that it wasn't actually Carmen who was at the other end, but Chris. Her heart leapt for joy at his solitary 'Hi babe!' but she felt that she dared not speak a word this time, even quietly, as she had always felt that her mother could hear soil creep.

'Tell her I'm going to be paying for the two of you,' Gwen announced, suddenly walking into the room, opening up the purse she held, and taking out two ten-pound notes. She placed them neatly on the bedside-table, and walked back out again, clearly not wishing to restrict her daughter from carrying on, what was after all, a private conversation, although, from Rhiannon's facial expression, it seemed to her that she might already have done. 'You'd best get moving, you know, Rhiannon,' Gwen called back, as she made her way downstairs. 'The bus'll be leaving in a couple of minutes. I dare say you can take your birds another time, perhaps.'

Rhiannon looked out of the window towards the terminus at the bottom end of the road, where no more than two or three people stood waiting, and wondered what on earth her mother could be chatting about this time. Birds! Birds, did she say? Rhiannon still hadn't yet fathomed out the *Excalibur*-nonsense, which, thankfully, the police hadn't chosen to investigate, or perhaps were still too totally baffled by, as she herself still was, to take seriously. But if one day they did manage to trace it all back to Pant, she thought, then her sick mother could either be arrested, or committed, or possibly both. At least I'm glad I managed to keep it all from my father, she told herself. He has his hands quite full enough at the moment, just looking after her.

Rhiannon spoke quietly into the phone. 'Where are you now?' she asked.

'I'm in the pub over the way,' Chris told her. *'The Pant-Cad-Ifor.* What can I get you to drink?'

Rhiannon laughed louder than she had for weeks. 'I'll have a W-K-D, if that's all right,' she told him, turning to check that her mother had definitely gone.

'Wicked!' he shot back, far from ingeniously. 'Look, I need to see you to tell you about something that happened last night,' he continued. 'Although, thankfully, it turned out O.K. in the end.'

'Well, I'm glad,' she told him, disinterested in any nighttime activities he got up to that didn't involve her. 'Chris, it's your lucky day, do you know that?'

'Why?' he replied. 'Don't tell me you're wearing those crotchless pants I once bought for you off that stall in the market?'

'No, I am certainly not!' the girl screamed back at him. She picked up the two notes her mother had left behind and placed them in her pocket. 'But perhaps I could do one day, I suppose.' She silently winced at her shameful wickedness. 'Are you saying that you and me are back together again, then?'

'Well, I hope so, babe,' he told her. 'I've already gone and bought you your drink, now.'

Rhiannon giggled. 'I see. Like I said, it's your lucky day, Chris.'

'And why is that, beautiful girl?' he asked.

She warmed inwardly at this unwarranted reply, recalling how he had said this to her a few times before, and once especially near there. 'Because, lover, for once I'm going to be paying.'

Less tham a minute later Rhiannon left the house and turned right to go off to meet Chris. But she suddenly saw that her mother, dressed now in a macintosh and scarf, and carrying something heavy with her in a polythene bag, had just emerged from the house and turned left, and was walking slowly up the narrow pavement of the winding road that led over *The Bryniau* moorland in the general direction of her school. Rather shocked, Rhiannon decided that she had best follow her, but at a safe distance. Since she realised she would be passing the field where her father's horses were kept, Rhiannon spun round and returned to the house, and fetched from the kitchen a bag of stale bread, then shut the front-door once again, and walked after her mother, en route phoning Chris to tell him exactly what she was doing.

Gwen soon approached the field in which the two old, wooden railway-carriages stood side- by-side, and which served as rudimentary stables for Gavin and Stacey. However, instead of continuing up the road, she eased her body through the low wire-fence, and, with her little booted feet pumping, marched right past the ageing, equine pair, and right up to the site of the two horse-boxes that were their neighbouring homes.

Rhiannon knelt low and hid behind a bush that grew beside the footpath, and stared after her poor mother with an anxious and terrified look. She soon saw her set the bag down on the grass, and take from it a paint-tin and brush, that were plainly different ones from those she had seen her using in town, and which, back then. she had left behind her at the scene of the crime.

'God! What on earth is she going to be writing this time!' Rhiannon uttered in dismay.

Just then Chris ran up the pavement and joined the girl just out of sight of her mother. 'I didn't know your Mam was a painter,' he told her, chuckling.

'She isn't,' replied Rhiannon. 'She's about to do some crazy graffiti if you want to know. God, this is so embarrassing, I tell you. Hey - there's nobody coming, is there, Chris?'

'Well, no, but I can see the bus comng over *The Bryniau*,' he told her. 'And it'll be driving past us any second now.'

'Oh, no!' stammered Rhiannon as, whirring loudly, the single-decker vehicle swung by. 'Chris - are there many people on it? Can you see?' she asked.

The red bus drove right past the crouching pair, carrying on it less than a dozen seated men and women, plus the driver. The passengers all turned and stared into the field to their right, but none seemed to raise so much as an eye-lid at the strange event that was nevertheless happening at the make-shift stables in the sheep-field that they no doubt passed twice daily.

Rhiannon puffed out her cheeks and blew heavily with relief. 'Thank God *they've* gone!' she told Chris. 'It'll be in Welsh, I bet you.'

'What will?' asked Chris, completely confused.

'The graffiti - the red writing she's doing,' Rhiannon told him, watching Gwen like a hawk, to see what words she was daubing on the side of Stacey's box. 'Look!' she stammered, 'it starts with double-L. What did I tell you? Say, Chris, how good is your Welsh?'

'Not bad,' Chris replied. 'But I've got Google on my i-phone. Just tell me what the word is, yeah?'

'L-L-A-M-R-A-I,' Rhiannon spelled out for him. 'What the hell is that? Llamrai? Don't tell me she's doing anagrams now.'

'Llamrai,' Chris repeated. 'Llamrai. In ancient legend Llamrai, or Llamrei with an 'e', is Arthur's trusty mare. Wow! This shit is fascinating.'

'Quiet!' Rhiannon told him. She's painting the other bloody box now. Here goes - H-E-N-G-R-O-E-N,' she spelled out. 'Hengroen!'

'Hengroen. Hengroen, as you can probably guess, my love, is the name of Arthur's stallion.'

'Oh, my God!' Rhiannon stammered. 'My mother's completely lost it!'

'Oh, I don't know about that,' Chris replied with a smile, putting his arm around his girl in an effort to console her. 'Because, after all, it is true, isn't it?'

'What is?' Rhiannon shot back.

'Well, the horses *are* both your dad Arthur's horses, right? Can you see what I'm saying?'

'Er - no!' she responded sharply, completely mystified, and looking it.

'O.K. But listen, Rhiannon,' Chris continued. 'Perhaps your mum just didn't like 'Gavin' and 'Stacey.' Yeah?' He smiled at her and added, 'I know for a fact it was ages before *I* did.'

Carla spun round and, standing still in the middle of the field, looked back at the upstairs-window in her father's house, waiting until she could at last see his familiar frame moving about once again, before taking hold of Chris's hand and setting off for their afternoon walk. The path they had chosen took them over the hill and through a coppice of trees, and then down a steep path into the wooded, youthful valley of the narrow stream, whose watercourse flowed away to the left of where they stood, on its route down into the '*Blue Pool*' in the River Taff proper, there swelling the main river's capacity not inconsiderably.

Late Spring in this part of Wales was customarily a season of wind and showers, but this had not been any customary year, pondered Carla, looking up. The skies were once again completely devoid of cloud, and the May temperatures were clearly more than ten degrees higher than one had any reason to expect at this time of year. She smiled, believing that the sunshine, which she already felt was warming her delightfully today, was just as likely to tan her skin as rapidly and as thoroughly as it did during the silent, blissful weeks when she got to stay at her little hill-top home in the village of Kalithea on the paradise island of Rhodes.

Chris looked over into Carla's face, and she could tell that he was about to pose the question she had hoped he might skip asking, at least for the first hour or so of their walk. There again, she thought, it might be best to make a clean breast of things to him, and let him see for himself that she was, when all was said and done, a genuinely good person, who was at least trying to lead a decent life these days, and not allow a situation to arise again where total strangers felt they had the right to point fingers in her direction and scoff. And what is more, now that she had returned to the land of her birth, she simply wanted to make her dear father's time a happy and comfortable one as his inevitable death drew ever nearer.

'Carla, what did the police find when they got to your house?' Chris enquired.

'You mean after the men ran off?' she asked.

'Oh, they'd disappeared, then?'

'Well, they must have,' she told him. 'I never saw hide nor hair of either of them. But I trusted that *you* had seen them, and I reacted straightaway, just the way you told me to.'

Chris bit into his lip. 'I - I knew one of them, you know,' he told her,

Carla halted and stared straight at him. 'Hey! How could you?' she asked, shocked at this.

'Well, at least I think I did,' he replied. 'I mean I believe I do, yes. The tall one who was standing back - the one that I saw was carrying a gun. I've never actually met him, of course, but I reckon it had to be him.'

'And who *is* he, then?' she asked.

'Well, you won't know him. His name is Volver,' Chris told her. 'He lives in England - Bristol, I believe - but he's originally from South Africa. He's an evil man, Carla. That I do know.'

'Is he really?' asked Carla, looking away. 'Then how would *you* know him, then? Surely you don't mix with people like that, do you, Chris? With people who are evil.'

'Of course I don't,' he retorted. 'But I hear things, you know. I got told that he was back in the area again. And, do you know Carla, it wouldn't surprise me one bit if it turned out that he was the guy who murdered that boy from my school.'

'Do you mean that Danny?' she asked, staring at him.

'Danny Flynn, yes. He was - he got stabbed with a knife.' Chris's voice was beginning to shudder. 'I know - I've heard - that this Volver guy always carries a blade and a gun with him in the dash-board of his Audi - in his car - in his bright-blue Audi that I heard that he drives.'

Carla studied her new friend closely. For some reason, his eyes seemed reluctant to fully meet her gaze. 'You say you don't know this Volver, Chris, yet you do know what car he drives,' she told him. 'Mm. Interesting, that. You know I'd wager a fortune that there's a lot more to all this than you're actually telling me, right? For a start I bet you know the Audi's registration. Yes? If you can recall it, then please tell me. *Can* you remember it, Chris?'

Chris looked into Carla's eyes. He decided to be part-way honest with her. 'Apparently, it's impossible not to,' he told her. 'I heard it's only got four digits.'

'It's a personalised one, you mean?'

'Yeah, and they are Dutch plates, not British.'

'How do you know that if you've - if you've never actually seen it?' Carla asked him.

'The - the colour, of course. I was told that they are both yellow, front and back, you see, with the letters N-L on the left side of each plate.'

'Shit Sherlock! I'd better watch out for you,' stammered Carla, mouth agape.

'Why's that?' he asked.

'Why? Well, I smoke drugs for a start,' Carla told him, smiling, and slapping him on the arm. But listen - you won't tell anyone will you?'

At this Chris laughed out loud. 'Well, I guess they already know, don't you? Look – let's be honest, shall we? I guess almost everyone alive on every continent must know that fact, Carla. I mean, isn't that why they wouldn't let you into the States that time to receive that big award?'

'Hey, I'm allowed in there now, remember,' she told him. 'I even have a house over in the States these days, you know. Perhaps you don't believe me, but it's true. Look - you can come over and visit some time if you like.'

'When?' asked Chris, excited.

'Well, when -' she began her reply. A cold tear suddenly welled up in the corner of her right eye. She rubbed it away with her thumb and prepared for the same event happening in her left. 'Look, I'll let you know when the best time to come is, O.K.? Trust me.'

'Well, this summer is bound to be the best time for me,' he told her. 'My final year in school starts in September. And it's already the middle of May.'

'Listen - do you trust me, Chris?' Carla asked, looking directly into the young man's eyes.

'You know I do,' he replied. '*And* I went and told you about Rhiannon and *everything*.'

'Well, if you do, then why don't you start telling me exactly what you know about this Volver guy you just mentioned? Because if you do that, and be totally straight with me about it, then I promise I'll be straight with you too. What do you say to that, Chris? Eh? Say. What's up? Pussy got your tongue?'

'Eugh! That sounds disgusting, especially coming from you,' retorted Chris, hoping that this might delay somewhat Carla's questioning.

'I tell you what,' she said. 'I'll start the balls rolling, shall I? Wait - that sounds almost as bad.'

The two of them giggled away, first pretending to poke each other in the general direction of the genitals, then grasping each other tightly by the arms so as to keep them from falling over on the steeply sloping field they stood in.

After walking on a distance, Carla put her arm round her friend's shoulder and spoke to him. 'That man you call Volver, Chris -' said Carla.

'What about him?' the boy asked.

'Well, he is actually called Kronfield,' she told him. 'And he certainly is very dangerous, you know. Extremely so. He's twice served prison-time in Holland, for a start. The truth is - he has been trying to blackmail me for years, and right now he has probably got easily enough on me - my unpaid taxes, my shameful term at Oxford, my drug habit, my sex life - I'm bi, you see, Chris - to succeed beyond his wildest dreams.'

Chris found that this was all too much for him to take in at once, but he still wanted to hear more. 'Go on,' he told her.

'Volver - Kronfield - had a young policeman killed in London a few weeks back, who had just stumbled upon the body of someone he'd once murdered, and was convinced he'd securely hidden away. Ironically it was my father who helped the young copper locate the body. Unluckily for the young copper, though, as it turned out.' Carla sighed deeply. 'You know, if I were Volver I think I'd be terrified of what else my father could reveal. Only he probably doesn't realise that my Dad was in any way involved. At least I hope not.' She turned to look into Chris's eyes. 'Right, now that I've got that lot off my chest, what is there that *you* would like to tell *me*, young man?'

Chris pondered Carla's words for a second or two, then decided he had no alternative but to take the plunge. 'The man's been buying my weed off me for several months now,' he told her.

Carla suddenly halted on the path. 'You mean Volver?' she asked, eyes wide.

'Yes, Volver. He has never actually met me, of course, just heard of me, you know, but he does know that the herb's quality is good. It's strictly business to him, you see. Strictly profits. He always buys it off me through two boys in my school, and it's they that do all the actual selling for him round here. There were three of them originally, you see, Carla, only - only one of them is dead now.' Chris gulped audibly, but forced himself to carry on.

'Jesus!' stammered Carla.

'But this Volver hasn't actually paid me a single penny for my crop yet - the bastard. He's just told me - through the two boys I mentioned - that I've got a big pay-day coming my way one day soon, and to keep my head down and keep on growing the stuff. And all the time I'm waiting for my dosh, Volver is trying to force the boys to sell a stack of cocaine for him. But Merthyr's not exactly Las Vegas, is it? It's not even Cardiff. And so they've found that they can't shift more than a few ounces of the stuff each week, and I gather the guy's not at all happy about it. People round here don't have that sort of money anyway these days, even if they had the inclination to use the stuff, which most don't. Carla, you see that, don't you?' She nodded. 'And, to top it all, the boys have just told me that Volver wants *me* to start helping them sell the coke, and now I fear I'm going to have to, otherwise I may not get to see any of the money I'm owed by him.'

'Christ alive!' exclaimed Carla. 'You've got yourself in a right pickle, haven't you, Chris?'

'A pickle! Is that what you call it?' he told her. 'I'd say it's a darn sight more than that. Listen, Carla - I feel really, really bad about what cocaine involves, you know. It's a whole other level, you get me? I mean, compared to blow, puff is nothing - it's just sort of recreational, isn't it? Whereas coke, and especially its variations, such as crack, well, it's - it's -'

'Reprehensible,' suggested Carla. 'Although I have to admit that that never seemed to stop me from indulging in the past, of course.'

'Well I feel it's almost worse than that, anyway,' retorted Chris. 'After all, you're a celebrity, aren't you? In the circles you mix in it's almost expected, right? Carla - look - can you help me, do you think? Because - because crack-cocaine isn't as yet such a big problem round these parts. And, worse than that even, I've already been handed the stuff, and I really haven't a clue what I should do with it.'

'You don't mean - so you mean it's all up in my dad's loft right now, then?' Carla asked him. 'The crack.' Rather sheepishly, Chris nodded. O.K., O.K. Then listen. I'll tell you what we'll do.'

'What?' he asked.

'I'll take the whole consignment off your hands,' she told him.

'You'll what!' stammered Chris, beaming, his mouth agape.

'You heard,' said Carla. 'And make sure you tell Volver that you sold it all, O.K.?'

'Tell *him*?' Chris asked, puzzled. 'But why - why is that important?'

'Just do as I say,' Carla told him. 'Listen - promise me you will, right, Chris?'

'Well, O.K., then. But the consignment of crack is on a sort of 'sale-or-return basis,' he protested. 'And Carla, I've literally got bags and bags of the stuff that I've never even opened!'

'Chris, listen - it's not a problem, so don't worry about it,' she reassured him, grasping his two trembling hands tightly in her own. 'And, anyway, I might discover that I have a genuine need for it all myself when my dad - you know, when my dad finally passes.'

Carla suddenly clasped Chris's lissome body tightly to her own, and the pair wept silently over each other's shoulders, and over each other's tribulations, in the cooling breeze that now blew down on them off the high, brown-tinged peaks of The Beacons.

'Gwen and Arthur,' my wife told the woman at the desk.

'I don't just mean *first names*,' she replied, without looking up from the register.

'The whole thing?' Gwen asked her. She shook her head around in frustration. She seemed to do a lot of that sort of thing these days, I'd noticed. 'Well, O.K., then. Best sharpen your pencil if I were you, girl.'

At this the woman looked up at us for the first time, and, with a wry smile, scanned closely, the (to her eyes,) rather obtuse married-couple who were her latest hospital arrivals of the day.

'Arthur Dylan Thomas Cook, fifty-six, and twelve stone three pounds in a good year, and any time but Christmas,' my wife informed her. 'And Gwen Hwyfar Ada Cook, fifty-three, and - well, quite a few pounds under that all year round.'

'You make it sound like a boxing-match, dear, with all the weights and all,' I told her, smiling. 'Fight night on Sky. The inter-sex, cruiser-weight championship of Wales over twelve rounds. And in the blue corner -'

'In the blue corner are the toilets and the baby-changing room,' the woman suddenly explained, clearly having paid little attention to anything I had said. 'The former are 'handicapped,' naturally, and we have to have the latter due to the silly new regulations they brought in, even though, you know -'

'I understand,' I told her, pointing to my right, towards the bright, red rectangle stuck firmly onto the bare wall. 'And in the red?'

'Refectory and day-lounge. And over there in the green corner -'

'There's a green?' I asked.

'And an orange,' she continued. 'And finally a lemon.'

'Five!' I stammered. 'But I've never known a rectangle with -'

She pointed at the yellow rectangle above her head. 'We're in it now, actually,' she announced. 'Very calming - lemon - don't you think? Tell me, Mr. Cook - has your wife gone on ahead of you, do you think? She shouldn't really have done that, you see.'

I looked around, but sadly my Gwen was nowhere to be seen. I quickly picked up the card I had brought along and made to go off and locate her, but the woman reached across and tugged at my sleeve.

'Just one last thing - is your wife's second name really *Hwyfar*?' she enquired, with a highly querulous look on her face. 'You see, I've checked our records and -'

'It isn't, no,' I told her, puzzled by the bizarre nature of what she had just said.

'Because I've worked here for ten years now, you see, and I've yet to encounter a *Hwyfar* in all that time.' She suddenly looked up at me. 'Did I hear you say it's *not* - her middle name, I mean.'

'Of course not. No. Gwen's middle-name is Ada,' I explained. 'Just Ada. A-D-A.'

'Oh, just Ada, is it? Well, that seems to be right, at any rate.'

'Yes, I guess it's very apt, in a way - Ada,' I retorted, grinning. 'Very short and sweet, you see. Just like my wife herself.'

'And I'm very happy for you, I'm sure, Mr. Cook,' she told me, rising. 'Excuse me! Madam! The reception is on this side if you don't mind!' she suddenly shrieked, at an elderly couple who had just arrived from the lobby. 'I can see you now. You see, this gentleman here is just leaving.'

Taking the woman's kind advice, I edged away from the desk and scanned the huge room, unsure as to which colour corner Gwen had actually wandered into. I knew her favourite colour was yellow, but, since I was already there, it was the red zone I decided to look in first, and so elected to wander into the refectory, where I was soon able to make her out, carrying two teas and two buns on a tray over to a table, at which already sat a middle-aged man, wearing a hat and sunglasses, who was chatting away to his wife. I wandered across there, and sat down opposite my wife and began sipping my hot tea.

I watched as Gwen bit into her bun, and became more than a trifle perplexed, on seeing her look up and survey her new neighbours with apparent disdain. She seemed particularly scornful of the gentleman sitting diagonally across from her, and kept staring at him, and tutting away to herself quite monotonously, and, for the pair of them, plainly annoyingly. I noticed that the poor man appeared to be doing his utmost to ignore my wife's unwarranted attention, but, in truth, he seemed to be fighting a losing battle.

My feelings of embarrassment were mixed with more than a tinge of pity for what seemed to be happening to the woman I had chosen to spend the remainder of my life with. I had already become seriously concerned with regard to the state of Gwen's mental health, and if my wife went around calling herself *Hwyfar* all the time, I thought - whatever that strange Welsh word was supposed to mean - then she clearly ran the risk of being kept in hospital permanently, instead of receiving help as an out-patient, as was currently the case.

The balding man across from us soon leaned in to his bleach-blond wife and whispered something, and then, in reply, I could hear her tell him, 'O.K., dear. If you think it's best,' and the two of them suddenly rose and carried their plastic trays over to a table close to the window, where they smartly turned their backs on the two of us, and carried on consuming their breakfast.

Who could blame them? I asked myself. Not me, for one. The couple clearly had the right to some peace and quiet, after all, as we ourselves did, in the precious minutes leading up to an appointment with a consultant, or a psychotherapist, or just a counsellor even, as was my Gwen's case. Attending just her second weekly-sesssion was understandably quite a stressful time for my wife, I felt, and keeping her calm, and relaxed, and under control was, for me at least, of paramount importance. Sadly what happened next caused me to re-jig our day's plans completely.

'Didn't we see her starring on '*My Granny Was A Tranny?*'' the woman with the bleach-blond bouffant loudly enquired of the bald man who was eating breakfast alongside her at the table that faced the window. 'I can well believe it,' I'm sure,' I heard the balding man reply. What the woman had said might simply have been a relatively hilarious aside had my Gwen not heard the comment; but unfortunately for the pair of them, she certainly had.

Rising up from our table, Gwen immediately seemed to look round for something to grasp hold of - a weapon, I sensed, any weapon - with which to wreak revenge on the woman who had insulted her, and, just as likely it seemed, to inflict harm too on the man who accompanied her, and whom she appeared to know, for reasons that, at the time, I had little idea about. Spotting a long roll of French bread on a nearby table, Gwen quickly grasped hold of it, and approached the window-table at a rush, with the yard-long flute held out firmly in her two hands, and borne before her almost as a knight might bear a lance.

Then it really kicked off. Receiving the sudden, piercing blow to the back of his bald head, the man's cup flew out before him across the table, spilling hot tea everywhere. Shocked, he turned, and then quickly ducked the second thrust, before a third, well-aimed blow from my better half connected with his bulky chest, and rendered him winded, and hopelessly draped across the cheap, plastic seat, and in dire need of medical assistance.

'You bloody nutter!' the bottle-blonde woman screamed. 'You've probably gone and killed my husband. He might have testicular cancer, you know. Dick!' she called out, leaning over him. 'Speak to me, Dick!'

My wife suddenly spun round and held her weapon triumphantly above her head. I found I was so thoroughly embarrassed at that moment tnat I didn't know where to look. 'If he's dead, then tell them he was killed by Ron!' Gwen screamed back at her, readying her imperious flute for yet another attack.

'Ron! Ron! But your old man is standing just over there, you old fool!' the panic-stricken woman screamed at her, pointing across at me. 'And you're still carrying the bloody weapon in your hand, aren't you? So how the hell can you suddenly blame it on him? Look - this is quite outrageous! Who the hell are you, anyway, for Christ's sake? Some crazy, demented, New-Age, battle freak?'

'My name is Gwen Hwyfar!' Gwen replied in an unfamiliar, stentorian voice I had never heard her use before. 'Gwen Hwyfar of Caerleon, is how my people know me.' She peered in my direction. 'And the old man you so rudely referred to is none other than Arthur himself,' she told her, pointing the crusty, flaking flute back at me. '*My* Arthur,' she went on. 'And this in my stout, right hand is Ron,' she added, holding the French-bread high, now clearly at least a couple of inches shorter than it had been before the battle commenced. 'If Dick is slain,' she told the woman, 'then tell all the world that the mighty lance of Arthur wreaked revenge for Gwen Hwyfar, and rightly, and summarily, slayed him.'

CHAPTER 12

Lying alone in his bed, sleep began to overtake him like a nerve-killing predator. Tom knew that he had to resist the impulse at the critical, final moment, and that only in this way would he be able to recall the main features of the dream that he had had - the numinous dream that he already knew was of significance, and so was therefore vital for him to recall. He kept his body as still as could be in the bed and allowed all traces of thought to simply drift away.

Time had to be ticking away, but Tom was determined that he wasn't even going to acknowledge the fact. He knew full well that the re-filling process was beginning to take place, but he was adamant that he wasn't going to terminate his present, perfectly relaxed state to even acknowledge that fact either. Instead he would focus on precisely nothing. That is on *no thing*. No, the very opposite of focusing was what was now going on, was already happening, he told himself, but he knew that it was best he shouldn't even resort to thinking about that!

The thinking process ceasing, 'emptying' was now taking place, and Tom was sure that the blessed 're-filling' was about to occur, however long that process might actually take. Yes, a solitary nerve somewhere in his being told him that the silent infusion had begun, but he decided he would wait until the very last second until he finally disturbed the process by even considering that it was occurring.

Just a while longer, he told himself; now just a while more. Soon he felt that he could hold on no more and would simply have to forgo his hard-won feeling of utter displacement, and surrender to the inevitable. There, he told himself with consummate relief, it was over. He inhaled deeply and slowly.

It was now the moment of revelation. What on earth had this dream of his been about? After another few seconds Tom allowed himself to think once again. Yes, he told himself, it had worked, just as it had done so many times before. The dream he had earlier had was back in place, and now every bit as powerfully real as when he had first dreamt it.

The little girl with the pig-tails in her hair ran out of the building. She stood in the school-yard, staring up at the black mountain above her. She pulled the black mackintosh she wore tightly round her, and did up the top button to keep out the pouring rain. The sound of thunder suddenly rang out above her. Without any lightning-flash it sounded again, then a third time, but a great deal closer this time. She could see that this was much more than just a storm.

The mountain began sliding towards her. The little girl reached her hand into her coat-pocket and took out a card. She studied it, then hurried away towards the gate. Swinging it closed behind her, she trotted off down the hill in the direction of the railway-station. Behind her the school grounds quickly became flooded in a black lake, whose putrefied liquid poured out, lapped over the pavement, and ran down the middle of the road towards her. She knew that the school-buildings had been engulfed and laid waste by the sludge and slurry, the dislodged trees, and the rolling boulders, that, having poured down the mountain, surged silently past her.

The steam-train pulled in to the station, and the little girl clambered down onto the platform and showed her ticket to the man, who quickly opened up the carriage-door for her and helped her to climb inside. Suddenly the whirring sound of a helicopter caused the man to look up into the overhead sky, but, due to the thickening clouds, he found he was unable to see a thing.

As the train pulled away round the bend, and chugged its way up the broad river-valley, the man on the platform walked back to the ticket-office, and sat at his desk to examine the ticket that the little girl had just given him. He flattened it out with his fingers, and laid it on the table-surface before him. It was a beige card depicting two rows of printed boxes of almost equal length, and which for all the world resembled two parallel rows of square teeth. There were one or two inked slashes scrawled upon it, and it bore the name '*Anne Morgan.*'

Tom knew that it was over. He slowly nodded his head and pondered over the contents of his dream that he had just recalled for the umpteenth time in almost forty-five years. God! How long ago that first time now seems! Tom told himself. Almost like a bygone age. And as stark and colourless now as it had been when it first came to me on that fateful, wet October night.

'Oh, not that pink stuff - please,' she protested. The young girl in the check skirt, white blouse, and pig-tails pursed her lips so that the man in the white coat couldn't possibly prise them apart and complete the torrid ritual. 'I shall 'appily go and have a filling or a 'straction, mister, but please don't feed me the poison.'

The man in white smiled at the little girl's comment and her panic-stricken expression, and led her by the wrist over to the desk where he had carefully laid out all his cards and records. 'What is your name, sweetheart?' he asked, donning his reading-glasses so as to verify her details.

'Anne Morgan,' the little girl announced, leaning her slim body forward, and twisting her neck in a vain attempt to make sense of the black crosses and slashes that sadly now disfigured the pretty, beige-coloured card that the man now sat studying closely, and which she knew had to be her own. She looked over and asked, 'Is that your daughter, Mister - Mister -'

'Davies. No, Anne, it isn't,' the man replied without looking up. 'It's my wife if you want to know.' He gazed into her little, pale face and smiled, and considered how sharp she was. 'I see you've noticed she's quite a bit younger than me, then.' He looked up at her once again. 'You're a clever one, you are, aren't you, Anne?'

'Am I?' she asked, a cheeky grin starting to form on her round, pale face. 'Well, yes I am, Mister Davies, as a matter of fact. I came top in the Reading-Test that we had this morning,

you know. I was the only one who could read *'idiosyncrasy.'*
It's true, honest.'

'Wow! And can you read this word, Anne?' he asked.
'No - 'No -' he helped her begin.

'Extractions,' Anne pronounced with ease, then smiled.
'Say - what does it all mean, then, Mr. Davies? Can you tell me?'

'It means you won't have to go to the clinic a week
Friday - that's all,' he replied.

'Well, thank heavens for that,' she exclaimed, blowing out
a great puff of air. 'Then I won't have to swallow any more of
that pink stuff, will I?'

'The pink poison?' he suggested, chuckling.

'Yeah, that's right. And I won't have to miss the net-ball
match, neither. You know, I picked up a niggle in the first leg.'

'Really? And which one is your first leg?' the man asked
her, looking down.

'The first leg. The first game of the tie, silly,' she replied,
smiling. We were practising for the second this morning, and I
fell and hurt my knee bad after scoring. Ooh! Do you want to
see it?'

'Not really,' replied Tom with a smile.

Anne's jaw dropped. 'But everybody else did!' she told him
sternly.

'Oh, all right, then,' Tom said, lifting his glasses, and peering
over the end of the desk as she lifted her check skirt to disclose
it. Tom winced. The round, red mark was truly a horrible sight.

'Oh, sorry, Mr. Davies - that's the wrong knee,' said Anne.
'I'm so stupid sometimes my Mam says. They both hurt really
bad today, see.'

'Wait! Is that a cigarette-burn there?' Tom enquired. 'It is,
isn't it?' The little girl's face flushed quickly and she turned to
look at the wall. 'Listen - you can tell me, you know, Anne,' he
told her.

The expression on Anne's face had changed within an
instant from one of joy to horror. 'No, Mr. Davies! No, I can't,
I really can't!' she yelled at him. 'If only he got to find out.' She
quickly pulled the hem of her skirt down, turned, and limped
off towards the door.

Tom lay snugly and silently beside his wife Carys in their great double-bed and stared at the two cotton curtains that were drawn closed, ten feet or so before him. The light that was beginning to seep through told him that, since it was mid-October, and the Autumn Equinox was soon to occur, it had to be about 6 a.m. Since he was usually awoken by the wind-up clock's shrill alarm each week-day at a-quarter-to-eight, he looked up and wondered what it was that had made him suddenly stir awake like this. He didn't think it was a strange, ethereal dream this time; that had happened around a week before. But he knew that something had definitely been gnawing at his sleeping brain for much of the preceding night, urgently demanding to be allowed inside.

In an instant Tom realised what it was. He then leapt out of bed and ran into the spare-bedroom across the hall to get dressed. Forgoing his customary morning-shave, he dashed downstairs and, rubbing his eyes, hurried into the large, rambling kitchen, where he threw some cold water on his stubbly face, and scoffed the two jaffa-cakes that his wife had foolishly left out on the kitchen-table the evening before.

Closing the front-door as quietly as he could manage, Tom hurried round the circular path that led to the garage, outside which his racing-green Austin Wolseley sat parked. As he climbed inside it, he felt the first drops of rain in the air, and cursed the fact that he had emerged from the house without his rain-coat. But there was scarce time for turning back now, he told himself, so urgent was the task that he had just set himself. No, that wasn't it, he mused. The task had really been set for him. Tom drove down the hill and accelerated through the sleeping village, where it appeared only the milk-man, and the Jersey cows that supplied him with his precious fare, looked to be up and moving around.

Tom began pondering over his bizarre new predicament. If He truly existed, as his brother frequently told him He did, then The Almighty had maybe set this agenda, he told himself. Tom realised that he would then be just a funnel. 'A funnel of love,' he thought, then laughed at the oddness of the expression he had just come up with, and which had always made him think of *Porthcawl Pleasure Park,* that sat in Sandy Bay, where he had first encountered his dear wife Carys. And it was in the back of her parents' caravan in Trecco Bay, he recalled, smiling, that she had patiently taught him how to play on the guitar and sing '*Wimoweh,*' and '*Love Me Tender,*' the latter soon becoming their own personal song-of-love.

'And if He's there, and if He cares for me, then one day He will bless us with the child we so desperately want,' Tom announced to the sheep he drove past, as he rounded the bend that took him towards Talybont. Then it would be His will, not mine, after all,' he told the dappled, Shetland pony that stood in his usual field at the foot of the steep, winding climb that would take him through The Beacons and into the upper Taff Valley. The creature blew clouds of steam from his nostrils in the direction he was aiming his speeding motor-car, on which the speedometer had once or twice read a staggering 'fifty.' 'His Will,' he repeated, smiling.

'I still have time,' Tom told himself, as he sped south, past the highest of the station halts called Torpantau, and then powered the car down past the stream, and onto the main road that ran past the two vast, linked, sinuous reservoirs, and on towards Pontsticill. 'Just as long as the letter gets there before she goes off to school, that's all,' he told himself with a forced smile.

The little girl's house was located quite high upon the hillside, well above the mining-village of Merthyr Vale, upon which it looked down through three square eyes and a door painted green, just like all the others alongside it. It was the lowest of a line of half-a-dozen identical cottages, quite plainly built to house the colliers, who dug and drilled for their bread daily, or nightly even, at the valley's coal-mine, which stood darkly, but stolidly, like a huge, latticed, capital-A, alongside the railway-line and its little station, and close to the road that ran away into Aberfan.

As Tom powered his saloon-car up the, now silent, street, he imagined how busy it would get in just a few hours time, when the local children hurried down the hill in the direction of the junior-school he knew so well, many of them hand-in-hand with their mothers, and others, like little Anne, he told himself, who went off to school alone, as he himself recalled he had once had to do in years now almost too far gone to remember. Yes, like Anne, he too had been brought up by just his mother, his cruel, alcoholic father having one day decided that he needed the love of a second wife to make up for the disapppointment and frustration he felt had been caused him by the first. Until the day he died, he had loved him dearly, Tom told himself, but things had never been the same, and his mother's lovely face, that he knew and loved, soon grew to be so lined and care-worn that his new friends took the dear woman to be his grand-mother.

Scaling the steep path to the little girl's front-door, and with the unsealed envelope in his hand, Tom noticed that there was already a scrap of paper folded up and gripped in the metal, spring-loaded flap of the green, wooden door's letter-box. Careful not to dislodge it, Tom held on to the paper while he deposited his own envelope inside the sleeping house.

But overcome with curiosity, Tom decided that little harm could be done by him peeking at its contents, and so he unfolded the grubby missive and began to read it. *'It's not true what the evil little witch told you, Bet. I never laid a hand on her, let alone burned her,'* was the sum of what was scribbled upon it. Tom straightaway felt he didn't need any confirmation that it had been written by none other than the little girl's father, although it was very doubtful she would get to read it once her mother had got to the door to collect up the morning's post. But sensing that there was nothing he could do, and that it wasn't really any of his business, Tom re-folded the dreadfully hand-written note, and placed it back precisely where he had found it, being extra careful now not to let the metal flap spring back vengefully with a house-wakening clack.

A whirring sound suddenly pierced the morning silence. Turning about and spying an orange helicopter retreating up the valley, Tom climbed into his car and drove off in the same direction.

Anne dangled her bare legs over the front of the stool and waited for her turn to go in to see the dentist. God, it was packed solid in there this morning, she thought, and all the best seats were already taken, so that only the high stool remained. She was confused as to why she was there at all, if truth be told, but glad that at least the bad weather had caused the netball-match she was due to play in to be postponed. Anne scratched her knees and wondered whether it was at last time for her to be able to safely scrape off the dark brown scab, and see fresh, white skin in its place underneath. Anne thought about the mess this might make and so instead pulled the hem of her skirt down once again.

The lady carrying the list of names came out of the room every few minutes to announce one and summon the next patient. Anne guessed that her name had to be near the very bottom of it, and, sadly, this turned out to be an optimistic guess, at best. After over two-and-a-half hours of patient waiting Anne made a decision, and climbed down off the stool, and, massaging her aching bottom, went and sat on the sofa in the waiting-room, that was by now deserted and silent. She studied the magazine on the long table before her and read about 'The Beatles' and 'The 'Rolling Stones,' and her personal favourites - 'The Searchers' - who had just released their latest record. She turned to the page which featured the *Pop Chart*. *Jim Reeves* was at number-one again, she noticed. God! How she hoped he would be overtaken by a much more exciting song the following week.

A second door suddenly opened and the sound of Jim Reeves singing 'Distant Drums' filled the room. The little girl winced. To Anne, this song had a mournful, scary feel to it, and so she walked over to close the door of the room from which the music was emanating. But before shutting it, Anne happened to look inside, and she noticed that there was a man in there, sitting silently at a desk, writing. Even from behind, she found that she recognised him immediately.

Anne tapped on the door and beamed her cheeriest smile at the man whom, by now, she felt she knew quite well. 'Mr. Davies!' she called out. 'Do you work *here*, then?'

'Oh, hello there,' the man replied. 'Yes, this is my office - my humble abode,' he told her, without looking up. For almost a minute the man continued with his work and ignored all of the girl's quizzical glances. To Anne's mind, he seemed curiously dismissive of her, and this made her feel quite uncomfortable, but she was determined that she wasn't going to show it. Just then though the man looked up and spoke.

'You had good news, then, young lady,' said Tom.

'I don't know. I haven't been in yet,' she replied, electing to sit down on the seat before him. 'How long do you think they'll be?' She and Tom sat and stared at each other. 'You know, Mr. Davies, I thought they might even be finished already, and had somehow forgotten all about me.'

'Yes, they do seem to have finished up, I'm afraid,' said Tom. 'But, you know, I can check your mouth myself, if you like.'

'But what if I need a filling or something?' she enquired.

'Oh, I'm sure you won't,' he told her. 'Do you remember a fortnight ago, when I checked your teeth in school? They were in excellent shape then, weren't they?'

'Yes, I guess.' replied Anne. She reached down and rubbed her knee. 'So why am I here, then?' Anne asked him. 'Didn't they trust you, Mr. Davies? Your boss never believed you, did he?' She giggled at the notion. 'And so I suppose that's why I'm here.'

Tom smiled at the little girl's unintended bluntness. 'Er - evidently they didn't,' he replied. 'I'm not a bona fide, fully qualified dentist, you see, Anne. But, you know, since everyone working here seems to be finished for the morning, why don't I take a little look, and tell you what I'm pretty sure *they* would have said if they'd examined you.' Anne considered this for a moment, then nodded. Tom stood up, walked towards her, and gently turned her shoulders round so that she now faced him. 'O.K. Open wide now then, and let me see, there's a good girl,' he told her.

Anne sat deeper in the chair, head tilted back, teeth bared, and listened as Mr. Davies counted that all her teeth were still there. She never realised that dentists did that, but, since one of the last of her milk-teeth had fallen out onto her pillow one night a few years before, perhaps it was understandable that a tooth-count was a vital element of the dental check-up.

Tom soon ceased his examination and turned her round to face him. 'The good news is that you have a very fine set of teeth, Anne,' he told her.

'And the bad news?' asked Anne.

Tom stared at her. 'What do you mean? There isn't any,' he replied. 'I think you should be very proud of yourself, all told, and very soon now you'll be able to make your way home again.'

Anne wasn't at all happy with this, and the glum look on her face plainly showed it. 'But I shall have to wait almost an hour now for the next train,' she said. 'And I'm sure I won't get back to school again until well into lunch-time at the earliest, and I just know I'll miss my turn for dinner.'

'Oh, so you're not going to be going straight home then,' said a concerned Tom. Anne shook her head. He sat thinking for a few moments, then said, 'Listen - I bet it's fish on Fridays, isn't it?' Anne nodded. 'Then let me take you to the fish-and-chip shop up the High Street here. I'm rather peckish myself, as it happens. Tell me - what's your favourite, Anne? Cod or hake?'

'Hake,' replied Anne. 'Ooh, it's fab, don't you think, Mr. Davies? I'll have hake-and-chips I will. And please can I have some of those mushy peas with it, too? Or is that too dear?'

'You can have anything you want,' Tom told her, smiling. 'You know, they've even got tomato-ketchup if you sit at a table. And would you like to do that? Eat at a table?' Anne nodded excitedly. 'Come on, then,' he told her. 'Let's go up the fish-and-chip shop now, shall we?'

The music from the transistor-radio in the corner suddenly stopped mid-track, and a BBC voice announced - *'We interrupt this broadcast to bring you a very important news-flash.'* Tom suddenly stared at Anne. He had listened to this stern announcement with horror three times already that morning, each time the death-toll figures doubling as the scale of the horrible event just down the valley developed from accident to tragedy. He switched it off and, open-mouthed, walked over to the hat-stand to collect his flat-cap and his, damp but drying, macintosh.

As Tom left the clinic and crossed the street, hand-in-hand with the little girl from Aberfan, he lowered his open umbrella a foot or two so that Anne and he could shelter together from the incessant rain that was falling on Merthyr, and that had been falling non-stop for almost a week now - the devilish downpour that he already realised had played an enormous role in the loosening of the stream-infused foundations of the twin, gigantic coal-tips that overlooked the mining-village the little girl came from, and that he knew full well had brought utter destruction upon the junior school that she attended, and clearly loved, but, sadly, would attend no more.

When Tom's foot haplessly landed four-square in the middle of a deep puddle, he stood stock-still, and winced with discomfort, and no small amount of embarrassment. Anne giggled loudly at the nice man's sorry predicament, and called across to him from the further pavement that she had run to, 'You know, you saved me from a drowning then, Mr. Davies. My Mam will be ever so pleased you did that.'

As the older people of the town gathered in tight-knit groups on street-corners to engage in mass head-shaking, and frenetic, but sombre conversation, Anne took no notice, and began laughing and singing to herself the fantastic new song about *Eleanor Rigby* that she loved so much, and proceeded to skip up Methyr High Street with consummate delight. 'My Mam says she keeps her face in a jar, too,' she announced to the rain-drenched world rushing past her.

Tom smiled and shook his head with amazement at Anne's innocent comments, her sweetly-sung song, and her comical antics. Yes, he was clearly right after all, he thought, to drag her into town that morning under wholly false pretences. He felt fully justified because he knew he had developed a strong paternal empathy for her ever since he had discovered, by chance, how she was suffering badly at home at the hands of her tyrannical and abusive father, who seemed to take out on his sweet, innocent young daughter the frustrations that he felt for his estranged wife. And, with bitter recollection, Tom still remembered clearly the effect that this same treatment had had on him when he was more or less the same age that Anne was now, and every bit as vulnerable; and especially how he had been forced to suffer the dreadful physical abuse of an alcoholic father, as well as the shameful neglect of a dangerously deranged mother.

Tom stood and watched Anne as she used both of her thumbs, as well as her impudent, pink tongue to create a monstrously funny face, then instantly smiled back at him from the doorway of the bustling fish-and-chip shop they were heading for. What was it that his religious wife Carys had recently told him Jesus had said about this? Tom asked himself, as he halted and took off his sopping shoe, and tapped it against the lamp-post, so as to shake out all the rain-water and the mud and grit that had silently worked its way deep inside. Standing on one leg, and leaning uncomfortably against the post, while gradually fitting the leather shoe back into place on his badly drenched foot, Tom suddenly recalled the precise text his mind was searching for, and said aloud to the wet, hunched-up folk of Merthyr Tydfil, who strode purposefully past him, *'In as much as you have done it for one of the least of these, you have done it for Me.'*

CHAPTER 13

'Stephen Hawking says that heaven is a fairy story for people afraid of the dark,' Drew announced with a blissful smile on his face, reading aloud from an article he had found on page-two of the newspaper. He turned and stared across at his wife who was sitting comfortably on the sofa watching '*The BBC News.*' 'So what do you think of that, babe?' he asked. She clearly wasn't listening, so he tried another tack. 'Do you sometimes feel scared some nights, Anne?'

'Only when you've been to town for a curry again after work,' she said, smirking, 'and your flatulence is keeping me awake.'

'Flatulence!' said Drew, feigning bemusement as to what she was referring. 'Moi - flatulent?'

'You could fart for Wales and you know it,' she told him. 'You scored a hat-trick the other night.'

'How gross you valley-girls are,' he told her. 'If only I'd taken that job in Barry, life could -'

'You could captain the team, *and* kick all the goals.,' she added. 'We had to move the budgie downstairs, remember. Poor Joey would have been a lot safer down a coal-mine, I reckon.'

'Is there anything else you'd like to have a go at me about, now you've started?' Drew asked, grasping the remote, and switching off the television. 'Well, I guess there must be something, because I can clearly see it in your face.' He sat down opposite his wife in the easy-chair, and stared directly into her eyes. 'Speak to me, my heart. What is it?'

'Why don't you try telling *me*?' his wife said, licking her lips nervously. 'Tell me what you're thinking now, for a start, why don't you?'

'All right, then,' Drew replied. He got up with a little leap and walked over to the cabinet in the corner of the room, pulled open a drawer in it, and brought out a sheet of paper, swiftly returning to Anne with it gripped in his hand. 'What on earth is this poem about, eh?' he asked her. 'Are you - tell me straight, have you been cheating on me, Anne?'

'Me!' she screamed.

'Why, yes,' Drew told her aggressively. 'Because I found this hidden away in your private drawer. Yes, you had no idea I looked in there sometimes, did you? It's very - it's quite passionate, wouldn't you say?' He dropped the paper into Anne's lap, and turned and walked boldly back to his seat. 'Tell me - who is this boy who's writing to you? Do I know him?'

'Boy!' shrieked Anne. She felt compromised and somewhat undone by his sudden action, and was furious with him for that too. 'Drew,' she began, 'I found that poem tucked away in *your* jacket-pocket. Yes, I did. Don't go pretending now. It's obviously from a girl who *you've* been seeing. Methinks a school-girl, yes?'

'A school-girl! You're crazy,' yelled Drew.

'No, I'm not,' Anne retorted. 'Listen - I recognise the handwriting. I do, you know. It's Rhiannon, isn't it?'

'Rhiannon!' yelled Drew. 'Rhiannon Cook! Don't be so stupid. You know, I reckon you're only saying that because *I* found it first.'

'No, *I* found it first,' she retorted. 'That's why it was in *my drawer*, remember.'

'As if. Look - who is the boy? Drew asked. 'Tell me, please, because I need to know. Not that fellow on work-experience at your care-home, surely. Steffan, is it?' Anne shook her head, but not in response to the question he had asked. 'Or one of the other two, maybe? Jake Haines, is it? Or - or that twat of a mate of their's, Danny Flynn?'

'Eh? That young boy is dead now, remember?' she told him.

'Oh, God!' Drew said. 'Yes of course, that's right. Danny Flynn in Year Ten. The poor bugger. Just imagine - they found his body in the old railway-tunnel. Mutilated, and - and a lot more besides. Shocking that is! Shocking! O.K., Anne. I take back what I said. Will you forgive me?'

'I will,' Anne responded.

Drew got up and crossed to her chair and embraced his wife. 'I've not been cheating on you, sweetheart, I swear. You just have to trust me on this. Where is Chris, by the way?' he asked.

'I don't know. Out larking with some girl or other, I suppose,' Anne told him. 'Or Rhiannon, even.'

Drew.dipped his head, and considered her words. 'I've just had a thought,' he said, suddenly turning to face his wife.

'What?' asked Anne, her mouth agape as she began to contemplate the very same thought.

'What if - what if the poem was -' he raised an eye-brow.

'For Chris,' said Anne, reading his mind while declaring her own.

Drew nodded. 'Yes. What if it was meant for him?'

Chris and Carla were sitting in Tom's living-room playing music together - she on guitar, he on electric-keyboards - and sharing a long, lumpy, hastily-rolled joint together. The pair forever kept stopping and re-starting the song that they were practising. They told each other repeatedly that they were beginning to get the hang of it, but, since the chord-changes were tricky, Carla patiently offered Chris plenty of helpful advice, and gently encouraged him every time he messed up. *'You could shake me from sleeping -'* they sang together, with a harmony that was, by this time, becoming quite accomplished - *'and I would tell you that I love you - for the very last time.'*

The pair looked up on hearing the sudden creak of a loose floor-board above their heads. Carla leaned across, switched off the tape-machine, and threw her guitar down on the sofa beside a few scattered reams of sheet-music that they had waded through earlier that evening, when Chris had tried to find some music that he actually knew.

Carla leaned back and dragged deeply from the thick spliff he had handed her. 'I'm sure you can see why I wasn't able to invite the police in here that night, Chris,' she told him. 'You see, everything was just lying around much as it is now, and Dad's room was smelling even more strongly of puff than this one is right now.' Chris dipped and shook his head a fraction and giggled at the queer picture she painted. 'And if I'd gone and got myself arrested, then you can be sure it would have been all over the papers within hours, and, as a result, I can tell you there would have been hell to pay.'

'Yes, maybe you're right.' Chris told her, rubbing his tired eyes in an effort to prolong his powers of concentration.

'You know, Chris, I suppose it was lucky in a way that the men managed to spot you standing back there on the bridge,' Carla told him. 'Even though I'm sure you must have been terrified, alone and exposed as you were. You see, arriving back home at just that moment, and from the direction you came, seems to have made the two men think twice about whatever evil act they'd got planned for me. And that alone I guess probably caused them to vanish back into the night.'

The door beside the pair suddenly opened, and a pale-faced Tom slowly walked into the room dressed only in a pair of well-worn, and crudely-buttoned, striped pyjamas. The two young people shot out of their seats to support him.

'Call the police for me, would you sweetness?' Tom told his daughter, before collapsing sideways onto the settee, scatttering cushions of varied colours and patterns all over the floor. 'Tell them there are bodies buried in a mass-grave, just up the road here, not far frm Vaynor.'

'Dead bodies, Dada!' ejaculated Carla.

'That's what I said, girl,' he told her, puffing from his exertions 'And that's what I saw.

'But in Vaynor!' stammered Chris, in a tone just as animated as the old man's.

'Yes,' Tom replied. He raised both his bony knees up close to his chest and began to shiver. 'And be sure to say that every one of them is male, won't you? And - and that the very weapons they were murdered with are buried there, in the shallow grave, right smack alongside them.'

The two young people exchanged horrified glances.

'What sort of weapons did you see, Dad?' Carla put in, trembling perceptibly at his startling declaration.

'What kind? Why, the usual, I'd say,' her dad replied, stretching out his hands to aid his description. 'They were long knives and machetes for the most part, and one great, long sword.'

'Do you mean a samurai-sword?' asked Chris. He had seen Steffan wielding one in the park one time, and it had badly scared him. He suddenly thought Volver might have done for him.

'I've no idea what the damn thing is called,' retorted Tom, 'but one poor blighter is lying there decapitated.'

On dry, clear days when the sun is shining - and there are surprisingly more of these than you might at first think in South Wales - for my money there is no more beautiful place on the face of God's Earth than the upper Taff Valley. On such mornings I often found myself circling the narrow roads and bushy lanes in my new firm's van, dropping off supplies for the building trade, while carrying out my prime job of checking that construction and renovation tasks on the various sites that we had were not falling behind schedule, and that the occupants of the homes and business premises we serviced were content that the work they were paying for was getting done, and progressing more or less as agreed.

My jobs done, I would invariably find myself pulling up at the gate of some lovely field or forest glade, and, from there, watching the different farm-animals, (among them the year's growing lambs,) going about their business, or simply surveying the lovely, rolling landscape that comprised these green and pleasant foothills of The Beacons.

On one such sunny morning in May I was driving down from the hill-top village of Pontsticill, and skirting past Vaynor, as one does, when I spied a fleet of cars coming towards me from the direction of the viaduct at *Gloryhole*, looking just like any other gleaming funeral-cortege that was making its winding way up towards Vaynor churchyard at a suitably crawling pace.

Then the sudden sight of the boy I had long ago learned was my own son, barely managing to ride his wobbling, red bicycle towards me on the wrong side of the road, took me completely by surprise, and, in my efforts to avoid him, almost caused me to collide with the first of the cars he was overtaking, whose driver I saw was a blond-haired policeman. It was then that I realised that they were police-cars, and the reason for their slow progress was the fact that they were lost. The first car appeared to contain within it a woman who looked remarkably like Carla Steel, along with a group of much older men, two of whom had white hair, and all of whom wore tired, harrowed expressions on their faces, that seemed to speak to me of world-weariness, and care, and, more than likely, unrequested overtime.

I drove on, but looked back at them in my rear-view mirror, fascinated enough to wish that I might have been invited to join them on their detective quest for whoever-knows-what.

Anne scuttled along the quiet High Street and tapped once on the door of the *Café Giotto,* then pushed on the latch and went inside. Through the glass panel she could see that the women were already there.

'Sorry, but is this where the witches' coven are meeting this week?' she asked with a grin.

Zeta quickly rose and beckoned her to come and join them. 'I'm glad you could make it Anne, love,' she told her. 'I know you've probably got a million-and-one things you'd rather be doing on the weekend.'

'Not really,' Anne replied. 'Apart from all the usual, that is. So what have I missed then? What were you girls discussing?'

'Well we were talking about Dick,' said Maggie Scratch, rubbing the glowing red patch on the back of her neck.

'Oh, my God!' shot back Anne. 'It's Sunday remember. If I'd known you were -'

'Dick Plant,' said Janie.

'As was,' said Bobbie. 'Since the fella calls himself Riccardo Pantheon these days, of course.'

'That was Gwen's first hubbie, you know,' chipped in Zeta, by way of clarification. 'Before she married Dyl Cook. I was just saying to the girls that the fellow was born a man.'

'He was born a -' Anne was convinced she had mis-heard the comment Zeta had just made. 'What you're trying to suggest, Zeta, is that he was born a woman, yes?'

'No, no!' exclaimed Zeta. 'Of course he wasn't born a woman. Does he look like he was?'

'Not at all,' said Maggie. 'He's male all right. Zeta was only telling us how he always seemed to have been a man virtually from the day he was born.'

'Do you understand now?' Zeta asked Anne. 'You see, I mean he sort of missed out on his childhood, if you like,' she told her friend. 'Mario's cousin in Genoa had the same problem, so his family say. Only he was gay with it.'

It was Bobbie's turn. 'I had an English pen-friend who was in school with him in Gloucester - Dick Plant, you know,' she told them. 'And as soon as he could read and write, and had learned how to do his adding and taking away, well, he was into his *Times*, wasn't he?' she told her.

'His times-tables, do you mean?' enquired Anne.

'No, no - '*The Times*,' ' replied Bobbie. 'The daily.'

'She means the broad-sheet newspaper that comes out every morning,' said Maggie. 'I heard there's a man in Cefn buys it regular. Even owns shares he does.'

'Oh, I get it now,' said Anne.

'Do you get it now, do you?' said Maggie. 'And so you see, Dick never really got to play like we did.'

'Or like our brothers did, she means,' added Zeta.

'Or with girls like us,' chipped in Loose Linda, who, up until then, had remained quiet, scoffing away at a sandwich. 'Because I was in school with a boy like him, you see, and God, I felt sorry for the poor mite, so I did. Never let me kiss him once.'

'So where's Gwen now?' asked Anne. 'I thought you told me you'd invited her round here too.'

'Well, I did.' Zeta told her. 'The same time as you.'

'But she'll be in church now, won't she?' said Maggie. 'God, you should have known that Zeta, shouldn't you?

You're a catholic yourself, right? You know, I'm surprised that you aren't there yourself, if I'm honest.'

'Maggie - don't be like that,' said Anne. 'You're allowed to miss once in a blue moon, right, Zet? The Pope's not going to come round with his purple dictate, now, is he?'

'Papal,' said Linda, correcting her.

'Oh, I'm sorry,' said Anne. 'Anyway, that long wooden thing he carries round with him that everyone scurries away from.'

The women around her all tried to visualize what Anne was referring to, but none of them could manage it with any success.

'If you want to know, I went with the kids at half-eight, like I always do,' replied Zeta. 'Leaving Martin to have a long sleep, you know. And when was the last time you saw the inside of a church, Maggie?'

'Me! You're picking on me now then, are you?' the woman said angrily. 'Just before Christmas, as a matter of fact,' she announced proudly. 'When I went to give blood. Unless you count '*Orlando Bingo*' Friday nights, of course, which use that big chapel down at the bottom of town. We go there together, regular, you see - Linda and me. Oh, it's lovely in there. He worked in there a couple of times, you know. Replacement staff during the hols, as I recall.'

'Who?' asked Anne.

'Why, Dick, of course,' she told her. 'He didn't call himself Riccardo Pantheon that night I can tell you.'

'Why? What was he called?' asked Zeta.

'I'm not sure now,' Maggie replied, thinking hard. 'Well, he was called a lot of things that particular night, if truth be told - the prizes weren't up to the usual standard you see. But I'm not going to be repeating them right here and right now, if you don't mind.'

'Oh, go on,' said Janie, encouraging her to come clean, and grinning mischievously.

'No way. I will not,' she said. 'It's Sunday morning, for God's sake.'

Anne clicked her fingers, recalling something important. 'Oh, I've just remembered girls. There's something I have to tell you about Gwen. Oh, you'll never believe it. Listen to this.'

'We're all ears,' said Loose Linda, tipping her plate of crusts into the bin, and rushing back.

'She only went and attacked a man and woman with a bread-roll in *Prince Charles Hospital*.'

'Gwen did!' a chorus of high-pitched voices cried out.

'Ooh, that's awful,' said Janie, shaking her head..

'I'd say, said Zeta. 'There's a terrible waste of bread. If I told you what my Martin pays for -'

'Aisht a minute, Zeta!' commanded Maggie. 'I need to ask Anne something. Listen, Anne. Her mother is up in *The Willows* with you, right? So I reckon you must see a lot of Gwen these days.' Anne nodded. 'Tell me, love - like me, do you think she's completely off her rocker?'

The large, black police-car pulled up just before a row of old cottages that stood winking back at them in the bright morning sunshine. Chris already stood waiting, just yards away, beside his gleaming, red push-bike, and lifted his hand and shaded his eyes, watching intently as a duffel-coated Carla helped her aged father step out of the vehicle, and edge down the narrow path, that Chris knew ran down towards the little stream and its bridge, and, continuing, then rose up once more as it approached Vaynor Church. This ancient edifice, with its distinctive, triangular-roofed bell-tower, he could just make out to his left, standing, partially hidden, amongst a clutter of lofty elms and horse-chestnuts, and enclosed within its twisted fence of iron-railings, and its ancient, crumbling walls of red-brown sandstone.

On the path the two policemen turned round to wait for father and daughter to catch up with them, then slowly led the way further along the track towards the location which Tom had assured them contained the dead bodies he had seen so vividly in his mind's eye just the previous day. The two uniformed men halted, looked at each other askance, and then began to laugh uncontrollably. Even from a distance, Chris found he could also now comprehend the mistake that the old man had clearly made, but he realised that, not being from the particular locality himself, it wasn't possible that Tom could have known an awful lot about it.

'What's this? Christ! It's just an ancient monument, old boy!' announced Sergeant Foley, reading the rudimentary sign that someone had fixed crookedly onto the fence with a folded piece of rusty wire. 'Little more than a hillock. No, not even that, I'd say,' he added. 'Just some grassy old tump in a field that I swear you'd miss completely if you weren't actually looking for it.'

'Sergeant, it's a mass grave from the twelfth century,' Chris announced, hurrying up on his bicycle and joining the group on the tight, narrow path. Dismounting, he spun round to address them all. 'You see, the fields round here were once the scene of a humungous battle between the local Welsh people and the English - the Normans invaders from the castle over there.' With this he pointed with his free arm directly into the sun's rays, where what little remained of the ancient limestone battlements on Morlais Hill now made a strange, dark shape in the morning sky that resembled, if anything at all, a great, black whale upon the sea.

'That's all well and good, young man,' the sergeant answered him, though the whole while maintaining his gaze on Tom and Carla, as he walked back along the path to join them. 'But we fully expected you to be taking us to the site of at least one *contemporary* corpse, Mr. Davies - the mortal, if not still warm, remains perhaps of a second local drug-dealer come to a sticky end.'

'Aye. Didn't you tell us there were a shed-load of them buried up here?' the second police-officer said. 'Christ alive, man! Don't you know that our whole forensics team have already been summoned here from Cardiff. It seems to me you could be losing your touch, old boy,' he declared in his strange, cockney accent. We'd just as well have listened to one of those manky sheep chewing their way through the grassy stump over there as listened to you.'

'Tump - Dawson. Tump,' the Welsh sergeant corrected him. 'When in Wales -'

'Tump, then,' said the detective, looking even more glum and disapproving than he did before. He nevertheless continued apace. 'Look - the next time you have a meaningful dream, old boy, or a nasty nightmare, or just wet the bed for that matter, I suggest you just get up and make yourself a cup of tea, like other folk do, or perhaps re-fill your hot-water bottle.'

'Or, better still, just turn over on your side and go back to sleep, eh?' Sergeant Foley chimed in, shaking his head at the embarrassing predicament the pensioner had just caused him.

'Just don't go calling *us* up and wasting *our* precious time, all right?' said D.I. Dawson. I can see now how the one in the tunnel was a complete fluke, the last time. Yes, I've no doubt we'd have found it ourselves within an hour or so of the canine arriving.'

'Oh, really? Well, that's not what you said at the time, I remember,' Carla told the pair angrily. She clutched her father round the shoulders, and turned up his coat-collar against the cool breeze that suddenly rose up from the direction of the river. 'You know, your gratitude astounds me. My father is dying, I'll have you know. He should be at home now and taking his paliative.'

'Paliative!' said the Welsh sergeant, chuckling to himself.

'Don't say no more, sweetheart,' Tom told his daughter. 'You've got enough trouble already, my love, what with me, and the house and all.'

'Yes, paliative,' said Carla boldly. 'Pain-killer, if you prefer. Because without it, I swear the acute pain caused by my father's condition might easily have finished him off by now.' Carla took a step towards them. 'It's quality marijuana, if you want to know, Sergeant Foley,' she told him. 'Not your common or garden green. 'High-grade herbal,' I believe you chaps call it. But *Respite*, is how my Dad describes it. Or *Welcome Respite* might be an even better name, right, Dad?'

Tom's concerned look for his daughter's sake suddenly dissipated. Now, by way of concurring, he just nodded. Chris saw this, and, out of empathy with him, nodded along too.

Carla turned and watched as the boy climbed back into the saddle of his bicycle and pedalled vigorously back up the path in the direction of the road and home. Chris clearly felt he had overstayed his welcome, now that the cat was out of the bag, she thought to herself, smiling. But, there again, some things just needed saying, didn't they? And, from as far back as she could remember, Carla knew she had never been one who was capable of shirking the truth.

'*Welcome Respite,*' Carla repeated, now turning back to face them, and grasping her ailing father's arm even more tightly than before. 'For us two, at least, that somehow seems to say it all.' But the policemen she addressed now seemed to be looking everywhere but back at her firm gaze. 'And, gentlemen,' she added, now ever so slightly baring her teeth, 'if we ever should branch out into sales one day, then that's definitely what we plan to call it.'

Merlyn Foley shook his head and walked up to D.I. Dawson and spoke to him. 'So what do you make of the occasion when we brought him in and he located for you the body of that dead black girl in London? Do we simply put that down to luck then? Or does the old man have a genuine gift, do you think, as a lot of people seem to reckon he has?'

'Look, there's something I've yet to tell you about that business,' said the cockney detective.

'What's that?' asked Foley, tilting his head so his good ear would be sure to apprehend it all.

'Well, they found out that that dead girl's female lover came from somewhere hereabouts. And it's that particular woman who I gather is now trying to bring up her orphaned child.'

'Eh? You don't say,' said a starled Foley, scratching the stubble on his chin and deliberating fast. 'The woman is from Merthyr do you mean?'

'That's what I heard, anyway,' said Dawson. 'I'll give you the confirmation just as soon as I get it. Yes, the plot thickens, sergeant, wouldn't you say?'

'Aye, it sounds like,' said Foley. 'A young officer gets himself needlessly killed in the performance of his duties, trying to discover where a dead woman's body has been hidden. Carla Steel happens to be living a few hundred yards away from the scene, and her father - her own father remember - tells us precisely where the girl's body has been hidden. Fishy or what?' he asked D.I.Dawson, sniffing raucously, and pointing down to the road. 'Jeff, I'll bet you half my pension that that girl knows an awful lot more about this whole grisly affair than she's prepared to let on.'

'I was only twenty when I decided to walk away from *Jesus*,' Carla told him, carefully placing the acoustic-guitar she held onto the floor beside her chair.

'Do you mean to say you were a Christian back then, then?' asked Chris.

'God - no! Although I did used to attend chapel with my mother when I was young, and my uncle on my father's side is a man of the cloth,' she went on. 'No, *Jesus*. It's a college at Oxford. God knows how, but I got to go there to study music. Apparently I was the first girl to ever get in there from Pennant. 'A superb achievement, Carla,' they told me at Speech-Day. 'You'll be a role-model for all our young women musicians.' Well, O.K. Nevertheless I just up and quit.'

'You walked away from Oxford University! Wow! But why?' asked Chris.

'Well, after being there for only a matter of weeks I felt like I was like a fish-out-of-water in the place. And then I made friends with a very bright, black, working-class girl from Yorkshire who seemed to be every bit as out of it as I was. Sadly both of the girl's male siblings had unexpectedly died in the space of just a few months, both stabbed, the younger one more than likely on account of the elder, if you get my drift. Well, not surprisingly the girl was seriously depressed, and close to suicidal, no longer seeing very much point in life, let alone in studying. And at Uni she didn't receive the support I felt she was entitled to, except the help our friends in the Socialist Soc. gave her, who were true to the end. Our political enemies not so, I'm afraid.'

'You had enemies there!' exclaimed Chris.

'Yes, we did,' Carla replied. 'Although I dare say they were very much of our own making in a way. This weird, second-year, Tory prick from Market Harborough, with a handle-bar moustache, a cravat, and horrendous acne came up to our table drunk one night in *'Brown's'* and thought it dreadfully clever to announce - 'While losing one brother is plainly a misfortune, Miss Boyce - that was Jackie's name, by the way - the loss of both might be regarded as plain carelessness.'

'Wilde,' said Chris.

'Much more vindictive than wild, I'd say,' said Carla. 'Sebastian Jarvis his name was, if I remember. Daddy was a banker - Mummy something in boutiques, I gather.'

'I mean he was quoting - misquoting, actually - a line by Lady Bracknell from an Oscar Wilde play,' said Chris, raising his eye-brows. 'GCSE English Lit. I got a B.'

'Oh, yes, I remember now. Wow! You're good, Master Cillick,' Carla told him with an admiring grin. 'Well, anyway, it wasn't so much his pompous comment that riled me, as the sneering guffaw that swiftly followed after it. I mean I thought, *what a nerve!*'

'Or, *what a nerd!*' cut in Chris.

'Quite,' said Carla. 'And what a total snob and a complete twat. Well, angry as I was, it appears I must have stood up and swung for the little man. I sent him flying into the patisseries.'

'You floored him!' ejaculated Chris.

'Sort of,' she replied. 'They told me later I had broken his nose with my watch-strap, and that his silver monocle went rolling round the room and was never found again. He said he planned to sue me, naturally.'

'Monocle! God! How pretentious your chap sounds,' said Chris.

'I know. Well, anyway, the college rag had a field day over it. It was all my fault, blah, blah. The articles they wrote, and their stupid banners. 'Left-wing fire-brand.' 'Violent Welsh hussy.' One even called me 'a Traveller,' for Pete's sake. There again, I suppose I was, in a way.'

'How do you mean?' Chris asked her.

'Well, you see, I was up and gone by the following Monday. First train out of town, you could say. Never travelled so fast in all my life.' Carla grinned.

'Not to Worthing, by any chance?' he asked, smiling.

'No, silly. Oh, I get it. Very droll. No. Heading to London, as a matter of fact. With my leather travelling-bag - baby-less, naturally - perched securely on the seat beside me.'

'And I guess, from that moment you never looked back,' Chris added, smiling thinly at his attempted musical reference.. 'You know, Bob Dylan might have described it like that.'

'No, not once did I look over my shoulder,' she retorted, looking down and recalling the moment. 'My varsity life was behind me and good riddance to it, I thought. I remember that when I dragged my bags from the train I was greeted by a statue of Paddington Bear, and, standing alongside it, a balding, male busker playing *'My Funny Valentine'* on a tenor sax, and I just knew, somehow, that I had come to the right place. And, believe it or not, within a fortnight I was strumming away at the very same song myself outside Fulham Broadway Tube-Station, and, though it seemed from that day on I was eternally shivering and penniless, I just loved life in 'the smoke,' and felt so, so at home there. 'Capital punishment' is how I recall Dylan described life in London. He and his wife lived there for quite a long time, you know. Lovesick, homeless, and about as penniless as I was.'

'*Bob Dylan* did!' stammered Chris, wincing in disbelief.

'No, Dylan Thomas, silly,' said Carla. 'It was during the war, you see, when Londoners, whatever nationality or faith they happened to be, or gender, or age, or sexual orientation - and as often as not that was carefully concealed - were united together in a way I am quite certain they have never ever been since.'

The big window behind Carla was lensed with rain. Chris smiled lovingly at the dusky, buxom, intriguing little woman, who was sitting cross-legged, and curled up before it. He was grateful to her for allowing him to call her his friend, but totally in awe of her unique and considerable musical talent, that seemed to enrich, not just his own life, but that of the whole world about him.

The singer slowly, methodically, rolled a joint that this time would be big enough, and would burn long enough, to enable the pair of musicians to kick back and relax from their musical exertions for a while. What had always made drugs so essential - so sexy - to Carla, she thought, was the very real opportunity to be *other*. She looked across and studied her new-found friend closely, and wondered if he might be experiencing much the same. Carla wasn't sure, but she sensed that the effect the drug was having on Chris was to liberate his mind, since his deep, brown eyes - the windows of his young soul - seemed to be panning, with no discernible focus, the dim, shadowy room they were presently sitting in, almost as if slowly scanning the new, yet tediously bland surface of another planet. She leaned across and took the joint from between his fingers, laying it carefully within the saucer on the floor, and spoke to him.

'Tell me, Chris,' she asked. 'At this moment is there a particularly significant girl in your life?'

'Well yes, I suppose there is,' he replied. 'But I'd hardly call my mother a girl.'

'*You* know what I mean, smart-ass,' she told him, smacking the gashed, denim-clad knee that now lay languidly rolled against her own.

Chris so wanted her to smack him again - anywhere, on his arm, his face, even on his bare behind. Why exactly, mattered not to him. All he knew was that he craved more of this blessed intimacy that the artistic, musical duo already seemed to share, but which he had not yet found with the young Rhiannon, with a lover, with any other person.

Through liquid, fast closing eyes, Chris watched as Carla lifted and cradled her instrument, and once more tried to complete the song that they had first devised together not yet an hour before. Entranced, he watched her fingers thrumb, her moist lips pout and part, and then he lay back and listened as her deep, mellifluous voice once more filled the whole house. How Chris envied the young woman's assuredness about all that she set her hand to, while he, sad failure that he felt he was, hadn't even been able to discover whether or not a single sound was emitted in the woods as a tree fell, and there was no one there to hear it.

As Chris saw it, Carla's largely solitary life in the British capital had seemed to provide her with the perfect opportunity - the ideal setting - to open her box of lyrical matches, ignite around a dozen of various colours, and set the musical world alight. Her first album-release had gone platinum after just a year, he recalled, the second - *Candice Farm* - in less than a month. Economy was clearly the singer's watchword, he mused. Why else had Carla lived apart from people these last years, he thought, if not to say not a syllable more than was in her songs.

Yes, in truth, Carla Steel was economy personified, Chris mused, blazing the cannabis joint he held. She *was* the song; vocal *and* guitar; three island-choruses with a bridge in between. And there she now sat, relaxed, suitably reclined, smiling serenely, at peace and buzzing, in fact every bit as stoned as he knew he plainly was. Plucking the strings of her battered old guitar, and seemingly fusing the chatged elements about her, the boy beheld Carla perform her musical alchemy, which, as ever, solidified in mere minutes into a hard, gleaming band of purest gold.

CHAPTER 14

'We were on a break, remember,' Chris told her.

'I thought it was a lunch-time,' replied Rhiannon.

'Not that kind of break, stupid,' he retorted, throwing his gum-ball across the room, and watching it soar straight into the bin, where it landed with a metallic clunk.

Deep within the bowels of the school-library the pair sat huddled together in matching, facing chairs, alongside them the shadowy light of late-afternoon lying captive in the window-wells. Things appeared to be looking up, each one was thinking independently. However, unbeknown to them, *Discordia*, the goddess of marital strife, was seemingly pulling strings in some other tender scenario, in another world completely.

'Listen we're talking about Pippa Jenkins here, for God's sake,' Chris told Rhiannon, opening up another wrapper and refilling his drying mouth.

'And?'

'Well, she isn't exactly - you know -' He paused for effect.

'Me?' said Rhiannon, following her pert comment with a beaming smile.

'Well, that too, of course.' said Chris, leaning across and making as if to kiss her, but instead dribbling his glob of chewing-gum onto her shiny nose. Despite herself, Rhiannon tried hard not to flinch. 'But she's not really my type, is she?' he told her, gobbling the sticky ball up again.

'Isn't she?' asked Rhiannon, making light of his childish action, and dipping, and rubbing her nose clean with a paper tissue she always kept in her sleeve.

'No, and she never was, if I'm honest,' he snapped back.

'I see. Well, Chris, I can understand why you say that.'

'Can you?' he asked. 'How?'

'My form-tutor - Mr. Hardiman - told us last week that if you sleep with dogs then you're sure to catch fleas. That's pretty apt under the circumstances, don't you think?'

'I'm not sure. I bet he doesn't even have a dog,' he teased her. 'That guy is seriously weird. if you ask me. In Maths earlier today he told us that there are ten sorts of people in the world. Those who understand Binary, and those who don't!' Chris smiled a wry smile, but Rhiannon's brows narrowed as she tried, unsuccessfully, to fathom its meaning. 'And you tell me the guy's your form-tutor!' said Chris. 'Do you know I feel sorry for you, I really do. Harry Hard-on takes teaching even less seriously than old Mrs. Tibbs and my dad do, and I know for a fact that *he* thinks school is a complete joke.'

'O.K., I hear you. Anyway, I've been told she's riddled,' Rhiannon told him.

'Who? Mrs. Tibbs!' ejaculated.Chris.

'No, silly. Pippa Jenkins,' retorted Rhiannon. '*And* her sister. And their - their long-haired brother Sam. If you ask me, the whole family are a bleedin' -'

'Flea Circus?' Chris suggested.

'Menagerie, I was going to say,' she told him, giggling.

'A what?'

'Well, isn't that what you call it?'

'It's called a menage-a-trois, stupid,' Chris teased her, looking down straightaway to hide his grinning face.

'Is it?' she asked. 'O.K., well, unlike you, I was never any good at Spanish, was I?'

Pippa Jenkins suddenly walked past the window, arm-in-arm with a tall boy in a duffel-coat.

'Slut!' they both called out simultaneously, and then collapsed laughing and squealing into each other's arms across the table-top.

The kiss that followed caused the watching librarian, Ms.Seccombe, to switch off every light, and call time on all the sundry coupling that was taking place in virtually every available nook and cranny, except, of course, the very area that she herself supervised - the crowded computer-suite, where *'Homework-Club'* had been proceeding apace for well over an hour now.

Brenda Seccombe logged off her own computer and gathered up the six or seven text-books that the club-kids had been using. Gone were the days, the woman told herself, when homework was something that all children undertook at home. And gone also were the days when canoodling was something carried out well away from the school, either in the woods, the park, or very occasionally behind the bike-sheds. There again, Brenda thought, the Deputy Head-Teacher was always banging on about how her library should become 'a centre for all aspects of learning,' wasn't he? So, she told herself, I figure if the old fool chose to walk in here right now, and witnessed all the clandestine fondlling and smooching that was going on, she could always tell him that she was simply fulfilling one of the key-objectives that, after all, the man had insisted she put in her departmental action-plan.

And even sex had to be learned somewhere, didn't it? Brenda contended, as if arguing the toss with her alter ego. Otherwise all schools would soon run short of pupils, and teachers, technicians and librarians alike would be thrown out onto the scrap-heap as a result. Yes, you had to learn about love and sex somewhere, she mused, smiling benignly, as she held open the swing-door so that a dozen students, including Chris and Rhiannon, could make their exit. And, with all these new-fangled, parental controls they've come up with in recent years, she pondered, as she took her car-keys from her drawer and twirled them round her finger, no longer did everyone around have access to as wide a selection of adult-porn at home as she did.

In the northern sky over Morlais Hill, and above the much closer burial-ground, the clouds were clearly breaking up, but the harsh, eye-shadow shades of robin's egg blue and lavender marked out the cutting-edge of the latest cold front that was fast arriving. I drew the curtains closed and walked over to the sofa, picked up the weekly TV-magazine that we took, and scanned it. 'There's a programme on the box I want to see called '*If Wales Could Talk.*' Fancy it, Gwen?' I asked. 'I imagine it's a new political show.'

Gwen looked up at me with a disconcerting look. 'Surely that must be *whales*,' she said. 'You know, the swimming, squirting kind. And if it is, well, you know I can't stand nature programmes.'

I held the page close up to my eyes, and squinted manfully so as to check out the spelling. 'Oh, no, sorry, love' I said. 'It's actually entitled '*If Walls Could Talk,*' and it's apparently a property show about home-renovations. You know, I guess I'll need that second cataract operation sooner than I thought,' I told her, feeling a complete fool.

'Well, I've been telling you for ages, haven't I?' she continued. 'Last month you went and sent the council-tax cheque off to British Gas, and we still don't know yet if they're going to cut us off or evict us. Get a new pair of reading-glasses, why don't you.'

'But we just don't have the money, love,' I told her. 'The pay-check from my part-time job barely gets us through the week, as it is. And then there's our utility bills, which have got completely out of control.' I waved my arms above my head to express my frustration, then gazed back at Gwen. 'How ironic is it, love, that, in an energy-rich country like ours, so many people last winter were too terrified to even turn on their heating. I feel what we need to be told is why the government can't just stop the energy companies ripping us all off as they're currently doing? Who is in charge in this country, for heaven;s sake? I reckon Mister Brylcreem and his pal living next-door are even oilier than we all feared. My God! I reckon that with the Con-Dems in charge up in London, the light at the end of the tunnel has effectively been turned off.'

'Ever the optimist, aren't you love?' said Gwen sarcastically, crossing her legs and plumping a couple of cushions with her tight little fist, so making room for me to join her on the sofa. 'I have only ever voted once in recent years, you know, and that was in the Referendum, and I wasn't really bothered who won then, either. Listen, my love,' she said, 'when I am tucked up in bed and fixing to die, I can assure you that the last sound you will hear from me will be that of Lady Conscience cracking her hollow whip.'

'Yet if you go first, Gwen, and I'm left here a widower, you'll already be a householder in heaven by the time I get there,' I told her, putting my arm round her shoulders, and kissing her cheek. A nose, the elaborate, bony edge of which forever called for a lover's finger to be drawn down along it, received its just desserts. 'And I feel He'll look after you,' I said. 'I've always told you how God is just.'

'Yeah, just not available when you need Him,' was her cute reply. 'Arthur, for all the trouble I am sometimes, I can say that you've never once been a burden to me, do you know that?'

I glared at her. I had finally endured enough. 'Gwen - why do you call me that?' I asked.

'Call you what, love?' she retorted, her eyes narrowing.

'Arthur. You called me Arthur again. You see, for all but the last two or three years you've been calling me Dyl, like everyone else does. Then one day, quite out of the blue -'

'God - you went on about this nonsense last week,' she told me. 'You know, I do believe that I've always called you Arthur, have I not? It *is* your first name, after all, right? And, when I asked Rhiannon, she told me she can't remember me calling you anything else.'

'Rhiannon said that!' I bawled back at her, instantly regretting my statement of doubt. I wondered about this for a few moments and came to the conclusion that it could only have been that my daughter wished to prolong familial harmony in the household by getting her mother to believe she was right, even though we had many times discussed this queer Arthur-business, and Rhiannon had told me how she had been struck by the eccentricity of it every bit as much as I had. Indeed, coupled with the horse-box graffiti, and the business down in town at the call-centre I heard about from someone in the pub, as well as her violent outburst with a crusty French-loaf in *Prince Charles* that time, Gwen's apparent fixation on King Arthur, (or the never-crowned, Welsh chief known as Arthur, as she had once insisted) was a fairly recent development, and one which I had to admit had come to blight our most recent days together.

'Arthur - pass me my catalogue, please,' Gwen asked, reaching for a felt-tip pen with which she liked to circle items she wanted to order, and which she felt we could just about afford.

I passed it to her with her glasses, and, dismayed, went off to the kitchen to make us tea.

'Ooh! There's some gorgeous baby-clothes in here, sweetheart,' I heard her say from the other room. 'Come and have a look, love.'

'Baby-clothes!' I screamed, almost spilling the kettle. 'I think we're a bit old for new additions to the Cook family, don't you think, dear?'

'Why is that?' she asked. 'I mean Rhiannon is already seventeen, and, personally, I'd like nothing better than to become a grand-mother before it's finally time for me to go. I'm surprised you don't feel the same, Arthur.'

I gritted my teeth. That bloody name again! 'Well, I don't!' I replied sharply.

'Our daughter is blooming right now,' she told me. 'And since she doesn't want to stay on at school much longer, well, I believe it would make good sense if she decided to settle down with some nice young man who felt likewise, don't you think? Just like I did all those years ago. I mean with Richard.'

I was stupefied by this. My daughter - a mother! I couldn't - no - I refused to see it.

'Our Rhiannon would make the most wonderful mother, I'm sure,' she went on. 'Yes, I was only seventeen when I first left home, and then my gorgeous Olwen was born less than a year later.'

By Olwen, Gwen was referring to her much older daughter, who she'd had with her first husband, Richard, and who had lived in London now for many years. Although the woman's first-name was Sarah, Olwen was her, rarely used, middle name. And I heard she now refused to retain her runaway-father's surname - Plant - and had reverted to her mother's original, Havard.

'These little jump-suits look adorable,' I soon heard Gwen declare. 'Oh, there's no point in telling you, I know, Arthur, but I must remember to show Rhiannon when she gets in. She'll love them, I just know she will.'

'And where has she gone tonight, anyway?' I enquired from the other room. 'I mean, I know summer is almost here, but -'

'Look, we both know she's out seeing that boy from *Gloryhole*, don't we?' she announced, 'even though she thinks we don't really know about it. And he's a nice enough chap, I suppose - that Christopher. Yes, I'd say that my darling girl seems about to start nesting, don't you think?'

'Nesting!' I bawled back. 'Our Rhiannon!'

'You heard me, dear.'

'Well, she's already off to a good start, if you ask me,' I told her, carrying a tray bearing two mugs and a full plate of biscuits back into the lounge. 'I mean, her bedroom already resembles a hole in a tree-trunk, stuffed full, as it is, with food wrapping, straws, and old newspapers.'

'I wonder how many she'll get to have in the end?' Gwen asked, closing her eyes.

'Newspapers, or boyfriends?' I enquired, chuckling.

'No - children, silly,' she retorted. 'Twins would be nice, don't you think, Arthur? But, there again, triplets would be even better.'

'I can see them all now,' I told Gwen, resuming my seat beside her.

'Can you, really?' she asked.

'Yes,' I told her, sipping my tea. 'The bigger ones pushing the little one out of the nest. Something off the *Nature Channel*, don't you think? Not very unlike this family of mine, really.'

'Oh, don't be like that, Arthur,' Gwen told me, smiling. 'I'd simply love to see Rhiannon's little fledgings emerging into the world. Yes, that would make me so happy, so blissfully happy. You see, wait for my Olwen and you'll wait forever.'

At least Gwen was right there, I thought. I'd been told by different people around town that her elder daughter was lesbian, although her mother had for long remained in denial of the fact. Perhaps, nowadays, I thought, Gwen was at last denying it no longer.

'The birds of Rhiannon!' Gwen suddenly exclaimed, slowly biting into her jaffa-cake, and sitting with her head thrown right back on the linen head-cloth, her eyes tightly closed. 'The glorious birds of Rhiannon! I have long felt I knew them, but how I'd love to see them now. Listen - do you think we soon will, Arthur? Tell me, honestly, now, my love. Do you think we soon will?'

Chris stood and watched as the sky stuck forks of lightning into the salad of trees on the distant horizon, and then set off, at a rambler's gait, to the meeting-place that he hadn't even known existed, with the drugs he had grown stuffed into a gore-tex bag strapped to his back. To Chris, at first, this excursion seemed a task as Sisyphean as attempting to repair all the things that were wrong with his parents' house, and which his step-father seemed disinclined to do anything about, but he had convinced himself that he had no alternative but to set off across the hills and try. He recalled how he had once smuggled two dozen lock-knives through Dover to supply all his classmates at *Pennant,* who told him they hadn't the sort of money that his own family clearly had to afford the History-trip to the World-War-One battle-grounds. And, having achieved his objective, he had then honoured the fallen in his own unique way, with the shallow trench he had dug in his neighbour's back-garden, the very night he returned to Wales, to conceal them all in.

Carla's very latest offer, to purchase from him all the crack-cocaine he had been lumbered with, as well as what remained of the bud crop he had managed to cultivate in their loft. was terribly unfair on her, in spite of her considerable wealth, he told himself, and inexcusable on his part too, in that he never wished to feel, or be seen to be, dependent on anyone in life, least of all a woman, and least of all this particular one. In truth, Chris was desperate to display to Carla just how independent and self-reliant he could actually be, and how ingenious and discreet were his skills of entrepreneurship, and his modus operandi, if not so, perhaps, his connections.

To Chris's mind, only returning along the same path later that afternoon bearing a fat handful of paper in his back-pocket would suffice. Such was his fresh sense of self-dependence, he mused. Rounding the curve that would lead him down into the tributary stream's shallow valley, he felt the first spots of cold rain collide with his bare fore-head, but, though foolishly under-dressed, alone, and lacking a map of any kind, he was still confident that he would pull it off.

The red tractor, that was the source of the incessant, whirring sound that interrupted his thoughts, could eventually be sighted between the trees, circling at speed round the enormous, field above and to the right of him. Without thinking, Chris waved nonchalantly at the bearded, middle-aged farmer who was driving it, just as he would have done a thousand times before. But on this particular, far from normal, occasion, he suddenly wished that he hadn't done.

A hundred yards further on, a mating pair of magpies landed on either side of the undulating track he was traversing, and, to Chris's dismay, declined to desert it, even though he trudged his heavy, laced-up boots as noisily as he could manage just yards between them. God! Is this an evil omen, then? Chris pondered, and suddenly remembered the Swansea City footballer, who, having forgotten his shin-guards, and having returned to the dressing-room to collect them, came out onto the pitch as last man in his team, and promptly suffered a broken-leg! 'Well, I won't *let it* be a wicked portent,' he announced to the wind, and, looking back, repeated in a shout to the two magpies, at which point the twin birds hopped once or twice, then took flight.

Following the stream north now, along its narrow, stony bed, that would normally be lying flooded in water, even this late in May, Chris felt in his jeans-pocket for some chocolate, a packet of mints, or some gum, in fact anything he could slip into his mouth for sustenance, but all that he could find was a folded piece of glossy paper that, when he opened it up, read - *'Play for free - Win for real.'* 'Yeah, and lose for certain!' Chris exclaimed with a sneer, rolling it into a ball, and throwing it into the gently flowing stream, and watching it drift slowly downstream.

Chris ran the fingers of both hands back through his hair, and told himself how he felt like he was a person of two dimensions seeking freedom in a third. Life in the U.K. was fast becoming devoid of hope for young people like himself, he mused. For a start, British TV had become just like radio, only a hundred times worse. The country that meekly followed every auto-tuned moment and every phony turn, of 'X-Factor,' while the world around it went up in flames, seemed fully deserving of the grim future that awaited it. It was no wonder young people like himself desired 'the quick fix.' Where were the jobs that David Cameron and his Con-Dem associates had promised would be created by them? he pondered. And what had happened to the free university-education Nick Clegg and his cabinet friends had put their signatures to less than a year earlier, and that it now seemed certain they had done just so they could reward themselves with the briefest, and thinnest sliver of political power? Chris feared this might cost him dear.

In fact, who *could* you trust these days? Chris asked himself, as the stream-bed suddenly came to an end, and he was forced to climb up between tangled branches of dwarf-oak that camouflaged the small cataract sitting beneath it, and pursue what was left of the watery track that led to the strange, secluded, rendez-vous point.

Very soon the stream itself could be seen to flow out from a perfectly formed, limestone cave that Chris felt he may have passed once or twice, but had never previously had the courage to enter, let alone explore. But this aperture into the mountain landscape now seemed to him to cry out to be penetrated fully at some future date, when he arrived at the scene better prepared than he was today, and could change into wellington-boots so as to wade inside, and, by the light of a torch, that he didn't presently possess, explore its deepest, and most tantalising extremities.

Quite alone, and around a mile or two from civilisation, an exuberant Chris chose to hold an animated conversation with himself. 'Wow! So this is what some people round here call *'Merlin's Cave!'* he called out. It's entrance may be narrow, he thought, but how perfect and symmetrical it is. And the sound that the clear, fresh-water stream makes as it seeps out, bubbling joyously into the bright daylight can't help but remind you of something out of *'The Arabian Nights.'* As Daddy Drew is often heard to say, these days it seems that the only place you can still find beauty is where its persecutors have somehow overlooked it.

Leaning on a boulder, Chris bent over and shook the stones from out of one of his boots, and then turned and proceeded to duck and weave his way further up the, now dry, valley in the hope that he might encounter the elusive pair, whom his parents had separately, and forcefully, warned him about - Steffan Jones and Jake Haines - who would, he believed, enable him to become financially solvent again, and perhaps help him set down the foundations for his intended, but, sadly these days, far from inexpensive, university education over the border in England. 'A lot hangs on what happens this afternoon,' he told himself. 'And if I have to stay here until it gets dark to earn my bread, then I'm pretty sure that that is what I shall do.'

An hour or so later, hearing not a sound except the constant babble of the pure, clear, emergent stream, as it coursed across the limestone pebbles towards him, and then turned to flow away down towards the riverside path by which he had arrived, Chris elected to approach the intriguing cave-entrance. He soon noticed that someone had written something in small, painted capitals on the sheer, calcareous wall to the right. In order to read what it said, Chris found that he needed to splay his legs, wide and uncomfortably, on two sharp, narrow rock-ledges that were cut into the walls on either side of the narrow stream. Eventually gaining the position he sought, Chris soon found that he was able to run the fingers of his right hand along the cold, dry text that sloped gently before his eyes, and almost instantly was able to decipher the Welsh words - *BEDD ARTHUR*.

Chris turned his awkwardly balanced torso round and peered deep into the hollow, watery darkness beyond him, and spoke the two words again, aloud this time. '*Bedd Arthur!*' he called out. The sound he made echoed eerily inside the cave. He repeated the action three or four more times, at varying volume and tone, then ceased, and began pondering the meaning of the bizarre inscription that he had found. How strange, Chris thought, that a local person might claim in this way that the so-called '*Merlin's Cave*' retained within its confines the actual resting place, and therefore the bodily remains, of the man the whole world knew, and revered, as King Arthur.

About two feet to the right of the strange, scarlet inscription, and much closer to the water level, Chris soon spied a name of some kind - most likely an ancient Welsh name, he thought, - a signature, seemingly handwritten on the cave-entrance in a flowing, feminine style, not unlike that of Rhiannon's, and done in the very same shade of red. The woman's name, that Chris soon deciphered, he quickly concluded meant nothing to him at all; it read - '*Gwen Hwyfar.*' But someone else - a male hand, he felt - had scrawled beneath it in black lettering, and this time in large brackets, the much more familiar name *GUINNEVERE*, and which a nodding Chris instantly understood to be, and to mean, one and the same.

When Carla met Sarah Havard in the bar of '*The Riverside Studios*' in Hammersmith, (where she had been playing a free-concert that summer afternoon,) it was hardly love at first sight. For a start, the musician had another chick in tow with her at the time, a much younger, black girl, called Jackie Boyce, who soon informed the older, plainer, girl from Merthyr, whom she was not displeased to meet, that she was a proud single-mum, and had known Carla since Oxford.

'Carla's done her very best recently to be my daughter's father, you know,' the young girl had told Sarah with a wry smile, 'and the press haven't yet managed to cotton on to that. But people are forever telling me that every child needs a proper dad - a male one I mean, and the *actual* dad, if he's up to it - and I guess one day that's what we'll do - her and me, me and Leila, I mean. Because Leila's dad only lives just round the corner from here, you see, in Hammersmith.' She drank up what remained of her glass of white wine and regarded the two Welsh women who shared her table, but whom she felt seemed to have virtually nothing else in common. 'I'd be living with him now, only I've found that I can no longer stand the sight of him. My Leila happens to be with her grandma at the moment, if that's what you're wondering, Sarah.'

Carla knew from that afternoon that she and Sarah would soon be getting together: there were some very clear signals she could see. The woman was Welsh, for a start. In fact she hailed from Merthyr, which, though Carla came from a village over a dozen miles to the north of the town, was the place where her dad had worked, and also where, heeding her father's wise advice during a fractious period, both at her school in Brecon, and domestically, she had gone, to study for her A-levels. The taller, stouter Sarah was a much older woman, and far more self-confident than Carla, and that happened to suit the singer's needs quite perfectly at the time.

So nobody was more surprised than young Jackie when Carla suggested that all three women might consider moving in to a flat together. But far from being upset when the colossal change in domestic arrangements eventually took place, Jackie accepted the offer gladly, and, perhaps becoming more and more dazzled by the singer's growing status, and quite possibly by the burgeoning cash-flow, which would now be coming in regularly, and which would no doubt keep all three women well fed and watered, asked if she could move in with the three of them her young daughter Leila. After meeting the child, Sarah swiftly agreed, and so, from that moment on, she and Carla slept in a pair of single beds in the largest of the bedrooms, while Jackie took residence in the second largest, with young Leila sleeping in the adjoining box-room.

The arrangement seemed to work very well for a couple of years. Carla's repute as 'a talented musician with something to say,' (as more than one musical publication described her) began to soar. Sarah found herself a new job in the Civil Service, and even Jackie was able to accumulate sufficient income, both to enable her to care for her three-year old child, and to pay her share of the rent. Little Leila seemed to be thriving, and so all four females were very happy.

Then one morning around 6 a.m. the Fulham flat they lived in was raided, and Jackie was arrested for drug-dealing. Not long after that she was sent to Holloway Prison for five years, this having been the second time that she had been convicted of the offence. This was the watershed moment that, for some considerable time, Carla had feared might one day happen, and, once she and Sarah were made fully aware of the situation, they wasted no time at all in stepping in, and, after first ensuring that she wasn't going to be taken into care, henceforth reared little Leila themselves, much as if she had been their very own sweet daughter.

Carrying a green rucksack on her back, Rhiannon had run most of the way from her parents' home over the *Bryniau* moorland, through the castle ruins, and down the secret path which her father had shown her in the steep, grey, shelved cliff, when, as a child, they had explored daily, throughout the school-holidays and at weekends, *'the green and pleasant land'* of her native homeland.

Almost getting hit by a speeding cyclist with no bell, who was tightly, and bizarrely, dressed in lurex clothing, far too bright and colourful for even her to contemplate wearing to a dance-class, Rhiannon jogged across the broad viaduct, and discovered that her handsome lover was already awaiting her arrival by the side of the wide track, where the old station-halt had once stood in times gone by, in *'the days of steam.'*

Chris kissed his lover on the mouth, and she quickly handed him, almost as a reward, a small chocolate-bar that she had kept for him in a polythene-bag, rolled up inside her coat-pocket.

'What else have you got in there?' he enquired, licking his lips in anticipation. 'You know I can't stand *Snickers*.'

'I didn't know that,' she told him, pouting a little, and putting it back. 'What is it you want?'

'I'm holding out for an aero!' he told her, smiling.

'Well, I don't have one,' she replied, searching through the bag, then, seeing his cheeky grin, eventually comprehending the witty remark he had made to tease her.

'Crème Egg?' asked Chris.

'Sorry. They all went at Easter.'

'Frere Rochet?'

'Fat chance.'

'Oh, give me the *Snickers*, then,' he told her, 'and I'll share your fruit-juice with you as well.'

'That's nice of you,' quipped Rhiannon, feigning disgust, but not quite succeeding. 'Don't your parents feed you, then, young man?'

'Well, not like you do, sweet,' Chris retorted.

'No, I can see that,' said Rhiannon, unscrewing the top off her bottle and handing it to him to drink from. 'Where exactly is this cave you mentioned, anyway? *Merlin's Cave!* How come you never told me about it before?'

'I never really discovered it before, that's why,' he told her, handing her back the bottle, his thirst suitably quenched. 'But you know I must have heard about it forever.'

'Chris - what's that you're listening to on your i-pod?' asked Rhiannon.

'Er - It's *'I don't know where we're going'* by *The Sat-Navs*,' he replied, biting his top lip and turning away.

'Really?' said Rhiannon, instantly falling for it. 'Well, that's appropriate, anyway, considering what our plans are. Give me one ear-piece so I can listen, would you?' Chris obliged, smiling wickedly. 'But surely - but surely that's Carla! That's Carla Steel, isn't it?' she told him. 'You know you're such a liar sometimes, Chris Cillick. You'll go to hell, you will.'

'Yeah, I know,' he replied, winking.

'Say, Chris - was your new neighbour ever on *'The X-Factor?'* she enquired.

'Carla! *X-Factor!* You most be joking. Can you ever see them uncovering a genuine star on that show?'

'Mm, not really,' she said. 'Though two of their girls have done pretty well for themselves.'

'I mean, can you imagine, Rhi? 'And the act I've decided to put through tonight, Dermot, is......... Bob Dylan!' Just imagine that, eh?' Chris chuckled at the thought.

Rhiannon giggled too and decided to have a go herself. 'And the act I've decided to put through tonight, Dermot, is ......Amy Winehouse!'

A smiling Chris continued the game. 'And the act I'm putting through tonight is John Lennon!'

'Is........Elton John!' announced Rhiannon.

'Jimi Hendrix!' shouted Chris, dancing about and playing air-guitar, left-handed.

The pair laughed away, holding on to each other's waists so as to stop them from falling over. Chris suddenly thought of another angle to it. 'And, sadly, folks, in the bottom two tonight, are........Paul Weller, and........wait for it........The Arctic Monkeys!'

'And in the bottom two tonight are......... Adele........and Coldplay!' chimed in Rhiannon. 'And sadly, one of these two will be going home.'

'Simon........and Garfunkel!' yelled Chris, dancing about with a microphone at his lips.

'Or when they come to Cardiff, maybe,' Rhiannon told him, 'Duffy, and The Manic Street Preachers.'

'Hang on. You're going overboard now, Rhiannon,' Chris told her. 'And the live-shows are never in Cardiff, are they?'

'I know. Sorry,' she retorted, writhing about strangely.

'What's up?' Chris asked.

'I've got a wedgy,' Rhiannon told him, wincing with pain and wriggling a bit more.

'Oh, so you went and wore that thong again, then?' he suggested, his brown eyes flashing.

'Well, you did tell me you liked it,' said Rhiannon, getting up and feeling around in places that even her mother had shunned venturing into.

'I know I did. I do.' said Chris. He gazed at her. 'I think I love you, you know, Rhi.' he told her.

'I love you too, Chris,' said Rhiannon, gathering his lithe, strong body in her arms and kissing him moistly on the lips, her pearly-white teeth quickly encirclng his tongue.

The besotted, young couple turned and walked on down the dusty track, then, curving off it right, to the north, the sun beating down on them, they wandered across the wide, green fields that ran away towards the mountains. Before very long the pair reached their destination.

For Chris the entrance to the limestone cave had a different atmosphere completely this morning. With the day's early, glaring sunshine, it now lay much more in shadow than it had done when he had ventured there two days earlier, and eventually conducted his drugs sale successfully with the two boys from Pant and Dowlais. The strange writing on the wall was now barely visible from the rock-ledge in the middle of the stream where they were standing, but, knowing that it was there, Chris easily managed to locate it, and, soon called Rhiannon across to join him, so that he could show it to her.

'Let me get my wellies on first,' Rhiannon told him, suddenly springing to her feet, and kicking twice - once for each foot - at the front of a gigantic boulder lying beside her, so as to get her curled toes as close as she could manage to the rounded, rubber ends. Then arms outstretched, and wading right into the heart of the stream, Rhiannon approached as close as she could to the grey, limestone wall, studied closely the neatly written, scarlet inscription, and announced excitedly,' Christ alive! My mother *ha*s been up here! How on earth did she manage that? And *why*, for heaven's sake? She's not really into walking these days, you know.'

'Then perhaps she came here a long while ago,' Chris told her. 'I say that only because the black writing in brackets beneath it is fading badly, and yet it had to have been written later than your Mam's writing, since it sort of explains it. Do you get me?'

'Yes, you're right,' said Rhiannon. 'The words '*BEDD ARTHUR*' - meaning Arthur's grave - was clearly written there by *Gwen Hwyfar* - who is unquestionably my dotty old Mam. Why, though? God only knows. Say - do you have any idea yourself, Chris?' She turned and looked at him askance. Chris - what the hell are you doing?' she asked.

'Stripping off to my trunks, of course,' he told her. 'It's eighty degrees celsius today, you know. Apparently this is the hottest Spring we've had in Britain since records began.'

'In that case I think I might join you,' she told him. 'My one-piece costume is in my bag. I'll just pop behind the tree and change, O.K.?' Rhiannon smiled at the shake of the head he gave her.

While Rhiannon changed into her swim-suit, Chris slowly waded into the cave, grasping onto any, and every, projecting portion of the cream-coloured walls on both sides, so as to help him stay upright, as the pure, spring-water gushed up exquisitely against his advancing legs, and surged between and around them. This was an experience that was entirely new to Chris, and quite a taxing one too, and so, after a dozen or so long, tiresome strides he halted and turned, and, motionong with his hand, encouraged Rhiannon to try to wade up alongside him.

'Give me your arm, Chris!' the pale, slim-hipped girl cried above the growing symphony of the cavern's tinkling, water-music. 'And turn your torch on, for God's sake, or we'll probably get lost.'

'How the hell are we going to get lost?' he asked her, holding out the torch anyway, and lighting up the narrow route ahead of them. 'There's only the one way in.'

'I can't hear you,' Rhiannon shouted. 'What did you say, love?'

'I said your Mam is your Dad, and Harry, your dad's goldfish, is your twin-sister,' Chris announced, turning and smiling serenely at her as if butter wouldn't melt.

'You don't get goldfish in here, do you?' Rhiannon enquired, catching just that single word from his mischievous statement.

Bare arm in bare arm, the young pair ploughed on into the grotto's deepening gloom. The coolness of the air caught them unawares, but they convinced themselves that this was a very welcome blessing after the stifling heat that they had had to contend with in the hot, humid cleft of the wooded valley that now lay somewhere far behind them, and which, to their young, perceptive minds, already seemed a different, forgotten world completely.

In the rising arc of the torch's light the stalactites hung down like skinny pillars on either side of them, gleaming pink and cream, lime-green and gold. Had there been cob-webs suspended around them too, then Rhiannon felt she might have been venturing on foot through the ghost-train she had always adored in 'Dreamland.' Chris, on the other hand, pondered on a lap-dancing club he had once inadvertently wandered into in Swansea, and promptly banged his right knee into a large rock.

Rhiannon turned so as to share with Chris her feelings, but, noticing his shocking, pudenda-pink lips, and his satanic black throat, she instantly fell silent, and, head down, clung to his waist instead, as if in dread, or desperation. Rhiannon squeezed his ice-cold hand within her own. She so loved to hold his lissome body next to hers, partly because he always felt to her so much like a greater portion of herself. Soon she could feel her heart beating faster. No, she thought, she still wasn't able to say no to the drug that was Chris: she found that, even now, or more especially now, she wanted his hands on her, and at her, and around her, and even inside her, and the cavern's rich, intoxicating atmosphere now only made her more aware of this fact.

The semi-naked pair waded on as one, and, minutes later, when they glimpsed the great, round pool, that lay bathed in shadow just ahead of them, they simply stood and stared, in awe of its serene, magical beauty. Here, beyond the initial tunnel they had traversed, in the very womb of the tubular grotto, the vast cavern's ribbed roof, which they peered at high above their heads, arched like that of a mosque, or the heart of some medieval cathedral. Tiny bats circled silently above them, and spun and swooped hypnotically, and seemed endlessly to inter-weave and fold over themselves, in the coal-black, velvet space that now gaped, and throbbed silently with tiny pistules of light above them.

Averting their upward gaze momentarily, and instead turning and staring into each other's eyes, the young pair held on to each other even more tightly and kissed. This was without question the world each one longed for, their firm embrace conveyed. Yes, this, for both Chris and Rhiannon, was life without care; pure bliss; their private, and, perhaps, future Eden.

Switching off the torch's light, and untying, or at least slipping aside, what little covered their willing torsos, the couple bent down and reclined their slim, young bodies alongside each other, and began to make urgent love on the grey, shingly beach which skirted the grotto's black, gleaming pool. At first a few sudden cries of pain alone were all that echoed through the hollow darkness, but before very long the familiar sounds of the delicious, excited love they made soon filled the sweet, cool air, penetrated every rising joint, every vertical crevice, each dark and hidden, rocky recess, and infused and enlivened thrillingly what seemed to each of them to be the recently vacated hall of some mysterious mountain-king.

'Volver's late again,' said Steffan through a mouthful of chicken-drumstick and chips. He swallowed hard, then wiped both of his greasy hands on the bleached thighs of his jeans. 'He said sale-or-return, didn't he?'

' *'Coffee-powered car breaks world speed record,'* ' Jake read aloud from the tabloid newspaper he held, adeptly balanced on the steering-wheel before him. He then began laughing wildly.

'Didn't you hear what I said, cloth-ears? I was talking about Volver. What is that shit, anyway?' Steffan asked him, ripping the paper away from him with both hands. 'Oh, it's the Daily Shite again. I thought so.' He read out the next headline hinself. ' *'OAP dies of spontaneous combustion in his living room.'* Wow! What a way to go, eh?'

'Poor old bastard,' chimed in Jake. 'I bet he didn't see that one coming.'

Steffan turned and stared at him. 'Well, of course he didn't see it coming, twat-head!' he yelled. 'That's the point of the story, innit? It was *spontaneous,* do you get me?'

Jake leaned across towards Steffan in the passenger-seat and read the headline that was nearest to him, ' *'Evil Sat Nav sends car into water-ditch.'* Christ! Just imagine that.' He picked up the sat-nav that was sitting on the dash-board before him and banged it a couple of times on the steering-wheel. 'We'd best keep an eye on this one, too, I reckon. Look where it's gone and brought us this time.' He gazed out of the window and shook his head from side to side.

'Yeah, just exactly where we asked it to go. You know, I bet it wasn't the sat-nav that sent that car into the ditch, though, like they're saying it did,' said Steffan. 'I bet you anything she was a female driver. That'd be par for the course for one of them, don't you think? Say - how about this one? *'Unmarried mother stole Facebook pictures to convince her ex her son was theirs.'* There you go, Jake. See how evil women are.'

'Yeah,' Jake concurred. 'You'd never catch a man doing that.'

'Er - men don't have babies, Jake,' said his friend. 'Listen - don't worry, mate. I'll tell you about it one day.'

'You're funny,' said Jake.

'Apparently, and with the minimum of effort,' Steffan replied. 'Listen to this, will you? *'Doctor claims he can turn brown eyes blue, but he can't change them back again.'* Good God!'

Jake began singing. 'Don't you make my brown eyes blue.' That was on *'The Voice,'* that one was.'

'You know, I reckon that's seriously colour-prejudiced, that is,' Steffan told him. 'Try this one. *'Dead Man had the words 'DO NOT RESUSCITATE' tattooed on his chest.'* '

'Eh? But why would somebody do that to him?' asked Jake. 'I mean kill him - yeah, if you have to, but don't go messing with his corpse, right? I mean, we'd never go doing stuff like that, would we? And anyway it would take at least an hour to complete the whole thing.' He stared down at the white, polystyrene container that his friend held, and at what were now the cold remains of barbecue-chicken-and-chips and a set of cheap, white, plastic cutlery splayed inside it. He eyed the leg of greasy chicken, that by now lay severed in two and half-consumed. 'Hey - give us a chip, mate,' he asked his friend.

'You can have them all, if you like,' Steffan replied, staring into his comrade's eyes.

There was something about the way his friend said this that made Jake reconsider. Although starving now worse than ever, he stared down at the takeaway-meal and decided that the chips looked remarkably like a troop of slain and decimated soldiers, lying around soon after a battle, and still oozing ketchup liberally at every knife-wound.

'Too late!' Steffan exclaimed. He decided he wouldn't oblige his friend, but instead wrapped the container inside the folded newspaper, rolled down the passenger-window, and threw the whole package out onto the farm-track that ran beside them.

A disappointed, still hungry, Jake resorted to turning on the car-radio instead. *'Labrinth!'* he cried. 'Yeah, man! I love *Urban.*'

'Jake - what do you know about *Urban?*' Steffan asked him, reaching down and switching it off again. 'Seriously, man. You're about as Urban as a second-home in Tuscany.'

But Jake wasn't listening to him any more. He had suddenly remembered something that was, to his mind, at least, far, far more important. 'You know, Steffan, he lied to us about what happened to Danny, didn't he?' he declared to his friend.

'Who? Volver?' asked Steffan. 'How do you reckon that?'

'Well, he told us he died of natural causes, didn't he?'

'Well, I guess he meant natural to the line of work he was in,' replied Steffan. 'Your pal Danny Flynn sold drugs, right? Coke, for starters.'

'Well, he dabbled, yeah,' Jake told him. 'Lots of guys dabble, don't they? I - we dabble, right? Still, whatever happened, he definitely didn't deserve to die with a knife through his lung did he? And with his own soddin' lunch-box stuffed inside his mouth. What the hell is *natural* about that?'

'But he must have upset Volver somehow,' replied Steffan. 'And how many times has he told Danny and the two of us how nobody does that to him and gets away with it. So I guess he was warned, wasn't he? And so I guess he probably got what was coming to him, don't you think?'

For almost a minute neither of them spoke. Then Jake switched on the radio again. This time it was '*Goldie Lookin Chain*' singing a song they knew well about Newport.

'Now this is what *I* call Urban,' said Steffan, grinning. 'An urban district council.'

Jake didn't get it, and soon posed his friend another question. 'Say, have you got any tattoos, Steffan?'

'No. Why?' enquired his colleague, smiling. 'Are you thinking of getting one?'

'Well, I admit I've just started thinking about it,' Jake replied. 'Just the one word, of course.'

'Do you mean one with Chinese characters?' Steffan asked him.

'Christ no!' cried Jake. 'It would have to be in English otherwise the paramedics would be bound to get confused.'

'Paramedics! I don't get it,' said Steffan. 'Do you mean it's for them? What on earth is it going to say, for Christ's sake?'

'Well, it's going to have to be in massive capitals, I reckon,' Jake announced. 'And it's going to read '*RESUSCITATE.*' '

The quilt of stars folded over the sleeping countryside, and the moon, to which filthy Trefechan seemed to have given hepatitis not very long after it rose, lit up the isolated farms and scattered hamlets which colonised the rolling hills between the Taff Valley and The Brecon Beacons, which lay beyond and to the north. Chris looked up briefly at the end-terrace home that his mother, his step-father and a major, recently recovered, bank owned, and wondered how he could possibly manage ro tell them the truth about what he and Rhiannon had discovered in the subterranean rock-pool, little more than a mile-and-a-half from Gloryhole.

To his mind Chris had already chickened out, and, dropping down once again onto the track he had been skirting, as he made his weary way back across the *Bryniau* moorland from seeing Rhiannon back home, and circling the silent house he lived in, he climbed over the fence into his back-garden, and began searching for an empty stretch of soil in which he might bury the stiff, cold body he held.

The kitchen-light came on. Chris quickly realised that he was left with nowhere to hide, and so, instead of skulking back over the fence once again, he rose meekly to his feet, and walked onto the patio, and watched, as his mother, dressed only in her silky, cerise dressing-gown and curlers, unbolted the back-door, and came outside to find out what all the noise was about.

'It's only me, Mam,' Chris told his mother, but decided that it was impossible for him to approach her, since the smell that had blown away behind him on his way home, was now infusing the night-air around the pair of them, and so had become impossible to conceal.

'What have you got in that bag, Chris?' Anne asked, folding her bare arms across her chest so as to fend off the cold breeze that blew up from the river.

Anne watched Chris gently slip the bag from his shoulders and lay it on the ground before them, then with two hands unclip the straps, open up the flaps, and lift from inside it the stretched-out torso of Emily the cat. She approached her son and, placing one arm on his shoulder, studied the almost unrecognizable head and patched colouring of her favourite pet.

'Oh, my God! Oh, my God! She's dead, yeah? Chris - where on earth did you find her?' Anne asked him, turning away, her whole body shaking.

'In the *'Merlin's Cave,'* ' he told her. 'She was just floating in the shadows in the great pool there. You know, Mam, it seems the old man was right, after all.'

'What old man?' asked his mother, stroking the, no-longer-sleek, but still dappled, body of her deceased cat.

'Tom, our would-be dentist, next door,' he replied, pointing at the fence. 'Carla's dad.'

'*He* told you she was there!' his mother asked, mouth agape.

'Well, not exactly,' Chris retorted. 'But everything he did tell me about her turned out to be true. That old guy has a genuine gift, I reckon. It makes you wonder what else he's predicted.'

'Does it?' asked Anne, suddenly feeling a shiver pass through her. 'Chris, let's just put the poor cat into a bag or a sack of some kind for the night, shall we? Then we can come out here and bury her properly in the morning.'

'O.K., then,' said Chris, going indoors to search for something suitable they might use.

Leaving the cat's curled torso lying on the patio, Anne walked slowly over to the fence, and peered through it into the lit-up kitchen of the house next door. Inside it she could make out the old man sitting in a wicker-chair, his thin, pale feet buried in a bowl of steaming water, and his daughter Carla, crouched on her knees before him, gently washing them. Anne watched as Carla lifted his dressing-gown from off his lower body, and gently, and ever so carefully, washed her father's thighs and genitals, and, after bidding him to stand, and rinsing out the sponge again in the bowl, washed his thin, white posterior and his lower-back. This was something she herself had to do all the time at work, Anne pondered, and so she empathised with Carla to the point of almost wishing to call out to her to let her come inside and finish the task for her.

Anne suddenly heard Tom cry out in pain, and she felt herself wince with the agony of it. Very soon she found herself beginning to weep, and, when her son returned outside to join her, Anne silently called him over to her, and showed him the touching, family scene being played out in the house next-door.

Chris sadly, and predictably, saw it from a different angle completely, soon telling his mother, 'Crikey! The man's not wearing any pants! Carla shouldn't have to do all that, should she? After all, she's a wealthy woman.'

'Chris,' his mother replied tenderly, 'she only does it because she wants to - do you understand? Because she loves him so. You don't know, my boy, but you might need to do the same for *your own* dear father one day.'

'My step-father, you mean,' he replied.

'Yes - Drew,' she answered. 'Or your real father, even, if one day you finally get to know him.'

'Who *is* my real dad, Mam?' Chris asked her. 'I know you don't want to tell me, but I'm determined to find out for myself one day, you know.' He gritted his teeth together. 'But, Mam, don't you think it would be so much easier for me if you were to just tell me right now?'

Anne cast a final look towards her new neighbours and considered her son's request, which at that particular moment seemed a not unreasonable one. 'Do you really want me to tell you who your dad is, then?' Anne asked her son, turning to gaze into his face to verify for herself the fact that the boy did indeed resemble him.

'Of course, I do,' Chris retorted. 'Look, I can understand you being reluctant to tell me when I was young, but I'm a lot older now, aren't I? More mature and everything.' Chris watched as his mother suddenly looked away again, seemingly to consider the matter, the moonlight lighting up her face quite alarmingly. But this time he was determined that he wasn't going to let it drop. 'You know, I think you just won't tell me because I might have a brother in my own class at school, or something. Say - is that true? Do I, Mam?' Anne turned to look back at him. 'Go on - tell me, Mam. Because now I know you can't possibly hurt me if you do. Please tell me. Please.'

'Darling, it's not a brother that you have at school,' Anne told Chris, trembling more than ever.

'Do you mean - do you mean I have a sister!' he cried. 'Oh, my God!'

'A younger one, yes,' Anne said, finding herself beginning to form her lips into a smile. 'Though rather less than a year.'

'You mean I've got a younger sister?' he asked her. 'Wow! You know, that's quite exciting, as it goes. Please, Mam - tell me what her name is. Go on. Don't be afraid.'

'Anne grasped Chris by the shoulders, and, smiling broadly now, and staring deeply into her son's dark eyes, she told him, 'It's Rhiannon.'

CHAPTER 15

It must be said that the Reverend Gary Davies seldom sang *The Blues,* but he was indeed a very real local personage, with an active spiritual presence, not only within, but beyond, the country parish that included the hamlets of Vaynor, Pontsticill and, of course, *Gloryhole.* And on the night on which Carla's father became confined to bed, for what she feared might be the very last time, it was the rural preacher whom Tom asked his daughter to summon: a Welsh uncle whom the singer had rarely seen, and, as far as she knew, as an adult had never spoken to.

Uncle Gary more or less saw his brief in this way: after initially reconciling with his sole living sibling, (and, of course, with his, now celebated, daughter,) to help, and offer comfort to, the far weaker man as he drew closer towards his final passing. And then, he mused more solemnly this time, to follow this up by hopefully aiding his estranged niece in finally committing Tom's body to the good Welsh earth in the very fashion that her father had requested of her.

But now that Carla's uncle was so frequently there at the house in *Gloryhole*, and despite the fact that she now had an extra pair of hands to help her in the domestic situation, the girl was starting to feel more than a little uneasy about his presence. It didn't take her long, for example, to discover that her Uncle Gary was most unlike her dear father. To Carla's mind, the strange, round, rosy-hued, bespectacled reverend seemed to be a tad too occupied with trying to create a personality around his pipe for her liking. Since her father had, by then, more or less given up smoking - some time during the Spring - tobacco was a substance, and an odour, that she had never come to associate with him, and now it seemed very strange, and incredibly infuriating, to see its grey, billowing coils transfuse his whole house so completely, and so toxically.

'This stuff is a lot worse than weed, as I'm sure you know,' Carla was brazen enough to remark to the man, with a cheeky grin that she turned away from him just in time. She sat a little away from her uncle with the back-door open, the pair of them watching the sparrows frantically flitting down to scoff the bread-crumbs she had, minutes before, scattered outside for their breakfast. By this time Carla had fed the household, and was flicking through a magazine and some Sunday newspapers, searching for items in them that related to her musical career, and which she could cut out and add to the large, flat scrap-book which, quite unbeknown to her, her father had diligently been keeping of her.

'What's the point of feeding the birds in your garden if you're feeding them to the cat?' the flush-faced, old man suddenly turned and asked her.

Carla glared across at him. 'I guess you must mean the neighbours' cat, then,' she told him. 'because we don't own one ourselves. But sadly I gather Emily's gone missing lately. I just hope she gets found soon, that's all.' Fearing the Cillicks might be able to hear her, Carla got up and closed the back-door. She sat herself down again and quickly changed the subject. 'Uncle Gary - what was my father like when you two were growing up?' she asked him.

'When we were boys?' he replied. Carla nodded. 'Well, Tom was always very different to the rest of us,' he told her. 'Intrinsically good, you know. Your Aunt Charlotte is dead now, of course.'

Carla stared at the white, plastic collar that encircled her strange uncle's throat. 'God fearing?' she enquired. She suddenly found a newspaper photograph that depicted herself playing at a festival the previous year at Leeds, and, mentally measuring it against the space she found on the next page of the scrap-book, decided that it would fit perfectly, and so went and searched in the table-drawer for a pair of scissors with which to trim it.

'God fearing? No, not at all,' her grey-eyed uncle retorted. 'Tom certainly wasn't pious, or weighed-down with any sense of religious duty, as I felt I most assuredly was, even as a child. And yet you know, Carla, it was always impossible for me to believe that my brother's ambition was for this life alone. And, although I haven't been here with him for very long as yet, I already happen to know that it isn't, praise God.' The holy man sucked at his pipe in a succession of quick spurts, and so let the infernal smoke-screen between them reform.

Carla's long scissors cut the paper, and with it the silence that had suddenly fallen. 'Really?' she asked, fully detaching the picture, while wondering how on earth the man had judged this to be the case, since she certainly hadn't noticed any discernible change in him herself. 'Well, that's good to know, anyway,' she told her uncle, smiling, despite herself.

'Carla dear, I dare say there must come a time in everyone's life when your ultimate destination, and the - the act of getting there, gradually begins to take precedence over everything else,' Gary told her. 'Do you understand, dear? So then you quite naturally start thinking about purchasing a ticket - *the ticket* - that you believe will hopefully take you there.'

Carla looked up at him. 'You make it sound almost like getting on a train,' she said. 'When in fact it's simply expiring, dying, wasting away, that you're talking about.'

'But, you know, when one is able to see the big picture for the first time, I happen to believe that it is very like that,' Gary told her. At these words Carla's eyes narrowed and her brows contorted strangely. 'And I believe that my brother is just beginning to do this, after decades when, despite his numerous talents, and his wisdom, and his love for his fellow man, he didn't ever want to acknowledge that any of these things either came from God, or had anything to do with a religious faith. Yes, it has always been that way with my brother, you see Carla. Unlike myself, Tom always appeared to feel that everything he achieved in his life was attained as a result of his own hard efforts, you know, so it's hardly surprising that he worked himself to the bone for virtually all of it, and agonised so fiercely over the times when he felt he failed.'

'Then, Gary, I dare say you must be pleased that my father is perhaps, at last, beginning to see what you call 'the big picture' for what it is,' said Carla, wishing to shake her head at its abject futility, but desisting until she had at least heard her uncle's response.

'I am, I really am,' the old man told her. 'Except that, if I am honest, there is still a very small part of me that, in some strange way, resents this change he is making. Carla, before I say any more, I think it's only fair that I tell you that I have possessed feelings of jealousy towards my brother ever since we were teenagers, or even earlier than that, if I'm being completely honest.'

'I never realised,' said Carla, pressing the paper-cutting into place, and then smiling at the effect she hoped, and anticipated, that this new addition to her dad's book would have for him.

'Oh, yes,' Gary told her, pouting a little. 'You know, despite my faith back then, and my unblemished church attendance, and my earnest, diligent service, etcetera, etcetera, I nevertheless always saw myself as the black sheep in our little family - still do, I guess. Tom is a few years younger than me, you see, and so I sort of took him under my wing from a very early age, and for a long time I suppose he must have taken all my kindness and solicitude awfully for granted.' He nodded, then sighed aloud. 'Yes, I dare say I begrudged him this,' he declared. 'Indeed, it wasn't until this very recent conversion of faith that has happened to him, and with which I am very glad I was able to help, that I have at last begun to see Tom for what he was.'

'Don't you mean - *for what he is?*' said Carla sharply, looking up at him.

'Quite,' her uncle concurred, grinning at her. 'Is. Well, both, as a matter of fact. Is, was. Your father is a truly wonderful man, Carla dear. He has a heart of gold that, in my opinion, he never accepted, or even recognised, that he possessed. And I put this down to the family breakdown that accompanied his divorce, and the self-blame that he has since daily scourged himself with.'

'Well, thank you for saying it,' Carla told her uncle, smiling. 'Because it seems to me that the longer I stay here with him, and, of course, the longer he stays with us, the more perfect that this - this final setting of his actually seems. I mean, the more this old place feels like a - like a blessed retreat of some kind, a hospice of sorts, somehow pefectly created just for him.'

'Yes, I think I know what you mean,' said Gary, looking about him. 'The house has the atmosphere, the sanctity, almost, of a - of a hospice,' he told her. 'And can I tell you, though I could quite easily forgive you for laughing at me for it, that I believe this house feels much more like a body - softer, more organic, more human, you know - than it does any building created in stone. Tell me - do you feel that at all, Carla?'

'Yes, I think I know what you mean,' Carla replied, smiling at him. She had herself already experienced a feeling very akin to this, and was glad to find that someone else sensed it too. 'Gary, did you know that it was Dad who was the one who found the house?' Carla asked him.

'Found it?' the man repeated, his brows raised somewhat comically.

'Well no, chose it, I mean,' said Carla. 'It wasn't anything to do with me at all. He has never told me why, though. Why he chose this house, I mean. Say - do you have any idea why?'

The country pastor chugged again at his curved, black pipe, and sat back and seemed to consider his niece's query for a while. 'Well, I think I might,' the man finally told her. 'And, to be frank, I'm rather surprised he hasn't told you himself. But I have no desire to shock you Carla, so I'll leave it lie, if you don't mind, dear.'

Carla sat up. 'What! But I'm more intrigued than ever now,' she remarked, smiling. But her uncle was loath to explain himself to her and so she left it hanging. Instead Carla quickly picked out something new to discuss with him. 'That car you've got outside looks rather nice,' she said.

'You'd think so, wouldn't you?' he retorted. 'But I had the distinct feeling that I had made a bad bargain when I noticed that the clock on the dash-board read seventy-five thousand while the milometer read quarter-past-two!' He sucked his, now un-lit, pipe between his pale, cracked lips, then stood up and banged it clean on the rim of the waste-paper bin in the corner of the room. 'It's an old Lada,' he informed her.

'Yes,' Carla replied looking past him. 'It's very handy having it, but Dad understandably keeps most stuff in his fridge these days.'

'The car,' said her uncle, smiling, then breaking out into a merry little laugh.

'Oh, I see,' said Carla, blushing. 'I thought you meant -'

'Well, I suppose it's a silly name for a car, really, isn't it?' he told her. 'Lada. I call it Trigger.'

'O.K.,' she replied, puzzled, but not sufficiently to ask the man why that was. She knew he would tell her the reason anyway.

'You see, I find it only runs when it's had a decent rest.' He took up his seat again. 'I'm very much the same myself as it goes, girl. In fact, that's probably why I bought it, I guess. Rule number-one - old people usually buy old cars. Now why do you suppose that is?' he asked her.

'Well, I've never given it much thought, to be honest,' Carla replied. 'Although I might one day I suppose. Give it some thought, I mean. Not buy an old car. I don't drive, you see,' she told him.

'Ah. I suppose other people do that sort of thing for you, dear. Correct?' he asked.

'Well, yes,' she answered. 'More often than not, anyway.'

'Chauffeurs?'

'No - cabbies.'

'Oh, I see,' the old man replied. 'I did that during the sixties, you know. Drove a big black cab, I did. London style, do you understand?'

'In London?'

'No, no - in Merthyr, and in Ebbw Vale, mainly. I did the bingo, and the working-men's clubs normally, and also most of the rugby games. Not much money involved, of course, but lots of free tickets, you know. 'Bloody tickets! We can't eat tickets!' my dear wife used to tell me. Bertha - your Aunt

Bertha - used to say. 'Well, they're currency of sorts,' I'd tell her. 'I bet they'd accept them down the Co-op.' And bugger me, do you know they usually did.' Reverend Gary returned to his seat and blew his nose in a great crumpled handkerchief that he dragged from his trouser-pocket. 'I used always to dress smart in my job back then, you know,' he continued. 'Never once went out to work without a tie. How about that? Yes, those were the days, eh? I can even remember how the robbers used to wear suits in court back then.'

'They still do, Uncle Gary,' Carla told him. 'Only now we call them lawyers, don't we?'

'Touch-e, young lady, touch-e,' said Gary, chuckling. He inclined his head strangely. 'He's sleeping well up there by the sound of it - your dad,' he told her. 'Very like a pig in shit, I'd say. Oh, I'm sorry, dear. I wasn't thinking.' He turned to face her and resumed his discourse. 'You know I suppose I'd better be going soon, my dear. I have a few parishioners to visit, you see. Do you know, Carla, a deaf woman I visit up in the village has just had this implant put in the side of her head that has enabled her to hear for the first time in her life.'

'How wonderful,' said Carla, smiling.

'Yes, it's a miracle - it really is,' he continued. 'She told me she must have been the only woman in Wales actually looking forward to hearing her husband snore.' The man stood up again and crossed the room to the back-door. 'You don't mind if I go outside again, do you?'

'Not at all,' Carla told him, clearing from the linen-covered table the cups and plates that they had been using.

The Reverend Gary Davies walked out into the garden and lit up his pipe once more. Then he strolled calmly around the perimeter of the property, much as if he owned the land himself, then, leaning upon the garden-fence, he gazed out at the viaduct that so majestically bestrode the verdant gorge before him, and which ran away from his viewpoint towards the eerie-looking, mammalian shape that was the familiar sight of *Morlais Hill* in the middle distance.

Gary straightened his spectacles and, with keen eyes, followed the course of the river's valley upstream to his left, to where it disappeared from view behind the hill, which his home - 'The Manse' - stood upon. He started thinking about where all of the river's water came from, not its origin in the clouds so much, but its basins and storage facilities on Earth. 'He - he drowned in the reservoir up there, didn't he, Carla?' her uncle asked Carla, without turning to meet her gaze.

'Yes,' she replied, stepping onto the door-step, and looking over in the same direction. 'That was an awful business that was.'

'Awful, yes,' he concurred, shaking his head from side to side, the silver reels of smoke rising.

Carla felt a sudden tightness in her throat, and looked side-long into the ice-blue eyes that were the facsimile of her father's, and told him, 'And, to this day, I still wholly blame myself for it.'

Her uncle turned and looked deep into Carla's own eyes, as if to challenge this assessment.

'I always have done, and I guess I always will,' continued Carla. 'If only I'd learned how to swim back then, I tell myself, then things might have turned out very differently. You know, I'm surprised our Mam coped with it as well as she did at the time, since I was the only sibling who survived. Although I suppose it was inevitable it would finally bring about the termination of my parents' marriage in the end. I mean, something had to give.' Carla suddenly remembered that she wanted to ask her uncle a question. 'Uncle, are you aware of my father's gift?' she asked.

'Tom's gift! How do you mean?' he replied. 'Because I'm pretty sure he hasn't sent me a solitary card, even on my birthday, since - since we were both teenagers.'

'I don't mean that kind of gift,' she told him, grinning. 'I mean his - you know, his power.'

'Oh, that. But of course I am,' he told her, smiling. Then gazing deeply into her eyes he added, 'You see, Carla, we two both happen to possess it.' His niece's mouth dropped open. 'Oh, yes, girl, it's true all right. You know, I've been told it might be that it's something that's inherited, but I really don't have an opinion on that, to be honest.'

'You mean you're actually telling me that you possess a gift too!' said Carla.

'For my sins, Carla, yes, I do,' the man replied, sucking deeply on his pipe and creating the first sizeable cloud the sky above *Gloryhole* had witnessed that day. 'And perhaps even more so than your father does.'

'More so!' she exclaimed. 'Good God!'

'Sure,' announced Gary. 'You sound shocked, my dear. But tell me, why is that so strange? We *are* brothers, after all,' he told her. 'Forgive me if I describe myself as such,' he added, 'but for a very long time now I have felt I was the Mycroft to my brother Tom's Sherlock.'

Riccardo Pantheon, the self-styled 'mind-reader, clairvoyant, hypnotist, conjuror, and ventiloquist' (real name, Richard Ian Plant,) lived relatively unhappily ten miles north of Cardiff with his one-quarter-Welsh, second wife, (the mother of his three teenage, Bluebirds-fanatic sons,) who, like him, had marginally failed to achieve the A-level grades she required to secure a university-education. This deficiency, however, he frequently told himself, unquestionably went on to blight his own life and career far more than it appeared to have bothered her.

Ever since starting at secondary school, Dick's ambition in life had been to one day go to university, Oxbridge or otherwise, major in British History, work hard day and night, and hopefully leave with a first-class honours degree. But now sadly he realised that in this respect he had underachieved drastically, since by 2011, although he could boast that he had actually been to Oxford, and worked hard well into the night on both occasions (at a social club on the *Blackbird Leyes* estate, as it happens) the only first-class thing he had left the place with was the trunk road he felt repeatedly tempted to speed along - the A.40, via Cheltenham and Gloucester, to be exact - and all he ever seemed to get awarded with each time he ventured there were three more penalty-points on his driving-licence.

Despite his marital connections, and, more likely, because of them, the stocky, dark-haired, but balding, man hated the

Welsh with as great a passion as he hated the Taliban, black people, Asians, the Labour Party, and Fred and Rosie West, the latter pair quite understandably, for the indelible shame he believed their actions had brought upon his home town of Gloucester; so much so, that, in recent days, when asked where he came from, he invariably answered 'The Forest of Dean,' or 'the West Country,' or even, one time, 'Swindon.'

The former bingo-caller's one remaining ambition in life was to one day hypnotise the entire Welsh race into believing that they were 'the spawn of the devil,' whose traditional tongue was of the forked variety, slavered, as he believed it was, from before the Dark Ages, with a liberal coating of malice, aggression, bellicosity, self-love and self-delusion. He felt that if any race on Earth had conceived original sin then it had to have been the Welsh, and he would frequently tell people the same. One day soon he would get to punish them all, Dick had promised himself, but when he might actually get round to doing that - now that his latest wife was on the point of presenting him with their fourth child in just seventeen years - he wasn't entirely sure.

Dick felt that, if he were a David Blaine, or a Derren Brown, perhaps, he might stand a serious chance of achieving his objective, but only if he were to be granted a booking to perform on television, (preferably by BBC Wales, or the Welsh equivalent of Channel 4 - *Sianel 4C*.) As for the time being, sadly, he had wreaked revenge on just the one - the woman he most despised above all others, and not just because she was quite a lot cleverer than him, especially in her knowledge and understanding of the subject that had brought them together, namely ancient British History, but that, contrary to his belief, and his repeated assertions, Gwen proved herself to be a woman who was courageous enough to walk away from the man. And this his former wife had deigned to do, he recalled, on a bitterly cold, winter's night outside their house on Cemetery Road, a brown cardboard-box filled with his clothes at her slippered feet, and with a rolling-pin gripped in her strong right-arm, and their only child - Sarah Olwen - in the other.

By the seventh day of his inaugural visits to his elder brother's new, rural home, the Reverend Gary Davies seemed to have developed sufficient confidence - one might even say, self-indulgence - to allow himself to begin waxing lyrical on matters which bore only a tangential relationship to Tom's tragic, terminal condition, yet which clearly had a great deal to do with metaphysics, with philosophy, and, in a general sense, with the meaning of life.

'And so, in much the same way that we tend to approach the dilemma of the wasp that gets trapped inside our window, God is not unlike us, in that He too wants to get us back out into the open air once again. And so, to make that happen, He opens up a window for us, you see. But crikey how we scream and we shout and complain, in utter frustration, as we repeatedly butt away with our heads and noses in all directions, and into all manner of solid objects round and about us, when what He is doing - all He is doing, in truth - is the very best for us. Yes, the *very* best. And, as people of God, what we need to realise, Carla, is that He won't allow anything or anyone to effectively harm us. It's that simple, you see, *really* it is. Whatever sorts of problems and tragedies beset us in our lives, and there isn't anyone alive who won't get to experience all these, we should be in no doubt that God will just keep on flipping that flipping door open for us.'

'Window,' said Carla.

'Yes - window, I mean,' Gary told her, smiling. 'But it is true, nonetheless, don't you think? The Man-upstairs just keeps flipping that window open for us day after day, week after week, winter, summer, rain or shine.' He pouted. 'But do we see it? Do we even look for it? Do we even sense that He might have already released us from our torment? Do we heck as like! No - we just keep telling ourselves that there is simply no way out for us. 'I'm trapped!' we scream. 'Life is crap!' we tell the world. 'Ooh, wait - I've got a spare minute so I think I'll just pop upstairs and kill myself.' He watched as Carla smiled. Yes, I know it sounds crazy, dear, but it's true nevertheless. Aren't people amazing? We're all seemingly content to believe that we're locked up in - in Wormwood

Scrubs, when, in reality, we're running about freely, with a box-kite and a lollipop, in the warm airy gusts of Richmond Park. No, better still, The Brecon Beacons.'

The drone and hiccup of the washer-dryer broke into the silence which followed the reverend's earnest speech concerning the infinite grace and mercy of his God. Carla was hoping that the spin-cycle might start right that moment, and drown out whatever similar diatribe her uncle planned to follow it up with. And, if the machine didn't start spinning soon, she thought, she might be forced to adopt plan-B, which would most likely involve opening up a window - a la God and the wasp, she mused - and, with much waving and blowing, drive her uncle, and of course his infernal pipe-smoke, out through it, perhaps with the aid of a handkerchief, or a wet towel, or, better still, she thought, the giant frying-pan that her father kept sitting on the cooker.

But although these were Carla's initial feelings, her uncle eventually began, little by little, and day by day, to wear the poor girl down. For some reason, which she couldn't fully comprehend, he did at least seem to revive, or, perhaps, re-instill in her, some of the spiritual feelings that she remembered having felt during her youth; the comforting view, for example, of the existence of 'a loving God,' who was both above you and all around you at the same time; who cared about you and about the things you got up to, and the warm, tender, fatherly aspects of the same. It also fascinated her almost as much that her aged uncle - himself a father, and a grandfather, even - still welcomed and embraced this paternal slant of his God just as much as she did. The image Carla often got in her mind's eye of an old man in a wheel-chair being stroked and cuddled by an even more ancient man with a long, white beard, who stood benevolently, 'on guard' almost, just behind him, was one that frequently made her smile, and, on occasions, even giggle over.

'Suffer all the oldies to come unto Me,' Carla whispered to herself, smiling broadly, as she climbed the stairs once more to check on her ailing, but presently slumbering, father. No, it didn't seem right to her, somehow, except that God was, of course, old enough to regard everyone who walked the Earth as children, however ancient and decrepit they might happen to be.

How old *was* God? Carla wondered, as she closed her father's bedroom-door, having tucked him in again. Well, I suppose he had to be time-less, she thought, since He'd obviously been there since long before people were created, and therefore even before age itself was invented. Indeed God must have invented age, much as He had invented everything else. Therefore I guess, since God can't have an age, He must never have enjoyed having a birthday, or a birthday-party even, she mused, or once been in receipt of anything resembling a genuine present, or any kind of heart-felt, celebratory gift. Carla winced at this, rather sad, discovery.

'Yes, how strange and how difficult it must be to be a deity,' Carla pondered aloud. 'I mean, as an artist, I have a pretty enormous fan-club, and occasionally I even get to enjoy fabulous celebrations in town. But a deity Who, after all, is probably the only true Deity, can't possibly have experienced any of these terrifically fun aspects of a life at the top. And this just doesn't seem fair somehow,' she told herself, creeping downstairs and walking back into the kitchen, 'but I'm sure He must get His thrills in countless other ways. In fact, unlike most of His creation, He might get a high from just seeing people hug, and cuddle, and love each other and what-not, much as my father claims he does from seeing me stroke and play with Emily, next-door's cat.'

The past winter's extreme weather had rendered the valley's roads so riddled by the cruel effects of frost that many of their tarmacadam surfaces lay pitted and pock-marked, as if by the night-time actions of a tribe of clandestine, pneumatic moles. Indeed certain routes in the so-called 'local road-network' were now little more than sinuous mole-carpets, their fine, ground-up fragments of tarmac either dispersed laterally onto the grass verges (or the narrow stone-pavements, where the latter did exist,) or gradually, silently, becoming embedded in the tyre-grooves of the wide variety of vehicles that daily traversed the area, and so being distributed liberally to countless other towns and cities nationwide; in a way very like Welsh water, which, although a major export, is one that earns the uncomplaining Welsh not a single penny.

Volver himself had exported a vast amount of the crushed tarmacadan that Spring, but his favourite freight by far was cocaine, and in a variety of commercial forms, which catered to the specific needs of consumers throughout south and west Wales, as well as a vast network of retailing outlets he had painstakingly developed for himself right across the West Midlands and the South West of England. The exports which Volver specialised in had their origin, rather like himself, in Holland, and earned him enough untaxed income to maintain expensive, fashionable homes in London and two other international cities, as well as his temporary bolt-hole in Bristol.

On occasions Volver reminded himself that he might easily have made a first-class youth-worker, or teacher, even. After all, in recent years he was sure he had developed the sort of relationship with young people everywhere which enabled him to exercise significant persuasion over them, and, when the occasion demanded, to compel them even, as to their future conduct. And, quite naturally, he had found that the outcome of his efforts was rarely anything but beneficial to his bank-balance. Volver's father - also named Abram - who had been a very popular rabbi in his native Durban, and himself had a knack for collaborating with young people, might perhaps have been proud of him after all, he thought. The Afrikaner winced a thin smile as he changed up and slowed to a crawl in order to make his way across the narrow, limestone bridge near *The Blue Pool,* and soon after climb the steep, winding hill to *Gloryhole* that skirted it on the river's northern side. Yes, in a way I suppose I'm basically a role-model for Britain's youth, Volver told himself, nodding at his smiling brown eyes in the rear-view mirror before him.

Abram Kronfield was a wealthy, self-made man, and was clearly admired by a number of very beautiful women, largely on account of that fact. But there was still one woman who had long been on the man's radar when he was living in London, but who had now mysteriously gone to ground, sadly, he had once thought, never to be seen again. Volver recalled how he had first met Carla Steel in a drug-den in Fulham, and, for some reason, that he could never seem to fathom, had let the attractive, talented woman slip right through his fingers. But nowasays, and ever since his two new compatriots, Steffan and Jake, had discovered that she had at last turned up in her, and their, home-town of Merthyr, of all places, he had been determined to try to kill two birds with one stone, on what was to be his latest visit to the land of their fathers. But unfortunately it hadn't quite turned out as planned, he reminded himself, as he reversed his gleaming, bright-blue Audi into the last remaining parking-space across from the rear-door of the large, rambling roadside-tavern, on the road from *Gloryhole* to Cefn, known as *The Railway Inn*.

Just then Volver remembered that the blond girl, whom he had taken to calling his 'Welsh bitch' on the last occasion he was up that way, was very likely going to be in the pub where he had arranged to meet up with the boys. After all, she did seem to sort of live there, he mused. Striding across the car-park, and removing his *Ray-Bans* and smoothing down his long hair and his short, black beard, he chuckled contentedly to himself. If his wife only knew what he had already done, or had any idea what his present plans were, he told himself, then she would most likely throttle him, then chop off his prunes, (as she had countless times before threatened to do,) and then, with an explanatory note attached, post them off to Jacob Zuma. 'Oh, come on, now, Agnetha,' he recalled telling her soon after they had first met in a street-bar in Amsterdam. 'What you don't know won't hurt you, surely, sweetheart.' But this lax comment had turned out to be very like a red rag to a bull, and so, ever since then he had kept his business dealings entirely to himself, and his testicles in an even tighter pair of jockey-pants.

Pushing open the translucent glass-door of the lounge-bar and sauntering inside, Volver smiled inwardly as he thought about the isolated, rural domain where he had spent the last three nights, and the deep, relieving sleep he had experienced while staying there. Who could guess that the latest supply of Class-A and -B drugs to the valleys of South Wales was presently being organised from such an innocuous location? he asked himself. And who could imagine that the drugs themselves were now stored deep in underground tunnels, not a million miles from where he was now standing, and were even being packaged there for distribution, then doled out by his two new young friends, and their own friends, and sold, both singly, as well as in bulk, from the small, two-up two-down, terraced houses that populated the nearby town?

But what only a very small, select group of people did know, however - of which, of course, he was now one - was that the second house this side of the road-bridge that ran across the *Taff Trail*, and almost backed on to its viaduct, and but a short way up the road from the very pub he was ordering himself a drink in, was the current domicile of the renowned, international singer-songwriter, and equally renowned drug-addict, Carla Steel.

Moving his filled glass to the much drier beer-mat nearer his elbow, and accepting his change with a forced grin, Volver asked the Irish landlord why his pub was called *The Railway*, when he had yet to see a single train, or even a yard of standard-width railway track, this side of Merthyr.

'Well, a double-line track used to run right through here around thirty or forty years ago,' the Kerry man told him. 'And this pub, you see, happens to be much older than that.'

'Oh, is that right?' Volver asked him, slipping a tiny pill into his glass then drinking from it.

'You must have seen the huge viaduct called *The Seven Arches* as you drove your car up here, surely?' the Irishman added, studying the raw, acne patch bordering the Afrikaner's beard.

'Do you mean that huge bridge over the valley that only cyclists seem to use,' said Volver, 'and whose track then passes under the road that this pub is on?'

'Aye, that's right,' the landlord told him. 'Well, just this side of the little road-bridge that they all cycle under is the terraced house where the singer Carla Steel and her old, sick father now live. '*Coral,*' I think they went and called the house soon after they moved in there,' he went on, 'though none of my customers seem to have the foggiest idea why they went and did that.'

'I may seem like a useless, washed-up, toneless, old tin-can to you, my girl, but didn't you know that God recycles trash?'

Seated just across the finished breakfast dishes from him, Carla shook her head at her father, more in pity than in desperation.

He pointed at the black rectangular object that had now taken up residence on the living-room table. 'For heaven's sake what good is that thing to an old man like me, eh?' he asked her.

Tom was sounding especially angry that morning. Despite the thick reefers his daughter regularly force-fed him twice-daily, his pains now seemed to be getting worse once again. 'When you called up from London and you told me you were getting me a new eye-pad,' he said, 'I certainly didn't think you were going to bring me a blasted computer! I recently had cataract surgery, remember, so you surely must have known I'd look damn silly with that enormous thing cellotaped to my forehead?' He lifted it up and flapped it against his temple to illustrate his point.

'I know, Dad, I know,' his giggling daughter replied. 'But I couldn't exactly see your face from my flat in London, could I? After all, you haven't got *Skype* like I have.'

'*Skype!* What the hell is that when it's at home?' asked Tom, rubbing his now aching chest. 'Anyway, I told you I can't stand that *Sky,* didn't I? Their TV-News always seems to me to be wtitten by that Dai Cameroon himself.'

Despite having only recently arrived in *Gloryhole*, and with a few of his boxes still unpacked, Tom Davies was now very much on his way out. It was a tragic situation, of course, but one that he had trained himself to become accustomed to, more or less understood, and, in recent days, with the invaluable, spiritual support his brother Gary provided him, now partially embraced.

Tom let his mind drift back to the preceding winter when he was living in a flat on the outskirts of Cardiff. He had first known that he was in serious trouble when he wasn't able to find his only pair of pyjamas for three days straight, and then one morning, on opening the cupboard at the top of the stairs to collect a fresh tea-towel, found them draped snugly, but, of course, far too warmly, over the immersion-heater that sat inside. And then one morning, and at least three days after he had ventured out for his shopping, he discovered that the red, plastic serving-spoon he had mysteriously mislaid was lying deeply submerged within its tin under more than half a pound of *Alpen*, which he quickly realised he must have stupidly poured right on top of it.

These two instances were just signs, it's true, thought Tom, but he knew full well the enormity of what they meant for him. And what they meant was that, sooner, rather than later, he would need to ring up, and perhaps even summon to him, his only daughter Carla, whom he hadn't seen for years, and who now lived up in London, where her musical career continued to flourish. And what he realised he would now be forced to tell her, he regretted far more than if he was once again having to report to her the sudden death of their much-loved, springer spaniel, Coral.

Tom's mind then drifted forward to just a week ago. One afternoon he had told his daughter, 'It's only Spring, Carla, and the people on the television-news seem to be going on and on about 'summer bed-linen.' Turn it over so I can watch '*Countdown*,' would you, there's a good girl.' Carla had slumped sideways on the sofa and laughed up at him. 'It was a man known as Osama Bin Laden that that they were all referring to, Dada,' she told him. 'American soldiers found him and killed him in some mansion he was hiding away in in northern Pakistan,' Carla had continued. 'And then they promptly buried him at sea, if you care to believe what they claim.'

Tom screwed up his eyes in his quaint, enigmatic fashion, and tried hard to make sense of the rather improbable geography that seemed to be involved in the unlikely tale his daughter had just related to him. But, irrespective of the particular spatial limitations involved, Tom soon had to admit that he simply wasn't capable of making head nor tail of it.

'It's called a '*Sidecar*,' ' Volver told him. 'That's brandy, cointreau and lemon-juice. Stick with me and you could be drinking them every night of the week, trust me. Hey, boys - are you listening?'

'I won't be a minute,' said Steffan, turning away from the older man and approaching the one-armed bandit that stood against the pub-wall. 'It's just that this machine took money off me last night, and I swear I'm just not having that.' He tossed a coin in the air, spun his body round once, and caught it. 'It's pay-back time!' he announced to the strange metal object with a growl.

'Shall I tell you what that's called, Steffan?' asked Volver, turning round to watch him.

'Determination?' the boy shot back.

'Just listen to yourself, will you? No, it's called addiction,' Volver told him. 'And if you happen to have got an addictive personality - and you clearly have, lad - then, I reckon you should save your addiction for the things that really matter in life. I mean, save it for fhe food you depend on.'

'Food!' exclaimed Steffan, dropping a coin into the machine and seeing how his luck was. 'By that I take it you mean drugs?' he enquired of the man in the shiny suit.

'Of course,' the South African replied, wishing his young, track-suited companion hadn't moved so far away from him, so that he could have slapped him squarely on the back. 'You and I should be grateful that drugs are so addictive, right, Steffan? If coke happens to be a man's food, then a man has got to eat, right?' Volver stepped away from the bar and moved closer to him. 'Listen. That mate of yours.' The Afrikaner paused for effect. 'He's a couple of sheets short of the full roll, if you ask me.' He lowered his head and sipped his drink, and waited to see the stocky boy's reaction. 'Where's he gone now, by the way? I just went and bought the twat a pint.'

'Are you talking about Jake?' Steffan asked distractedly. 'Why, he's gone to get the food,' he told him, pulling once again on the obtuse-angled lever of the big, illuminated object, then flashing the older man a smile. The first coin he dropped plainly sank without trace, and the second quickly went the same way, but the third brought him three plums, and, as if so much fresh fruit had upset the very bowels of the machine, it suddenly belched like a mis-firing piston, and spewed out from its nether regions a gush of steaming silver.

'Wow! I see slot-machines just buckle in your hands, lad,' said Volver, grinning admiringly.

'I don't think it's so much the machine, per se,' Steffan told him, bending low, and gathering up all the money in two separate hands, then sifting it carefully, coin by grubby coin, through his fingers, and then down into the side-pockets of his jacket. 'No, I believe it's the fruit.'

'The fruit!' ejaculated the South African, looking down at him.

'Yeah. For some reason, fruit always seem to - to melt in my hands.'

'Melt!' exclaimed Volver, not catching the boy's drift, fearing it might be some new item of street-speak English he had missed out on, but still determined to press home the point. 'Please tell me, if you can, Steffan, how the hell fruit can melt, would you?'

'Crumble then,' said Steffan. 'Yeah, crumble I mean.' He made a determined effort to smile back at Volver, but suddenly felt something deep within his guts that prevented him. Yes, the boy realised that he had probably made an error in insisting that his school-mate Jake join the rich man's gang, but he didn't take kindly to the smug way in which the suited man seemed always to want to drive home, at their expense, his sense of superiority. Steffan felt it might be the kind of drugs the tall, bearded man was hooked on that made him act like that, or maybe that's just how he was by nature. Either way, Steffan knew that he didn't like it. 'They're just fruit, aren't they?' he told Volver. 'And didn't we hear the man on the news just say that this was likely to be the year when *Blackberry* and *Apple* crumbled? Or one of the buggers at least.'

Tom was lying on his back in bed with an open bible propped up, and supported vertically, in his thin, frail fingers, against the first fold of the thick blanket that Carla had turned back lovingly for him across the top of his shiny, green eiderdown. With the aid of his reading-glasses, which sat, unbalanced and askew, just below the bridge of his long, hooked nose, he was endeavouring to read a passage from *The New Testament* which he found had recently begun to mean the world to him, and which seemed especially pertinent at this, the crucial, pivotal juncture in his long, but now plainly ending, life.

Tom's reading was a silent, joyous task; these days, perhaps it was his only one. A blind person could not have heard the ailing man turn his pages, nor a deaf person have perceived the tiny tears that soon began to fill up the dark, inner corners of the old man's weary eyes. The door of his room slowly opened and he looked up and saw his lovely daughter walk over and sit herself down close beside the gentle, shiny hillock that was his slender, covered frame. Tom read on. He realised that, by now, Carla was as accustomed to the idea of the inevitable happening as was he himself, and, now that his reverend brother was present in the house with him most evenings, and also during the daytime hours when his work didn't call him away, Tom felt it far easier to accept, and even to corroborate without undue anguish, the undeniable fact that he had, by now, reached the final, wafer-thin pages of his very own *Book of Revelation*.

Though ever present, thoroughly devoted, and constant in her many, and varied, tasks of administering to him, at times Carla's mind couldn't help but be gripped with the sad, unfortunate image of the dying astronaut lying abed, and respiring over-loudly, in the film '*2001: A Space Odyssey*.' The man even looked like my dad, she mused. There again, that fictional figure had aged and died utterly alone and abandoned, she told herself, while her father, now at least, had around him all of the living members that remained of his once-close, but still cherished, family.

Yes, Carla pondered, as she watched her dear father's flickering pupils scan the brief lines of the numbered verses that he read without speaking, a once-loving family had sprung out of a small village embedded in the lush, green pastures of the Vale of Usk, and had travelled the wide world, seemingly making at least some difference to the lives of people of all ages, and of a variety of different creeds and cultures. And her dear father could feel rightly proud of his contribution in this respect, she told herself, nodding. While her own efforts had unquestionably entertained, and perhaps, to some degree, enriched, the lives of millions of music-lovers on six different continents - and many might claim that this was a very laudable achievement in itself - her father's efforts, and not just his medical work, but the actions that followed from the application of his *'gift,'* had actually *saved* lives. And so to Carla's mind there was little doubt as to whose lifetime achievements she considered by far the more worthy and meritorious.

Not many weeks after Carla had returned again to Wales, Death - that overseas relation, that foul-breathed reclamation-bailiff - had powerfully, but stealthily, appeared on the scene, and had now dealt his drastic, penultimate blow, which had all but taken from her father's, already withering, frame what pulsing life his lungs and limbs still possessed.

The old man now lay almost constantly horizontal and enfeebled, but, thankfully, still in possession of a brain that could apprehend the tragic, physical drama that was enfolding about him, accept it - both in its power, and in its finality - and, unlikely as it appeared to Carla at first, was still able, by intermittent, selected reading, to shape it to his own spiritual needs; hence the orange-covered, hard-back book he now gripped onto as tightly as the tendons in his frail, trembling digits allowed; hence the silent whisper of the magical words of Jesus, which she recalled her first pastor had ofttimes claimed saved a man afresh each time he read them. Carla watched lovingly as, after several futile attempts, the frail man finally found the diaphanous, curved corner, and turned over the page, knowing how this meant her father would now be able to finish reading the multi-versed passage he had begun, and which he had no doubt been recommended to read by his more knowledgeable younger brother.

Presently Tom closed the book and looked about him. His only daughter's lovely blue eyes were once more what he first caught sight of, and he smiled serenely in their direction. Yes, Tom told himself, he felt that he had lived a life that was packed full of love, even one punctuated liberally with single moments of heightened joy, and yet he realised that many other folk had been much less fortunate. In recent years he had seen first-hand what could happen to a nation when the world economy took its gloves off. And so, out of empathy for a people, who, in recent days, had felt cruelly traduced by those in whom, at the ballot-box, they had placed their trust, Tom was at least glad that it was at this gloomy time that he was being summoned to depart this life, on board the last, and final, train, fluorescently emblazoned, 'Bound For Gloryhole.'

The sound of the door-bell chimed three times throughout the house. Carla bent her head and listened, as the front-door was opened by her uncle, and then a woman, whose voice was, by now, very familiar to her, could be heard requesting entrance, and, not very many seconds after that, could be heard climbing the stairs towards them. Her Uncle Gary soon sent the uninvited guest into the bedroom ahead of him, and, very like a female sleep-walker, standing spellbound before them all in a plain skirt, jumper, and heels, their next-door neighbour, Anne Cillick, looked all about her in the interior gloom, then slowly approached the old man's bed.

The light emanating from the single bulb above their heads spread like a pale, watery paint across Anne's plain face. Seeing, and then suddenly recognising, precisely who his visitor happened to be, Tom let the orange-covered tome topple heavily to the carpeted floor. In an apparent effort to recover it, he forced his feeble torso to turn and swivel, his free arm very soon hanging low over the bedside, dripping thin, twitching fingers beneath it. But Carla, sensing the man's desperation, lifted his body back into place again, and quickly reached down and secured the precious book for him, placing it, now closed and safe again, alongside his crumpled knees.

Carla turned and stared up at Anne, plainly unsure as to why it was that the older woman had disturbed them with her presence. She waited for an explanation, any explanation, but, when it eventually came, she was aghast to hear her ailing father deliver it from behind her back.

'You finally came, then, girl,' said Tom. 'I knew - I just knew you would. Eventually, I mean.'

'Yes. I hope you don't mind,' Anne replied, quickly glancing at Carla, and then at the reverend, both of whom she sensed might already know why she had arrived to see their reclining host. 'I had just come home, you see, and had switched off the music that someone had left playing, and the computer, and the lights when - when you - when the call came.'

'I'm sorry. Do you mean somebody phoned you?' asked Carla, clearly perplexed. 'Please take a seat,' she said, pointing to the wooden rocking-chair that stood at an angle to the bed.

'Thank you, dear. Yes. No,' Anne told them senselessly, retreating unsteadily, then sitting down. 'No - it wasn't the phone. I think I must have fallen asleep in the chair for a moment, if I'm honest. Then I - then I heard the words.'

'Words!' repeated Carla.

'Yes,' Anne told her. 'At first I thought my boy Chris was calling out for me - from inside this house, you know? But I can see now that - that he's obviously not here.'

'Well, he *was* here much earlier,' Carla told her. Just then she heard the sound of a floor- board creaking overhead, and suddenly thought that he might now be moving around up above them in the loft, and perhaps even listening in to their queer conversation. 'But I haven't a clue where Chris is now, I'm sure,' Carla told her.

'Why, the young lad's just tending the farm, I guess,' Tom suddenly remarked with a grin, turning onto his side the better to see them, and then, from Catla's look, suddenly realising the folly of the comment he had just made in the presence of the boy's own mother. 'Oh, I'm sorry.'

'Farm! But we don't own any farm,' Anne told the old man, smiling. 'I'm Anne from next-door, dear, remember. Anne Cillick.' Then turning to his daughter, she remarked. 'Your father seems a lot more fatigued tonight, don't you think, Carla?'

Tom focused his ice-blue eyes on the visitor's face. 'But I recall you lived - you lived quite close to one back then, didn't you?' the man continued. 'A little sheep-farm, wasn't it?'

'Back then? Oh, I guess you must mean in *The Sixties,*' Anne told him. 'Yes, that's right, I did,' said Anne, intrigued now, and pulling her chair a little closer to the old man's bed.

'Where, if I recall, and please forgive me for my bluntness, dear, I recall that your parents - well, your father, at any rate - often maltreated you quite appallingly, yes?'

Anne bit sharply into her lip at the sudden, painful memory of it. 'Why, yes,' she retorted.

'Because back then I seem to remember you had cigarette-burns all over you,' Tom continued. 'Not to mention how terribly under-nourished you seemed to be for a girl of eleven.'

'Yes, I guess I was rather skinny, but I don't remember any burns,' Anne replied, wincing.

Tom stared directly at her. 'And yet you had the most perfect teeth, isn't that right?' he asked. He began to smile serenely as he gazed into the woman's face, and at the little red mouth, whose teeth he was sure he knew almost as well as his own. 'Not a single filling required, let alone a *'straction,'* he said. Tom smiled, then closed his eyes, recollecting it even more vividly.

'Yes, that's true,' said Anne, shaking her head from side to side. 'So it *is* you, then,' she said, trembling. 'You know, I had this odd feeling it might be when you - when you first moved in here.'

'My dad is *who*, exactly?' enquired Carla, her mouth agape, her blue eyes bulging, and now darting rapidly from one to the other. 'Would someone kindly tell me what this is all about?'

Tom leaned across and smiled at his daughter. 'Sweetheart, I was the man who checked Anne's teeth in that junior-school back then. You know, in *The Sixties,* back in Aberfan.'

'Oh, is that all?' said Carla. 'But what a fuss you seem to be making about it, Dad, since I guess you must have checked thousands of children's teeth over the years, including many who came from there. And now that I recall it, didn't you say you even checked many of the children who tragically got killed on that awful day in nineteen-sixty-six. Yes, I'm quite sure I remember you telling me that.' Her father nodded in acquiescence of the fact. 'Say, how sad is that, eh?'

'Yes, he did,' remarked Anne, turning away from Carla, and gazing lovingly into the sick man's eyes, that she could see were lined and cracked far more deeply than were her own. 'Twice every year, wasn't it, Mr. Davies? A small, sinister spoon in one hand, and a bottle of pink poison in the other.' She smiled at the distant memory her mind had just then recalled for her, then turned to look into the eyes of the old man's daughter. And, taking the pretty girl's pale, trembling hands between her own, she said, 'But Carla, dear - much more importantly, your father was the man who saved my life.'

CHAPTER 16

Leone Lewis wasn't the young, bleach-blonde girl's name when she got christened by her Gran in St. Helen's Catholic Church back in her native Caerphilly, although it might easily have been. After all, many girls got given strange names in the early nineties, she told herself, like Sinead, and Peaches, and, of course, Madonna. But, either way, ever since the very first day she left home, and moved into a flat on a vast, windswept housing-estate in Merthyr, Leone was the name that everyone came to know her by, on the net, on the phone, and on the street.

And, in Leone's case, that was the order in which things usually happened for her - work-wise, that is. I mean that was the way that she usually discovered that she was in demand, then confirmed she would be turning up to party, and then, well, partied hard and fast, invariably armed with at least one spare thong, a pair of thick, suspender-tights for cold surfaces, the obligatory maxi-pack of condoms (one size fits all), and, as a back-stop, a tab or two of morning-after pills. Designer-drugs she almost always left to her evening's date to supply, and in this respect she rarely found herself let down. To Leone, going out partying was very like going into battle, and, just like war itself, it often turned out to be a highly profitable business for all parties concerned.

Volver usually rang up Leone whenever he found himself in Merthyr, and, on the occasions when he didn't, and word of his presence reached her, far from feeling angry with him for his forgetfulness, or his indifference, she knew precisely how she could get hold of the man herself, and always ensured that she did. Leone knew only too well that the tall, rugged looking, South African drug-dealer made very good money, and, irrespective of where it actually came from, or of its general legality, Leone was determined that she would be getting her cut, her slice of it.

Although a woman around fifteen years Volver's junior, the positive side of being desired by someone older, Leone thought, was that she now felt less like the ungendered marionette she had always believed herself to have been while a school-girl, and also throughout the two, mind-numbing years that followed, when she was employed stitching knickers and bras for a pittance at *Blossom's* on the local industrial-estate, and awaiting, with growing anticipation, her land-mark, eighteenth birthday.

'It's not a bald patch at all, love. It's a solar panel for a sex-machine,' she suddenly heard Volver tell the fat, young barmaid in the tight top. Yes, she could easily tell that Gwenda Reilly was as smitten with her man as she was. What a plank the thick-hipped girl was though, she told herself; as out of shape as she was plainly out of her depth.

Boys! mused Leone in bewilderment. Though they seemed to want everything, what the boys her own age wanted she had never quite been able to work out. To be frank, she didn't even think they had much idea themselves of what it was they were really after. On receiving the customary, leering stare from some horny, downy-faced, eighteen-year old, Leone invariably felt almost as if someone was having a party in her own home without inviting her along to share the experience. And yes, too often it simply wasn't a two-way thing at all. And two-ways was how it had to be for Leone to be happy. Providing she had that two-way thing going on with a man, she knew she would be minded to agree to just about any suggestion that he might put to her. And with an older guy like Volver it thankfully always did go two-ways. Although, if asked himself, the lanky South African would most likely claim that the only choice involved was his own. You see, as Volver saw it, and was ever keen to claim, it had always been his way or the highway.

'If she hadn't been a nurse, I'd have felt a lot worse,' Leone heard Volver declare loudly, on his return from the bar, armed with more drinks all round.

'What was that, babe?' she asked him. But she quickly saw how he seemed far too excited with it all to be interested in even listening to anything she had to say today, let alone replying.

'You're a bloody poet and you didn't know it, Volve,' Steffan told the man, with smile, taking his frothy pint off the small, round tray he held, and handing another one over to Jake. 'Nurse and worse, I mean.'

Hangers-on, thought Leone, dragging from her Silk-Cut. Don't they just make you sick! Were these two youngsters planning on staying around all night, then? she mused. She sincerely hoped not. You see, Leone had serious plans for tonight, and they certainly didn't involve more than the one man - although, she mused, that sort of arrangement could always be accommodated at the right price, and in the right conditions. But these clearly weren't the right sort of men, she told herself, grinning. No sir-ee. Neither one seemed older than her younger brother, for a start.

Leone moved her busty body much closer to Volver, placed both her hands around his hips, and cushioned her head on his muscular chest. She nuzzled there for five seconds or more, but, from the man's total lack of reaction, she felt compelled to desist, smile up sweetly at him, then step back again. She quickly clocked that the coke the man had taken in the car had, by this time, fully kicked in, and so he didn't seem able to keep his gob shut even for a minute.

'I once got home from work and found my wife wearing this slinky number,' Volver was telling the two boys. 'I wasn't impressed, I can tell you.'

'Really? Why's that?' Jake asked him.

'Well, as I told her, I reckon it only really worked when she was going downstairs.' Volver sipped his drink, then looked from one to the other of them, then back round again. 'Don't you get it, lads?' he asked. Steffan nodded, smiling.

'Not really,' admitted Jake.

'Slinky number?' said Steffan, staring into his friend's eyes. 'Slinky, yeah? Going downstairs? Oh, forget it, Jake. You know, sometimes I reckon he's only interested in the universe, Volve.'

'Then that must mean I'm interested in absolutely everything there is, wouldn't you say?' said Jake, grinning.

Running his wet, beery fingers through his straight, dark hair, Volver eyed Jake warily. This guy was a liability if ever there was one, the Afrikaner was thinking. He would probably need to put him in the front-line sooner rather than later, he told himself. He had misgivings about it for Steffan's sake, but it was clear that, at the end of the day, Jake would prove to be a sacrifice worth making. Yes, the South African felt quite sure of this fact, and, if truth be told, he could even foresee in his mind's eye the scenario in which Jake's demise was most likely to occur. He just hoped it wouldn't need to be as messy, or as time-consuming, as the last time, that's all.

Volver turned to watch Leone's nervous movements, which, for some reason, seemed more frenetic than ever tonight. Witnessing at first-hand the racing metabolism that had kept her figure movie-actress thin, and barely weathering the tear-gas attack of her latest perfume, he listened with a certain admiration, as she loudly berated the behaviour of a scrawny, gangly youth who was standing sheepishly behind her at the pool-table, and who had most likely run his four-foot cue up her mini-skirt. Volver turned away and sipped his drink, feeling that he couldn't really blame the guy, since the Welsh girl, standing hand-on-hip before him, was clearly dressed to kill tonight, and, from her reactions at the pool-table, most likely wouldn't hesitate to do so.

It could easily be on account of the quantity and the variety of drink he had consumed this evening, Volver mused, but large, white, cartoon puffs of steam appeared to be shooting out of the petite girl's ears as she spun round and bawled for, what seemed, the final time at her callow-faced, local adversary. The South African watched keenly as Leone suddenly turned and reached for the pool-cue herself, and, grabbing it firmly in both hands, and, waving it just the once, struck the hapless youth a smack on the side of the head that made his knees buckle. Simply smiling over at the abrupt onslaught, Volver felt that the poor man's subsequent crash to the floor might easily have been mistaken for the last bar of a Bartok concerto, or the final, atonal chord of a symphony by Stockhausen. Yes, Leone was some tough cookie, and no mistake, the Afrkaner concluded, and so the pretty Welsh girl was just as much a liability to his future plans as was poor Jake, and, as a result, he would almost certainly have to let her go too.

But informing Steffan of Jake's expendability could well backfire on him in the long run, he told himself, whereas hinting as much to the boy about Leone was unlikely to create such a problem. Either way, he thought, to avoid complicating his plans disastrously, he would be best advised to keep his feelings about the pair of them strictly to himself for the forseeable future. And anyway, he didn't want anything to have the effect of unsaddling his present hurtling gallop towards hedonistic oblivion. There would come a time when he could unburden himself to Steffan, Volver told himself, but until that time arrived, his intention was only to consume as much of Leone as his precious time, and his folded tab of viagra, would that evening allow.

No, Volver thought, it was clearly best for the time being that Leone continue to presume she still held before her the prospect of a future with him, even though he had already judged her to be past her best physically at just nineteen years young, and so her chances were already hopelessly shot. Ah, well, he pondered, Man had always been the un-fairer sex, had he not? And, in truth, it had always been thus, and so he understandably felt he had a long and proud tradition to uphold in this regard. And so, winking across at Jake, and with this final thought in mind, Volver spun round and finished off what remained of his *Sidecar*, and swiftly forgave himself, well ahead of time, for the utter carnage he most assuredly knew lay ahead of them.

Considering the strange, unexpected response Chris had just given her, the middle-aged spinster in the squeaky court-shoes, chequered skirt-suit, and polo-neck sweater, from whose scrawny neck hung a chain-tag whose card read 'Stella Probert,' carefully placed her round, silver-framed, spectacles on the small table that sat between them, and regarded the uniformed student thoughfully.

'*Nothing can deform the human race like to The Armour's tight embrace,*' she told him slowly, simulating a stern countenance throughout, while beating out an iambic metre on the table-top with two of her long, but unpolished, finger-nails on a left-hand that bore no ring.

'Rhod Gilbert, yes?' asked Chris, arching his brows.

'Really? I thought it was William Blake,' Stella told him, squinting suddenly and sitting back, so betraying more than just a faint sign of disappointment at his quirky response. 'I'm sorry but isn't Rhod Gilbert a comedian?' she asked.

Chris nodded in reply. God, man! All he had done was to express to the woman an interest in joining *The Army* when he left school, Chris told himself. Of course, he wasn't being serious, but he figured that this thin, rather emaciated, lady from the county's *Careers Service,* (who looked for all the world like some pale-faced minion from *The Treasury*, and who, like him, probably hadn't done a proper day's work in her entire life,) would either be impressed by his reply and compliment him accordingly, or have a slight fit and respond in much the same way as she had in fact just done, except with far less cultivation and artistic awareness than she had actually managed. Well, there you go, thought Chris, it did seem that there were some women from the Rhymney Valley who were quite erudite after all.

'Blake - of course,' he said, grinning, having no idea whether it was or not. 'I was only jesting. And if I'm not mistaken, I do believe he wrote that particular ditty not very long before he set off for the New Jerusalem. I'm right, aren't I?' This statement of his was, of course, complete garbage, but Chris was very interested to see how the geeky-looking woman responded

'Yes, I dare say you're right,' the careers-officer replied, leaning her round, bunned-head on one side and beaming across at him.

Watching the woman fiddle nervously with her pen, as her eyes moved up, then down, his youthful body, Chris asked himself why it was that spinster-virgins were so easy to spot these days, and then wondered how many liquid *Stellas* he'd need to consume in a row before finally consenting to do this one. He chuckled inwardly. Well, she could certainly benefit from a piercing or two, he mused, smiling thinly, as well as perhaps a lot more besides.

'Chris - what are you thinking right now?' the woman suddenly asked him.

'Oh, I was just wondering what - what exactly you had against the military?' he replied. In truth Chris was actually ruminating over whether or not she had ever given head. 'The pointy weapons, perhaps?' he asked, pursing his lips. 'The night-manoeuvres? All that banging?'

'No, it's not that at all,' Stella told him, repeatedly licking her lips on the occasions when he wasn't watching. 'It's just that, however hard I try, I just can't seem to visualize you in fatigues, Christopher. You don't really seem to fit the type somehow.' The girl nevertheless attempted it.

Chris didn't at all like being judged in this way, especially as he thought he looked rather hot on days when he donned his green combats, and so he planned a little further revenge. 'I guess - like a lot of other people - I think I just want to join the Army to forget,' he informed her.

'To forget? To forget what?' she asked, tilting her head to the side.

Yes, she had fallen for it all right. 'Mm,' Chris retorted. 'I can't seem to remember now.'

'Very funny, Chris. Ha, ha,' said Stella. 'You'll be telling me next, that you want to join the Foreign Legion, or some such thing,' she said, putting her glasses back on, then leaning forward and scribbling something down on the one-page form that sat before her, and which Chris could see bore his full name, written in particularly large capitals, across the top.

Chris wasn't at all happy with this either, and tried hard to read what the woman was jotting down, twisting his head round almost in a full circle to do so. But so illegible did he find Stella's writing to be that he wasn't able to make out a single scrawled word of it. Chris leaned back in his chair again and inhaled deeply. He hadn't quite finished with this infernal, dowdy throw-back yet, he told himself. 'But that's French, isn't it? The Foreign Legion, I mean,' Chris told her, affecting a glum expression. 'You know, I think I'd much prefer working in the British Legion.'

'What on earth do you mean, you silly boy? There's no such thing,' Stella replied, giggling.

'There is. There's one at the bottom of town,' he countered. 'Just imagine the fun it would be to work there. I bet I could pull pints, serve spirits, and even get to sell those little red poppies all at the same time.' He bit into his lip again to stop himself from creasing up.

Stella Probert finally realised what was happening, and she decided that didn't like it one bit. 'Stop it, Chris!' she told him. 'Come on, now, think. There must be something you could actually see yourself doing?'

'Do you mean like installing mirrors?' he replied, screwing up his mouth so as to stifle the short guffaw that very soon came out anyway.

'Well, do you think you'd like that?' she asked, completely oblivious to his latest jest.

'Not really, no,' Chris responded. 'Look - I really can't see how you're going to be able to find a career for me, Miss Probert. I remember my sister was in the same boat when she left this place. Bethan. Do you remember? You interviewed her too, you know, when you first got your job here. She told me you reminded her of Thatcher.' He saw how Stella was shocked by this. 'But please don't feel offended. You see - we both have the same problem with authority figures.'

'Oh, do you think so?' asked Stella, leaning forward and scribbling on the form again.

'To be honest, yes,' he told her. 'Though I must admit Bethan's a lot worse than me. She quit her job at the helium-gas factory on the very first day.'

'Oh? And why was that?' asked Stella.

'She told the manager she refused to be spoken to in that tone.' Chris leaned right forward, bending his torso up double in gloating euphoria.

'O.K., that's quite enough,' remarked Stella. 'You're just making fun of me now, right?'

'Does the Pope shit in the woods?' Chris retorted cryptically.

Stella stared at him, non-plussed by his response. 'I wouldn't know, does he?' she asked, getting to her feet and walking over to a filing-cabinet near the large, single-pane window, through which Chris could see a school's cricket-match taking place in the sunny distance, and which summer-term fixture, right now, he should have been taking part in. 'But, whatever effect I had on your sister, I can tell you now I refuse to be treated in this way.' She spun round and stared in his direction, looked at the clock on the wall, and, professional to the end, decided to press on regardless of the palpable anger that she was now desperately trying to quell within her. 'Tell me Chris - have you seriously not got an ambition that you would like to fulfill in life?'

'Yes I have, as a matter of fact,' he told her.

'And what is it?' she asked, standing above him, hands-on-hips.

'I want to be a rock-star, and be incredibly rich,' said Chris. 'You know, like Carla Steel.'

'Like Carla Steel!' the woman repeated, pouting manically.

'Yes,' he told her. 'Though God only knows what advice you gave *her*.'

As Stella scribbled his response down, she pondered this, and surmised that her predecessor Bryn had probably met with her. 'O.K. Well, all right then,' she told him. 'Now that wasn't hard, was it?' Stella picked up the form, pocketed it, placed her brief-case under her arm, and opened the door to leave. 'I shall send you some leaflets re your choice within the next seven working days, Christopher. Although, I must say, rock-star isn't one that I find I encounter most days.'

'Mm, I can understand that,' Chris told her, getting to his feet and loosening the tie that he now didn't require out on the field. He watched the woman's eyes drift down as he unfastened three buttons on his tight, white shirt and went for the fourth. 'But that could be because the boys see you as a bit of a prude, Miss Probert, you know, and they don't want to say anything that might - might shock your pants off.' He beamed a sharp smile and unbuttoned on.

Studying him from behind, Stella was suddenly feeling flushed, and so took the top off her water-bottle and swallowed a mouthful. Screwing the top on, she turned away but stared surrepticiously as Chris pulled his white, short-sleeved cricket-shirt down over his slim, tanned torso. 'By the way, Christopher,' said Stella, 'the reason I wasn't able to help your sister Bethan, I remember, was that she told me, plain and simple, that she wanted to find the right man, have lots and lots of kids, and live the rest of her life on benefits. And, I'm sure that even you can appreciate that we simply don't issue any leaflets on that.'

'I see. Well, you might like to know that she managed to achieve it anyway,' Chris told her, smiling a thin, pinched smile. 'Three at the latest count.'

'Children?' enquired Stella.

'No, no - partners,' Chris replied. 'But I have five lovely nephews and nieces now, and I look forward to having more as the years go by.'

Stella glared at him, trying to imagine the poverty and the shame this all entailed, and which she had successfully managed to avoid during her life, though quite naturally at a cost in terms of love and sex and motherhood - a bargain which she felt - no, she knew - she would always feel was well worth the making.

Stella Probert continued to study him closely - by now Chris had slipped off his shoes and socks - and licked her thin, parched lips for the final time. 'Well, goodbye now, Chris,' she told him, with a brief, manufactured smile that she felt suited all sorts of occasions, and clients of both genders. She then walked her squeaky little court-shoe-d feet out into the noisy, school-corridor, and, with a final, sly peek, pulled the heavy, window-less door tightly closed behind her.

For much of the time that Padraig stood pulling pints behind the bar he seemed to be delivering a virtual monologue, which normally comprised an ironic, barbed commentary, filled with inimitable, trade-mark interjections, that seemed to his customers very like a train that, if they chose to, they could hop on and ride for a while, then leap from once again, to continue conducting their business - their social interaction - on the bar-room platform that ran alongside.

This, you could say, was the Irish landlord's trade-mark managerial style, and, by the evidence of the crowds, both young and old, who flocked to *The Railway* nightly, and throughout the afternoon, it was one of which the locals seemed to mightily approve. And yet, although respected for the quality of his beer and stout, his boisterous, self-effacing humour, and his passion for international rugby, boxing and football, the one thing about Padraig of which people didn't approve was his over-use of the word *'fucking'* in general conversations, as an intensifier.

'Craig - you fucking eejit - what the fuck are you talking about?' the short, stocky, thick-jowled, man bawled out from behind the beer-mat strewn bar-counter. 'God's own people indeed. The damned Scots were a fuckin' *Irish tribe,* remember,' Padraig told the young Scotsman with an aggressive, somewhat sarcastic laugh.

'And what the hell have you got to laugh at, Paddy?' Craig retorted, a blue Rangers' baseball-cap perched slightly askew on his dark, curly forehead. 'It's a known fact that St. Patrick came from Wales.'

'Don't fuck with me now!' Padraig warned him, threatening to blast him in the face with a wet, scrunched-up dish-cloth.

'But he's absolutely right,' I told them both, with a smile, but ducking as I did so, just in case, as did the wiry Scotsman to my left. 'Whisked off the South Wales coast by a band of Irish pirates so the story goes, or so my wife tells me, anyway. Soon after that to become an eminent cleric in Ireland, of course, and later to be sent off to see the pope in Rome on behalf of the Irish people, and the rest, as they say, is history.'

'History! Bull-crap! You're fuckin' wid me again, Dyl!' Padraig rudely, but typically, retorted. 'And I was considering getting you both a pint, as well you know. But you've gone and missed out there, I can tell you,' he announced, turning away from us and shaking his over-large head about.

'I'll venture your missus is no more an authority on Celtic History than you are, damn you. Or me, for that matter. Yes, you've gone too far, now, boyo. And just you wait till the Rugby World Cup comes round in September, old man. We're gonna bounce your red, spotty, Welsh arses out the whole fuckin' competition, so we are.'

'Fat chance of that, I'd say,' I retorted, 'what with all those talented youngsters we've got coming through.' This didn't please the Munster man one bit, and I felt I'd overdone it. 'Look - I'll get them in, Paddy,' I said, waving my beer-mat in his direction. 'It's my turn, anyway, as I recall.'

'I'd get a round in myself but I'm well nigh broke today,' Craig countered. 'Do you know that energy costs have shot up so high these days I can barely keep all my farms going!'

'Farms, you say? Really, Craig? Sheep or cows?' I asked him, chuckling.

'Er, neither, as a matter of fact,' he replied, smiling. 'Small, sort of highly intensive, *interior* farms, is what I'm referring to, you know.'

'Interior farms! What the hell are they?' I enquired, thoroughly confused by what the Scotsman was telling me.

'Weed.' he said, winking oddly with his good eye.

'Have you?' I asked, stepping back. He grinned and shook his capped head from side to side in frustration. 'Oh, *weed*,' I continued. 'I see. And what exactly do you feed that to? Seagulls?'

'Well, people, generally,' he replied, smiling, and giving me a somewhat quizzical look. 'Dyl, do you know, you come across as incredibly naive sometimes, wouldn't you say? You should try to get out of Pant more often, if you ask me. I reckon it's a bit like a coffin that's restraining your spirit of adventure. I had a similar feeling when I used to live in Swansea, you know. Though being stuck in the city's jail for most of the time didn't help, I admit.'

Yes, Craig was clearly right about me and Pant, and about getting out a bit more. Sadly, it dawned on me far too late what it was he was really talking about to start making any plans, but, either way, I thought it best to change the subject.

'Talking of feed,' I said. 'When I was driving down here from *'The Butcher's'* this evening I saw that stupid neighbour of yours - Mervyn, you know - nicking hay from a farm this side of Pontsticill. What a prat he is, wouldn't you say? I guess I could get him arrested, couldn't I?'

'Well, yes you could, I suppose, but he'd be sure to get bail,' Padraig shot back with a broad grin. 'Bail. Do you get it, Dyl? Ha Ha. No - I don't suppose you do.'

Yes, occasionally I still find that I can be the butt of other people's jokes, but much more frequently at *The Railway,* I find, than at *The Butcher's Arms.* Now I wonder why that is? I wondered, rubbing my eyes, and blinking, in an effort to stabilise my focus.

Appreciating how the ale had got to me, Craig took the opportunity to go for a leak. I was left with nobody to talk to, so I just allowed my thoughts to drift off to wherever they wanted to take me. I believe my son Chris - a son who has never known his real dad - me - sometimes goes off there too, I thought. But, in his case, I recently discovered he usually smokes cannabis to see it. Weed's the key to *his* door. That's the way his cat-flap gets opened up, even though he might not actually know it yet. But, in stark contrast with Chris, I find I don't need to smoke or ingest a damn thing. No. In my case I just have to think it, to see it. *Think it, to see it, to be it,* in fact, is how the whole thing seems to work for me, I told my flushed face in the mirror behind the bar.

I looked down at my pint-glass which, though sitting perfectly still, was ever so slightly wobbling on the counter before me. Is this bitter starting to get a lot stronger, then? I pondered to myself. Or is this some sort of after-shock of a minor earthquake caused by the afternoon's blasting at the limestone-quarry just down the road? Or could this even be my brother Sam, finally fulfilling his pledge to get back to me about the existence, or otherwise, of the after-life.

A thought suddenly hit me. Unlike the vast majority of my friends and family, including, of course, my wife Gwen, I had long felt convinced of the existence of *the supernatural world.* To me it seemed obvious that, rather like icebergs, all things material continued on down below the surface of our world, as much as nine-tenths of their reality concealed from the sight and senses of us plain, rudimentary folk.

I recalled how it had occurred to me one Sunday morning, much as an icicle occurs to a branch after a cold, hard night of constant dripping, that, in contrast to general opinion, our dead and departed are hardly departed very far from us at all, but instead, hover about us, almost entirely unobserved, in the high, shadowy corners of the rooms we inhabit, constantly open to oral, as well as wordless, thought-exchange, if not to direct consultation. 'No, this isn't just the ale talking this time,' I explained to my long-dead brother Sam, who I felt I could sense shaking his head at me from the far, upper corner of the bar, a foot or so above the clock. 'This is me telling you how it really is, Brawd. Though, being where you are, I guess I shouldn't need to!'

Tom was feeling dreadfully weary once again, and so he carefully placed his copy of Kahlil Gibran's '*The Prophet*' on the kitchen-table beside his rocking-chair and, folding up his glasses and placing them alongside it, gazed through tired eyes out across the verdant, tree-filled valley that was now thriving in its summer best, and then to his left at the great, stone viaduct that bestrode it, and which for many decades had carried the coal-powered steam-trains on a double-railway track right the way across it, and that he had had the pleasure of riding upon on a multitude of occasions in the days before he could afford a car, when he daily commuted to work in Merthyr from his boy-hood home in a village near Brecon to the north.

Tom took up the slim volume he dearly treasured once again and sought out the brief passage that had, just minutes before, moved him so much. He read it through one more time. Have I remembrances? Have I memories? he asked himself. Those glimmering arches that span the summit of my mind? He considered this and nodded. Yes. Yes, I truly believe I have, he answered, with a thoughtful smile. A great many wonderful memories, as a matter of fact, that are worth more to me now than any other thing in my life, except, of course, my Carla.'

Tom could still recall the first time he had leaned out through his carriage-window to gaze down into the Taff River, winding and carving its course through the deep cleft beneath him, and almost came to grief when the door suddenly slipped open, and he was forced to hang onto the leather window-belt for dear life. He was probably no more than twenty at the time, he mused, and, if his memory served him well, he was on his way to Merthyr to take his driving-test.

Tom found that many similar, but contrasting, experiences could be summoned up just as easily in his mind if he so chose to do, a number of them esconced in torrential rain, others, as today, bathed in warm, bright sunshine. The old man believed he could even remember being aboard the very last steam-train that passed through the halt that had stood alongside *Gloryhole's* only road, and which had traversed the *Seven Arches* at a much slower speed than was usual, perhaps because the train-driver and his fire-man were as conscious, as was Tom himself, of the significance of the sad, but momentous occasion. Quite soon Tom fell asleep, his bald head sunk back onto the chair's wooden back, and dreamed of those happier, sunnier days, probably the happiest of his life, a long time before his debilitating sickness took root.

Carla had been pottering about in her room, and decided to go downstairs to the kitchen to check on how her father was, and to see if he had finished any of his breakfast. To her eyes he thankfully now seemed comfortable and thoroughly fed, serene even, while taking nis customary nap. Suddenly, seeing the bright morning sunshine outside the window, Carla opened the back- door and stepped out onto the stone patio. 'Wow! What a crazy door-mat,' she exclaimed, stepping off it once again so as to study it closely. ' '*God Is Love*!' What's this Dada?' she whispered, bending low, then turning and holding it up before her, so that her father, if still awake, might see from the kitchen-table.

Blinking, Tom smiled at the sight, and answered, 'Oh, the mat,' he said. 'Well, if you must know, when you went down to Cardiff the other day I ordered it especially for you. Jack Belt brought it up in his van this morning, along with the cheese and the box of fuses.'

'Well, I'm not going to quibble about the message,' said Carla, shaking off the dirt that had already gathered upon it, and laying it back in place. 'I'm thrilled that you've seen the light at last. But on a door-mat, Dada! I mean, isn't that a bit silly?' She entered again and shut the door.

'Call me silly if you want,' he said, 'but I got it so you'd always have a scripture to stand on.'

Carla smiled at his comment, and surveyed the small, prickly, white beard that by now had begun to adorn her father's thin face since he had finally refrained from shaving daily, as had always been his custom as a younger, healthier man. Isn't it strange, Carla mused, how, as a middle-aged father, the beard he had worn back then had made him look twenty years older, and her mother had eventually made him shave it off, but now, as he neared the end of his days, the exact same beard, though much greyer, naturally, now made him look a good deal younger.

To the good folk of Gloryhole, Vaynor and Pontsticill, and of all the farms, inns, cottages and parsonages scattered around, about and in between, Jack Belt was much, much more than just a milkman. Old Jack was a travelling grocer, greengrocer, florist, pharmacist and tobacconist, who also operated an informal, though very highly valued, postal service, the continued operation of which was dependent on tips, gifts, gratuities, in other words on the anticipated, grateful benevolence of the receiver. On occasions, bottles of wine, bottled, home-made beers, home-made pies and pasties, and even cooked breakfasts were gratefully accepted by Jack, and frequently consumed in his van. Yes, in his daily travels around the northern, rural fringes of the Merthyr Valley, Jack Belt constantly felt like he led the sort of fulfilled and happy life that he had long hoped to. And, what is more, from his consistently happy, smiling disposition, the people of the quiet, green valley could quite easily see and tell as much.

Since the sliding-door on Jack's green Volkswagen *'Camper-Van'* would never shut properly, and the wind coming off the Beacons was invariably strong and fierce, more often than not Jack Belt could clearly be heard approaching his intended destination from as far as a mile away. On apprehending the strange, unique sound, local children would often hide behind walls and trees, and much older people would run back indoors, telling each other excitedly that *'Jack's banshee-van'* was coming; while well-travelled pensioners even reported how his eccentric, whistling vehicle sounded far more like a 'ghost-train' than the real thing in *Porthcawl Pleasure Park* had ever managed to, even in its hey-day in the nineteen-sixties.

Life-long bachelor Jack was an inveterate story-teller, who seemed to have very little trouble in detaining on her door-step any single, widowed, or divorced home-owner for anything up to an hour or more. He may have been small, bald, and ever so slightly bowed in carriage, but Jack Belt was as busy and urgent as a stoat, or a grey squirrel, or an upland badger even, and with the help of his natural vigour, his large, calloused hands, his over-tanned, nut-brown face, his single, silver ear-ring, and his broad, but gapped, smile, he certainly succeeded in capturing many a female's custom without even trying, and very often within the fluttering of a heart-string.

One of the more famous tales Jack was wont to tell his customers was how, as a boy of sixteen, who had mysteriously, and, most probably, mistakenly, got himself accepted into the town's *'County Grammar School,'* he had fared so atrociously in his only two 'O' level examinations - Physics and Latin - that when the the examination-board's letter came back the following August, he discovered that they had awarded him CSE's in Woodwork and Welsh! The gob-smacked Jack was naturally more than thrilled at this laudable, but highly unexpected outcome, and spent the rest of the day drinking celebratory rounds with his mates, in the public- bar of *The Quarryman's Arms* in Pant, and yet he still asked his Auntie Jean to hide the certificate somewhere in her cellar, so that there was no chance it might pop up again unexpectedly, and compromise whatever career it might be that he chose to turn his hand to.

But Jack soon discovered.that he needn't have overly concerned himself on that account, since he and Snowy Evans were appointed the town's official rat-catchers, and went on to hold their esteemed positions for well over twenty years, before Jack finally summoned up sufficient courage to finally bid farewell to the council, and to his generous, blond-haired compatriot, and set off in his recently recovered, second-hand, twice written-off, VW *'Camper-Van,'* to rent an isolated cottage, and its adjoining, former cattle-shed just north of *Caeracca*, and so try to live the airy, liberated life of the mythical, gipsy king, which Jack had for many years longed to be.

Goya's *'Colossus'* had been hanging on the wall in the living-room of Tom's house for some months now, having been brought there in the furniture-van along with everything else he had had the men pack for him on the bright, March morning when he had first arrived. Asking Carla to go downstairs and get it for him took the girl quite by surprise, but she nevertheless concurred with her father's request, and was soon entering his bedroom once more, this time with the large, glass-covered print held securely up against her front. When she turned it round to show him, Tom at first gawped, open-mouthed, at the utter beauty of the strange, powerful subject it depicted, but then lay back down again and smiled serenely, almost as if its arrival within the scene of his imminent demise was, in some way at least, a partial justification for the same.

'Yes - hang it up just there, would you, my love,' said Tom, lifting a thin, veined, wavering arm and pointing to the section of the bare wall immediately across from his bed, and wishing that he still had the energy to climb out of it to assist her in the task his daughter was confronted with.

Carla stepped out of her slippers, stood up on the wobbly, three-legged stool, and, with a minimum of fuss, and just the one solitary readjustment for form's sake, securely attached the great picture to a single hook, located centrally on the, otherwise bland, flock-papered surface.

'How is that, Dada?' she asked, hopping nimbly back to the floor, spinning round, and wiping her dusty fingers on the rear of her jeans. 'Now are you sure he's not going to scare you?'

'The Colossus! Heavens no! Why should he?' Tom asked, carefully sitting up against his pillows so as to experience the full aura of the cloud-covered, Iberian rural-scene now displayed before him, with its great, bearded colossus strangely turned away from it, his broad, muscle-bound back exposed and looming, and his powerful left arm poised, flexed and threatening.

'Well, I can well empathise with all the Spanish folk running for their lives to escape him,' Carla told her father. 'They are understandably all panic-stricken if you ask me. I'm terrified too just looking at it, if truth be told. That scary giant is one frightening sight, and no mistake, yeah?'

The two locked glances for a moment, while the elder probed deeply for the reply that would speak his mind and, at least partially, express the wit and weight of his experience. 'And am *I* a frightening sight?' the old man suddenly enquired, looking straight into Carla's sparkling eyes.

'What do you mean!' she asked, confused, and somewhat flustered by his strange riposte. 'Of course not, Dad. Why?'

'Because - well, because,' Tom replied, struggling to put his elusive thoughts into words that were comprehensible to her. 'Look - you're a clever, artistic soul, aren't you, my sweet?' he said. 'Why don't you come and sit down here next to me and tell me exactly what it is that Goya's great painting says to you. Yes? Would you kindly do that for me?'

Carla smiled at him and nodded, then, slipping her purple foot-wear back onto her feet, she crossed over towards the bed, and gently sat herself down alongside her father's thin, silk-covered knees. She stared down at the floor for a few seconds, nervously pinching her top lip between her teeth, then suddenly looked up and scanned the enthralling sight which now brightened up, indeed transformed, the rectangular wall before her. The questions the painting posed in Carla's brain were many and varied, and one or two were deeply, deeply harrowing for her to contemplate. She decided to ask her father just the one she felt would insult him least.

'Dad - why do you think you're a frightening sight?' Carla asked him, tenderly stroking the silky, arched projection that was his bony knee. 'You're not a frightening sight at all, you know, but *he* certainly is and no mistake.' She pointed across the room so as to emphasise the point.

'What! That pussycat?' her father replied, his grey brows arched. 'Look again, Carla, would you? The great Colossus is not at all what he at first seems, you know,' he told her. At this she screwed up her eyes and studied the painting even more closely than before. 'You know, dear, I guess you probably see him as a terrible giant scaring all the poor Spanish people away from him, very like the French general Napoleon, with his great armies, did in real life in Spain around that time.'

'Well, yes, I do,' Carla replied, turning towards him. 'Something very like that, at any rate.'

'Well, that's understandable,' said Tom. 'You know, I felt much the same way the first time I saw it all those years ago in Madrid. The original, you know. But you see the painter is actually trying to show us something very profound here.'

'Well, I realised he wasn't showing us the burly prop-forward Adam Jones celebrating one of his tries at Twickenham,' Carla retorted, giggling, both at her comment, and at the look of incredulity it had suddenly summoned to her father's coarsely-lined face. 'Though it could quite easily be a depiction of that, don't you think?'

'Well, now that you say so -' said Tom, pondering the matter and smiling.

'But to be serious, Dad, just tell me what the painting says to you, yes?' Carla told him, turning and gazing into his ancient, veined, and woefully blood-shot grey eyes. 'After all, you say you've owned it for years and years.'

The old man stroked his daughter's side lovingly, and began his explanation. 'Well, for a start, the great Colossus we can see towering above them doesn't really seem to be threatening any of the fleeing people, does he, my love? I mean, after all, he's not even looking at them, is he?'

'Mm. Well, I suppose that's true,' said Carla. 'But there's no doubt they are all terrified of something.'

'Oh, yes. The people are terrified, all right,' Tom replied. 'But just look at how the giant floats mysteriously above the landscape that they all inhabit, but yet is, in no way, rooted in it.'

'In no way is he rooted in it,' repeated Carla, straining her eyes now to comprehend it. 'Yes, I see that, yes. O.K., Dad. I think I can concur with you on that one.'

'You see, my love, he's not *the source* of their fear at all,' Tom went on. 'No. The way I see it, he really seems to embody fear himself, do you see? He represents, to my mind at any rate, that awful dread that we all get to feel at least once in our long lives, sooner, or later. The naked man whom Goya has seen fit to set before us most surely is, I feel - and most surely represents - the generic fear that *we all* experience, and which goes hand-in-hand with being a mortal creature that will one day most assuredly grow old and die.'

Carla turned to look at him. 'Do you mean - you surely don't mean *like you*, Dad?' she said.

'Yes, that's right, my love,' Tom replied. 'Like me. And like Francisco de Goya, himself, too.'

Carla pondered this. 'Well, then very like me, as well, I guess,' she added.

'One day - yes, one day you're almost certainly going to feel it too,' he told her. 'Hopefully, many moons from now, of course.' Tom suddenly sensed his daughter's body tense up as she plainly imagined it already happening. 'You don't have to be sad, you know, my love,' he said. Because, you see, this is in no way a despairing picture that Goya has painted for us here. I believe that it is the deaf, world-weary, old painter's own personal suffering - his own fear - that he has depicted up there, looming so powerfully and majestically above us all, and it is precisely this that he is telling us that he has, at last, managed to come to terms with.'

Carla rubbed an errant tear away from her cheek and looked into his eyes. 'Just as you seem to have, do you mean, Dad?' she asked.

'Yes, my love. Just as I now have,' replied Tom, smiling. He reached out and caught his daughter's slender hand and gripped it firmly within his own. 'You see, the giant - Goya's Colossus - now accepts his fate - indeed has seized it firmly in his fist - and so, you see, my love, the painting, to me at least, is nothing more, nothing less, than a clear, unqualified statement of hope. The dreadful Colossus whom we see there embodies for all of us this hope.'

'So you mean, he is triumphant,' she told him, her voice now croaking with palpable emotion.

'Yes, he is triumphant, Carla,' Tom told her, 'because, you see, he has conquered fear once and for all. But he is exquisitely beautiful too, don't you think?'

'Yes, he is - he truly is,' she told him. 'And I guess even Adam Jones in the after-game shower was never quite that rugged and handsome, even after winning the Grand-Slam.' The girl laughed a frenetic, joyful laugh at last.

Carla's father smiled his tender love back at her, and then, leaning back to rest his head deeply amongst the pillows that she had minutes before mounted behind him, and gazing at the masterpiece which she had generously carried upstairs and arrayed before him, spoke softly, as if to sum up how he felt about the death that was very soon to come his way. 'And so the fear that is made beautiful,' he whispered to her, 'is now forever overcome.'

By the dull, orange tone of the lights outside the window on Cemetery Road, they could tell it was already evening. Still attired in school-uniform, Rhiannon and her closest friend Carmen were sat alongside each other, reading at the large, round table in the front-parlour of *Caerleon*.

'Who is that in the photograph over the fire, Rhiannon?' Carmen asked her friend, looking up.

'Oh, that's my Uncle Sam,' Rhiannon told her. 'My Dad's brother, you know. I never got to meet him as he got killed a long time before I was born.

'He was killed you say!' exclaimed Carmen. 'But how?'

'On the railway,' her friend responded.

'Do you mean he worked on the trains?'

'No, I don't think so, Carmen,' Rhiannon replied. 'His body was found lying on the line that ran from Dowlais and Pant up to *Gloryhole*, where the tunnel emerges above the river-bend, apparently. There was some sort of controversy about his death back then, I gather.'

'Controversy! How do you mean, Rhi?' asked Carmen, clearly aroused by the mysterious aspect of the tale.

'Well, I don't really know,' she replied. 'My father still won't tell me anything about it. I'm too young to be told, apparently. But the authorities demanded his body be dug up recently so that extra tests could be taken, to see if they could draw any new conclusions. But sadly to no effect.'

'Oh, that's too bad,' Carmen replied, switching her attention back to the magazine she was reading, and that lay across her homework. 'Hey, listen to this, Rhi! The shortest story ever written was by Ernest Hemmingway,' Carmen told her. 'Say - do you want to hear it?' Rhiannon nodded. "*For sale: baby shoes never worn.*" Carmen paused for effect. Wow! Isn't that cool?'

'What a strange title,' said Rhiannon, smiling at her across the table.

'Oh, that wasn't the title,' Carmen told her friend. 'That's the whole thing! Truly. The entire story. That's how it's the shortest story ever, see. Get it? '*For sale: baby shoes never worn.*' '

'Baloney!' ejaculated Rhiannon. 'Are you serious? Really? Well, I bet you I could write a shorter one than that if I tried,' she went on. 'If I had the time, I mean. As it is, this blasted homework is taking -'

'But why would you need time, Rhiannon?' said Carmen. 'How long does anyone need to write five or six words? Eh? You call yourself a writer, yes? Well, I bet that story took Hemmingway a whole minute to conceive it, at most. So don't you reckon you could match that?'

'You betcha!' retorted Rhiannon fiercely. 'Check your watch, Carmen, and time me.'

'O.K., then,' said Carmen, folding the sleeve of her sweater back to reveal her pink wrist-watch. 'I'll give you exactly a minute, right? Ready? Three - two - one - go!'

Silence fell on Rhiannon's home. Rhiannon looked blankly at her friend's annoyingly wincing face, and desperately scanned her brain for inspiration. What could she write about? What were the issues that were on her mind at present, and which one of them bothered her most? And, even more to the point, how could she then abbreviate it?

'Ten - nine - eight,' said Carmen, mischievously

'*Un-buttoned tree-feller caught short and killed*,' Rhiannon suddenly announced triumphantly.

Carmen looked up at her, mouth wide open. 'What the hell is that!' she screamed. '*And* it sounds disgusting, too. Anyway, I make that seven words, Rhiannon, and you had six to beat, remember.'

'Start again,' Rhiannon commanded.

'O.K. Go!'

Again today, Rhiannon's thoughts seemed to be all about Chris. She hadn't seen him for a couple of weeks now, and when she glimpsed him he always seemed to be in the company of Carla Steel, of all people, either with a guitar apiece in the same woods that they had once tenderly explored together, or walking around over the lightly wooded limestone foothills of The Beacons that ranged to the north and west of the boy's home.

"*Cat hunting caver washed away*," she suddenly called out.

'What the hell!' ejaculated Carmen. 'Er - five words. Not bad.'

'Drowned!' shrieked Rhiannon, her mouth agape, her body trembling. 'Drowned! *Cat hunting caver drowned*.' Four words must be the winner, surely.'

'Do you think? But I bet I could match that,' said Carmen, gritting her teeth. She pointed at Rhiannon's wrist-watch, and said, 'Ready?'

'Ready, steady, go!' said Rhiannon, biting her lip tensely. The flame-haired girl watched her friend's brown eyes sparkle, as she gazed out of the front parlour-window, and endeavoured to conjure up a brief, record-busting tale of her own. 'Ten seconds left!' she announced excitedly.

"*Cemetery killing taken no further*", Carmen told her. 'Do you get it? They're already there, see!'

'Yes, but where's the story?' enquired Rhiannon. 'Carmen - look yours is more like a dumb newspaper headline in *The Sun*, or even some morbid sort of joke, don't you think?'

'O.K., then. '*Cemetery killer buried at work,*''

'Mmm, I don't know. 'Smothered with work' is cleverer, in my opinion,' chipped in Rhiannon. 'How about '*Cemetery killer smothered with work.*' There. That's almost perfect, don't you think? Humorous, too. Or better again, I think - '*Grave-digging killer smothered with work.*'

'Yes, all right. I think I could settle for that,' said Carmen. '*Grave-digging killer smothered with work.*' You win. Six, no five. And every bit as good as the Hemingway, I believe. It was a joint venture, too, so it kind of feels right.' Hey, Rhiannon. Do you hope he gets drowned, then?'

'Who?' asked Rhiannon.

'*You* know who,' Carmen replied, carefully avoiding her best friend's gaze. 'The two of them, perhaps, if they continue hanging round together all the time. And are you sure you're not sort of *willing their demise*? You know, like - like Abigail Williams.'

'Abigail in Year Ten?' enquired Rhiannon, puzzled. 'Why on earth -'

'No, Abigail Williams in '*The Crucible,*' silly,' said Carmen. 'You must remember her, surely?. You know, the play we studied in English before Christmas.'

'Oh, that,' her red-haired companion replied. Rhiannon deliberated for a moment, trying to visualize clearly the particular female her friend was referring to. 'So are you calling me a witch now, then, Carmen?' she asked pointedly. Carmen quickly shook her head. 'No,' continued Rhiannon, 'as a matter of fact I am actually very glad that Chris is seeing –'

'Seeing!' ejaculated Carmen, covering her mouth to indicate her friend's faux-pas.

' - I mean, spending - spending quality time...with Carla Steel. You see, Carmen, it is bound to help him in the long run, isn't it?'

'Is it?' asked Carmen, puzzled by her comment.

'Well, there's no doubt she has been playing a lot longer than he has, right?'

'I don't doubt it for a moment,' retorted Carmen, her mind busy steaming up a different track.

'So I guess his finger-work has to be improving every day, don't you think?'

'I - I'd rather not think about it, actually, if you don't mind,' Carmen answered, this time her hand fully across her mouth.

'Carmen - what on earth are you trying to say?' asked Rhiannon, suddenly springing to her feet. 'I think - I think I know what you're trying to suggest, you know, and you are being truly disgusting, as usual, so you are. Ooh!'

'I am not!' protested Carmen.

'Remember she's a lot older than he is, right? Almost twice Chris's age. And you're supposed to be my best friend, too. How could you! Look - I demand you take it back.'

'But what have I said, Rhiannon?' pleaded Carmen. 'I've said nothing. I mean, *you've* done almost all the talking.'

'What you've been thinking, I mean,' said Rhiannon. 'Take it back, Carmen. Right now.'

'What I've been thinking!'

'Take it back, I command you,' insisted Rhiannon, her shoulders thrust back, and quivering.

'You command me! Just listen to yourself, Rhiannon,' said Carmen, smarting.

Carmen watched, alarmed, as Rhiannon spun round and ran to the door, and then listened, open-mouthed, as her feet pounded their way up the stairs. Forlornly Carmen picked up her magazine and her school-books, and, stuffing them inside her bag, made her way to the front-door, opened it, and slipped quietly outside.

As Carmen walked across the yard towards the gate in the late-evening twilight she turned and saw Rhiannon's mother standing at the side-door of the house, dressed in what looked like a flowing, sky-blue, silken shift, a pointed, cream-coloured hat, and with tight, well-worn, and desperately patchy, cream ballet-shoes squeezed onto her bunnion-ed feet.

She was throwing half a dozen or so full, knotted, polythene-bags into the trash-bin, but acting, for all the world. as if the strange garb she was attired in were her usual, everyday house-clothes.

'My God! It's the Lady of Shallot,' said Carmen under her breath. 'Mrs. Cook! I'm leaving now!' she cried, as she closed the wide, iron gate behind her.

'All right, love,' Gwen replied, turning. 'I suppose it's warm enough for you to walk home tonight, yeah? Mind you go safely now. You don't know what strange people are out at this time of night, do you love?'

'O.K., bye,' the school-girl replied. 'You, for a start, you crazy old bat,' whispered Carmen to herself, fixing the heavy school-bag onto her slim shoulders and setting off along the pavement. As she walked along, she watched with a sideward glance as Rhiannon's mother went inside the house again and pulled the side-door tightly closed behind her.

Walking up the road past the field that contained the two boxes where Rhiannon's horses were kept, Carmen could still just about make out the tarnished, rain-washed words that Rhiannon had told her her mother had daubed on them with red paint some time back in the Spring. Intrigued, she climbed through the wire-fence, and, carefully stepping by the two standing horses, who were busy chewing what little grass there was left there, approached the pair of makeshift stables that stood side by side in the middle of the field.

'*Llamrai,* and *Hengroen,*' Carmen read aloud in her finest Welsh accent. '*The Bounder*, and *The Old Skin*. The supposed names of King Arthur's two horses. But why on earth would the old bat have done such a crazy thing?' she asked herself. 'And why the weird clothes? Does she - does she think she was alive and living her life back then, or something? Back in the days before the Angles and the Saxons had arrived on this island, or at least before they had united, and inter-bred, and began taking over most of the British mainland. Does she - surely she can't think she was some lady, or some queen even, in a former life, back in the deep and distant Dark Ages? Well, you know, maybe she actually does. Some past-life regression perhaps!' Carmen suddenly let out a raucous laugh, and then spun round nervously to happily discover that only the horses had heard her.

'Oh, my God! The poor woman,' she went on. 'No. Poor Rhiannon, I should say. Yes, poor Rhiannon. Because, if it's really true, then she's the one who is really going to need my help right now. Yes, I'll be sure to ring her and make up with her the minute I get back home,' she told herself. 'And to think that *I* feel embarrassed because my mother works as a school-dinner lady.'

Carmen smiled at her rather comical observation, patted the mare, then the stallion, on the side of the head, then climbed back through the fence, and set off along the main road again. She hooked her bag behind her over both her shoulders, gritted her teeth, and made her way up the hill and across *The Bryniau,* but this time at a much faster speed, and in a far more determined frame of mind than was the case just four or five minutes before.

The sound of the toilet flushing in the bathroom across the hall woke the old man from his slumber. Deep within the dark room Tom looked up and spoke. 'He is a man who stands in the sunlight, but with his back to the sun,' he called out hoarsely. After the pause that followed, his deep, but brittle, voice called out once again. 'He sees only his shadows, and these shadows are his only laws.'

'Who, Dada?' asked the rudely awoken Carla, pushing the open door further ajar, and stepping lightly into her father's bedroom.

Sitting up, but leaning towards his daughter on one elbow, Tom repeated exactly what he had said before, but this time more slowly and much louder. 'He is a man who stands in the sunlight, but with his back to the sun. He sees only his shadows, and these shadows are his only laws.'

Knowing full well that the vision her father had just seen, or the inspiration he had received, had to be of crucial significance, Carla walked over and sat on the bed, and grasped her father's arm with her hand, and cradled his soft-bearded face with the other. 'Is he evil, then, Dada?' she asked him, biting painfully into her lip. 'The man you've seen - that you're describing. Is he?'

'That man is the devil,' her father told her, his wrinkled eyes still tightly shut. 'He is surely Satan himself.'

Carla's brain was racing. 'If he's the devil - if he *is* Satan - then what is his name, Dada?' she asked him, her bright eyes sparkling. 'How will people know him?'

'I keep doing what I do,' Tom replied.

'What? No, Dada, not you,' said Carla. 'What is this wicked man called, so that we'll know him, should we meet him?'

' '*I keep doing what I do*,' they call him,' her father replied.

'His name, Dada. Just say his name,' she said once more.

'I just told you, didn't I?' Tom told her, breathing heavily now. 'His name is - his name means '*I continue in my wicked ways*.' Because, you see, that man cannot help himself, and what's more he doesn't *care* to. Even though - even though for many years he grew up with Him,'

'The man grew up with who, Dada?' asked Carla.

There followed a minute or so of silence while Tom stretched his bent body back on the bed. By now warm tears were pouring from his eyes, and, at the sight of them, and of the terrifying way his twisted, bony frame shuddered, as if with a mysterious power, Carla grew afraid that her dear father was about to die. Then suddenly the old man's eyes opened wide again, and he spoke, but much quieter, and far more controlled, this time. 'He chooses to continue in his wicked ways, Carla, my love, even though - even though the man was born to a God-fearing family, and was raised - yes even raised -'

'Raised where, Dada?' asked Carla, by now recognising precisely who the evil man was that her father was describing.

'And raised, in great fear and trembling, in the House of God.'

CHAPTER 17

Now that she had finished her first joint of the morning, and had carefully washed her face and hands, Carla let go of the soft, blue, woollen towel she had used to dry herself, and, leaning her head to within just a few steamy inches of its surface moisture, stared intently at the pallid, pillow-creased face that now looked back at her forlornly from the oblong mirror that hung over the wash-basin. She moved her chin into a variety of positions, and in this way did her utmost to properly assess the sorry situation.

'Well, thank God I'm not touring these days, at least,' she told herself, clenching her pearly-white teeth into a painful, but somewhat comical, grimace, and, with her small, delicate fingers placed on either side of her skull, stretching her taut, pulsing scalp back as far as it would go. She maintained the same position until she was confident she could now sum up matters to her satisfaction, then let go. Yes, for the first time in her exciting, but turbulent, young life Carla now felt like tearing her hair out, and, the more she inspected her forehead and hair-line, the more she felt convinced that she might quite easily have already begun.

Suddenly hearing a deep, tremulous, but familiar voice barely calling out her name from the next room, Carla bit tightly into her bottom lip, then felt a single tear spring onto her cheek. She reached out and swiftly wiped it away with the hand-towel, and, dipping her head so as to listen more intently, turned round and sat on the rim of the bath. She fully realised that she couldn't bare to see her dear father as sick and wasted as he had now plainly become. These days even the action of getting him to his feet again, after a prolonged period of time seated, or lying abed, often now took as long as a minute or more, and the experience often shocked her immensely, rendering her incredulous and weak. But her reaction was more than she felt she was prepared to let her father see, especially at a time like this, when what she believed he truly needed was measured, if banal, consistency, an appropriare degree of empathy, and, above all, pure love.

But what was to be done? she asked herself, letting her head loll before her. Her father was the master of his own destiny, his own mortality, and, as long as she could remember, he always had been. And if, as he had suggested some time during the previous fortnight, the time had come for him to finally act, and act decisively, and set about the dreadfully calculated, fraudulent process of taking his own life, then *so be it*. Carla looked round and, recognising the sound, turned off the tap behind her right hip that was emitting but the merest of drips. She sensed that she could feel the washer within it scream silently as she repeated the same action on the cold-tap, subconsciously, perhaps, seeking a closure that was, at least relatively, eternal.

Carla recalled how, only days before, she had discovered the strange words 'AS EASY AS AS' roughly scribbled in capitals in the top-left corner of the frontispiece page of her dad's favourite bible - an orange-covered, King James' authorized-version, which he had once been awarded as a prize for scholastic achievement. And the writing she had found she recognised as being unquestionably his own. After first believing that he might simply have omitted the word *PIE* from the tail of it, Carla had decided to give his queer statement a little more thought. Then, after puzzling over it at length, she finally managed to decipher what the last two capitals in the cryptic line almost certainlly referred to. She had then shook her head from side to side and smiled thinly at the strange irony that appeared to be involved in it.

'*Assisted Suicide* couldn't possibly be permissible to the Christian Church, could it?' Carla recalled she had asked herself. After all, largely due to her Uncle Gary's staunch efforts, her father had certainly seemed to have undertaken a belated, but wholly creditable, conversion, that meant that he fully embraced the Christian faith these days. I wonder if my uncle even knows what his brother has written in there, she pondered, and in the holy book of all places. Well, if he doesn't know yet, then the next time I see Gary I must remember to tell him.

'Carla!' her father's voice called out again. 'I can't seem to lift myself out of the rocker at all now. Can you come in and help, do you think?' Yes, she could forgive her father for his innocent thoughts and his idle jottings, but, having not long since lost her mother, she certainly felt in no mood to contemplate aiding and abetting him in the direction of euthenasia, she told herself.

'Tell me - what poem were you reading, Dad?' Carla asked him a few minutes later.

Tom looked down at the weighty black tome so as to refresh his memory. 'The Sea-Nymph's Farting,' by Landor,' he told her, without a single slither of humour, not even a smile.

Carla moved closer to his chair, tilted her head to one side, then lifted up the large, leather, hard-back book so as to read it for herself. 'Parting, Dad,' she told him. 'Parting.'

'That's what I said, didn't I?' he replied, looking up with a startlingly innocent, childlike pose.

'No, you said - well, you said something else completely,' she told him.

'Eh? What are you talking about, silly? I'm not losing my marbles just yet, you know,' he replied.

'No, I know that, Dad,' mumbled Carla, suddenly biting her lip with tangible emotion.

'But when I do, girl, then you'll have to be very, very careful round here,' he told her.

'Oh? Why's that?' she asked.

'Well, isn't it obvious?' he shot back. 'Because they'll be rolling about all over the floor, won't they? Like - like marbles they will.' His hollow face made a silent laugh at her. 'That's if there are any in there to begin with,' he added, pointing at his temple and simulating a doltish pose.

'Oh, Dad,' said Carla, welling up suddenly, and turning away so as not to show him her tears. 'Whatever are we going to do?'

It was Saturday afternoon, and Chris was seated alone in the first-floor of *Merthyr Library* doing some last-minute revision for his first examination of the summer. He tried to concentrate while the two girls at the adjacent table to his own chatted away merrily. Chris knew that the one with the fair, curly hair, who was currently speaking, was called Wendy Rees, and that she was a year below him, and in Rhiannon's Art class, and, in his opinion, was almost as pretty, but the other, a tall, dark-haired girl, he didn't think he knew at all.

'Bloody exams!' Wendy announced loudly, then sipping her carton of juice through a straw. 'You know, I wish I was still in the first-year, Avril. Don't you? School was a lot more fun back then, don't you think?'

'Tell me about it,' responded Avril, turning the page of her text-book and reading on.

'Teachers weren't as predictable and boring for a start. Hey - do you remember that student-teacher we once had in Science,' Wendy continued. 'I mean the one who switched on the DVD-player on his classroom white-board and over thirty of us saw him having sex with his retriever?'

'God! How could I forget?' Avril shot back, giggling. 'I was sat right in the front.'

'Everyone was totally shocked, weren't they? You know, Av, I never even knew he was gay, I swear.

'What? Gay!' said Avril. 'But he wasn't - stupid.'

'He wasn't!' exclaimed Wendy, scrunching up her nose.

'Course not,' her friend replied, smiling. 'You see, his dog was a bitch.'

Wendy slurped loudly with surprise. 'The dog was....Oh, I see. Well, how could I tell that?' she asked. 'I was sat at the back in the corner. And I was never much good at Science, was I?'

'Well, that's true at least,' said Avril.

Wendy continued. 'Do you remember that time in Year-Seven when I sucked in a lung-full from that helium balloon you brought in on your birthday and just passed out on the floor? The ambulance-driver said I'd had a narrow escape, but I still remember he could barely stop laughing.' She slurped the last dregs out. 'Say - whatever happened to him, do you reckon?'

'The ambulance driver?' asked Avril.

'No, no. That teacher, I mean.'

'Oh - the teacher! Mister Jarvis? What a twat, eh?' observed Avril, placing her book down and regarding her friend. 'Well, I heard he's a Deputy-Head these days.'

'Really?' exclaimed Wendy. She crushed up the carton in her fist and threw it straight into the waste-paper bin in the corner of the room.

'Yeah - down the Vale of Glamorgan somewhere, so I was told,' said Avril.

'Never?' said Wendy, open-mouthed, eyes wide. 'God - he did well for himself, then, didn't he?

'Didn't he just,' her friend concurred.

Wendy looked over in Chris's direction and spoke quietly. 'Then you know I'm glad we never shopped him for it, eh? For that dog thing - that bitch thing, I mean,' she said. 'I used to really like his Science lessons, I really did. Except for *that one*, of course. And he always dressed fit, didn't he? Even out of school. You know, Av, my eldest brother wears the same pair of pyjamas that he's got.'

'How do you -? Oh, I see,' said Avril, grinning. 'Is that right?'

'Yeah. Candy-stripe pink - I think it's called. Mind you, he *is* gay, of course.'

'Your brother? Yeah, I know - you told me,' said Avril. 'You know, I'm sure that if he ever went on *'Big Brother'* -'

' - then I bet you he'd win it,' cut in Wendy, excitedly.

'I bet he would. He would, I'm telling you,' Avril repeated, smiling. 'The boy's rude enough for a start. And you say he's got piercings in unmentionable places too. And you certainly need them.'

'Yeah. And I'd make sure he packed those pyjamas too. If only to have some sweet boy rip them off him in the bedroom on *live-feed*.' The two girls suddenly began hooting with laughter.

Hands over his head, Chris decided that he couldn't take any more, so he promptly got to his feet, pushed all of his books and files deep into his shoulder-bag, attached it securely, and made for the stairs. It would be a lot busier downstairs, of course, he thought, what with the *'Celtic History Exhibition'* that was taking place in the side-room, but surely it couldn't be any noisier than this; or, even if it was, then certainly not half as infuriating.

Once on the ground-floor Chris spun round and marched straight into the lending-library, and soon found a small, wooden desk with its own seat, neatly tucked in between two enormous book-shelves, where, although the light was limited, he at least found he had space enough to resume his work. Yet no sooner had he settled down once again but his happy sense of splendid isolation was severely compromised by the arrival of a tiny, middle-aged woman at the complementary desk-and-chair set directly opposite him. She suddenly smiled sweetly at him, and it was then that he realised that the new arrival was none other than Rhiannon's mother, Gwen, whom he was always careful to address formally on the rare occasions when they met.

'Mrs. Cook!' exclaimed a stupefied Chris. 'How - how nice to see you.'

'You, likewise, young man,' the little woman retorted. 'Hey, there's no need to look so shocked, you know, Chris, because I swear I'm not following you around or anything.'

'I never thought -' Chris stammered, squirming slightly, and beginning to feel uncomfortable, while flushing up accordingly.

'You see, I work in here these days,' she told him, proudly holding up the red, rectangular badge that hung suspended round her neck on a gold-coloured chain. 'Part-time, anyway.'

'Oh, that must be nice,' Chris told her, not knowing what else to say that might make her think he was calm, and responsible, and possibly a charming young man, who couldn't possibly have been taking outrageous liberties with her sweet, angelic daughter. But, irrespective of what he chose to say or do, Chris could already tell, by Gwen's attitude and posture, that she wasn't intending to get up any time soon and leave him to get on with his school-work. What was the dotty old biddy planning on doing? he asked himself. Well, within a minute or two he got the answer he was seeking, and it wasn't at all what he was expecting.

Gwen suddenly leaned forward towards him, her shoulders and chin almost touching the surface of her desk, and smiled at him disarmingly, and told him the last thing he really wanted to hear at that moment.

'You know your father is holding court in the next room,' said Gwen, grinning. 'Say - do you want to see him?'

'Eh? I thought he was at home,' Chris replied, puzzled. 'Oh, then he must be working on the exhibition. I know he was here with some kids yesterday, mounting some of the paintings they'd been working on in his lessons.' But Gwen grinned on. 'Holding court, did you say? Yeah, I guess he just loves all the attention he gets, don't you think? He is a teacher, after all.'

'Your dad!' exclaimed Gwen, wide-eyed. 'But he's not a teacher.'

'Oh, he is, you know,' Chris told her. 'He teaches Art. I – I thought you knew. He teaches Rhiannon.'

'Your father has a multitude of talents, young man, but I don't think teaching Art is one of them,' announced Gwen in a calm, reassuring tone, and with a perky smile on her wizened face.

'He's even got the name for it,' Chris added with a smile.

'Arthur?' exclaimed Gwen.

'No - Drew. Arthur! Who's Arthur?' asked Chris, wrinkling up his face with puzzlement.

'But Drew is not your real dad, Chris,' Gwen told him. 'You did know that, didn't you?'

'Yes, yes, I know that,' the boy replied, beginning now to flush up warmly.

'He's your step-father.'

'Yes, I know. My mother told me years ago.'

'Chris - listen to me,' Gwen continued. 'Your father - your real dad - is *my Arthur*.'

'What do you mean - *your Arthur?*' ejaculated Chris. 'I thought Rhiannon's dad was -'

'It's true, you know. Cross my heart.' Gwen paused to minimise the likely effect of her next comment. 'You and my Rhiannon -'

'No. Please don't tell me - please don't say that we're siblings,' shot back a troubled Chris.

'Why not?' asked Gwen.

'Just don't, please. I just can't get my head round Rhiannon and me being brother and sister.'

'Oh, I see,' said Gwen. She smiled benignly at him. 'But you're not, Chris.'

'We're not!' exclaimed Chris. 'Did you say that we're not? What? Wow! Well, thank God for -'

'No - you're *half* brother and sister.'

'We're what?' ejaculated Chris, thinking fast. 'Yes, I see what you're -'

'You're half siblings,' Gwen told him. 'You share the same father, you see. And that man, happens to be my Arthur. And, as if by magic, Chris, he happens to be in the next room.' Gwen paused again as Chris turned his head to stare at the book-case beside him, in an attempt to piece together all the mystifying stuff that he was hearing. 'I know!' said Gwen excitedly. 'Let me take you to see him, Chris. Yes? Please. Don't go being afraid. I'm sure you're old enough to deal with it all now, aren't you? *And* it makes good sense, don't you think?'

'What? Now?' said Chris re-focusing, and staring back at her.

'Yes. Why not?' Gwen replied. 'Say - what's wrong, Chris? You know I do believe you're trembling with fear. Look - I know people say Arthur has a fierce temper, but you don't need to be -'

'Does he? Does he really?' asked Chris.

'Well, yes, he does, actually,' the little woman responded swiftly.

'No - I mean - tell me, Mrs. Cook - does he know about me and Rhiannon?' Chris enquired.

'Well, of course,' the woman replied, smiling again. 'Arthur has a right to know everything.'

'But I mean about us - you know, about us being -'

'Half siblings, yes,' said Gwen, misunderstanding his concern. 'And he knows an awful lot more than that, too, I can tell you.' She suddenly hurried round to the side of the book-shelf that Chris was on, and, crouching down, took him firmly by the arm. 'Look - come with me, Chris. Come on! You needn't be so scared, you know. Big lad like you. You know, I believe it's high time you faced up to the facts, young man - faced up to your - your heritage.'

'Is it? Do you think so?' Chris asked her. 'Well, all right, then. It's now or never, I suppose.'

The two boys at the door of the side-room jingled their tins at Chris for an entry-donation of sorts, but, though he dipped a hand in his pocket, he found himself being pulled right past them by Gwen, and at an almost uncontrollable speed. The little woman dragged him along past countless figures and faces, both young and old, and then past long trestle-tables that were filled with artefacts, jewelled merchandise, and books and maps, both large and small. She then dragged him past a massive painted sign on a pole proclaiming *'The Welsh - the indigenous people of Britain,'* until they reached the furthest wall of the great room, on which was pinned an enormous portrait-painting that Chris had last seen during the previous week, lying horizontally, in four separated sections, on the large central table in Drew's Art Room. The vigorous, rather frightening, representation of the renowned British chieftain - his Celtic sword of judgement grasped firmly in his right hand, the cross of Christ, with which to terrify the heathen Saxon invader, emblazoned on his shield - which the colossal mural before them forcefully depicted for all who chose to admire it, at last seemed to begin to make a modicum of sense to him.

Newly released, Chris edged forward, then spun round to observe what had become of the dotty old woman whose short, powerful arms had quite easily managed to drag him all the way there. He saw Gwen Cook standing in the middle of the room, alone, trembling, and grasping her chubby, tanned, left hand tightly inside her right. It seemed to him that she might also be crying. Chris watched her intently as she repeatedly, remorselessly even, turned her gold wedding-band round and round between her thumb and forefinger, while gazing admiringly, seemingly entranced, at the life-size image portrayed on the wall before her, that was surrounded by a dramatically curved, gold pennant bearing the italic, barely legible, inscription, *'Hammer of the Saxons.'*

As Chris watched her, he realised that Gwen seemed now to have forgotten completely all about his presence, while at the same time he began to sense that there was something strange, almost remarkable, about her that, as yet, he could not fully comprehend.

Chris stepped forward towards the bottom-right corner of the great picture so that he could discover for himself the precise identity of its subject, and also its creator. Bending his head low, he soon deciphered, then read out silently to himself, the words that he found stencilled there on a small, white card that was crudely glued on. *'ARTHUR OF THE BRITONS - by Wendy Rees and Avril Humphreys,'* he read.

Carla sat herself down cross-legged on the bedroom-carpet, and watched her Uncle Gary at rest, reclining, as he frequently did, his torso draped over the bed's pillows, while her father sat in his customary seated position in the rocking-chair across from, and facing, the pair of them.

'Brawd - do you believe that you possess a *secular* consciousness or a *sacred* one?' Gary asked his brother, grinning a little, but clearly deadly serious in his enquiry. He anticipated no quick reply. 'Because I believe that, unlike me, you possess the former, and that is what is at the heart of this silly euthenasia nonsense that I hear you've recently become obsessed with.'

'Oh, you think so, do you?' Tom responded, adjusting slightly the two cushions that had been helpfully placed behind him, and now sitting back even more deeply in his chair, so letting Gary know that he was ready, and willing, for him to do his worst, and fill him in - perhaps, literally - on this new and vital matter that had clearly fomented in his brilliant mind, and which he plainly could not resist sharing with his closest and dearest. 'And if I do possess *a secular consciousness*, as you call it, then what of it?' Tom added. 'After all, it is mine, right?'

'Then it figures that you clearly believe yourself to be the centre of your world,' said Gary. 'Your universe, you know.' His brother looked up and frowned at him. 'When, in fact, you are, if you'll forgive me saying so, just one of over seven billion human beings scratching out a moderately miserable existence on the surface of one of nine planets -'

'Eight, Uncle' interjected Carla.

'Eight? O.K. then - eight planets,' said Gary, 'that are, when all is said and done, but mere components of a tiny, spinning solar system within just one galaxy amongst millions of others.'

'Wow! That's quite a mouthful even for you, Brother Preacher Man,' Tom told him, grinning.

'And, like you, almost every other human being alive believes similarly that he or she is the centre of this universe. And so, as a consequence, intelligent people like ourselves understandably have a tendency to feel rather lost and forlorn amongst all this - this hugeness.'

'Well, that figures I guess,' said Carla, so far managing to follow her uncle's analysis.

'And, despite their supposed centrality, it is quite understandable, is it not, that they can all be forgiven for experiencing a sense of - of meaninglessness and - and -'

'Insignificance, perhaps,' his niece added once more. Though surprised by Carla's second interjection, Gary nodded at her by way of acquiescence with her chosen expression.

Tom watched his two closest living relatives.seemingly collaborating quite amicably before him and already realised that contradiction would likely be pointless. 'And *you*, dear brother,' he nevertheless countered, staring across at Gary's flushed, but scholarly, face. 'Or, should I say, he of *'the sacred consciousness.'* What of him, then? What of that man, if I might be so bold?'

'Well, irrespective of the numerous faults and shortcomings which the man has,' his elder brother replied with a smile, of course referring to himself, 'in no way does he need to view himself at the centre of *any* universe, because, you see, he understands perfectly well that the centre of *his universe* happens to reside elsewhere, specifically in God. In the sacred - do you see?' Ice-blue eyes flickering, Tom sat impassive and unmoving before him, considering deeply the point that Gary was making. 'And interestingly, with his lack of centrality, he is happily much less likely than the secularist -'

'Me,' said Tom, winking across at Carla.

'Yes, you, Brawd - to experience those terrible feelings of meaninglessness and insignificance. Because, you see, he sees himself in a meaningful relaionship *with* this Sacred Other - *with* this all-powerful, central force.'

'God,' said Tom.

'Yes - God,' said Gary.

'Then I'd much rather you called Him by His proper name,' the seated man retorted, 'rather than some *Sacred Other* nonsense, which, after all, only serves to confuse everyone.' Tom turned to his daughter for approval on this point. 'If He's God then He's God, right Carla?'

Carla smiled benvolently back at him, and also at this very welcome evidence of her ailing father's still sharp, perceptive mind, and silently thanked her Sacred Other for the same.

'And so, what I hear you saying,' Tom continued, a finger now circularly scouring his right ear, 'is that the man with the sacred, rather than the secular, consciousness - namely *you*, Brawd - derives his sense of importance and his sense of meaning solely *from* that relationship, right?'

'Why, yes. That is it precisely,' replied Gary, with a smile. 'And it is to your eternal credit that you appreciate the point.'

'To my eternal credit!' repeated Tom. He glanced at Carla, brows raised. 'Pray, how, exactly?'

'Well, as you can imagine, and knowing me as you do, from this basic premise, that you plainly appear now to have accepted, a very great deal must follow.'

'Oh! Oh, does it?' said Tom, pouting. 'Then I guess you must want to unburden yourself of it.'

'Then let me make us another pot of tea,' said Carla, rising, 'because I get the feeling that this discussion might go on for some little while yet.'

The two young people lay side-by-side on their stomachs in the long grass, the breeze from the high peaks blowing loose, curly strands of hair right across both their tanned faces.

'Teasing you about sex! Carmen!' exclaimed Chris. 'But she's just a child. She thinks BDSM is a Driving-School in Glebeland Street.'

'Well, isn't it? I'm sure I had two of my very first lessons with them.' Rhiannon told him, stroking his hand.

'Not in driving, you didn't,' he quipped grinning, then sitting up and gazing down at her. 'Er - is there anything you want to share with me, Rhiannon?'

'Like what?' she asked him, not yet apprehending the cause of his jollity. 'It was just before the nights started closing in. Then my father took over.'

'Now that's what I call too much information,' said Chris, moving his forehead just out of range of the sudden slap she attempted to give him. 'Why are you trying to hit me?' he asked.

'I'm not quite sure,' replied Rhiannon, this time suddenly catching him on the end of his nose. 'But you probably deserve a proper spanking.'

'Oh my God!' cried Chris, rolling over onto his back, and grasping his nose to verify that it was still attached. 'You bitch! Rhiannon. Spanking, did you say? You've gone all BDSM all of a sudden. Why is that? Whatever next? Rubber masks? Whips and clamps?'

'Stop it, Chris!' exclaimed Rhiannon, knowing full well she had hurt him, and leaning on her elbow so as to tenderly cradle his face between her slender fingers.

'Testicular teasing?'

'That's enough, now,' she told him, kissing his head. 'And you're not really hurt, anyway, are you? It was only - it was only -'

'My nose,' he told her, grimacing, then seeking out her lovely blue eyes to check that his teasing hadn't hurt her. 'Look - I know it's hardly a prize feature. I got it from my mother, after all, and definitely not from Arthur.' Shocked at his own sudden utterance, the boy rolled away a few feet, and turned his back fully on her. At this a skylark shot out of its nest on the hillside not far from where they were, and, catching the thermal, and rising, sped higher and higher into the wide, blue cosmos, where the naked eye was hard pushed to catch sight of it, the golden bird's song now a mad, rushed cadenza.

'Who did you say?' exclaimed Rhiannon, suddenly sitting up straight, and gazing after him with furrowed brow. 'Is that your real dad's name, then? Arthur.' Rhiannon paused. She felt that, for some reason, Chris didn't seem to want to reply to her. 'Is it?' she asked again. 'Say - Chris. And however did you manage to find out about him? Tell me, won't you.' Rhiannon crawled on her bare knees over to where Chris lay and waited. 'And how strange that it's the very same name as *my* dad,' she told him. 'Though most people, except my mum that is, usually call him, Dyl, of course. So your dad is an Arthur, too, then?' She smiled as she pondered this. 'God! That must be a thousand-to-one chance at the very least, don't you think?' Chris didn't reply, and Rhiannon was beginning to feel a little cross with him. 'Say - why won't you look at me, Chris?' she asked. 'What have I done? What have I said? Tell me, won't you!'

Chris responded without looking directly at her, his voice barely audible above the background chorus of the searing birdsong. 'Rhiannon - I met your mum in town last Saturday,' he told her.

'So what?' she asked. 'She's got a part-time job in the library these days.' He didn't reply. 'And? Did you warn you off me or something? She did, didn't she? Chris - you can tell me, you know. You truly can.'

'Well, not directly, no,' he told her, staring at the ground, and pulling clumps of grass from it with both hands, and flinging them as far as he could manage down the sloping field before him.

'Well, you simply must tell me, Chris,' she continued. 'Else I'm bound to start thinking the very worst, aren't I?'

'It *is* the worst,' Chris told her.

'Eh? What was that?' she asked him, reaching out and grasping him round the waist. 'Come on. Let's have it. What did she tell you to break us up?'

There followed ten to fifteen seconds of silence, broken only by the sound of the skylark overhead, trilling away to the big, blinding sun and the bright, blue sky that presently encompassed them all around. 'About Arthur,' Chris eventually said, turning, and slowly, furtively seeking out Rhiannon's eyes, so as to witness for himself the desperately sad sight that he felt he already knew the sweet, red-headed girl would make at the coming denouement.

'What about him?' Rhiannon asked, continuing to massage his tight abdomen, but stroking him more urgently now, the more confused she found herself becoming. 'What about my dad? Eh? What has *he* got against us? Oh, hang on. Or do you mean *your Arthur*?' she asked him. 'Because now I'm getting really confused. Which is it? Tell me, Chris.'

The singing lark suddenly swooped so low to the ground that the final words he told her she lip-read more than heard him say.

'He's one and the same,' Chris told her, averting his gaze again, finding now that he couldn't bear to watch her, as he felt her slowly release the hold she had on his hand and edge away.

To scatter the maddening lark-song that filled his head, as much as to hide himself away, Chris leapt to his feet, and began sprinting headlong down the steep, grassy slope that ran towards the hazel-wood, and the narrow-gauge railway which threaded its way right through it. Leaping its line, he sprinted across the narrow country-road that lay just beyond that, and then hurtled down the steep, stony escarpment beyond and below that again.

Finally, his head dipped low, and throbbing madly from the sudden, jolting deceleration, the boy waded slowly, but determinedly, into the brown-hued, bubbling river - The

Taff - whose fresh water swept along on its ancient, relentless course: a winding course that discharged its waters from The Beacons above him and to the north, down through *Gloryhole* and the Merthyr Valley, then on towards the Bristol Channel at its mouth, then into the Irish Sea, and finally into the vast, broad, fathomless Atlantic Ocean that lay yet further west again, and where the waters of all the world's western lands finally became one and the same.

And Chris urged himself, between great gulps of air, and spurts of salty tears that criss-crossed his scorching cheeks before becoming washed away in the turgid stream, not to call a halt until his entire body was fully submerged within its deep and fearful flow.

Anne sighed quietly to herself and put down the newspaper for someone else to look at. She then stood up and moved to the bright side of the room, and looked out of the window at the lovely rose-garden of *The Willows,* where her thoughts often seemed to reside, whatever monotonous, depressing, or depraved task she happened to find herself having to carry out. Yes, the Spring just gone had unquestionably been the warmest on record, she thought. Even *The Sun* had said so! And, as summer was ushered in, there was still little sign of the rain that was desperately needed to top up the valley's many lakes and reservoirs, and guarantee its local gardeners a second, consecutive summer without a hose-pipe ban.

'Listen to this, Anne,' said a young black woman called Sharon, who, clad in overalls, and seated beside her elder sister, was reading a small headline from the tabloid newspaper on the table before her. ' *'As unemployment rockets and the economy goes onto recession, David Cameron tells us to read to our children.'* Well, I'll tell you this, Mister Prime Minister, my little girl can already read my Jobseekers' booklet better than I can, thank you very much, and she has even been practising signing her name on the dotted line on the back in the most beautiful, flowing script you've ever seen. So there can be little doubt I'm playing my part in the national literacy drive, wouldn't you say?'

'No doubt about it, girl,' her sister Evy told her with an encouraging smile.

'And I see *'The Dai Jones Index'* is tumbling down, and austerity's the only game in town -.'

'Christ, Sharon!' Anne exclaimed, grinning. 'You're a poet, and you didn't even know it, girl.'

'I thought it was called *'The Dow Jones,'* I did,' an elderly lady in a wheel-chair who was wearing a thick, grey mud-pack informed them. 'Although I know they do speak funny down in Cardiff, don't they?'

'Care-diff,' said Evy.

'No - Karr-diff, said the lady.'

'No, it's Keir-diff,' said Sharon.

'There's a lovely dressing-gown you're wearing, Angharad,' said Anne, feeling compelled to intervene, and striding away from the window to push the woman through the open doorway and in the direction of the common-room. But by her action she was just as determined to put a halt to the endless tirade, that occurred at least twice every week these days, regarding the nation's capital city, and which, to her mind, whether innocently expressed or otherwise, cast an undeserved aspersion on her husband, who most folk in the care-home knew full well hailed from there. 'A very nice robe indeed, sweetheart, if you don't mind me saying. Though yellow is a colour that rarely works on most women, I find. In my case I feel it makes me look jaundiced. And as for the push-up brassiere your daughter bought you.'

'I know what you're all thinking, you know,' Angharad replied without turning. 'Listen - I believe my body is my temple. And right now my temple needs redecoratng, O.K.?'

Seeking to avoid further confrontation, Anne accelerated Angharad's rubber-rimmed vehicle down the corridor, and right the way round to the day-lounge where Gareth presently was. He was just about the only person in the place Anne felt she could have a serious conversation with these days, and she always found that the afternoon was the most suitable time for that.

'I'll never manage to finish this crossword, Gareth, however many times you urge me to attempt it,' an old man was saying. 'Like Tom Cruise in a foot-spa, I feel totally out of my depth.'

'Nice one, Bernard,' said an old man nearer the piano.

'Shall I start it for you?' asked Gareth, sitting himself down in the next seat to Bernard's, and studying the book carefully. 'What's that you wrote down for 'condition of a cancer - six letters?'

'*Malign,*' said Bernard. 'It's definitely right because my old lady died from one of them, see.'

'Mm. Well, I think it might have been '*benign,*' Gareth told him, smiling.

'No, no, I remember it well,' Bernard told him. 'She only got diagnosed in the Autumn and - bugger me - the girl was gone by Christmas.'

'Yes, I know,' Gareth told him. 'O.K., so do you want to write down '*malign*' then? Do you?'

'How do you mean? No. I want to get it right,' replied Bernard. 'Otherwise I'm going to bugger it up good and proper, then, aren't I?'

'You know you seem to love that particular six-letter word, Bernard,' Anne told him, settling Angharad into her new location near the window.

'*Benign*, do you mean?' asked Bernard.

Not *benign,* no - another B-word completely, I'm talking about,' Anne told him, shaking her head. 'But you're not going to get me to say it this time, you crafty old thing, after I went and fell for that far more disgusting one you made me write down for you in your puzzle last week, right?'

'Hey? What was that, love?' asked Bernard, grinning innocently.

'You know right well what it was,' said Anne, making as stern a face as she could compose, and waiting until he had finally seen it before relaxing her face-muscles once again.

'*Erection!*' called out Angharad from across the way.

'Aye, it was, Angharad,' said Anne, turning round and shaking her head at the old woman's candour. 'But the right eight-letter answer happened to be *building*, as it goes. But don't go encouraging him now, will you, there's a good girl.'

'Encourage Bernard! Fat chance of me doing that,' she exclaimed, chuckling wickedly. 'How on earth can you encourage someone who never has a full - a full - what-do-you-call-it?'

'Breakfast,' said Gareth helpfully.

Anne stared at him, admiring of his clever ruse. 'That's right, Gareth,' she said, smiling. 'I find I can barely do any work myself without a full breakfast, let alone -'

'Fuck!' the two old folk chimed in together. They stared at each other and chuckled heartily at their sudden, unexpected harmony.

'Right - that's it!' exclaimed Anne. 'Poker is banned this evening. If I've told you two once, then I must have told you a thousand times.'

'Oh, don't be like that, Anne,' Bernard pleaded, looking from one to the other. 'Gareth - please. I promise I'll even let you win tonight.'

But Gareth was standing firm, and, to show his solidarity with the colleague he secretly adored, he took Anne's hand in his and squeezed it. Recalling the last time this had happened, and the embrace in the medical-room that soon followed, Anne squeezed Gareth's hand just as tightly, taking care not to let the two old folk see what they were doing.

'Christ, Anne!' exclaimed Angharad, tossing the pack of playing-cards into the tray where the multi-coloured chips lay loose, and scattering most of them across the floor, then glaring up at her from her mobile chair. 'You know, sometimes I reckon you're bloody worse than my mother.'

Her Uncle Gary shuffled his way across to where Carla was sitting on the garden-bench in the sun, stroked a few times his fast-reddening, bald-pate, then covered it smartly with his cream- coloured, straw hat, and sat down beside her. He smiled at her serenely, and then handed her the tumbler of orange-juice she had requested he brought her, with an additional chocolate- biscuit which was his own idea. 'You know, in a way your dad was right in what he said to you, Carla,' Gary told her. 'When I was younger I certainly attended more rugby internationals in Cardiff than he did, and, in all probability, more than almost any Welsh fan ever managed to.'

'Oh, you mean that that was true what he said then,' she told him. 'And I thought Dad was joking, because I wasn't even aware you liked sport, Uncle.'

'No - that's right. I don't as it goes,' he replied oddly. 'You see, I never once ventured inside.'

'You never went inside the stadium!' stammered Carla, her brows raised. 'But how on earth -'

'No - each time I went - which was every single home-game as it goes - I stood just outside the ground, bible in hand, preaching The Word to everyone who passed me as they exited, whether they happened to be joyous at that moment or despondent, having won or having lost. And more often than not I stayed there until the very last spectator was making his way home.'

'God - Uncle Gary. Even I got to go inside there one time,' said Carla, 'although it was to sing the anthem on the pitch with the brass-band. I had no intention of watching the game, of course, which I could easily have done if I'd wanted, although I'm sure I saw the highlights back at the hotel later on that night. You know, I can't even remember who we were playing, to be honest.'

'Well I certainly remember that day, Carla.' Reverend Gary told his niece, smiling. 'It was France if you recall. And we were all incredibly proud of you. You know, I'm sure I've still got the video-tape at home somewhere.'

Carla sipped her juice and sat back in the sun's warm, healing rays, and closed her eyes. 'You know, Uncle Gary,' she began, 'although I'm sure I can appreciate why rugby means so much to us Welsh people, the sheer physicality involved, and the passion, and the bright-red, scarlet jersey are all, in my eyes, reminiscent of a torrid, bloody battle fought out in some grassy field somewhere. But, like you, I can't say the game of rugby itself means an awful lot to me.'

'Well, you're a girl, for a start,' he told her.

'No, it's not that, Uncle Gary,' responded Carla.

'Rugby football simply isn't your passion, is it, sweetheart?' he told her. 'I can remember that from a young age your interests were always of the artistic kind, you know.'

'Yes, I guess that's true,' she replied, nodding.

'Why should you need to know anything about scrums and mauls, eh? Music was always your game.'

Carla smiled across at him. 'You know, as a young Welsh girl, and I'm a tad embarrassed to admit this, Uncle, but I always thought a prop was something that held up the washing-line.'

'It is,' chimed back Gary. 'And you know there's a great big one leaning against the wall over there,' he told her, smiling. 'I see there's even a line out today. Ha, ha.'

'Well, I can see that,' Carla told him, not even close to getting his joke. 'And as for rucks. Well, I've seen a fair few of those in my time, I'm afraid, most notably outside a host of different clubs in London I once used to frequent. And sadly, even at one or two of my concerts, too. And, you know, very often they needed the police to sort them out, with their pepper-sprays, and their truncheons, and their tazers even.'

'Well, in rugby union it's the referee that gets to do all that, and with just his little whistle to help him,' Gary told her. 'Though he can, just occasionally, get himself knocked over in the process. Accidentally, mind, and without any malice intended.'

In the bright sky above them the sun passed behind a cloud temporarily.

'Uncle Gary - would you tell me something?' Carla asked him. 'How is it that you became a religious man, while your only brother - my father - remained relatively agnostic for most of his life, and apparently, you tell us, seemed to revel in all things secular?'

'But that's where you're wrong, you see, Carla,' the old man responded. 'I agree that you're dad was never an overtly religious man, but, in my opinion, he was always deeply spiritual.'

'Hey! Do you really mean that?' she asked him, glancing into his bulging eyes over the top of her sunglasses.

'I certainly do,' Gary told her, leaning forward. 'And you know Carla, I'm sure that you - being a chip off the old block, so to speak - are most definitely a spiritual soul too.'

'But I bet you're just saying that because of the - the expressive element in many of my songs,' she replied.

'Well, there's that, too, of course, my dear,' Gary told her. 'But, to my mind, it's quite apparent in your nature, too, and in the things you do, often at times when you aren't even thinking about it.' Gary placed his hand on her arm. 'In fact, I wouldn't be at all surprised if you left Oxford largely because your soul took action.'

'Because my soul took action!' exclaimed Carla. 'Uncle Gary - are you being serious?'

'Of course I am. One hundred per cent, in fact,' he told her. 'For you, I believe that Oxford was really a sort of lay-by for your talents on the main road to London. Look - talent like yours, my love, couldn't ever have seen the light of day in academia, could it? Oxbridge has never produced someone of your ilk, Carla, nor ever will. Or an Amy Winehouse, or an Adele, or a Kate Bush, even. An English or Music degree does absolutely nothing for someone's - for someone's creative ability, does it? It might prepare the groundwork for somebody to become a - a teacher, or a political lobbyist, or a research student, or a civil servant, or a newsreader, or a -'

'Or a journalist,' said Carla.

'Quite. And perhaps even a journalist in a respected music magazine who, one day, if they're really lucky, gets to meet and write a piece about a real, bona fide musical genius, whose soul at one time led her to reject academia -'

'Uncle Gary,' said Carla, smiling at his sly, unexpected compliment.

' - along with its cold mediocrity, and its barren, outdated trappings and traditions, in order to set the whole world alight from the most unlikely of settings, namely a damp, poky little one-bedroom flat in Hammersmith.'

'Fulham,' cut in Carla. 'And it was just a little bed-sit to begin with, remember.'

'Sorry - Fulham,' Gary announced, happily corrected. 'From a bed-sit in a very strangely-painted house in a little terraced-street very close to the river, that she could barely afford, and where, hour after hour, and day after day, she sat alone with her acoustic guitar and her second-hand, upright-piano, and composed the unforgettable *'Candice Farm,'* and - and -'

'Purple Home,' she reminded him, beaming out her most adorable smile .

'Purple Home - yes, of course. How on earth could I have forgotten that third album of yours, dear?' He squeezed her round the shoulders. 'And so realised her lifetime's ambition to perform music, and sell records, and top the charts, and tour the world, and show everyone what an ordinary, humble young girl from a bog-standard comprehensive school in a tin-pot, Welsh-valley town can achieve when she is as infused with music as you are, and really puts her mind to it.'

Carla found she wasn't able to contain her laughter any longer, and so flopped her lolling head onto her roly-poly uncle's barrel-chest, and, punctuated with sundry bouts of coughing and spluttering, split her sides uncontrollably for a minute or more, until an agonised cry suddenly rang out from upstairs. Getting up and leaving her uncle's side, Carla hurried inside, only to find, when she arrived at her father's room, that, thankfully, it was just another problem with a bed-pan. Just minutes later the girl reappeared in the garden, and, sitting down once more across from her uncle, found that she needed to ask him if he remembered what the cause of her earlier merriment happened to have been. Modest as ever, Gary responded that he didn't.

CHAPTER 18

The two uniformed policemen approached with care the gnarled, knotted door of the square, wooden shed that sat ungainly on the lip of the steep slope which ran down to the river. Their much heavier companion, who followed behind them, tried his best to keep up, but found this well nigh impossible on account of the considerable burden that his two brawny arms, held out quivering before him, were carrying.

'What's a hot spot not?' the sergeant suddenly asked the bleach-blond constable who was walking alongside him with his black, yellow-striped tazer ready for action, poised as it was in the young man's right hand.

'Well, I guess I might have known the answer to that when I once watched that infernal TV show on '*Dave*,' ' the blond bobby replied, 'but I very much doubt I can remember it now.'

'Cabbages,' the sergeant told him.

'Cabbages!' the other asked, bemused.

'Or cauliflowers, Ben. Cabbages or cauliflowers, or any other type of fruit and veg for that matter.'

'Really? So what *is* a hot spot, then, Sergeant Foley?' Ben enquired.

Turning, the white-haired sergeant signalled briefly to the heavy-set constable at his rear, and with a great, sweeping thud of his big red key, the huge man suddenly split apart, and forced open, the wooden door of the shed. 'This is what a hot spot is,' Foley told them, pointing ahead of him into the darkness. 'Just smell that, would you? That's prime skunk - that's what that is. A bleedin' shed-full of the stuff. I guess those young whipper-snappers must have thought they were home-free, but you can't expect to fool the heli-cops,

406

can you? That heat-seeking camera they've got is truly amazing, wouldn't you say? You know boys, if you shat in a wheelie-bin and tossed it in the river, then those boys would be sure to find it.'

'As you know, Sarge, I'm a police-interceptor these days,' Ben told him, with a wicked grin. 'So, naturally, I crap in the woods like everyone else.'

Suddenly a small form in dark clothes shot out of the shadows and ran straight past them. The sergeant turned and watched as the two younger, fitter officers chased after, then pounced upon, the running boy's back, flattening him out like a pancake on the wet ground.

'Put both your hands behind you - now!' Sergeant Foley bellowed at him, hurrying over to join them. 'Say - have you got anything on you that you shouldn't have?'

'Er, yeah - police. At least two of 'em, by the feel of it.' the face-down boy replied. 'Yaah! Hey - that bloody hurts.'

'Stop resisting!' the burly Constable Llewellyn shouted at him, twisting the boy's skinny, bare arm right up his back.

'Yeah - stop resisting!' Ben Thomas repeated, reaching down and curling up the boy's calves from the knees, so that any notion he had of fleeing from them was now out of the question..

'How the hell can I resist?' said the boy, spitting grass and twigs out before him. 'The two of you must weigh half-a-ton each at least.' He turned his head back and bit into his lip. 'No offence intended, of course, lads. Aah! O.K., O.K. - I admit that was a bit below the belt. You probably both go to '*Weight-watchers.*' '

'You carrying needles?' Llewellyn asked him.

'What! Yeah - a couple. I was just knitting a sweater when you drove up, as a matter of fact.'

'Oh - is that right?' said Sergeant Foley, stepping, ever so gently, on the boy's back so as not to be left out, and adroitly removing a set of handcuffs from off his belt.

'Yeah. I was planning on doing you all one, as it goes,' the boy continued. 'You don't mind black, do you, lads? I figured it was bound to go well with your riot-gear.'

'Hey - pencil-dick!' Llewellyn bawled at him. 'You probably think you're funny, don't you? When the only thing remotely funny about you, butty, is your face.'

The boy sniffed in a couple of times. 'Well, you did just manage to re-break my nose for me, big boy,' he responded, turning his head from side to side, and trying hard to breathe normally.

'Thanks for that, by the way, 'cos it's incredibly painful when you have to do it yourself, like.'

'O.K. Let's get him in the van, Dan,' Sergeant Foley told the larger constable.

'Van Damme! God - he's not here, is he?' the boy shot back, rolling over onto his back and looking up at them with terrified eyes.

'Shut it!' Sergeant Foley told him. 'Now bring yours knees up to your chin and get to your feet. O.K. Right - now stand with your feet wide apart. Wider! Search him, Thomas. Say - why's there blood pouring from your nose?'

'Oh, I guess I must have stuck a needle up it,' the lad retorted. 'Knitting's so bloody complicated these days, I find, don't you?'

Merlyn Foley placed his huge, lined forehead up against the young chap's face, 'Well, get any of it on my uniform and I'll bloody hammer you, butt. Compris?' He then spun the youth's body round and snapped the hand-cuffs on him securely.

'Received,' the boy replied, staring down at the wet ground and beginning to shiver.

'Right. Now walk over to the car.'

The police-men retraced their steps, ushering their puny, young prisoner ahead of them.

Arriving first, and opening the back-door, Sergeant Foley addressed the boy. 'Now turn round and slide your skinny arse across the back-seat,' he commanded. 'And don't go trying to conceal anything neither, because that won't work. We only cleaned the car out last Wednesday, so any drugs or weapons that we happen to find in there -'

'Must have been left there since Thursday, right?' said the boy, attempting a thin smile as he slid his way inside.

'No - must have been left there by you!' Foley told him firmly.

'Oh, really?' said the boy.

'Listen, ass-wipe - so far we're only planning on charging you with possession. O.K.?'

'Possession of what?' the boy asked. 'You can't mean drugs 'cos I haven't got any. Hey - what the fuck's that?' the lad asked, looking up and seeing what Constable Thomas now held up in the palm of his hand.

'Drugs,' Thomas told him.

'Your drugs,' Sergeant Foley clarified for him.

'Show me,' said the boy leaning closer. 'But we don't deal in amphets. You must know that, boys.'

'Well, you do tonight, butt,' Foley told him. Then more quietly, ''Cos that's all we brought with us, see.'

'Fuck me!' the boy exclaimed, shaking his head about. 'Where's the barrel, boys? 'Cos I figure I'd best start lying over it.'

'Hey. Don't go playing the victim, now, sonny,' Sergeant Foley told him. 'You're lucky we're not charging you with evading, or obstructing.'

'But I'm in cuffs, for Christ's sake,' the lad replied.

'Your hands are, yeah. But you've still got legs, right? You could easily have fled, do you get me?'

'Fled!'

'Exactly,' Sergeant Foley told him. 'And run headlong down to the river like a - like a headless chicken.'

'But I'd have drowned,' the boy shot back.

'Not a bit of it,' Foley continued. ''Cos, seeing you struggling, we all dragged you out and *saved* your arse, see.' The older man illustrated this with a powerful tugging motion.

'Hey?'

'And did CPR. on you and everything,' said the sergeant. 'And, even though you told us plainly you'd rather have died, we courageously carried on anyway.'

'But how the hell could -'

'Which would explain all the bruises on your body, and the broken nose.'

'Bruises! What bruises?' the boy asked. He turned his head, first to the left, then to the right, then addressed them all. 'Oh, I get it now - I get it.'

The grey-haired officer carried on, in no way pausing to acknowledge the young lad's comment. 'And went and won ourselves a medal apiece for it too.' He then stopped and smiled broadly at his two younger colleagues who quickly shot smiles back at him.

'I remember winning one of those in school once,' Ben told them. 'They presented me with it under the diving-boards at the deep end. It was a bronze with a pin in the back. Only I was in pyjamas at the time.'

'Ooh! Sounds painful does that,' said the sergeant, chuckling.

'Hey. What the hell's that fella talking about?' the boy asked the sergeant.

'I've no idea,' Foley retorted, chuckling away.

'Great story, fella,' the boy told them. 'Got any more?'

'I'm glad you liked it,' Constable Thomas told him, shaking his blond head back, his face flushing a bright, rose colour. 'Now shut your cake-hole 'til we get you down the station, yeah?'

The boy stared up at him. 'Aw, don't tell me you're going to be putting me on a - on a - on one of those things,' he said.

'On a what?' asked Thomas.

'On a train,' the youngster retorted, laughing heartily.

'Very funny,' Sergeant Foley told him, 'But Ben was referring to the police-station actually.' Foley reached out his arm and slammed the door on the boy, and then turned where he stood and watched admiringly as Llewellyn-the-Great, (as his colleagues often called Dan,) lifted up, then tossed, the large, red enforcer back into the trunk of the police-car.

Llewellyn climbed into the front-seat, and frowned aggressively across at his bleach-blond, uniformed colleague as the latter started the engine with a sudden jolt that shook all four men about like a jelly, and betrayed the fact he had left the car in gear.

'Twat!' Sergeant Foley told the driver emphatically, from behind, leaning forward.

But, after a combined shake of heads, both beside and behind him, and a second attempt by the young constable, which this time proved more successful, Constable Thomas at last managed to engage the vehicle's transmission and manoeuvred the large, black car back onto the narrow, muddy track they had arrived by. Then seconds later, in a loud and shuddering first-gear, he proceeded to drive them up the steep, grassy hill, and from there across the field of newly-sheared, and plainly terrified, sheep, and off towards the crescent-shaped horizon.

Chris had found out from the school's web-site that it was the morning of Rhiannon's final GCSE examination, and, although he tried his utmost not to, he had snuck along to Pennant to catch a glimpse of her, as she came out of the main-gate and crossed the road to get her bus home. But determined not to be seen, especially not knowing how she had taken his earth-shattering news, Chris lay flat on his stomach on the small grassy knoll across the road from the main-entrance, and from this vantage-point, elbows stretched out in front of him, and his interlaced fingers supporting his stubbly chin, gazed over at the cluster of small buildings, willing Rhiannon to emerge, but knowing that he had almost an hour more to wait before she would in fact do so.

Soon Chris fell asleep. In the dream, (that he now had for the second time,) he was speaking to some people in town beside his new, white car, which was parked alongside him on Brecon Road. Completing his conversation, he decided to proceed on down the hill towards Pontmorlais and Merthyr High Street, and so squeezed the stick-like remote he was holding in his hand, and made the car proceed along the road before him, but under his full control. Chris manoeuvred the white car round the bend and onto the downslope of the main road when he suddenly noticed that it was beginning to run away from him. Despite his urgent fiddling with the controls in a vain attempt to slow it down, he realised that the car was getting farther and farther away from him, and that it was already merging in with lots of other cars, many of which were also white, that were also passing through the green traffic-light, then making their way north towards Dowlais. Chris saw that there was no hope of catching up with it, and so he ran into a nearby office, found a phone, and rang up the police, and told them that his white car had been stolen.

A noisy lorry suddenly disturbed him, and, on waking, Chris immediately thought of Rhiannon. The fact was - and Chris knew it well - that the membrane between his waking and his sleeping self was so thin that he often seemed to have little trouble discerning the meaning, and even the significance, of some of the things that he dreamed. Yes, he told himself, the white car was definitely Rhiannon. It wasn't just her pale, white skin that suggested this, but Rhiannon had also once told him that she habitually wore white underwear in the days before the two of them started going out together: a habit she had retained from childhood, he assumed.

The sun emerged from behind a small cumulus-cloud to his right and so Chris shaded his face with his hand, closed his eyes, and thought about Rhiannon. He wet his lips as he considered her slim, white form, and the beautiful pair of sweet, pert, damson-like breasts that had poked out at him on the occasions when he had undressed her. No girl he had ever known possessed the unusually broad, pink nipples that she did, and, to him, this was a secret treasure that Chris felt sure only he had yet discovered, and that only he had teased and made love to.

Discomforted more than a little by what this wonderful thought provoked, Chris rolled over onto his back and peered up at the blue-and-white sky that lay spread out above him. Through half-closed lashes he recalled the way Rhiannon had often cupped in one of her hands his penis and testicles, and lifted, and squeezed, and kneaded the fleshy prize firmly, but gently, almost as if she was transplanting into fresh soil some garden-shrub she had brought home from the garden-centre, and was now pointing in the direction she was encouraging it to grow. At this quirky, outlandish, but erotic thought Chris chuckled deeply to himself. Taken aback by it, he knew only too well that his brain was on fire, and so he turned his head to the side and allowed his face to bask in the warm glow that the late-morning sun threw down upon him.

The blow that suddenly struck Chris on the side of the head spun his trunk round in a full circle, and caused him a pain the like of which he had never before experienced, even at the bottom of a ruck. Finding himself face down in the grass, he shot his right hand up to his temple and was shocked to find hot blood freely gushing out. Turning to face towards the sun again, and seeing two great, dark figures looming over him, Chris realised that he needed to get up right that instant and run, but he wasn't at all sure that he had the strength to bring it off.

'You went and shopped him didn't you, Clicker?' said Steffan, clumping Chris a second time with the baseball-bat, but this time in the guts. The heavy-set boy grinned widely as his hapless victim doubled up beneath him.

'Who - who are you talking about?' asked a wincing Chris, turning onto his side, breathing heavily, and clutching his lower abdomen with both hands.

'My older brother,' said Steffan. 'Don't go pretending you don't know now.'

'Brynmor, you know,' said Jake, clearly not as one-hundred-per-cent certain, as his friend clearly was, that they had found the right culprit. .

'Do you mean they found your farm?' enquired Chris, climbing onto his knees in preparation for standing up. But his words and his actions clearly weren't to Steffan's satisfaction, and the third, and final, strike he received from the solid, wooden weapon landed flush across his jaw.

Half-an-hour or so later, when Chris next woke up, he slowly turned his aching head and saw the red, single-decker bus, bearing a gorgeous, white-dressed Rhiannon, driving off towards Pant. She was seated at the rear of the vehicle, next to an enormous lad in the year above him who played lock-forward in the school's rugby team, and whom he knew was soon going to be leaving for university. The sudden sight of the girl Chris loved, as well as the fact that he himself was completely covered in blood, caused him to lie low for a while and conceal his gory face.

As the roaring bus climbed the steep hill and rounded the bend, Chris got unsteadily to his feet, and, his head still swimming, made his weary way back home again, now for the very first time beginning to fully accept that, as his dream had plainly told him, he would no longer be able to be intimate again with the adorable, flame-haired girl his body plainly still yearned for, despite the fact that he realised she was his half-sister.

The young constable smoothed down his bleach-blond fringe, then, seeing the wink his superior gave him, switched on the tape-machine that would now record the interview.

'You saw the CCTV-DVD as we all did, Brynmor,' said Sergeant Foley, waving the small case that now contained it in front of the young man's face. 'Have you got anything to say about it?'

Brynmor considered the question for a moment then spoke. 'B-G-I-P,' he replied, waving his open hand back at him in a similar fashion.

'What?' asked Foley, his grey brows raised, his head tilted to the side.

'Bloody good in parts,' the skinny lad told him, smiling. 'Except for the bits I'm in, of course. The action seemed to sag a little there, don't you reckon?'

Sergeant Foley spun round and frowned at his two colleagues, as if to suggest this wasn't likely to be an easy interrogation, then stared at the interviewee, who now sat slumped in his seat, and asked his key question. 'As you're no longer attending Pennant Comprehensive, Brynmor, what reason do you have for being outside the school-gates at that time of the day?'

'Well, that's my effin' - er - no comment,' said Brynmor, checking himself, and sniffing the air.

The three police-officers exchanged glances once again.

'Can you tell us why you ran away when the police arrived?' enquired the sergeant.

'No comment,' Brynmor replied, removing and lifting up his trainer in both hands, and sniffing it, thereby verifying that there was nothing attached to the sole.

Sergeant Foley wasn't to be de-railed by his response and ploughed on regardless. 'And, when you were - er - persuaded out of the car, why did you have so much cash in your pocket?'

The young man shook his head and sniggered, then responded, 'No comment.'

'Four hundred smackers to be exact, I understand.'

'No comment,' said Brynmor.

'Brynmor - tell me - were you selling something?'

The boy looked down at the surface of the table that separated them and said, 'No comment.'

'Were you selling something illegal?'

He yawned, then decided to check the state of his finger-nails. 'No comment.'

'Were you selling drugs?'

Biting one that seemed to him a little long. 'No comment.'

'Were you selling the school-pupils drugs, young man?'

'No comment,' said Brynmor.

'Well, I put it to you that that is exactly what you were doing,' said Sergeant Foley, leaning forward.

'No comment.'

'And who bought you the flash car that you were driving? Because, you see, we've established that it's not nicked.'

'No comment.'

'Well, it's neither yours nor your brother Steffan's, that's for sure. It's top-of-the-range for a start, and it was purchased for cash from a large garage in Bristol just a month ago.'

'No comment.'

'Mm. And whose shed is it we caught you in today? Eh? Yours, or your brother Steffan's?'

'No comment.'

'Because it's my belief that it's neither. 'Because, you see, I reckon you're both being bank-rolled by some city big-fish from England, and the Volvo you were in was part-payment.'

'Did you say Volvo?' asked Brynmor, looking alarmed. 'Er - no comment.'

'Say - do you think, young man, that refusing to answer my questions is going to get you released from custody?'

'You betcha!' exclaimed Brynmor, glancing up. 'Er, sorry - no comment.'

'Look - I don't see much point in persisting with all these questions, sergeant,' said D.I.Dawson, pushing open the door and joining them. 'Because we know what his answer is going to be. And I suppose in a while we'll just have to release him on bail.'

'Told ya!' said Brynmor.

'What was that, lad?' asked Dawson.

'I said - I said - 'No comment.' '

'No, after that, he means, lad,' cut in Sergeant Foley. He and Dawson stared down at the boy and waited.

Brynmor leaned his head to the side and checked out what quantity of wax he could manage to eke out of his left ear with his littlest finger, then did the same to the right. He then looked up and smiled at the pair of senior officers poised before him. 'What? Er - no comment,' he said. 'As I keep on telling you guys, 'no comment.' '

The sergeant turned round to address his Cockney colleague. 'Look - I hear what you're saying Jeff, but just let me put a few more questions to him, yeah?' Then turning back once again to the boy they had arrested by stealth just hours before, he said, 'And what's the point, do you think, of all the stupid answers you keep giving to my questions, such as -?'

'No comment?' ventured Brynmor.

'Precisely. I mean, what is the point of it all?'

'No comment.'

'Listen - I was just being rhetorical that time.' Foley stared down at the empty plate that lay before the arrested man and pondered his next move. 'Say - Brynmor - which is your favourite sandwich, eh? Ham, egg, or cheese?'

'No comment.'

'I see. And which is your favourite car?'

'No comment.'

'T.V. channel?'

'No comment.'

'Comic?'

'No comic.'

'Comment,' the sergeant corrected him.

'Comment - sorry. No comment.' Brynmor smiled a pinched smile at his error.

'And your favourite newspaper?'

'No comment.'

'Oh, you mean the F.T.?' asked the constable from the corner.

'No comment.'

'F.T. - No comment,' said Dawson, chuckling loudly. 'Nice one, Thomas.'

Sergeant Foley turned and signalled to Constable Thomas for him to switch off the tape-machine. Then after hearing the click sound, he said, 'Look - you wouldn't describe yourself as mentally challenged exactly, would you now, Brynmor?' The confused boy stared up at him, brows narrowed. 'Undiscerning, I mean. Feeble-minded, you get me?'

'Er - no comment,' Brynmor responded once again.

'Oh, go easy, Sergeant, please,' said Dawson, slowly shaking his head from side to side.

'What? Oh, I see,' said Foley. 'Then I'll try and make it simpler for you, shall I? Be more - more monosyllabic, perhaps.'

Brynmor stared up at him. 'You know, that's always bothered me, that has,' said the boy.

'Sorry?' said Foley, somewhat shocked at the normal conversational response he had just received, and quickly opening up his note-book.

'What has?' asked Dawson.

'Why *monosyllabic* is such a bloody long word. Say - why do you think that is, Sergeant?'

Foley tapped his pencil on the table a few times, considering his comment. 'Brynmor - I see that you've at last begun answering my questions. Now that we've switched the tape off, I mean.'

'Yes, I must admit I'd noticed that myself, officer,' Brynmor answered him, smiling.

The sergeant signalled to the constable to press the on-switch again, then smiled back at the boy. 'You do realise, young man, you already possess a criminal record, don't you?' he told him.

'No comment,' came the lad's reply.

The sergeant closed his eyes and let his head fall heavily onto the table. The thud this made caused his two colleagues to suddenly jump to their feet.

Dawson patted Foley on the back and said, 'I can see you're getting rather tired, sergeant. Look - let's wrap it up for the day, shall we?'

'No comment,' said the sergeant.

'What!' stammered Dawson.

'What?' exclaimed Brynmor, breaking into a laugh.

'Sorry, boys,' the sergeant replied, sitting up once again and rubbing his weary eyes. 'Look - in six months time I plan to retire for good, as you guys very well know. And I'd - and I'd just like to go out with one final success, you know. Just one.' Then much louder, 'Is that too much to ask do you think? Eh? And don't any of you guys dare say 'No comment.' '

Carla had received written confirmation from her bank that they had transfered a five-figure sum from her private account to a small company in Switzerland. She didn't like seeing her father suffering and dying like this, and had told him again and again that she was prepared to bring into the house a carer who lived in the locality, or even one who was happy to have the box-room as a bed-sitting room for as long as he remained alive. But it was her father, who, having read about the activities of the private clinic in Zurich, and after tearfully explaining to Carla that her *Welcome Respite* medication no longer worked for him, made his decisive, heartbreaking decision, and told her that, as long as she was prepared to fund it and arrange it for him, and promised not to question his decision, then this was how he wanted to go.

Hearing her Uncle Gary in earnest conversation with her dad, Carla, slipped on her slippers and crept upstairs. But discerning the topic they were busy discussing before she reached the top, she paused for a moment, then sat herself down on a triangular step where the staircase doubled back on itself, and listened intently to the conversation that the pair were having.

'But don't you feel, Tom, that our God is as much a stake-holder in our lives as we are?' she heard her uncle telling her father.

'Gary, I'm not sure what you mean exactly,' she heard her father reply hoarsely. 'But I'd be glad if you'd kindly explain yourself.'

After so many years, Carla told herself, when the behaviour and antics of these two elderly brothers had seemed to a large extent to disprove the theory of relativity, it would now appear that they had become just about as close as two, quite unalike, nay, two radically different, brothers ever could be.

'Well, since we all have free will,' remarked Gary, 'we clearly have the power in our possession to kill ourselves, right?'

'Right, I see that,' responded her dad, suddenly breaking out into a harsh cough.

Gary waited for him to settle, then continued, 'But do you really believe we have the moral right so to do?'

'I don't think I've properly considered it,' Carla heard her father reply.

'Well, consider it now, then, would you, Tom,' said Gary. 'Because, personally, I believe that we don't.'

'You think we don't have that right?' asked Tom.

'No I don't,' Gary replied. 'And, by electing to commit suicide, to me you're simply snatching the reins out of the hands of God, basically choosing to set the timing of your termination - of your death - without any reference, or deference for that matter, to the life-giver Himself.'

There followed a protracted pause, then Tom said, 'Yes, I can see what you're saying, Gary, but I'm afraid you still have a way to go to convince me to even consider putting the matter off.'

'But wait, Brawd - there's a whole other issue completely that is involved here, you know.'

'Can you feed me my milk?' his ailing brother asked him, ignoring his words.

Gary dutifully performed the required task, which involved a loud gurgling sound, then carried on explaing to his brother what was in the forefront of his mind. 'You know I believe that we have a great deal to learn from the actual process of dying - of dying a *natural* death, I mean,' he said.

'Oh, really?' said Tom. 'From dying! You mean from dying!

'Why, of course,' said Gary.

'And how on earth would you know that?' Tom asked him. 'When did *you* ever go through it?' There being no response, Tom added, 'I rest my case.'

'Hey! You can't just say that,' countered Gary.

'But, Brawd, you aren't the one lying here in terrifying pain every day of the week, are you?'

'I know, but -'

'Unable even to get up, let alone go to the toilet in the normal way. It's thoroughly humiliating is what it is Gary, especially when you and Carla aren't here to help me.'

'Yes, I know, Tom, but -'

'Then why should I listen to you? Eh? Aside from the fact you're a lot cleverer than I am, I mean. Why should I accept any of your advice on this particular subject? Anything else, maybe, but not on this.'

'Why!' repeated Gary. 'I'll tell you why. Because it's right. How about that, for a start?'

'Listen to me, Gary. I've thought long and hard about this, and I fully intend to choose euthenasia.' Tom broke out into a cough again. 'And - and if *you* won't assist me, then I know for sure that my Carla will. You see, I think it might have been her idea to begin with.'

Gary wasn't surprised at this, but at the same time wasn't prepared to put his young niece down. When you've got as much wealth as she has, he thought, then there is no limitation to the range of options on offer. 'Then tell me, Tom,' he began, 'Are you seriously telling me that you would actually want to short-change yourself of that learning?' he said.

'That learning!' exclaimed Tom, scrunching up his nose.

Carla smiled at her father's anger with Gary's words. She imagined the fiery look he must have given him, then shivered from the sudden draught that swept up the stairs from behind her.

'Yes - that crucial learning,' replied Gary. 'That knowledge of - that learning about the vital, vibrant, existential suffering involved in the process of normal ageing, and equally normal dying.'

'What! Are you being serious?' asked Tom. 'But why shouldn't I want to avoid the suffering? What on earth is to be learned from going through it - from just - just putting up with it all?'

'Look I realise I'm not ill, Brawd,' replied Gary. 'So I'm not in your shoes - and so, frankly, I wouldn't know exactly, and I am prepared to acknowledge that. But what I do know is that, however painful or drawn out the process of dying might turn out to be, when it comes to me - when my turn comes round - and it will - then I fully intend to stay the whole course and find out.'

'Find out! Let me get this right,' said Tom. 'Are you trying to tell me that you've already decided that, however bad things get, you're going to be choosing knowledge over - over pain!'

'Yes, that's right,' Carla heard Gary tell him, perhaps through gritted teeth. 'I certainly am.'

Tom laughed heartily at him, then summoned up, and spat into a bowl beside his bed, some phlegm that this action had created. 'I wonder, Gary,' he continued, 'if you'll actually live up to those brave, commendable intentions of yours when *your* time comes, if come it does, or - or whether you will just forget you were once so inclined, and, like me, choose the easier way out.'

'But, Tom, I don't think you fully understand what I'm saying,' Gary pleaded.

'Well, tell me then' Tom shot back. 'Go on.'

'It's that - it's just that I really don't feel I have *the right* to do such a thing - take my own life, I mean,' Gary told him.

Tom paused for a moment then spoke. 'You know, I shouldn't really be so surprised that you are saying all this,' he said.

'What do you mean by that?' enquired Gary, feeling he knew more or less what his brother was about to say.

'Well, you are an ordained minister, after all, aren't you?' said Tom.

'Listen - it's not because of my religious vocation that I'm telling you this, Brawd,' replied Gary. 'And nobody ever taught me it, either. I say it simply because I - because I am *a man* - a human being, Brawd, who, like you, was created in my Great Father's image. And it is my God who created me - supplying me, as He did, with that very first gulping breath of life I inhaled in the vast, new, stranger-than-strange, ocean-like atmosphere that my tiny, helpless body fell into from our dear mother's birth-canal. And Who, even now, continues to deliver to me the very same blessed draft, because - well, because He commited Himself so to do on my behalf for every single, lung-filled, breath-taking moment of my long, painful, arduous, but wonderful life.'

Carla got up and stood at the door, and watched her father's eyes wander about as he considered the words her uncle had just spoken. 'Do you mean to say, Gary - are you telling me that you believe Our Maker has made a binding commitment to keep us alive until the moment - that crucial moment - when He elects - when He - chooses to take our life away from us again?'

'Yes, I do believe it,' Gary answered, clasping his brother's blue, vein-ridged hand in his.

Tom gazed lovingly into his elder brother's eyes. *'Out of a misty dream our path emeges for a while, then closes within a dream,'* he said, his eyes shut tight.

Encouraged by the poem's lines that he knew so well, Gary smiled back at his brother through a stream of tears that suddenly began to flow down his face like warm, trickling rain. 'And that moment - that crucial moment, my brother - was set in stone and decided a long, long time before either of us was even born.'

'Before we were even conceived, are you saying?' said Tom.

'Yes,' said Gary. 'Most likely far, far earlier than that, even. Eons before, I'd say. You see, Tom, I have long believed that the very moment of our demise was written down by Him at the start of time, in the great *Book Of Life*.'

Tom lay his head back on the pillow and stared straight up at the ceiling. 'Now I understand what you are saying, Gary,' he told him. 'And yes, like you, I admit I too believe that it's true. I too believe that He promised to be with us, and care for us, and sustain us right from the moment of our very first breath of life, in this world that He created for us, right up until our last.'

'Womb to tomb,' said Gary, suddenly recalling how he had once sung a part alongside his brother in a school-production of '*West Side Story*,' and even believed he might still have the cool, red Jets-jacket he wore in that performance buried somewhere in his glass, walk-in wardrobe back at home.

'Birth to earth,' said Tom, smiling at the mutual recollection he realised he and his sibling had just enjoyed.

'Between the forceps and the stone,' a tearful Carla whispered in the doorway, recalling the iconic lyrics of Joni Mitchell that she had once sung at a concert, and yet again wishing that they could have been her own. She could already tell from her father's discussion with her uncle that her trip to the bank the previous week had plainly proved a pointless one. The money itself meant nothing to her, of course, she told herself, wiping the streaming tears from her face into the white handkerchief that she had earlier unfolded, and now held, pressed tightly to her cheek. But the sudden failure of the intricate plan she had devised, with her dad's enthusiastic help, relating to his sad, but imminent, demise, had plainly taken the wind from her sails, and now left her feeling downcast and depressed.

Carla slowly crossed the threshold of the shadow-strewn bedroom and took in the sight of the two aged brothers on the bed, hugging each other's contrasting frames, and looking almost as if they had lived their long lives together, and had never once been apart.

'It is the choice a Christian has to make and it's the right one,' she heard her uncle's deep, mellifluous voice tell her supine, nodding father, as he lay cradled and supported by Gary's strong left arm, encircling firmly and fully, as it did, both of his bony, pointed shoulders.

Tom once again emitted a hoarse, painful cough, then replied to him, and to the whole wide world, 'And what the dear Lord gives us, only the dear Lord Himself has the right to take away.'

Carmen and Rhiannon were sitting on the grass revelling in the powerful rays of the morning sun.

'Good at English! Pippa Jenkins!' ejaculated Carmen. 'I don't think so, somehow. Last week she told Mrs. Jarman she thought '*subordinate clauses*' might be Santa's little helpers. She did, Rhi, I swear!'

Rhiannon turned to her friend and said, 'Chris told me he can't stand her any more. She's got horrific personal B.O. too, he told me.'

Carmen considered this news. 'Doesn't surprise me a bit,' she told her friend, giggling.

'And do you know what else he told me? He told me she's got so much vagazzle going on down there, he said it didn't - well, he didn't feel right.'

'What a bloody waste of money,' said Carmen. 'She should have got a tattoo on her forehead instead, I reckon.'

'A tattoo!' said Rhiannon. 'What sort of tattoo?'

'One saying '*I badly need doing,*' Carmen told her. 'It would definitely save time, don't you think? *And* it wouldn't rust.'

Carmen went back to reading the joke-page in her magazine. After a minute or so she turned to Rhiannon to share what she had gleaned from it. 'If *The Grim Reaper* comes for you, whatever you do don't go hitting him with the vacuum-cleaner, Rhi,' said Carmen.

'And why is that?' asked Rhiannon.

'You could be Dyson with death,' She paused for her friend to ponder it. 'Dyson with death - do you get it?' Then the two girls rolled about laughing.

All of a sudden Pippa Jenkins and a group of her associates walked past, totally ignoring the two of them as usual.

The friends watched them go by, then Carmen sat up. 'You know, I sometimes wish I had bigger boobs like you've got

Pippa,' bellowed Carmen, easily loud enough for the whole group to hear her.

'Really?' replied a shocked Pippa, turning, approaching, and then perching herself down on the wall, facing them. Rhiannon spun round to face her friend, open-mouthed, clearly not expecting this.

'Yeah, just sometimes, I mean,' said Carmen, grinning. 'No - occasionally I wish I had. No, I lie - I did once, then I thought better of it.'

Pippa stared at her. 'Well, what you should do, Carmen, is get some really soft tissue-paper, darling, and, once a day if possible, rub it firmly back-and-fro between your breasts. You know, down the cleavage like this.' She opened her blazer and imitated the action required.

'You being serious!' said a shocked Carmen. 'And how the hell is that supposed to work, you daft bat?'

'Well, I don't rightly know, but it cetainly worked on your arse,' replied Pippa, smiling broadly, then getting up and hurrying away to join her friends again, who were already laughing themselves silly.

Watching Pippa scamper off, Carmen waited a while. Then, when the group had turned the corner of the main building, she jumped to her feet. 'I want to ask you something, Rhi,' she said. 'because you're my dearest friend.'

Anticipating the question that was coming, Rhiannon told her, 'No, it doesn't look big at all in that skirt. I don't know how many times I've told you.'

'It's nothing to do with my arse,' said Carmen. 'It's about my mother.'

'What about her?' asked Rhiannon.

'Well, you know how she works evenings in the Labour Club?

'Behind the bar, yeah.'

'Right. Well, she told me this morning how she met your Mam's husband in there doing a show.'

'My dad!' exclaimed Rhiannon. 'But he works part-time driving a van for a living, Carmen. I thought you knew that.'

'She meant your Mam's first husband, Rhi. Er - Dick something or other.'

'You mean - oh, you mean Dick Plant!' said Rhiannon. 'Oh my God!'

'Yeah, that's what she called him. I thought she was having a laugh, like, or maybe that it was the lager talking. But, no. Dick Plant is what she called the fella. She said she saw him on stage performing, though what it was he was doing she never told me. Say - what was he like, Rhi?'

'How would I know?' replied Rhiannon. 'I never met the bloke, though there's a couple of snaps of him in the first part of the photo-album. My dad says he pissed off when Sarah, my half-sister, was still in her teens.'

'Then do you reckon that's why she's a - why she likes the women, do you think?' enquired Carmen.

'Sarah? I haven't a clue,' replied Rhiannon. 'You see, I haven't seen her in years. She lives and works in London these days, doing something or other for the government I gather. And Dad says she only seems to come back home again for funerals.'

'Well, listen, Rhi. If you fancy seeing your sister's dad - this Dick bloke - in action, well, my Mam says he's working there every day this week,' Carmen told her.

'I don't know,' said Rhiannon, pondering the matter. 'But I do know I wouldn't go down there on my own. And anyway, it might be expensive.'

'True, but you never know, my Mam might be able to get us in there for nothing,' her friend replied. 'Say - would you like me to ask her?'

The burly police-officer placed the heavy, red enforcer on the door-step outside Anne's home and joined his two uniformed colleagues inside.

'Llew!' yelled Sergeant Foley from above, 'Get up these stairs now and lift Ben up into the loft, will you?'

'Thank God I was in to open the door for you, that's all I can say. And mind the aspidistra!' Anne told them, to absolutely no effect, edging down the stairs, and then bending low to catch the slowly tumbling pot, but sadly not much of the soil it contained, and which soon became scattered all over her floor.

'Grab the torch, boy!' the sergeant urged the young constable, who had already reached the very top of the step-ladder, but discovered that he was still a foot or so short of being able to scramble up into the loft on his own.

Llew-the-Great grasped Ben's calves in both arms and hoisted him high.

'O.K., O.K.!' blurted Thomas, stretching out both his arms to seek some lateral support. 'Don't send me into orbit, for God's sake!'

'Aye, you're not practising the line-out now, you know, Llew,' said Sergeant Foley, peering up, and rubbing dust from out of his thinning, grey hair. 'Say - what can you see up there, lad?'

'What the hell's to see?' asked Anne from the foot of the stairs. 'The lost continent? Listen - if you're looking for a box of Christmas decorations and a couple of broken chairs then I reckon you boys have hit the jackpot.'

'What's in there, Ben?' asked Constable Llewellyn, ignoring the home-owner's comments.

'Bugger all, that I can see,' replied the muffled voice of young Thomas. 'A large box of Christmas decorations and a couple of broken chairs is all I can make out.'

'You mean there's no drugs?' asked Sergeant Foley, holding firmly onto the step-ladder and peering up again.

'Well, none that I can see,' said Thomas.

'Drugs!' screamed Anne. 'Why the hell would we have got any drugs up there?'

'Well, you see, we were anticipating a small farm,' Sergeant Foley told her.

'But does my house look like a farm?'

'No - I mean up there, ma'am,' he told her.

'A farm! In my loft!' exclaimed Anne, sitting down on a step and rubbing her temple with the tea-towel she was holding. 'But God alive, man! Don't you think we'd have noticed if we had any sheep up there? We'd have heard them, wouldn't we? And the only thing bleating in this house these days is my husband.'

'He means cannabis, Mrs. Cillick,' Llewellyn told her, by way of calming her fears. 'Weed, you know.'

'Well, I've got a garden full of those if that's what you're after,' she told him, breathing in deeply, and gripping her forearm so as to check her pulse. 'Shall I take you out front and show you? Say - who the hell told you my boy was up to no good, anyway?'

'Er - one of his friends squealed,' said Llewellyn.

'Squealed! Why? You didn't sit on him, did you?'

'No,' the constable retorted sharply, then looked over at his sergeant.

'The fact is - a lot of them shopped him, Mrs. Cillick,' said Sergeant Foley. 'So we had to pay you a visit, see.'

'Aah! Found some,' they heard Thomas report, ducking his head back into view once again.

'What have you got?' asked Foley.

'Coffee-beans,' the constable told them, holding up two large bags and smiling at his new discovery.

'Oh, is that all?' asked Anne, getting to her feet and mounting the stairs again. 'They're my boy's, they are. There's probably tons of them up there. He bought them in bulk months ago.'

'But why would he have them, ma'am? That's what I'd like to know,' Sergeant Foley asked her.

'Well, why does anybody have them?' countered Anne, suddenly catching sight of her injured son standing just outside the open front-door, and watching him turn and run back down the footpath he had just arrived by. 'To - to make bloody coffee, innit?' she announced sarcastically, edging cunningly towards the front-door and then peering out.

'What is it, Mrs. Cillick?' asked Sergeant Foley, making his way down the stairs to join her.

'Oh, I - I was just checking on those weeds I mentioned,' she told him, shuffling from one foot to the other on the threshold, hoping to block the large man who approached from being able to stand alongside her, and, at the same time as her, watch Chris speeding down the road away in the direction of '*the ninety-nine steps*.' 'And don't think It's just my son, you know,' she announced.

'How do you mean?' enquired Sergeant Foley, becoming more than a little intrigued, and squeezing up behind Anne, and seeking to follow her gaze down the hill, where now nothing and nobody could be seen moving or breathing.

Biting her lip nervously, Anne swiftly edged away from his bulky, uniformed torso, and bent over on the lawn to search for a weed or two that she could pull up in her hand and show him. 'What I mean is, even my husband can't get enough of it, you know,' Anne told the sergeant, without turning. 'He even has someone at work who grinds it for him, he told me.'

'Grinds it for him!' asked Foley, initially picturing in his mind's eye a cannabis-grinder, but soon feeling strangely hot and flustered, as he stood at Anne's front-door, staring down at the woman's bent body, her tanned, exposed knees, and shapely buttocks, and trembling perceptibly. He felt queasy, then a thought hit him. 'Oh, for the coffee, you mean?' he said.

'Of course, for coffee,' said Anne, glancing back at the man, and, suddenly sensing her exposed position, swiftly straightening up her body and adjusting her skirt. 'What on earth did you thnk I meant, officer? Cannabis? Or that damned marijuana, even?' She glanced down just to check that her cleavage was also now suitably covered, but elected to fasten another blouse- button anyway. 'You know, I'll be honest with you, Sergeant Foley,' Anne continued, far less inclined now to seek out the man's gaze for fear she might discern that same look she saw for many years in her young husband's eyes, but these days only seemed to see in Gareth's. 'I wouldn't be at all surprised if, like Chris, my Drew has become totally addicted.'

'What goes round the world but stays in a corner?' was the riddle her Uncle Gary had posed, and left for Carla to try to resolve the night before he had set off with his second Mrs. Davies for his annual fortnight's break at a small hotel in the west of Cornwall. Carla was determined to work it out by the time he returned, and spent days pondering the solution, until one morning, after hearing the letter-box rattle, she bent down and saw the bright, red-and-white postage-stamp, featuring a famous Welsh castle, to the top-right of her name and her father's address, on the long, white envelope that lay on the mat. Carla smiled, emitted a quiet chuckle, and told herself that she would be sure to let her uncle know that she had found out the answer on the very next occasion he rang up to check how his ailing brother was faring.

Carla walked into the living-room, pulled back the curtains, and sat down on the sofa, so allowing the light from outside to illuminate the envelope's contents. The letter that arrived for her was one of the first she had received since taking up residence at her father's home in *Gloryhole*, and she was even more surprised that, far from having circled the globe to get there, it had barely travelled the length of the road outside her window; in fact, she mused, noting the outrageous lean on the tower of Caerphilly's famous fortress, a costly postage-stamp was barely required, or a post-man even, as Jack Belt himself could have picked it up in his van, and delivered it through their front-door in less than five minutes flat.

Carla didn't know who was behind the forthcoming gig at '*The Railway*' - a pub that she could only recall having been inside on one or two occasions, since, to her mind, it wasn't the sort of place you would elect to visit if peace and quiet were what you were seeking. She noticed that the signature at the foot of the page was that of a certain Paddy Docherty, whom she knew managed the premises, and was an Irishman whom most local people spoke well of.

Although she hadn't played in public for almost a year, and her band was currently in Europe backing another singer, it took Carla just seconds to decide that she would most certainly grace the gig with her presence, at the very least, and that she wouldn't ask for a penny as payment if she did play. This wasn't just because it was billed as a charity-concert, but because it had been hastily put together as a sort of tribute to the singer Amy Winehouse, who had mysteriously died just a week or so before, and whom Carla had met on more than one occasion, and for whom she had tremendous respect, both as a fellow artist and as an inspiration to singers like herself and Adele, and Duffy, and Lily, and Marina, all of whom, strangely, she suddenly thought, smiling, either came from Wales, as she did, or had strong Welsh family-connections.

Carla left the letter on the table and got up and went into the kitchen to take a pair of her father's trousers off the drying-rail. Pulling the zip up tightly, she then folded them very neatly and placed them in the airing-cupboard, in a way that she would never dream of doing with respect to her own clothes, but, because this was how her father had done it before she had arrived to help him, she now felt a sense of duty to carry out the exact same task on his behalf.

Carla suddenly paused, and then dashed over to the kitchen-table to scribble on a piece of scrap-paper a question that had just posed itself in her mind, in much the same way as she found a line of a song-lyric was apt to do on occasions. 'What has two legs, no wings, but flies?' she wrote down, giggling, then went upstairs to check on her father.

After tending to him, Carla decided to go and have forty-winks on her single-bed, and so, removing her slippers, and sipping some water from the tumbler she had brought upstairs with her, she turned away from her window, which looked out over *The Seven Arches,* and instead faced towards the wall, feeling sure that this would most likely speed up the intended process.

Soon Carla began to recall the day she had first arrived at this little, three-bedroomed cottage in the foothills of The Beacons, after having chosen to spend her first night back in Wales in a motel amongst the range's peaks. On climbing the stairs that first time, she recalled, she hadn't needed telling which bedroom her father had selected as hers, for, apart from the small, wooden-framed bed, the pale-blue quilt, and the double pillows that were there for necessity's sake, on the wall alongside it, and that she now lay looking at, hung a large print of a stunning painting by the Dutch master Gerard Ter Borch entitled *'Parental Admonition.'* I dare say my dad probably wished to convey to me something about my lifestyle in London, but felt he couldn't quite bring himself to say it, Carla had concluded with a wry smile at the time. But whether that were the case or not, regarding the painting now from her reclining position she concluded that it was certainly a very attractive picture to look at.

In the household scene depicted colourfully before her, Carla could see the stern father waving his finger reprovingly at the tall, slender figure of his daughter, whose tearful face is understandably hidden from sight. Her mother is simply seated at the father's side, not even engaging her daughter with her gaze, plainly preferring to let the head-of-the-household, youthful though he appeared to be compared with herself, Carla thought, deal with whatever misdemeanour their troublesome offspring had got up to.

Despite the painting's serious subject-matter, Carla had been so enchanted by the oyster-satin dress which the daughter wore that she had sought out and purchased in Cardiff a very similar one for herself, and it was this shiny, new purchase which now hung, loosely but elegantly, and still within its polythene covering, from a hanger inside her wardrobe. Carla felt that she simply couldn't wait for the moment when she would get to wear it outside for the first time, and now, as she lay there, she began to consider that she might actually chance her arm by wearing it for the forthcoming charity-gig down the road at 'The Railway.'

After her brief nap, Carla awoke with a sort of disconcerted feeling that she couldn't seem able to explain. Then, sipping from her glass of water, and rising and kneeling on the duvet, she decided to study more closely the scene depicted in the painting on the wall across from her, and was soon shocked when she noticed in it something rather alarming. It seemed to her that, far from simply waving an admonishing finger at the young girl standing meekly before him, Carla could plainly see that the seated man's hand contained a coin!

'Oh, my God!' exclaimed Carla, jumping to the floor and nimbly dragging her bed further from the wall so that she could study the painting even more intently. 'Parental Admonition -

my arse!' she told herself. 'It's nothing but a - a common brothel - that's what this supposed family- household actually is. And the older lady sipping from a glass of wine, and sitting, eyes down, alongside the seated man, far from being the girl's mother, is - is nothing other than 'the Madame' of the sordid establishment!' Carla moved to the side and stared at the print from a different perspective. 'And, of course, the man sitting in the seat and gesticulating at the poor girl, far from being her father, is nothing but a common patron of the gaudy boudoir, clearly attempting, with his proffered coin, to purchase for himself the female's services.' Carla smiled at the budget trousers and the horrid, sagging socks that the young man was wearing, now feeling sure that they alone went most of the way to confirming her fresh assessment.

Carla opened the door of her wardrobe so as to gaze at the oyster-satin dress that she had purchased at a leading department-store, and straightaway realised that she now viewed it in a completely different light. She quickly reached in, and, elbows pumping, deposited the covered dress much farther back on the sliding-rail, burying it deeply behind all manner of older, cheaper garments. 'There's just no way I'm going to be wearing that on the night,' she told herself. 'No - it'll have to be jeans and a t-shirt once again, I'm afraid, and the punters will just have to put up with it. And, yes, I'm quite sure that Amy herself would very much approve of that decision.'

CHAPTER 19

The burly police-officer flashed down the saloon-car and pulled up just behind it. He applied the hand-brake and then spoke into his radio. 'Hello Control! Hello! Doris! Yeah, Llew here. O.K., I'll shout then. I've just stopped a black Maestro on the main road south of Merthyr, love!'

'What do you mean black?' the middle-aged, male driver suddenly bellowed over his shoulder at the constable parked behind him, whom he could easily hear. 'Do I look black to you?'

Having checked that he was wearing his hat, and that his tazer-gun was fixed securely on his belt, the police-officer got out of his car and approached the door of the obliquely parked-up Maestro. He soon noticed that, far from being worried about the situation, the driver seemed to be smiling away, and singing along to the music that was playing on his car-stereo system.

'Do you think you could turn off the engine, Sir,' Constable Llewellyn asked. The engine-noise ceased as the driver obliged. 'Say - what's your name, chap?'

'Frank Sinatra,' the man replied, with a loud belch.

'Frank -' The burly police-officer shook his head briefly, leaned closer, and sniffed the man's breath. 'Say - have you been drinking, Sir?'

'I've had a few,' the driver replied, a starry glint in his eye.

'Mm, I thought so,' said the constable, nodding.

'But, there again, too few to mention.'

'I think I'll be the judge of that, Sir.' the officer replied, pausing to think for a moment. 'Oh, I see, I see. But please don't start singing it again, Sir,' the officer warned him. 'Just hand me the keys, would you. And kindly stay in the car, if you don't mind. You see, I like to do it my way.'

The man began to sing once again, only this time at the top of his voice. 'I'll do it my way!'

'Christ! I said no singing, Sir! Do as I say, please, or you'll certainly have regrets when we get down the station.' The officer adroitly slipped a white tube into the driver's mouth and ordered him to blow. 'Harder, harder, harder!' he commanded at increasing volume. 'Right, that's enough.' He flicked the tube onto the ground and studied the reading. 'One-two-three,' the officer told the man.

'Four, five, six,' the man replied, chuckling, 'I remember I did a test like this to get in the navy one time. You know the kind of thing. They say 'rum,' and you say 'breakfast.' Right, officer - can I go now, please?' He made a sudden grab for the keys but failed, as Llewellyn closed his massive fist around them.

'Tough titty, Carlos. The motor is coming with us,' the constable told him. 'And you're under arrest, by the way.' Llew unclipped a set of handcuffs from his belt and began to secure the driver in the front.

'Wait! Wait - damn you! I've got a question,' said the driver.

'Fire away,' said the officer.

The man belched again. 'Say - why are you calling me Carlos?'

'Why? Well, think about it for a minute,' said the constable, flashing his newly acquired set of keys at him and smiling. He then tightened up the cuffs and opened the man's car-door.

'Oh, I get it now,' said the man, putting a leg out.

'Oh, you get it now, do you?' asked the constable, helping the driver to climb out of the car.

'You think I'm Spanish, right?'

'Are you Spanish?' asked the constable, turning the standing man round, and slamming, and locking the door.

'I am, I am,' the man responded. 'And what's more, I demand that you take me to the embassy.'

'In Madrid, Sir?' the constable asked, forcing the driver ahead of him along the footpath..

'Yeah. Or in London,' the man replied, lurching from side to side. 'Whichever is closer.'

As the pair approached nearer to the police-car Constable Llewellyn lifted his radio to let control know that the Maestro he had stopped needed recovering to the pound, and that he had carried out an arrest, but then realised he still didn't know who the man was. 'Say - what did you say your name was, Sir?' he asked.

'I never did,' the man replied.

'Because I bet it isn't really Spanish, is it?'

''Course not, silly. Dick,' the man told him.

Llewellyn tugged at the man's cuffs, halting him in his tracks. Then he stood before him and pressed his huge forehead right up against the man's face. 'What did you just call me!' he bellowed.

'Wait! I'm telling you the truth, officer!' the terrified man responded. 'I said 'Dick' because, you see, that's my name. In full it's Richard, you see. That is my name, honestly - Richard.'

'Really? Richard what?' asked Llewellyn.

There followed a pause, during which the man dropped his head, clearly thinking fast. 'Plant,' the man announced. I am called 'Richard Plant,' though people generally call me 'Dick Plant.'

' 'Dick Plant!' repeated the police officer, clearly not happy with this response. 'Really, Sir? And are you sure it's not 'Dick Transplant?' Because I'd be much more likely to believe you if you said that. Say - have you got ID on you?'

'My card is in my back-pocket,' the man told him, bending slightly. 'That'll show you I'm precisely who I say I am.'

Constable Llewellyn reached into the man's back-pocket and took out a whole bunch of business-cards. He read one. ' 'Riccardo Pantheon!' ' he exclaimed. ' 'Riccardo!' So you are a bloody Spaniard after all, then.'

'No, that's just my stage-name,' the man told him. 'I've just come from doing a show, you see. In The Merthyr Labour Club.'

'Really? And what do you do? Impersonations?' quipped Llewellyn, grinning.

'Very funny,' the man replied. 'Look - if you care to read the card, then you'll see my job-title.'

'Christ! You do all this?' asked Llewellyn.

'I do,' the man replied. 'Though I can't throw my voice like I once could, so I've knocked the ventriloquism on the head.'

'Really?' said the constable, seating the man in the back seat of his patrol-car. 'Well, perhaps you shouldn't have done that.'

'Why's that?' asked the man, looking up.

'Well, that's assault with a deadly weapon, that is, you see,' Llewellyn told him, grinning. 'And you're in enough trouble as it is tonight with the - with the D.U.I., as they say on *'Cops.'* '

'Now stop crying this instant,' Tom commanded, looking up at her from his pillow. 'You don't need to feel anything but joy for me, Carla,' her dad told her, perspiring freely now, and, to her eyes, looking more gaunt than ever he had before.

'If that's what you want, Dada,' Carla told him, clasping his thin, veined hand in hers, and, though biting into her top lip, attempting to smile back at him,

'You know sweetheart, during the last few weeks your Uncle Gary has helped me to understand and appreciate a great many things.'

'Really?' asked a not wholly convinced Carla. 'Such as what, exactly?'

'Well, amongst other things, he showed me how you can't hope to learn anything from the process of dying unless you first accept the fact that you are, in fact, 'on the way out.' Denial, after all, is senseless, as it simply arrests the learning process.'

'Is that right?' Carla replied, seeing that her father seemed determined that what could be their final serious conversation together was going to be on his terms, and his terms alone. 'Yes, I think I can see what you're saying now. And what else have you learned? Because I've noticed he has been reading to you an awful lot these past weeks.'

'Well, for example, did you know that, almost two thousand years ago, the Roman sage Seneca said that 'throughout the whole of our lives we need to keep on continuing to learn how to live, while at the same time continuing to learn how to die.' '

Carla's tears now began to roll freely down her cheeks. 'And what else did Uncle Gary tell you, Dad?' she asked him, turning to look towards the door.

'Well, he not so much told me, sweetheart, as showed me. For example, he showed me how major learning is a lot like dying.'

'And how is that?'

Tom coughed phlegm into the basin that his daughter patiently held out before him, then, in a hoarser, lower tone, slowly answered her. 'Well, you see, in order to learn something significant we must first unlearn the old, wonderfully familiar, but ultimately useless, things that we do know. And this self-emptying process is - is what Gary has now, thank God, helped me to achieve.'

'This self-emptying,' said a trembling Carla. 'Tell me - what has that been like to go through?'

'Well, it feels an awful lot like annihilation,' replied Tom, 'And it can scare the shit out of you too, if you'll pardon my language. The ancients had a word for it. They - they called it *kenosis*.'

'Did you say *kenosis*?' asked Carla, gazing into his eyes. 'You know, I think I might have heard of that.'

'And the purpose of this *kenosis*, this self-emptying process, is not simply to have an empty mind, or empty soul if you prefer, but to make room there for the new and the more vital. No, the more vibrant, is probably what I mean, darling.' Tom looked up to see that she was still listening. 'What I now understand, since, you see, I believe I have managed to achieve it, sweetness, is that we can empty ourselves sufficiently of ego, so that we might then become truly spirit-filled.'

'Spirit-filled! How wonderful. Then I am so happy for you that you've achieved it, Dad,' Carla told him, through sobs that now broke from her like loud rollers on the Cambrian coast, and which echoed through the house very like a banshee's wailing. 'Yes I am - I truly am, Dada.'

'The goal we seek is not the obliteration of the soul, after all, Carla, but its expansion, do you see?'

'Yes, I think I see it now,' she told him, noting how dreadfully weary his words seemed to be making him. 'But just lie back now, and rest for a little while, there's a love.'

In the silent moments that followed Carla wiped all the tears from her eyes and tried to pull herself together. She stared down at her father's thin, drawn face, and his perspiring forehead, that remained unmoving, and the pulse on his neck that rocked apace quite independently of it. She felt completely taken aback, and humbled, by her father's earnest efforts to seek to self-improve himself, so late in life, indeed, so very near to the time of his fast-approacing death.

Tom's lips suddenly quivered, and Carla could tell that he had something important he wanted to tell her. 'Carla dear,' his hushed, hoarse voice whispered. 'I realise now that my goal is beyond.'

Carla considered this, then, while patiently and lovingly drying the gleaming drops that lay on his brow, told him, 'Then I'm pretty sure that mine is too.'

The bleach-blond police-officer looked across the top of the bulky, cream-coloured machine at his big, burly, uniformed colleague, who, to his eyes, in some strange way resembled it, and who was again distracted from his work by the gleaming pool-table that they had had to store in the little room from lack of space. There again, Llew is far more like a filing-cabinet, in my opinion, Ben told himself, grinning. Solid and square, and every bit as sturdy, but open a drawer and. there's virtually nothing on the inside. He chuckled lightly. He decided to induce his colleague back on task, so nudged his elbow just as he was lining up a shot to the corner-pocket

'Sorry Llew! 'I didn't see you there,' said Ben, holding in a laugh.'

'Shit! I think I've gone and ripped the cloth,' Llew told him. 'Bugger! There's only the table-tennis left now, and we haven't got the balls for that.'

'Say - do you think this chap was behaving illegally tonight, then?' he asked him.

'Of course he was. I could have brought him in for his singing alone, you know,' the sturdy constable replied, 'but it was clipping that bollard near *'Hoovers'* that clinched it for me.'

'Say - did I tell you how last week I caught an under-taker doing forty in a bus-lane,' said Ben.

'What the hell was he doing in a bus-lane?' Constable Llewellyn asked him.

'What was he doing?' said Constable Thomas, raising his brows. 'Why - he was under-taking, like I said.'

'In a hearse?' asked Llewellyn.

'A hearse! Who the hell mentioned a hearse?' Thomas cut back. 'No - a white-van, as it goes. It seems the driver reckoned a lorry had dropped its load in the middle-lane, but when I checked up there wasn't any mess to clear up, and no lorry either. Some people will make up any old shit just to get out of trouble, don't you think?'

'Oh, he was under-taking?' said Constable Llewellyn, chuckling. 'I get what you're saying now.'

A young female P.C. walked into the room and handed a plastic cup containing hot, steaming tea to the driver the officers had earlier arrested, and who she thought seemed to have a terribly confused look on his lined face. 'I thought you might like a change after all that coffee,' she said.

'The higher of the two readings was a-hundred-and-one, but the lower I gather is considerably better,' Constable Llewellyn told the bald man. And, of course, that's the one we always take account of.'

'Thank God for that,' said Dick Plant, smiling thinly. 'What figure was it?'

'Ninety-nine,' said the blond-haired constable standing beside him, and who was leaning over the table to make it out.

'Bloody hell!' exclaimed Dick, grasping what little hair he still possessed in his two fat hands, and shaking his head from side to side.

'Yep - you failed on *'the roadside,'* and you've failed again on *'the intoxicator'* too, I'm afraid, Riccardo, mate,' said

Constable Llewellyn, waving in his hand the tiny slip of paper he had just torn off the machine, 'And that reading is nearly three times the limit, you know, despite the two hours or more that have passed since you had your last drink.'

'So, naturally, you're going to be charged with *'Drink-Driving,'* and you'll be staying in a cell for the rest of the night to sleep it off,' added Constable Thomas.

'Well, bang goes my job then, boys,' said Dick, wincing sharply at the thought.

'Well, we're very sorry about that, Sir,' said Thomas. 'But that's how it goes, you see. He rolled his bottom-lip over, and gurned his face into his sympathy-look. 'Yes, you're going to lose your licence, I'm afraid, Riccardo,' he continued. 'But your car will naturally be released any time you want, and will be available to be driven away by any licence-holder that you nominate.'

'Your wife perhaps?' suggested Llewellyn.

'Great,' said Dick, shaking his head. 'Then you boys will need to park it on the roadside with the door open and the engine started or Vera won't even bother to get in it. She drives a smart-car normally, you see. She'd never manage to get my big one out of the car-park.'

'My wife's just the same,' chimed in Thomas, chuckling. 'Drives a rusty, green Micra. Nothing remotely smart about that that I can see.'

'But Riccardo mate, at least there's some good news for you,' Llewellyn told the man, creating a broad, beaming smile out of virtually nothing.

'There is?' Dick asked in reply, looking up at him. 'And what's that then?'

'Well, you'll still get to walk round to *The Labour Club* for you final show there tomorrow night, won't you?' the burly copper told him. 'And so there'll be no need to worry your head about the state of the traffic coming up from Cardiff, or the road conditions - it's going to piss down tomorrow, see - or the cost of the petrol to get there, or finding somewhere to park, even.'

'Yeah, well we've at least got that last one covered for you,' added Thomas.

'And we can recommend a nice little restaurant where you can have a pleasant meal before your show starts, too,' said Llewellyn. 'Tell me - do you like Italian?'

A giggling sound suddenly filled the night air, and small puffs of smoke could be seen emerging from a black saloon-car parked some distance behind the pub. The group of young men who were slowly walking in that direction quickly caught on that there were two people lying on the back-seat of the Vauxhall Vectra, (that was parked tightly up against the fence,) with their faces pressed close together. The back-window of the car was slightly open, so that the couple's conversation could easily be heard by them. The men stayed quiet and crept up to the vehicle to witness what was happening inside.

'Damn buttons and metal-clips,' the boy could be heard telling the woman. 'I'm - I'm a bit new to all this, you know. *And* I'm only a poor farmer's boy, so maybe I should -'

'Plough me!' the much older woman told him, laughing aloud in a deep voice, then leaning her head so far back that it banged loudly against the car-door. 'Shit!' she yelled.

'Are you O.K.?' the young man asked.

'Sure. But don't stop. It's only my head,' she told him. 'But thanks for asking, anyway. You're really sweet, you are, aren't you, bach?. Come here.' She kissed him passionately on the lips. 'O.K. Now, like I said - plough me good - cow-boy!'

To the pair of lovers inside it, the car seemed to be rocking a heck of a lot more than they had anticipated, but they weren't overly interested in that. However the rocking-motion soon became so extreme that two of the doors soon flew open and the back-bumper dropped off.

'Christ! What have you been drinking, love?' the woman was heard to enquire.

'Just the usual,' the boy told her. 'Why?'

'Well, I must try some of that, whatever it is,' she told him. 'You know you'll be sure to make the London Olympics next year if you keep this up.'

The three men, who were soon sitting on the low wall near the pub, holding white, plastic spoons in their hands, and munching their take-away Indian from three separate brown, paper bags, went on witnessing what was happening in the car they had been rocking and that sat in the shadows to their right, but, following Volver's lead, now did their best to ignore them.

'Did you guys ever see that film *'Dead Man Walking?'* asked the Afrikaner. 'Guy out walking one night comes across two dirty bastards, much like that pair there, and decides to put the pair of them out of their misery. If you ask me, he performed a great service for society that day. But what did that society do to the poor bastard? They went and executed his arse with a lethat dose, that's what they did. Can you believe it? You know, I could easily go over there right now and put paid to the pair of them in seconds, and then come back and finish my food with the very same knife - wiped clean, naturally. But hey - let's let sleeping dogs lie, yeah? And judging by the fact we can't hear their rutting racket any more, then I take it they've just dropped off.'

The South African's two dining colleagues inclined their heads, nodded their agreement, and chewed on.

'You know, for a number of years I used to live in London,' Volver told them. 'Did I tell you that? And one wet, windy night in Hammersmith I was forced to stab this druggie who kept giving me the v-sign all the time, and screaming abuse as he was buying gear off my mate.' The two boys turned and stared at him. 'Imagine. The cock. Well, I waited until he paid me, obviously, then, as change, I slipped a four-inch blade through his belly-button.'

'Wow! Now that's one slow way to do it, I heard,' said Steffan, holding before him a curry-stained hand, and then twisting it maliciously. 'The guy had no respect, yeah?'

'You know, that's exactly what I told my buddy as he dragged him into the river. Sank in seconds, he did, and without a single rock being laid on him. A bit weird that, I thought at the time.'

'Yeah, I'd say that's unusually fast,' said Jake.

'I guess,' said Volver. 'My buddy told me later that he had tourettes. Well, hey-ho! He's cured now, I told him.' The

Afrikaner spooned up a mouthful of curry, swallowed it, and carried on. 'Funny but I can't remember his name any more. Fetched up in Margate, he did, a fortnight later. The dog-fish down there had made a right fish-supper out of him so I gather. Kent Police thought he'd come across from France, of course. Thought he was continental, you know.'

'Of course, he might have visited the place and then drifted back,' said Jake, smiling.

'Either way, it's nice that he got to see the world a bit,' said Steffan, munching away. 'Don't you think?'

'Yeah, I suppose so,' said Volver. 'Because prior to that I very much doubt if he'd ever been out of west London. But I can tell you his girl was totally devastated when I told her he had run off with somebody else.' He turned to Steffan, grinned, then slapped him on the back, as the boy and Jake swiftly visualized the funny side to their boss's callous and cold-blooded, yet incredibly hilarious actions, and then broke out laughing accordingly..

Now that her father was asleep, Carla returned downstairs to where Chris sat awaiting her return, inspecting her strange wind-up wristwatch that was shaped and coloured like a goldfish.

'Are you going to be singing *Acapulco*?' Chris asked her. 'Because I really love it when you do that.'

'*Acapulco!* No, silly,' replied Carla, wondering why he'd asked her that. 'Chris - are you high already? I think you'll find that that's an Elvis song. She took the spliff from his fingers and drew it in deeply, then coughed with sudden, comical recognition. 'Oh, you mean *acapella*?' said Carla. She shook her head about and giggled at him. 'No, on Sunday I'm going to be accompanying myself on the acoustic guitar all evening, as I heard that the bar is a bit small for my Fender. For the sound, I mean. And anyway there going to be no band there, so I guess I've got little choice.' She handed the joint to Chris who took his turn.

'I googled you this morning, you know, Carla,' he suddenly announced, smiling.

'Well, I didn't feel anything,' she replied, eye-brows raised, and affecting surprise.

'Ha, ha,' he said, then waited for her to return to being Carla once again. 'Do you realise that you're currently the eleventh most google-d person on the face of the Earth?'

'I never knew that,' she told him, picking up some ash from the carpet. 'Who is number-one?'

'Michael Jackson,' said Chris.

'O.K., that figures,' she said. 'And second?'

'I'm not sure, but I think it's Justin Bieber.'

'Dear, dear. And you said I was eleventh? So who is tenth?' she asked

'Oh, I do remember that one,' he replied, grinning. 'It's Jesus Christ.'

'Really!' exclaimed Carla, her mouth falling open.

'Er - the very same,' said Chris, beaming out a smile at her. 'And you are only one place behind him. Say - isn't that amazing?'

'No, it's not at all,' shot back Carla sharply. 'The whole notion is absurd. Do you want to know what's amazing, Chris? Yeah? What's amazing is that you bothered.' Carla took the spliff from him, but instead of dragging on it, she quickly put it out in the ash-tray that lay beside her.

'Oh, I'm sorry if I offended you,' he told her, instantly regretting that he had brought it up.

Carla reached out a hand and stroked away his budding shame. 'Oh, you haven't offended me,' she told him. 'I realise that it's tempting to go on-line and do what you did. Millions do it, don't they? I'm just glad I wasn't ninth, that's all.'

The pair glanced at each other and laughed.

'What the hell is *Google* anyway?' said Carla. 'If I curse Michael Jackson today - out loud, or under my breath, or The Good Lord Himself for that matter - then I bet there's sure to be thousands upon thousands of unfathomable, throw-away pages that refer solely to my supposed slur, in a hundred-and-one different cultural, scientific and psychological contexts, recorded on it before six o'clock tomorrow morning.'

'I believe it, Carla,' said Chris, grinning. 'If you so much as fart it seems to circle the world.'

'Well, I could easily take exception to that comment, young man, but I won't,' she told him. 'Though it's an interesting way to put it nevertheless. And as for *Twitter* and *Facebook* - those twin cess-pools of fuckery and self-delusion that I've always detested with a passion, and shun at all costs - please do me the kindness of never mentioning either one of them in my presence.'

'Well, I'll do my best,' he replied. 'though I don't reckon I've alluded to them even once up to now. But hang on, Carla - you've always had a *MySpace* page, haven't you?' he countered. 'So aren't you being a teeny bit hypocritical here?'

'What do you mean?' she cried. 'The *MySpace* was never ever *my* space at all. Not really. Since every other artist they represented or endorsed was already on it, both my management and the record-company simply demanded I follow suit. And I basically just let them get on with it. That's all it was, Chris, I swear.'

'You know, I believe you,' said Chris.

'Pass me the bottle of wine, would you?' Carla asked him. Taking it from Chris, she unscrewed the top and filled to the brim both glasses that sat on the table between them. Then watching Chris swiftly grab hold of his glass and swallow a goodly portion, she sat back in her chair and sipped her own more decorously. 'You know, I read that a scientific study made using a series of detailed brain scans has revealed that alcohol doesn't actually cause us to behave badly, it just stops us from caring about embarrassing ourselves when *we are* behaving badly.'

'Is that right?' said Chris.

'Apparently,' she went on. 'A classic depressant like alcohol can suppress shame and inhibitions for a time. But what I say to that is - just witness the remorse when 'the high' wears off. And remember it was me that told you this when you look in the mirror tomorrow morning.'

I had gone into '*Poundland*' out of the rain to see if they had a video of '*Four Weddings And A Funeral*' that my wife Gwen desperately wanted to watch, and I was standing in front of the shelf that displayed them all for sale, at a pound a piece, when a young man came and stood next to me. I glanced briefly to my side, but quickly realised that I didn't know him.

The black cases were all lined up completely haphazardly in one long row, not even sorted by stars or genre, with '*Lock Stock And Two Smoking Barrels*' propping up '*The Sound Of Music*' and '*Silence Of The Lambs*' right next to '*Bambi,*' when the guy chose to pounce.

Plonking a large, unzipped hold-all on the floor before him, the young man in the dufffel-coat and trilby reached out with both arms, and grabbed hold of, then tossed, the entire contents of the shelf inside, then zipped up the now bulging container, and, heaving it onto his shoulder, spun round, and dashed straight past the check-outs and out of the shop.

However the thief had missed one, which he had dropped on the floor, and which now lay under my feet, so I picked it up and walked with it over to the young girl who sat at the cash-till, who was engaged in serving a customer. 'Did you see that?' I asked her.

'What?' she replied.

'That young chap just nicked all the videos you had in the shop. But it's O.K., you'll probably have him on CCTV, for sure.'

'Please, mister,' said the girl. 'This is *Poundland*. They can't even provide us with proper toilets.'

'Or radiators,' said the woman she was serving, who picked up her purchase, smiled at me, and walked out into the rain..

'So what are you going to be doing about it?' I asked the cashier.

'Well, I'll report it, naturally,' she told me, searching for her note-book. 'Say - did he take the video you were after, then?'

'*Four Weddings And A Funeral*'? Yeah, he did, as a matter of fact,' I replied. 'Now I suppuse I'll have to watch this one. It's the only one left.'

'Well, I'm sorry about that,' she told me, smiling thinly. 'Shall I pop it in a bag for you?'

I was still stunned and pretty incensed at the outrageous nature of the crime I'd just witnessed. 'And you mean - and you mean that's it!' I exclaimed, mouth agape.

'Well, what else is there I can do?' the cashier asked me. 'Perhaps you could have stopped him yourself.'

'Have you any idea how old I am?' I asked her. 'If I had it could have been my own funeral you'd be seeing, if you'll pardon my pun. The chap could have been my grandson.'

'And is that who he was, then?' she asked, pausing from her scribbling.

'No, of course not,' I replied. 'I don't have a grandson, as it goes, and if I did I'd be sure to have him locked up for doing something like that.'

'Wow! You'd do that?' exclaimed the girl, clearly shocked. 'Your own grandson too! I'm shocked. Anyway, that's none of my business, I suppose. You're taking the video yeah?'

'Well, yes, I suppose I'd better,' I replied, placing a pound-coin on the counter. 'After all, it's the only one you've got left.' I let out a chuckle, then turned to see if any of the customers queueing up behind me found it as humorous as I did, but I could tell straightaway that they weren't in the least bit interested in the conversation I was having, or even knew that a theft had just occurred while they were in the shop.

'And do you want it wrapped?' the girl at the counter asked.

'Aye, go on,' I said, watching her place the video in the polythene-bag. 'After all it's chucking it down out there. Do you know, I haven't even read what it's called yet.'

The girl turned the package round so she could read the label. 'Oh, it's one of my favourites,' she told me, smiling. 'And quite appropriate too under the circumstances.'

'Why? What's it called?' I asked.

'*Gone In Sixty Seconds*,' she responded, grinning. 'Vinnie Jones. Love him. Next, please.'

The bald, hatless man I saw walking into *Lloyds Bank,* with his right hand buried deep in his coat-pocket, didn't look very like a robber to me, but after my recent experience just down

'How come?' I asked.

'Well, it's a long story, but I spent the night at Her Majesty's pleasure, I'm afraid,' he told me, wincing, and running a hand down his back. 'And they made me leave the car in the police-pound, etcetera, etcetera.'

'Oh, I get it,' I said. 'You were on the sauce last night, yeah?' Dick nodded. 'And you failed a breath-test on your way home to Ponty.'

'In a nut-shell,' he told me, dropping his head onto his chest. 'I sucked on a two-pence coin, for all the good it did me, and I drank all the coffee I could scrounge, but it had no effect at all.'

'No, it doesn't, because I tried all that stuff one time,' I told him. 'As well as sucking on the tube instead of blowing, and pretending to be knocked-out, in the hope they'd take me off to *Prince Charles* in an ambulance, and I could get up unnoticed and dash off home again. I got myself a three-year ban a long time ago, so I know just what you're feeling, Dick. What beer were you drinking? A strong one?' I enquired.

'Yeah, the strongest you can get,' Dick replied, chuckling. 'Cognac.'

'Oh, dear,' I responded, shaking my head. 'God! You don't want to be doing that, man. Not if you need your car for your job, I mean. And do you? What do you do these days, Dick? Still on the bingo, are you?'

'No, that all went tits up donkeys years ago, that did, Dyl,' he explained. 'I just do the performing these days,' Dick told me. 'On stage, you understand?' I didn't. 'Which reminds me, Dyl, I'm working at *The Labour Club* again in a few hours time. That's if I've dried out enough by then, I mean.'

'Say, I'll tell you what you need, butty boy,' I said. 'A nice hot cappuccino, eh?'

'Well, I wouldn't turn one down right now,' he replied, smiling thinly at me.

'Be my guest, then, Dick,' I said, standing. 'Say - you ever been to the *Café Giotto*?'

'No, I don't believe so,' Dick replied, rising too, and running his hands through what little hair he still possessed.

450

the road I couldn't really be sure, so I studied him closely
behind. There was something familiar-looking about
I thought, but wasn't at all sure what it was, so I decide
go inside.

The drying queue at the ATM machine was breaking up,
I approached and soon took out some money in ten-pou
notes. As I turned and folded the money, and then placed
safely in my trouser-pocket, I saw the man wandering ove
towards the long seat in the corner, where he took off his
dripping overcoat, then sat down, and, making use of a
crumpled handkerchief that he drew from his pocket, began to
to mop the raindrops off his face, and the two little puddles off
the leather upper of each of his sopping shoes.

Well, he had certainly put the wrong coat on this morning,
I pondered, watching him sympathetically from across the
large room. How on earth could that have happened? After
all, he clearly wasn't blind, and the incessant rain that was
falling had started the previous night.

It was just then that I remembered who the chap was: he
was my Gwen's first husband - Dick Plant! I chuckled briefly
at the thought I had that this was one plant that had been
grossly over-watered, and no mistake.

Disregarding our unusual, rather obtuse, relationship, (and
the fact that we had never even once met in person,) I decided
to go over and greet the man, whom I figured might easily have
already recognised me anyway, and was simply feeling
hesitant about making the first move. I sat myself down beside
the bald-headed man and stared into his eyes. He recognised
me straightaway.

'God Streuth!' Dick bellowed. 'It's Dyl Cook, isn't it? Long
time no see, pal.'

'We've never actually met, Dick,' I reminded him. 'It was
the pictures in Gwen's album that clinched it for me. If it
wasn't for those then I might have thought you were the god
Neptune, just popped up to see what life on land was like.'
I smiled at the queer picture I had created.

'Aye, I must admit I wasn't prepared for this downpour
today,' he said, drying his knees.

'Although I believe one of the coppers recommended I try that place.'

'Aye, they do a stunning cappuccino in there, they do,' I told him. 'And it's only just across the road too. Come on. And I bet you must be starving too.'

As usual, the meat-balls were epic. The balding, former marital partner of Gwen Plant, as was, and I wiped our stained mouths simultaneously with the white, cotton napkins provided, then exchanged eye-watering glances that spoke volumes about the quality of the food and the tastiness of the meat-ball sauce we had just consumed. I burped loudly, as was my custom at such times, and, though a little taken aback by this at first, my English-born guest smiled, then sat back snugly in his booth-seat and, though a little less discreetly than myself I felt, unashamedly followed my lead.

'My Vera can cook, don't get me wrong,' Dick Plant told me. 'But she's never once made me a meal like that.'

'But you love her all the same, yeah?' I proffered. 'It's just that some women weren't born to cook meals, right?'

'No, I guess,' he said.

'And I imagine your Vera's talents run in other directions,' I said hesitantly, but with a smile. Dick looked at me almost as if I were conversing with him in a separate language. 'I mean, on days when I'm not working - I'm presently working part-time, see - I do most of the cooking in our house. Whereas Monday to Wednesday, when I'm at work, Gwen does it all. I'm not saying she enjoys doing it, of course, unlike my daughter Rhiannon, who, like me, loves to experiment with new recipes, but Gwen manages to carry out her side of the marital contract, so to speak.'

'Let there be spaces in your togetherness, and let the winds of the heavens dance between you,' Dick suddenly exclaimed, beaming a smile across at me. 'Sorry, but I don't think I remember the rest.'

'And stand together, yet not too near together, for the pillars of the temple stand apart, and the oak tree and the cypress grow not in each other's shadow,' I said completing it for him. 'Gibran,' I told him, quoting from memory a portion of the book I endeavoured to read at least once every year..

'It is indeed,' said Dick. 'My. Who'd have thought that the two husbands of Gwen Havard would have read the very same book. Then turning, Dick called out over his shoulder, 'Waiter!'

'Waitress, you mean,' I told him. 'She's called Zeta, you see, and she's really nice.'

'Well, she cerainly wasn't around when we came in, was she?' Dick announced with a pout. 'Didn't we have to find our own table? I believe we did.'

Dick was right. Zeta hadn't moved from her seat at the far end of the room - where she sat with her back directly to us - in all the time we had been there, and I felt that that was a very odd thing, she normally being the supreme hostess during all my previous visits.

Martin arrived at the table, a little, pink tea-towel draped over his muscular forearm, looking for all the world like a professional boxer carrying a copy of 'Little Women.' 'Did you enjoy your meal, then, Dyl?' he asked, with a pinched grin, lifting, then adeptly balancing our two dinner-plates in one hand, while shifting the sugar-bowl, the flower-glass and the condiments back into place with the other.

'Yes, very tasty it was,' I told him, glancing across and seeing my table-guest nodding in agreement with me. 'Say, Martin - where's the missus today then?' I enquired, already knowing the answer before I even asked.

'Oh, she's over there on the phone, she is,' he replied. 'I try my best not to disturb her when she sits facing the clock like that. Do you know what I mean, Dyl?'

I didn't, but still nodded at him my full understanding of the matter.

'I dare say she's busy calling her friends,' he continued, dabbing with his towel, then straightening the crumpled, dreadfully gore-stained table-cloth. 'But I'll be sure to tell her you asked after her.'

'Aye, do that, would you,' I told him. 'I'm sure my Gwen'll pop in to see her some time during the week, if ever this horrendous weather lets up and she decides to come in to town.'

Gwen had just taken a refreshing shower, and now, clothed only in a belted, white robe and the obligatory towel twisted round her head, was lying flat on her back on top of her eiderdown, taking a nap. Her little pink nose was twitching, not just from the contralto snore she was not infrequently given to emitting, but almost as if somewhere in the wide world about her someone very close to her was trying to make contact, but was finding it impossible to do so.

Odd though it might seem to some, Gwen and her husband Dyl had never once owned a mobile-phone between the pair of them. Each one, of course, had known of this fact from the start, and had happily approved of it; indeed it was one of the things that had brought the pair together, and which had probably helped keep them together, during good times and bad, through sickness and health, and right up to the present moment, when her warm, dignified, and splendid isolation meant that her friend Zeta couldn't reach her with news that would no doubt force her to rise up straightaway and address it.

But the actual cause of the problem in *Caerleon* which prevented her friend Zeta from being able to establish contact was a simple one, but one that neither woman knew the slightest thing about. Gwen had accidentally dislodged the receiver on the house-phone in the lounge downstairs, and it wasn't until long after she had gone upstairs that the strange whining noise, that signified a problem with the telephone's connectivity, began to sound off.

Inside the little bathroom a naked Gwen had drawn the plastic curtain closed soon after having climbed inside. Under the hot, gushing stream she was in heaven, despite the fact that her bath-tub shower was of the old-fashioned, dripping kind, which understandably annoyed Rhiannon far more than it ever did herself, the mother, unlike the daughter, having never once experienced the holistic wonders of the power-shower. What you've never had, you never miss, Gwen might have remarked, by way of explanation, had anyone ever bothered to ask her for her explanation for this life-style omission, which, of course, was just one of many.

It was past seven p.m., that is when her daughter Rhiannon finally arrived home, that contact with civilisation was finally restored.

'Mam! Why is the phone off the hook?' the red-haired girl bellowed up the stairs, rushing to the side-door to open it, so as to let some fresh air inside. 'You must have banged into it again, you know.' Then silently, to herself, 'I bet it's been screaming like that for hours.' She bent down and replaced the receiver again. 'Mam! Where's Dad? Hasn't he come back yet? I'm starving.'

Just then the telephone rang, and Rhiannon sat herself down on the sofa and answered it. It was Zeta Jones from Café Giotto in town, a woman she barely knew, and so Rhiannon galloped up the staircase to wake her mother, and to get her to come down to talk with her.

Barely a half-an-hour later, and Dyl not having returned home to make the Friday evening dinner, mother and daughter got dressed in long and short raincoats, and polythene and cotton hats respectively, and, dashing from the garden-gate to Rhiannon's yellow Fiesta, very like a pair of contestants in the *Le Mans* road-race, took off in the driving rain for Merthyr town-centre.

Without doubt it had been an unseasonably hot Spring, 'almost as if *The Maker* had left his great oven-door open as He was cooking us all breakfast,' her Uncle Gary had recently told her. But now that Spring was past, Summer was being much more its usual self again, Carla pondered, almost as if He had shut the oven again, but this time left the fridge-door a little ajar as He was fetching everyone afternoon drinks. If there indeed *was* a God, then He was undoubtedly male, she thought.

And here was two-thousand-and-eleven gradually uncoiling itself before our very eyes, Carla mused, her head deeply buried beneath the duvet, just as predictably, and every bit as disappointingly, as any year already passed. She mentally flicked up the four numeric flash-cards in the red-black, swirling pool behind her lightly-clenched eye-lids. *2-0-1-1* it flashed. Just another prime number amidst a whole millennium of them, she told herself. But, as her father and uncle had recently told her, in the very year when the world's most renowned scientists undertook a frantic, but effectively abject, search for a God-particle, the actual Living God gazed down with open hands extended, and pleaded for us to quite simply look to Him in this most seductive, shameful, and ultimately satanic of times.

In the last few days the Libyan capital Tripoli had been liberated and the tyrant Gaddafi effectively overthrown, and yet, unbeknown to Carla, he was, not very long after, to be pulled from a rat infested sewage-pipe and summarily shot, as adults and children across the world witnessed the Muslim country's despotic head-of-state starring in his very own snuff-movie.

And within weeks, and totally unrelated to these events, a thick, pyroclastic cloud of over a thousand hooded, urban looters and wreckers would have had their state-of-the-art i-pads and x-boxes, and brand new track-suits and trainers, ripped off them, and returned and re-packaged for sale, by the police constabulary, and been fast-tracked through the English court system, and ultimately locked away in jail for many months, for partaking in, what soon became known as, *'The English Riots.'*

2011 was a year when the stock-exchange was almost permanently in free-fall, and the UK economy - already in a total mess since the worldwide banking crisis - found itself in the pale, feeble hands of the aptly named Con-Demns - a Coalition Government that even the Tories' own Boris Johnson was soon to claim was 'doomed to succeed.' Yes, this oily-tongued, shower of posh boys, whom even their most ardent supporters freely admit couldn't tell you the price of a pint of milk, (or the cost of a litre of unleaded petrol, for that matter, since it seemed to rise almost daily,) gripped and squeezed ever more tightly, with thin, manicured hands that were greedy for power and wealth, and soon bore even more up-to-date, gleaming Cartier watches on their puny, pen-pushing wrists as evidence that they had achieved it. Knowing who the nation's real wreckers were in 2011 had now become a far simpler matter, Carla mused.

But it was the recent, sudden death - the (for too long a time) unexplained, and initially, misreported, death - of twenty-seven year old Amy Winehouse, which easily disquieted Carla the most about 2011; yes, the Camden singer-songwriting legend, whom she had had the good fortine to meet on a handful of occasions, but alas never got to sing with, except one wet, windy, otherwise largely uneventful Tuesday night, when the slight, dark pair, jointly intoxicated, and seated facing each other, at a small, round, table in a corner of *'The Jazz Café'* in Parkway, wiled away a couple of hours together. Like myself, Amy may have had her problems of the addictive kind, thought Carla, but psychologically, she certainly hadn't seemed to have displayed any manifestations of the kind of issues Carla believed she herself had been confronted with.

A tall, willowy, black woman on the stage nearby had sung to them that night, Carla recalled, and to less than a dozen other customers scattered about the dark, tinkling room. But, if truth be told, Amy just hadn't seemed overly interested, and instead shared some of her personal feelings with her. 'Do you know, Carla, I quite often feel like a black boy in a white girl's body,' she had declared between sips of vodka-and-tonic.

'You know, I believe I know what you mean,' Carla had replied, nodding, and biting her top lip in her unique, but unattractive fashion, and shuddering somewhat from the stark honesty, and the effortless poetry, of the plainly tipsy, but deeply sensitive, Cockney girl's admission. That year *'Back To Black'* had taken the album-charts by storm right across the world, she recalled, and, quite literally, had altered the musical landscape for ever, and Carla simply ached within to create for herself a similarly spectacular album, that would be just as blessed with its own unique, enigmatic, life-changing sound.

Carla recalled how a man across from them - who looked for all the world like a twin-brother of the chancellor, George

Osborne, - had suddenly bellowed to his equally posh friends how he believed that the only thing wrong with the death-penalty was that it hadn't been used often enough. When they all laughed in unison with him, Carla remembered how Amy had turned her chair to face them, and, in her distinctive, deep, urban drawl had asked the man if he didn't think it might be a great idea if he took himself out the back and tried it for himself. She'd gladly let him borrow her belt, since he didn't appear to be wearing one of his own, she told him, suddenly ripping the thin, white one from the ringlets in her own waist-band, and presenting it to him.

The group at the man's table had all wanted to laugh at Amy's comment, but, out of loyalty to their male companion, had bitten their tongues, and gazed long and hard into their drinks instead, clearly waiting for their friend to reassert himself, and be the first to break the eerie silence that, by now, had ensued. It goes without saying that the chap never did. The group all knew, as the two singers themselves knew, and as the rich boy himself plainly did, that he simply wasn't up to it. The beads of perspiration on his temple betrayed the fact that he had plainly floundered out of his depth in an ocean of confusion and dread; he was lost; sunk. After all Amy - this diminutive, dusky-headed girl before him - was *The Queen of Camden*, and possessed both the wisdom of Solomon and the balls of Heracles; and those Berkshire buffoons were on *her* manor. With just a quiet word, and an arch of her long black brows, she had swiftly turned them all to stone.

During her initial period in London, Carla faithfully believed that the road of excess leads to the palace of wisdom. And unsurprisingly, in the aftermath of leaving Oxford she had convinced herself that she wanted to open up her mind and experience much more of life than she had managed hitherto, and to do this she felt tempted to sample practically every substance that she encountered, including almost every type of religious belief, life-style, body-art, food, drink, vitamin, and, of course, drug.

It was during this critical, 'blue period' of her life that Carla had first met Abram Kronfield, and at the time she was quite naturally elated to do so, since she found he was a man with access to a great many of the things that she patently desired. It is fair to say that the Afrikaner's arrival on the scene was critical to her, to an extent at least, in that he was to prove instrumental in helping Carla achieve so many of her early ambitions. The man had, for example, sundry contacts in club-world, amongst other things, and being certain in his mind of her continuing, indeed burgeoning, success, he was no longer shy about using them.

And it wasn't very long before Carla was to sign the record-deal that catapulted her to musical prominence; and, for much of the time, there beside her in many of the publicity snaps, CD signings, and magazine-interviews, if not as yet in her bed, was that same Abram Kronfield.

When Rhiannon arrived at the café ahead of her ambling mother she could sense that something strange was going on. The coven of gross, middle-aged women staring in her direction, for a start, seated, as they were, round two adjoining tables, and smoking cigarettes they all seemed to be holding up before them, less than three feet beneath a sign she was currently unable to read for the clouds of smoke, and which she knew plainly forbade them.

'Is she with you?' asked Zeta Jones, leaping to her feet, and approaching Rhiannon to relieve her of her dribbling brolly.

'My mother? Yes. She's just coming. She sent me on ahead to tell you 'two teas, both with milk and one sugar.' Why? What's happening? Tell me, please!'

'Martin - did you get that?' exclaimed Zeta to her nodding husband, taking Rhiannon gently, but firmly, by the arm, and escorting her past her group of female friends and all the other customers towards the Ladies' loos, that stood at the far end of the long room. 'There's just something I need to tell you, love, that's all,' Zeta told her, closing the door tightly behind them. 'Before your mother gets here, I mean.'

If truth be told, the music being pumped out from the quadraphonic sound-system around me was a little too loud for my liking, although I admit there must be times when a smattering of *Bonnie Tyler, Tom Jones* and *The Manic Street Preachers* was exactly what was needed on a Friday night in the *Merthyr Labour Club,* so as to raise the general level of excitement and fan the flames of mass anticipation. But, though being admiring of all three musical acts, it is just that I wasn't at all sure that they were what was required on that particular night.

I took my pint of bitter off the tide-washed counter and turned and sought out my seat at the very back of the hall. The excited buzz in the audience was, I felt, understandable, most of the crowd there I'm sure, like myself, having never before attended, or perhaps never had the courage to attend, a live show of this type. Sitting myself down next to a couple in matching blue blazers and mullets, I took a large sip of my ale, and then, ever so carefully, placed the pint-glass under my chair, and equidistant between my two, carefully planted, feet.

I looked about me. The group of women I had met in the café had insisted I accompanied my English companion to the club, which I had done, and also helpfully informed me of a man in the bar who would be able to furnish me with a ticket. But where were those women now? I wondered. After telling me that something would be taking place tonight that would both shock me and gratify me, my mind was understandably filled with a whole pauperie of notions, of sorcery, of self-embarrassment, and possible sexual malpractice. And, in a strange way, with regard to all three, I soon discovered that on that particular night I wasn't about to be disappointed.

The soprano was dreadfully flat, both in bust and pitch, the sparkly dancer less than exotic, and the comic nothing to laugh about, but, in all fairness, the animated crowd that filled *The Labour Club* that night definitely hadn't bought tickets to see any of them. Their *piece de resistance* was still to come. The lights were dimmed again, and then onto the stage came my new friend, Dick - the 'Riccardo Pantheon' who was headlining the show.

The porn-star shades, the anthracite-black dinner-jacket, and the pearly-white dicky-bow were a complete shock to my eyes, and even more so the song - *'Hit The Road Jack'* - with which the performer began his set, and which, for all I could tell, seemed to bear no link whatsoever to what the man had prepared for our entertainment. But, after that harmless, toneless distraction, it was soon straight down to business.

'I am looking for six volunteers from the audience tonight,' Dick announced. 'Brave, or stupid, it doesn't really matter.' The audience erupted. The first four individuals who rose from their seats appeared largely to be either pushed or bullied into coming forward, but came forward nevertheless. The fifth - a young man, probably no older than sixteen, and very unsteady on his feet, and whom Dick straightaway rejected - was replaced by an attractive young woman with bleach-blond hair, a shoe-shine tan, frighteningly white teeth, and a massive tattoo of a constricting snake all the way down one leg. The sixth and last volunteer I saw was a middle-aged woman in a long, black dress, who, to my eyes, looked remarkably like Zeta Jones from the café where Dick and I had eaten no more than two short hours before. I gazed at the row she had emerged from. The sight of Maggie Scratch and Bobbie Hole - the latter woman's real name - both of whom had gone to junior-school with my Gwen, leaping to their feet, and cheering her on, told me instantly that it was indeed Martin's better half who had presented herself as the willing focus for our evening's amusement, and, just as likely, I thought, our abuse.

In less than ten seconds - or at least the time it took me to sip my beer and store it away safely again - it appeared that Riccardo Pantheon had hypnotized the whole lot of them, and very soon had them sit down on a row of six chairs that faced the audience and himself. Thereafter he had each of them perform - unknowingly, of course - sundry acts of humiliation, self-degradation, even self-flagellation, the like of which I had never before witnessed, and, quite frankly, never wished to witness again. First there was 'a public caning in school' - on the bottom, naturally - where schoolboys screamed out from imaginary pain, and their tearful lovers chased the teacher in and out of the club's loos before administering on the caner a dose of the same medicine. And then there was a take on the television show 'The Voice,' where two women turned their revolving chairs round to discover Michael Jackson and Elvis just yards away, singing for a shot at fame, and thereafter rushing on-stage to rip imaginary tight clothing off the two equally imaginary, and wholly dead, stars. Watching the poor girls take off their own blouses and slacks to don the same perhaps went a little too far for my palette, I felt, but clearly not so for the bulk of the inebriated audience, who, quite literally, seemed to lap it up, and even cried out for more.

After forty-five minutes or so, the show appeared to be nearing its conclusion. But before galloping off to the lounge-bar to hand out imaginary Christmas presents to unsuspecting regular customers, the two-legged, but tightly manacled, male reindeer had had same-gender sex with a yielding, smiling Father Christmas. Yet not long after that, unmoved and unscathed, his pretend antlers throbbing, he emerged once again from out of the imaginary chimney-piece into the bedroom of a family-home, soon to roger the euthymolised, tanned wife, who shocked us all by causing her fine, long legs - snake and all - to securely pin her supine partner to the ground in the sort of rutting position I could never imagine a reindeer ever managing to achieve, with, or indeed without, the aid of his bearded master. But then again the unlikely pair seemed more than overjoyed when Santa himself, this time without any encouragement from the crowd that whooped and screamed, did in fact elect to assist in the human rut, and, after pushing and squeezing them into genuine, eye-popping ecstacy, he finally wrapped up the beast-with-two-backs in yards and yards of imaginary cellotape and acres of human-sized wrapping-paper, and left them, struggling hopelessly on the floor, for their imaginary kids to discover, and no doubt prise apart, very early the following morning.

Yes, the show that Riccardo Pantheon put on at *Merthyr Labour Club* that night was nothing less than scandalous mayhem, and, though clearly of the kind the audience, who paid good money to see it, had craved, it certainly wasn't at all to my taste. I did, however, screw up my own eyes and whoop loudly when I spied my wife Gwen sitting on one of three empty chairs that I quickly assumed her friends must have vacated. I was naturally very shocked by this; after all, there was I, thinking that I was the dirty stop-out, and that Gwen was at home, patiently awaiting my return, when all the time she was out for the night partying, and doing precisely what I was doing. Whether this was fair or unfair I was largely undecided, but, either way, I simply couldn't believe it.

When the crucial moment came for the six dazed volunteers to be snapped out of the spell Riccardo had put them under, I noticed that it was Zeta whom he chose to de-hypnotize first. Looking all about her as she started coming to, and recognizing where it was she was standing, (if not what ignominies she had been performing for us,) she suddenly ran back to where my Gwen was seated, and, taking her by the hand, led her out swiftly to join the five others who were all standing in a line. Presently Riccardo came to Gwen, and, no doubt assuming she too had taken part in the crazy actions along with her friends, waved his hand across her face too, and uttered the same words he had used on them.

As the lights went up, and the audience stood, applauded, and bellowed out their appreciation, all four women quickly returned to their seats, gathered up their bags and coats, and made their way out to the bar. For myself, I found I was too gob-smacked to follow after them, and so, instead, made my way outside to my car. and drove back home to Pant.

What my Rhiannon told me as I made my way upstairs - about the unexpected phone-call she had received from Zeta, and about her and her mother's trip to the *Café Giotto* (not long after Dick and I had left) - still didn't furnish me with the whole story, and sadly that had to wait until quite early the following morning, when Zeta's husband Martin and his meddling, but ingenious, Italian wife delivered my stop-out wife back home to me. And what Rhiannon chose not to tell me was that she and her friend Carmen had themselves turned up to watch the show that night as well, having been informed by Zeta that it was quite likely to be life-changing.

To say that my Gwen was, from that night on, a changed woman was, I would say, certainly no gross overstatement, but it was undeniably the last that either Rhiannon or I heard from her about any great Welsh chieftain called Arthur, or about his family. his horses, or indeed the weapons he was said to have possessed and intermittently wielded. And, thankfully, Gwen returned to addressing me by the name with which she had hitherto always called me - Dyl.

CHAPTER 20

It was August, and the school-library was open for the very
last time before finally closing for the last fortnight of the
school holidays, and the two best friends decided it would be
a great place for a natter about their plans for the rest of the
summer, about boys, and about life in general. Rhiannon was
in the process of combing her long hair and pinning it back in
place, while across the table from her Carmen was reading a
newspaper. She suddenly looked up at her red-haured friend,
and said, "Teenagers are like insects, in that they can't stop
grooming so as to get near the opposite sex."

'Speak for yourself,' retorted Rhiannon, clearly offended.

'But Rhi, it's just a story in the paper, that's all,' said
Carmen. 'There's no need to get arsey, you know. It's nothing
personal.'

'All right. But if you have to read one, read me a normal
one,' Rhiannon told her, 'and not one that's almost bound to
offend me.'

'O.K.,' said Carmen. Then, after a short pause, she
announced, 'Mankind is a plague on the Earth says Wildlife
legend David -'

'Carmen!' exclaimed Rhiannon. 'You're only offending
everybody who's alive this time. Look - there has to be
something in today's *Mail* that is uplifting. And I don't mean
like that either.'

Carmen grinned a wicked grin, then read on. "Sperm
quality has declined by a third in a decade," she announced.
'Are diet and lifestyle to blame? 'asks -"

Rhiannon grabbed hold of the newspaper and threw it
onto the floor. 'Carmen - I'd like you to do what that ad says

on the TV. 'Break the habit of a lunch-time.' Now I'm sure you can do that.'

'But I've given up chips,' said Carmen. 'And come September -'

Rhiannon wasn't interested, and her mind drifted onto other things. 'Carmen - does it make me a prude that I don't like things like nipple-clamps, butt-plugs, whips or vagazzles?' she asked.

'I don't see why,' said Carmen. 'I'm not a bit prudish, right? And I've never once been whipped, or plugged in the butt, that I remember, anyway.' She took another toffee from the box sitting before them, unwrapped it, and popped it in her mouth. 'Or clamped even. Except that time I parked my dad's car under that awning down the market. Christ, it was pouring down! 'So how else am I supposed to get those dresses in my boot?' I asked the little parking-officer in the turban.' She took a second toffee from the container and tossed it before her friend. 'And the only thing's ever been up *my* bum, Rhi, is a pessary, and that just an itsy-bitzy one.'

Rhiannon would normally have quizzed Carmen on the details of this queer, last statement, but just then she wasn't listening. 'Or that I only want to make love with just the one man?' she went on. 'Say - Carmen. Do you think that makes me a prude? Just Chris, I mean. And now I'm practically a virgin reincarnated, you see, since, for some reason, he simply won't anymore.'

'He's a bastard, isn't he?' said Carmen, smiling. 'Chris, I mean, not the traffic-warden. I mean *they're* on a whole other level completely, don't you think?'

'Something has happened to make him act like that, I feel,' said Rhiannon.

'I reckon it might be how little we pay them,' retorted Carmen. Her friend suddenly stared at her. 'Hey - do you mean the warden, now, or Chris?'

'No - Chris, I'm talking about,' said Rhiannon. 'Keep focused, will you?'

'Well, I don't know,' said Carmen. 'You know him so much better than I do, right?'

Rhiannon suddenly placed her finger across her lips, and then pointed to the table in the corner where her class-mate Jake Haines sat reading some newspapers. The two girls hadn't even noticed that he was there, or perhaps, Rhiannon thought, the strange boy might have snuck in while they were engrossed in conversation. Why is he there? she was thinking.

'Blimey, it's Jake Haines. Why do you think he's here?' said Carmen, her mouth falling open.

'Perhaps he's come to see you,' suggested Rhiannon. 'He knows you fancy him, for sure.'

'I did!' her friend snapped back. 'But you know he hangs round with some right nasty people these days. Total idiots, some of them.'

'Most of them,' added Rhiannon. 'And they treat Chris like he's their junior, when in fact -'

'Look what he's doing,' said Carmen. 'Now listen - nobody could read newspapers that fast. Not even Chris's dad.'

'I bet he could,' said Rhiannon, picturing her favourite teacher skimming through the dailies at his classroom desk. 'Mister Cillick does everything fast.'

'And how would you know? I'm not sure I want to hear any more,' said Carmen, giggling.

'Stop it!' exclaimed Rhiannon. 'We don't want him to hear us.'

'But he's probably in *Gloryhole* painting in his garden right now,' Carmen suggested.

'Not him - Jake,' Rhiannon snapped back. 'Say - let's wait until he's gone, then we'll go over and see what it is he's been up to, yeah? You know, I bet it's something illegal.'

'Oh, look how quick you are to judge, Rhiannon,' said Carmen, frowning. 'You should be ashamed of yourself, girl. I can tell he's only cutting out little pictures with a scissors. Bless.'

'Bloody tiny pictures, if you ask me,' Rhiannon told her, screwing up her eyes so as to see better. 'Look - he's getting up to leave! Pretend you're reading!'

Jake Haines got up and carried the pile of newspapers over to the waste-paper bin, folded them once, then stuffed them deep inside. Passing the two girls without even a glance, he then made his way out. After a few seconds Carmen and Rhiannon jumped up, the former heading for the bin, the latter for the vacant table. Carmen pulled out the folded pile of papers and carried them across to her friend. Meanwhile Rhiannon dived down onto her knees and began scooping up from the carpet every single scrap of litter that the boy had accidentally dropped there. They then sat on either side of the boy's table and discussed what it was each of them had found.

Unbeknown to either girl, the librarian, Brenda Seccombe, head surreptitiously bowed, was observing their every move from her desk at the very front of the room. After a few minutes the woman smiled broadly and whispered, 'Out of such mischief and downright nosiness real detectives are made.' Strangely, on this occasion, she was actually referring to the two school-friends, busy burrowing about in the corner, and not to herself.

'Letters! What do you mean - letters?' a white-shirted, white-trousered Chris asked them, his uni-brow suddenly forming alarmingly, and frightening the pair of them.

'You know, *the alphabet*,' said Carmen.

'Of course I do,' he replied aggressively. 'Are you trying to be funny, Carmen McGrath?'

'She means cut-out letters,' said Rhiannon. 'Jake must have dropped at least a couple of dozen of them on the floor while he was at it.' She smiled, an idea forming itself in her mind. 'You know, I reckon that if we lay them all out together here on the bench -'

' - then we could see if they make words. Ingenious, right?' added Carmen.

'Stupid, you mean,' snapped back Chris.

'Why so?' asked Carmen, making a face that seemed to impugn his sanity.

'Well, isn't it obvious?' said Chris. 'If he was actually writing something with them, then he wouldn't have any use for the ones he threw on the floor, would he? It stands to reason, right?'

A stiff silence, broken only by the sharp thwack of willow on ball, filled the air around them.

'Yeah, that's what I thought,' said Carmen, taking out a handkerchief and blowing her nose.

'No, you didn't, you little liar,' said Rhiannon, slapping her friend on the arm. 'You're perfectly right, of course, Chris,' she went on. 'We two are just a bit thick, that's all.'

Chris seemed to stare at a point in the air just above their heads. 'But if only we could find the newspapers they came from, then we might be in business,' said Chris. 'Carmen - what's that?' he enquired.

'The pile of newspapers they all came from,' said Carmen, smiling. 'I took them from out the bin. You know, I reckon that if we were to identify all the cut-outs that Jake made -'

' - then subtract all the ones that I found on the floor,' added Rhiannon, 'then we should discover every one of the letters that he must have chosen to take away with him. That makes sense, don't you think, Chris?' She beamed her most perfectly formed smile at him.

'It certainly does,' said Chris, hugging Rhiannon towards him in excitement, but then only pecking her gently on the cheek.

'Hey - it was me that figured it out,' said Carmen.

'Yeah, but he's not going to kiss you, is he Carmen?' said Rhiannon, trying to make herself feel a little better about the partial snub she felt she had suffered at Chris's hands.

'Too right I'm not. I can see she's got another scabby cold-sore coming,' retorted Chris. He then ducked fast as Carmen swung a hefty left hook at him, which thankfully missed, swiftly followed by a slash with the thick roll of newspapers she held in the other hand, and which not only landed, but very nearly took the boy's head off.

The afternoon sun beamed down on them as the three school-friends sat, three-in-a-row together, with the male of the group seated judiciously in between, on the green, wooden bench that looked out onto the cricket-field. Far out on the pitch, two cricket sides, dressed in all colours, including white, were attempting to knock six bells out of a cricket-ball that was yellow in colour, and no longer even close to round. The two girls suddenly glanced up at each other.

'Have you written them all down, then, Rhiannon?' asked Carmen. 'Yeah? Right, let's see.'

'God - there's got to be thirty-five or more, by the look of it,' said Chris, moving the sheet the flame-haired girl had been writing on round and round on the grass below them until all three could see it clearly. 'I reckon this is going to be a real nightmare trying to work out,' he told them.

'No it's not,' said Rhiannon. 'I reckon it's just a sort of cross between a normal crossword puzzle and that *Enigma-Code* thing in the magazine, and that's quite a lot harder. But recently I've been getting much better at solving that one, and so I feel sure that we'll be able to do it.'

The cricket-teams had racked up forty overs, trooped off, changed pads, and returned for their second innings minus Chris, before the three friends managed to solve it. But solve it they did.

'As I said earlier, I think it's definitely a ransom-note for a kidnapping,' Chris told them, biting his thumb-nail nervously. 'What else *could* it be?'

Rhiannon read out for them the strange sentence that the three teenagers had finally managed to uncover and piece together. "*Want her back live or in a box? Gonna cost you 500K in used or else too bad.*" Rhiannon looked up. 'God, to think he's in the same English set as me. Who the hell could Jake Haines have kidnapped for heaven's sake? His baby sister? And, you know, I doubt if she's worth five-hundred p.'

'Ooh, that's cruel, Rhi,' said Carmen. 'The girl's only in Year Eight, remember. And it's not her fault she dresses like her gran.'

Chris, of course, felt he knew exactly who the ransom-note related to, but he wasn't about to tell even Rhiannon about it. He was just hoping that the kidnapping hadn't happened yet. Chris looked across to the wicket and recalled vividly the night, just a couple of months earlier, when his timely arrival from Rhiannon's had prevented certain harm from being done to his new neighbour, Carla Steel. She was the one whom he felt needed to be told about what the trio had just discovered, Chris told himself. But just then, he recalled how Carla had asked him not to bother her at all that day, or the next, on account of her having to rehearse for the benefit-gig at *The Railway* which was taking place that Sunday evening. And so, getting to his feet, folding up the sheet of paper and popping it inside his bag, which he swiftly shouldered, he made the decision to tell Carla about it as early as he possibly could the morning after next, and, leaving the two girls sitting on the grass, hurried home.

Perched high on a rickety, brown stool placed in front of the bar, her short, slim, denim-clad legs crossed, and with just her battered acoustic-guitar to accompany her, Carla bent her head slightly and tightened a couple of strings, then looked up and smiled just once at the three-score faces in the semi-darkness before her, as she waited until their opening applause fell away. She then proceeded to play, one after the other, each of the songs she had composed for her latest, and, as yet, unreleased, fourth album - *'Two Birds - One Stone'* - which, of course, no one there knew, and so, perhaps unsurprisingly, many of the more inebriated, especially in the blind corners, and in the adjoining back-lounge, whose door stood wide open, began to whistle at quite loudly.

'Listen, everyone,' announced Carla, around a half-a-dozen songs into her performace, 'if you guys just stick with me a little while longer, then I promise you at the end I'll play you only songs you've heard.' At this welcome news the audience briefly cheered again, and, seemingly much comforted, once again settled down. Then, when she had finished performing all ten tracks, the singer began playing the very same songs from the first half all over again!

Beaten to the punch, what could the Welsh crowd do but admire the singer's balls. After all, they hadn't paid more than a small donation for the privilege of seeing and hearing her. And this was how Carla Steel was, after all, they concluded, and everyone right across the musical world knew it, and, yes, loved her for it. The feisty, little Welsh girl took no shit, but, if some ever got hurled in her direction, then she knew exactly how to fling it back.

Carla also seemed to know better than anyone how 'a prophet has no honour in her own country,' and she certainly expected nothing less than what she got from her humble, but fiercely proud, native audience. Yet, as the evening wore on, and unsurprisingly, given her awesome talent, the largely young crowd in *'The Railway'* that night appeared to revel in it just the same, and soon screamed and whistled up the singer for a couple of encores. Carla, being Carla, did just the one - the song she had started the evening with - then, guitar in one hand, and a bottle of *Stella* in the other, nonchalantly disappeared into 'The Ladies' for a well-earned pee, a cold beer, and the trademark joint.

Around ten minutes later, a woman entered the stall next-door to Carla's, and straightaway began a conversation with her. 'Imagine that! Carla Steel playing *'The Railway!'* Whatever next,' she said, in between a host of other sounds. 'Lovely voice, that girl has, hasn't she?' Carla heard her say. 'Though I wish she'd done my favourite song.'

'Which one is that then?' an intrigued Carla decided to ask her.

'It's the one my old man calls 'the clinic song.' the woman told her. Then she suddenly began singing it. ' *'Sometimes it dah-dee-dah-dee-dah, and sometimes it hurts instead.'* Oh, I love that one, I really do.'

'It's not one of hers, I'm afraid,' said Carla, smiling to herself, and shaking her head from side to side.

'Is it not?' asked the woman, who then tutted disappointedly, promptly flushed, and went out again.

Later Carla was to acknowledge that she should really have slipped out the side-door after that and made her way straight home, since events that fateful night were, sadly, to take another turn completely.

'What the hell bloody name is that?' Jack asked the dark stranger, loud enough so that he could be heard above the blare of the loud music that was hammering out from the two vast speakers alongside them. 'My girl had one of those that I recall being partial to once,' he told him, grinning.

'It's his name, so just leave it,' Steffan told the wind-blown Welshman, swiftly moving in between the pair of them, and then aggressively staring him down.

'You can't be serious,' Jack told him, shaking his head in disbelief at the tall man with the beard, then smiling at them both, but failing utterly to suppress the loud belch that followed, and was, for him, the inevitable result of drinking far too much lager and omitting to eat.

'*You* can talk, pal,' Jake told him, moving ahead of Steffan, so that he too could be heard. 'Jack Belt! What sort of a name is that, for Christ's sake? Jack Belt!' he repeated, smiling. 'I mean, isn't that something you get given for martial arts?'

'What! I'll have you know I've never dabbled in any of those,' Jack replied angrily. 'And I tell you I never will. There was one of those crazy covens operating up in Cefn one time. Up near the golf-course, it was. And I got given a parcel to deliver to one of them - one of their - their wicker-men they had up there, but I just couldn't bring myself to do it. I had to pass up the commission, like. You see, I get scared shitless by all that kind of stuff, I really do. And in the end I had to let the Royal Mail deliver it instead. Imagine that. I know you probably can't believe it, but I even paid them the proper postage and everything. I swear I'd never had to do that before. I even post all my own Christmas cards normally, and always have done.'

Volver gently eased his two side-men out of the way, and confronted the speaker he couldn't understand, just as a second belch emerged from his mouth and blasted him in the face like a sharp gust of wind, which, of course, is exactly what it was; except the Afrikaner with the weird name didn't quite see it like that, in fact, he appeared to view it as some kind of personal slight, which was a first for Jack Belt, who had never slighted a single soul in his entire life. And this was unfortunate for Jack, as things went. In fact, the whole evening quickly turned into one massive, great regret for the man, if truth be told, and he soon wished that martial arts were

472

something he'd decided to look into after all. No - won a belt of some kind in, he told herself. Preferably a big black one.

'I've got a job for you,' said Volver.

'I start work at six in the morning,' Jack answered, sipping his drink.

'Well, it needs doing tonight,' the South African told him. This statement he repeated, a lot more firmly the second time, just in case the tipsy Welshman hadn't managed to catch it.

'Well, I'd be interested,' Jack told him, 'but you see, I don't drink and drive as a general rule.' Which response, sadly, turned out to be the wrong answer completely as far as Volver was concerned. And everyone in the group surrounding Jack knew that instantly, and, at first smiled at him benignly, and then shook their heads from side to side and chuckled loudly over it.

And, seeing this, Jack suddenly sensed that, against his better judgement, he might be about to do some drink-driving that night after all! And, given that, he would therefore need to refrain from drinking any more of the *Stella* tonight, and stay awake, so as to endeavour to concentrate on whatever he was going to be asked to do when the time came for him to be asked to do it.

And, some time between eleven p.m. and midnight, while taking a much needed leak in *Les Messieurs* alongside his three new compatriots, an inebriated Jack somewhat inexplicably realised that, in the circumstances, his CSE's in Woodwork and Welsh might not turn out to be a great deal of help to him that night. He had cause to smile at this bizarre observation, which seemed to him to have entered his brain from the gushing water-tank above his head, and, looking up, and chuckling raucously at the sheer impossibility of it, promptly soaked his trainers.

'Bloody hell, Jack!' cried Jake, climbing aboard. 'Say - why has your camper-van got a big, round hole in the floor, for God's sake?'

'Air-conditioniong, is it?' asked Volver, peering over his friend's shoulder.

'It's so his passengers can take a dump en route, I bet.' Steffan announced, climbing into the passenger-seat instead, and moving up, so that the South African could slip in alongside him.

'No, it's not that, guys,' Jack Belt told them, climbing into the driving-seat and switching on the lights. 'I bought it off this bloke who used to use it to knick man-hole covers, you know.'

'God Streuth!' cried Jake, suddenly losing his footing in the back, and almost falling through.

Jack Belt continued with his tale. 'Yeah. People used to wonder why he and his lovely Missus used to park up on different parts of the Heads-of-the-Valleys Road at odd hours of the night. Together I mean. Folk deliberately stayed out of his way, of course, as any normal person would, you know. Even the police, as it turned out. The chap's a millionaire now, they tell me.'

'Metal thieves, eh?' said Volver. 'They're a damn sight worse than terrorists, if you ask me. I'm thinking it won't be the bloody terrorists who put a halt to the Olympics next year, guys, you get me?' With a bout of hearty guffaws the other three men concurred.

'You know those five rings they normally put up outside the stadium?' said Steffan, his eyes suddenly sparkling. 'Well, I bet you Steptoe-and-Son will have melted them down before the opening ceremony's even started.'

'And God help 'em in the pole-vault,' said Jake. 'They jump up, and, blimey, the bar's gone!'

'And the same goes for them in the hammer,' said Steffan. 'And the discus, and the shot.'

'Do you want to buy some big ball-bearings, mister?' added Volver, grinning. 'Fell off the back of a Russian. Know what I mean, guys?' They all laughed again at this.

'And Usain Bolt might have to change his name, don't you reckon?' chipped in Jake.

Nobody laughed at this one except Jake himself. Instead Volver and Steffan turned their heads round as Jack became fully occupied in trying to reverse his van out. In his drunken state he managed to scrape against two neighbouring cars, and so opened his door to climb out and assess the damage. But before he could do so, he found himself crudely grabbed at the collar.

'Where do you think you're going, dumb-fuck?' shrieked Volver. 'So they've got a small scratch on them. They should be so lucky. That's what you call superficial damage, right? Then we'll send 'em a cheque in the post.'

Jack turned and looked into the wild eyes of the bearded South African sitting beside him, and quickly realised the futility of taking issue with him. Volver was clearly the govenor of this crew, Jack told himself. And what he said you'd best do, it seemed, even inside your own camper-van.

You know, I really loved your set,' said Steffan. 'But it's a shame you didn't get to do the gang-bang song.'

'Gang-bang song!' said a mystified Carla from out of the shadows. 'Whatever do you mean?'

'You know the one,' he told her, suddenly beginning to sing - *'Sometimes I'm last to love, but often I'm first instead.'* His sneering tone was evident as he went on to justify his random, but malicious comment. 'I just love that one. I can sort of identify with it, if you know what I mean.'

'Sadly, I believe I can,' said Carla, cringing at what she took as the creepy lad's foul attempt to intimidate her, and quickly turning her head aside to look out of the window. 'But that's definitely not one of mine, I'm afraid,' she told the boy.

'Oh, is it not?' quipped Steffan, beginning to relish the power he felt he now had over this acclaimed, yet still only female and diminutive, musical icon.

'So is that what you pulled me in here for, then?' Carla asked. 'Is it, Abram? A gang-bang.'

'Abram!' stammered Steffan in response, turning smartly so as to register the expression on his governor's face. 'Magic!'

'Abram-cadabram!' said Jake, chuckling loudly behind them, but swiftly realising that he may have gone just a little too far.

'Stick to *Volver*, please, Carla,' the Afrikaner responded slowly, and with obvious authority. 'We're not in London now, my girl. And you're no longer head down like some rutting rodent, clambering around in the gutter outside '*The Half Moon*' in Putney for the greasy tab you were too fuckin' spaced-out to hold onto.'

Carla closed her eyes at the memory of it. She straightaway regretted even mentioning his name.

'And it's a long while now since you were forever calling me up in the middle of the night, and screaming out for it. 'Oh, please Abram! Please!' '

'Sex, do you mean?' asked an intrigued Steffan, spinning round to see the look on Carla's shadow-strewn face. 'Famous singer or not, she certainly does look the type who'd scream out.'

'Smack,' said Volver. 'Yeah - you guys heard right - smack. And coke, of course, and ketamin. You know, Carla, my business back in the smoke might easily have gone tits-up without your new record-deal to keep me going.'

'Ain't that the truth?' quipped Carla, trying her best to match the cocky, masculine tone that pervaded the gloomy, rattling van, but clearly falling short. She elected to try a different tack. 'But, you see, things are a damn sight different now, aren't they? I mean, since I stopped touring, and then returned home again.'

'Are they?' retorted Volver derisively, spitting a thread of tobacco from his mouth at the windscreen before him, almost as if he were answering his own question. 'I don't really see how, do you? My contacts in the smoke all tell me you've still been using again this year, Carla. And, as you well know, every single penny you've been shelling out on the stuff only helps to fatten up my wallet in the end.' He spun his head round. 'And you know what they say, don't you, boys?'

'What's that?' asked Jake.

'Once a smack-head, always a smack-head,' Volver told them. 'That's rule number-one in my book, boys. Follow that and you won't go far wrong, I can tell you. I got to learn it a very long time ago, and that's why I can afford to drive two top-of-the-range sports cars at the same time.'

'Wow! That's bit of a stretch, isn't it?' said Jake, smiling, and imitating the trick with his two hands held out before him.

'Well, his driving can't be any worse than when he's sitting in just the one car,' said Carla, emitting a low chuckle. 'And nobody would ever know that he's officially banned from driving, would they? Still, it's common knowledge that Abram Volver changes his number-plates almost as often as he changes his boxers, these days, and so I guess there's little chance he's ever going to get stopped by the police.'

'O.K. You can shut up now, Carla,' said Volver, staring through the rear-view mirror into the eyes of the petite, but feisty girl sitting behind him, and gritting his teeth aggressively.

'Say, where are you taking me, by the way?' Carla asked them. 'And why is there a dirty, great hole in the floor? I can't believe none of you guys have even bothered to mention that.'

'Oh, I can explain that, love,' Jack Belt told her. But, as it turned out, he didn't get the chance. One sudden, side-long glance from Volver and the van-driver quickly froze. Yes, although inebriated, and terribly worn out after another twelve-hour shift, even Jack could work out what was likely to happen if he elected to say another word.

Carla was gradually getting more and more concerned for her safety, as the rattling van rolled past her father's home, and ploughed on out of *Gloryhole* - its enormous, arched viaduct barely visible now in the darkness to her right - and soon rounded the tight, left-hand bend, and rose up the hill, past Vaynor, with its own tight bends, and on towards the hill-top village of Pontsticill.

There, receiving instructions from the Afrikaner to carry straight on, Jack Belt took the broader road to the left, which headed north, and rose even higher, rather than take the right-turn that led down towards the dam of the great reservoir and its gloomy tower, under the shadow of which Carla had once watched helplessly as her brother Will had tragically drowned. Gazing out of the left-hand window at the group of wild horses which stood together grazing on the skyline, the singer was glad at least of this particular twist, since she had no desire to re-visit that site again so late at night, and in the company of her current drunken male companions.

'Go faster, would you, old boy,' Volver commanded the driver. 'We're late already.'

'Late for what?' asked Carla, staring into the rear-view mirror so as to seek out his eyes, but failing, and now starting to shiver noticeably. 'Where the hell are you taking me?'

Steffan suddenly spun round so that he could take in the expression of panic on the singer's pale, but pretty face. 'Didn't you say she knows it well?' he asked Volver, who also studied her reaction when she got told of their destination. '*Cwm Scwt!*' Steffan announced to her shrilly.

'Or, as you know it, *Candice Farm*,' Volver told the girl, grinning. Carla shook her head in astonishment. 'Yes, I knew you'd be shocked. And that was the title you gave your second album, wasn't it, Carla? Tell me, won't you - *why was that*, exactly?' But he saw there was no hint of a reply. 'It wasn't on account of the magic-mushrooms growing round the place, was it? Or the day-night, summer rave-parties that were said to have taken place there, and to which you regularly got invited? The owner of the place sadly passed away, you know, Carla.'

'Emlyn Hughes is dead!' she suddenly stammered, eyes bulging, mouth wide open.

'Apparently,' answered Volver, looking all round him to work out just how close they were now getting to the farm's location. 'An accident with a fire-arm, I understand.'

'So listen - how the hell can we be going there?' Carla asked him, biting into her lip, and believing that, even if she thought about it for just two or three seconds, she would be sure to know the answer. 'And at this time of night, too. Does the owner know we're coming? I mean, who owns the place these days?'

'Who owns it?' repeated Volver. 'Who do you think owns it, Carla? Why, I do, of course,' he said, turning to face her again. 'You didn't know that, did you? Well, of course you wouldn't, would you? I mean I didn't exactly go out of my way to publicize the fact, did I? Would you?'

'Well, I don't sell class-A drugs like you do, do I, Abram?' she responded fiercely.

'No, but you're still thoroughly hooked on them, aren't you?' he told her, grinning. 'I mean, I happen to know that just now you're still taking a whole variety of them. Of course I could never blame you for it. I'd be a complete hypocrite if I did that. But *now*, Carla, I gather you're sharing your drugs with under-age school-boys, of all people. Not very clever, that, as it goes. Don't you agree, Carla? Not terribly wise with the - with the sort of profile you're desperate to maintain, anyway. If word of that ever got out, girl - well, I mean, it could have serious repercussions for your career, don't you think? Our Carla - back in the pit *yet again*.' He shook his head about.

Carla was beginning to see where all this was heading, and she felt her body shiver much more deeply this time, but still decided to do her utmost not to let them see it.

'Take a right turn soon after this second big lake, Jack,' said Volver. 'Then, in the dip near the stream, straightaway take another. You know, boys, what I especially like about the place we're going to be staying at is its complete and utter isolation. Don't you agree, Carla? Up here in the wild, green foothills of The Brecon Beacons even a shrieking owl won't ever wake a soul.'

'And how would you know that?' Carla asked him. 'City boy that you are, I mean.'

'How do I know? I'll tell you how I know, girl.' said Volver. He then forced his hand into his coat-packet and took out a revolver. 'I know because last night I found I couldn't get to sleep for the second night running. The evil, hooting bastard! So, naturally, I had to go out and kill one.'

Tossing his head back, the Afrikaner's abrasive laugh rang out loudly and raucously from the passenger-window. Scanning the grassy slopes on both sides of her, Carla pondered how, to the sheep who lived out there, the man's voice must surely sound like the harrying sound of a goshawk, a buzzard or a falcon, selfishly intruding on their lifetime pasture. In fact, she mused, one could be forgiven for thinking that that was precisely what the evil man was, as it was likely he had only come to Wales to pursue her, but that while here he certainly wasted no time in doing his utmost to wreak havoc on the people living in the peaceful communities round about.

The van turned right at the junction, and drifted silently down into the narrow valley, then made its way up the opposing slope again, soon disappearing into the grey mist that was, by this time, fast gathering for the chillier than usual August night that Carla felt must surely lie ahead.

A valid argument need not be a sound one. All dogs have four legs -cats have four legs - therefore all dogs are cats. Er - I don't think so, somehow. Either way, although invalid, unsound, and well wide of the mark, I quite naturally, no, forgivably, assumed that Chris, although almost fifteen years her junior, was, in fact, the step-brother of Carla Steel, who was presumably the daughter of Drew, that refractory, half-English, Cardiff-reared, mad-arsed, loose-cannon of an Art teacher at *Pennant School*. There had, you see, long been rumours that, some time before his marriage to Anne, Drew had fathered another child with some other woman while living alone in the Welsh capital, but, for some reason that I simply can't explain, I had always assumed the child to be male.

But, mistaken though I later found out I was, it certainly did appear to me that 'Drew-the-Art' - as parents and pupils at the school frequently called him - was the father of the young woman whom the whole world admired, even loved, and knew as Carla Steel. Well, I concluded at the time, the pair of them were both artistically inclined after all, and so I wasn't persuaded to even question the sudden discovery I had made, even though I still decided not to share it with another living soul, not even my daughter Rhiannon, no, especially not Rhiannon, at least until I had myself confirmed its veracity.

But, as luck would have it, in the end it was my daughter herself who, one quiet evening, settled the issue, and so dispelled my supposedly well-considered conclusion, (wholly without knowing of it herself,) by informing me that Carla

Steel was living slap next-door to her school-friend Chris Cillick, and so therefore not in the same house as him. Well, I was genuinely glad to hear that, I can tell you, because I wasn't at all sure I wanted my seventeen year-old daughter, through the auspices of young Chris, consorting with someone known right across the world, not just for her musical talents, but also for the kind of social behaviour that I hoped and trusted Rhiannon would continue to shun for the remainder of her life.

And then one Sunday morning I had occasion to pay a visit to the tiny village of *Gloryhole*, not to call at the home of my one-time lover, Anne, but the house two doors down, since I had to drop off some building-supplies for the owner of the house that stood on the other side of the one where Carla's dad lived. There was, of course, nobody living there at the time, but a married couple from Merthyr, that I met through Zeta's husband Martin, were then in the process of renovating it, with a view to hopefully moving in there permanently some time in 2012.

There I was in the process of re-locking the front-door of the property, with the intention of going off right away on a separate call, when I happened to hear a deep, male voice scream out. At first I thought it might have been the sound of an animal of some kind being attacked in the vicinity of the viaduct at the rear of the property, but the second scream, which followed soon after the first, told me that it was coming from the house in the middle of the three, called 'Coral.'

I hurried round to the front of the terraced property and rapped at the door. There was no reply, so I rapped again. This time I thought I heard a voice from inside calling out 'God Help me!' or perhaps just 'Help me!' Well, I didn't require a second invitation. Trying the door and finding it locked, I put my shoulder to its upper portion and burst the little lock right off. I dashed inside, then through the ground-floor into the back-kitchen. It was there that I found the prostrate man - the aged, skeletal-framed father of Carla Davies.

Lying face-down on the linoleum-covered floor, and dressed only in striped pyjamas and a loosely fitted robe, the bare-headed gentleman turned his neck round and spoke. 'Dylan!' he called out. 'Why, it's you, my man.'

'Yes, it's me,' I retorted, thinking fast. 'But I'm sure I don't know you, old boy, do I?' I told him. 'Except that I understand your daughter is staying here with you, so you must be her father, Mr. Davies, Sir. What has happened? Tell me.'

'I don't really know,' he replied. 'Carla's not here, and I very much doubt she'll be returning.'

'Oh, why is that? Has she gone back to London, then?' I enquired, kneeling on the floor beside him, and trying to assess the ailing man's physical state.

'She's been taken off to the hills,' he stammered.

'Do you mean on a day-trip?' I asked.

'No, no. Totally against her will, Dylan,' he told me. 'She was performing at *The Railway* last night, you see. Playing her music, I mean. But now she *and* her guitar have been whisked away.'

'You don't mean - surely you don't mean *kidnapped*?' I asked.

'Well, what do *you* think?' he retorted, laying his head back on the hard floor, and looking up into my face. 'She didn't come home last night, you see, and she was supposed to.'

'But that's hardly proof, is it?' I told him. 'Your daughter is a grown woman. She might have made other plans. She might even still be there.'

'Well, I don't know about that, I'm sure,' he answered glumly.

'Either way, I can see that you definitely need medical assistance,' I said. 'Where's your house-phone, Mr. Davies?' I enquired, looking round.

'I'm Tom,' he replied. 'It's out in the lounge. But don't leave me, Dylan.'

'Dyl.'

'Dyl. You see - you see I know that this is the end for me now. Oh yes. And, you see, I always knew I would be on my own when it - when the time came. That - that I was going to die alone.'

'But you're not alone,' I told him. 'And very soon there'll be some other people here too, to help you. Just you hang on now.'

'No, no,' he urged me. 'Please don't go ringing them, Dyl. Promise me that you won't. The last thing I want is for someone to start banging me on the back and pumping on my chest singing songs by the blasted *Bee Gees*.' I had to smile at this. 'When I need to go I'll go, right? And anyway, I'll be gone before anybody gets here. I'll be gone just like - just like your brother.

'Sam!' I exclaimed, taken aback by this.

'Left to be run over -'

'He wasn't run over,' I told him.

'Run down, then, by a train that never even came his way, and so never even touched him.'

'Why Sam died exactly they didn't know - and now they'll never know,' I explained to him.

'Young Sam heard a train coming, Dyl,' the old man whispered.

'You what!' I interjected, my mouth suddenly falling open.

'From the tunnel-entrance he heard the noise the train made as it got closer and closer, coming up the valley from the viaduct here, you see? And so - and so he naturally assumed -'

My head was spinning. 'That it was going to proceed into the tunnel -' I said.

'Where his three friends had just minutes earlier tied him securely to one or more of the raised sleepers in the track. In jest, of course, Dyl, purely in jest. They never meant Sam any harm, I swear. They were all his friends, and it was his twenty-first birthday, after all, right?'

'Yes, it was,' I told him, the tears now welling up in my eyes, my breathing becoming laboured, the hands with which I gripped the old man's shoulders now trembling with trepidation - with fear of the unwinding narrative he un-spun for me - the awful truth that he was revealing. 'But wait! What

about the horrible cuts and bruises they found on his torso?'
I asked.

'Oh, don't think he didn't try to get away, Dyl, because he
most certainly did, boy,' Tom said. 'Sam tugged, and pulled,
and screamed, and pulled again at the tethers that held him,
the wooden sleepers becoming tremendously shaken around
by it all, and yet just too firmly fixed beneath the rails to come
away and free him.'

I mulled over every single point that he related. 'Yes, I recall
now how one of the sleepers, where they found Sam's body,
did seem a lot looser than all the rest,' I told him. 'And yet the
fact must have been deemed irrelevant by the police, since no
rope was ever found there, nor did anyone even so much as
suggest he might have been secured to the track. Rather that
Sam was just discovered lying there, dead from a sudden heart-
attack they concluded.'

'You know, you and I can barely imagine the sort of colossal
efforts that your brother made to break free, Dyl,' the old man
announced. 'Such panic would do for most of us, I can tell you.'

'I see. And his friends, Tom?' I asked. 'Surely they had to
have heard him scream out?'

'No, Dyl,' Tom replied. 'By then they had already run up
the slope and along the path to the prince's seat. You see that
was where they'd parked their car, on the grass-verge by the
double-bend. And then the driver among them drove it a little
way further down the road so as to - to -'

'To compound the joke they were all playing on him,
right?' I said.

'Yes, I guess that's what it was, Dyl,' said Tom. 'I ask you -
how could they possibly have known that there would be a
train coming up the line that day of all days? After all, there
hadn't been one up that way for ages had there? And so, when
a train trundled up the valley from *The Seven Arches*, its
whistle sounding shrilly, the noise of its engine and its wheels
growing louder and louder by the second, then rounded the
bend close to where Sam lay bound, the young man
understandably feared for his life, and soon expired, knowing
there could be no escape from it.'

'Great God in Heaven!' I cursed, visualising my brother's terrible plight before my eyes.

'But, you see, Dyl, he was never to know that the points were set the other way, was he? And that the train therefore would roar past the tunnel-entrance, just inside which his three best friends had trussed him up. All three of them loved Sam like a brother too, Dyl,' he added. 'Just as you did.'

'You mean with ropes?' I interjected. 'You say they had bound Sam up with ropes?'

'Yes, with yards and yards of coloured rope they'd brought along specially in the boot of the car. And of course poor Sam wasn't to know of the playful prank they had planned for him.'

'My God!' I said, now shedding tears freely.

'Very much as we might bind a birthday gift in loops and bows of coloured ribbon, Dyl,' the old man added. 'But, you see, the group had temporarily taken the car just a bit too far down the way from where they had left him to hear that any train was coming, and so sense danger.'

'It just doesn't bear thinking about,' I told him, now able to see clearly in my mind's eye the very scene that had occurred back then. 'And I bet, even if they'd seen the train trundle past, they would never have guessed it could possibly have harmed Sam, would they? When, in fact, it killed him, as you rightly said, without even touching him - without even coming close to him.'

'Quite so, Dyl,' said Tom. 'And then, perhaps just minutes later, when the group drove back to the prince's seat, and parked up the car as before, and merrily trotted back down the slope once again to release their much-loved, birthday victim, they - well, they no doubt expected -'

'That Sam would find it just as funny as they did,' I told him.

Tom nodded, and continued, 'The three of them walked up to the tunnel-entrance, only to discover that their dearest friend seemed to have burst his little heart asunder in his strenuous efforts to avoid being crushed alive.'

Gripping my top lip tightly between my teeth, I ducked my head and wept. 'Can you - can you see it all, then, Tom?' I asked the frail old man.

'I can, Dyl,' he replied, reaching up and stroking my temple with his bony hand. 'But, you know, your brother wants you to know he made it there after all, Dyl. I guess he means *heaven*, right?' I nodded, recalling the unique pledge my brother had made to me all those years before. 'Yes, Sam wants you to know that he made it, and that he's in heaven right now,' the old man told me. 'And he's saying - he's telling you right now, Dyl - 'I'm in the wonderful arms of Jesus.' '

CHAPTER 21

A loud crack suddenly sounded, and Carla's deep reverie was rudely ended. She pulled the duvet from off her head and, sitting up on the bed, stared wildly about her. For two or three seconds she had absolutely no idea where the large, dark room was that she found herself in, or what the cause of the scary noise might have been that had awoken her. Then, on jumping down onto the bare floor and staring out of the grimy window, the sight of Abram Volver on a grassy patch of ground about thirty or so yards away, showing Jake and Steffan how to load and shoot his revolver, told her all that she had no wish to know. The previous night's crazy events suddenly flashed back into Carla's mind - the gig, the abduction, the van with the great hole through its floor - and, paralysed with fear, she bent her knees, and crouched out of sight on the floor-boards beside a smashed-up guitar that still bore her monogram and smiley face.

'And there was that night behind *The Riverside Studios* in Hammersmith,' Volver was telling them, 'I stabbed this druggie to death who kept giving me the v-sign and swearing at me all the time he was buying off me. Oh, I think I told you guys about it, didn't I?'

'Yeah, but like I told you then, the dumb guy was showing you no respect, right?' snarled Steffan, whipping out a knife from his back-pocket, and switching it deftly from hand to hand.

Volver took hold of Steffan's knife and straightaway threw it, powerfully and accurately, and spinning wildly over and over itself, into the trunk of a tree ten yards or so away from them. He then calmly walked over to the tree and, with his left hand pressed against its bark as a fulcrum, pulled the knife out again. 'And it wouldn't surprise me if he's still a fully-functioning part of the estuarine food-chain, boys,' he told them. 'Primary consumer level, naturally.'

'Hey - I never knew you were a fuckin' environmentalist,' said Steffan, chuckling maliciously

'Producer layer,' said Jake.

'What's that?' asked Volver, gazing across at the skinny Welsh boy who was still standing on the yard in front of the house.

'He'd be the producer layer,' said Jake.

'Naturally. He's hardly consuming a lot, right?' said Volver, laughing. 'Producing, yeah. Cronin.'

'Cronin?' asked Steffan, puzzled.

'Yeah - Cronin, I was told the dead guy's name was. The name suddenly came back to me.' He handed the knife back to Steffan. 'Yeah - Dave Cronin. That's it.'

At this, the seated Carla winced painfully, as if she too had been stabbed right through the gut. She rolled over onto her side, and began to cry her eyes out on the thread-bare carpet, whose loosened threads cut into her face like glass-paper, causing a pain she could not feel.

'Don't go letting on to you-know-who, though, right?' added Volver, more quietly now, and pointing at the first-floor window overhead, behind which Carla lay, and which he imagined was shut tight. 'Because those two had a sort of thing going for a couple of years, as I recall. Hit her really badly, it did, if truth be told.' Volver looked up at the sky and smiled at the memory. 'Then, within just a month or two she was living with me. Christ! Women, eh?'

My flapping, human burden held out before me, (a weight, incidentally, considerably less than that of my daughter Rhiannon,) I climbed the creaking stairs, and carried the old man through towards the bedroom that sat at the front of the house, its white door already wide open, as if welcoming us.

'Dyl, let me look for one last time, would you?' Tom whispered, his blood-red eyes staring up at me, and so I spun my feet round, and instead walked him across the hall and into the back-bedroom, clearly his daughter Carla's room, and where items of her clothing hung from hangers and hooks in all corners. From the window there we were both now able to look out and view the great, grey viaduct that straddled the wooded valley below us in all its morning glory. Never did it quite look as majestic as it did that day, I thought, or indeed the cream-coloured castle that sat perched on *Morlais Hill,* some way above and behind it.

'O.K., Dyl. Best now take me back to my own room at the front,' said Tom, and so I turned and carried him into the larger bedroom across the hallway. Placing the old man's slight, robed torso gently upon the bed before me, and easing his small, grey head back onto the double- pillow, I lifted a glass from the bedside table to offer him some water. He declined it and looked away.

'Take the Spaniard off the wall for me, would you Dyl?' he asked, pointing up at a large, colourful picture behind me. 'Old Francisco is me, you see, when all is said and done,' he added.

'I turned about and approached the large print that hung on the wall, and, lifting it high, brought it over to him.

'Place it here on the floor against the wall so that I can see it properly, there's a good man,' Tom told me. 'That's right, Dyl,' he said, approving my effort. 'Bless you, my friend. You see, now I can touch it.'

The old man lifted a trembling arm, and, turning his body round, used his thin, brown-speckled fingers to stroke the hirsute giant's broad, rippling shoulders, then opened his hand as wide as he could so as to span the crowd of men and women who appeared to be fleeing the rustic scene of fearful death. 'And the sheer power of it infuses me,' he whispered, 'and its message inspires me.' Soon after he looked up at me. 'And it is good,' he said, smiling.

Reading the title, I asked, 'And what message does the Goya Colossus give you, then, Tom?'

'Its message? Well, like me, Dyl, he has gripped his fear of death within his fist, and sqeezed hard, and wrung from it every drop of its terrifying power. And so, you see, mortal man is triumphant, and can leave this world unafraid, the moment that his God summons him.'

Inebriated, and perspiring profusely, Volver put his bottle down on the trestle-table next to the others, and handed a roll of bank-notes to Steffan, then smiled at Jake, who quickly realised that he would have to wait until a later date to get his cut from his governor and colleague in crime.

'You know, quite soon, now, boys, I plan to be going straght.' announced Volver.

'You - straight! As if,' said Jake, for whom the alcohol he had consumed seemed unquestionably to have gone to his head.

'No, you don't understand, buddy,' said Volver. 'I intend getting into *'legal highs'* big time, and I have plans to set up a network of shops across South Wales and the west of England in which to legitimately sell them all.'

'Yeah, *'legal highs'* is where the money's going to be made in the future,' said Steffan. 'That's what I heard anyway. Although I must admit we seem to be doing pretty well right now with the other kind.' He waved his roll of notes in the air and grinned broadly at the pair of them.

'Yeah, you guys seem to have done very well through your association with me,' said Volver.

'That's not even it, Boo,' Jake told the Afrikaner.

Volver stabbed him with a look. 'Boo! Why boo! Are you trying to scare me or something, bell-end?'

'Yeah man!' the boy retorted, smiling broadly, believing, mistakenly, that his harmless comment had been one that the Afrikaner was, in reality, amused by.

'Only scary thing about you is your pimply-ass face,' said Volver. The other two males laughed loudly at this, and Jake swiftly responded by flushing a rose colour, and turning round and walking back inside the farmhouse. As he retreated up the hall, sniffing repeatedly, he pondered how he had felt this way several times before, and almost always when his head was befuddled with drink, but, for some reason he couldn't fathom, this occasion seemed a lot worse. He felt he urgently needed to talk with someone about it, but since Steffan seemed to be treating him in much the same way that Volver was, he felt he was left with little choice.

Jake climbed the stairs and tried the wooden door at the end of the shadowy hall, but found it locked. He remembered why, then, pausing to consider the situation, he went to the hall-cupboard and collected the key that he knew was presently stored on a hook there. Then he went back and opened up the door, quickly locking it behind him, before approaching the grubby spot on the floor of the room where he saw Carla was lying. He prodded the toe of his trainer into her side. 'Hey, get up!' Jake exclaimed, moving round her prostrate torso so as to look into the girl's face with the window's light behind him. He quickly saw that she was sobbing, and he felt uneasy with the sight. 'I wanted to speak to you, Carla!' Jake began. You don't mind do you?'

'Carla rolled onto her back, and then, straining her stomach-muscles to the limit, sat up. Remaining reclined wasn't an option, she thought. She wasn't sure how much of a threat this skinny lad was to her on his own, but she wanted to be prepared for the worst, just in case.

' *'Don't walk on by me,'* said Jake, seating himself on the small table. 'That's not really what you called your latest single, is it?'

'Well, yes,' replied Carla, drying her eyes with the corners of her fists. 'What about it?'

'Hardly what you might call an edifying title is it?'

Carla gazed up at him. 'How do you mean?' she asked, puzzled.

'Well, isn't it just an unashamed appeal to folk passing by to fork out their hard-earned money on the single and buy it?'

She blinked momentarily, then looked up into the boy's eyes. 'You mean *'Don't walk on by me?'* ' she asked, ruminating. Then she suddenly announced in a comic voice. 'Don't walk on, mister! Buy me, please.' Carla chuckled once. 'Yes, I guess you're right. Though it went and reached number-five in The States, so I figure its title was probably justified.'

'And what number is it here?' asked Jake. 'In the U.K.?'

'It hasn't been released yet,' she told him.

'No?'

'No. That all very much depends - well -' Carla raised her knees up to her chin.

'On you getting out of here, and back up the smoke. To where - to where the action is.'

'Quite,' she replied. 'And do you happen to know when that might be?'

'The note hasn't even been delivered yet,' he told her.

'You mean - do you mean a ransom-note?' Carla asked, her mouth falling open.

'That's right,' he replied. 'Just a short one, but very much to the point, you know.'

'You mean *you* wrote it?' she asked him.

Jake licked his lips. His mouth was getting very dry. How the hell was she to know that? he asked himself. Jake feared that he might be telling the woman too much, but he recalled how, the night before, Volver had been so familiar with the singer in Jack's van that he, Jake, had quite naturally assumed that he could be too. But perhaps he was wrong on that score after all, Jake mused, biting into his lip. And worse, by what he'd just said, let slip, perhaps he had spoiled the Afrikaner's plan, whatever that might turn out to be.

Snatching a glance at the door-key he held in his fist, Carla said, 'You're Jake, aren't you?'

Jake nodded. Yes, he definitely felt he wanted to be known by her, he thought. Who wouldn't want it? This was Carla Steel, after all, he told himself. This was the singer off the TV. The girl who had enthralled *The Railway*-crowd without even trying, in fact, by deliberately *not* trying to. She had gripped them all as firmly, and as completely, as she had gripped the neck of her guitar. And she was lovely too; very lovely. No, there was no point in denying that, Jake reflected.

'My name's Carla,' the singer said. 'In truth it's Carla Davies, you know. That wouldn't be your name, would it?' She smiled at him. 'Davies, I mean. No?'

Jake felt his face getting uncomfortably warm, his hands begin to shake of their own accord, a sudden movement perhaps in the leg of his jeans, which made him lift one of his feet up onto the table for shame's sake. 'No, my surname's Haines,' he told her, then thought - was that wise? But the woman wanted to know who I was, and so I told her. That's no great shakes, surely. He licked his lips again. 'You know, it's easy to see why people like you,' he told her.

'Aw, what a lovely thing to say,' said Carla, smiling once again.

'Do you think so?' he enquired, smiling back, though not quite as masterfully.

'Yes, I do, Jake,' she told him. 'That, I believe, was a really *genuine compliment.*'

Jake paused to consider this. 'From the heart,' he said, grinning tenuously, scratching his cheek with the sharp prongs of the key.

'Yes, from the heart,' she told him, grinning too. 'At least I took it as such. And so rare are they these days that you could be sending unicorns out to find them.' A beaming smile this time.

Jake's face changed to a blank. 'Unicorns!' he stammered. 'I certainly don't believe in those.'

'Do you not?' asked Carla, not at all expecting that particular response. She thought fast. 'Then do you believe in - in monsters?'

'Well, dinosaurs, yes,' he responded. 'And pterosaurs, too, of course. Although a great, big, massive asteroid put paid to the whole lot of them.'

'O.K.,' she said, not having been aware of that fact. 'Then how about angels?'

Jake stared at the woman's lovely pink cheeks, and then at her soft, wavy, black hair, desiring to stroke it, and said, 'Human angels do you mean?' Carla could tell instantly from his spaced-out look that he was possibly thinking of her. 'I've seen a few human ones,' he told her.

'Girls?' she asked, raising her brows mischievously.

'Yes, girls,' he retorted. He considered this for a moment. 'And I've even told them so.'

'That they were angels?' asked Carla, beginning to understand. 'Have you really, Jake?'

The boy nodded, then looked down at his foot. 'But for some reason they never seem to think the same about me. You know, one day I intend to figure that out.'

Carla suddenly got this image of the boy doing it on a calculator, and so almost giggled and gave the game away. 'So do you believe in love, Jake?' she asked him, taking care not to make eye-contact.

'Not now,' he answered. 'Definitely not any more.'

Carla could see that the boy had been deeply hurt by someone in his past. 'Well, if you don't believe in love, Jake, then - then why don't you tell me what you do believe in,' she asked him.

'O.K., if you like,' said Jake. He looked up and gazed into her eyes. 'So I'll do that, shall I?' Carla nodded. The boy looked about him, then turned and stared out of the window that sat, uncurtained behind him. 'See that pale sphere up there?' he asked her, pointing into the distance.

'I do,' Carla answered, shifting her position on the floor a little, the better to see it. 'The sun, you mean?'

'Well, it's the moon, actually,' he told her. 'I know it's only the afternoon, but, trust me, that's the moon.' He chuckled. 'If it were the sun then I doubt we could just stare straight at it, right?'

'Yeah, I guess that's true, Jake,' she said. 'Silly me. Now I can see clearly that *it is* the moon.'

'And, do you know, Carla, that altogether twelve men have been there and walked across its stony surface?' he told her.

'Is that right?' she asked him. 'Twelve in total? Twelve Americans I guess, yeah?'

'That's right,' he said. 'In pairs, of course - they all landed in pairs each time. The third guy didn't get to land, you see.'

'Do you mean the pair landed with the third man on each mission going round and round the moon waiting for them to fire off from the lunar surface and link up with him?' she asked, smiling.

'That's right,' said Jake, more than a little surprised that she knew this. 'But do you want to know what one of the men said on his return?' he asked.

'Tell me,' said Carla. 'Because I think I can feel a song coming.' She smiled at him, but noticed that he didn't react to this jocular aside. No, he was gone - too far gone - Carla thought. Jake's mind was transported in time and in space, and Carla could see this clearly happening.

'Back then,' Jake told the singer, 'this one astronaut was said to have claimed he felt there had been a third man on the moon along with the two of them, when they were walking about there, you know, and doing their exploring and what-not.'

'Did he really?' asked Carla, tilting her head quizzically. 'You know, I never heard about that.'

'Well, he did,' said Jake. 'But of course he couldn't say anthing about this while he was on the surface, when he and his suited and helmet-ed companion were bouncing around, doing what they had been commanded to do. You could be court-marshalled for less than that, I'm sure.'

'Yes, I guess you could,' said Carla. 'But *you* believe him, don't you, Jake?' she asked.

'Well, yes, I do, as a matter of fact,' he replied, blinking, once again taken aback at how the famous singer he was conversing with could possibly know this.

'And who do you think that man was?' asked Carla. 'Who do you think that had to be who was walking around with them in that dusty, crater-ed, dreadfully hostile world out there?' She pointed up at the disc above his shoulder. 'Tell me, Jake.'

'*Tell* you?' said Jake. 'Well, you know, I've thought long and hard about who it might have been,' he said, 'even searched the internet for answers, but, do you know, I'm still clueless.'

Sensing her power over the boy, Carla got to her feet and walked across to him. She noticed that her head barely reached up to his chin 'Think Jake!' exclaimed Carla. 'Think! Go on!' Suddenly she reached out and gripped his hand in her own, and stared into his blinking eyes.

'I don't know,' said Jake. 'How *would* I know?' He gazed into Carla's eyes. 'But - but I guess you do, don't you?' he said. The girl nodded and smiled sweetly at him. 'Who was it, Carla?' asked Jake, his mouth open, his eyes wide and burning. 'You see, I've always wanted to know.'

'It was Jesus,' she told him.

I stayed, hand-in-hand, with Tom all day, waiting for the moment when, in his words, he would 'breathe his last.' He had insisted that I remain with him and 'see it through,' and I must say I felt privileged so to do. His daughter Carla had still not come home, but I knew that any attempt to ring her from there would have proved futile since the old man and I had already seen that her mobile-phone had been left lying on the table beside her bed. On a personal note, I was very sad that Carla was not there to assist her father at this time, to help, empathise with him, and love him. And yet I got the distinct impression from Tom that he knew full well that she would not be returning, and was looking to me to be the final companion that he conversed with in this life.

A loud bang sounded on the floor overhead. 'Who's that in your loft?' I asked the old man.

Silence followed. Tom, seeming to apprehend my words more slowly than before, asked, 'Did you hear someone, Dyl?' I nodded. 'Oh, then that'll be the boy next door, that will,' he told me. 'Young Chris. He and my daughter have been storing their - their weed up there, see.' He pointed to the end portion of a spliff in an ash-tray on his dressing-table. 'You know, unless we want the two of them to come to serious harm, then I'm afraid you shall need to climb up there, Dyl, and clean out what the boy's created.'

'My son has a farm in your loft!' I exclaimed.

'Carla told me that Chris has been cultivating his plants up in the loft of this house for a lot longer than I have been living here,' he told me. I shook my head in dismay at this news. 'But on the other matter, I'm afraid you're mistaken, Dyl.'

'Mistaken! How do you mean? About what?' I enquired.

'I mean about you being the boy's father,' Tom replied. 'Because I can assure you, Dyl, that you certainly aren't that.'

'Am I not!' I ejaculated. 'Then you - then I guess you must know who is then?'

The old man shook his head, smiled weakly, and stared up strangely into my eyes. 'You and I share a name, I believe,' he suddenly announced.

'No, I don't think - oh, you mean Thomas,' I replied. 'Yes, that's my third Christian name as it goes,' I told him. 'So yes, we do share a name. But tell me, Tom,' I enquired, 'how on earth did you know that?'.

'Will you clear the loft for me?' the old man asked. I smiled, then nodded. 'Then I think you'll find that the step-ladder is currently downstairs somewhere, possibly in the kitchen. I guess you can probably dispose of the plants over the fence out back. But as for all the equipment, well -'

'Don't worry your head about that, my friend,' I told him. 'I'll transport it all away in my van and later on take it to the dump. I will. I give you my word,' I added. 'Nobody will ever know a thing,'

His life's work now accomplished, his long day done, Tom, who had once visualized a tranquil, rural idyll stretched out ahead of him, knew that his God had had other plans. And now that it was coming to an end, the man certainly wasn't planning to fight it, fight against its dying light, as he recalled another Thomas had said, and many years before that man's own young flame had been extinguished, in a way drowned, in a cold room in a street off East River, New York.

Fight it? Why? And with what? he mused. That was back then. Not any more. No, Tom accepted that his hour had come. And very soon now he realised that he would leave behind him the shell that was his frail, tortured body, and rise up to the ceiling of the room, formless and invisible, to gaze down upon his modest legacy, and the kind, undoubting man who had comforted him when he most needed it, and so helped him to step away.

The sudden tapping sound echoed round the house. 'Tom - if you can hear me -' I said. Tom could hear me clearly enough, I felt, but most likely found that he could no longer look up. 'Hold on, brother,' I told him. 'It's Carla!' I said. 'There is someone knocking at the door. I'll just go down and let her in, O.K.? Just wait there now, old buddy.'

I rose from the bedside and let the old man's thin, blue-veined hand fall onto the silky, cool eiderdown that otherwise completely covered him. I made my way downstairs and approached the front-door. Through the glass panel I could plainly see that there was no one standing outside, but noticed a small brown envelope lying on the mat. I picked it up and opened the flap. '*Want her back live or in a box? Gonna cost you 500K in used or else too bad.*' the glued-on assortment of printed letters, that constituted the ransom-note, read.

I immediately opened the door and stepped out into the glaring southern sun. I noticed Jack Belt's old, green van trundling down the hill in the direction of the *Blue Pool*, but, apart from that, I could see nobody about. Someone must have come here on foot, I told himself, and is probably right this minute scuttling away across the viaduct. And so I rushed out onto the road and made my way down onto the old railway-halt, and then turned and walked back under the road-bridge to see what I could make out on the surface of the old track that spanned *The Seven Arches* and ran away from me towards the east. I could see that there wasn't a soul upon it, not even a solitary cyclist traversing *The Taff Trail* in either direction. But low in the distant sky beside the castle I saw the sphere of the full moon gleaming dimly down at me through a thin veil of clouds.

I felt I had no choice but to retrace my steps and go back. But when I returned to the front of the terraced house called *Coral* I noticed that the door was now wide open, and that the breeze, which now swept in from outside, and down the hallway to the kitchen and out through the open back-door, had toppled over a pot of dry flowers onto the carpet. I picked them up and replaced them in the pot, then saw a woman's skirted legs coming down the stairs to greet me, and naturally thought it must be Carla.

'Thank God you've come,' I bellowed. 'He needs you now more than ever.'

But instead a voice I knew so well said, 'The old man's gone, Dyl. He has passed away.'

'Anne!' I exclaimed. 'What are you -'

'You and I have an awful lot to do now, you know,' she told me

'Yes, I dare say,' I said, climbing the stairs, and joining her. Then I remembered something. 'But before we call a doctor I think we first need to clear out the loft.'

'Yes, we'll certainly need to do that, I know,' she replied, biting her lip. 'I was up there earlier on, and it's very like something out of *'Ali Baba And The Forty Thieves.'* I smiled back and nodded. 'But you know first we will have to dress the body.'

For a moment I considered this. 'Like - like the miners' wives used to do, you mean,' I said, 'when their menfolk got killed down the pit?'

'And as they did again when we were young in Aberfan, Dyl. Do you remember? But, thankfully, it's a task I've done many times before in *The Willows,* so don't concern yourself. Say - why don't you go and bring the step-ladder and a torch up here, and I'll go down and boil a kettle. You won't need to go back into him, Dyl. I've just done everything that was needed doing.'

'Anne, you're as wonderfully kind as you always were,' I told her, almost tearfully.

Ignoring my comment, and looking down at the cloth she held, she continued, 'And if Carla gets back, then leave her to me, will you? It's bound to be a terrible shock for the girl. But somehow, Dyl, I don't believe she's going to be coming back any time soon. What do you think?'

In the northern sky slate-grey clouds stacked, then shifted on the serrated, mountainous horizon. By this time the moon was long gone from sight, and the early evening breeze swirled noisily, cantering like a pony across the cobble-stone yard that lay just in front of the farm. Jack's van was back and was the only vehicle that was parked out front, Volver's Audi and his new four-by-four sitting snugly, and well hidden away, in the double-garage round the back.

The door of the farmhouse opened and out walked Jack, dipping his head as he walked, to count all the notes he had just been given, and then folding them in two so that they would slide easily into his front trouser-pocket where he buried them. Slidng the side-door of his iconic, green camper-van closed, he climbed into the driving-seat and drove away down the narrow track towards the main road, where, at the junction, a small, wooden sign on a post, bearing just a white-painted arrow and the words *Cwm Scwt,* were all there was to inform any passing motorist that a building of any kind, much less a farm, nestled there among the hillside's trees.

The falsetto voice of Leone Lewis soon called out Jack Belt's name, and the front-door of the farm-house opened a second time, but by now the man she sought was long gone. 'Oh, fuck!' Leone cursed, looking out, fixing a small paper-bag between her teeth so that she could tie a shame-saving knot in the satin robe she was barely wearing. Taking the bag in her hand again, she said, 'He forgot to take his drugs with him, the old twat.'

'Jack doesn't do drugs,' called a voice from behind her that was Steffan's. 'What were you thinking?'

'Oh, well. Do *you* want them?' she asked, turning.

'What the fuck *are* they?'

'Viagara,' she replied.

'What are you doing giving him them for?' bellowed Volver, suddenly appearing on the door-step beside her, and grabbing her by the arm. 'Jack doesn't need those, you air-head. He lives in an isolated house on his own.'

'Then all the more reason,' she answered. 'Look - the man's hardly a pensioner, is he?'

'Jack's seventy if he's a day,' said Volver. 'Jeez! What are you like girl, eh?'

'I'm sorry,' she told him. 'Look - I'm sorry, O.K.? How was I to know, babe?'

'Give 'em here,' commanded Volver. 'The boys will know someone who'll buy 'em. Failing that they can take them down that care-home they used to work at. The last load they took there caused a bigger stir than a Barry Manilow concert I heard. Now, Leone, piss off inside and get the girl upstairs undressed and showered, O.K.? Then get some fucking clothes on.'

The blond-haired girl did as she was asked, but with her head thrown back confidently, and a swift turn of the hips as she cast an impish glance behind her. Volver opened up the bag, examined the contents, and detached a single tablet from its sachet. He then snapped the tab into two separate halves between his fingers and swallowed one. 'Your things are all in the dryer, right?'

'My thongs?' called back Leone from the door-step, giggling.

'Your things, I said,' he replied. 'And be careful with Carla in the bathroom too. She's taken so much dope today she could easily fall over and hurt herself. Again, I mean.'

Cigarette in hand, Steffan stepped out and joined his older compatriot on the door-step. 'What time do you reckon we need to be up for tomorrow, boss?' he asked him.

'Let's think. Tomorrow is Tuesday. We're going to have to call up the old man early before he'll have worked out what to do about his dirty stop-out of a daughter. Then we'll wait here for the return call on the new mobile. I guess it's then that the real fun will start. But no worries. It's all going to work out fine, I promise you. Although I guess it's possible that one of you two might have to help the old fella get the money out of the bank. What do you think?'

'One of us!' exclaimed Steffan. 'How the hell do you figure that?'

'Hey. Don't go wetting yourself now,' the Afrikaner replied, raising his head. 'After all it might not come to that. But the geezer's a hell of a lot older and frailer than our Jack is, right? How is he going to collect the dosh from a bank on his own?'

'But we could use Jack again, couldn't we?' said Steffan. 'The old man trusts him, doesn't he? *And* he's got the transport.'

'Yeah, but I already paid Jack off,' said Volver. 'He's been told now he's finished with.'

'Well tell him again,' said Steffan. 'Or if you don't want to, I will. Look - you don't want to have me and Jake hanging round *Gloryhole,* for Christ's sake. Not now. His neighbour - Bed-pan Anne - knows the two of us from our time at *The Willows.* She works there, remember. No, it's definitely best if Jack does it. Unless, of course, the old man gets out of bed and goes and gets the money on his own.' Steffan chuckled and threw his cigarette-end onto the dusty surface of the yard, that stretched away to the trees before him.

Volver nodded, slapped Steffan on the shoulder, and went inside with him, shutting the front-door firmly behind him, and locking it.

Within seconds, and even before the light in the hall had been extinguished, a group of squirrels had run out from the cover of the trees, and began picking at the rubbish and remnants of food that had been thrown out front over the last few hours by the raucous band of newcomers. One of the squirrels had even retrieved the cigarette-butt that Steffan had thrown, but soon dashed it down once again on discovering that it was still alight.

Tom looked down from the top-corner of the only window in the room. He gazed below him and to his left at a large bee that was sitting perched on a short horizontal strip of the wooden window-frame. He knew that soon it was going to leap up insanely and attack the glass in its mad, insatiable quest to get outside. When it did so, albeit with a far greater volume of irascible frustration than he had imagined, Tom smiled inwardly at his newly-found power of prediction.

The bumble-bee sat and rested silently on the ledge just above the one that he had left. Tom could see that the black-and-tan creature was now located just a few short inches below the large opening gap from which it seemed incapable of sensing the in-rush of a breeze that he himself could see was clearly bending inwards the corner's cobwebs, and fluttering the curled edges of the flock wall-paper where it was no longer stuck down. Tom vowed that he would make sure he attended to this defect the next time he got the opportunity.

Tom decided to give his friend the bumble-bee a bit of a hand by pushing the window-frame down a little, and ever so gently, so that the insect wouldn't be unsettled, and could achieve its greatest desire and fly out. So he turned, and, facing the gap above the window, made the usual, necessary effort, but nothing happened. Tom tried again, but to no avail. Shocked beyond belief, he looked about him, and searched high and low, but however hard he tried, and wherever he looked, he quickly discovered that he possessed no arms with which to accomplish it; nor legs; nor a body of any kind, for that matter. As a last resort, Tom made an attempt to close his eyes, but, to his sheer delight, found that not a single lash now obscured his sight.

Suddenly sensing what had happened to him, Tom smiled, inwardly, and majestically, at his good fortune. His brain was whirring. A pertinent thought arrived. 'Then - I saw as through a glass darkly,' he told himself. 'Only now -'

But before he could complete his final words, the orange-and-black bee leapt up from its ledge and flew straight out of the window. For a brief moment Tom watched it soar off over the road and the corner of the green field across from the house, then hover briefly above the site of the old station-halt, where Tom saw that no train could possibly stop, and then, as if spotting the huge orange sun setting in the distance, soared away again along the course of the old railway-line that ran away west towards it. Amazed, and earnestly desiring the same, Tom leapt up and, passing swiftly through the same gap in the window, soared away there too.

The telephone in the lounge of *Coral* had been ringing for some time. But the old man who lay upstairs wasn't going to be getting out of his bed to answer it this evening, or going anywhere else for that matter, least of all to the bank. No, the lately-bathed shell that had been Tom Davies, and which, just a matter of hours earlier, had encased his very soul, now lay covered with a clean, white bed-sheet on his still, white-sheeted double-bed.

I had been up since five that Monday morning - a day that I rarely worked - and had, at last, manged to empty the loft completely of its rickety, rudimentary farm. The plants I had found there, and that I had painstakingly carried downstairs, were now all lying, confused and rootless, on their sides amongst the trees and the bushes on the steep, grassy slope that ran from the back of the house down to the river; and all the glass, and all the plastic and metallic trays and equipment that Chris had been using to cultivate his crop had been taken away for good and safely dumped at the council's recycling plant in Dowlais. And so now, with this done, I felt that Chris was safe from any possible threat, or accusation even, that might otherwise be made against him, once Anne and I had called up the authorities, which we still hadn't yet done, to report that a death had taken place in *Gloryhole*.

As I walked up the path from my parked van I could easily hear the telephone ringing inside. To me it seemed that it could have been ringing for some time, because I noticed that Anne was there waiting at the lounge-window of her home next-door, the curtains drawn, looking anxiously in my direction. I waved towards her, beckoning her to come and join me, unlocked the door, and, with her alongside me, made my way inside Tom's house once more.

Even before I got through the door, Anne dashed in to the lounge and sat on the sofa beside the phone. I glanced at her, and, without further delay, I picked up the receiver. We had each expected, and of course hoped, to hear Carla's voice on the other end of the line, but instead we listened as a gruff-voiced man proceeded to speak and, quite frankly, terrify the pair of us.

'Take down this number old man!' the stranger bellowed, clearly thinking that it was Tom who had answered the phone. Anne passed me a pen and paper and I hastily scribbled down the eleven digits he recited. 'If you don't ring back within the hour, then we'll know you don't care about what is going to happen to your daughter. But that's all right, geezer, because it so happens that we don't either.' That was all the man said before he ended the call, not even providing me with the chance to ask him any questions.

'God, that was cold!' said Anne.

'Yeah, short and sweet, but to the point,' I added. 'They would seem to have all the angles covered, don't you think? And it's even possible they knew about Chris's skunk-farm in the loft, and so knew how unlikely it was her dad would call in the police to conduct a search for Carla.'

'Yes, I see what you mean,' said Anne. Then grasping my hand, she added, 'Listen - you've done really well, Dyl, you really have. I feel sure Tom would have been very proud of you for all your kind efforts. And you were there with him at the end too, weren't you, and so at least he had someone present to unburden himself to, and to share his fears.'

'Which reminds me, Anne,' I said. 'Before Tom died he told me something that was, to say the least, a shock for me. Though how on earth he knew about it, to even tell me, I've no idea.'

'What was it?' asked Anne, her mouth falling open.

'Well, he told me that your boy Chris wasn't my son after all. Say - how about that?'

'Did he really say that?' she asked, plainly astonished. 'My God!' She paused and stared down at her lap to consider this. 'And did he - did he say who he thought I'd been - I'd been, you know, carrying on with? Because, apart from you, Dyl, I don't believe there was ever anyone.'

'Anne - are you sure about that?' I asked her.

'Yes, of course,' she replied. 'Well, apart from a bit of fun I once had at work around Christmas one year, or maybe it was New Year. It might have been.'

'Oh. With Gareth, was it?' I enquired.

'How the hell would you know that, Dyl?' she replied.

'Well, I didn't,' I told her. 'But I do now, girl.' I grinned mischievously.

'Oh, hell!' exclaimed Anne, getting up and walking away from me, and then down the hall into the kitchen. 'And I thought - I stupidly thought I'd never have to tell a soul about that.'

I got up and trailed after her. 'The person you actually need to tell, love, is Gareth,' I said.

Anne slowly poured herself a glass of water from the tap, sipped some of it, then spun round to face me. '*And* Chris,' she said. 'I need to tell him just as much. He thinks you're his dad, you see. That's what Drew and I have just told him, anyway.'

'Well, now you're going to have to tell him he isn't my son,' I said. 'And do you know what? You can be sure he'll be overjoyed when he discovers that, after all, Rhiannon *isn't* his sister.'

'Look - Dyl. I don't mind telling the boy that,' she went on, 'but telling him that one of my colleagues at work is his real father - well, that is going to be a real block-buster for him to take, don't you think?'

'Nevertheless it has to be done,' I told her. 'And then, when you've done that, you will need to talk to Gareth.'

'Oh, hell's bells!' she exclaimed. 'And what if he doesn't believe me?'

'Look - don't go fearing the worst,' I told her. 'It'll be fine. But then there's Drew, of course.' I watched, as Anne dipped her head low and covered it with both hands. I smiled at her child-like timidity. 'You know, love, I reckon this might have to be a job for D.N.A. in the end,' I said.

'And maybe for Jeremy Kyle, too,' Anne added, spinning round in a full circle, and uttering, at the top of her voice, by far the most vulgar curse imaginable to womankind, plainly visualizing the future prospect of what she felt her immediate family would most likely make of it all.

CHAPTER 22

The crazies that the Welsh singer-songwriter encountered in the pubs of west London eyed her at first like schoolboy butterfly-collectors might eye a *'Painted Lady'* or a *'Camberwell Beauty'* on the wing. And Carla wasn't usually displeased that they had, and quite often was not averse to calling for a drink at the bar for such admirers, or even, on occasions, asking them to join her at her table, if they weren't already inebriated, or looked the type to provoke her unduly with innocent-sounding conversation about music, or politics, or Wales, or women's rights. Carla couldn't count the number of times she had fallen foul of this sly tactic, and frequently felt regretful of her youthful naivety, and her predictable, helplessly ingrained, gregarious nature.

Rarely questioning her habitual use of alcohol as a daily shock-absorber, and recreational drugs as sleep-defying stimulants, too often for Carla the webs of the past night's dreams and follies were recalled, and painfully disentangled, amidst a drawn-out, wakeful reverie that usually extended way past the point when the hands of her digital wall-clock had crossed the vertical plane. And, once the stinging rays of the afternoon sun had managed to slide past the ends of her thick bedroom-curtains, she invariably found herself forced to turn her body round in the bed, and occasionally even to rise and face courageously what little was left of the capital's day.

Well, musicians, artists and writers are not exactly an abstemious lot, thought Carla, one reason obviously being the acute mental pressure that goes hand in hand with the act of creation. Since the singer-songwriter's basic raw materials were, more often than not, her own personality, her own thoughts, emotions, and state of mind, she found that she could not be easily shut away from her work, as say a scientist could close behind her the laboratory door, or a lawyer might lock up her briefs for the night, perhaps in her knicker-drawer, or her boyfriend's even. She giggled at the schoolgirl humour involved in this last thought.

And very soon Carla was to come to the conclusion that her situation was fast becoming much worse, indeed intolerable. Four individuals eking out their existence in a flat built for two was always going to be far from ideal, but now, as Leila grew older, and therefore bigger and more demanding, the more hampered Carla felt in a creative sense, and the more her thoughts seemed to turn to the notion of moving out, if only to give her two adult friends a lot more space. But the notion of Carla proceeding in this way was not lightly countenanced by the others, for self-centred reasons, she felt, rather than for financial, or indeed any other justifications.

As far as men were concerned, at that time it was a wonderfully talented busking musician called Dave Cronin who seemed to float Carla's boat for her, she recalled. Though suffering dreadfully from a demeaning tic, which seemed to disfigure almost every conversation the young man had with members of the public, Carla considered the singer-guitarist both a hunk and a genius - that combination which women, especially her type of woman, often found irresistible.

The two years that followed, spent sharing Dave's humble garden-flat in Chelsea with him, were, for the Celtic song-bird, a time of love as well as good fortune; after all, the pair seemed to complement each other in a whole host of ways, not least in their addictions. And so, whenever they chose to consider their prospects for the future, they unsurprisingly looked no further than to each other. And then one night Dave went out to get a fix, but failed to return home, and with the whereabouts of the amiable singer with Tourrettes being a complete mystery, and a body never being discovered, Carla's ideal life was brought to a swift and abrupt end.

It was around this time that Abram Kronfield came to intervene in Carla's life once more, and, within weeks, the singer's magnetic pole became shifted around half a degree west, or, more accurately, to the handsome, sleek South African's roof-top, riverside penthouse just a short distance from the south side of Hammersmith Bridge, and, unbeknown to Carla, within but a stone's throw of the scene of Dave's callous murder.

And so the autumn of 2006 proved to be a climacteric in Carla's young life. Sharing a home once again, and, by definition, a double-bed, with a member of the opposing gender, at a time when her notoriety was soaring, and the public demands on her time and person had reached the sort of pinnacle that would send the average human into depression, proved more than even the feisty young singer from Wales could handle. Quite soon valium began to appear on her shopping-list almost as frequently as did face-wipes and marmalade. And then, suddenly finding herself pregnant for the first time in her life, it was hardly surprising that the poor girl ceased her recording and touring completely, and, pulling her phone from its socket, cracked up big time.

'I'm not going to do it!' shrieked Leone. 'I've been a blonde ever since I was twelve. Why the bloody hell are you trying to make me dye my hair?'

'But you won't be dyeing it, sugar, just washing that blasted colour out,' Volver told her. 'Look - the roots are going already, can't you see that? And didn't you once tell me you were a natural brunette?'

'At one time, baby, yeah. But I detest black and I always have. My entire bloody family are black. Even the tom-cat and my dad's dying Labrador were black. Though he's dead now.'

Volver gripped the girl's arm, opened the kitchen-door, and silently led her over to the sink, where Steffan stood waiting, having already prepared the lotion. 'Didn't you say last night you loved me?' the South African asked her.

'And didn't you say the same?' she countered, smiling thinly, but trembling like a leaf.

'But you see it's something that I really want you to do for me, sugar' he continued. 'And you know - you already know - I'll make it well worth your while.'

The girl stared into Volver's eyes for a few moments then winced. 'All right, then.' Leone told him. 'But if you find you don't like it, babe, promise me you'll let me dye it back, yeah?'

Projecting a taut smile, Volver nodded, then manoeuvred into position the squat, busty girl he still gripped onto, so that Steffan, resplendent now in a yellow, plastic apron and green marigolds, could force her head down into the basin which he had carefully prepared in the kitchen-sink, and, with his stubby, nail-bitten fingers and thumbs working furiously, attack with real venom the poor girl's two-tone, wire-like, blond tresses.

'If you'd - ouch! - if you'd only told me over the phone, babe, I'd have - I'd have got it done for you last week in *Gaston's*,' Leone stammered loudly, between head-wrenching jerks and repeated gasps of pain. She then let out a drum-bursting scream as Steffan suddenly turned on the cold tap, instead of the hot, in his understandable haste to finish up the despicable task.

'What the hell was that?' said Carla in her locked room on the floor above, where she was sitting, cross-legged, on the edge of the bed.

'Sounded like a banshee,' said Jake from his position by the window, from where he had long been staring out at the night-sky. 'Or maybe the aliens out there have finally landed at last.'

Carla shook her head at his odd remark. 'I understand the Americans are sending a robot to Mars soon,' she told him. 'And a few months ago they asked my people would I be interested in becoming the very first singer whose voice would get to be broadcast on another planet.'

'Wow!' ejaculated Jake, spinning round to face her. 'What an honour that must have been.'

She smiled back at the boy, seeing how passionately he seemed to regard what was, for her, simply a boring topic. 'But of course I said no,' she told him.

'You said no! But why would you do that?' exclaimed Jake, his eyes wide and gleaming.

'Well, for a start, I didn't require the publicity that the stunt offered half as much as some others probably did,' Carla told him.

'Really?' he asked, considering her comment. 'O.K.'

'But far more importantly, since everyone knows there's nobody living on the surface of Mars to hear it,' she went on, 'then obviously no sound would actually occur, would it? You understand that, right? A friend of mine taught me that.' Jake looked down, then nodded. 'So, you see, to my mind, letting them do it seemed about as pointless as - oh, I don't know -'

'As recording your next single in the shower?' asked Jake.

'Well, yes, that's a pretty good analogy,' Carla told him, smiling. 'Or maybe doing my one and only live gig this year on a wet Sunday night at *The Railway* pub in *Gloryhole*, a venue your average music critic would understandably be too terrified to even venture to, and where the only news-report covering it would most likely appear in the once-weekly *Merthyr Express*.'

'That was a great idea of Volver's, though, don't you think?' said Jake.

'What was?' asked Carla, glaring at him. 'What was a great idea?' She watched as Jake suddenly turned round and walked back over to the window, his head dipped this time, and not really looking out at all. 'Are you saying - are you telling me that the charity gig for Amy was - was Volver's idea, then? Oh my God! Oh my Great God! Yes, of course it was,' she yelled. The singer suddenly covered her dark head with her hands. 'And how stupid of me not to have seen that. Yes. It was by far the easiest way that he could have set me up for - for this. What a slimy bastard, eh? He took advantage of my kindness - god-dammit - knowing all the time how I knew and - and respected the singer so much, and knowing full well that I could never turn it down.'

Jake spun round and stared down at the woman, who was, by now, lying crumpled up on her side on the bed. 'Please promise me you won't tell him, though, Carla,' he pleaded, slowly moving closer to the bed, then parking his bottom on the very edge of the mattress.

'Tell him what?' asked Carla, suddenly sitting up, a pillow grasped tightly in her hands. 'That you just dropped this bombshell on me?' She pondered this carefully for several seconds, then responded. 'Listen - don't worry yourself, Jake, I won't.' She moved her body round so that she could sit alongside him. 'And what does it matter anyway that I know about it? Since there's precious little I can do about it either way, wouldn't you say? If the wicked devil means to kill me, then I guess he's going to do it anyway.'

'But he's unlikely to do that,' said Jake. 'After all, to Volver this is just a money-making exercise. Nothing more, nothing less. Trust me.'

'I would,' she told him, 'I would, Jake, except that - except that by now he probably realises that I know how it was him who murdered someone I knew less than a year ago. Someone very, very dear to me, as it goes. Yes, I'm absolutely certain the guy must realise that.'

'Who *was* that?' enquired Jake.

'A girl, Jake. Not many years younger than me, if you want to know,' she told him. 'Yet another poor victim of Abram Kronfield's intricate web of induced - no, enforced - narcotic addiction, and subsequent human helplessness, that at one time had included myself.' She dragged her crumpled handkerchief across her weeping eyes, then continued. 'But you know a very strange thing happened in here - in this very room - last night, Jake,' she told him.

'What was that?' enquired Jake.

'Well, I dreamed that the lovely young girl with the tight, black plaits walked right in here, bold as brass, in her red leather jacket and her Doctor Martins, and asked me where her lovely daughter was.' Carla bit sharply into her top lip, then broke down sobbing. As she did so, the young man sitting alongside her, (who was fast beginning to seem to her like the only friend she had left in the whole world,) put his arm round her shoulder to comfort her, and began to rock her gently back and forth. Quite soon, however, Jake was forced to turn his head away from her for fear that Carla might see just how deeply her sad and heart-rending news had affected him.

Drew brought in the steaming teapot from the kitchen and placed it on the table beside the family's Sunday tea-set. Then, through lack of seats rather than marital fidelity, he carefully parked his bottom down on the arm-rest of the easy-chair his wife Anne was occupying, her hands gripping tightly the paper-tissue she was using when the conversation regarding her deceased neighbour and his famous, but missing, daughter became too harrowing, or involved her having to recall to mind, and then to relate to everyone what she and I had gone through in the last twenty-four hours.

'Wow! That's some powerful brew you've made there, Sir,' said P.C.Ben Thomas, sniffing the rising steam like a mountain hare. 'I guess it's one of those new-fangled fruit teas is it?'

Anne and Drew turned towards each other and exchanged quizzical glances that suggested they couldn't understand what the young, bottle-blond officer was talking about. '

'Yes, it's bouquet is not unlike that of a certain plant we recently thought your boy might have been cultivating here,' said Sergeant Foley, with a thin smile. 'Right, Thomas? Look - I'll just have a cup of milk myself, if it's not too much trouble, Mrs. Cillick.'

Anne winced a little, but ceased pouring out tea for everyone, and poured the officer a cup of milk instead, and placed it on the table in front of him. 'Here you go, Sergeant,' she said, 'though I can't think what you find unusual about our *PG Tips*. You know, I imagine it's possible you brought the queer smell you mentioned in with you. It happened once before, as I recall.'

Ignoring the woman's implication, Sergeant Foley threw back his head and eagerly drank up all the milk in the cup, which he then placed back on its saucer, and, with his large, creased handkerchief, carefully wiped away the cream moustache that he knew he had to have deposited across his top lip.

'Now that Mr. Davies' body has been taken off to the morgue, Dyl,' Sergeant Foley said, gazing in my direction, 'and you and Mrs. Cillick here have been kind enough to describe for us in full the circumstances surrounding the old man's death, perhaps you might like to show us the note that got pushed through their letter-box. You do have it with you, don't you?'

'Anne has it,' I told him.

'Yes, it's upstairs,' said Anne, rising. 'I'll just pop up to get it, shall I?'

I wasn't sure why, but I stood up too, and walked over to the door as Anne went out into the hall and began climbing the staircase to retrieve it. The strange sound of scurrying bodies on the upper floor took me somewhat by surprise, and so I quickly followed her up to the landing, where we soon discovered her son Chris, accompanied by my red-faced daughter Rhiannon, sitting, huddled together on the carpeted step, holding hands, and plainly listening in to the conversation that had been going on for some time in the lounge below.

'What on earth do you two think you're doing?' exclaimed Anne, shaking her head about.

'Just listening,' replied Chris. 'I can do that, can't I, Mam? I do live here, you know.'

'Well why don't the two of you come down and join us if you want?' she asked. 'You've got nothing to fear from the police have you?' There was a pause during which the two youngsters gazed at each other. 'Or have you?' asked Anne. 'Look - tell me Chris. What have you done?'

'I've done nothing, if you want to know,' he told her. 'But - but there's something in the corner of our lounge I suggest you move to another room when you go back down.' At this Rhiannon smirked, and began giggling, and very soon Chris found that he couldn't help but follow her lead.

'Aisht now! Look I haven't got time for all this silliness,' Anne told him, as she disappeared into a bedroom to fetch the ransom-note from her bedside drawer.

'What is it in your lounge that needs moving?' I asked the boy quietly.

'It's the potted plant,' replied Chris. 'Mam thinks it's from the rainforest.'

'Well, it is in a way,' said Rhiannon, grinning. 'It's certainly not native to Britain anyway.'

I shook my head at the pair of them, realising what sort of plant they must ne referring to, and why it was that the police-officers had stunned Anne by questioning her choice of scented tea.

'It's not in here!' bellowed Anne, soon emerging onto the landing once again and staring at me in desperation. 'Somebody must have moved it.'

'Chris!' I said, eye-balling the boy. 'Would you happen to know anything about this?'

Rhiannon suddenly fetched the note from the pocket of her jacket and handed it to me. I smiled back my gratitude, and then opened it up to check that it was what we were after. Happily it was, and so I passed it over to Anne, who edged past the young couple and made her way downstairs again.

'We happen to know who wrote it, Dad,' said Rhiannon.

Plainly shocked, Chris turned and stared at her, then up at me. 'But we're not going to tell the police,' he added, 'because - well, well because.'

'Because we don't believe he's the one to blame for Carla's kidnap,' Rhiannon told me. 'We think he may have been forced to write it. You see, he's just not that kind of boy at all, really.'

'Man,' said Chris.

'Man,' said a surprised Rhiannon, shutting her eyes and wincing. 'Oh, hell!'

Frowning, and shaking my head at their hapless folly, I turned and walked down the stairs, and made my way back to Anne's lounge. I then walked into the corner of the room and stood in front of the potted plant that Chris had referred to, in an attempt to conceal it from view. But it wasn't long before the distinctive odour it emitted began to fill my own nostrils and affect my brain, and I was suddenly forced to sneeze out loud. I nevertheless lifted the plant-pot, and, turning the knob with my left hand, carried it out of the door and down the step into the Cillicks' kitchen. But finding the back-door of the house locked, and not knowing where the key might be, I placed the cannabis-plant securely on the kitchen-table and returned to the lounge, on this occasion to resume my original seat much closer to everyone else.

'Have either of you got any idea who brought this note to the door?' asked P.C.Thomas, turning the paper over to examine it properly.

'No,' I replied. 'There wasn't a single soul out on the road when I collected it, and the only passing motorist I saw nearby was Jack Belt, doing the usual rounds in his noisy, green van.'

'Jack Belt, do you say?' said Foley, pouting as he contemplated this, then scribbling the name down in his open pocket-book.

'Yeah, but he's harmless, he is,' I told him. 'I can't for the life of me imagine that Jack Belt, of all people, could be involved in any of this.'

However the strange looks and the prolonged silence that followed my remarks suggested I should perhaps reconsider this.

'He's no longer just involved in, what you might call, *'the black market'* these days, I'm afraid,' said young Thomas, rubbing his face in his hands. 'We've cut the old fella a load of slack in that regard for a number of years now.'

'He's right, Dyl,' said the sergeant, smiling. 'My wife certainly couldn't manage without the cheap fags from the continent she gets off him every week. But ever since the Cambornes have been in power up in London, and money round here is tighter than ever, we've noticed he's started keeping company with some of the young lads in the valley who are dealing drugs.'

'They live over in Pant and Dowlais mainly,' Thomas added. 'Say - you live over that way, don't you, Dyl?'

'I do,' I told him. 'But listen - I hope you're not suggesting -'

'Ben - button it!' the sergeant bellowed at him. 'Sorry, Dyl. The boy's so keen to hoover up all the narcotics round hereabouts it wouldn't surprise me if he confiscated your *Sanatogen* next.' He glared at the young man who quickly flushed up. 'Anyway, now that we know that Carla Steel is definitely missing we can't afford to leave a single stone unturned, right? First of all, I can guarantee you that our old friend Jack Belt will very soon be coming in for questioning.

Do you mind if I use your toilet, Mrs. Cillick?' the sergeant suddenly asked Anne, getting up.

'Not at all, officer,' she replied. 'There's one through the door there, just off the kitchen.'

The officer disappeared out of the room, and I stared across at the unorthodoxly seated Drew, wondering how any man could remain so incredibly quiet in the supposed comfort of his own home. I began to sense that it might well have something to do with me, and specifically with the fact that one of his wife's old flames had seemed to have unexpectedly come back into her life. But whether this was true or not, I can't say that I felt at all sorry for the man. After all, I posed the man no threat, and so I felt he could, and should, have conducted himself far more confidently and hospitably. Unless, of course, I thought, his wife had gone and told him about what happened many years before between her and Gareth at the care-home around Christmas-time. Yes, that could be the cause of it, I told myself, smiling.

Sergeant Foley soon returned to the room, thanked us all for our kind cooperation, and invited his younger colleague to accompany him to the front-door. I wasn't able to make out most of the small talk that the police-officer shared with the Cillicks out in the hall, nor did I try to, but I became rather alarmed when I did manage to hear the grey-haired sergeant tell Anne, 'Might I suggest you throw it over the back-fence with all the others, Mrs. Cillick, before you find you have the law come calling.' With this the grey-haired, old fox smiled at Anne, and walked out of the front-door to join his younger colleague inside the black squad-car. 'Do you know, Ben,' I heard him tell the younger officer as he climbed in, 'I think it's high time we called up Dawson in the smoke, to come down here again and help us out.'

'But will he want to come, I wonder?' asked Ben. 'On account of the last time we took him to a murder-scene just up the road there, that turned out to be just a tump-ful of medieval corpses?'

'No, he'll come,' Sergeant Foley told him, grinning. 'After all, the guy's been trying to pin something on the great Carla

Steel for almost a decade now. And a little matter of a kidnapping is unlikely to deter him in that respect, I bet.'

'O.K., if you say so,' said Ben grinning back at his superior and starting up the engine.

'Hang on a minute!' the sergeant suddenly told his young colleague, before climbing back out of the car. 'Mrs. Cillick - can you tell Dyl I want a word with him,' he told her.

Hearing this, I walked down the path and joined the sergeant beside his car.

'There's something I forgot to tell you, Dyl,' said Foley.

'What's that then?' I asked him.

'You must know that your Gwen has a daughter much older than Rhiannon, yes?' he said.

'Of course,' I replied. 'She's called Sarah, and she lives in London. God, she must be around forty, now, I guess, though we haven't seen the girl for ages now.'

'Really?' said Foley. 'Then it might interest you to know that she and Carla Steel were lovers up until quite recently. Shared a flat and all. Even brought up a little girl together, I understand.'

'What! Are you being serious?' I asked the sergeant, stunned beyond measure.

'Never been more so as it goes,' he said. 'A little black girl called Leila, so I gather. Her real mother got sent to jail for a stretch, and even got herself sent back there again. Well, soon after being releasd she disappeared, and was later found dead, you see. Her decomposed body was only discovered just a few short months ago, concealed in a locked coal-hole in west London.'

'Well I never!' I said, shaking my head. 'And where's the little girl now?' I asked him.

'Social Services took Leila away with them initially,' he replied. 'But I gather she's back living with Sarah in their flat in Fulham again these days.'

'Thank God for that,' I said. 'I guess I'll need to get my Gwen to contact Sarah now, yes?'

Foley nodded, then added, 'But listen, Dyl - you'll never guess who helped us find the body of the mother of the child that your Sarah and Carla Steel have been playing parents to?'

I thought for a moment, then pointed towards the door of *Coral* just behind me. 'Something tells me it was the old man here,' I told him.

'Blimey! You've got it in one, Dyl,' said Foley, turning towards his partner in the car, his mouth wide open. 'But how on earth would you know that?'

I said nothing in reply, but simply stepped away from the car, and let Foley climb back inside again. Waving once, I stood and watched the pair of officers drive off.

Not feeling able to trust the August weather half as much as Chris did, Rhiannon insisted on taking her cagoule along, and, after tossing it onto the back-seat of the yellow Fiesta, she climbed into the driving-seat and drove her on-off boyfriend and her off along the road that ran due north out of Pant.

'Your cagoule! Why the heck are you bringing that along?' Chris soon asked her, as they sped past the *Pant Cad Ifor* pub and then the extensive, packed car-park that served the narrow-gauge railway station. 'How do you figure you're going to get wet today of all days?' He shook his head at her. 'And what's this music you're playing? I didn't know you liked rap.'

'It's Radio-One,' Rhiannon told him, quickly reaching her hand down and switching it off. 'You know, there are some CD's in the drawer there. Get one out and put it on if you like.'

Chris opened the dash-board drawer and found sitting there four discs which he took out and inspected. '*Twenty-one*' and '*Nineteen*,' he told her scowling. 'What happened to Twenty, then?

'What do you mean?' Rhiannon asked him, smiling.

'Well, I always buy raffle-tickets in strips of three, you see. Don't you?'

'They're *Adele*, silly,' Rhiannon told him. 'There's a *Marina* and at least one *Carla* in there too, if I'm not mistaken.'

Chris took the Carla Steel disc out of its case and popped it into the player. Carla's voice immediately started singing the title-track. He listened attentively then gazed across at his companion. 'Hey this is crazy, don't you think?' he asked.

'What is?' enquired Rhiannon, changing down to second-gear to negotiate the steep slope that descended past the tinkling freshwater spring to their right, (which poured off the steep slope then passed under the road,) towards the low, stone railway-bridge that sat ahead of them.

'Well, here we are, venturing out, intent on finding the kidnapped Carla Steel, and she's clearly encouraging us in song along the way.' Chris grinned from ear to ear.

Rhiannon suddenly turned and gazed into Chris's face just as she drove her car into the darkness and sought to negotiate the awkward double-bend that sat beneath the bridge, before emerging once again into the dappled sunlight that lay beyond. But, having forgotten to sound her horn on approach, she was quickly confronted by a large black van that was approaching the bend from the opposite direction, and which very nearly collided with them. In panic Rhiannon steered to the left, and all but hit a large tree which stood at the junction with the narrow, tributary road that descended left, towards the river. The music ceased as the Fiesta came to a sudden halt, and the pair were thrown forward in their seats. Seconds later, and gazing about them in wonder, the couple soon agreed that a serious accident had been narrowly averted.

'What do you think you're doing!' Chris screamed. 'You very nearly killed us there!'

'I know -'

'I know too,' said Chris, mouth open wide.

'No, you don't understand,' said Rhiannon. 'I know, at least I believe I know, where Carla could be - *right now*.'

'You - you know where she could be!' stammered Chris. 'What are you - some sort of clairvoyant or something?'

'No, I'm not saying that,' she told him. 'I'm nothing like her father, Chris, you know that.'

'And I'm glad to hear it,' he said, taking Rhiannon's trembling hand in his, and stroking it lovingly, recalling how it was only very recently that she had returned once again into his life, into his arms, his heart. 'So tell me, sweet, where is it you think Carla might be then?' he asked, lifting with an index-finger the curly, red strands of hair that the car's jolt had suddenly formed into a rudimentary fringe across Rhiannon's forehead and nose, then tenderly running the adjoining thumb along her pale, perspiration-speckled, brow.

Rhiannon stared into her lover's eyes and said, '*Candice Farm.*'

Having stopped the car on the narrow road that ran along the crest of the great dam, just short of Pontsticill village, the young couple dashed across to the wall, where Chris effortlessly lifted Rhiannon up onto its summit, then climbed up it himself to join her there. The pair soon sat with their legs dangling over the edge, and, facing due north, surveyed the gleaming surface of the vast lake that stretched out for close to four sinuous miles before them, after that almost seeming to merge into the golden, serrated skyline that was *The Brecon Beacons* proper.

'But even if she were there we don't have a clue where *Candice Farm* might be,' said Chris. 'It could be anywhere out there,' he told her, pointing. 'On the bare hills, or hidden among the forests, or in the valley on either side, or behind us even.'

'But it couldn't be behind us, Chris,' said Rhiannon. 'You see, in the song she says that it's 'halfway to town,' right? And as the town was almost certainly *Merthyr*, since she went to the same school that we did, then if we could discover where her home was, then we could maybe pin-point the area that we ought to focus our search on. Chris - what are you doing?'

'Doing a search on-line,' he told her, staring intently at the tiny screen of his mobile-phone. 'There's only mention of '*Candice Farm*' on here as a song, babe, and none of the farms mentioned with that name are to be found in this part of the country.'

'Listen - Chris. Find out where her home-village was, if you can,' said Rhiannon, looking over his shoulder. 'I'm sure it has to be on there, she being such a big star and all.'

'*Talybont-on-Usk*' said Chris. 'Her father's home where she grew up was in *Talybont-on-Usk*.' He looked up. 'God, I used to go camping by the canal in Talybont when I was in Scouts,' he announced. 'I never knew she came from *there*.'

'And how many miles is that from here?' asked Rhiannon.

'From Merthyr, you mean,' Chris corrected her, since we've established that that's what the song says. Well this web-site claims it's around fourteen miles, so that means the farm she named the song after -'

' - which almost certainly doesn't have that name today, by the way -'

' - and quite probably never did have,' Chris added, 'is around five or six miles from where we are sitting right now.'

The couple looked up at the breathtaking vista before them. Chris turned his head and gazed to his left at the tower that stood, like the great, brown head of a wading bird, in the midst of the dark, still water, and recalled the night some months before when he had met Carla there to sell her his weed. He then turned and gazed at Rhiannon, and told himself that there were plainly things she need never know about him, especially if, this time, he intended to hold onto her love.

'Do you know that there's a little village down there somewhere, that new History-teacher told us,' Rhiannon informed him. 'Buried deep beneath the water, since the day, around a century ago, when they flooded this valley for water for homes and industries in the Valleys and Cardiff.

'Oh, I get it now,' said Chris. 'That's why you brought your waterproof coat along, right? You mean to swim down and search for Carla down there.' He arched his brows and smiled at her.

Rhiannon slapped him gently on the shoulder then smiled at the notion. Becoming more serious again, she said, 'Still her body could easily be swirling about in this lake somewhere.' Her pretty mouth fell open as she contemplated this. 'Chris - just imagine that!' she exclaimed.

'You know, Rhiannon, she once told me that her brother Will drowned while swimming in here many years ago,' said Chris. 'And, what's more, she holds herself totally responsible for it.'

'What *did* happen?' asked Rhiannon.

'Carla told me he cooked her a meal on a primus stove, and, because she didn't like the taste of it, and sulked about it, he chose to teach her a lesson about gratitude and selflessness, and ate her portion of the meal along with his own. Later that afternoon, while swimming alone somewhere out there, he sadly got his foot caught in an underwater branch of a floating tree, and, despite all his best, most strenuous efforts, and possibly on account of the amount of food he'd consumed, couldn't free himself, and so drowned.'

'Oh my God! How utterly awful!' said Rhiannon. 'What - what did Carla do?'

'There was little she could do,' he told her. 'Carla was only about eight at the time, you see, couldn't swim, and obviously panicked, and somehow ended up falling down and knocking herself out. Well, by the time help finally arrived, and they revived her again, Will was long dead.'

'Oh, that's dreadful,' said Rhiannon. 'And Carla such a young girl as well.' Her eyes narrowed as she considered this. 'But you know, Chris, I think that might go some way to explaining the theme of another track on her debut album, the title of which escapes me at the moment.'

'You know, I don't really want to know, babe,' Chris told her. You see I imagine Carla has most probably been haunted by the guilt of what happened here right through her entire life. I know *I* would have. And to be honest, could anyone really blame her for experimenting with the array of drugs she got into while trying to develop for herself a career in music. You know, Rhi, I feel this whole business is just so sad that all I want to do is simply set off and find her. And you know I'd go right this second if only I knew which direction to take.'

'Clutching her lover's arm, and placing her head on his chest, Rhiannon said, 'Well, there is only the one main road that we *can* take to drive towards Talybont, Chris,' she told him. 'So let's just drive along it and see where it takes us, shall we?'

'Yeah, O.K. That's a sound idea,' Chris told his lover, kissing her softly on the cheek. 'Only let me drive the car this time, would you, babe? Look - I know I haven't passed my test yet, but you must admit I've actually been driving cars a lot longer than you have.'

Rhiannon gazed into Chris's eyes. 'Well O.K., then,' she said. 'But I'll need to pop the L-plates on just in case, yeah?'

'Just in case of what? No, please don't Rhiannon,' Chris pleaded. 'Who the hell is going to stop me up here, do you reckon?' he asked pointing along the lake shore. 'A fisherman? A lumberjack? A sheep farmer? Or one of the sheep, perhaps?'

Knowing he had won the argument, Chris jumped down onto the road, reached up his strong arms, then snatched up and carried Rhiannon, kicking, but definitely not screaming, back towards their little yellow car. Within seconds the young couple had slammed the doors and set off in it in the direction of the brownstone tower at the end of the dam, and then sped past it into the upland village, where the sharp right-turn, and the Talybont-posted road that led away from it into the heart of the mountains, seemed magically to beckon them on.

Unbeknown to the Merthyr police, D.I.Dawson was already in town, having been called up at his office in west London early on the Monday morning by a gruff-throated Welshman, whose identity was withheld, and whose voice he wasn't able to recognise, or, more importantly, record on tape, when the man informed him curtly that Carla Steel had disappeared.

However, despite the singular anonymity of the messenger, Dawson made immediate arrangements to drive down to Merthyr, and, just a few hours later, accompanied by a young Asian constable called Shah, whom he now frequently worked alongside, he drove due west down the M.4 motorway. Flashing his warrant-card as he sacheted through the bridge-tolls, and exceeding the speed-limit at every available opportunity, he got them to Wales by lunch-time, later that day to accommodate himself and his companion in adjoining single-rooms in the same motel in The Beacons where Carla Steel had spent a solitary night no more than five months before; not that Dawson or Shah were ever likely to discover this curious fact of course, (the proprietor appreciating the importance of secrecy far more than she believed the police-service did,) otherwise it is quite likely that the younger officer would have transferred his personal belongings, and his Carla-fronted copy of *Rolling Stone,* to that very same room.

Dawson recalled how he had first become embroiled in the matter of Carla Steel when the body of a relatively young black, female addict and ex-con called Jackie Boyce was found to have mysteriouly disappeared from the home she lived in with a middle-aged, Welsh woman in Fulham - a woman whom Dawson had found was the owner-occupier of a property which was actually registered as belonging to Carla Steel. Then, if the recent discovery of Jackie's stabbed body in a locked-up room in sheltered accommodation in Putney wasn't enough, the fact that Carla's own father, whom she was living with at the time, had located it for them, suggested to him that Carla herself might well have played a role of sorts in the poor woman's demise. The coincidence involved was far too great to actually be one, Dawson felt, and so, ever since then, he had focused his efforts on trying to uncover the nature of the singer's involvement in Jackie's murder, and even in its bizarre concealment just across the river from where she lived.

P.C.Vic Shah, who was lying flat-out on his bed, happily sampling the cold contents of his mini-bar, was an officer who knew all there was to know about narcotics, and had been a crucial part of the team that had succeeded in finally getting Carla Steel convicted for possession of class-A just a few years before. So it came as no surprise to Shah that he was the man whom D.I.Dawson turned to when he found out that the singer had gone missing in Wales.

Initially the young detective had, like Dawson, believed that Carla Steel might be one of the perpetrators of the heinous crime that had shocked west London, but recent events had now suggested to him that this was probably not the case. To the young officer's mind it seemed that there was a very unusual, and probably highly significant, link, or, at least, a correspondence, between the abduction and murder of Jackie Boyce in 2010, and what seemed to have just taken place here in Merthyr. And the conclusion Shah had come to, on discussing the matter, at great length, while travelling in the car with D.I.Dawson, was that someone whom both women - both drug-users - knew, was most likely to be at the heart of both events, and was also likely to be the man who had covered up his evil tracks by murdering the young policeman, Darim Ahmed, whose final words seemed to suggest that he had recognised him. But who that dangerous man might actually be, neither he nor Dawson seemed to have the foggiest notion.

A firm double-knock on the door told Vic that his superior had come calling. Quickly sitting up, and placing his can of lager on the bedside-table, he called out, 'The door is open, Sir!'

'Vic, I told you before you can call me Jeff, you know,' the officer replied, opening the mini-bar and taking out a can for himself. He smiled at the younger man, turned a wooden chair right round, and sat his legs astride it. 'I need to let you know something that I only just found out,' the older man said. 'The morning after Carla Steel disappeared, her father Tom passed away.'

'Really?' said Vic. He thought for a moment, then said, 'The two events couldn't be linked, could they?'

'I can't see how,' Dawson told him. 'In fact I can't imagine Carla is even likely to know of this.'

'Oh, I see,' the young man replied. 'Say, but wasn't he the chap who seemed to know poor P.C.Ahmed was about to cop it just before he did?'

'He certainly was,' said Dawson, recalling the strange, terrifying evening in Merthyr Police Station. 'You know, I shall never be able to forget how the old man cringed up his face and covered his ears just a second or two before the two shots were fired. It was quite astounding.'

Vic Shah pondered this. 'Then I guess, Sir, the old man might have known that he himself was about to kick the bucket,' he announced, arching his brows, then smiling at his companion.

'Yes, I suppose that's quite possible,' said Dawson, breaking into a laugh. 'You're a clever lad, do you know that, Vic? I feel we always seem to work really well together, don't we? And, if truth be told, I'd like to see you get yourself the credit for tracking Carla down, I really would.'

'You mean share the credit, yeah?' the constable replied, smiling.

'Well yes, of course,' said Dawson. 'But I've cracked a lot of big cases over the years, you see, whereas you, Vic, have yet to pop your cherry, if you get my drift. Yes, I should really like to see you get promoted, I really would, lad. And if we find Carla Steel, and bring the woman back home in one piece, then I can promise you that your life is unlikely to be the same again.'

'You know, I have never yet met the girl,' said Vic. 'Say - what is she like, Sir?'

'Jeff, remember, Jeff. To look at, do you mean?' the older man asked.

'That, too,' said Vic, grinning.

'Well, if you like the bi-sexual look, then I'm sure she could easily be your Miss World. Or Miss Wales, anyway.' He chuckled. 'She's got millions in the bank, of course, so if, like me, you prefer another type of female completely, then you could do a lot worse than spend some of Carla's cash on finding that one instead.'

The two men laughed heartily at this.

'Jeff, can I tell you a little confession?' the young man asked.

'Of course you can, lad,' replied Dawson.

'Well, I've had a crush on Carla Steel since I was in sixth-form in Peckham. I swear it's true. And despite what you've said, I reckon she's sexier than Katy Perry and Lady Gaga combined.'

'Wow! That's an interesting concoction, if ever there was one,' said Dawson.

'I've got every song the singer ever recorded, I really have,' Vic told him. 'And I know all the words to most of them.'

'O.K.,' said Dawson, surprised more than intrigued. 'Hey, you don't mind if I test you, do you?'

'Fire away,' the young man retorted.

'So where the hell is *Candice Farm* then? Because it sure as hell ain't on any map, I can tell you.'

'You know, Jeff, I haven't a clue about that myself,' replied Vic. 'But, you know, while I'm down here, I'd sure like to find out. You see, Jeff, according to the song's lyrics, Carla and her friends seem to have achieved a large measure of, what she calls 'enlightenment' there, when they were all still quite young.'

'Lost their cherries there, she means, then, yeah?' said Dawson, grinning.

'Well, that as well, I bet,' replied Vic. 'But to my mind I believe a great deal more must have happened out on that farm during those balmy, summer holidays.'

'Christ, Vic, you're beginning to get *me* interested now,' said Dawson, shifting in his seat. 'Listen, I bet you any money old Sergeant Foley knows where *Candice Farm* is. And if he does, then trust me, I'll be sure to get it out of him, so I will. Then, perhaps, when Carla is out of harm's way once again, you and I could take a trip out there. Blimey, did I say *trip?*' exclaimed Dawson, chuckling away merrily at what he regarded as one of his finest jokes.

Vic watched his D.I., but decided he wouldn't be joining in with him this time. 'You know what I hope happens, Jeff?' said the young man.

'What's that?' asked Dawson.

'That Carla Steel might be so grateful to us, after we've rescued her I mean, that she offers to take us there herself. Now that *would* be worth doing, don't you think?'

'Hey, I wouldn't want to play gooseberry, Vic lad,' said Dawson, smiling. 'After all, I'm a lot older than you two are, and a married man to boot. And booted is how I feel a lot of the time, I can tell you. What I mean is, you two being about the same age and all, I'm sure the pair of you would really value a little trip out to that place together. '*Make hay, not war,*' yeah? as that blond Welsh bird used to sing back in my day. Say, what the hell was her name again, I wonder? 'Cos she certainly did it for me back then, I can tell you.'

'We must have come off the *Talybont* road some way back there, I reckon,' said Rhiannon, throwing the folded map down into the foot-well and frowning.

'But I thought you were navigating, babe,' yelled Chris, slowing down the yellow Fiesta as they traversed a stone bridge yards away from a picturesque little waterfall just off the carriageway, that delivered cool, cascading water down to the Taff River from the high, angular peaks known as *The Fans,* that had, by now, quickly become a solid, foreboding presence round and about them, as they bounced along the narrow, rising, stone-strewn, road.

'Where are you taking us to?' enquired Rhiannon.

'Look, I can't turn the car round here,' retorted Chris, becoming more than a little impatient with the unfamiliar terrain which unsurprisingly put a considerable strain on his inexperienced driving skills. 'I'll just have to drive on a bit further, O.K., Rhi? Though something tells me this road will turn out to be a dead-end before very long.'

Chris was right. The car that contained the pair of young lovers soon emerged from the cover of thick trees into the bright sunlight, and the full majesty of the serrated peaks, that formed the backbone of the Beacons massif, could be properly assessed.

'Hey, I recognise where we've come now,' exclaimed an excited Rhiannon. 'I think my Dad has driven Mam and me up this route once before. I can remember her telling us how this is the ancient Roman Road which, because of the high terrain, had to become a narrow track along here, so allowing their legions to march over the mountains, then descend to their fort in Brecon. You know, Chris, we'd need to be in a four-by-four if we we wanted to do the same right now.'

'Well there's no sense in us getting out and walking any further north,' said Chris. 'We should probably stop somewhere around here and eat something, don't you think, Rhi? I could murder a sandwich right now, couldn't you?'

'I certainly could,' she told him. 'I know, let's go back to that waterfall, shall we?' said Rhiannon. 'It looked really nice back there.'

Before long the teenage couple had returned, and parked up by the little stone bridge that bestrode the stream, and sat alongside the tumbling cataract that discharged its flow underneath it, happily sharing together the food they had brought along, and, of course, the genuine love they had by this time developed for each other. Their bare calves swirling around in the stream's cool, rushing water, Chris and Rhiannon drank from the bottle they had brought with them, and discussed the worrying matter of Carla's disappearance against the cacophonous back-drop of the waterfall, and the sweet sounds that the summer's songbirds made, as they swooped down upon the crumbs and tit-bits the pair joyously dispersed around for them.

Above the serene sound of nature at play the low drone of a whirring vehicle somewhere high in the sky above them could soon be clearly heard. The barefoot couple waited patiently for the flying craft to enter the gap between the tall trees on either side of the watercourse, and so at last become visible to them. When it finally did, they were able to clearly see that it was a bright orange helicopter that had suddenly disturbed their peace, and was now swooping low and, its black, fish-net tail spinning right and left, gliding its way along the flanks of the mountains. Suddenly turning clockwise, the orange craft advanced towards them, and, as it did so, seeming almost to skim the crowns of the diaphanous, green conifers all about them, that liberally coated the valley proper in these wild, upper reaches of the Taff river-basin.

'You know, Rhi, I - I'm sure I saw this once before!' exclaimed Chris, jumping up and standing on the bare sandstone boulder that lay behind them.

'Really? When?' asked Rhiannon.

'I'm pretty sure it was the day that Carla's dad first arrived in Gloryhole in the spring,' he told her. 'You know, the day he moved in next-door. I never found out why it was buzzing about the place then, and I'm just as puzzled as to why the thing is back now.' He suddenly ran across to his bag, and from inside it brought out the binoculars he always carried with him, then standing completely still, his sturdy legs akimbo, he carefully focused his sights on the wild, flying craft.

'But it's surely got to be the police,' said Rhiannon, clambering up out of the stream herself and joining him. 'Like us, they're probably out searching for Carla, don't you think?'

'No, I don't,' said Chris, straining his eyes to try to make out what letters or numbers there might be on the helicopter's roof or side, but quickly discovering that there didn't appear to be any. 'For a start it's the wrong colour to be one of theirs,' he told her. 'And it's definitely not a mountain-rescue craft either. No, this is - this one is something completely different if you ask me. You know, Rhi, to be frank, I seriously don't know *what* to make of it.'

Rhiannon contemplated this for a moment, as she watched the strange, insect-like shape hover off into the distance, soon to disappear completely into the eastern sky high above distant Talybont; Talybont, the village which had given birth to both Tom Davies and his talenred daughter, she told herself. Then she suddenly looked up into her lover's eyes and gripped him firmly by the arm. 'Hey, I think I get it now, Chris,' she exclaimed. 'Wow! Isn't that out of this world!'

'What is?' asked Chris, tucking the field-glasses back in their holder, and clearly confused by her comment. 'Explain, would you, because I don't understand what you're talking about.'

'Well, don't you see, Chris?' said Rhiannon, waving her arms about in her excitement. 'This strange craft - this mysterious, orange helicopter, which, more than likely, no one had ever seen before - appears for the first time the very moment that Tom arrives in *Gloryhole*, yeah? Months go by, during which time he shares a new life - a wonderful, new, loving relationship - with his gifted daughter, who had previously severed all ties with him. Not long after that he informs you that poor Emily is dead, and even tells you where to find her.'

'Not really, no,' protested Chris. 'He just said she was in a tunnel, and would soon float out.'

But Rhiannon wasn't listening to him, and continued much as before. 'Later on he tells my dad what really happened to my Uncle Sam when, almost fifty years before, they found him mysteriously killed on the railway. And, from what you've told me, he even told your mother things which convince her that he had played a key role in saving her life way back in the sixties, when she was in school with my dad, and the terrible disaster happened.' By now Rhiannon could feel tears welling up from deep inside her. 'And just to cap it all, the next time you see the mysterious orange-and-black helicopter is when the man concerned has just passed away.'

'And?' said Chris, turning to Rhiannon and making a face at her. 'Wait. Are you suggesting - surely you're not suggesting that the old man next-door was some sort of *special man* - some sage, or prophet, or some guru or such like? God! What was in that sandwich you ate just now, Rhiannon?' he asked her, smiling. 'Because, if you ask me, it sure as hell wasn't ham.'

Rhiannon was beginning to feel frustrated that Chris wasn't on the same wave-length as she was; in truth, she thought, he didn't seem prepared to even consider what she felt she was now beginning to see very clearly indeed. 'But Chris,' she continued, 'to my mind it all seems to be much more than just an odd coincidence, don't you think? At the very least, you have to admit yourself that the whole thing is quite creepy.'

'Creepy!' echoed Chris.

'Well, maybe that's not the best word,' said Rhiannon. 'How about uncanny? Or - or supernatural? Or transcendental even?'

'Babe, are you seriously trying to tell me that - are you saying that you believe the orange helicopter that we just saw flying over us could be - could be carrying the old man away somewhere? Tell me - Rhiannon! Are you trying to say that? But that's preposterous, isn't it?'

'Why is it?' she asked, staring into his eyes, her brows lowering.

'Because I'll remind you that Tom's body is at present lying, awaiting burial, in a Cardiff morgue. 'That's why,' he told her, grinning.

'Yes, I know - I understand all that,' she responded, wringing her hands, and thinking furiously. 'But the question I have is - is that really Tom that's laid out down there?' she asked him. 'Chris - do you think it is? Because - well, because I don't.'

'You don't!' Chris yelled at her. 'You don't believe he's there? You don't think he's In Cardiff!'

'No,' she told him, then, raising her gaze, staring right into him.

Chris suddenly felt afraid of her. 'So - so where the hell is he, then!' he asked her.

'Chris - I can't believe you're saying that you believe he will always remain in that stiff, broken, old body that your mam and my dad discovered? Do you believe that, Chris? Tell me.'

'Chris looked down, clearly trying to comprehend Rhiannon's words, and piece together all the facts - the separate, confusing facts - that pertained to the matter that so engrossed her.

'And anyway, what would be the sense in that?' Rhiannon asked him, taking his two hands in hers, pleading. 'Is that where the great dead go, Chris? Do you think they are still buried in soil? Under our feet? Boxed in like - like ancient turnips, and just rotting away? The wonderful dead? Pl-ease.' Seeing Chris unable to respond, Rhiannon decided to develop even further the point she was making. 'Or is the soul of a man able to soar, as some people say, do you think?'

'So - so is that what you believe, Rhiannon?' Chris asked her slowly.

'It is,' she replied, smiling. 'That's precisely what I believe.' Then squeezing his hands tightly within her own, she asked him, 'And what do you believe, Chris? Tell me. No, don't be afraid.'

Chris was feeling seriously challenged, and more than a little confused, by what Rhiannon was telling him. He suddenly became aware that his lips had gone terribly dry, and so he licked at them furiously with his tongue, if only to facilitate the words he now felt desperate to express. 'I have to tell you, Rhiannon,' he said, his two hands moving down and tightly gripping her sides, 'that it worries me greatly that you seem to believe that this - this strange orange craft we just saw was - well, that it was transporting the old man's soul. That's right, isn't it? His soul.'

Resting her head gently on Chris's shoulder, by way of showing him that, whatever he believed, she still loved him dearly, Rhiannon stood completely still, and allowed the power she felt she knew existed above her, around her, within her, to act, to perform whatever miracle of faith it wished to. Or, if this doesn't work, and if I am deceived, she told herself, then - then a motor-car will pass, a sheep nearby will bleat, or some wind, or breeze even, will blow on my face, and then I shall know to drop it, and let it lie, and life will simply carry on just as before.

Embracing her tightly, Chris's thumb suddenly detected a pulse throbbing away urgently in Rhiannon's chest, and almost straightaway he realised that this had to be her heart. Instinctively he reached the same hand down and felt his own, and was shocked to discover that it was pounding away at the exact same pace.

'Tell me, my love - is that what you truly believe, then?' Chris asked Rhiannon, trembling slightly. 'We just saw the soul of a great man returning home?' His lover didn't reply, or even move a muscle. 'You know, normally, babe, I'd - I'd blast you, and - and castigate you for saying something like that,' he told her. 'But, you know, when I looked up at the orange helicopter through my binoculars just now, I remember clearly thinking - why is it that I can't see any pilot?'

CHAPTER 23

'Look, we're starting to get very tired of this, now, Jack,' said Sergeant Foley. 'And I gather from my colleagues that you've obstructed the police before, right?'

Jack Belt stared up at the officer with a blank look on his dirty, round face that screamed - 'what the hell are you talking about?'

'I'm thinking of that pigeon-coop the court said you had to get rid of,' Foley went on. 'Have you done what you were told yet, Jack? Or are you still keeping your homing-pigeons?'

'I smashed up the coop - yes I did, Mr. Foley,' the skinny, straggly-haired man replied.

'Oh, really!' exclaimed Foley. 'Because *we* recently discovered you're still keeping them'

'Well, aye,' said Jack. 'But what can I do? They just keep coming back, don't they?'

Next-door Officers Dawson and Shah began laughing so loud that the noise could clearly be heard inside the interview-room.'

Merlyn Foley walked out of the room and called the two London detectives into the corridor. Dawson and Shah quickly joined him there.

'As you can see, boys, Jack's denying everything,' said Foley. 'He even claims he doesn't know where Carla Steel lives, for a start, though he accepts for months now he's been delivering all sorts of stuff to her dad. Drill-bits, razor-blades, fish-fingers, an enormous coloured print of a French brothel, a religious door-mat, all sorts of things. He did say weed at first, but corrected himself. I said why, he said because the old man seemed to have got stacks of the stuff already.'

535

'Carla could easily have turned up from London with a suitcase-full of skunk, or, as you told us, even bought it off the boy next-door,' said Dawson. 'It seems he even grew it in his front-room, remember.'

'So what do we do next, then, boys?' asked Foley.

The three officers strolled into the room they had emerged from and stared through the pane of glass at Jack Belt's queer, seated frame. The man sat forward in his chair scratching what little hair he had left, the dry skin from his scalp dropping to the linoleum-floor like falling snow. 'The rattling van-man' - as he was known to those who didn't shop with him - reached over to the table for his cap, but Constable Llewellyn got there before him.

'Later,' the seated officer told him in his deepest voice. 'We haven't finished with you yet.'

'You gonna arrest me?' Jack asked him.

'That's for the sergeant to decide,' said Llewellyn. 'He's probably considering it right now.'

'Well, I wish he'd get a move on,' said Jack. 'I've got customers waiting, you know. Two garden-loungers and a deck-chair for an old couple in *Dowlais Top* to be dropped off before two.' He looked up and glared into the one-way mirror on the wall before him that he knew full well Sergeant Foley and his pals were presently standing behind observing him. He grasped his broken nose, flattened it like a pan-cake, and gurned at them his prime facial contortion. He paused a few seconds, then with his fingers rubbed the folds of his face back into place again.

The constable sitting alongside shook his head at him. 'And we noticed your van's holding a massive home-cannabis kit that was built in the Czech Republic. Do you want to tell us anything about that, Jack? No? I thought not. They're illegal these days, by the way, even if some of our own ones aren't.'

'Illegal! I recommend you check up on that. Say, did you see what I did there, bach?' asked Jack, smiling. 'Because I already have checked up, you know. Listen - I clear over a dozen of those things every month in the Merthyr Valley alone. I'm sure those ministers in the government would give me an award if ever they found out.'

'And how do you figure that out?' asked Llewellyn.

'Because the weed-sellers are what the government calls small businesses, that's why.'

'Funny. We've always called them joint enterprises,' the burly officer told him, grinning.

'You're funny, Llew,' said Jack. 'Anyway we're all entrepreneurs, yeah? So therefore we're self-dependent, and no burden on the welfare-state. Look - I can avoid tax as well as anyone if I want, and some of the buggers are devious. Some bloke told me the other day, that if you want to find out who the best tax-avoiders are, you just get on your computer, go to Google, and -'

'And just stay there. Yeah, I've heard it,' Llew replied, smiling. 'Can I ask you one final question, Jack?' the burly constable asked him.

'Of course you can,' Jack answered, checking his watch.

'Say - why did you never get a job? You've been unemployed for almost three decades now, mate, according to our computer.'

'Then you need a new one, don't you, bach?' Jack retorted sharply. 'Listen, I can do you a good deal on a second-hand computer if that one you've got has started playing up.' He grinned at this. 'Listen, big boy - I'll have you know I can't possibly be *unemployed* for the very good reason that I have never really *been* employed,' he told him. 'I've worked my whole entire life, so I have. If you trust that record you have on me, then you need to add on it that never in history has an unemployed man been as busy as I currently am. I mean, look at last Christmas, Llew. When I took over that bus-shelter in Pant I was bleedin' run off my feet with business, so I was.'

'Yeah, but almost all the gifts you had in your sack had instructions in Russian, and that Santa outfit you were wearing didn't suit you at all. Black's your colour, Jack. Always has been.'

In the room next-door D.I.Dawson decided it was time he assumed control. He looked into Sergeant Foley's eyes and said, 'O.K., now's the time for us to take charge of the kidnap investigation, Merlyn. Trust me, Jack Belt is about to tell us every single thing he knows.'

'But we've had him in custody for hours now,' the Welshman told him. 'And he hasn't come out with a damn thing we didn't already know.'

Detective Constable Shah moved closer to them. 'Look, Sergeant - the man has said enough in the short time *we've* been watching him that could have him put away for months,' he said. 'I believe he needs to be told this up front, even if it's us just being optimistic.'

'And you don't bake a cake without breaking a few eggs, right?' added Dawson, grinning. 'Look, I'll go in there and break the bad news to the man. Vic - as usual, you play good cop, O.K.?' The detective gave out a beaming smile. 'Let's just see what transpires, shall we, chaps?'

It was 'flying-ant day,' thought Rhiannon, but this time she had forgotten to get a card - to swipe them away with that is! Giggling to herself, she recalled how she must have killed well over a dozen on the same occasion the previous August, having that day armed herself to the hilt with an assortment of cards, when she set off from home to go shopping in town with her friends. She sat up on the grass and flailed her two arms about wildly, but to no avail. 'Chris - help me!' she screamed, but her dreamy, love-drained companion slept on, his sun-hat draped over his sleeping head, seemingly held captive somewhere between the Kalahari Desert and Christmas.

The young couple had lain together in the long grass that clothed the mountainside for well over an hour, and, after replacing their discarded clothes, which took far longer than expected, they soon felt that it was high time they descended into the wooded valley once more, and drove their little yellow car away from their waterfall base, and so continue their search for Carla. Above them the bright blue, afternoon sky now bore no trace of aviation craft, not even a lofty vapour-trail; instead it seemed vast, and calm, and but lightly streaked with loosened, cirrus cotton-buds and curls.

This time Rhiannon chose to drive, and she held the car in third-gear all the way back to the fork in the road where the wooden sign-post pointed off left for Talybont to the east. She turned her car in the same direction and was suddenly overtaken on the narrow, country road by a white Vivaro van, doing well over sixty, on the back of which was emblazoned a picture of a gap-toothed, growling, one-eyed pirate. '*Captain Morgan's Sandwiches*' it broadcast colourfully, but gaudily. '*Is my driving good? Bet it's not a patch on our sarnies - Arrh!*'

Then coasting gently along beside the bubbling stream, a white Escort SRi with the words '*Attention Whore*' emblazoned across its windscreen soon approached them on its way back to Merthyr, and seered by them at stupendous speed, its passing very like the slap of a white-water wave against Rhiannon's frail, yellow dinghy. Taken aback by the sudden arrival of fast, noisy traffic once again, she changed down and turned off the road onto a narrow track which led uphill into the trees, and before long brought the car to a halt at a small fork.

'Why did we come up here?' asked Chris angrily. 'There's bugger all up here that I can see but squirrels and trees and fallen logs.'

'I know but isn't this the sort of place you'd take Carla if you had kidnapped her and wanted to keep her out of sight for a long while?' she asked him. 'Just look - the tree-cover is so thick up here that it probably seems like night-time for the best part of the day, I shouldn't wonder.'

Chris suddenly climbed out of the car and began to walk to the left, up the steeper of the two tracks that lay before him. Puzzled, Rhiannon tried driving along behind him, but soon she found that the hill's gradient had become too steep even for her to make any progress in first gear.

'Park up and join me!' yelled Chris above the thunderous roar from the Fiesta's engine.

Rhiannon turned the car round, pointed it downhill, then switched off, and secured the hand-brake with the gear set in reverse, just as her dad had always shown her she should do when parking on a steep slope. Locking the car, she got out and asked Chris why he had chosen to venture up the steeper of the two tracks.

'I'd like to get well above the tree-line if we can,' he told her. 'We could barely see the flippin' helicopter above us when we were down in the valley earlier, let alone any of the farms and barns and other buildings that are dotted round the place here. You see, I have a feeling that, in the end, *they* are where we shall need to focus our search.'

'Say, this climb could take us a while,' said an already puffing Rhiannon, doing her best to keep up, 'but I'm up for it if you are.'

'Let's go,' said Chris, taking Rhiannon's hand in his and forging ahead.

Clinging firmly to each other even when the going got tough, the young pair set off up the slope, and, on rounding a fern-tangled bend to the right, soon discovered that the track they were following was becoming progressively narrower, eventually terminating as a routeway altogether, instead becoming a barely visible path, which zig-zagged madly between trees, then rocks, then trees again. After clambering across a rushing stream by way of its scattered rocks that supplied a sort of make-shift causeway, the couple finally reached the summit of a high, grassy hill that could only support the growth of long, parched grass and a few stunted trees.

'Oh, bloody hell! I forgot my binoculars,' said Chris, angrily, turning to Rhiannon.

'No, I have them here,' Rhiannon told him, smiling. She took the case from her shoulder and handed it over to him, and watched as Chris dashed a few paces from her, and, clambering up onto a large boulder, and with the field-glasses pressed tightly to his head, began to survey the undulating landscape that encircled them, and with which neither of them was at all familiar.

'What can you see?' asked Rhiannon, eventually climbing up onto the same boulder. 'Where's the nearest building? Can you see any?'

'No, I can't see a single one round here,' he told Rhiannon, handing her the binoculars so that she could try her luck.

'Apart from the forestry-sheds, I bet there are only a few scattered sheep-farms within a square-mile of here.'

'Despite what you're telling us, Jack, we happen to know that your van has just returned from the Beacons,' said D.I.Dawson.

'But I swear I haven't been up that way,' the straggly-headed man in the macintosh told him.

'Oh, yes, you have,' the officer continued. 'Our forensic chap confirmed that your tyres are covered in red-sandstone soil, for a start. And I gather you can't pick that up round here.'

'*I* could,' said Jack, grinning. 'I can pick up anything at all. White goods, metal goods, plastic goods, rubber goods. Car-tyres even. Red soil wouldn't be a problem. Car-tyres with red soil on - a piece of cake. How many do you want?'

Dawson slapped his forehead in frustration. 'You know, I think it's over to you at this point, Vic,' he told his young friend. 'Mental health issues aren't my strong point, I'm afraid.'

'Yes, I see the man's answers are about as meaninglful as a Sanskrit limerick,' the young Asian detective replied, smiling. He slowly approached Jack's seat and, placing his plate of white and brown sandwiches on the table to the side, gazed down at him. 'Look, Mr. Belt,' he began.

'Jack - please,' the man shot back.

'Jack,' said Shah, watching the Welshman turning his head nervously so as to eye his food.

'God, there's a fine tan you've got there, boy,' said Jack, smiling. 'From Swamsea, are you? No, hang on. It's got to be further west than that, right? I can tell by your accent, see.'

'My accent!' said D.C.Shah, grinning as he spun round to face his Cockney companion. 'I'm afraid I hail from a place a lot further east than Swansea.'

'Porthcawl, then, yeah?' asked Jack. 'My sister lives by the sea down there, but, try as she might, she can never seem to get herself a tan like what you've got.'

'He seems convinced you're Welsh, Vic,' said Dawson. 'And I must say, I can definitely hear a remarkable similarity between your Indian accent and old Jack's here.' He watched the young officer's eyebrows droop. 'Anyway, don't let it bother you, lad. Crack on with your questions.'

Vic Shah turned back to face the strange man in the long mac and jeans who sat before him. 'The penalty for selling drugs is normally jail-time, you do know that don't you, Jack? Now you wouldn't want to go down that road, would you?' he asked him.

'I certainly wouldn't,' said Jack. 'One of my nearest neighbours went down for doing that, see. He had a big caravan up on the mountain, he did. Until they caught him, of course. Poor sod.'

'Oh? Who was that then?' asked Shah.

'Humphreys, his name was. Though you'd no doubt know him as Inspector Humphreys. Nice man. Once a month I used to get him some Polish fags and viagara, you know. He was seeing my niece for a while, you see. She was his common-law wife, well, as she saw it, anyway. And blimey, that's all she was left with when they came and took him away.'

'What? The caravan?' asked Shah.

'No, the viagara. And a lot of good that is to you, I told her. So naturally -'

'You sold it?'

'Well, aye,' he said. 'And the fags. Though they're a bit chesty, if you want my opinion. Say - you don't know anyone who wants to buy a caravan, do you? 'I reckon it could provide you with the sort of field-base you need in your search for Carla Steel. I'll take five K. No - go on, four.'

'Have you met Carla Steel, then?' Shah asked him.

'Who? Are you kidding? No, not at all. Never even seen the girl,' Jack Belt told him, with an angry stare that seemed to the detective to wither within seconds of it being applied. Noticing this, Vic Shah chose this moment to go on the attack.

'But you did attend the Sunday-night gig she took part in at *The Railway*, I understand.'

'I never,' retorted Jack. 'Who the hell told you that?'

'Then this isn't you in the picture in The Merthyr Express?' Vic asked him, proffering a large, shiny, printed photograph.

Jack stared down at it, and the plate full of sandwiches alongside it, and licked his lips. 'And your van wasn't parked up on the pavement outside, so preventing the pub-manager from bringing up to the door the extra casks of lager he needed to unload.'

'It had to have been another van completely,' said Jack, handing the officer his picture back, only to be handed another, similar-sized image, that he once again studied carefully with ever more darkening eyes.

'Do you know what 'crank' is, Jack?' enquired Vic, calmly taking a bite from a cheese-sandwich.

Jack watched him closely, salivating with envy. 'Crank, you say? Er - the noise my engine makes?' he asked. 'I can tell you straight it's been mis-firing for years now.'

'Skunk?' the officer asked.

'Now there's no need to get insulting, now, is there, Mr. Shah?' retorted Jack.

'Blow?'

Jack's mouth fell open. 'Beg pardon, young man, but I hardly know you.'

'White? Brown?'

Jack leaned forward, smiled, and shook the officer by the hand. 'I'll take the white, if you don't mind, Mr. Shah. But I hope you've gone easy on the butter.'

'No, no!' said Shah, removing his sandwich-plate from the man's clutches. 'Brown and White happen to be drugs, Jack, as you very well know. And drugs that you've been known to be delivering in your van for very many months now, I understand.'

'Me! You're saying *I* do that! Says who?' asked Jack.

'Could you pass me the list,' said Shah, turning to his superior.

'No, don't bother,' said Jack, looking down. 'Merthyr people are too honest for their own good, if you ask me.' He grimaced. 'Look - basically I'm stuffed, right, Mr. Shah? And, you can see very well I'm desperate for a sandwich.' He looked up. 'Or a chicken curry if you've got one.'

'Funny you should say that,' Shah told him, grinning. 'You see my family happen to run an Indian restaurant.'

'Really? Then I'm sure we could go into business together,' said Jack, smiling. 'I once delivered pizzas in my van, you know. Only I had to knock it on the head, you see, as I found they got in the way of all the perishables and - and all the goldfish.'

Stifling a laugh, Vic said, 'You must know, Jack, there's enough evidence, in this room alone, to put you away for quite a stretch. Only in jail I'm sure you wouldn't get the preferential that your old mate Humphreys most probably gets.'

'Well, I realise that,' said Jack. 'He's one of your own, after all.'

'But, you know, friend, if you were to - if you *were* to - to play fair with us, Jack, then -'

'Oh, I see,' said the Welshman. He rolled his bottom-lip outwards in deep contemplation. 'But, you know, if I did, Sir, would I - I mean, would I get prosecuted?'

'Prosecuted! Good heavens, no. For what?' asked Vic, grinning. 'Parking on the pavement?'

'Unlike you, Rhiannon, I agree with Buddha that the essence of life is evil,' said Chris, lying back on the short grass, and inhaling from his six-inch reefer.

Rhiannon knelt before him, watching his every action. 'But that doesn't mean you must seek to embrace it yourself, does it?' she told him. 'I mean, I believe I could accept your need to smoke a joint on occasions,' she continued, 'although I'm not sure how much that is just a pose of yours to be honest. But it would be a totally different matter if you ever began *selling* drugs.' She suddenly had a thought. 'Tell me, Chris, you'd never do that would you? Sell drugs. And go getting yourself a criminal record before you've even found a job?'

Chris exhaled a cloud of smoke into the summer air. 'You know, I don't know what I want,' he replied, only half understanding what she was saying, or even trying to.

'My dad says there are people round here who have started to retire before they've even started work,' said Rhiannon. 'They line up every signing-day and squander the lot in the pubs in double-quick time, with precious little left over to hand to their longsuffering partners, and so feed their children. I tell you straight, Chris, I'm never going to live like that.'

'Nobody is asking you to,' said Chris, suddenly feeling cross with her for appearing to be comparing him with his sister. 'I know you, Rhiannon. You'll probably go and find yourself some decent, hard-working, hard-saving, soft-bellied, soft-hearted sucker of a man, who'll take out for you a mortgage on some three-bedroom semi in Brecon Rise, and fly you and your two-point-four kids off to Tenerife every August without fail, to see the sun and get himself a tan, and Orlando every five or six years so the kids can see Mickey Mouse and Spiderman, and get himself a burger.'

'Chris!' yelled Rhiannon.

'Can't you see just how meaningless and pointless all that is, Rhiannon?' he asked her. 'I'm telling you that guy I'm describing could never be me.'

'So you think I could settle for someone soft-bellied and soft-hearted, then, do you, Mister Buddha? Because I assure you I find it every bit as repulsive as you do. Look - if you'd like to know, it's - it's you that I want Chris Cillick. Faults and all. Joints, even.'

'Yeah, you say that,' he told her, sitting up, and dabbing out his spliff to smoke it later. 'But you don't really want me, babe, I know that. I bet you you'd run a mile if you had any idea what I'd got up to in my, close on, eighteen short years on this planet.'

'Oh, you think so, do you?' she respondesd spunkily. 'Try me, then. Go on. What *have* you done? What have you got up to that is so, so bad? Say. I bet you I don't even blink an eye.'

'You certainly will if I told you it all,' he told her, nodding.

'Try me - I said. Go on!' she insisted.

The wind swept in on them for the first time that day, causing their open shirts to flap about madly. Rhiannon tried to tuck hers in, but failed.

'O.K., then,' said Chris, sitting up much closer to her, so that he could register even the slightest flickering of an eye-blink. 'Steffan, Jake and I spiked cakes with cannabis in Food Tech. one time. Half the class had to be taken to Casualty.'

'That was you!' yelled Rhiannon. 'Carmen nearly died that day!' She contemplated this most shocking of revelations. 'My God! I'm shocked! But you haven't made me blink yet, have you?'

'I probably have,' Chris replied, smiling. 'But let me tell you another that definitely will make you blink, shall I?' Rhiannon nodded. 'I grew cannabis plants in a clearing in Vaynor Woods.'

'Well, I guessed that,' said Rhiannon, smiling. 'You practically lived there all last summer. My friends were convinced you had turned gay. Me, too, as it goes.' She giggled.

'*And* in my neighbour's loft.' He bit his top lip, knowing that this would surprise her.

'Wow! Now that's pretty awesome,' she retorted, thinking furiously. 'Though that explains a lot, I reckon. Your phone being off for hours on end. Your clothes stinking so bad.'

'Oh, thanks,' he replied.

'Don't mention it.'

'And I thought you liked coffee.'

'I do when it's wet and steaming,' said Rhiannon. She smiled serenely at him. 'And I guess all that time you spent with Carla upstairs in her home, the two of you were - were running a farm. And you told me it was music practice. Dear, dear. O.K., next. Where else did you grow it?'

'In a small patch in *Pant Cemetery*, just over the wall from yours.' He tried to stifle a laugh.

'You're lying!' Chris nodded that he wasn't. 'What!' she screamed. 'A young grave-digger called Evan got the sack for that, you monster!'

'Colossal blink there, I see,' Chris told her, grinning.

'God! What is it about you and skunk cannabis, Chris Cillick?' she asked him. 'Sounds very much like you love weed more than anything, and a great deal more than you love me.'

'Rhiannon, babe, your love *is* my drug,' he announced. 'You must know that.'

'Ha! Gotcha!' she yelled. 'That just proves you're fake. *Roxy Music* that is, yeah? My dad's got that one on vinyl.'

'But that doesn't mean I don't mean it,' he told her, reaching out a hand to stroke her curls.

Rhiannon pulled away. 'Gotcha again!' she shrieked. 'Two *means* in the same sentence that time. Dead give-away, right? You're such a charlatan, do you know that, Chris?'

A loud gun-shot rang out.

Both young people ducked and rolled over in the grass, Chris soon pressing his body over Rhiannon's to protect her. They listened to the silence that ensued, broken only by the sounds of the birds squawking madly in the trees down below them.

'There's just one more thing I must tell you, babe. You ready?' he asked, then pausing for full effect. 'And I was Carla's dealer for the last four months,'

Trembling with fear now, and staring up into his big brown eyes, Rhiannon asked him, 'Chris, why are you telling me this? You - you know you never had to.'

'Because - well, because these could be the very last words I *ever* tell you,' he replied, biting into his top-lip.

It occurred to Rhiannon that the gun-shot had quite possibly been meant to strike down her lover, and she suddenly became terrified. 'Mine, too, then,' she told him, shaking.

'Yours, too,' he concurred.

'Chris - I love you so much,' whispered Rhiannon, a tear filling up her left eye.

'I know. And I love you, too, Rhi,' he told her, hugging her slim, wondrous body tightly to him, warm hands exploring freely between the folds of her madly flapping shirt and his own.

'Right now Venus is hurtling like a blue tennis-ball across the black Cosmos,' announced Jake, looking up at the fast-darkening sky above them.

'Venus Williams?' asked Leone, staring through the same, open, window but at the yard below.

'No - fluff-head. The planet Venus, I'm saying,' said Jake. It might look still enough in that patch of sky over where the sun just went down, but, in fact, it is shooting along at break-neck speed, just as we are zooming along too. The major difference being that we - the Earth - are spinning round once a day, while that little planet barely rotates at all. Hence the enormous temperature contrasts on its surface.'

'You've lost me eons back,' said Leone, her mouth falling open in a yawn. 'My brain can't possibly take in all that space.' She looked down and regarded her new, black hair in her mirror.

Carla however nodded, appreciating fully the information that the simple, but knowledgeable, kid was dispensing, which kind she was often wont to process swiftly within her own smart brain, the result being that it often emerged again, not many moons after, in a musical form.

Jake looked across at Carla and each one smiled, aware they were exchanging a common thought about their relative insignificance in the wondrous universe they were barely a part of.

A loud gun-shot suddenly rang out.

'Not another one!' shrieked Leone. 'What the fuck does he think he's doing now? I hope he's not trying to impress me. Who the fuck loves pigeon-pie anyway? And I already told him I was vegetarian.'

'Leone - do you love Volver?' Carla asked her, looking up again at the twilight sky for fear the younger girl might sense her query had significance.

'Of course I do,' she answered, staring at the singer. 'He's one hell of a catch if you ask me. He could have any girl he wants he could, I bet. All my best mates for a start. And do you know, I heard that, in total, he's got three different houses and four different cars? *And* a platinum card too. And he's never been to prison neither. Christ, that's a first for me, that is.'

Carla smiled. To her mind Leone seemed so wedded to the evil man she clearly knew better than her that there was little point in even trying to enlist the young girl on her side. Young Jake, on the other hand, was proving a completely different matter, she thought. He had wavered like a candle-flame in a windy corridor the previous night, then finally succumbed to her finest, almost effortless, endeavours. Yes, it appeared

Pennant School musical-theatre had served her really well after all, thought Carla. And, having virtually won Jake over, she realised only too well that she couldn't afford to lose him now otherwise she herself would be lost; lost completely.

A car's engine could suddenly be heard approaching the farm along the track from the main road. When the vehicle finally got parked up outside the front-door Carla recognised it straightaway as belonging to Chris's girlfriend Rhiannon. Wow! This was an interesting development, she mused, but one that she knew she was going to have to keep to herself. If the car was here, then where was Rhiannon? Carla asked herself. She now began to fear for the young girl's safety; after all, like Chris she was only seventeen years old, and possibly alone.

Seconds before Leone and Jake had rushed downstairs, and both soon emerged onto the front-yard, illuminated in the little car's headlights. 'Where did you get the car?' Leone asked Steffan, who soon leapt out of the driving-seat and thrust up the bonnet. 'You didn't get it for me, did you? I loves yellow, I do. Only nobody ever taught me how to drive, see. Unless *you* want to.'

'And why would I want to do that?' asked Steffan, slamming the bonnet down. 'You have enough trouble walking, the shoes you wear.'

'Fun-ny,' said Leone. 'Hey - did you buy it, or is it nicked?' she asked him, as Volver walked across from the trees to join them, a rifle gripped under each arm.

'It was left parked up on the hill path,' the boy told Volver. 'No keys in, of course. So I punched the ignition and brought it down here.'

'What do you want to do that for?' yelled Volver, throwing his weapons down. 'Do you want to bring the cops here? Because that's what's going to happen now if we don't get rid of it.'

'Aw, can't I even have one ride in it?' pleaded Leone. 'Please, babe.'

Completely ignoring her, Volver continued. 'You need to take it somewhere where they can easily find it,' he told the boy. 'You and Jake go and dump it somewhere right now.'

'Like where?' asked Steffan.

'Take it down as far as that bridge that separates the two reservoirs at that Dolygaer place,' Volver told him. 'Then walk back on this side of the lake, along the old railway-track that runs past here towards Talybont and Brecon. That way nobody will see you.'

The two boys jumped into the car straightaway and sped off, and, seconds later, Carla watched as the yellow Fiesta hurtled down the track towards civilization once again. The singer watched its red back-lights vanish amongst the trees, then rushed over to try the door, only to find it locked as usual. She then returned to the window and waited for a few minutes until she felt sure she had caught sight of its headlights travelling south again on the road in the distance.

Carla closed the window, lay back on the bed, and began to cry. Rhiannon was out there, with or without Chris, she thought, and the temperature in this upland terrain was now starting to drop fast. If the girl happened to wander into *Candice Farm* looking for sanctuary, then there was no doubt that she would seriously regret it. Why ever did I call it *Candice Farm* just then? Carla asked herself. After all, it was called *Cwm Scwt* these days, and that was what the wooden sign back at the junction on the main road declared to all the travellers who passed by. And passed by they clearly did, she thought, since not a single soul had turned off the main road and driven up the narrow trackway to the farm in the best part of forty-eight hours.

Candice Farm had been very different about fifteen years ago, recalled Carla, around the time when she had first been invited along to sample the fun, and the music, and the accompanying excess that, on specific occasions, went on there. She couldn't actually remember having ventured into the house itself more than perhaps once or twice, she thought, since the real action, including the musical gang-bang that she had participated in, had definitely taken place in a barn somewhere thereabouts, which she recalled had sat partially hidden amongst the conifers quite some distance to the rear of the farmhouse-building she now lay abed in. Carla then suddenly remembered that she had lost her virginity in the cool, shadowy woods nearby, although, with whom, she couldn't actually say.

Carla began to think about Leila and Jackie Boyce, wondering whether the tragedy that had happened to the mother might not one day become erased in the mind of her poor daughter. She felt sure that Jackie's killing had been purely a vile act of vengeance perpetrated on the woman on account of Carla's love for her. And although she realised that it was Volver who had clearly been behind it, Carla herself felt a terrible responsibility for what had taken place

The singer then began thinking about her poor father back home in *Gloryhole*. Who was looking after him now, she wondered, now that she was no longer there to help him? Was Chris or his mother able to spend time with him, and meet the bulk of his daily needs? She hoped they were. And was Rhiannon helping out too? she wondered. A feeling of horror suddenly came over her, wondering where the sweet young girl with the heart of gold could be right that moment, now that she had become sadly separated from the safety of her motor-car.

At the first and only phone-booth the two boys came to, they found the instrument to be wholly castrated, its twisted, coloured tassels all that were left at the end of its, normally vocal, cords.

'Where is your mobile-phone again?' asked Steffan.

'Like I told you, I'm not sure,' said Jake. 'You know, it could even be upstairs in her room. But I hope not.'

'What! I tell you if Carla has got it then you're toast, pal,' Steffan told him, chuckling maliciously. 'Just you wait 'til Volver finds out.'

Jake suddenly felt he wanted to strike his companion with his fist, but knew from painful experience that such a course of action was totally out of the question. Instead he turned his head to the side, and stared blankly at the gleaming, anthracite surface of the vast, serpentine lake that extended south from them all the way back to the dam and the tower at Pontsticill.

'Hey! There's no need to cry about it,' said Steffan. He wandered over towards a low wall and picked up a few slabs of rock, then steadied himself and hurled one point-blank at the open door of the phone-box, then another at its side, smashing a glass panel to smithereens. He then threw a third at its other side. 'I didn't have any coins on me, anyway,' he told Jake, grinning.

'But why are you trying to ring him?' asked Jake. 'I'm pretty sure he wouldn't have driven down here to get us anyway because he already told us to return along the old railway-track. And it's probably quicker than walking back along the road we drove down on, don't you think?

'Do you know that railway route, then?' asked Steffan. 'Because I've never been along it before. Say - what's up?'

'My phone,' said Jake, baring his teeth. 'I remember now I left it on the dash-board of the Fiesta.'

'You did what!' yelled Steffan. 'You numbskull! We can't let the fuzz find that. Now we have to go back to the bridge and get it. Shit! Well, come on - let's go.'

The two boys strode down the hill again in the dark. When they reached the parked-up Fiesta, Steffan leaned in through the broken, passenger-side window and collected the phone, then threw it to Jake.

The unmarked police-car that approached, lighting up the two boys clearly, was driven by D.I.Dawson, and navigated by his colleague D.C.Shah, (who had missed the left-hand turn for The Beacons and Talybont,) and so the car they were in coasted round the lakeside bend and up to the bridge. Seeing two boys standing beside a car with a smashed window, they pulled up, climbed out of the car, and walked quickly towards them.

'What's up boys?' Dawson asked them, illuminating their faces in the beam of his torch.

'We noticed this car parked up here, guv,' said Steffan, thinking fast. 'It's a stupid place to leave your car, don't you think? Well, I mean there's criminals and all sorts living round here, and you never know who could be walking past, do you?'

'So it looks like,' said Shah, smiling.

'Do you know whose car it is?' enquired Dawson, inspecting the damage to the window and the bust ignition. The boys shrugged their shoulders and shook their heads in reply. 'Because it looks to me like the criminals have only just finished with it.'

'It's been sitting there for ages, man,' said Jake. 'We noticed it from up on the hill over there, so naturally we came down to take a look.'

Shah felt the bonnet with his palm, then checked the car's front-tyres. 'It's still hot,' he told his colleague.

'And do you lads live round here, then?' Dawson asked them.

'Not exactly,' said Steffan.

'How far from here?' asked Shah.

The two boys looked at each other. 'Probably about five or six miles,' replied Steffan.

'Really? And how were you intending to get back there?' the young officer continued. 'Wouldn't be in a yellow Fiesta, would it?'

'We're planning to walk back,' said Steffan. 'Even without hurrying, we're sure to be home again soon after midnight.'

'Well, it all looks mighty suspicious to me,' said Dawson. 'What's your name, lad?' he asked Steffan.

'Barlow,' Steffan answered, gritting his teeth.

Dawson made a note of this in his pocket-book. 'First name?'

'Er - Gareth,' said Steffan, looking away.

'O.K. And you?' he asked Jake.

'Me? Er - Walsh,' replied Jake.

'First name?' asked Dawson. He looked up. 'It wouldn't be Louis, would it? Or Lewis, perhaps, more like?' He and Shah exchanged knowing glances.

'I don't understand,' said Jake. 'My first name's Simon, actually. Always has been.'

Dawson wrote this down. 'Are either of you known to police, then, lads?' he asked. Both boys shook their heads. 'Right, then I'll just go and run your names through,' said

Dawson, walking back to the police-car. Suddenly spinning round, he yelled, 'And if everything checks out, and the computer tells me neither of you has warrants, then I dare say you'll be free to continue your night-time yomp.'

'Hey - see if you can find out who owns the Fiesta while you're at it, Sir,' shouted Shah.

Chris and Rhiannon woke up to the sound of a genuine, ear-piercing, country cockerel. They looked about them and saw that the barn they had broken into the previous evening now seemed much larger in the cold light of day. And cold it certainly still was, despite their noticing through the broken panels in the arched roof that day had clearly broken.

'I still can't believe that my car has gone,' said Rhiannon. 'My dad will be furious.'

'I guess so,' said Chris, picking something up from amongst the bed of straw upon which his body, and that of his girlfriend, lay.

'Show it me,' she said. 'And tell me again how you know it's Steffan's.'

Chris held up the small, green, plaid scarf. 'Oh, it's his all right. I don't know anyone else who wears a muffler like this,' he told her. 'And if you still don't believe me, then check out the initials on the underside. Oh, it's Steffan's, all right. No doubt about that.'

They suddenly heard a strange noise that sounded like the whirr of a helicopter hovering close by, then crossing over the sky above them, and so jumped up and hurried towards the closed barn-door. But soon, emerging into the morning sunlight, they found that they were too late, as the craft they sought to catch a glimpse of had already passed them by.

'Did you see it?' asked Rhiannon, running about to get a clearer view of the sky.

'No, I didn't,' said Chris. 'But this one was almost certainly the police searching the hills for Carla. But they obviously haven't got a clue where she might be, so that's probably why they are flying so fast.'

'Well, do *we* have any better idea where she is, then?' asked Rhiannon.

Chris rolled his bottom-lip and considered her question. 'Well, at least we know that Steffan is around here,' he told her. 'And I dare say that means that Volver has to be in the vicinity too.'

'Well, if that's true, then Carla must be not far away, either,' added Rhiannon, 'since I guess they have to have her incarcerated close to where they are.'

'Then let's not waste any time,' said Chris. 'With or without your car, let's go off and continue searching for her, shall we?'

Initially Carla thought that the weird sound she heard outside the window might be an articulated lorry on the main road that ran away towards her childhood home-village, but quickly realising how impossible that would be on a route as narrow, steep and undulating as the road that traversed the mountain-pass, and then descended in a series of crazy double-bends towards Talybont, she began to consider that it might actually be a helicopter or a low-flying aeroplane.

Carla walked over to the window and lifted the lower half of it up a foot or so, and was straightaway taken aback by the strength of the cool breeze that flew inside, bringing a host of flying insects with it. Had the weather changed suddenly, then? she asked herself. She leaned her head outside to see, and quickly saw that thin, grey clouds now lay over the plateau to the west like an immense dust-sheet over a grand piano. It was plain that today was likely to be a lot more like the August days of a year ago, when some of the outdoor gigs she was invited to perform at, on her circuit of British summer-festivals, had either had to be curtailed, or forced to take place on dull, uninspiring days, often plagued with sodden ground and leaking tents.

Turning to walk away from the window, Carla suddenly saw that a man had entered the room, and now stood looking across at her from the farthest, dimmest corner. She blinked, then rubbed her fingers across her eyes, so as to better validate her observation. Yes, it seemed that this was truly happening, she told herself, although how exactly she hadn't a notion. Though fitter, more handsome, and far younger than she could ever remember him, there was no doubt in her mind that the man who stood gazing at her across her un-made bed was none other than her dear father.

Mouth agape, her body trembling, Carla continued to stare at Tom, now standing tall before her in his best black suit and black tie, with his hands down at his sides, his broad head steady, his ice-blue eyes fixed firmly upon hers, his lips moving, as if speaking, though strangely silent. For a few short seconds Carla thought her father well, and unquestionably alive, and the rush of pure joy she felt was palpable. But then, as he remained firmly fixed to the spot, and the sound of his lovely, lilting voice didn't reach her ears, the thought suddenly crossed her mind that the exact opposite might in fact be the case, and that he was alive no longer. And, to Carla's great sadness, it was this latter notion which before long triumphed in her consciousness and consumed her, and that caused her eyes to bulge out, as if on stalks, her mouth to quiver like jelly, and her ankles and feet to shake beneath her.

'Oh, Dad - I feel that you have passed,' whispered Carla, knowing it a fact, but hoping that her saddest of claims might yet prove untrue. At these words, her father seemed to nod to her just once, then disappeared completely from sight. Astounded by this, and more distressed than at any time in her life, Carla crumpled helplessly to her knees on the bedroom floor, and, her bare arms outstretched and shuddering wildly before her, her head forced into the duvet on her bed, she screamed out a strange, squealing sound that her body had never emitted even once before, but which for Carla spoke powerfully and expressively to the world of the living, of which she was still a tragic, moving part, of the heart-rending sorrow and anguish she now felt at her dear father's last departure, at his leaving her, unsupported and alone, to board his long-awaited, final train.

CHAPTER 24

'Don't be so bloody negative, for God's sake. Almost everything can be turned round, lads. Out of every ditch a path, if only one could see it.' These were the words of Sergeant Foley from the back-seat of his police-car, that Constable Ben Thomas was driving, and Constable Llewellyn was patiently navigating, with the aid of an old, coffee-stained, over-folded and badly split, ordnance-survey map, that they had always kept in the passenger-door pocket.

As if by some magic spell, all three officers suddenly stared across to their right at Pontsticill Reservoir, its surface now glistening majestically in the early morning sunlight, as they sped past it on the road which ran north, towards the peaks, and ultimately to Talybont and Brecon.

'That's where the tragedy happened - just there,' said Sergeant Foley, pointing at the water.

'Tragedy? You can't mean the village in the valley that was buried by this lake over a century ago,' said Llewellyn, 'because I don't imagine anybody got killed back then, did they, Sarge?'

'I'm talking about Carla's Steel's brother, boys,' Foley told them, grimacing. 'That was a very bad business that was, I can tell you. Drowned in the very middle of it while out swimming he was, and she, poor dab, his only hope for life. God, I remember it like it was yesterday. The poor young girl could play every scale known to man, on piano and guitar, and Handel's *Water Music* too, I shouldn't wonder, but could she swim? Not a yard. Jesus, I can't imagine she will ever forgive herself for that, you know. It's little wonder she took to drugs if you ask me.'

'*And* went off to England,' added Llewellyn.

'Aye, to England. To it's capital city too,' said Foley. 'Mind you, that alone would have certainly turned me to drugs, I can tell you. Though I'd have drawn the line at turning bi-sexual, naturally.' He smiled. 'We blame the English for an awful lot sometimes, I feel, but we can hardly blame them for doing that. After all, lads, they do have something that nobody else has got that sort of mitigates against it ever happening.'

'And what's that?' asked Llewellyn, turning round to face him.

'Kelly Brook,' the sergeant told him.

'Kelly Brook!' said Thomas, changing gear to round a tight bend as they neared Dolygaer. 'Agyness Deyn, more like.'

'Agyness Deyn!' yelled Llewellyn. 'God, it's legs all day with you, Ben, isn't it? Imogen Thomas for me, any day. Now there's a real woman.'

'But she's one of us, you damn fool,' said Foley. 'Her dad grew up in the same town as I did. Wow! Just look at that trout jump! Did you see that, boys?'

'I missed it,' said Llewellyn.

'And I'm driving the car, Sarge,' said Ben.

'Too bad. My, it's a lovely sight up here this time of the morning, don't you think? Reminds me of something my old dad used to say to me, God rest his Celtic soul, when I was just a boy, and we were out fishing. 'Cast thy bread upon the waters,' he used to tell me, 'and it shall come back to thee with knobs on.' And I tell you what, lads, I've never forgotten it, either.'

The two young constables turned slowly and regarded each other.

'Hey, there's Dyl's van parked-up on the verge!' yelled the sergeant. 'This is a bit early in the day even for him, wouldn't you say? Stop here for a minute, Ben.'

I saw the police-car pull up just ahead of me. Sergeant Foley was in the rear, and he it was who soon wound down his window and yelled out to me.

'What the hell are you doing up here so early, Dyl?' he asked.

I got out of the van and walked ahead of it to speak with the man. 'My daughter Rhiannon never came home last night,' I told him. 'And Chris - the boy from Gloryhole she's seeing - still hasn't returned either. I just went and checked with his mother. In short, I'm very worried.'

'Are they likely to be in a car?' asked Foley.

'She took her yellow Fiesta,' I told him. 'So that's what I'm presently out looking for.'

'Well, we can certainly help you there,' said Constable Llewellyn from the front. 'It's parked-up near the bridge just up ahead of us. We're going round there now to check it out, as it goes.'

'Why don't you follow us down there, Dyl,' said Foley, smiling.

And so I did. Within minutes of setting out in tandem we reached the little yellow car I had purchased only months before, as a reward for my daughter passing her driving-test at her first attempt. From the outside it looked quite damaged, but I was hopeful that the engine was still fully intact and in as good order as I had left it a week or so before.

'Two of our boys stopped a couple of local lads messing about round it last night,' Merlyn Foley told me. 'But we didn't have grounds to hold them, you know. They claimed they had only arrived to look at it just minutes before our officers got there.'

'Who were these boys?' I asked, ducking my head inside the car, and seeing how it had clearly been hot-wired and taken, praying that Rhiannon hadn't been inside it when it happened, and that she and Chris hadn't suffered a car-jacking.

'Well, they gave my two London colleagues the run-around I'm afraid, Dyl,' Foley replied, 'with their false names and alibis, you know, that any of us local coppers would have kicked into touch within minutes.'

'Seconds,' added Llewellyn.

'Then they just let the buggers go. But, if it's any consolation, their descriptions suggest to me they were almost certainly that - that Steffan Jones from Pant and his lanky Dowlais mate.'

'Jake Haines,' I told him.

'That's the one,' said Foley. 'The odd chap who seems to go round wearing a different coloured planet on his t-shirts every bleeding day of the week. Last night it appears he was a Venus in blue jeans. Hang on, Dyl - I'm almost sure I bought that record once.'

'Me, too, Merlyn,' I told him, smiling. 'Mark Wynter, wasn't it? And I'm pretty sure I went out with that girl he was singing about, too. She lived in a pre-fab in Dowlais Top around that time.'

Sergeant Foley and I enjoyed a little laugh about this, but not much more than that, since I could see that this whole business was starting to look a very serious one indeed. First a kidnapped singer, then two police-officers who had come down all the way from London to aid the investigation, two missing young people, a stolen car, and now two local tearaways who seemed to be somehow mixed up in it all. Yes, I was becoming very worried indeed, and, apart from retrieving the Fiesta again, and perhaps towing it home, I didn't really know what to do.

'Do you know the forested land up here very well, Dyl?' the sergeant asked me.

'Well, about as well as anyone from Merthyr, I suppose,' I told him. 'Why, Merlyn? Do you want me to join the search with you then?'

'Well, you won't be able to get your Fiesta back yet anyway,' he told me, 'because it's about to get lifted back to the station, but you could do a lot worse than follow behind us on the road through The Beacons if you like, and down towards Talybont. How about it? Just beep or flash us if you want us to stop, or think we ought to be turning off somewhere.'

I agreed to the sergeant's proposal, and within seconds we had gone back to the junction, turned right, and, speeding up the hill, drove northwards along the narrow, winding road that led us into the heart of the mountains, where it now appeared that the two missing young people, and possibly Carla Steel herself, might well be. As I drove past the tiny church and then down the steep hill to skirt the water's edge again, it suddenly occurred to me that all three young people might now be being held together against their will in the very same place, but, as this notion seemed to be more a product of my paternal fears rather than anything more concrete, I quickly cast it aside, and instead tried to focus my attention on the roads, and the side-lanes, and the narrow track-ways that we repeatedly came across, and which seemed to open up unexpectedly all about us in a sort of haphazard, geometric progression, very like the minor tributaries of a river, as the high, shadowy peaks of The Beacons loomed much closer in the early morning light.

Carla was beginning to fear the worst. Jake hadn't spoken a word to her since early that morning, and, although she offered to wash his blue, Venus t-shirt for him, having helpfully pointed out to him how grubby it had become from his unexplained excursion the night before, the boy declined, and then swiftly went off and washed and dried it himself. Even Leone didn't knock on Carla's door for their customary morning chit-chat regarding hair-care and shower- times, instead remaining downstairs in the large farmhouse kitchen, where the boys almost always hung out, presumably catering to their daily needs. Yes, something was definitely afoot, thought Carla.

She moved across the room and pressed her temple to the door and listened. The few sounds she managed to make out on the floor below were no longer those of high-jinks and excitement, but rather those of ill-temper and dissension. Most likely, Carla told herself, Volver's efforts to secure a large ransom for her safe return had capitulated, or, much more likely perhaps, were being frustrated by delay. Yes, she pondered, delay did seem to be the usual tactic pursued by the police in cases such as these, and Carla was certain that, by now, they must be deeply involved in a thorough search for the kidnap-location. She was hopeful that a yellow police-helicopter might soon roar like a hungry lion in the sky above her, and might even fly close by her window; or that she would catch sight of a police-car flashing its spinning, blue light as it swerved and coasted like a rally-car along the main road in the valley below.

But when would that be? Carla wondered, if happen it ever did. Or could it be that the farmhouse she was trapped in by a gun-toting megalomaniac, former boyfriend - an Afrikaner madman with a real axe to grind - lay too far from the road, and too greatly hidden by the high conifers that clothed the lower mountain slopes, that a potential rescue was out of the question.

The late morning sun - Carla's second visitor so far that day - now began to fire its searing rays into the room, but knowing that it was unlikely to bring her anything resembling comfort or consolation, she quickly walked across and adjusted the curtain so as to shade her eyes. She raised the window's base, however, and began peering out. She could see that the distant road was again empty of traffic, and she realised that, even if vehicles were presently passing by, there would be little point in screaming out, as, apart from the fact that everyone in the building would hear her, there was no possibility that her voice could carry that far.

It was just then that Carla caught sight of her two young friends. She blinked and stared ahead of her, fearing that her eyes might be playing tricks on her, and yet Carla felt sure that, somewhere amidst the branches of the spruce and fir trees that grew on the downward valley slope before her, she could make out the forms of Chris and Rhiannon, standing slightly apart, and peering back up in the direction of the farmhouse she was currently detained in.

After half a minute or so had passed by, Carla came to realise that it was inconceivable that the pair could make out her form anything like as clearly as she was now able to see them. She began to wrack her brain for a means by which she might be able to attract the pair's attention. There seemed little within the actual room that she felt she could use to assist her, but the window's curtains were a different matter. Carla quickly stood on a chair and opened up the top half of the window, then grasped one of the long, brown curtains, and, bit by bit, fed it out through the gap into the morning breeze outside.

Fully four or five minutes must have passed by before either of the two young people in Carla's line of sight seemed to notice any discernible change. Then she suddenly saw Rhiannon attracting her lover's attention, then pointing up the slope towards her. She watched as the pair got together, conversed, then, hand-in-hand, ducked nimbly out of sight amongst the conifers. It was done, thought Carla. She beamed out a broad smile that she hoped the pair might make out, but, whether they were able to or no, she turned round and began gambolling about the room like a Spring fawn, soon after climbing onto the bed, and, curled up in a tight ball, began deliberating on whether there might be anything she could still do that she hadn't yet done.

It was quite a while before Carla remembered the curtain, its flapping sound suddenly attracting her attention. Carla began to fear that during that time she might have drifted off to sleep, so, leaping up, she ran to the window to pull the flapping cloth inside. But she soon saw that it was too late. Looking down, Carla noticed that all four of her kidnappers were presently standing in the yard below, gazing up, one or two shaking their heads, the others laughing loudly at her sorry efforts. Scared, she leapt away from the window and thought about Chris and Rhiannon, and especially the fact that they too were now so perilously close to being captured.

Carla began trembling with fear, and, eyes wide, stared down helplessly at her shaking hands. Feeling dreadfully alone and powerless, she sank to her knees, and began to pray to the God that her mother, her Uncle Gary, and, yes, in recent times, even her father had instilled in her. She prayed that her dad was now safe in heaven in the arms of his late wife - her mother Carys - and that the mightier Father she hoped was still available to her, might use His great power to free her from the clutches of Abram Kronfield - that serial murderer and insane instrument of Satan, who had kidnapped her just two days before, and whom she knew would happily snuff out her life as he would a candle's flame, and as he had already done, at the slightest provocation, to the wonderful, spirited lives of her dear, departed friends Dave Cronin and Jackie Boyce.

The old, crumbling, brownstone wall behind which Chris and Rhiannon took refuge was no more than fifty yards from the farmhouse, but, having succeeded in not betraying their presence when the strange group of people they partially recognised came outside and took note of Carla's signal, the young couple at least felt relatively safe there. The pair were also out of sight of the track-way that ran up from *Cwm Scwt* to the road-junction off to their left, and also screened off by more trees from the main road itself, which wound its way through the narrow valley some distance behind and below them.

But, now that the two young people had managed to locate Carla, more by luck than judgement it seemed, deciding what to do next was far from an easy matter. After all, without a charged mobile-phone between them, by which to contact the police, (or indeed anyone else for that matter,) and fearing that the kidnappers would discover them, they felt that venturing down the grassy slope towards the road, and attempting to stop passing traffic, would most likely place them in harm's way.

'I've got an idea,' said Rhiannon, grasping Chris by the arm and staring into his big brown eyes. 'Why don't I stand on the down-slope side of one of these trees here and wave a flag of some kind at a car as it's passing by?' Or my blouse or something?'

'And why don't flash your rear end at them while you're at it?' said Chris, shaking his head about. 'Because I guess they'll be certain to stop then.' At this, Rhiannon pouted, let go of his arm and looked away. 'Don't you see, Rhiannon, that if just one driver chooses to stop his car on the road down there, then the kidnappers at the farm would most likely see it too,' he told her, pointing up at *Cwm Scwt*, 'and then that could put us in real danger. After all, they can clearly see the road from the farmhouse. And anyway, what if the car that stops turns out to be one of theirs? Hey? Then we're really done for, right?'

'Yes, but what if it's a police-car?' asked Rhiannon.

'Well, wouldn't that be fantastic,' replied Chris. 'But tell me, have we seen one yet? No, babe, we need to stay put behind this wall here and see what happens. If a police-car or helicopter gets here, well, then we can probably make our presence known to them somehow. But that man in the shades we saw earlier happens to be called Volver, and I know for sure he'll stop at nothing to get his ransom demand for Carla met. And, you see, that could mean taking us out.'

'But how do you know this Volver man?' asked Rhiannon. 'After all, he's a criminal, right?'

'Well, earlier this year I sort of got very involved with Jake and Steffan,' Chris told her.

'Do you mean selling drugs?' asked Rhiannon. 'Because everyone says that's what *they* do.'

'Well weed, yes,' said Chris. 'But I never got involved with anything else, I swear.'

'So you sold drugs, yes?' said Rhiannon, staring fixedly at him. 'And not just to Carla, right? Look - you might as well be honest with me, Chris. If you really love me, as you say you do, then I know you'll want to come clean about it.'

Chris bit into his lip, then raised his lowered head to look at her. 'I grew cannabis in Tom's loft, and then, when it was mature, I cut it and sold it to that man Volver,' he told her, pointing to the farmhouse. 'It was he who used Steffan, Jake and the Flynn boys to sell it round the town. But it's all been cleared out now.'

'Oh, really?' she said. 'And why should I believe you?'

'Why? Well, because your father did it, that's why,' said Chris.

'My father!' exclaimed Rhiannon.

'That's right,' Chris told her. 'You see, when he discovered that Tom had died he dumped everything that was up there to save the family from any grief. The lights, the transformers, the timing-unit and filters for the hydroponics, and of course all the pots of weed that were growing.'

'My dad did all that!' exclaimed Rhiannon, her eyes wide.

'Yes, he did,' Chris told her. 'I wasn't at home that day, you see, and he and my mother did it to - well, to cover up for me.'

'You know, I guess it's pretty clear now my dad happens to like you, Chris,' said Rhiannon.

'Well, yes, it seems he does,' Chris told her, smiling thinly.

Rhiannon suddenly looked away. 'But, you know, I'm not at all sure I can put up with all this - all this crap,' she told him, then looking back into his eyes again. 'Because that's what it is, right? And anyway, why should I? You know, Chris, I always believed you were a lot better than that.'

A helicopter could be heard flying towards them from the mountain peaks to the north. The two young people turned and gazed up at the whirring, black-and-yellow craft, that seemed to Rhiannon to resemble a very noisy wasp on the rampage through a country picnic. It approached at speed, its four rotor-blades spinning at such a velocity that they might have been the spin-cycle of her mother's washing-machine. At the last moment the craft veered away from them to the right, to the east, and flew at low altitude through the high pass of Torpantau, then, with a markedly decreasing volume, disappeared down the widening valley in the direction of Talybont Reservoir, the village, and the verdant Usk Valley that lay beyond that.

His police-radio blaring madly, and his brawny, shirt-sleeved arms full of bulging, white paper-bags, Constable Llewellyn emerged from *Nice Baps* and walked slowly into the main road, causing traffic on both sides to halt and wait for him to cross. He suddenly turned and glared at the driver of the one solitary car that dared sound its horn at him.

'I'm a copper on a double-shift, mate, O.K.?' he told the fuming driver, staring at him with a sadistic smirk through the man's passenger-window. 'And that there's a bakery. Do you get it? Good. Have a nice day now.'

Llew stood and watched the man drive away, then turned and approached the two cars his colleagues were sitting in, parked behind one another in the lay-by of the bus-stop just across from the shop, each officer patiently awaiting his return.

'Cheeky bugger! I'm surprised you didn't hurl a jam-doughnut in his chops,' said Sergeant Foley, chuckling. 'Yours, of course.'

'In his cake-hole, yeah?' said Ben, smiling benignly from the driver-seat.

'I felt sorry for the bloke, actually,' Llew replied, handing all the bags he was carrying to his bottle-blond, fellow constable to distribute.

'Oh? Why was that?' asked Ben, climbing out of the car to make the task easier.

'Well, his road-tax was more than six months out of date, and he works in the garage opposite mine,' Llew told him. 'So tomorrow the short-arsed Celt should be getting a little visit from me, know what I mean? And you never know, if all goes well I might soon be getting a free quote for my next service and M.O.T.'

'You scratch my back,' said Sergeant Foley, licking his lips as he opened up his paper-bag of treats.

'Exactly,' said Llew, smiling. 'And those tinted windows he was sporting could be worth a nice soft hand-wash or two, don't you reckon?'

'And there's me thinking you had a wife who did all that,' Ben told him, trying hard to contain a laugh, as he moved on to serve the officers in the second car with their savoury brunch.

Llew turned and glared at his colleague's fast-retreating back. 'For my Volvo, dip-stick,' he told him. The burly constable got into the passenger-seat of the car, and wasted not a second in biting deeply into his steaming-hot pasty. 'God! What I'd give for some ketchup right now, Sarge,' he announced. 'How's yours?'

'Beautiful, boy bach,' Foley told his bulkier colleague. 'You can't beat a piping hot sausage-roll, I reckon. What did you get the cockneys, by the way? Jellied eels?' Foley laughed merrily.

'Two meat-pies,' said Llew. 'They're not going to be happy, I'm afraid. They weren't half as hot, see. And I hope to God there's no pork in them.'

'Mind you, our pies are probably not half as bad as you get up in that London,' said Foley.

D.C. Shah approached the window of their car. Leaning on it, a bag of crisps in his other hand, he began to address them. 'I was just telling Ben, we managed to find out from the station where that *Candice Fatm* actually is.'

'But *I* could have told you that,' Foley told him. 'Why did you want to know anyway?'

'Well, I know it's a long shot, Sergeant,' said Shah, 'but the D.I. and I reckon that's where Carla Steel might be. Ironical, you might say, but a possibility, yeah? Say - would you know how to get there, Sergeant?'

'But of course,' said Foley. 'Tell Mister Dawson I'd be glad to take him up there. Just let us finish our grub first, there's a good boy. And, you know lads, I do believe I'm going to need something to wash this lot down with, too. Hey Llew - pop in the pub for a couple of bottles of stout for me, would you? Look, I know they're not open yet, but just tell Jean who it's for, O.K., and have her put it on the tab.'

Pasty already eaten, Constable Llewellyn climbed out of the car and disappeared into the nearest building to the bus-stop, where the delivery men from the brewery had already pulled up the cellar-cover, and were busy with ropes, dropping large barrels below ground.

'I can see *those chaps* have already had a pint, see, Ben,' Foley told his uniformed colleague sitting in front of him. 'So a couple of bottles shouldn't be a problem, right? Hey, I hope you're picking all this up, by the way, Ben, because I won't be here next year to teach you, you know.'

'Where do you plan to be next summer, then, Sarge?' asked the bleach-blond constable, chewing the last remnants of his brunch.

'Where? Me and the missus will hopefully be sunning ourselves down the Gower Peninsula, by then, lad. Yes, weather permitting, I intend to be lying on a sea-facing slope in my khaki shorts and vest, slapping masses of sun-cream on *The Worm's Head*.'

P.C. Thomas looked at his sergeant in the rear-view mirror. 'That's a damn funny name to be calling the wife, 'innit Sarge?'he said, swiftly ducking to avoid the heavy clout to the back of his head that he knew full well would be coming his way. Thankfully the older man's aim wasn't true, but the second swipe, which Ben wasn't at all expecting, caught him smartly in the ear, and rendered him helpless, bent double, and impotent, beneath the car's steering-wheel.

After circling the village of Talybont (where Tom had told me his family had lived decades earlier), and seeing nothing remotely of interest, I drove my van back westwards past the great, serpentine Talybont Reservoir, then sped along the remaining section of the relatively straight road that ran west, right up to the foot of the steep, zig-zag section that wound its way right up to the high pass through the Beacons at Torpantau. The steep gradient of this tricky climb meant that I took each and every one of its double-bends in first-gear, dodging numerous families of dozy, newly-sheered sheep at each and every turn.

As I drove past the site of the old station-halt, and slid down alongside the mountain stream, I suddenly saw someone who looked remarkably like my daughter sitting amongst the conifers that grew upon the steep, grassy slope to my left. I slowed the vehicle down and peered across to see more clearly, and saw that it was indeed her, and that she had by now stood up and seemed to be furiously waving me on, as was an even more excited Chris Cillick, who was standing behind her. Despite still feeling I must stop, I drove on slowly, and soon rose up the hill to the junction with the Roman Road, that took off right, and made its way deep into the heart of the peaks. Not knowing what best to do, I waited at the signpost for fully half a minute, then turned off left onto the road that went south towards Pontsticill, Merthyr, and my home.

I soon parked up in the first lay-by I encountered, and then decided to get out of the van and walk back a few hundred yards or so to peer back through the trees towards the site where I had just seen the two young people standing. But, unsurprisingly, I discovered that the pair now appeared to be completely out of sight, and so I turned and walked briskly back along the road towards my vehicle, picked up my mobile-phone, and rang Merthyr police. The lady who answered my call told me that two of their cars were fast approaching along the road where I was parked, and so I climbed back into the van and waited for them to arrive at the scene, which, minutes later, they did.

The two cars slowed and halted in the middle of the carriageway. In the marked car sat the corpulent Sergeant Foley, and it was he who told me that they had arrived to check out a local farm called *Cwm Scwt*, which lay some short distance away, and he suggested that, rather than follow after them, I remain where I was, and wait for them to get back to me.

But when the two police-cars drove off, I nevertheless decided to make a turn in the road and shadow them. Defying police instructions wasn't normally a course of action I would take, naturally, but I told myself that my daughter's safety was involved here, and so my decision seemed quite a straightforward one.

Reaching the road-junction again, and its sign-post for Talybont, our entourage suddenly halted. I looked across the narrow valley once more and could see that the young couple were definitely no longer in the location in which they had been when I saw them. Then I suddenly remembered that perhaps the police up ahead of me hadn't been told about the presence of Rhiannon and Chris, and so I climbed out of my van to approach them and let them know. But as I edged along the carriageway towards the junction, it was precisely then that something rather extraordinary happened.

Approaching us up the steep slope, its iconic rattling and whistling sound heralding its arrival, came Jack Belt's old, green camper-van, with Jack himself seated in it at the wheel. Seemingly oblivious to the three cars halted at the junction, he indicated, and slowly turned left, then, without making eye-contact with anyone, drove straight past us in the direction from which we had all just arrived. Unsurprisingly, and almost immediately, the two police-cars ahead of me circled the mini-roundabout and, accelerating fast, headed southwards straight after him.

Thinking about Rhiannon and Chris, and especially the fact that I hadn't informed Foley and his colleagues of their presence, I decided it might be best to remain where I was and await their return. But, after sitting in the road for some time, I began to think that this could take forever, and so, largely out of boredom, I stepped out of the van, and walked slowly along the road that ran downhill into the shallow vale, and towards the spot in the trees where I had earlier seen the young pair standing.

'You know, I bet you probably can't remember the first time you met me, can you, Carla?' said Volver, looking up from the wheel to the rear-view mirror, and staring directly through it into the singer's drawn and weary looking face, cramped and scared as she clearly was from sitting between two males in the back seat of his brand-new, and scarily silent-running, Range Rover.

Rather than reply to his question, the diminutive, curly-headed singer sighed, and then closed her tired eyes, and rubbed the sleep from them with her short, ringless fingers. At a second glance the South African told himself that she must be screaming back at him under her breath, 'Why the hell would I want to remember when that event happened?' But being the man, and unquestionably being the one in total charge right now, Volver decided to make her anyway.

'Those were the days, eh, girl?' he remarked, 'as that Mary Hopkin bird once sang out from some valley hereabouts.' The two boys turned and glanced uncomprehendingly at each other across the face of Carla, and in the front-seat Leone turned sideways to look at him, being every bit as clueless on the subject. 'You know, when boys were clearly boys, and girls looked more like women than rag-dolls. And when the powder-room really was a room for actually powdering in, if you know what I mean.' Volver chuckled at his ingenuity. 'In those days they certainly wouldn't have let you sit in there for hours on end with your daddling mates, missy.'

Carla huffed at his comment. 'And when girls often loved their boys enough to be willing to keep their criminal activities under wraps for them, you mean,' she said, looking to her side at the sign they sped past which she was shocked to see now announce '*Cwm Scwt*' when she had fully expected it to still read '*Candice Farm,*' as it had done in days gone by, and would continue to say for all time in her dreams, and in the song-book of her creative mind.

Miffed at Carla's sharp response, Volver turned his proud head and sniffed the air that blew in from the spruce trees that rushed by his window, rather than encounter her dark, accusing eyes again in the small, convex glass, and so acknowlege the truth the singer spoke. 'And when, I well recall, some girls loved other girls a lot more than they did their own boyfriends,' he told her, smiling at her the kind of forced grin it pained the muscles of his jaw to hold in place. 'And enough, I recall, to get a young black one to take the fucking rap for one more famous one, yes?'

'Jackie did it to save you, you liar,' retorted Carla. 'And Sarah and I had to step in to save her Leila from being taken away. Yes, we did it for *your* daughter, Abram,' she added. 'Because Leila is your child, as you certainly must know by now. And Jackie would never have got locked up at all if you'd had the balls to admit to the cops what it was that you and your pals were up to. But bravery was something you clearly left behind you in Durban, along with your twelve-bore and your saddle-bag. Around the time you proudly told us all how you ran a scam there escorting English and American tourists, with more money than sense, on shooting safaris round a one-lion enclosure you fraudulently set up with miles of chicken-wire, on a farm you bought from - stole from, more like - a poor, black family, whose crop that year had failed in the drought.'

'Wow, what a memory you've, got girl!' the Afrikaner told her. 'I see now there are things I should never have shared with you back then, Carla dear. When you were my bed companion as well as the love of my life. Well, one of them anyway.'

'Which fact I very soon gleaned from Jackie. Yes, she found out a lot about you for me when she worked in that lap-dancing club you ran in Hammersmith as a cover for your drug-empire.'

Volver gritted his teeth. 'But still I got my revenge, I guess,' he snarled back.

'Yes, you certainly did that, didn't you, Abram?' replied Carla. 'When you and that ape you consorted with at the time killed our best friend Dave Cronin, the only man I can say I ever truly loved. And then, years later, poor Jackie herself. Christ, you went and murdered a young, black mother over a few bags of dope, leaving her young daughter an orphan. Wow! That must make you feel very proud, eh? You're a low-down scum-bag and you know it, Abram Kronfield.'

'Ah, but there was a principle involved, wasn't there?' Volver retorted. 'And anyway, Jackie wasn't just a dancer and an addict, was she?' said Volver. 'Your Jackie friend was a common-or-garden prostitute. And let's be honest, she wasn't at all particular where she did it, was she? On the common, or in the garden.' The South African bellowed out his loudest laugh yet.

'You sound pathetic trying to slander the name of an innocent young addict,' retorted Carla. 'The mother of your daughter, too. And now she's just another of your long list of dead victims.'

'Yeah, so you say,' said Volver. 'And anyway Dave Cronin was her pimp, plain and simple. Let's be honest - the pair of them were the scum of the earth, and killing them was probably doing a tremendous service to the good folk of west London. A sort of ethnic cleansing you could say, only without the ethnic.'

'Oh, it was *ethnic* all right,' snapped Carla. 'The wonder of it all is that you haven't had Leila, your daughter, killed too, her skin being the colour that it is.'

Volver ignored her comment and, thinking fast, sped the SUV round a bend. 'Incidentally, Carla, your dad is certainly taking enormous risks with your safety by refusing to meet our demands, wouldn't you say? I mean, he's had our ransom-note for days now and we still haven't heard a word. Are you sure the man even loves you?'

Carla considered for a moment how she should reply. 'My dad is a very sick old man, you know,' she told him. 'If he'd finally passed away, do you think you guys would even get to hear about it?'

'Oh, now surely you're not telling me that missing you for a few days is likely to finish the old boy off, are you?' sneered Volver. 'Do me a favour, Carla. I mean how many years is it since you were last back here to see the old codger? Ages, right? He probably loves his budgie more.'

Carla suddenly recalled the chilling moment that her dead father had appeared to her in the upstairs-room where she had been incarcerated. Eerie, and incredibly sad, though it clearly was, the strange event seemed to offer her a hope that she felt desperately in need of just then. Gazing at the light gleaming on the great lake to her left, she quickly thanked God for the same.

A mobile-phone started ringing in the front of the vehicle. Volver picked it up and answered it without slowing the vehicle. 'Who's that?' he called out. 'Jack? Jack - where are you? The police have stopped you! Really? Good. Well, that's why we decided to send you on ahead, isn't it? How the hell else could we get a clear passage? *Who's* dead? *Who? Dead!* Don't fuck with me. You're fucking with me, Jack.' Volver glanced up into the rear-view mirror and, quickly clocking Carla's feigned lack of interest in the news he was receiving, began suspecting that she almost certainly must have known that her father's life had come to an end.

The South African halted the car on the roadside, secured the hand-brake, and spun his leather-jacketed body right round. 'You two get out of the car now,' he ordered Steffan and Jake. 'No - wait! Jake - you stay there with Leone. And don't you take your eyes off Carla, O.K.?'

Leaving Carla in the middle of the rear-seat, sat next to Jake, Steffan climbed out of the car and followed Volver across the tarmac to the other side of the road. They stood looking across at the Range Rover and the three people who were still sitting inside it, and began discussing the news that Volver had that minute gleaned from Jack Belt.

'You know, I can tell that Carla already knew that her dad was dead,' said Volver. 'And it wasn't you or me that told her, right? And Leone just about knows what day of the week it is, so that leaves just the one possibility, you get me?' He locked stares with Steffan. 'Yeah, it had to have been Jake, right?'

'Well, I guess it must have been,' Steffan told him. 'Though how he could have found what had happened I really haven't a clue. You know, I suppose Jack had to have told him.'

'Maybe. Yeah, I think you're right,' said Volver. 'Well, the pair of them can rot in hell now as far as I'm concerned. Listen - I'll take care of Jake soon after we get there. But can I ask you to do the same for Jack the next time you see him?' He made a shooting action with his right hand.

Steffan curled his lip for a moment as he considered exactly what was being asked of him, then nodded back his consent. 'Don't worry, you can count on me, boss,' he declared.

'That's what I wanted to hear, mate,' Volver told the much younger man, slapping him firmly on the back, fully realising that this would be the first time for Steffan to actually take someone's life. He recalled the first time he had squeezed the trigger of a gun, as he pointed it at the back of a rival dealer in Shepherds Bush. It had taken an element of courage, yes, but in the long run, and in the wider realm of things, it had enabled him to take a much firmer grip on the control of the drug trade in that particular part of west London. 'You know, you and I are going to come out of this well ahead, Steffan, don't you worry, mate,' the Afrikaner continued, feigning a smile.

Steffan gritted his teeth, then curled up his lips into a malicious looking grin that he soon noticed closely resembled the one he was staring at, and nodded his approval.

'But I guess your old mate Jake has decided to betray the pair of us and play us both for fools,' Volver told the boy angrily. 'And for that, well, for doing something as traitorous as that, I'm afraid he's going to have to die.'

'Rams wrapped in thermogene beget no lambs,' said Chris, throwing a piece of wood at the fearsome, horned creature who now stood blocking their path to the farmhouse-door. 'Say - where did I read that?'

The queer statement was familiar to Rhiannon too, and she dipped her pretty head to properly consider the puzzle he had set her. 'I think it must have been in that book we studied together for GCSE English, just before I got put back a year,' she told him. 'It was either by Lawrence or Orwell or Huxley, I believe. Though I'm not sure which.'

'Ah, yes,' said Chris. 'It might have been the latter, I guess.'

Rhiannon stepped back behind her lover just in case the ram decided to bolt towards them rather than run away. 'You know, Chris, this horny old fellow looks like he might be related to the one we saw outside the railway-tunnel near Pant that night, don't you think? That night we -'

'Oh, yes, I remember now,' Chris told her, recalling it well. He took aim and threw a second, much thicker, branch ahead of him, and this time it landed plumb on the creature's head, and bounced away onto the ground before him. The ram seemed to ruminate over the meaning of this for a moment or two, then slowly walked off into the trees, no doubt with the extreme pain gradually overtaking his ailing brain.

The young pair gripped hands and walked gingerly up the grassy slope towards the, now empty, yard in front of *Cwm Scwt*, and then approached its peeling front-door. As they had expected, on reaching the farmhouse they found the deserted building locked. Chris turned and smiled at Rhiannon, then lifted a booted foot and, with just one single, upward swing of his heel, kicked in the wooden door.

Hand-in-trembling-hand, and more than a little nervously, the young couple entered the farmhouse, and then moved about it carefully, from room to shady room, in search of anything that would implicate the trio of men who had kidnapped Carla, and were now holding her against her will in an SUV that they had minutes before seen driving away from the location in a southerly direction. The couple had sincerely hoped they might find their stolen Fiesta, but soon discovered that it wasn't anywhere around. They also discovered that the old building didn't even have its own land-line, by which they had hoped they could phone the police and report to them what they had seen go down there from their warm, but fly-infested, nest amongst the trees.

With diminishing stride, and ever-shortening intakes of breath, I managed to stumble my way up the steep, grassy slope into the eerie shade of the scattered spruce-trees, and became immediately confronted with a wooden sign-on-a-pole beside the track that announced that the farm some distance off to my right was called '*Cwm Scwt.*' I turned and walked in that direction towards the open, disabled gate that I could see up ahead of me, which led the visitor into a grey-brown, stony yard, and soon saw the farmhouse loom up amongst the shadows to my left.

There was no one around that I could see, not even a dog or two to challenge my approach, and this fact I immediately sensed signified that the farmhouse might well be vacant, or at least vacated. Approaching the entrance, I soon found the front-door to be broken open, and so, a little tremulously I admit, I wandered inside and looked around.

I hoped to find some evidence that people had been staying there and, to my dismay, this I not long after discovered. My daughter Rhiannon's monogrammed, handkerchief lay suspended from a hot-water pipe, barely off the floor, in a corner of the kitchen, and, in bending to collect it, I discovered Chris's felt hat sitting on a chair nearby. A busted-up guitar, stuffed in a large bin in the opposite corner of the room caused me almost as much dismay, especially as it looked as if it could easily have been rendered like that by having been wrapped round someone's poor head. Selfishly perhaps, I just hoped it hadn't been Rhiannon's.

It was when I began climbing the stairs that I heard the noise. My first thought was that it may have been a cat which was trapped up there, perhaps even too scared to venture down to greet a noisy newcomer. But hearing voices, then the sound of 'Dad!' being yelled out, told me instantly that my daughter Rhiannon and her boyfriend Chris were up there somewhere. She called again for me to join them, and, after rounding the bannister and walking down a dark, uncarpeted corridor, I soon found the two of them at the end of it, standing at the door of a bedroom, and holding up for me to see some items which they said they had just that moment discovered, and that proved that Carla Steel had been held against her will there.

'But where is she now, then?' I asked, hugging to me the pair of them, and no doubt shedding a tear or two at my good fortune at having been reunited with Rhiannon, the apple of my eye.

'She's been taken off by a really wicked monster, Dad,' she told me. 'His name is Volver, and, now that her dad is dead, and can't supply him with the fortune in ransom money that the man wants for her, then he is almost certainly planning to do her harm. We really need to find her, Dad, before it's too late. Can we go after them with you in the van?'

In the back of the Range Rover Carla looked across at Jake and decided that now had to be the time, and that she had nothing to lose by trying. 'Can you lip-read?' she asked him.

'No - can you, then?' the boy asked her nervously, his narrow mouth dropping open as he awaited her reply.

Carla couldn't, of course, and decided she wasn't going to lie to him, but still she felt disinclined to avert his fears that she might possess such a power. 'Well, I can see it's not me they're gabbling on about, I can tell you,' she said. 'And just look how angry the pair are getting.'

'Perhaps I'd better get out and join them then,' he said. 'Don't you think?'

'You know, Jake, I wouldn't if I were you. Not right now, anyway.'

'Say - is it true what people say about your father, Carla?' he asked her. 'That he has a gift?'

Carla nodded. 'Yes, it's true,' she told him. 'Had one, anyway.'

'Had one!' exclaimed Jake, a look of complete puzzlement on his thin, but swarthy face. 'You mean you can lose it!'

'No, you don't understand, Jake,' said Carla, slapping the boy gently on his thigh. 'Mt father is dead now, you see.'

'Oh, I'm sorry to hear that,' said Jake, without thinking.

'His MS had become very critical,' she announced, watching his eyes dart about as his brain sought to make sense of the information he was assembling. 'He passed away two days ago.'

'O.K. But how - then how would you know he'd died?' he asked her, his eyes bulging.

'Well, you see, my father came and visited me in the farmhouse,' she told him, emitting the thinnest of smiles. 'Do you understand what I'm saying?'

There was a three-second pause. 'Sort of,' Jake replied. She saw that he had begun to fidget around in his seat very much as if he had haemorrhoids. 'So are you saying your dead dad came back to see you!' exclaimed Jake, wobbling around worse than ever now.

'You mean you don't think that that's possible, Jake,' she said, witnessing the boy's confusion, but knowing full well of the thrill it gave him to again have her speak his name.

'Well, I do believe that tele-porting is possible,' he replied. 'Is that what you're suggesting?'

Carla was tempted to tell him that, yes, it was. But resisting the notion, she declared, 'No, I mean that his soul - you know, Jake, his spirit - returned to tell me something.'

'What?' asked Jake, trembling, a dribble of saliva leaking out of the corner of his mouth. 'To tell you what?'

Carla suddenly realised that she was deceiving him with this comment, as her father hadn't actually said anything to her, just nodded at her as if he wanted her to acknowledge his express departure to the other side. She felt that Jake didn't deserve to be lied to, so she decided to let him know only the true facts of what had really taken place. 'My dad flew in to me through the open window of my room upstairs,' she told the boy slowly. 'You see, he wanted me to know that he had passed, and - and that, despite my kidnapping, that - that everything would be all right.'

'But, Carla, don't you realise they plan to kill you if he doesn't pay them the half-a-million quid they've demanded. And now that your father's dead, then I guess he won't be able to.'

'You sound like you'd be awfully sad to see them do that to me, Jake,' she told him, smiling.

'I don't want to see you get hurt,' said Jake, touching her arm. 'If your dead father is tele-porting around the place, and returning to tell you all the crucial stuff that you will need to know, then - then Volver's plans are plainly doomed, and no mistake. And, if only for that reason, I certainly don't want a part in them.'

'Really? So are you going to help me then?' Carla asked him.

'You know, Carla, I don't see how I daren't,' he replied. 'I mean, he could quite easily fly down here right now and destroy the two of them across the road with a - with the kind of weapon that nobody on Earth will ever have seen before. I know I would.' Jake let the dusky singer take both his hands in hers and shake them with obvious excitement. He looked into her laughing eyes and knew within himself that he was making the right choice, both for hmself, and for her. How this would play out he didn't know, but even if the two armed guys huddled together outside were planning to desert him, or even to do for him, he felt that he now had *'the old man with the gift'* on his side - the man who had conquered death to return to reassure his lovely daughter, and so would clearly also wish to protect whomsoever was committed to protecting her.

Outside the vehicle the distinctive whirr of a helicopter crossed the morning sky above them. Unable to view it, however hard she tried, Carla turned and looked out of the window at the two evil men who stood together across the road, and who now shaded their eyes with their hands from the harsh morning sunlight as they peered upwards in its direction.

'It's the police!' yelled Steffan.

'But it can't be. After all, it's orange, not yellow,' shouted Volver, the volume of the craft rising sharply as it scooped down low from the north, and banked, as if to pause for a moment to gaze at them all, and then spun itself round, and carried on threading its way southwards through the wooded, mountain vale, finally rising up high again into the azure sky, and then flying off in the direction of the southern of the two reservoirs, and towards the villages of Pontsticill and Vaynor and the town of Merthyr that lay some way beyond that.

D.I. Dawson parked his car at the rear of the police-station, crossed the yard, and peered in through the open window of Sergeant Foley's police-car, quickly noting from his hang-dog expression just how tired the Welshman seemed to have become of wearing his famous, iconic black uniform with the shiny buttons. 'What's afoot, Sherlock?' the Londoner asked Foley with a smile.

'Oh, about twelve inches,' Foley replied. 'You know, I'm very surprised you didn't know that, Jeff, to be honest. I thought you must have had some knowledge of what life was like pre-decimalization, even if you weren't born 'til after it.' Then, spotting the cockney detective's Asian side-kick so close by he could easily have kicked him in the side, added, 'What is it you guys actually get up to in that London then, when you aren't detecting stuff I mean? And don't tell me terrorising innocent black folk, phone-hacking, and working incognito for the Sunday tabloids, because we already know about all that.'

A Polish registered Micra, with its carbon-footprint trailing out of its exhaust-pipe, suddenly turned the corner and sped past them. The three officers turned and watched it go for a few moments, then, turning back and regarding each other afresh, resumed their conversation.

And it was Sergeant Foley who hadn't finished. 'Listen, chaps, I reckon I owe you an apology,' he began. 'I'm awfully sorry we went and let you follow Jack Belt into that storage-unit up in Dowlais. I mean you two weren't to know that it was un-staffed and had a timed gate, were you? Or that Jack was going to swipe his card in the machine, circle round the yard once, count to nineteen, then leave your sorry arses locked up inside.' Constable Thomas, sitting beside him, guffawed at the words his sergeant had just expressed, which hardly resembled an atonement.

The two Londoners turned and gazed at each other in an effort to share, and perhaps somehow, dilute, the embarrassment each felt at this un-solicited speech the sergeant made.

'But, you know, if we three hadn't gone off and left you there for the next couple of hours,' Foley added, 'then I feel sure we would never have caught up with old Jack, would we? That camper-van might look slow at first sight, you know, but it's almost super-sonic going downhill.'

'So what finally stopped Jack in the end, then?' asked Dawson.

'He collided with Steve Davies's ice-cream van just below *The Guest Club,* didn't he?'

'Not the snooker player, I hope?' said D.C.Shah, smiling.

'Good heavens, no,' said Foley. 'Our Steve is anything but forgettable, or boring, or ginger. For a start he's completely bald, generally only plays Frank Zappa through his loud-speaker on a normal day, and his strawberry-splits and ninety-nines are legendary.'

'Well, at least you caught him,' said Dawson, deciding it was now best to draw a line under the matter. 'Although I take it neither Carla Steel nor anyone else was in the back of his van.'

'No thanks to you, I gather,' replied Foley. 'Didn't you hint that you'd struck a deal with the fella before you told us to let him go?'

'O.K., so we did,' the cockney detective replied. 'And, in hindsight, perhaps we might have been better advised to have held onto him a bit longer, or at least put a tail on him following his release.' He watched as Shah nodded in agreement. 'So what is Jack saying now?'

'Nothing yet. But we're going to interview him again very soon,' Foley told him. 'Only this time we're going to do it the Welsh way, O.K.? And threaten to lock him up for a few days without even a biscuit for grub. Never fails. So now that you two unfortunate souls have finally made it back, why don't you come up and join us, eh? There's even some sandwiches left over from earlier today, if I remember.'

'But look - you're a rooster one day, a feather duster the next,' said Rhiannon. I laughed, but when I looked to my side I saw that Chris didn't seem at all happy with my daughter's comment.'

'But you haven't met the man,' he said to the girl he loved, and who presently sat bouncing around on his lap. 'If he's a rooster, then there's never been one like *him*, I'm sure of that,' he told her. 'If you ask me, that man is as used to crushing souls as - as a judge on X-Factor. And with Steffan there to help him, well, I'd say he is capable of doing just about anything for the stack of money that Carla Steel could potentially bring him. And I reckon he's sure to have done this sort of thing before, or worse, maybe. Why do you think the man is so wealthy, Rhiannon?'

'Aye, Chris is probably right, girl,' I told my daughter. 'What did my old chum Balzac tell us?'

'I wouldn't know, Dad,' replied Rhiannon. 'I haven't really met a lot of your drinking friends.'

Chris laughed hilariously at Rhiannon's reply to me.

''Behind every great fortune there is a crime,' the Frenchman told me one evening over a pint of bitter in *"The Butchers,"* I said, smiling into her blue, flashing eyes, then steering sharply to the right, to avoid flattening a ewe that was rolling awkwardly over a cattle-grid, but was finding the manoeuvre a lot more difficult, indeed more perilous, now that she had been sheared. 'God! That was a close shave,' I said.

'Well, they get one every summer round here, don't they?' said Rhiannon.

'I didn't actually mean it like that, love,' I told her. 'My girl's a genius, don't you think, Chris?' I proffered. He didn't reply. 'Say, kids - how many were in the SUV that we're after?' I asked them.

Rhiannon raised a hand and began counting on her fingers. 'Well, let's see - it had to have been Carla in the back, squashed between Steffan and Jake, and then, of course, the Volver man himself driving. So I suppose that makes four altogether, right Chris?'

'But didn't you see there was someone else sitting beside him in the front?' Chris asked her. Rhiannon looked non-plussed. 'Well, there was, babe,' he told her. 'Although I didn't get a decent look at them. In fact, I think he was probably ducking down when they accelerated past.'

As we coasted round a bend a slow farm-vehicle virtually halted our progress. I realised that it would almost certainly have slowed down any vehicle that preceded us too, and so I decided to be absolutely sure about the fact. 'Chris - jump out and ask the driver if any cars have squeezed past him in the last few minutes, would you?' I asked him. Seconds later the boy was back telling us that the driver had verified that no vehicles had even approached him from behind, let alone overtaken him, and so I halted straightaway and turned the van round.

'What are we going to do, Dad?' asked Rhiannon.

'Well, they must have turned off somewhere, mustn't they, love?' I replied. 'So don't you think it makes good sense for us to go back a way and see whether we can discover where that was?'

CHAPTER 25

From the brown sandstone outcrop on the highest point of the plateau the unsheared, hoary old ram could see for miles in all directions. Master of all he surveyed, he bleated out loud basso profundo. He knew his home well; in the summertime he expected sun, green grass, wind, and a quantity of warm, showery rain, and in no year that he could recall had he ever been disappointed. On the high slopes he expected his belly to be full and his annual rut to be awesome. But what the great-grandfather of thousands certainly didn't expect up there was a motor-car.

The Abraham-of-Sheep was used to dogs, large and small, eluding their slack owners, and noisily giving chase to him and his tribe across the broad, verdant pastures, and the practically indiscernible, methane-rich marshes of this, his promised land; and, as ever, with insufficient sense to suppose the main-course they sought for their dinner might not be the least bit scared of them, and might instead elect to spin round at any moment and sniff what the breeze might recommend, rather than meekly take to his two-toed heels and flee. Yes, out of bitter experience Abe anticipated the unexpected incursions that were made into his kingdom, and, more often than not, relished, the defensive campaign that swiftly ensued. But what the ovine patriarch could never in a month of Sundays have anticipated was that a bullet would ricochet off the rock he was currently resting his ancient loins upon, then spin off it to land, smoking off its excess powder, in the short, stubby grass that he had, just seconds before, been chewing.

'Lamb of God! It's those blasted humans again,' Abe cursed, this time vacating his stony throne, and, after thrusting up a cloud of grassy soil with his hind feet, galloping a dozen or so yards to a less lofty ledge, where he could now view the brainless invader askance from out the corner of a broad, blood-shot eye, and liberally berate the same in male baritone sheep-speak.

The Afrikaner of the very same name strode ever closer to him up the high, slippery slope, his black, gleaming, chariot-of-fire roaring like a lion, yet, strangely, now as still as a boulder, far behind him on the lower. He viewed the ram before him as an enemy rather than a dinner, and soon halted, set his feet, and steadied his rifle accordingly. Eyeing the animal's solid form intently through the metal sight, and already picturing him dead, the man fired. When the bullet went right through the beast, and it failed to have its gaze disturbed, let alone drop, he could be forgiven for not knowing that the shot he had dispatched had simply pierced his shaggy fleece.

'You mean you missed!' screamed Steffan, bravely castigating the South African from afar, then hurrying up the slope to do the same again, this time with a choice facial expression or two.

'The bastard must have moved!' yelled Volver, watching as the ram now turned to face him square-on, and half-fearing that he was about to charge. His poised hands now visibly shaking, the second shot he fired missed the ram's eye by less than a centimetre, but was, without question, another abject failure. 'Christ! Now I'll have to re-load!' he told the Welsh boy.

'Hey, let me have a go,' said Steffan, approaching the Afrikaner from the side, and touching his shoulder so as to make him aware of his presence. 'I reckon I'm sure to hit him.'

'Get off!' Volver told him, re-loading. 'This has never happened to me before, I swear. Steffan - tell me if the bastard decides to charge us, yeah?' The South African carefully took aim again.

Steffan stood back a yard, and, covering his ears, waited. Seconds later he spoke. 'You know, mate, I reckon you keep missing because you're not used to your target threatening you back.' Then, sensing the ironic humour in his, otherwise innocent, aside, he began to chuckle loudly.

Volver ceased aiming, and turned and stared at Steffan with pure venom in his eyes. 'What the fuck are you trying to say?' he asked the boy.

'Fuck all!' said Steffan. 'Why? What do you think I'm saying? God - man. Anyone can miss, can't they? Jake missed that apple in the tree yesterday and he was practically touching it.'

'Yeah, but I'm not Jake, am I? Jake is a cock,' Volver told him, beaming a malevolent stare at the boy who was, of course, the cock's best friend.

The shaggy, old ram, most likely bored, awaiting, what must have seemed forever, his imminent slaughter, and understandably having other things in life he wished to be doing, promptly turned and scampered up over the summit of the hill, and down into the dip on the other side. The two humans watched him go, and soon began laughing at the sight, yet each one for diametrically opposite reasons.

'Listen - we've got far more important things to do than chase sheep,' announced Volver, shouldering his weapon, and spinning round to gaze anew into the far distance. 'Just a mile or so more and we'll be there, you know. You did bring all the wet-suits, didn't you?'

'Yeah, but we're one short, remember,' Steffan told him.

'No, we're not,' replied Volver, his top lip soon curling up into a sadistic sneer. The two males stood and studied each other. Then they began emitting a second, hearty laugh, but this time for the very same reason.

The large wooden gate lay busted open, hanging as it now did on just the one iron hinge, and rather disconsolately folded over itself, its component parts pointing in several different directions all at once. The muddy ground, churned up by flocks of sheep that had recently been siphoned through at this point for the summer shearing, had, by this time, become dried hard in the August sunshine. This meant that I was now able to drive my van through, which I quickly did, then, by steering it sharply to the right, and putting my foot to the floor, managed to negotiate in first-gear the grassy slope that rose up steeply towards the plateau to the west.

The mad, bumpy ride that ensued was such that Rhiannon decided the time had come for her to climb over the seat into the back of the vehicle, where she soon sat side-on, her back to the van's metal side, clutching on to Chris's neck, and watching fearfully our shuddering progress. I continued to accelerate hard, and, with little alternative open to me, used all my skill to force the roaring vehicle up and along the twisting tract of land which offered us the least hazardous gradient, a process which quickly saw us slewing left, then right, to best ensure that we made it. And made it we eventually did, the naked, summer-slim, newly-branded sheep staring over at us with inscrutable incredulity, before electing to scatter as one in an almighty ovine charge.

The van's engine idling, its chassis vibrating madly, but sitting still at long last on a high, level tract, I climbed out of the driving-seat and looked about us. It had been months since I had ventured this high up, I thought, and nothing had really changed. This was a beautiful, but treacherous, landscape, that clearly favoured the walker over the runner, the bike-scrambler over the motorist, I mused, its only paths being narrow, twisted ones, that could only have been trodden out over the centuries by the sure-footed sheep for whom it had always been both sanctuary and home.

While Rhiannon climbed over and re-joined Chris again in the passenger-seat, I considered whether or not we were any closer to finding the kidnapped Carla Steel. Given our isolation, and the silence that now reigned all about us, I was forced to ask myself whether the SUV we had been pursuing, without once having caught sight of it, had actually driven up onto the plateau in the first place. I had a strong feeling that it had, of course, and soon, thankfully, my suspicions were to be confirmed.

What little breeze there was was blowing towards us out of the west, and, but for that, I certainly wouldn't have been able to hear the high, buzzing sound of an engine a mile or so away from us. The young people soon jumped out of the van and ran round to join me, having heard the strange sound too, and, with the aid of his pair of binoculars, Chris was soon able to confirm that the black spot we soon saw moving left on the distant horizon was indeed the vehicle that we were desperately seeking.

'Where on earth can that crazy man be taking her?' asked Chris. 'There's nothing to speak of over that way, except masses of sheep, some tumbled rocks, and the vast limestone-quarry way beyond them in the valley. You know, I reckon Carla must be petrified.'

'I know *I* would be,' said Rhiannon, grabbing the field-glasses from the boy and, straightening up her slim back, peering deeply into the western horizon, her long, red hair fluttering behind her in the bustling breeze. 'Hey! They've stopped, you know!' she suddenly announced. 'And - and I do believe that Carla is off running! Yes, she is you know! Go - girl! Yah!'

Within seconds of confirming that what my girl had seen was indeed true, we were all three back inside my van, and careering off westwards at speed, dodging boulders and thick patches of heather all the way, while carefully skirting the great, dark-green marsh that, barring a prolonged drought, or a fourth Ice-Age, would more than likely sit, perched on this sloping hillside, for the rest of time.

Whle still proceeding apace, we agreed that the singer had elected to flee up to the highest point of the land in order to evade recapture, and we watched admiringly as she clambered up the hill, which stood ahead and to our right, as nimbly and as swiftly as her legs could carry her.

'Christ! They've decided to drive off!' Chris suddenly yelled out jubilantly, staring through his binoculars. 'So Carla has escaped!'

'Let me see,' said Rhiannon. 'Yes, Dad - it's true. Oh my God! Then let's drive over there and pick her up, shall we?'

I didn't require a second invitation. Veering away towards the north-west, I powered my van in the direction to which Carla was fleeing. Then, as we approached her, I rolled down my window and began screaming at her to stop, and instead to run across and join us. But it seemed that this wasn't something the singer was at all keen on doing. And so instead

I brought the van to a halt, allowing Chris to dash out and attempt to overtake her. But the boy wasn't to know that she would ignore his repeated appeals too, and instead endeavour to climb higher and higher, until at last she had rounded the hill and completely disappeared from our sight.

Rhiannon and I decided to remain in the van and wait, but it must have been fully five minutes before Chris finally reappeared, this time pulling his famous friend along by the arm.

As confused as I was, Rhiannon snatched up the binoculars again and began studying their approach, and then, to my horror, announced, 'Dad - it's not her!'

It certainly wasn't a cave, in fact it seemed little more than a small, insubstantial fracture in the creamy-coloured, limestone landscape, that the three males and one terrified female approached at a trot from the Range Rover, that they had minutes before left behind them, locked up securely and hidden, in the small barn of a long-abandoned sheep farm.

'Where on earth are you thinking of taking me?' implored Carla, surveying with horror the small, dark crack that lay beside her foot. 'It's little more than a hole in the ground if you ask me. I'd have as much chance of squeezing myself down the toilet as of getting down there. What the hell's down there anyway? A fox? Someone's grave? Purgatory? All three, I shouldn't wonder.'

'Well, it's very tight to start with, and you certainly won't be able to turn round, but it gets bigger and wider the further you descend,' said Jake. 'I found it for us a long while ago, and now all three of us know it well, so don't get alarmed, O.K.? This is definitely not a time to panic.'

'Then I'll have to have a word with my psyche,' said Carla. 'Tell it it's a wendy-house, maybe.'

Volver ignored the singer's sarcastic aside. 'You're going down it second, incidentally,' he told her, 'with Steffan at the front, leading the way, and myself bringing up the rear. I've got the weapon you see,' he added, placing his hand in his jacket-pocket. 'So just do as you're told and keep moving along,

O.K.? And if anyone were stupid enough to think about coming down there after us - well -' Volver didn't need to tell Carla, or anyone else, another word.

Below them, a kneeling Steffan poked his head and shoulders through the tight gap and was soon gone. Then, with a stifled call, he beckoned Carla to follow him. The singer got down on her knees, zipped up her jacket, smoothed back her hair, and then leaned forward and slowly edged her slim frame into the hole before her, through which she soon found she needed to slither like a snake so as to progress. When Carla had disappeared, the other two quickly followed, and very soon the south-facing slope of the green hillside was as empty as it had been just minutes earlier, its utopian silence broken only by the intermittent bleating of the sheep, both from round about the hidden aperture, and, more high-pitched again, from off the mountain.

'If I put my shoulder to it, then I reckon it should open,' I told the three young people, and sure enough, one great thrust and we were inside. The black Range Rover stood before us in the shadows of the barn, its wheels still warm, its engine as hot as burning coals. Let's leave the door open for the cops to see it, shall we?' I suggested. Rhiannon liked the idea and nodded.

'If they ever get here,' said Chris, a glum look on his face, and still firmly holding onto his diminutive, dip-dyed, female prisoner, as though she had just murdered his celebrated next-door neighbour rather than simply impersonated her.

'You're hurting my arm, you know!' yelled Leone. 'Mister - tell your son to leave me alone.'

'Chris isn't my son,' I told her, recalling straightaway how just weeks before I had been almost certain that he was. I looked into the handsome boy's face. 'Though one day I have serious hopes that he might be,' I added, turning to smile at Rhiannon, and noting the blush that swiftly claimed her.

Once we had forced the barn-door as far back as it would go, Chris said, 'I feel we should get back in the van now and drive south after them.'

'Really?' I replied. 'But do either of you know this area?' The blank faces told me all I needed to know. 'Then I suggest we wait here until the police arrive,' I said. 'We've rung up twice now and told them where we went, so I guess the helicopter should be flying over here soon, even if the cops don't actually get here on the ground until a little later.'

'Dad - I think Chris is right,' said Rhiannon. 'When was the last time we saw the helicopter? When we were back by the reservoir, right? But that was ages ago. Hang round here, and we could find ourselves waiting here for hours, don't you think? I feel we'd be mad if we don't do something ourselves, and soon.'

'Rhiannon's right,' said Chris. 'We're the ones who saw the kidnappers last, and now that we've found their car, and they've got no transport of any kind, then we might still be able to overtake them before they get to wherever the hell it is that they're heading.'

'Well, O.K., then,' I told them. 'But the surface-rock is limestone fom here on, remember, and the boulders and blocks lying about look like they're getting thicker and thicker, so I know I shall have to drive very, very slowly.'

Ten minutes later, the sound of a pierced and deflating tyre came as absolutely no surprise to me. The four of us climbed out of the stricken van and prepared ourselves for the long walk that we fully expected lay ahead. The route we four followed was a southerly one, and, quite soon we encountered a tract of limestone-pavement, on which even walking was hazardous, and, for the two females amongst us, well nigh impossible.

Chris now permitted the girl we had captured, whose name she had eventually told us was Leone, to walk along on her own, and quite soon she began to drop behind us, claiming she was getting weary. But turning to help her, Rhiannon spotted the girl picking something up off the ground close to a small crevice in the rock, and quickly brought the matter to my attention.

'Dad - Leone has found something!' she told me. 'Look!'

Chris walked back to where the girl was standing and snatched the item from out of her hand. He then approached me and showed me what it was she had found. 'It's Carla's own purse,' Chris announced. He opened it up. 'Her photo-ID is in it and everything. You know, this means we must be getting closer. In fact -'

Chris knelt down and thrust his hand inside a large, shiny crack in the rock. 'You know, I do believe they may even have gone down here,' he announced, smiling strangely.

'What!' yelled Rhiannon, arching her body right over. 'Down there? But that's impossible.'

'Wait,' the boy replied, ducking his head and shoulders inside it, then poking his head out again to speak to us. 'I'm sitting in the opening to a cave,' he told us. I'm sure they must have gone down here - they must have. Come on you lot - get in and join me. I'll try and lead the way.'

'You won't catch me going down there,' said Leone.

'Then we're going to have to leave you here, I'm afraid, young lady,' I told her. 'And don't worry too much about that ram over there.' The two girls turned swiftly to study it. 'I doubt that it's brave enough to charge a whole group of people.'

Rhiannon smiled at me, then knelt down and slithered into the cave-opening in the limesone bedrock, if only to be with Chris. Then Leone quickly hurried ahead of me and did exactly the same. When she was gone, I stood upright and looked about me. Thick clouds were gathering. There was no sign of a helicopter anywhere that I could see, and no sound of an engine either.

So we had made our decision and had chosen our route, I told myself. 'Is it the right one, old boy?' I enquired of the ram, gazing in admiration at the hoary old fellow's stolid, obdurate stance, his unshorn flanks, his strangely unmoving skull, and the two gnarled, asymmetrical horns that projected, spiralling forwards and upwards, from out of a tangled mane of coarse wool round his head, that oddly reminded me of what I, as a young male, used to look like first thing in the morning.

The moment of shared understanding between the two of us was brief but uncanny. I repeated my question to him and waited. 'Is it the right one, old man?' But the only response

I received came, not from the ram, but from the thickening clouds above us, as rain suddenly began to pelt down all around. And so I quickly got down and clambered on all fours, and before long, albeit with far less ease than anyone ahead of me, eventually succeeded in squeezing, first my shoulders, then the rest of my body, all the way inside the shiny, tight crevice in the rock.

Whirring like a dervish above the uniformed group, the black and yellow helicopter completed its wide, sweeping circle about the green hillside, then set off westwards to search for the second, larger vehicle it had been despatched to find.

'O.K. So here is Dyl's van, but where the hell is the man himself?' Jeff Dawson asked the other policemen who were gathered round him. 'And where on earth is the vehicle he was supposed to be pursuing? If it is in fact a Range Rover. And why the hell did he stop phoning?'

'Well, it's obvious, isn't it?' replied Vic Shah. 'He and his daughter and her boyfriend have gone and got themselves captured by Volver too, the twats. And didn't we tell the man repeatedly to sit tight and wait for us to get here?' He spun round. 'I remember you voicing your opinion that he was a stable sort of chap, didn't you, sergeant?'

'Yeah, would you care to amend that now?' asked Dawson.

'I won't amend a word I said,' Foley told them. 'If you want my opinion, Dyl Cook is the sort of bloke you'd definitely bank on in a tight spot, and even in a dangerous, unpredictable situation like this.' Dawson and Shah turned and stared at each other in disbelief, but constables Llewellyn and Thomas gazed across at Foley and nodded their agreement with their superior's assessment. 'You know, boys, it could easily be a foot-chase he's involved in, for all we know.'

'Well, if it is, let's hope the 'copter can tell us as much before very long,' said Dawson. 'Because, apart from further west, there's nowhere else they could have gone, is there? Unless they've all vanished down a bleedin' rabbit-hole with Alice.'

'Alice!' said the two Welsh constables in unison.

594

'Or maybe the Pied Piper of Merthyr waltzed them all off into the mountain,' said Shah, smiling at his senior officer.

'But until we hear from the air-cops again, then I suppose the only thing we can do is sit down here and wait,' Dawson told them, turning about and parking his backside on a boulder.

'Yeah, and twiddle our thumbs, maybe,' said Shah, sitting beside him, and contemplating attempting the queer action he had just suggested.

'Or count to one-thousand,' said Llewellyn. 'Considering we could be here a while.'

'A million, more like,' said Thomas, grinning.

'Yeah? Well just do your best not to fall asleep, guys, that's all,' remarked Dawson.

'Fall asleep! My boys? Why the hell would they?' Foley asked him.

'Yeah, why would we?' asked Llewellyn, raising his big head aggressively, and proceeding to stare out the two cockney officers who were now beginning to get on his wick.

'Isn't it obvious?' said Dawson. The man spun round, and pointing, told them, 'I reckon there's enough bleedin' sheep up here that, if you counted them, they'd be bound to send us all into a coma.'

As I pulled and dragged and twisted myself, on my elbows and knees, along the dark, narrow limestone passage that seemed to slope ever downwards, all that I could make out before me were the tiny, muddy heels of Leone Lewis, and those only when Chris elected to stop and flash his torch back along the line. Most of the time I crawled blind, then halted to take a few deep breaths, then endeavoured to crawl some more in an effort to catch up again.

On occasions I could hear Chris's voice ahead of me telling us how, though we still weren't able to turn our bodies round, the cave seemed to be getting a little wider, but in all honesty that wasn't my experience at all, and was most likely the boy's method of trying to keep all our spirits up. In truth I felt that, if anything, the passage seemed to be getting tighter, and, the way I looked at it, we seemed to be gradually decending from the broader trachea into the narrower bronchus of some great black lung, whose multi-branched, ever-tightening bronchioles still lay ahead of us and no doubt deeper still, and where, ironically, and before too long a time elapsed I feared, we would all four most likely asphyxiate and die.

When I caught sight of Chris's torch-lit face in the gap ahead of me I was quite shocked, not least because this could only mean that he had at last managed to turn his body round. I waited until it was my turn to reach him, and then looked up and saw that the two girls had now squeezed past him, and were seated together in a small round chamber with their backs to the crusty, crinkled wall, looking ruddy-faced and excited, but rather weary.

'Perhaps we should rest here for a while,' I told them, being suddenly conscious of my age and of my questionable condition. 'Is this where they've taken Carla, then? Is it, girl?' I asked Leone. She shrugged her shoulders in response, then let her head fall back and rest on the rock-wall, as if it was her intention to take a nap.

'You can stay here by all means, Dyl,' said Chris, 'but I need to be sure whether we're in fact heading the right way, or if this is just a wild goose-chase.' With that he turned and set off crawling along one of the two tunnels that branched off from the chamber we currently occupied. It wasn't long before we realised that, without the only torch we had to light us up, which was of course his, we would soon resort to counting down the seconds until his return. But, if a count took place, then it couldn't have lasted for long, because the girls and I all quickly fell asleep where we sat, and so, when Chris returned again and roused us, we had absolutely no idea how long the boy had been gone.

'Hey - there's a pool down there!' Chris yelled as soon as he had flopped down beside us.

'Well, I hope you haven't been in it,' said Rhiannon, her mouth agape.

'Of course not,' he replied. 'But you'll never guess what I found beside it.'

'A deck-chair,' suggested Leone, seemingly being serious.

'Not that sort of pool, silly,' he told her.

'A whale,' I suggested, smiling.

'Yeah sure. Let's free Willy, shall we?' he continued, laughing aloud.

'A fish,' my daughter proffered.

'Well, not quite,' responded Chris, teasing her with his eyebrows raised.

'So I'm close then?' she enquired.

'Sort of,' he said. 'It's now in my jacket-pocket, so how about that?' Rhiannon seemed none the wiser. Chris smacked its location with his hand, then he squeezed the object with his fingers.

'Eugh! That's disgusting,' said Rhiannon, sniffing deeply. 'A fish in your pocket!'

Leone chanced her arm. 'A wrist-watch in the shape of a goldfish,' she told him quietly.

Chris stared at the girl. 'That's exactly what it is,' he announced, taking the gleaming object out of his pocket and showing it to us. 'So I guess Carla must have let you see it then, Leone?'

'No. No, I saw it on the chair beside her bed when she went - when she was asleep,' Leone told us. 'Even tried it on once, I did. It's beautiful, isn't it? She must have taken it off to save it - to - oh, I don't know.'

'From getting wet,' I suggested, gazing over at Chris and seeing him nod. 'She left it behind to save it from being destroyed as they forced her along, didn't she? You see it's a sixties' time-piece,' I told them, holding it between my fingers, and twirling it round in the narrow beam of light which emanated from Chris's torch, and that instantly seemed to transform its golden-orange form into something wondrous and alive. 'And they didn't make watches water-proof back then, you see. I know because I ruined a fair few of them by stupidly soaking them back in the day, and not all of them mine, too.' I handed the orange timepiece back to Chris, who wrapped it up very tightly inside a polythene bag.

'Didn't Mam once have one just like that, Dad?' Rhiannon asked me. You know I'm sure I saw it in that photo she has of her and - you know.' I knew exactly who she meant, but decided just to nod my aquiescence rather than talk about who she was referring to.

'Sarah?' asked Leone. 'Is it Sarah you mean?' Rhiannon looked at me, then turned back and stared at the black-haired girl, and nodded to her ever so slightly. 'Then that's who gave it to Carla then. When they shared a place together up in London. And I happen to know that Carla loved the woman. And so that's who she got it from, you see. Volver - Volver told us all about it.'

'Told you what exactly?' my daughter asked her. 'Do you mean - you don't mean about my half-sister?' I gritted my teeth and winced, as I felt I knew what was coming.

'Yeah. The two of them were lesbians, you know,' announced Leone. 'It's true, girl - I swear.'

Chris leaned forward and handed me the wrist-watch. 'You look after it, Dyl,' he said to me with a smile. Then he turned his body round and told everyone, 'Carla happens to be bi if you want to know, girls. She told me a long time ago. And, you know, I reckon that that's what makes her such a fantastic artist, to be frank. It follows, don't you see? I mean, to have experienced all that she has - her schooldays in Merthyr, her formative times in Oxford and London, her amorous relationships with people of both genders, her mother's sad death, I mean everything she's ever been through, including her substance-abuse, and even, in recent days, her dad's terminal illness - and to be able to make it *real* for us, in the most - in the most poetic, powerful, visceral way possible. Few could surely have achieved musically what Carla has.'

I carefully tucked the twisted polythene-bag that held the wrist-watch inside my waistband, then watched as Rhiannon looked lovingly into Chris's eyes, then laid her head gently on his lap. I inhaled deeply and smiled at the pair of them, sitting sweetly as they did before me. Just then I felt so utterly glad that the boy who had said those profound, heartfelt words, and who had bravely led us deep inside the bowels of a mountain, in pursuit of a madman who had kidnapped a legend, clearly loved my daughter every bit as much as I knew I did myself.

While the police search for the kidnappers moved off towards Trefechan and Cefn, and the even smaller villages that lay further off to the west, we four, who knew next to nothing of this, and who sat in the heart of a nameless cave-system on an inglorious, unsung Welsh mountain-side, were the only ones who knew where the miscreants whom they sought had gone. But there was a world of difference between having that critical, new knowledge we had acquired and possesssing the means by which to follow after them, let alone capture them.

Having now followed Chris down to the pool where he had found Carla's wrist-watch, we four all stood, circled round it in the torch-light, wondering how the four we were chasing after had managed to progress beyond it.

'They must have had wet-suits and ropes and oxygen and the rest, right Leone?' said Chris, trying hard to form his facial features into a look that might frighten the Welsh girl into concurring. Unlikely though that appeared, it seemed to work.

'Only for four people, though,' Leone told him. 'And Volver already knew I wasn't up for it anyway - the deepwater diving, I mean - although that didn't seem to matter in the end as things turned out, thank God.'

'Well, I can tell you I'm definitely going down there,' said Chris, pointing into the freshwater pool, whose unseen depth we could only guess at.

'But you haven't even got a swimming-costume, sweetheart,' Rhiannon told him. 'And it's probably a lot deeper in there than it looks, you know.'

I thought about what my daughter had just said, and looked around me at the water trickling into the pool from the rounded walls of the chasm we were all standing in, and asked Chris, 'Is the pool deeper now than it was the first time, do you think?'

'Maybe a foot or so,' he told us. 'No, I'd say a little more than that. Two feet, perhaps. If it weren't dry above ground then I guess we could be faced with a real dilemma.'

'Then I think we all might need to take a decision right now,' I told them. 'You see it starting raining heavily just after you all crawled into the cave, and, if it hasn't yet stopped, then I imagine this chamber could easily begin to -'

'Fill up!' yelled a horrified Rhiannon, her hand across her mouth.

'Yes, I fear so,' I told them.

'Even more reason then for me to go down there,' said Chris, 'if only to see if I can surface again somewhere further along.'

'Are you a nut?' asked Leone. 'How on earth are you going to be able to see where you're going for a start?'

'But this torch I'm holding is totally water-proof,' said Chris, holding it aloft. 'And I can hold my breath for two minutes on a good day, can't I Rhi?'

'Oh, yeah? And *is it* a good day?' asked Leone, wobbling her little head about as if it mattered a fig. Straightaway she could tell that Chris wasn't going to bother replying to her. 'Girl - you should tell your boyfriend to wise up if you ask me,' she told Rhiannon. 'After all, who does he think he is? James Bond? God - isn't he still at school?'

Chris quickly tore off his clothes and shoes, and then sat himself down on the rocky rim of the pool with his two feet dangling in the water. He dipped his torch below the surface to prove to us that what he had previously said was true, then he jumped in, and, inhaling deeply, dove straight under. I had a watch on, but I didn't once feel inclined to count off the seconds, for fear Rhiannon would become even more scared than she already appeared. But once I was sure that two minutes had most certainly come and gone, I edged over towards my daughter and, wrapping my arm around her shoulder, gripped her tightly to me.

Finally, after what must have been at least a five-minute lapse, Chris's head surfaced again.

'The - the next chamber is much bigger than - than this one,' he announced, between intakes of enormous gulps of air. 'And the - and the roof is far higher, too, so it has to be much safer than where we are now. I suggest you all get your kit off and follow me. There's no one in there, by the way, although there's plenty of evidence that the kidnappers stayed there a while.'

Not wanting us to leave anything behind, I encouraged Chris to put his clothes back on, and when, like us, he was fully dressed, he leapt back into the water and led the way, showing us how we could best swim under the great neck of limestone that looked like it fully confined us, but which had simply obscured our view of the stream's actual cave-system which lay ahead.

Around fifteen minutes later we had all managed to swim singly beneath through the submerged archway, and so succeeded in manoeuvring our way past what had at first appeared an impassible obstruction. Surfacing now in a new, much larger cavern, we each climbed out of the swirling water, and, sitting in a curved line on the rim of the pool, began to survey our new, albeit temporary, domicile.

'Where's Leone?' I asked everyone. 'Oh my God! It looks like she didn't make it. I'm going to have to go back to find her.'

'She told me she couldn't do it, Dad,' Rhiannon replied, taking my hand. 'After you dived in I watched her crawl back up the tunnel. I nearly joined her myself, to be honest, when I saw how dreadfully hard it looked. She'll be above ground again very soon, I'm sure.'

I considered this new situation. 'Well, there's very little we can do about it now, I suppose,' I said, gazing at Chris. 'Say - what is it that you found in here?' I soon asked the boy.

He rose and tentatively approached a shadowy corner in which lay an object he seemed very reluctant to let Rhiannon see. I joined him. 'It's a white, American-style, pocket t-shirt,' he told me,' and there's blood all over it.' I looked into his eyes. 'It's Carla's,' he added, gritting his teeth. 'She told me she would be wearing it to the gig at *The Railway*, the night she got abducted. Dyl, I can't hang around here a minute longer, I really can't. I've got to swim on further, and right now.'

'Well, you're not going on alone,' I told him, clamping my hand on his shoulder. You take the lead as you've been doing, and I'll do my best to make sure that we all keep up.'

Once more we waited until Chris rerturned from under the submerged arch which sat ahead of us, and then, on hearing him state that our next planned movement was achievable, we three swam through in single file, not long after re-surfacing in an even larger chamber again. But this new arched room I saw was very different to the others we had already travelled through in one important aspect - it contained a large number of crates and boxes, stacked in a corner to one side, each one closed tight, and bound, in the form of a cross, with a long, thin chain and padlock.

Rhiannon dashed over and began examining them. 'What can be in them?' she asked.

'I've got a fair idea,' I told her.

'So have I,' said Chris, using his hands to push a chain to the side of one box, so that he could flip open a corner and examine the contents. 'Wow! I don't need to delve any deeper inside,' he told us. 'The smell is enough.'

'Is it drugs?' my daughter asked him.

Chris nodded. 'It's literally tons of cocaine,' he told us. 'This must be the stuff that Volver wanted the local lads to start selling for him. But why on earth would they store it up here?'

'Well, it's relatively secure, isn't it?' I replied. 'And they probably take it out of here a box at a time, and, since they're wooden boxes, and as long as they're not too full -'

'Then they could probably float them out,' said Rhiannon, smiling.

'But that's a long way to transport a large box, don't you think?' asked Chris, pointing upstream. 'I mean, just on our own, and carrying nothing at all it must have taken us a good hour or two.

'But they wouldn't be taking the boxes upstream, would they?' I told him. 'Unless there's a much bigger cave opening back there. No, my guess is that they follow the natural stream-flow, and take the drugs out into the valley somewhere below us, and wherever this cave-system eventually comes to an end.'

Minutes later we were all ducking and diving beneath yet another submerged archway, then swimming slowly and carefully downstream, for what must have been a considerable distance, along a tunnel where we could only surface safely at selected points, chosen by our leader Chris, where isolated air-pockets existed above the, still clearly rising, water-level.

When we had reached as far as our energy-levels would allow, we rested for some minutes, by hanging onto a half-submerged wall of limestone, then swam on a little further again until we reached a point where Chris suddenly popped his head up, and commanded us to be as quiet as we could possibly be.

'There is a light just ahead of us,' he announced. 'So I had to turn round and swim back.'

'Then It has to be them,' I told him. 'Listen - don't go doing anything rash now, Chris. Remember they are most probably armed, while we haven't even got a chisel. And there's just you and me, while there's three of them.' Chris nodded. 'I reckon we had better decide our next step very, very carefully.'

'Yes, but we can't very well stay here, can we?' said Chris. 'There isn't anywhere for us to sit for a start. We're just treading water and getting more and more weary. We had better go back a way I think.'

So that is what we did, and, minutes later, we pulled ourselves up onto a narrow ledge just above water-level, and a proper discussion then ensued about what we should do next. But quite soon we were to discover that our hand had been forced: as the level of the rushing water in the cave-system could now be clearly seen to be rising to alarming heights, and we could tell that, unless we elected to swim on into the lit cave downstream of us then we would unquestionably be drowned.

And so beneath the arch we three dove, and quite soon we resurfaced again inside a vast chamber where we were thrilled to be able to climb out of the swirling water and walk around, for the first time in a long while, on a broad, solid, rocky floor. We saw there was a lamp hanging from a hook in a corner, which cast sufficient light for us, and so Chris decided to switch off his torch.

'But you know I'm sure I know this place!' exclaimed a wide-eyed Rhiannon.

'Me, too,' said Chris. 'We came here once before, remember Rhi? Only back then there was no lamp or light of any kind in here, was there?'

'No,' Rhiannon replied, walking over to join him, and taking his hand in hers. 'But the place was very like a fairies' grotto back then, don't you think? A kind of magic kingdom. Ethereal, you know.'

Chris nodded, then suddenly recalled how the pair of them had made love in the cave's darkness, in the very shingle alongside the glistening pool that they were currently standing upon, and instinctively he looked down at it in awe, his bright eyes searching along its rippling contours for signs of their coupling, or their footprints even, and, seeing none remaining, closing them as tightly as he could, and trying hard to relive the intimacy of that moment, and that experience.

'The sort of place lovers steal away to,' I whispered, looking up, and glimpsing above our heads the lofty, arched roof of what might easily have been the crypt of some great chief's, or monarch's, mighty palace. The gleaming surface of the same was ribbed liberally with pastel-coloured stalactites, some short, some long, that dripped alternately, and that we could observe being repeatedly criss-crossed and bisected by streams and streams of endlessly circling, silently fluttering, bats.

'Do you remember the way you got out of here?' I asked the young pair a few moments later.

'It's that way, Dad,' Rhiannon replied, pointing to where the water streaming from the pool we were standing beside slithered right, then left, before disappearing beneath the arched entrance to what appeared to be a low-roofed tunnel.

I decided to leave the others and wander off alone towards it. Peering down the stream's narrow tunnel, I could clearly see a tiny circle of light some distance away, which I felt had to signify the outside world. But if that was true, I thought, and our salvation was so near at hand, then plainly we could be just as close to the dangerous, villainous man we were chasing after, namely Abram Volver. And it was more than likely, given what we knew about him, that the South African was armed with at least one fire-arm, I told myself; and, as I had once heard someone tell me in the pub, 'if all you have is a gun, then everything around you is a target.'

Carla had spent at least half-an-hour trying to stymie the blood-flow, initially in a cave somewhere upstream from where she now lay, but now, for a second time, much nearer to the cave-entrance. Since no one else was prepared to help her back there, she had had to use her own t-shirt, and, very quickly saturated in blood, she had then discarded it on the ground.

Jake cried out again. 'My best mate!' he yelled. 'How can your best mate just stab you with a knife like that?' He winced with pain. 'And I had no idea it was coming, either.'

Carla recalled how she hadn't actually seen it happen - she was being forced to swim ahead of them at the time - but soon after they had climbed out of the water, Jake had rushed up to her, much as a boy is inclined to do to his own mother, and had shown her the wound in his side that Steffan had just inflicted. The blood was simply pouring out from it, and Carla suddenly had this feeling that, if Volver saw it, he would most likely shoot the boy, if only to save himself from the hassle that this would now create for him. And so she took Jake off to a shadowy corner to see how she could help him, soon tearing off her own t-shirt to use it as a makeshift tourniquet.

And now, lying alongside him in only her bra and jeans, and on a hard, but dry, platform of rock, hidden away, six or seven feet or so above the swelling stream that ran on noisily towards the cave-entrance close by, Carla felt that she might possibly have saved the unfortunate boy's life.

'God! I should have noticed how eager Steffan was to swim last,' Jake told the singer, sobbing heavily, and still grasping Carla's arm for dear life. 'And do you know he was only inches away with his second thrust!'

'Hush! Don't think about it any longer, Jake,' Carla told him. 'You're going to be O.K., I swear.'

'But how do you know that?' asked Jake. Then much quieter, 'The very next moment they wonder where we've disappeared off to, and climb up here looking, could easily be my last, you know.'

'But they've got more important things to do right now,' said Carla. 'They've gone outside to check that the coast is clear so they can make their getaway. And anyway, where is your faith, Jake?'

'At home with her mum, I hope,' he replied.

'I think you could be getting a little delirious,' Carla told him, stroking the boy's cold temple.

'I'm not,' the boy replied. 'Faith is the littlest of our cat's kittens at home. And I wish to God I was with them right now, I can tell you. Hey - what's that?'

The pair had heard a sound. Carla crept over to the top of the limestone chimney up which they had climbed to get their wet bodies into the dry, stone chamber in which they now lay. She could hear someone wading through the water six feet or so below her, and, anticipating Volver's arrival, silently crept back to link hands with her terrified, supine companion.

Seconds later a head popped up before her, but, in the chamber's gloom, she found that she wasn't able to make out whose it was. Carla and Jake lay as still as death and waited for it to go. Then voices could be heard below in the water, and one of these voices belonged to a girl.

'It's Leone,' whispered Jake.

Carla wasn't convinced and shook her head. She got up and, edging her torso across the bare rock once more, looked down the chimney to where the afternoon light from outside the cave-entrance lit up a tiny sliver of the narrow channel down which poured the, now gushing, stream. She and Jake were barely ten yards from freedom, she thought, but she was just as convinced that they were still a very long way from safety.

A torch-light suddenly flashed up the limestone chimney towards her. Terrified, Carla ducked back inside, and lay still in a prone position on the striated, rocky surface, an arm across her injured companion, hoping and praying that the unknown intruder would fail to see them there and disappear down again.

As our group of three waded our weary way down the ever-deepening, final stretch of stream, towards the disc of light that signified the welcome end to the grotto's cave-system, Rhiannon suddenly noticed a gap above her head. She pulled on Chris's shoulder, and asked him to shine his torch up in that direction, and the boy duly halted, turned back a few steps, and obliged.

'You're not climbing up there, Rhi,' Chris told her. 'You could easily fall. Look - if you're so inquisitive I'll go up there myself and take a look if you like.'

I watched from ahead of them, as Chris handed his torch to my daughter to hold for him so that he might climb up unencumbered. Raising, then spreading his two feet wide apart, and using his elbows to lever his body aloft, he soon disappeared up into a narrow vertical space that none of us had previously any idea was there.

Not long after I heard a woman's voice yelling, 'Chris!' Then, as my daughter and I stood together in the deep, churning water, peering up into the semi-darkness above our heads, we could faintly make out a conversation taking place. It was Chris who first leapt down again, and then, reaching his arms above him, carefully lifted down a boy's torso, and supported him as he did his utmost to stand up, four-square, in the deep, swirling stream. When the boy spun round to face me, with the beam of light now full across his face, I could see clearly that it was Jake.

'Jake!' I yelled.'What the hell are you doing up there?'

'I don't really know, to be honest,' he replied strangely. 'But listen - Carla is up there with me!'

'Did the two of them leave you behind then?' Chris asked the boy, then staring up the chimney once again, in preparation for a second scaling. 'And has she lost a tremendous lot of blood do you think?'

But, after listening to his puzzling words, Jake smiled thinly at his old school-friend, then swooned, and fell, head first, straight into the water.

Carla leapt straight down into the stream to help, and between the four of us we managed to raise Jake up to his feet, and walk him, very slowly and carefully, down the channel and out into the open air, the thickening clouds overhead suggesting that even more rain was arriving.

As we trudged wearily down the wet, narrow path that ran alongside the stream, a black-and-yellow helicopter could be seen circling in the valley to the south of us, and, on spotting our approach, it flew upstream in our direction, and hovered, noisily above us. A small carriage was soon lowered down towards us by which to lift Jake, but, as it descended, we could clearly see that someone, almost certainly a female, was already sitting inside it.

'It's most likely a nurse,' I told the others, seeing the carriage collide with a tree and almost toss the poor woman out. But when it finally reached the ground we could all tell that it wasn't a medical person that it had been transporting, but Leone.

'They picked me up in the pouring rain back up on the mountain,' she announced as she leapt out and joined us. 'And so I told them where you had all gone to, and they seemed to have a fair idea where you might all come out again. And bloody hell, it seems they were right!'

We all helped Jake climb into the carrriage, and then sent him aloft to the helicopter that we knew would transport him straight off to hospital.

'And what about Volver and Steffan?' Carla asked Leone. 'Have they got away?'

'They probably think they have, especially now that evening is setting in,' she told us, hugging Carla tightly round the neck, then Rhiannon, as if they were long-lost sisters just returned from another land, and as if she had never even been involved in the singer's abduction. 'But that pilot showed me his big, heat-seeking camera, you know,' she added, giggling, 'and, boy, you couldn't help but be impressed.'

The singer held up the extraordinary golden wrist-watch I had just handed her, and let the gold-fish embellished on its back catch the light. 'Yes, it belonged to Sarah,' she told us, smiling. 'Isn't it beautiful? It's one of a great many things she gave me, you know.' She raised her head and looked over at my daughter. 'Your half-sister is a wonderful human-being, you know, Rhiannon. She really is. Although I can easily understand how you couldn't possibly know that. You see, Sarah told me more than once that, when you were born, she felt quite - well, quite -'

'Jealous,' said Rhiannon. She bit into her lip. 'You see, Carla, I'm beginning to understand now. Especially as I had a mum *and* a dad at home, while Sarah obviously had to make do with just a mum. And my mum has her moments, as I'm sure you've heard.'

The two girls smiled at each other.

'And a step-father she couldn't possibly feel close to,' I added, rubbing my eyes with the towel I had earlier used to dry my hair. 'She used to come back for holidays for a few years, you know,' I added, 'and on the few occasions I met her I tried to get to know her, of course, but it felt like I was just banging my head on a brick-wall. The girl is head-strong, and, in all honesty, I can't say I blame her for deciding to go off to the smoke when she did.' I felt myself beginning to fill up. 'And after that even her occasional visits home came to an abrupt end.'

'Do you know, perhaps that was when I first met her,' said Carla, taking my hand and squeezing it. 'For a very long time Sarah was my soul-mate, my lover, my friend. We went through so much together, we really did, that - that sometimes I felt she was the other half of me. But it became particularly bad when our closest friend Jackie disappeared, and poor little Leila was forced to look upon Sarah as her mother. Of course we weren't to know that her mother had been brutally murdered, or that Abram Kronfield - an erstwhile friend of mine, whom you probably know better as Volver - was the man who engineered it.'

A haggard Sergeant Foley walked across the room from the filing-cabinet in the corner. 'Well, he's in custody tonight, Miss,' he said, pouring the Welsh-born singer a second glass of whisky.

'Yes I know,' said Carla. 'And I thank God for it.' She looked around her. 'And do you know that it was in this very room that my father managed to locate Jackie's body.' She shook her head. 'Though sadly the discovery did cost one poor London bobby his life.'

'And at the hands of a wicked old man called Michael Ryan, as it turned out, Miss,' added Foley, 'whom this Volver paid very generously over a long period to suppress his crime.'

'Since the two of them had most likely murdered her together at Ryan's almshouse home in Putney,' said Vic Shah.

'By the way, we have since heard that that Ryan man is currently on the run in the west of Ireland, and we're confident that, with the Garda hot on his tail, and the fact that he's travelling in a horse-drawn carriage, it won't be long before he's captured.' The police-officers all laughed.

'Then you'll need to add to Mike Ryan's crime-sheet the murder of a fellow Irishman of his called Dave Cronin,' said Carla, 'whom Volver stabbed, and Ryan drowned and disposed of.'

'Dave Cronin?' said a pensive Jeff Dawson. 'Ah, yes, I remember him. He had a very bad habit, he did. But what a terrific guitarist nevertheless. A sort of Irish Johnny Winter, as I recall.'

I smiled on recalling the talented albino musician from the seventies who was his prototype.

'Yes, handsome, gentle Dave Cronin,' Carla told him, dipping her head in the recalling. 'Who sang to thousands every day on the London Underground, and spurned every one of the pleas that came his way from the reality-show circus. A dedicated musician and a man of principle. A generous man who serenaded me nightly in our little flat with a music that was truly his own.'

'Rhiannon looked over at Chris and smiled that smile I'd seen her give him in the cave a number of times earlier that day.

'And the only man I've truly loved,' added Carla, leaving none of us in doubt that these words she spoke were the murdered man's real epitaph.

'You're still very young, Miss,' said Sergeant Foley. 'You just haven't found the right one yet.'

'You may be right,' Carla told him, raising her eye-brows suggestively, then stifling a burp. 'I'm sorry, but I fear the whisky is making me rather hungry.'

'Well, let's all adjourn to Zeta's, shall we?' said Foley, swigging what little was now left of his whisky by the neck. 'Their meat-balls are legendary, you know, and I'd say the very thing to take your mind off men.'

'Oh, would you now?' said Carla, flushing brightly. 'Meat-balls! I beg to differ.' At this everyone laughed.

'There seem to be an awful lot of people in town tonight, don't you think?' said Rhiannon, as she walked up Merthyr High Street hand-in-hand with Chris and me, as we all made our way, behind Carla and the small group of police-officers that comprised her escort, towards *The Cafe Giotto*.

'The last train from Cardiff has just come in, Miss,' Sergeant Foley told her, turning about. 'And a lot of them I reckon are Fleet Street paps that I fear, Carla, you're bound to have to face tomorrow morning.'

'But not all of them,' Jeff Dawson told him, gripping his arm and winking.

'No, not all. I never said that, did I?' said Foley, grinning back at him.

When we entered the restaurant I straightaway saw my wife Gwen sitting at the farthest table, chatting with our host Zeta, and with Anne, and some other women I vaguely knew who were seated alongside them. I must admit I was somewhat taken aback when Carla suddenly dashed across the room towards them, and leaned over and hugged a woman sitting across from Gwen, who seemed to have just arrived, and, like us, had yet to take her coat off. We made our way over towards them and, as she turned, I could clearly see that it was my estranged step-daughter Sarah whom the singer had greeted so warmly, and I swiftly guessed that the pretty, smiling, mixed-race girl sitting alongside her, and whose hand she tightly held, had to be Leila.

Despite the intense excitement and the understandable emotion in the air, before very long everyone managed to sit themselves down at the two large tables that our hosts had generously placed together for us.

'Here's to British Rail for getting you both here so fast,' said Gwen, raising her glass of wine, and smiling at her prodigal daughter, and at the enchanting little girl who was sitting quietly beside her. Everyone raised their glasses, and nodded and smiled in agreement.

'But Gwen - it's not called that any longer,' said Zeta. 'Is it Anne?'

'I wouldn't know to be honest,' Anne retorted, stroking Zeta's new Siamese kitten as it sat placidly, purring loudly on her lap. 'You see, these days I usually let the car take the strain.'

'Well, how about we toast Jones and Trevithick then,' Gwen suggested. 'For they started it all, didn't they? Trains, I mean. The original iron men those two were. Way back in 1804, and here in Merthyr too.'

'Though my wife and I can't actually remember that far back, naturally,' I added, smiling.

'To Jones and Trevithick,' everyone cried, glasses held aloft and clinking.

'Aye, wonderful half-backs they were, as I recall,' said Foley, smiling. 'But not the best.' We all laughed.

'No, that's true,' said Martin-the-Caff, getting what for him was a brain-wave. 'To Gareth Edwards and Barry John,' he exclaimed proudly. Gleefully, we all repeated that toast too.

'Joe Calzhage and that gorgeous Johnny Owen,' said his wife Zeta, raising her little fist and punching the air above her. 'They've both been in here, you know, when they weren't in training of course.' A smiling Martin nodded by way of confirmation.

'To David and Lloyd George - a fine Coalition!' shouted a drunken man at the counter, who promptly knocked his change from off the surface and right across the floor, and swiftly set about chasing it, on his hands and knees, in the direction of the door. We laughed again, only this time with pure gusto at the sight of it, then slowly composed ourselves once more as the first plates of meat-balls began to arrive at the table.

Rhiannon lifted her glass and looked around. 'To Carla and Sarah,' she said, a tear clearly forming in the corner of her eye. Chris leaned over, smiled, then tilted his head and kissed her.

'Yes, to Carla and Sarah,' said Leila, in a sweet, high voice, who, sitting between them, very soon found herself getting tightly hugged to bursting by the pair of them. To the rest of us the genuine tender love that plainly existed between the three females was palpable and a genuine sight to see.

'Say - where are we going to be staying, now we've finally arrived in Merthyr, then, Auntie Carla?' the little girl asked, just failing to stifle a yawn, and twirling in her little fingers the red and green, Welsh-Dragon flag that Sarah had bought for her many hours before in the little shop on Paddington Station.

'Why, that's very easy,' said Gwen, smiling across at them. 'Isn't it, Anne?'

'That's right,' said Anne, grinning from ear to ear. 'There's a lovely house that's just been cleaned afresh, with beds aired and everything. And I believe it's called *Coral*, right Gwen?'

My wife nodded. 'Yes, it is,' she said. '*Coral* is the place for you three tonight and no mistake.'

The young girl considered the words the two women imparted for a moment. 'And is it near here?' she asked, now emitting a full-blown yawn. 'Or do we take another train to get there?'

'No, love, there are no trains that go through there any longer,' Carla told her, a bright image of *The Seven Arches* suddenly flashing up before her eyes. 'But it's not far. It's in a little place called *Gloryhole*, is where it is, sweetheart. And, you know, if you and Sarah really like it there, then I don't see any reason why we shouldn't stay there for an extended holiday, or even - or even a little while longer perhaps.' She reached over and squeezed Sarah's hand below the pale -blue table-cloth, and mouthed a faint kiss to her.

Espying, with sleep-defying eyes, their timid embrace, Leila picked up the goldfish wrist-watch, and, sitting far back in her seat, twirled it round and round in her tiny fingers before her captivated, twinkling eyes. She soon turned and smiled at Carla whose watch she knew it was.

'And that is a little present from me to you, Leila,' the singer told her, smiling broadly.

The little girl's brown eyes lit up. 'Ooh! Thank you, Auntie Carla,' she said, gritting her cutely spaced, white teeth together tightly in sheer excitement. 'This is my bestest present ever for sure. Want to know cause why?'

'Why?' asked Carla, smiling at the simple, childish words which her tender heart had for too long missed.

'Because I can see now how, like your daddy, orange is my favourite colour too.' Her words and smiling countenance almost brought Carla to tears.

Then Leila had a bright idea, and, leaping to her feet, and lifting the bright, shining timepiece high above her, and opening her little mouth and whirring loudly like some high-pitched, tropical bird, she flew the magical orange object round and round about our heads, to loud, joyous whooping, and general acclaim. Then, finally, sweeping it down low once more at the end of her thin, brown, outstretched arm, and making it look for all the world like an African flamingo returning home once more to its vast, blue lake, Leila landed it, safe and sound, and with a timely whoosh!, in the very middle of our table.

THE END

Lightning Source UK Ltd.
Milton Keynes UK
UKOW04f0606240913

217764UK00001B/1/P